THE PUBLIC BURNING

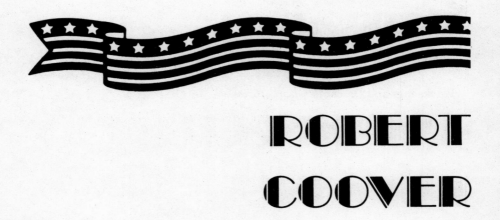

ROBERT
COOVER

THE PUBLIC

BURNING

A RICHARD SEAVER BOOK
THE VIKING PRESS   NEW YORK

A Richard Seaver Book/The Viking Press
First published in 1977 by The Viking Press
625 Madison Avenue, New York, N.Y. 10022
Published simultaneously in Canada by
Penguin Books Canada Limited

LIBRARY OF CONGRESS CATALOGING IN PUBLICATION DATA
Coover, Robert.
  The public burning.
  "A Richard Seaver book."
  I. Title.
PZ4.C78Pu [PS3553.0633]   813′.5′4   77-4923
ISBN 0-670-58200-X

Printed in the United States of America
Set in Linotype Bodoni

ACKNOWLEDGMENTS:
  Fred Rose Music, Inc.: From "Hey, Good
Lookin' " by Hank Williams, © Copyright 1951
Fred Rose Music, Inc.; all rights reserved.
From "Ramblin' Man" by Hank Williams,
© Copyright 1951 Fred Rose Music, Inc.; all
rights reserved. Both used by permission of the
publisher.
  United Artists: Lyrics on Pages 241 and 243
from "High Noon" by Ned Washington and
Dimitri Tiomkin, Copyright © 1952 Leo Feist,
Inc.
  Warner Bros. Music: From "42nd Street" by
Harry Warren and Al Dubin, © 1932 Warner
Bros. Inc.; Copyright renewed; all rights
reserved; used by permission.

  I wish to thank the Guggenheim and
Rockefeller foundations for grants which were
of great help in writing this book.
                                        —R. C.

For the sixth time, the mousy little engineer and his wife, waiting in Sing Sing's death house, had petitioned the highest tribunal. . . . For the sixth time, a majority of the nine Justices rejected a Rosenberg appeal. . . . Then, as the clock ticked on toward 11 p.m. Thursday, the hour of death for the spies, Supreme Court Justice William Douglas acted alone. Unexpectedly, the court having recessed for the summer, he granted the stay of execution that the full court had denied. That touched off, within the next 24 hours, one of the most dramatic and novel episodes in all the august annals of the U.S. Supreme Court. . . .

> —"The Last Appeal,"
> TIME, June 29, 1953

That's what I'm counting on most of all—the stories.
> —JOSEPHINE PARIS (as played by Ethel Rosenberg) in *The Valiant*, by H. E. Porter and Robert Middlemass

Of course, none of us had much money at the time, so we would just meet at someone's house after skating and have food, a spaghetti dinner or something of that type, and then we would sit around and tell stories and laugh. Dick was always the highlight of the party because he has a wonderful sense of humor. He would keep everybody in stitches. Sometimes we would even act out parts. I will never forget one night when we did "Beauty and the Beast." Dick was the Beast, and one of the other men dressed up like Beauty. This sounds rather silly to be telling it now, but in those days we were all very young. . . . It was good, clean fun, and we had loads of laughs.
> —MRS. RICHARD NIXON

All my humor is situation stuff. . . .
> —MR. RICHARD NIXON

I did not come to tell you things that you know as well as I.
> —DWIGHT DAVID EISENHOWER
> April 7, 1953

FOR JUSTICE WILLIAM O. DOUGLAS,
who exchanged a greeting with me while
out walking on the old canal towpath
one day not long after these events . . .

Contents

PROLOGUE

Groun'-Hog Hunt

On June 24, 1950, less than five years after the end of World War II, the Korean War begins, American boys are again sent off in uniforms to die for Liberty, and a few weeks later, two New York City Jews, Julius and Ethel Rosenberg, are arrested by the FBI and charged with having conspired to steal atomic secrets and pass them to the Russians. They are tried, found guilty, and on April 5, 1951, sentenced by the Judge to die—thieves of light to be burned by light—in the electric chair, for it is written that "any man who is dominated by demonic spirits to the extent that he gives voice to apostasy is to be subject to the judgment upon sorcerers and wizards." Then, after the usual series of permissible sophistries, the various delaying moves and light-restoring counter-moves, their fate—as the U.S. Supreme Court refuses for the sixth and last time to hear the case, locks its doors, and goes off on holiday—is at last sealed, and it is determined to burn them in New York City's Times Square on the night of their fourteenth wedding anniversary, Thursday, June 18, 1953.

There are reasons for this: theatrical, political, whimsical. It is thought that such an event might provoke open confessions: the Rosenbergs, until now tight-lipped and unrepentant, might at last, once on stage and the lights up, perceive their national role and fulfill it, freeing themselves before their deaths from the Phantom's dark mysterious power, unburdening themselves for the people, and might thereby bring others as well—to the altar, as it were—to cleanse their souls of the Phantom's taint. Many believe, moreover, that such a communal pageant is just what the troubled nation needs right now to renew its sinking spirit. Something archetypal, tragic, exemplary. Things have not been too good since the new war began—especially since the Chinese Reds came swarming across the Yalu and put our boys to rout—there's a need for distractions, and who knows? done right, it could bring a new excitement into the world, lift hearts, get things moving again, maybe even bring victory to the Free Peoples of Asia, courage to the rioting workers in enslaved Eastern Europe, fertility and tax reductions to the nation, all this is possible. And though the delays in the courts have at times perhaps been worrying, it is all coming together now in this time and place like magic. Fourteen, after all, symbolizes fusion and organization, justice and temperament; the City is this year celebrating the tercentenary of its own founding as New Amsterdam, its axis the Times Tower is in its Silver Anniversary year, and the Statue of Liberty—Our Lady of the Harbor, Refuge of the Destitute, Ark of the Covenant, Regina Coeli, Mother Full of Goodness, Star of the Sea and Gem of the Ocean—is sixty-nine; Times Square itself is an American holy place long associated with festivals of rebirth; and spring is still in the air. It is even hoped that a fierce public exorcism right now might flush the Phantom from his underground cells, force him to materialize, show himself plainly in the honest electrical glow of an all-American night-on-the-town, give Uncle Sam something to swing at besides a lot of remote gooks.

Weeks before, the designated area is cordoned off with police barricades and a stage is erected at the intersection of Broadway and Seventh Avenue on top of the information kiosk. This stage is built to simulate the Death House at Sing Sing, its walls whitewashed and glaringly lit, furnished simply with the old oaken electric chair, cables and heating pipes, a fire extinguisher, a mop and bucket for cleaning up the involuntary evacuations of the victims, and a trolley for carting the corpses off. The switch is visible through an open door, stage right, illuminated by a hanging spot. Other elegantly paneled doors, right, exit off to press and autopsy rooms, and upstage left another door leads in from the "Last Mile," or "Dance Hall." Over this entry, which the Rosenbergs will use, a sign is tacked up that reads: SILENCE. Details from the set of the Warden's Office in *The Valiant*, a one-act melodrama by Holworthy Hall (*pseud.*) and Robert Middlemass about a condemned man wrongly accused, produced in the early thirties by the Clark House Players on the Lower East Side and featuring starry-eyed sixteen-year-old Ethel Greenglass, are incorporated (a telephone instrument, a row of electric bell buttons, a bundle of forty or fifty letters, etc.), partly to make Ethel feel more at home, partly to impress upon her the ironies of her situation, partly just to surprise her with a little jolt of déjà vu.

Special seating sections are set up out front, camera platforms are built, backstage VIP passageways, wedding altars, sideshows, special light and sound systems. The streets funneling into Times Square are hung with bunting (the Square is not a square at all, of course, and from above the decorated area looks a little like a red-white-and-blue Star of David); traffic is rerouted so as to cause maximum congestion and rage, a solid belt of fury at the periphery being an essential liturgical complement to the melting calm at the center; and billboards and theater marquees, the principal topographical feature of the district, are consecrated to the display of homespun American wisdom:

EVERY MAN MUST CARRY HIS OWN HIDE TO THE TANNER

OUR LIVES ARE MERELY STRANGE DARK INTERLUDES
IN THE ELECTRICAL DISPLAY OF GOD THE FATHER!

AMERICA THE HOPE OF THE WORLD

NICE GUYS FINISH LAST

THREE MAY KEEP A SECRET IF TWO OF THEM ARE DEAD

An Entertainment Committee is appointed, chairmanned by Cecil B. De Mille, whose latest success was last year's Oscar-winning *Greatest Show on Earth*, with assistance from Sol Hurok, Dan Topping, Bernard Baruch, the AEC and Betty Crocker, Conrad Hilton, whose Albuquerque hotel figured prominently in the prosecution's case against the Rosenbergs, Sam Goldwyn and Walt Disney, Ed Sullivan, the director of the Mormon Tabernacle Choir, the various chiefs of staff, Sing Sing Warden Wilfred Denno, the Holy Six, and many more. They audition vocalists, disk jockeys, preachers, and stand-up comics, view rushes of Uncle Sam's new documentary on the two little Rosenberg boys intended as a back projection for the burnings, commission Oliver Allstorm and His Pentagon Patriots to compose a special pageant theme song, assign a task force of experienced sachems to work up a few spontaneous demonstrations, and hire a Texas high-school marching band to play "One Fine Day" from *Madame Butterfly*, "The Anniversary Waltz," and the theme from *High Noon*, said to be a particular favorite these days of President Eisenhower. The President, just back from a week of moralizing and whoopee in the Badlands and Oyster Bay, has been visited at the White House this week by the Singing Cowboy Gene Autry, and Gene has been invited to render "When It's

Twilight on the Trail" and "Back in the Saddle Again" at the electrocutions. TIME, the National Poet Laureate, celebrating this spring his own thirtieth birthday, is asked by the Committee to read a commemorative poem, an American middleweight championship bout between Bobo Olson and Paddy Young is appended to the program, and someone hires Harry James and His Orchestra to play overhead on the Astor Roof. Efforts are made to rush through a new ordinance allowing the sale of liquor in city theaters, and thus by extension in Times Square on Thursday night. The weather has turned hot, and in such a pack-up it will help if there's something with which to wet the whistle. As the day draws near, a massive contingent of New York State Troopers is dispatched to Ossining to relieve the 290 overworked prison police now guarding the Rosenbergs and to escort the atom spies to the city—and all of the other principals in the case are to be brought here as well: the Judge and jury, prosecution team and witnesses, including Ethel Rosenberg's kid brother David Greenglass, the Los Alamos soldier whose self-incriminating evidence almost single-handedly brought about the convictions of Ethel and her husband and got them condemned to the electric chair. This chair, now looming stark and fearful on the Times Square stage, is the singular responsibility of State Executioner Joseph P. Francel, World War I veteran and Cairo, New York, electrician. Francel, who was badly gassed in the war, is a professional who has hastened hundreds of malefactors to their deaths—in fact, he is celebrating his own fourteenth anniversary this year as Sing Sing Executioner, having first been appointed on Columbus Day, 1939, and will receive a bonus $300 for this double bill. All of this is taken as a good omen.

Not that Americans are superstitious, of course. How could they be, citizens of this, the most rational nation (under God) on earth? They need no omens to pull a switch, turn a buck, or change the world, for these are the elected sons and daughters of Uncle Sam, né Sam Slick, that wily Yankee Peddler who, much like that ballsy Greek girl of long ago, popped virgin-born and fully constituted from the shattered seed-poll of the very Enlightenment—"slick," as the Evangels put it, "as a snake out of a black skin!" Young Sam, "lank as a leafless elm," already chin-whiskered and plug-hatted and all rigged out in his long-tailed blue and his striped pantaloons, his pockets stuffed with pitches, patents, and pyrotechnics, burst upon the withering Old World like a Fourth of July skyrocket, snorting and neighing like a wild horse: "Who—Whoo—*Whoop!* Who'll come gouge with me? Who'll come bite with me? Rowff—Yough—Snort—*YAHOO!* In the name of the great Jehovah and the Continental Congress, I have passed the Rubicon—swim or sink, live or die, survive or perish, I'm in fer a fight, I'll go my death on a fight, and with a firm reliance on the pertection of divine protestants, a fight I must have, or else I'll have to be salted down to save me from spilin'! You hear me over thar, you washed-up varmints? This is the hope of the world talkin' to you! I am Sam Slick the Yankee Peddler—I can ride on a flash of lightnin', catch a thunderbolt in my fist, swaller niggers whole, raw or cooked, slip without a scratch down a honey locust, whup my weight in wildcats and redcoats, squeeze blood out of a turnip and cold cash out of a parson, and out-inscrutabullize the heathen Chinee—so whar's that Johnny Bull to stomp his hoof or quiver his hindquarters at *my* Proklymation? Whoo-*oop!* we love our cuppa tea, boys, but we love our freedom more, so bow yore necks and spread, you Hottentots, it is vain to extenuate the matter, the kingdom of sorrow's a-comin' and the Child of Calamity with her, and may Great Britain rue the day her hostile bands come hither! Lo, I say unto you, I have put a crimp in a cat-a-mount with my bare hands, hugged a cinnamon b'ar to death, and made a grizzly sing 'Jesus, Lover of My Soul' in a painful duet with his own arsehole—*and I have not yet begun to fight!* Yippee! I'm wild and woolly and fulla fleas, ain't never been curried below the knees, so if you wish to avoid foreign collision you had better abandon the ocean, women and children first! For we hold these truths to be self-evident: that God helps them what helps themselves, it's a mere matter of marchin'; that idleness is emptiness and he who lives on hope will die with his foot in his mouth; that no nation was ever ruint by trade; and that nothin' is sartin but death, taxes, God's glowin' Covenant, enlightened self-interest, certain unalienated rights, and woods, woods, woods, as far as the world extends!"

The American Autolycus, they called him in the Gospels, referring to his cunning powers of conjuration, transmutation, and magical consumption (he can play the shell game, not with a mere pea, but with whole tin mines, forests, oil fields, mountain ranges, and just before Thanksgiving this past year made an entire island disappear!), and it's been said that when he steps across the continent and sits down on Pike's Peak, and snorts in his handkerchief of red, white, and blue, the earth quakes and monarchs tremble on their thrones. . . .

"Oh, we must fight! I repeat it, sir, I am feelin' awesome wolfy about the head and shoulders and I must have a fight, those who expects to reap the blessings of freedom must, like men, undergo the fatigue of twistin' noses and scrougin' eyeballs and rib-brakin' and massacreein'! So carry the flag, you sons a Liberty, hang on to yer balls and keep step to the music of the Union, our brethren are already in the field, why stand we here idle? Time is money! No pent-up Utica contracts our powers, but the whole boundless continent is ours, it's as much a law of nature as that the Mississippi should flow to the sea or that trade follers the flag! *Fear* is the fundament of most guvvamints, so let's get the boot in, boys, and listen to 'em scream, let us anny-mate and encourage each other—*whoo-PEE!*—and show the whole world that a Freeman, contendin' for Liberty on his own ground, can out-run, out-dance, out-jump, chaw more tobacky and spit less, out-drink, out-holler, out-finagle and out-lick any yaller, brown, red, black, or white thing in the shape of human that's ever set his onfortunate kickers on Yankee soil! It is our manifest dust-in-yer-eye to overspread the continent allotted by Providence for the free development of our yearly multiplyin' millions, so damn the torpedoes and full steam ahead, fellow ripstavers, we cannot escape history! Boliterate 'em we must, for our cause it is just what the doctor ordered, logic is logic, that's all I say, and remember, if you will not hear Reason, she will surely rap yore knuckles! I tell you, we want *elbow-room*—the continent—the *whole* continent—and nothin' *but* the continent! And—by gum!—we will *have* it!"

And thus it was that the mighty Sam Slick, star-spangled Superhero and knuckle-rapping Yankee Peddler, lit upon the Western World in all his rugged strength and radiant beauty, expounding what the Disciple Rufus Choate called "the glittering and sounding generalities of natural right which make up the Declaration of Independence," sharpening his wits on the hard flint of war and property speculation, and honing his first principles by skinning the savages and backwoods scavengers and picking the pockets of the thieving princes of Europe. He's been committed ever since to propagating the Doctrine of Self-Determination and Free Will and bringing the Light of Reason to the benighted and superstitious nations of the earth, still groping clumsily out of the Dark Ages like breech births from a mother turned to stone, so neither he nor his kith can be easily overawed by this or that putative portent.

Nevertheless, as General George Washington himself—who as the Primordial Incarnation had led the nation in its escape from what he called "a gloomy age of ignorance and superstition"—once put it: "No people can be bound to acknowledge and adore the invisible hand which conducts the affairs of men more than the people of the United States. Every step, by which they have advanced to the character of an independent nation, seems to have been distinguished by some token of providential agency!" This was true then, it is true now. Throughout the solemn unfolding of the American miracle, men have noticed this remarkable phenomenon: what at the moment seems to be nothing more than the random rise and fall of men and ideas, false starts and sudden brainstorms, erratic bursts of passion and apathy, brief setbacks and partial victories, is later discovered to be—in the light of America's gradual unveiling as the New Athens, New Rome, and New Jerusalem all in one—a necessary and inevitable sequence of interlocking events, a divine code, as it were, bringing the Glad Tidings of America's election, and fulfilling the oracles of every tout from John the Seer and Nostradamus to Joseph and Adam Smith. The American Prophet S. D. Baldwin summed it up in a nutshell in the title of his 1854 classic: *Armageddon: or the Overthrow of Romanism and Monarchy; the Existence of the United States Foretold in the Bible, Its Future Greatness; Invasion by Allied Europe; Annihilation of Monarchy; Expansion into the Millennial Republic, and Its Dominion over the Whole World.* All Incarnations of Uncle Sam have noticed this and been humbled by it, and Dwight Eisenhower, the newest, is no exception. Speaking in Abilene just last fall, the Man of Destiny revealed his own brush with Illuminating Grace: "This day eight years ago, I made the most agonizing decision of my life. I had to decide to postpone by at least twenty-four hours the most formidable array of fighting ships and of fighting men that was ever launched across the sea against a hostile shore. The consequences of that decision at that moment could not have been foreseen by anyone. If there were nothing else in my life to prove the existence of an almighty and merciful God, the events of the next twenty-four hours did it. . . . The greatest break in a terrible outlay of weather occurred the next day and allowed that great invasion to proceed, with losses far below those we had anticipated!" No, friends, America has not arisen: *it has been called forth!* It's like the Divine Hawthorne once said: "There is a fatality, a feeling so irresistible and inevitable that it has the force of doom . . . !"

Something like that force seems to have been at work all over the world these past few weeks: everything tumbling irresistibly into place. Not without a bit of push and shove from Uncle Sam, of course: red-and-white striped hat cocked jauntily, blue cutaway coattails fluttering behind him like a wartorn battle flag, he's been advancing on all fronts, sweeping away the hostile shadows of the world, stemming the Red Tide, producing miracles with gamma globulin, chlorophyll, and laminated iron duck underpants for American Marines to keep their balls safe from flying mortar fragments, securing the resources of poor nations from the Phantom's greed, sprinkling the spirit of truth and plutocracy on the world like a purifying fallout. But some days it seems to work and some it doesn't, and right now it's working. That force. He has overseen the patient extermination by saturation bombing of a thousand Mau Mau terrorists, a movement described by the British Colonial Secretary as "perverted nationalism and a sort of nostalgia for barbarism," and then back home has flown out to that wide open country that he loves, and crying out, *I lift my lamp beside the golden door!*", has struck the match that set off the most powerful A-bomb of all time: a frame house ten miles away collapses, acres of Joshua trees and sagebrush burst into flames, the flash is observed a thousand miles away in Canada and Mexico, and residents of Southern California feel the shock twenty minutes after the blast. Atomic Energy Commissioner Gordon Dean, admiring the 40,000-foot-high cloud of radioactive dust, reflects on the infancy of Hiroshima's "Little Boy" and says that this year will see Atomic Power come of age. In Korea Uncle Sam has broken the intransigence of the Reds, bringing them to the conference table if not to their knees, while further down the coast pro-French candidates have won all localities except Hanoi in the first real democratic election those little yellow people of Indochina have ever known. Not far away, the fifth year of the Red War in Malaya ends symbolically with the extermination of five guerrillas, British High Commissioner General Sir Gerald Templer expressing "satisfaction" over the kill and declaring: "The struggle goes on and it will go on until we have eliminated all traces of militant Communism from this country!"

No less a struggle is being waged in America. Police juvenile officers warn teen-age clubs in Columbus, Ohio, to be suspicious of "any new member of a group whose background is not an open book," and in Birmingham, Alabama, the city fathers push through an ordinance banishing from the city "anyone caught talking to a Communist in a 'non-public place,' or anyone who passed out literature that could be traced, even remotely, to a Communist hand." The home of the State Secretary of the Communist Party in Houston, Texas, is stoned, and outside a plant in Los Angeles, surprised workers get the piss beat out of them by a gang of aroused patriots calling themselves "Crusade Against Communism." There's been an abortive effort to muzzle Senator Joe McCarthy, but the Fighting Marine has hit back, seeing to it that the worst of his enemies are kicked out of Congress by the people and, if possible, ruined for life, and now his metaphors grip the national imagination utterly. Rare is that politician who fails to pay at least passing homage to the "crimson clique," "left-wing bleeding hearts of the press," "front men for traitors," and "stained with the blood of our boys in Korea." Joe launches a whole series of new investigations into heresy in high places, becoming one of the most celebrated orators in the nation. Some people believe he might even be the secret Incarnation of Uncle Sam—a heresy in itself perhaps, but one long tolerated in the democratic tradition. He is hailed by J. Edgar Hoover for his "Americanism," cheered on by his colleagues, and awarded a "National Americanism Award" by the Marine Corps League for his heroic actions in "rousing the nation to the menace of bad security risks in our government." The American Civil Liberties Union reports that twenty-six of the forty-eight states now have laws designed to bar Reds from running for public office, twenty-eight have laws denying them state or local civil-service jobs, thirty-two require loyalty oaths from their teachers, and across the country, suspected Comsymps are prevented from living in federally aided low-income housing projects, getting passports, holding office in labor unions, or in some states, drawing unemployment compensation. Congressman James Van Zandt of Pennsylvania asks for swift deportation to the Soviet Union of all alien Communists and fellow travelers, in or out of government. Private travel into Phantom-land is simultaneously banned and infiltration from abroad is blocked, J. Edgar Hoover's budget is increased, and Senator Harley Kilgore of West Virginia drafts a bill to "grant the FBI war emergency powers to throw all Communists into concentration camps!"

And so it goes, from one end of the world to the other, because, as Dr. Norman Vincent Peale has written in his book of Yankee Peddler's proverbs, *The Power of Positive Thinking*, America's runaway number one best seller for the thirty-second week running: "This is the one lesson history teaches . . . The good never loses!" Fulgencio Batista regains control of Cuba and General Rojas Pinilla, who fought with Uncle Sam as a staff officer with the first contingent of Colombian troops to Korea in 1951, pulls a quick coup in his country and ousts Laureano Gomez, who as TIME say: "slid like a wilted leaf down / history's drainpipe." From the Dominican Republic Generalissimo Trujillo ("an illustrious ruler," the young Vice President Richard Nixon has called him) sends a priest as delegate to the United Nations, explaining that his country intends to use "the arms of faith and Christian charity to combat the poisonous Communist doctrine in the international organization," and on television the Reverend Billy Graham backs him up: "Communism is a fanatical religion," he declares, "a great sinister anti-

Christian movement masterminded by Satan, that has declared war upon the Christian God! Only as millions of Americans turn to Jesus Christ can the nation be spared the onslaught of a demon-possessed Communism!" Yes, Daniel Webster expressed it long ago: *"Whatever makes men good Christians, makes them good citizens!"* A survey by the *Catholic Digest* shows that 89 percent of all Americans, including Jews, believe in the Blessed Trinity, and 99 percent believe in God—get rid of that one percent, it's said, and the Phantom's had it!

Not even the innermost precincts of the Phantomized world have been immune. In the Soviet Union Josef Stalin's heart "has stopped beating," and his presumptive heirs—Beria, Molotov, Malenkov, and Khrushchev—are said to be at each other's throats. As though in sympathy, Czech Puppet Klement Gottwald has "died of a cold," and strikes and riots have crippled the country. And now, overnight, with the Rosenberg executions just a day away, the big breakthrough comes: the East Germans, who until now have been fleeing Westward at the rate of nearly fifty thousand a month, suddenly stop, as though on cue, turn back, and confront their masters . . .

> barehanded they gathered in the grey
> morning rain—masons in white
> carpenters in black day laborers
> and factory hands in hobnailed
>   boots and raveled suits
>
> in mumbling columns that suggested
> disconnected centipede legs groping
> for a body they streamed from all
> directions toward the center where
>   the communist proconsuls rule
>
> shopkeepers clanged down shutters peered
> through the slits children on bicycles
> circled in front trucks twisted through
> the crowd nose to tail like a team
>   of prodding sheep dogs
>
> an east german perched shakily
> on an idle cement mixer
> pointed with a sneer at a tall vopo
> "hello long one!" he cried "your
>   pants are open!"

anger scudded in like a rain cloud
"freedom" they chanted thousands
began chanting the forbidden anthem
deutschland deutschland über alles
über alles in der welt!

on both sides of the iron curtain
the world heard with a thrill
of east berlin's

rebellion in the rain . . .

"The Rebellion in the Rain": no wonder TIME's been inspired! This uprising in Berlin, which soon spreads to Magdeburg, Jena, Chemnitz, Rathenow, Leipzig, Halle—in Brandenburg, workers maul the Red D.A. to death on top of a police car and rip the ear off a "people's judge," while Czechs are pissing in Pilsen on portraits of dead Puppet Gottwald—is Uncle Sam's crowning touch to over two years of stagecraft, prayer, and arm-to-arm Injun rassling with the Phantom's ubiquitous agents.

But it has not always been easy, not even for America's mighty Superhero. The tag end of the 1940s, which began so well, has seen the Red Tide swallow up half of Europe, sweep through Cathay and threaten all of South Asia, batter at the shores of Africa, Byzantium, and Latin America.

How did it happen?

The score in the middle of the decade is 1,625,000,000 people for Uncle Sam, only 180,000,000 for the Phantom, and most of them in declining health, thanks to Overlord, German tanks, and the A-bomb. What's more, no sooner has Uncle Sam, virtually single-handed, won the war and saved humanity but what he's out inventing the United Nations, unleashing television, laying a dose of freedom and morality on the Hottentots, funding the World Bank, and humbly taking over the world for its own good—he's had to use up one of his best Incarnations of all time to do it, but it's worth it. With the bodies of the Nazi hoodlums still dangling warm on their ropes, Ely Culbertson the Bridge Wizard can announce to the world: "God and the politicians willing, the United States can declare peace on the world and win it!" That's mainly because the U.S. is holding trumps, of course—and keeping them. As Harry Truman, Uncle Sam's unusual new disguise, puts it: "The atomic bomb is too dangerous to be let loose in a lawless world. That is why Great Britain, Canada, and the United States, who have the secret of its production, do not intend to reveal that secret until means have been found to control the bomb." It seems like the Golden Age—like Mother Luce's dream of "The American Century" come true!

And yet, suddenly, by the end of the decade, the Phantom has a score of 800,000,000 to Uncle Sam's 540,000,000 and the rest—about 600,000,-000 so-called neutrals—are adrift. What went wrong? Who's responsible? People wonder if this is what the astronomers are talking about when they speak of the "red shift": God drifting away and losing touch. The Phantom's dark gospel has spread throughout the world, he has acquired dozens of new disguises and devices, Uncle Sam's most private councils have been infiltrated. Not that the American Superchief and his Sons of Light have been idle—the Truman Doctrine has wrested Greece and Turkey from the Phantom's grasp, the Marshall Plan has saved Christianity in Europe, West Germany and South Korea have been improvised, staffed, and armed, the Strategic Air Command has been revved up with atomic weapons and NATO created, and Point Four is spreading the American Dream upon the Yahoos like manna—but you can't argue with the scoreline. "In 1944," as Congressman Richard Nixon of California sums it up, "the odds were nine to one in our favor. Today . . . the odds are five to three against us!" And worse to come: in a few short weeks, before the 1949 World Series has even begun, Mao Tse-tung chases Chiang Kai-shek's bony behind off to Formosa and the Reds take over all of China, America is hit by its first postwar recession, the U.S. Secretary of Defense commits suicide, and on top of it all, Russia explodes her first atomic bomb!

The news rocks the nation. *"Treason!"* cries the press. Others agree. "If the President says the American people are entitled to know all the facts," declares Congressman Nixon, "I feel the American people are also entitled to know the facts about the espionage ring which was responsible for turning over information on the atom bomb to agents of the Russian government!" *Espionage ring?!* Here Uncle Sam's been seeding the rubes gathering outside his tent all these years with whole pressruns of fresh greenbacks, and now that his wares are out on the table and it's time for the payoff, not only have they pocketed the bait and wandered off, making ungrateful ridicule the while of his "Yankee notions," but some bastard's even picked his pockets while he was watching them go! *"Sweet Betsey from Pike, I been hit by a pooper!"* cries Uncle Sam as the Russian bomb mushrooms into the ether. *"Thar she blows, goddamn it, our just and lasting peace with honor in our time, shot to shit, it's most enough to make a deacon swear! Ed-GAR!"*

Deep in the inner sanctum of the Federal Bureau of Investigation, high up on the fifth floor, J. Edgar Hoover, the world's most famous policeman, lost for a moment in reverie and congratulatory telegrams (he is this year celebrating his Silver Anniversary as America's Top Cop, his career being contemporaneous with that of Mickey Mouse), jumps clean out of his chair. What? What! He stumbles about confusedly, scattering dossiers, old $2 betting stubs, and comic books depicting his own life saga every which way. Holy Moley! This is terrible! His heart is palpitating, his florid face is splotchy, his trigger finger has gone cold and limp as a wet noodle. It's times like these when John Edgar Hoover of the FBI wishes his mother were still alive. Of course it's a spy ring, has to be, it always is. I *mean*, there's only one secret, isn't there? We had it, now they've got it, it's that simple. He's been warning them this would happen since 1937. The enemy within. Now, just look! Jumping Jehoshaphat! And if they could penetrate Los Alamos, they could penetrate Congress or the White House, or even—he pushes the thought out of his mind and, glancing edgily over his shoulder, scrambles frantically for the intercom buttons. Goodness! he's all thumbs! This is worse than the day he tried to put the cuffs on Old Creepy Karpis! He whacks the intercom with his thick fists and cries: "The secret of the atom bomb has been stolen! Mobilize every resource! Find the thieves!" He cries:

> Call up yer dog, O call up yer dog,
> Le's go a-huntin' to ketch a groun'-hog!

> Whet up ye knife an' loaden up ye gun,
> Away to the hills to have some fun!

Up on Capitol Hill, Early Warning Sentinels Mundt, Bridges, Nixon, and Hickenlooper take up the chorus: "To-my-rang-tang-a-whaddle-linky-dey!" It mushrooms into a countrywide singalong, orchestrated by the national press. G-men, whistling along softly, scurry through the FBI building and out secret exits, buttoning up their trench coats . . .

> They picked up their guns an' went to the brash,
> By dam, Joe, here's the hog sign fraish!

> Git away, Sam, an' lemme load my gun,
> The groun'-hog hunt has jist begun!

FBI double agent Herbert Philbrick breaks his cover, and eleven top U.S. Communists are nailed as fanatical schismatics. Spying charges and naughty rumors are slapped on Judy Coplon from Justice and a Russian plant in the U.N. Wartime New Dealers are implicated, and the shadow of suspicion falls heavily on apostate Henry Wallace—once but a heart-beat away from the Incarnation—plus the million people who voted for him in 1948. And, thanks to the untiring vigilance of Congressman Nixon—who has already helped to sanitize Hollywood and the labor unions, and co-sponsored a tough-fisted Communist registration bill, which even Harry Truman has to admit is the equal of the Alien and Sedition Act of John Adams's heyday—the slippery Alger Hiss is run to ground at last . . .

> He's in here, boys, the hole's wore slick!
> Run here, Sam, with ye forkéd stick!

> Stand back, boys, an' le's be wise,
> Fer I think I see his beaded eyes!

"The only sensible and courageous way to deal with Communists in our midst," declares Hearst columnist Westbrook Pegler, "is to make membership in Communist organizations or covert subsidies a capital offense and shoot or otherwise put to death all persons convicted of such!" Congressman Harold Velde, an ex–FBI agent elected to the House on the slogan GET THE REDS OUT OF WASHINGTON AND WASHINGTON OUT OF THE RED, has a celebrated vision of Russian espionage agents running amok all over the country, and his Pennsylvania colleague Bob Rich, speaking in tongues, lets fly the suspicion that Secretary of State Dean Acheson *might* be working for Stalin himself! "The great lesson which should be learned from the Alger Hiss case," Dick Nixon warns, "is that we are not just dealing with espionage agents who get thirty pieces of silver to obtain the blueprint of a new weapon . . . but this is a far more sinister type of activity, because it permits the enemy to guide and shape our policy!" To that, Mr. Republican himself, Senator Bob Taft, says: "Hey! to-my-whang-fol-doodle-daddy-*dey*, Dick!" And in Wheeling, West Virginia, Senator Joe McCarthy, the Fighting Marine, waves a piece of paper—"I have here in my hand a list . . . !"—and launches an Era . . .

> Up jumped Joe with a ten-foot pole,
> He roused it in that groun'-hog's hole!

"A list," says he, "of two hundred and five . . . card-carrying Communists in the State Department!" He says: "Commiecrats! Prisoners of a bureaucratic Communistic Frankenstein! Parlor pinks and parlor punks! Prancing mimics of the Moscow party line in the *State* Department!" Oh yes! "Egg-sucking phony liberals," says he, whose "pitiful squealing . . . would hold sacrosanct those Communists and queers" who had sold China into "atheistic slavery!" He says: "A conspiracy so immense and an infamy so black as to dwarf any previous such venture in the history of man!" He says:

> Stand back, boys, an' gimme a little air,
> I've got a little o' the groun'-hog's hair!
>
> I heard 'im give a whistle an' a wail,
> I've wound my stick right in his tail!

"I thank God," cries the Reverend Billy Graham, "for men who in the face of public denouncement and ridicule go loyally on in their work of exposing the pinks, the lavenders, and the reds who have sought refuge beneath the wings of the American eagle, and from that vantage point try in every subtle, undercover way to bring comfort, aid and help to the greatest enemy we have ever known, Communism!" And then, while Bible-belters, ex–FBI agents, Catholic hardliners and anti-Zionists, ladies' clubs, Hearst newsmen, the legendary China Lobby, patriotic queer-bashers, and most of the Republican and Democratic parties surge around Joe to get a piece of History, the besieged President, egged on by Bernard Baruch, Edward Teller, Columbia University's Dwight Eisenhower, and an uptight Dean Acheson, overrules the Atomic Energy Commission and sets in motion a new crash program: TRUMAN ORDERS HELL BOMB BUILT! "I wasn't going to be one of your arm-rolling cheek-kissing mollycoddles!" says Harry. Du Pont gets the H-bomb contract, cash on the line. But already it may be too late . . .

> Stand back, boys, an' lemme git my breath,
> Ketchin' this groun'-hog's might nigh death!
> To-my-wham-bam-diddle-all-the-day . . . !

Up on the fifth floor of the FBI buildings, surrounded by souvenirs from his epic past and autographed photos from the radio stars of "The FBI in Peace and War," Crimebuster J. Edgar Hoover, hand-in-hand with his bachelor friend Clyde Tolson, oversees the spy-ring hunt. "Clyde," he says, feeling a bit giddy, unable to suppress a soft little giggle, "this is the Crime of the Century!" "You said it, Eddie," says Clyde. The entire FBI is mobilized for the hunt. They are digging into records at Los Alamos, poring through AEC personnel files, badgering a few old suspects, interviewing hundreds of people. Others, disguised as tourists, slip catlike through the ghettos of the nation's cities, in deep where the unassimilated live, speaking alien tongues, eating weird shit, their seed still frothy with unhomogenized Old World discontents; 90 percent of all Commies in this country, as every G-man knows, are foreign-born or were dropped by foreign-born parents. But chasing them down is like falling down a well: there are nearly forty million of these yahooskis in the U.S., plus all their goddamn kids—over three hundred thousand Russians in New York City alone—it's an impossible job. Knock knock! Who's dere? Police! Police who? Uh, police tuh meet yuh, lady. Thistle be quick. Chester routine inquiry. Hassan a body here seen a spy ring? We all aspiring, mister, it's a Mary kin way! Clem the ladder of success, you know? Gopher broke. Hokay? Well, yeah, but . . . C'mon, Thomas money, copper, and Eisenhower late as it is! Yes'm, Czar Rhee tuh bother yuh. Dewey have your pardon? Sure, son, Hiss all right, to err is Truman. Better luck on the—knock knock!— Nixon . . .

But then suddenly Scotland Yard of Great Britain arrests a high-domed bespectacled atomic scientist named Klaus Emil Julius Fuchs, and Fuchs confirms the darkest of Patriot visions: while working on the Manhattan Project in New York and Los Alamos, *he stole atomic secrets for the Russians!* It's all true! As *Newsweek* says: ". . . the fantastic is beginning to be accepted as fact. There are men like Fuchs and Hiss!" Fuchs describes his U.S. contact as a man "from 40 to 45 years of age, possibly five feet ten inches tall, broad build," and the FBI promptly arrests a soft little five-foot-six Russian immigrant ten years younger than that named Harry Gold, who quickly acknowledges that he is Dr. Fuchs's mystery man. His family is amazed by this confession of a ro-mantic double life, since Harry, who likes to amuse himself through the long nights with a little parlor baseball game played with a deck of cards, has never really left home. TIME say:

> why had harry gold done it?
> he could only mutter a line which
> a thousand sinners had muttered
> before "I must have been crazy"

While Harry embroiders on his saga and crystal-balls the American League pennant race for his captors, other agents interrogate a young ex-GI, a ne'er-do-well ghetto Jew and ex-Commie (pieces all falling into place), suspected of stealing uranium and other valuables during his days as a mechanic at Los Alamos. He doesn't want to talk about the thefts, but he *is* willing, when invited, to say he spied for the Russians. In prison, Harry Gold confers with the FBI and then tells his lawyer that he thinks there's going to be something extra about a GI in Albuquer-que: "Ah . . . This event, as I said, was—I'm not being—I'm being deadly serious when I say it was an extra added attraction. I use the term, as I said, not in any joking manner—because this is no joking matter—but simply because I believe it best describes the affair . . . Yakovlev told me that . . . after I had seen Klaus Fuchs I was to see another man. I don't remember the name of the street. We, uh, I think that their principal talk . . . concerned the difficulty of getting Jewish food, delicatessen, in a place like Albuquerque and a mention by the man that his family or possibly her family regularly sent them packages including salami . . . Yakovlev said we could forget all about him . . . apparently the information received had not been of very much consequence at all . . ." He doesn't remember the GI's name, some kind of mental block, but a couple of days later, after David Greenglass has been formally arrested, it comes to him: David Greenglass. Also, perhaps he was wrong about what Yakovlev said, probably. David is very contrite. He says his sister Ethel and her husband, Julius Rosenberg, made him do it. They had a kind of power over him. Harry Gold had forgotten about this connection, but with the FBI's help he begins to remember. Maybe that's who was sending the salami.

The net goes out and draws in Julius and Ethel Rosenberg, described by J. Edgar Hoover in one of his daily press releases as "important links in the Soviet espionage apparatus"—Rosenberg, Hoover declares the day he arrests him, had "aggressively sought ways and means to secretly conspire with the Soviet Government to the detriment of his own country!" Fuchs to Gold to Greenglass to Rosenberg—quadruple play!—and now what next? Praise pours in. "No finer body of men in all of the world," says a new federal judge. The FBI is getting its biggest headlines since the vintage years of the 1930s, and the Boss is exultant. He's reminded of a recurrent dream in which he's pulling on a kind of rope coming out of the ground, something like a navel-string, and the more he pulls out, the more there is. "We're going to need a new building, Clyde," he titters, and cracks open a celebrative bottle of Jack Daniel's. Walter Winchell invites him out to dinner at the Stork Club. People smile wherever he goes. Cabdrivers give him racing tips. Waiters bow. The cigarette girl thanks him from the bottom of her heart: "We're all praying for you, sir!" "You do that, miss," he replies gravely. "Suppose *every* American spent a little time each day, less than the time demanded by the Communists, in studying the Bible and the basic documents of American history, government, and culture? The result would be a new America, vigilant, strong, but ever humble in the service of God! All we need is faith, miss, *real faith!*" She swoons at his feet. As he steps around her, he thinks: This is a lot better than being a Presbyterian minister, I'm glad I changed my mind about that, after all. Only one momentary snag spoils an otherwise perfect evening: the Rosenbergs don't seem to know what everybody is talking about. But they give themselves away: they keep insisting on their "rights." Well, remind them they can rightfully get the chair for this, see what that does for their memory.

Meanwhile, former friends and ex-classmates of Rosenberg are tailed and questioned. Not much happens until it's discovered that one of them, a radar man named Morton Sobell, has apparently whipped off to Mexico in a wild blue funk: aha. Can't risk extraditing him, he might slip behind the Iron Curtain before those dumb greasers have got the papers processed, a goon squad has to be used. A bit irregular maybe, but when you're up against the Phantom, the rulebook goes out the window. Sobell is snatched and dragged, kicking and screaming like Jimmy Cagney in *Angels with Dirty Faces* (they have to bludgeon the *hijo de puta* to keep him in line), across the Rio Grande in the dead of the night to Laredo, where he's delivered to a waiting G-man—"Knock knock!" *Eh? Who dere?* "Grassy!" *Grassy? Grassy quién?* "Grassy-*ass*, amigos! Mooch-ass grassy-ass!" *Ha ha, de nada, jefe!*

> They took 'im by the tail an' wagged 'im to a log,
> An' swore by gum! he's a hell-of-a-'hog!

> Carried 'im to the house an' skinned 'im out to bile,
> I bet you forty dollars you could smell 'im fifty mile!

Smell him maybe, but you can't hear him: he's as adamantly uncooperative as the Rosenbergs—but no more kid gloves, no more time for pussyfooting, for Sam Slick is suddenly in a pot of trouble himself, more hogs than even he can boil: not only has the Phantom got Eastern Europe, China, veto power in the U.N., and the atomic bomb, but on the 24th day of June, 1950, precisely at two p.m. in the middle of Uncle Sam's Big Roundup, hot war has broken out in Korea! "Yowee! take thy beak from out my heart!" yelps Uncle Sam. "Blow the strumpet to arms! Strike up the band! We gotta raise the beacon-light o' triumph, snouse the citadel of the aggressor, and press onward to liberty and the Injun Ocean before that bluebellied bloodsuckin' scalawag snatches us bald-headed! Whoo-oop! Hang onto yore hats, boys, we're ridin' a tiger!"

Hastily, the Seventh Fleet hightails it out of Pearl Harbor, a trial date is set, troops are rushed to Korea. Greenglass and Gold are lodged together on the eleventh floor of the Tombs prison in New York, where they can help stimulate each other's recall powers. The Rosenbergs are separated for, obversely, the same reason. An ad appears in *The New York Times:* "From now on, let us make no mistake about it: the war is on, the chips are down. Those among us who defend Russia or Communism are enemies of freedom and traitors to the United Nations and the

United States. American soldiers are dying . . . every man's house will be in a target area before this ends!" The Yankee Peddler, turning to meet this new challenge in Asia, is knocked reeling—invading North Koreans cross the 38th Parallel and roll south; Americans land at Inchon, cross the 38th Parallel, and roll north; the Chinese People's Volunteers cross the Manchurian border and roll south—and by the time the clerk in Room 110 of the Foley Square Courthouse in New York City is ready to step forward on Tuesday morning, March 6, 1951, to call out the case of "the United States *versus* Julius Rosenberg, Ethel Rosenberg, and Morton Sobell, et al.," the whole scene is in great disarray, Uncle Sam doesn't know whether he's coming or going, the Mongol hordes of Red China have overrun Tibet as well as Korea and are pressing out in all directions like a bursting waterbag, the Russians are arrogantly lighting up the sky with atomic-bomb tests, the President and his General are at loggerheads, and Nightmare Alley—the escape route out of the Korean hills to the south—is littered with frozen American dead. "We have met the enemy," cries Uncle Sam, gasping for breath, "and bile me fer a seahorse if I wouldn't ruther crawl into a nest o' wildcats, heels foremost, than be cotched alone in the nighttime with one o' them heathen buggers again!" TIME's Mother Luce, who, perhaps inspired by the early successes, has been urging her son to push the idea of living with perpetual war as part of the American Way of Life, now writes despondently:

I had a call from John Foster Dulles, a very special assistant to Secretary of State Acheson. Dulles said he was at his home in New York and could I come after dinner. When I got there I found Foster and Brother Allen and a foreign service officer. The atmosphere was solemn. Foster Dulles put the situation to me concisely and precisely. He said the American army had been surrounded and a Marine division too. "It is," said Dulles, "the only army we have. And the question is: shall we ask for terms?" I could hardly believe my ears and that is what I said. . . .

As the brightly badged bailiff enters from the Judge's chambers and faces the packed courtroom in Foley Square, TIME's visionary kid brother is declaring: "LIFE sees no choice but to acknowledge the existence of war with Red China and to set about its defeat, in full awareness that this course will probably involve war with the Soviet Union as well!" Work on the H-bomb proceeds feverishly, but there are fears the Russians may have stolen that one before it's even been invented. Joe McCarthy, the Fighting Marine, demands that General MacArthur, who is widely reported to be "the greatest man alive," be given the discretionary authority in Asia for "speedy action of the roughest and toughest kind of which we are capable!" The bailiff pounds his knuckled fist on the door three times and calls out: *"Everybody please rise!"* There's a scraping of chairs, a scuffling of feet, the Strategic Air Command is put on alert, the Communist program for world domination is released by the House Un-American Activities Committee. A *New York Times* headline announces: DANGER OF ATOM BOMB ATTACK IS GREATEST IN PERIOD UP TO THIS FALL! The Judge enters—a ripple of surprise: Uncle Sam has chosen for his Easter Trial little Irving Kaufman, the Boy Judge, a stubby Park Avenue Jew and Tammany Hall Democrat who looks a little like a groundhog himself with his plastered-down hair, thick bumpy nose, and damp beady eyes. Old-time court buffs, however, glance at each other and wink knowingly. Not only are they great admirers of the Boy Judge's fine voice and his activist take-no-shit style of conducting a trial, but they know something most other people in the courtroom don't: that Irving Kaufman's own wife is a Rosenberg! They also know that Irving's an orphan, and though a Jew, a whizkid law-school graduate of Fordham University, the Roman Catholic farm for FBI agents (his classmates called him Pope Kaufman after he aced Christian Doctrine with a 99); that he was once a shrewd prosecutor, one of the original "Foley Squareheads," an admiring student of the tough-fisted tactics of the Fighting D.A. Tom Dewey, and the first prosecuting attorney in the district to use a wiretap as a weapon in a federal prosecution; and that when his appointment, sponsored by Carmine DeSapio, to become the youngest federal judge in the country was held up eighteen months ago, it was J. Edgar Hoover himself who came to the rescue. He mounts the steps to the bench, dragging his robes behind him, and stands there, peering over the top like Kilroy, while the court clerk announces that the court is now in session: IF SOVIETS START WAR, ATOMIC BOMB ATTACK EXPECTED ON NEW YORK FIRST, says the *Journal-American*. "All ye having business before this Court, come forward and ye shall be heard!" Julius and Ethel glance at each other, GIs lose another hill in Korea, and East Berlin policemen fire openly on U.S. Army sightseeing buses. The Russians are said to be massing troops on the Manchurian border. "God bless the United States of America!" cries the clerk. "Nobody will have to run if H-bombs start detonating. A big black cloud full of radioactive particles will get you even if . . . you happen to be browsing around the bottom of an abandoned lead mine!" Behind the Courthouse on Duane Street, the bells of St. Andrew's Church are striking the half hour. *"God bless this Honorable Court!"* There are fervent whispers of "Amen!" in the crowded courtroom. The Judge climbs up into the big leather chair

and sits down. Schoolchildren scramble under their desks in an atom
bomb drill, and an entire Yank company is bogged down in a Korean
rice paddy. "The District Attorney moves the case for trial," says the
Prosecutor gravely, adjusting his wire-rimmed glasses on his long nose,
"and is ready to proceed." He glances severely at the suspects who sit
stiffly in their chairs. ATOM BOMB SHELTERS FOR CITY AT COST OF $450,000,-
000 URGED.

If the choice of Judge is somewhat unexpected, the choice of Prosecutor is not: though a Tammany Hall ethnic like the Judge, Irving Saypol
is not only big in the Boy Scouts, Salvation Army, and Knights of Pythias,
he is also, as the National Poet Laureate says: "the nation's number /
one legal hunter of top / communists." Devious, hardboiled, fast on his
feet, he's a tough man to beat. This, however, is the most critical case of
Irving Saypol's career. American casualties in Korea are approaching the
one-hundred-thousand mark when he rises, tall, hard, and graying, to
make his opening statement. There are fears of imminent war everywhere
in Europe. He shuffles his thick sheaf of papers, smooths down the
pocket flap on his double-breasted suit jacket. Irving Saypol is a sonuvabitch at gin rummy, but does he hold the cards? The Speaker of the U.S.
House of Representatives warns that a third world war may be just
around the corner. Julius Rosenberg drums on the counsel table with
long nervous fingers, President Truman calls on all police officers and
citizens to be watchful for spies, saboteurs, and subversive activities. Saypol's gaggle of assistants and FBI investigators huddle close together,
watching their man. TENSION IS GRAVER THAN IN NOVEMBER, MARSHALL'S
BELIEF. Ethel Rosenberg edges forward on her chair, little worry lines
crossing her face, as she struggles to hear Prosecutor Saypol's muffled
low-key delivery: in soft flat tones he is accusing her of "the most serious
crime which can be committed against the people of this country."
Morton Sobell strokes his jaw, licks his lips, wrinkles his nose, confers
nervously with his lawyers. David Greenglass and Harry Gold come down
from the Tombs and, assisted by David's wife, Ruth, confess to spying,
perjury, conspiracy, and the lot, and then the Greenglasses say the
Rosenbergs were behind it all. Twenty other witnesses corroborate
minor details of their story—including Liz Bentley the Red Spy Queen,
who adds a bit of swish and dash to the proceedings. Julius and Ethel
take the stand and say it isn't so. When they're asked if they're Communists, though, they duck behind the Fifth Amendment. Morton Sobell,
who has been largely ignored in the testimony, figures they must have
forgotten about him and keeps his mouth shut. The members of the
jury, mostly accountants and auditors, retire and tote up the witness

score: 23 to 2 with 1 abstention. They return with a guilty verdict for all three, and the Judge says: "My own opinion is that your verdict is a correct verdict. . . . The thought that citizens of our country would lend themselves to destruction of their own country by the most destructive weapon known to man is so shocking that I can't find words to describe this loathsome offense! *God bless you all!*" He goes off to the Park Avenue Synagogue to pray and sneak a quick American cheese sandwich. TIME say:

it

was a

sickening and

to americans almost

incredible history of men

so fanatical that they would destroy

their own countries & col

leagues to serve a

treacherous

utopi

a

The Free Nations of the World, bracing for the holocaust, are fragmented and exhausted. Even sturdy little Judge Kaufman seems suddenly drawn and haggard, aged past his years, as he emerges from the synagogue, mounts the three steps to the bench, and in a hoarse faint voice charged with repugnance and something bordering on panic, tells the packed galleries: "These defendants made a choice of devoting themselves to the Russian ideology of denial of God, denial of the sanctity of the individual, and aggression against free men everywhere! I feel that I must pass such sentence upon the principals in this diabolical conspiracy to destroy a God-fearing nation, which will demonstrate with finality that this nation's security must remain inviolate!" This is true; the nation assents: "Wickedness must be humbled and left without remnant!" The tumult of the cries of the common people resounds in the Courthouse at Foley Square. *"No survivor shall remain of the Sons of Darkness!"* Julius sways slowly back and forth on the balls of his feet; Ethel's right hand is clasped in a white-knuckled grip on the chair before her. It is High Noon, and the bells of St. Andrew's are tolling deep vibrating peals, as Judge Irving Kaufman turns to the atom spies standing mutely before him. *"Plain, deliberate, contemplated murder is dwarfed in magnitude by comparison with the crime you have committed!"* the Boy Judge rasps grimly, stretching forward so as to be able to see over the top of the high bench, and shouting now over the clanging bells:

I believe your conduct in putting into the hands of the Russians the
   A-bomb years before our best
Scientists predicted Russia would perfect the bomb has already
Caused, in my opinion, the Communist
Aggression in Korea, with the
Resultant casualties exceeding fifty thousand and who knows but
   millions more of
Innocent people may pay the price
Of your treason. Indeed by your betrayal *you undoubtedly have altered
The course of history* to the disadvantage of our country!

The Sons of Light fall to their knees: "O Lord, how long shall we cry, and thou wilt not hear?" Behind the fading echoes of the noontime bells can be heard the distant evil laughter of the Phantom. The whole world seems to be falling down, imploding upon Room 110 of the Foley Square Courthouse! But then Judge Kaufman gathers up his strength and says: "I have deliberated! It is not in *my* power, Julius and Ethel Rosenberg, to forgive you—only the Lord can find mercy for what you have done! The sentence of the Court upon Julius and Ethel Rosenberg is that, for their crime, *they are sentenced to death!*" And then Uncle Sam says: "Those who have cast their lot with me shall come to dominion! Those who have cast it with the Phantom shall get their ass stacked!" And then the people say: "Bless Uncle Sam and all His unerring works!" And then Julius turns to Ethel and sings "The Battle Hymn of the Republic." It's as though a great weight has been lifted from the courtroom. *"Mine eyes have seen the glory!"* They all join in. All except Morton Sobell, ever the spoilsport, now in a deep sulk over being sentenced to thirty years in Alcatraz. *"Glory, glory, hallelujah!"* At the conclusion of which, Rabbi William Rosenblum of New York's Temple Israel, soon to enter History as the first of the Holy Six, steps forward and delivers a "Worse Than Murder" sermon, declaring that the death sentence would be applauded by all decent Americans . . .

Such acts of treason . . . are always an invitation to our enemies to attack us in the hope that they will find countless others who are ready to sell us down the river! However, equally guilty with these atomic spies, though they are rarely brought before the courts, are the men in our arts, science and even the clergy, who are constantly making appeals for appeasement of those foreign nations which any schoolboy knows are just waiting for a propitious moment to unleash their weapons against us! Judge Kaufman has done the American people a great service!

The Boy Judge accepts the many honors due him, gives his wife and J. Edgar Hoover a hug, then goes fishing off Palm Beach with Thomas Dodd, leans back, lights a cigar, and while the rest of the nation settles back to await the inevitable finale, lands a five-foot wahoo. . . .

So, Sam cocked his gun an' Dave pulled the trigger,
But the one killed the 'hog was old Joe Digger!

The chil'ren screamed an' the chil'ren cried,
They love groun'-hog cooked an' fried!
To-my-ring-a-ding-doodle-all-DAY!

PART ONE

WEDNESDAY-THURSDAY

1.

President Eisenhower's News Conference

I was with the President at his news conference that Wednesday morning when the maverick Supreme Court Justice William Douglas dropped his bombshell in the Rosenberg case. Everything had been proceeding according to plan, the appeals had been exhausted, the Rosenbergs were due to be executed the next night, and Eisenhower had called the news conference the day before to confirm the details and remind the nation: "I think I am as implacable a foe of the Communistic theory as there is in this world!" The General had been submitting himself to these confrontations at the rate of nearly three a month since taking office in January, and this worried me. They exercised a visible drain on his powers, he seemed almost to deflate, to simplify, from beginning to end, and from one news conference to the next. As a precaution, we had begun weighing him—down to 180 already—but I didn't need medical proofs, I could see for myself. He won't last, I thought. Not at this rate. Can the Phantom see this? Am I ready, if it comes to that?

The President was talking now about the so-called book-burning scandal—Roy Cohn, Joe McCarthy's right-hand man and one of the guys who had helped Irving Saypol send the Rosenbergs to the Death House in the first place, had been flying around Europe with his buddy G. David Schine, purging U.S. libraries there of what they considered dangerous authors—people like Howard Fast, Mrs. Clifton Fadiman, Theodore White, Bert Andrews, Dashiell Hammett—and yukking it up in their peejays with hotel clerks and cub reporters. Foster Dulles had had to admit that as a result somebody over there had actually set fire to eleven of the damned books, and now the press was in an uproar about it. The President was clearly confused on this issue. This was because, except for the odd western, he'd never read books, and so respected them more than he ought. Even the westerns were just part of the exercises associated with the reinforcement of his superpowers—he usually skipped past all the technicalities about such things as horse-breeding, trial procedures, and prospecting, all the interesting parts. As for the book-burners themselves, well, Roy's devices were crude maybe, but after all they were also consistent, just like his courtroom prosecutions and his cloak-and-dagger work for McCarthy's committee. Roy was smart and close to the hot center, but like Joe, he lacked real cunning. This was ironical because this is just what they were always accused of. They looked mean and shrewd—but they always outreached themselves. I warned Joe about this three years ago, but he wouldn't listen, he was too excited. In the end, through excess and discredit, they served the Phantom. Risks of the holy encounter. Well, a Jew, a Catholic—maybe they lacked certain defenses, being spiritual outsiders, not quite true full-blooded Americans—too fearful of being misunderstood, of being victimized. Probably. Also Joe was piling up a lot of dough through privileged information—that was okay, but you couldn't do that and be a crusader, too.

The President was saying: "By no means am I talking, when I talk about books or the right of dissemination of knowledge, am I talking about any document, or any other kind of thing that attempts to persuade, or propagandize America into Communism, so manifestly, I am not talking about that kind of thing when I talk about free access to knowledge."

His clumsiness, I thought, is part of his disguise, part of his armor, a kind of self-defense mechanism—he seems most sincere just when he makes the least sense. I knew I still had much to learn. People still took me for a carnival barker, a used-car salesman, a fast-buck lawyer—I was still too fluent, too intense, too logical. I had to study this awkward confusion, this easy stupid grin, this casual good-natured gruffness that blunted all the questions. It angered me that Eisenhower had seemed to come by all this naturally. He'd never had to study for anything, not even war. Who else in all history had ever become the world's greatest living military hero without so much as firing a shot or suffering a wound, without so much as a field command, a single battle, even five minutes of real combat? I was no hero, but at least I'd got sent to the goddamn South Pacific and had had a pretty frantic month on Bougainville, while the nearest Ike had ever got to real battle was the White House Egg Roll this year. He was a lucky man. They all said this, it was true. It all seemed to fall in his lap. How could you imitate something like that? I felt cheated. I'd been studying all my life, and I still wasn't there. I worried that I'd never learn enough, worried that Uncle Sam would never use me, and then worried about the worrying. Eisenhower, damn him, never worried at all.

Maybe inquiry, self-consciousness, impeded the process. Maybe Uncle Sam needed vacuity for an easy passage. Certainly, the President never risked clogging the mechanism with idle curiosities of the intellect. He'd had to lean all his life on his little brother Milton whenever it came to thinking (which was something of a closet problem for the Republican Party, Milton having rubbed shoulders with old Henry Wallace during the New Deal days), and as for reading, more than a page and he went blind. The only TV program he was known to watch was "The Fred Waring Show," which he took to be a classical-music program. He sometimes liked to take in a movie in the White House basement, but generally snored through them, *High Noon* being one of the few that seemed to keep him awake. More or less awake: he tended to doze off during the kissing scenes (did he resent it that the wife was a Quaker?), then would wake up snorting: "What time is it?"—meaning, Is it noon yet? There was a motto inscribed on a small black piece of wood on his desk, SUAVITER IN MODO FORTITER IN RE, which he thought was Spanish and pronounced like a Texan. Of course, it was true, he had taken up painting of late, and the room across the hall from his bedroom, I was told, had even been converted into a studio, but other people generally drew the pictures and he just filled in the colors—he was always lamenting that he knew nothing about the chemistry of paints, next to nothing about anatomy (he would wink slyly over my head at some crony or other), and draftsmanship was the one subject that nearly got him flunked out of West Point. He was happiest with eight or ten buddies, broiling steaks and roasting corn in their husks on the grill up in the solarium on the White House roof, or else having some old cronies over for a stag dinner of pheasant in the State Dining Room, then sitting around in a circle in his oval study after, talking about fishing or women or war.

I was not included in these parties. He didn't really like me. I was a "politician." American adversary politics, the kind I knew how to fight and fight well, was nothing better than a childish gutter-brawl to Eisenhower: "If it takes that kind of foolishness to get elected, let them find someone else for the job!" Yet it was I, not he, who had whipped Adlai Stevenson last fall—Eisenhower won the election, because he couldn't help it; but it was I who beat the other guy. Slogans of his like "Heart, Determination, and Productivity" did no harm—indeed they put people to sleep, and in this day of the hovering Bomb we could all be grateful for that—but people don't vote *for* things, they vote *against* them, take it from W. C. Fields, and when they went to the polls it was my K_1C_3 formula they remembered, scrawling their X's against "Korea, Communism, Corruption, and Controls." (If some people were reminded of the old Klan slogan "Kill the Kikes, Koons, and Katholics," it was not necessarily an accident; Eisenhower wasn't the only campaigner who knew how to stir up a little useful nostalgia for the primitive and virtuous village life of the past.) Ike had come home from his imperial life abroad, picked up the cross, and launched his "Great Crusade," but I was the poor sonuvabitch who had had to get down in the ditches and fight the Turks. He seemed to think there was something shameful about this, about being a shameless politician, and always gazed at me as though he saw shit on my face. Yet at the same time he expected me to keep the politicians in Congress in line and got annoyed with me when they deserted him to cater to the home-town vote. His program over on the Hill was faltering. Even his Defense Department reorganization bill was under attack—and if a General didn't know about defense, then what the hell was he good for? That "bunch of clowns" in Congress was concentrating on headline-grabbing investigations instead of constructive legislation, as he liked to call it, something which amazed and confounded this Living Legend—a man rich from birth astonished by thieves. And somehow all this was my fault. He maybe even thought I was betraying him. He was a Superhero, wasn't he? Then why weren't they doing what he asked them to do? Somebody must be messing with the message on its way over there. Thus, he didn't even understand his own role. In a real sense, *I* was the old man, *he* the boy. Even Stevenson saw this.

This is an irony I have learned to live with. Old men, liking me, tended to make the paradoxical assumption that I could win votes among the young and women voters, the province of happy-go-lucky studs like Eisenhower—just as it had been my experience, and not Ike's, that had kept our Party's professionals, the old boys, from bolting the ticket last fall. They had made the obvious surface choices at the Convention last summer: Eisenhower was the candidate of the Eastern Establishment, so a Westerner was needed for balance. Eisenhower was old and easy-going and had lived much of his life abroad, he needed a sidekick who was, as Herb Brownell described me, "a young aggressive fellow who knew the domestic issues—the President could be presented to the country as one who would stand up against the Communists in the international sphere, and Nixon would lead the fight in the discussion of the domestic issues."

But in fact, though all too few understood this, it went much deeper than that. Likable Ike's open-faced friendliness and easy smile won a lot of votes, but some people began to suspect he might be a little simple. Any man on the street past thirty knows there's a lot more to politics— at home and abroad—than plain talk and friendly handshakes. Here is a political truth: Deviousness wins votes. Dishonesty is often the best policy. We all know this: politics is a dirty, combative, dangerous game, it's not something to grin at like a doped monkey. A beloved leader is no leader at all. Gregariousness is a liability if you live close to the center. Crusaders all make one mistake: they leave home. Optimists buy the wrong used cars, take it from a guy who's sold them. And never trust any man who's "clean as a hound's tooth": it's clear he's never been out in the real world when the shit's hit the fan.

So everybody liked Ike, that casual straightforward bumbler—me they called Tricky Dick. I hated this at first, it was a brutal thing to fight, but eventually I discovered it won votes. Uncle Sam probably didn't like being called Yankee Doodle at first either, but eventually he stuck a feather in his cap and called it macaroni. And as these plays on my name got filthier, I even started picking up some votes among women and young people. I'm not very interested in the philosophy of any gimmick or policy, only its efficacy. It's not the content that counts, but the impact— and that attitude itself is efficacious at the polls. Ike was so accustomed to being loved, even apathy offended him. When some guy up in Racine, Wisconsin, borrowing from the 1948 campaign, invented the phrase "Phewey on Eisenhewey!", the General was genuinely upset and wouldn't associate with Tom Dewey for days. If the Democrats had hit him hard enough, portrayed him as a pompous disloyal fraud and something of a helpless moron to boot, if they'd ridiculed his cronies and dragged old Mamie through the mud as they should have, he'd have probably quit. In fact, I knew he could still quit, any day, he was already losing interest.

"I believe the United States is strong enough to expose to the world," he was saying now, "its differing viewpoints, from those of what we call almost the man who has Socialist leanings to the man who is so far to the extreme right that it takes a telescope to find him, but that is America and let's don't be afraid to show it, to the world, because we believe that form of government, those facts, that kind of thinking, that kind of combination of things has produced the greatest system of government that the world has produced, that is what we believe, that is what I am talking about."

Raymond Brandt of the *St. Louis Post-Dispatch,* one of the weak links in the American press system, was trying in his tenacious hangdog way to stir up trouble with further questions about this, when Herb Brownell, the Attorney General, came in, looking dark and secretive. Of course, this was easy for Brownell with that high dome and fixed gaze, he always gave you the impression there was nothing he didn't know, even when he was half dozing, but today he looked less cool and collected than usual. He motioned me aside. We huddled, scowling importantly, and the newsguys watched us; I was beginning to catch on to some of these angles. "Pete Brandt's trying to get up a fight between Ike and Joe," I whispered.

Herb didn't seem to hear me. Up close, I realized he was very agitated. "It's all off, Dick!" he whined. "Douglas called it off!"

"Off?" I said. "What's off, Herb?"

"The executions! The Rosenbergs! The anniversary! Tomorrow night!"

My heart jumped, seemed to lodge in my throat. I worried that the reporters would notice this, but there was nothing I could do about it. I'd been very tense about this thing since that golf game with Uncle Sam over the weekend, and I wasn't sure whether this new situation was good or bad. I was pretty sure Uncle Sam wouldn't like it—we'd been building up toward this thing for two years, everything was ready up in Times Square, we'd thought the last hurdle had been cleared: and now this! The fat was really in the fire! Or rather, it wasn't. . . . There'd been delays before, of course—Uncle Sam had originally scheduled the executions just before the balloon drop at our Inaugural Ball last January—but none so shocking as this. On the other hand, I realized, it at least gave me more time. I'd been pressing very hard, going over everything, and I still hadn't figured out what it was Uncle Sam wanted me to do. I'd thought I was safe, I who'd single-handedly vanquished Alger Hiss and put Voorhis and the Pink Lady to rout, but now I was feeling vulnerable again.

"But I . . . I thought the Supreme Court had recessed!" I whispered.

"They *have!*" wheezed Herb. "Douglas waited until all the other Justices had left town on their vacations, and then issued a stay of execution! It's a helluva mess!"

"We've got to get word to the General, before one of these organ grinders asks the wrong question," I said.

"Generally speaking," the President was saying, "that is exactly what I believe. But I do say I don't have to be a party to my own self-destruction, that is the limit and the other limit I draw is decency, we have certain books we bar from the mails, and all that sort of thing, I think that is perfectly proper and I would do it now, I don't believe that standards of essential human dignity ought to be violated in these things. And human decency."

I scratched out a note: ROSENBERG EXECUTIONS CALLED OFF! and passed it to the press secretary, Jim Hagerty. Hagerty blanched, seemed uncertain what to do with it. I motioned toward the President, but Jim seemed reluctant to pass it on. Probably afraid the Old Man would read it out loud like an announcement. Or get confused and become completely unintelligible. Maybe even blow his stack.

"How many of you have read Stalin's *Problems of Leninism?*" the President was asking the reporters. We didn't even know he knew the title. "How many of you have really studied Karl Marx and looked at the evolution of the Marxian theory down to the present application?" Everybody thought he had said "Martian theory" and he was getting a lot of laughs. This was very successful, the reporters had completely forgotten what they'd asked him, but I thought: My God, I could never do this! I wrote a new note: URGENT BUSINESS! BRING THIS CONFERENCE TO A CLOSE!, and handed it to Jim. Jim added in PLEASE and AS SOON AS POSSIBLE, passed it on to the General, who was just saying: "Of course we shouldn't give that text to a Communist teacher and say, Now. Take your students off, and try to lead them astray any more than you would give them, let us say Al Capone's book on how to be a crook!" Nobody knew any longer what text he was talking about.

When the news conference was over and we'd cleared everybody out of there, Herb sprang the news.

The President drew himself up—a tall man, after all, and strong—in fact, his countenance was already changing—and with jaw set and fists clenched, yet with perfect composure, perfect equanimity, said simply:

"Friends, this is a job for Uncle Sam!"

2.

A Rash of Evil Doings

A United States Supreme Court Justice—himself a controversial appointee from the Era of Compromise—thwarts the long-planned execution of the atom spies, disappears.

Two ore tankers go aground in the mud of St. Clair, Canada.

A coffee plot is uncovered in Brazil.

Russian tanks tool up, roll toward East Berlin.

From North Korea come horrific images of brainwashed GIs staring vapidly and twitching like zombies, while in the South, the port of the capital is bombed and underground rumors abound of trouble afoot, strange stirrings in the prisoner compounds.

In Times Square, the "c" has vanished from the SILENCE sign tacked up over the stage door of the execution chamber mock-up, and the letters are scrambled to spell SENILE, a cross-eyed Uncle Sam chalked crudely on the wall above it. The electrical sign reading AMERICA THE HOPE OF THE WORLD has been altered to AMERICA THE DOPE OF THE WORLD, and now, metamorphosing a letter at a time right before the eyes of astonished passersby, becomes:

AMERICA THE ROPE OF THE WORLD

AMERICA THE RAPE OF THE WORLD

What's happening?!?

The men of Local 333 of the United Marine Division of the International Longshoreman's Association strike the two boats that take sightseers out to Bedloe's Island, throwing up what *The New York Times* calls "an iron curtain around the Statue of Liberty!"

Judge Irving Kaufman, now guarded day and night by FBI in mufti and twelve boys in blue at his Park Avenue home, receives two bomb threats against his life, and total strangers send him telegrams: "May your children become orphans!"

British Foreign Secretary Anthony Eden, the heir-designate to Prime Minister Churchill, is struck down in London, taken to the hospital for a gall bladder operation, and fire breaks out in the key U.S. military port of Whittier, Alaska.

AMERICA THE RAKE OF THE WORLD
AMERICA THE FAKE OF THE WORLD

King Sihanouk of Cambodia, having fled to Thailand, takes encouragement from the sudden dissolution and demands from the French full independence for Cambodia. The French will to stand firm falters.

The Phantomized Guatemalan regime seizes lands belonging to Uncle Sam's United Fruit Company, redistributes them to greedy and incompetent peasants.

Francis Cardinal Spellman's tireless epistolary efforts to the contrary notwithstanding, Italy, without a government, slips to the left, just as the body of a twenty-year-old student in the Passionists' seminary at Caravete is found in the woods, skull smashed by a stone. There have been fires in the convent library, two watchdogs have been poisoned, and all the Passionist brothers and pupils found potassium cyanide in their morning espresso one morning of late. The village's small community of newly-converted Protestants is suspected; anti-American feeling grows apace.

AMERICA THE FATE OF THE WORLD
AMERICA THE HATE OF THE WORLD

Something passes like a cold unseasonal wind through Times Square, tipping over police barricades, blowing holes in the set, and stripping away all the white and blue bunting in the streets, leaving—from a Busby Berkeley overview—a tattered crimson star fluttering in its wake. This same wind blows through Whittier, Alaska, fanning the flames, spreading the fire through docks and warehouses, forcing back the hundreds of stevedore troops battling the blaze, and then through Africa, stirring the blacks in Kenya, Northern Rhodesia, and South Africa to rebellion. It whistles through the Federal Council of Italian Evangelical

Churches, which cables President Eisenhower "to be great in your mercy and spare the lives of the Rosenbergs," and it even touches the Kingdoms of Great Britain and Nepal: they erupt into a sudden feud over the exploits of Heroes Edmund Hillary and his guide Tensing Norkay, now down off the roof of the world, the British claiming that Hillary had to drag the reluctant Sherpa (they persist, out of habit, in calling him "the native") up Everest's summit behind him, while the Nepalese, who have declared May 29 a new national holiday—Tensing Day—retort that in fact it was their man who had to carry the fagged white man up on his back. An international crisis develops, and America seems unable to do anything about it.

Elsewhere, the Phantom strikes out even more boldly, using every weapon from hysteria to hyperbole, tanks to terrorism. In Korea, firing thousands of artillery and mortar rounds, the Phantom's troops attack along a broad front, capturing Finger Ridge and Capitol Hill, breaking through Allied lines near Outpost Texas, scattering chickenshit ROKs and exhausted GIs in all directions. "If this is getting ready for peace," bitches a shot-up U.S. rifleman as they cart him away on his stretcher, "I'd just as soon go back to the old war!" TIME, the National Poet Laureate, records this sentiment for immortality, then adds:

> americans could not forget
> korea and it spoiled
> some of their pleasure in
> tv sets and cadillacs

Uncle Sam wants the hell out of this war, but Syngman Rhee is threatening it go it alone. He sends mobs of schoolgirls out in the streets to attack the GIs from the rear in protest against the truce negotiations under way. Key to these negotiations are the North Korean prisoners of war in South Korean compounds, most of whom are said to be anti-Communist. "Just so Rhee don't go berserk," mutters a U.S. negotiator, "and let them prisoners go!"

Almost as a kind of reflex, the guard is doubled on the Rosenbergs at Sing Sing. The Rosenbergs are said to be gloating over their new stay of execution. The Phantom whips up anti-American demonstrations in their behalf in Milan, Toronto, Jakarta, Genoa, Paris, London, and swamps the White House with protest letters—nearly ten thousand letters asking Eisenhower to spare the couple are passing like stuffed ballots across his desk every day now. The Rosenberg lawyers, augmented by a gang of last-minute interlopers, are scrambling frantically through

ancient lawbooks in search of any new shyster tactic that might confound Uncle Sam.

To gain time, the Phantom sends his terrorists into action in Malaya
and French Indochina, and his tanks into East Berlin. The Russian T-
34s come clattering in over the cobblestones, "rocking and snarling," as
TIME say, wagging their big 85-mm guns about like magic wands . . .

> the machine guns and submachine guns
> began chattering the crowds broke threw
> themselves into gutters and down subway
> stair wells to dodge the bullets but
> not all made it . . .

Some run, some stand, some die, many are glad they stayed at home,
most are frightened, and everyone soon vanishes, as the Rebellion in the
Rain gutters out, all of it watched morosely by Uncle Sam, sitting helplessly on his blistered duff on the wrong side of Potsdamer Platz. Soon,
nothing can be heard in the divided city but the soft dripping of rain-
water, the clink of knives through the evening rituals of black bread,
butter, cheese, and sausage, the odd Soviet firing squad off in the
fields. . . .

> AMERICA THE NATE OF THE WORLD
> AMERICA THE NITE OF THE WORLD

> it was a quiet rainy night in
> prisoner of war camp number nine
> under the brow of a green hill in
> pusan
> at 2:30 a.m.
> pfc willie buhan was reading
> a book in the "maximum security"
> compound (for prisoners who had broken
> minor rules)
> he wasn't
> worried much though vaguely aware
> that his two rok buddies on guard
> duty had been acting sort of
> "funny"
> the next thing
> he knew he was looking down
> the barrels of two carbines

one garand rifle and one pistol
all in the hands of

rok guards . . .

They're gone: some twenty-five thousand of them. Dashing out into open fields, remote villages, the alleyways of Pusan: Rhee, the obstreperous old bastard, has pulled the straw mat out from under Uncle Sam's feet and let his prisoners go.

By Thursday, peace hopes have been dashed in Korea, the East German freedom fighters have been crushed, and all preparations for the great atom-spy pageant have been thrown into utter confusion. The wires have been pulled on the electric chair and a manikin has been strapped into the seat, dressed up to look like Uncle Sam with a Hitler moustache. Bombastic handbills, instruction sheets for clemency vigils, tattered bunting, and dirty pictures showing President Eisenhower and all his Cabinet in compromising positions litter the streets.

The fire in Alaska is quenched at last, after millions of dollars of damage to military installations and supplies, but simultaneously the new $3,000,000 U.S. Embassy in Rio de Janeiro bursts into flames. Smaller fires break out in a random pattern across New York City—on Fourth Avenue, West Thirteenth, Eldridge, and East Forty-ninth in Manhattan, Fulton and West Eighth in Brooklyn—and during a demonstration at Fort Dix, a mortar shell explodes, injuring sixteen American GIs and killing Private Frank X. Zirnheld, 20, of Buffalo. Adlai Stevenson travels all the way to Turkey to praise the Turkish troops fighting in Korea, but his words are drowned out by earthquakes that rock Adrianople; he sighs, remarks on his usual luck, and goes for a hopeful swim in the Bosporus.

Three Israelis are slain by a Jordanian patrol, three Home Guards by terrorists in Malaya. The Red Chinese crack down on the last of the Roman Catholic missions, arresting eleven priests in Shanghai, ten in Tientsin, more in Canton, as "well-known spies." Indonesian terrorists kill 60 villagers and burn 800 homes in a raid on 4 villages south of Jakarta, leaving 3500 homeless. U.S. casualties in Korea shoot up to 136,029, while at home 305 new polio cases are reported for the week, bringing the year's total to 3124. These numbers rattle through the streets like apocalyptic codes, signals of some numerological conundrum, resolving itself toward catastrophe. Broadway bookies now give the Rosenbergs a fifty-fifty chance of survival, which is better than they're giving the best horse running that day. The local boatmen, holding out for another thirty-five cents, still refuse to take pilgrims over to Miss

Liberty on Bedloe's Island. Clemency floats containing photographic blow-ups of new documents brazenly stolen from the office of the Green-glasses' lawyer, purporting to prove that major prosecution witnesses lied against the Rosenbergs, roll into Times Square. Enraged loyalists try to smash up the floats and fights ensue. AMERICA THE BITE OF THE WORLD, the sign reads. BILE. PILE. PULE. PUKE. JUKE. What kind of game IS this?

AMERICA THE JOKE OF THE WORLD!

There seems no stopping the Phantom in his blasphemy. It's almost as if he has been playing dead all this time, like those inscrutable Japs used to do in all the World War II movies, lying in ambush, flat out, with a pile of hand grenades tucked under their yellow bellies. It's not even clear who Uncle Sam's friends are. The French, facing the most serious crisis in the dismal history of the Fourth Republic, are losing their nerve in Indochina, and everybody from President Auriol on down is protesting the Rosenberg executions. So are the Scandinavians, and the Pope is not exactly standing up and cheering for the Sons of Light. Churchill has talked about withdrawing British troops from Korea, where only 40,000 outside forces now support the 460,000 ROKs and 250,000 American GIs in this so-called United Nations action as it is. "United Nations, my ass!" Uncle Sam is heard to mutter, trying to find a toehold along Finger Ridge. "Hal-lucy-nations, more like it! In-subordy-nations!" India and Switzerland actually threaten to quit the commission to supervise repatriation of war prisoners in Korea, confirming Uncle Sam's mistrust of "neutralism," and there are suggestions—even at home in the Americas!—that Red China be admitted to the United Nations. TIME say: "SHADOW OF THE RED DRAGON!"

Not only are the North Korean hostages out of the prison camps and living like the golden boys of Pusan, heroes of the local dongs, but women and children are out in the streets, screaming insults at the Americans for failing to unify the nation, and mutilated veterans are staging a very unappealing lie-down strike on Pusan's main drag. Syngman Rhee smiles at Uncle Sam's discomfiture. Says a soldier-friend of TIME: "We came over here to help him, and now he's kicked us in the face."

It's a scandal, just like the strikes, the rising prices, the legal shenanigans, the erratic weather, the clemency appeals. The Red Puppets of Poland insolently offer political asylum for the Rosenbergs. France's *Le Monde* says Uncle Sam is "disturbed" and accuses him of planning a "ritual murder." "More and more," says *Le Monde*, "the Rosenbergs seem to us like the expiatory victims of the cold war . . ."

Many of America's own atomic scientists, led by Nobel Prize-winner Harold Urey, seem to be siding openly with the spies, claiming that there *is* no secret to the atom bomb in the first place (but this is a lie—Harry Truman said there was a secret, and so did J. Edgar Hoover), and now the granddaddy of them all, Albert Einstein, writes to a teacher just fired by the City Board of Education for refusing to answer questions about his connections with the Phantom: "The reactionary politicians have managed to instill suspicion of all intellectual efforts into the public by dangling before their eyes a danger from without. . . . They are now proceeding to suppress the freedom of teaching and to deprive of their positions all those who do not prove submissive. What ought the minority of intellectuals to do against this evil? Frankly, I can only see the revolutionary way of non-cooperation. . . ." New apostates are being won and the letters keep coming in. From Netherlands Women, British Railwaymen, French Lawyers, and the Uruguayan Chamber of Deputies. Clerics, novelists, schoolteachers, and 2200 Melbourne ladies. The British *Electrical* Union! All writing to the President, all urging clemency for the atom spies. Even their sons—which prompts President Eisenhower to complain in a sputtering rage that "they have even stooped to dragging in young and innocent children in order to serve their own purpose!"

If he is offended by the boys' appeals, he is even more outraged when Ethel Rosenberg's latest letter to her two sons is flashed on the moving electric sign on the Times Tower: Christ on the mountain! he can just feel the damned Phantom's power radiate through the spellbound crowds in the Square . . .

My Dearest Darlings,
This is the process known as "sweating it out," and it's tough, that's for sure. At the same time, we can't let a lot of chickens that go about their business without panic, even when something's frightening them—we can't let them put us to shame, can we . . . ?

What's that about chickens? The people duck their heads and peer nervously up at the sky. Is this it, then?

. . . Maybe you thought that I didn't feel like crying too when we were hugging and kissing goodbye, huh, even though I'm slightly older than 10. Darlings, that would have been so easy, far too easy on myself . . .

What's to be done? The National Maritime Union's strike spreads like a virus, tying up hundreds of ships, and the U.S. Post Office announces a 36 percent rise in parcel post rates. Pickets appear: NEW EVIDENCE SHOWS PERJURY!

. . . but it would not have been any kindness at all. So I took the hard way instead of the easy . . .

The Reds walk out of the Korean peace talks, accuse Uncle Sam of bad faith. The Chinese breach the ROK defenses north of the Hwachon Reservoir. Soviet occupation troops raid workers' homes in East Berlin and mark some thirty thousand ex–Wehrmacht officers for automatic arrest.

. . . because I love you more than myself, and because I know you needed that love far more than I needed the relief of crying . . .

Mrs. Sarah Brock Dodge, U.S. Army nurse in the Spanish-American War, and later personal nurse for General Douglas MacArthur and the Taft family, drops dead as a doornail . . .

. . . We need to try to remain calm and free from panic, so that we can do all we can to help one another to see this thing through!

. . . and then in Japan, an Air Force Globemaster transport with 129 American servicemen aboard falls right out of the sky, the worst disaster in the history of flight! Those damn chickens! "East and West," TIME say, "from within & without / news crashed / upon the U.S. . . ."

> for 120 seconds
> the rows of servicemen
> held fast to their seat-
> belts as the plane lurched
> and swayed towards the
> air base
>   some prayed
> one boy clutched his
> rosary
>   a second engine
> failed & the plane began
> to lose altitude more
> rapidly
>   four miles short
> of the base the globemaster
> slammed steeply into a watermelon

patch broke up & caught
fire skittering bits of
burning metal at a frightened japanese farmer who stood
nearby
        most if not all
of the men were killed
on impact which was so great
that many bodies were torn
from their boots
                they were
returning to korea to defend
the embittered koreans against
the great conspiracy that
the rosenbergs had served . . .

. . . All my love and all my kisses!

Mommy

Demonstrators march in broad daylight through the streets with signs
that read: THE ELECTRIC CHAIR CAN'T KILL THE DOUBTS IN THE ROSENBERG
CASE! ROK troops fall back in Korea in the biggest retreat in two years.
An anonymous caller tells the police that a bomb is set to go off in
Public School 187 in the north part of the city. There are rumors of an
all-out strategic exchange. Scrawled across the whitewashed walls of the
Sing Sing Death House set atop the information kiosk: WHAT THE BOUR-
GEOISIE, THEREFORE, PRODUCES, ABOVE ALL, IS ITS OWN GRAVEDIGGERS. Then
somebody sabotages the stage and the whole business collapses into the
street. And in Vienna, three beetle-browed Russians force their way past
the landlady and drag Czech refugee Jaroslav Lukas out of his flat.
Strange perspectives, weird watching faces, peculiar zither music—an
Austrian policeman intervenes and a four-man (French, English, American, Russian) Allied Military Patrol speeds to the scene. They block the
kidnappers' escape route, leap out of the car with weapons at the ready.
But the Soviet member of the FEAR Patrol commandeers the patrol car,
shoves Lukas and his kidnappers in, leaps into the driver's seat himself,
slams into reverse, rams two civilian cars, shifts back into first—for
God's sake!

STAND BY TO CRASH!

—*Where Is Uncle Sam?*

3.

Idle Banter: The Fighting Quaker Among Saints and Sinners

My old California colleague Bill Knowland was in trouble in his first test as the new Republican floor leader in the Senate, so on the way back to my office Thursday from the emergency meeting of the National Security Council at the White House, I stopped by the Capitol to see if I could be of help. The Hill and Mall were swarming with demonstrators, counterdemonstrators, tourists, cops, dogs, kids, and there were expressions of worry, gloom, apprehension, uncertainty everywhere. There'd been too many setbacks. In the middle of all this, Knowland had decided to pull a fast one: after having told the Minority Leader Lyndon Johnson earlier that there'd be nothing more controversial today than the call of the calendar—which few Senators even bother to show up for—he'd suddenly decided to interrupt the call with an aggressive attempt to ram our new controls bill through and catch the Democrats flatfooted. I wasn't sure Bill was doing the smart thing, but I understood his motives and had to admire them: he'd just taken over from the ailing Bob Taft, and he was trying hard to put his personal stamp on the leadership job, make it his through partisan conflict. It wasn't easy to follow a living legend like Taft, Bill had to do something audacious to signal the change and establish his authority. Of course, he could blow it, too, and the chances were just about fifty-fifty—with Wayne Morse now voting with the Democrats, there were forty-eight votes on each side of the aisle, and my vote was the tie-breaker. I was eager to get back to the Rosenberg case, things were in a mess now, thanks to Douglas, and I didn't know what the hell was going on or what I was supposed to do, but Eisenhower's relationship with Congressional Republicans was so fragile, we couldn't afford to antagonize them in any way—I had no choice but to be on hand and save the day for Knowland if need be. Besides, it was just the kind of political battle I loved: nobody gave a shit about the bill itself, it was a straight-out power struggle, raw and pure, like a move in chess.

On the way in, I saw Bob Taft. The poor bastard, he looked like hell. Mr. Republican. Fighting Bob. The Go-It-Alone Man. He was going it alone now, all right: he was dying, hip cancer apparently, probably wouldn't last the year out. On the side of the angels now. There were some reporters hovering around him, looking very sympathetic, and since sympathy from those sonsabitches was something I rarely enjoyed, I decided Fighting Bob could share a little of it with me, he wasn't going to need it much longer anyway. "Say, Bob," I called out, moving in, "I have news for you!" Taft knew where I'd been that morning, knew about the Korean and German and Rosenberg crises—the whole Capitol was obviously ass-deep in the usual rumors, prophecies, and panic—and so of course he was all ears. He was on crutches and appeared to have lost a lot of weight (which was maybe why he seemed to be "all ears"), but he stretched forward eagerly as though reaching for a cure. The newsguys all turned to me, grabbing for the pencils tucked behind their ears, and photographers snatched up their cameras—I quickly lifted my chin and raised my eyebrows, conscious that my stern Quaker eyes and heavy cheeks often gave me an unfortunate scowly sinister look, putting a whole different slant on what I was saying (isn't that a hell of a thing—that the fate of a great country can depend on camera angles?), and said: "I broke a hundred at Burning Tree Sunday, Bob!"

The Senator shrank back as though suddenly aged, but he smiled and congratulated me. I bowed acknowledgments, smiling generously, trying to make the best of it, but I was suddenly sorry for him, felt suddenly like a brother, regretted my little joke—hadn't he said when he fell ill that the first thing he'd noticed was a great weariness when he started "whaling golf balls" early last spring? Shit, I was just rubbing it in. I wanted to reach out and embrace him, give him my shoulder to lean on instead of those damned crutches, make him well again, make him President or something.

We went on talking about golf, he seemed cheerful enough, but I felt like hell. I saw that the news reporters had stopped grinning, too, most of them had turned away, I'd been misunderstood again. I'd only wanted to give Taft something to laugh about in these troubled times, I'd meant no harm. He was one of the few guys, after all, who'd stood by me through the Fund Crisis last fall—even if the reason was that he was afraid Bill Knowland would be the guy to take my place. Taft had made a lot of mistakes, but he still might have gone to the White House if he hadn't opposed NATO and collective security in Europe—what the hell, let's face it, he would have gotten there anyway if a few of us hadn't axed him, he could have won last year, that was clear now. And but a few short weeks ago, he was the most powerful man outside the White House in all America—maybe the most powerful Senator in history. Cut down. Last summer he'd been my enemy. It was I who'd busted up the unity of the California delegation and so assured Eisenhower of the Party's nomination, had beat him out myself for the vice-presidential nomination—but now, looking at him there, shrunken, held up by those crutches, smiling gamely, his belly hanging low in his pants, I thought: Jesus, he's a goddamn saint! I wanted to tell him everything, about the National Security Council meeting, about my talks with Uncle Sam, about the moves soon to be made, about the Rosenberg letters strewn around my office, about my hopes, my fears, the whole works.

I remembered the time he came to my office and asked for my support for the Party's presidential nomination—me, just a green junior Senator from California—and I'd had to put him off. I think in part I objected to the fact he'd asked me. As though he'd demeaned himself. It was too personal, coming to my office like that. It embarrassed me—it flattered me, too, but mostly it made me uneasy, and I didn't want to have anything more to do with him. Besides, with him I had no shot at something bigger myself. It must have been a terribly difficult thing for him to do, I could never do it, I could never walk into some other guy's office and ask him to help make me President, any more than I could fly. I could send somebody else, but I could never do it myself. But now, if he'd come today, I thought, I'd have said yes. Now that it was too late. He smiled feebly but kindly, adjusted his clear horn-rimmed spectacles, said we'd have to get up a game soon, shifted his weight, and hobbled away on his crutches, showing me his bald spot like a kind of halo. Was *he* needling *me* now? I wanted to call out to him, but I didn't.

This often happened to me, this sudden flush of warmth, even love, toward the people I defeat. It worried me, worries me still. It could backfire someday. Back when I was in the Navy, I wrote a note to myself on the subject, I have it still, taped inside my desk drawer: DON'T BE-COME OVERGENEROUS ON THE SPUR OF THE MOMENT! But I kept forgetting. It was a weakness. Already some people were complaining I'd made too much of the tragic side of the Alger Hiss case, been too insistent in pointing out his intelligence, sensitivity, idealism, should never have said that I thought he was sincerely dedicated to the concepts of peace and of bettering the lot of the common man, of people generally—I might as well say as much for the goddamn Phantom. But once it was over, once I'd nailed the lying supercilious bastard for good, I couldn't help myself. There's something that makes me want the happy ending. Most conflicts are irresolvable, I know that, someone wins and someone loses, someone's on the right side, someone's on the other side, and what resolutions are possible are got afterwards by way of the emotions. I learned that way back in the seventh grade, first time I beat those girls in the now-famous Insect Debate. I'm no believer in dialectics, material or otherwise, let me be absolutely clear about that, I wouldn't be Vice President of the United States of America if I was, it's either/or as far as I'm concerned and let the best man win so long as it's me. But I want these emotional resolutions when the fights are over.

People misunderstand me. They think it's all vindictiveness. It isn't. Personal hatred is a big waste, it's as simple as that. Issues are everything, even when they're meaningless—these other things like emotions and personalities just blur the picture and make it difficult to operate. But it feels good to indulge in them when it no longer matters. I've often said that the only time to lose your temper in politics is when it's deliberate and useful. I don't always live up to that, I'm human, but I still believe it. I'm a tough sonuvabitch to run against in an election, everyone knows that by now, they say I'm a buzzsaw opponent, ruthless and even unscrupulous, they say I go for the jugular, no holds barred, or as Stevenson put it, "Nixonland is the land of smash and grab and anything to win," and discounting the partisan hyperbole, that's largely true, I guess. You've got to win, or the rest doesn't matter. I believe in fighting it out, in hitting back, giving as good as you get, you've got to be a politician before you can be a statesman, I've said that and it's so. No ruffed-shirt, kid-glove, peanut politics for me. As Uncle Sam once told me: "Politics is the only game played with real blood." I didn't want to believe him at the time, I wanted it to be played with rhetoric and industry, yet down deep I knew that even at its most trivial, politics flirted with murder and mayhem, theft and cannibalism.

But—maybe because I do know that—I've always thought of myself as a healer as well. I was always breaking up fights between my brothers, saving them from Dad's whippings, calming tempers at school, it was I who stopped that ugly brawl between Joe McCarthy and Drew Pearson in the Sulgrave Club washroom two and a half years ago (people thought I was siding with Joe, but actually I was saving Pearson's life: Joe had heard from some Indian that if you kneed a guy hard enough in the nuts, blood would come out of his eyes, and he was eager to test this out), and it was I who bridged the generations in the Republican Party and brought its warring sides together for victory at last this past fall, I who now kept the peace between the President and a truculent Congress. I was Eisenhower's salesman in the Cloakrooms, that was my job, I was the political broker between the patsies and the neanderthals, I had to cool the barnburners, soften up the hardshells, keep the hunkers and cowboys in line, mollify the soreheads and baby tinhorn egos, I was the flak runner, the wheelhorse, I had to mend the fences and bind up the wounds. Yes, bind up the wounds: I'm a lot like Lincoln, I guess, who was kind and compassionate on the one hand, and strong and competitive on the other. I gave Voorhis no quarter, for example, when I beat him for his seat in Congress in 1946; I called him a puppet of the Communists, hit him with dirty broadsides, anonymous phone calls, the whole lot, and if I hadn't played it that way I wouldn't be where I was now, America's history and that of the entire world would have run a different course, the Phantom might well have had his way with us, maybe none of us would even be here now. But afterwards I went to the bastard's office and smiled and shook his hand, spent nearly an hour with him, and I meant it when I said there was scarcely ever a man with higher ideals than old Jerry Voorhis, even if, like Alger Hiss and a lot of other insolent bums I've run into out here, he did come from Yale.

Probably I got this from my mother. My father was a scrapper, a very competitive man, cantankerous even and aggressive, he loved to argue with anybody about anything, and he always instilled this competitive feeling in all of us, we owed him a lot, my brothers and I, even if sometimes we hated his guts. But my mother was just the opposite, a Quaker, a peacemaker, and she taught us—showed us—charity and tolerance and the need to keep your feelings about people separate from your feelings about moral questions. People were weak, of course they were, but that didn't mean you were supposed to stop loving them, even as you punished them. When my father's Black Irish temper reared up inside him and he went for his strap or rod, she wouldn't interfere, she understood the need for rules and the need for punishment and stood by watching while he laid it on (Jesus! he could really set your ass on fire, he scared the hell out of me early on and I learned how to avoid the beatings, even if I had to lie or throw off on others, but he pounded Don's butt to leather and I used to worry he'd broken poor Harold's health and crushed little Arthur's spirit, I still have nightmares about it), but afterwards she always made him forgive us—some of our best family moments came after the strappings were over and Mother was getting us all together again. I suppose I've got something of both of them in me—"The Fighting Quaker." TIME had called me after my nomination last summer, and that was probably the closest anyone had ever got to summing me up. "Richard M. Nixon: Change Trains for the Future." I liked that touch, it took me back to my childhood in Yorba Linda, and identified me with the westward sweep of Uncle Sam's evangel. Of course, there were the Democrats' inevitable malicious jokes later about "the crash of the Federal Express" after the trainwreck here in Washington. And I wasn't too happy about the anonymous parody I got in the mail shortly after that, titled "The Farting Quacker," with a picture of me like a train engine chugging butt-backwards—was it my fault I had stomach problems? Some agent of the Phantom, I supposed, like all pornographers and irreligionists. I was used to it by now, I'd been called just about everything as far back as I could remember. When I was in high school, our Latin class put on a play based on Virgil's *Aeneid*, it was maybe the most romantic thing that ever happened to me—I was Aeneas and Ola was Queen Dido and we wore white gowns and fell in love—but even then they started called me "Anus" and not even Ola could keep from giggling. Years later, when I was in the Navy, I realized we could have called her Queen Dildo, but we were all too green at the time to know about that. It was amazing we knew about anuses.

I stopped in the Chamber but things were dead in there. Bill Langer was reading off a list of aliens who were being let into the country as permanent residents, and George Smathers and silver-headed old Pat McCarran were making wisecracks about all the goofy names. When Langer was done, Smathers got the floor and announced: "I wish to commend the distinguished Senator from North Dakota for his linguistic ability!" The farmers up in the gallery laughed. Smathers waved at me, and I nodded. He was maybe the best friend I had over here, even if he was a Democrat. We were Senate classmates. In the Florida spring primaries, he'd defeated Senator Claude Pepper by calling him Red Pepper and a nigger-lover. I'd studied his techniques and turned them against the Pink Lady in California, a "brilliant campaign," as Herb Brownell said, that laid the groundwork for our Party's national success last fall. Smathers was apparently filling in today as Minority Leader while Lyndon Johnson was out getting his troops formed up for the vote to come—he was showing a lot of promise. Knowland was absent as well, Bob Hendrickson doing the Leader's job for us. Things were quiet yet stirring. Even with the Chamber at low tide, you could smell the impending battle. My own presence here was electrifying in itself.

I let Bill Purtell, the acting pro tem, know I was around, then wandered back to the Republican Cloakroom. Ev Dirksen, another classmate of mine, was in there, and when he saw me he hunched his shoulders and snarled like a lion—with that curly hair, he looked like one, too! I grabbed up a chair as though to fend him off, cracked an imaginary whip. This got a lot of laughs from the old boys standing around (I have a sense of humor like everybody else, I don't know why people doubt this), and Ev shrank back, making a sad face like the Cowardly Lion. He was making fun of course of all the pictures in newspapers and magazines of late showing me in the lion's cage with Sheba, part of my initiation into the Saints & Sinners Club of circus fans. I had suggested through intermediaries that this would be a good year for my old law school at Duke to give me an honorary doctorate, but for some goddamn reason they'd refused me—me, the Vice President of the United States! Some malicious left-wing Democratic cabal on the faculty, I assumed. The rumor I heard was that it was because of the Dean's Office break-in when I was in my last year there, but that was a lot of sanctimonious bullshit—every student breaks into the Dean's Office to steal exams or find out results, most common prank in the world, it was just an excuse. So hurriedly, since I'd left this gap in my schedule, we'd arranged this initiation into the Saints & Sinners. Just as well. I'd got a lot more publicity out of it. Though not all the photos were flattering: when Sheba took offense—maybe at the smell of Checkers on me—my own reflexes had been pretty quick, and the newsguys had unfortunately caught the moment of panic. Later, they told me she'd only been yawning, but I didn't believe it.

"Hey," Ev rumbled, "I guess you heard about the Rosenbergs taking the Fifth Amendment . . . ?"

"Oh yeah?"

We all perked up.

"Yes, they refused to answer on the grounds that it might tend to incinerate them!"

Dirksen grimaced comically and we all responded with groans and laughter. Dirksen had a wonderfully expressive face, it was a delight to watch it, just the opposite of mine, a real clown's face—and he knew how to use his hands, too. He had produced one of the great gestures of all time at our Convention last summer, when he'd turned on Tom Dewey, pointing his finger at him and bellowing out as though in mortal pain: *"We followed you before!"* The finger was pointing all right, and in Dewey's direction, but it was also as limp as a wet noodle, quivering slightly as though straining feebly and ineffectually to overcome its impotence. He'd given the crowd of delegates plenty of time to stare at that drooping digit and then to roar and moan, before continuing: *"And you took us down the road to defeat!"* I hoped he'd never turn that finger on me.

"Say," he continued now, rolling his eyes, "you know what you get when you cross Little Miss Muffet with Red Riding Hood?"

"Naw," laughed Gene Millikin, "whaddaya get, Ev?"

"A curd-carrying Communist!"

There were a lot of snorts and guffaws, and then Ev trundled off toward the Senate lavatory. I realized I badly needed to piss myself and I probably should have gone along with him, but not only did I feel out of place in there, never having really become a member of this private club (I often got odd surprised stares from other Senators in there, even the janitors were more welcome than I), but also to get to it you had to go through the President's Room where all the news reporters hung out. According to the legend, the best news sources have always been Senators with "weak bladders and strong minds"—all the more so when the bladders have been weakened by bourbon. There were even women journalists out there, laughing as the Senators hurried through clutching their nuts. To me it was a real indignity, but most Senators didn't seem to mind, even enjoyed the notoriety of it. It was said that during the debate on the Tidelands Oil Bill, Lyndon Johnson had got trapped by a young socialite reporter and had agreed to an interview provided only she'd come in and hold his pecker for him while he peed—which presumably she did. Scoop of the year. Or, as Lyndon was said to have remarked at the urinal, "Lady, you just struck a gusher!"

Homer Capehart came into the Cloakroom and started complaining loudly about the collapse of the workers' riots in East Berlin. "First Czechoslovakia, and now this!" he snapped, glowering narrowly in my direction. Homer seemed edgier than usual today, and for good reason: if Bill Knowland succeeded in getting the controls bill past the Democrats and out on the floor this afternoon, it would be Capehart's duty to defend it. "Why the hell is it we can't seem to *capitalize* on these things?"

I worked up what I hoped was an enigmatic smile, meaning to suggest that there was more to what was going on behind the Curtain than met the eye, but in truth I was pretty disappointed myself. I remembered the day three months earlier when we heard that Stalin had suffered a stroke—if that was all he'd suffered—and was dying. It had been a raw day, one of those gray March mornings that makes the Capital look like a city in Central Europe, and a bunch of the boys had gathered early in the President's office, waiting for the Old Man to come down. He'd come striding in, wearing a tan polo coat and a brown hat with the brim snapped far down over his eyes, like a Marine on shore-patrol duty. "Well," he'd barked, making us jump, "what do you think we can do about *this?*" So we'd thought up a few things and done them. And this was what it had come to. You couldn't help but feel the frustration of it. And I could see that some of these guys had had their confidence shaken. Though many of them had decried Uncle Sam's vulnerability as a campaign tactic, none had truly believed it, but now they had seen for themselves: even Uncle Sam could get left with his finger up his ass.

"Give us time," I said, "it's a tough ballgame. But we've got them on the ropes, it's the beginning of the end. The seed has been sown, they've had a taste of freedom and they won't soon forget it. It's like George Humphrey says, 'You can't set a hen in the morning and have chicken salad for lunch!'" Which reminded me: I was pretty goddamn hungry. Homer nodded solemnly, shrugged ambiguously, gazed off. Herman Welker, who had joined us, seemed less convinced, belching sourly. He said that over in the House Don Wheeler was outraged by the fact that Justice Douglas had "taken unto himself the authority to grant amnesty to two proven spies," and was drafting an impeachment proposal, and Bourke Hickenlooper looked up from the old sofa where he was sprawled, going through his morning's mail, to say that he hoped they smeared that butternut once and forever. Maybe I should find a page, I thought, and send him down for a sandwich.

Uncle Sam had actually prepared me for this crisis during our last match at Burning Tree Golf Club, but I had not understood. Had not taken it all in. I knew now he'd been telling me a lot of things—about history, about guilt and innocence, death and regeneration, about the security of the whole nation and the cause of free men everywhere—but I'd been too abashed by my transparent ignorance, too upset by the coincidence of anniversaries and by my fluffed drives, to think clearly. The only accurate description is that I was probably in a momentary state of shock. I had failed to heed one of Eisenhower's favorite admonitions (which, in fact, he rarely heeded himself): "Always take your job, but never yourself, seriously." Even the anniversary remark I'd misread—when he'd said that all judges were cabalists at heart, I'd thought he was talking about Kaufman, not Douglas.

Fourteen. Fourteen years ago today Julius Rosenberg and Ethel Greenglass were married. That was the same summer, fourteen years ago, that Hitler and Stalin signed their pact: yes, it was a year for weddings. Hitler had seized Czechoslovakia, annexed Danzig, and invaded Poland, divvying it up with Stalin, while Britain and France were celebrating a short-lived marriage of their own. But I was courting Pat at the time, could think of nothing else, hardly noticed the world falling down about my ears (how far away it seemed then!), I thought I'd go to Cuba to get rich or else to the opening of the New York World's Fair, or freeze orange juice and start a company. If only I could win Pat. It wasn't easy. She laughed at me when I proposed, made fun of me in public, it was humiliating as hell. She was so goddamned cool, she seemed to know everything, and all I could do was pretend. She tried to put me off, made me drive her into Los Angeles for dates with other guys, kept me on the leash for over two years before she finally gave in—and even then it was possible she capitulated only because she was getting on in years and I was the only real prospect still around. But I didn't care, as long as I got her. I needed the win and she was it. I felt like a champ—like the Brown Bomber himself, who was ripping up Arturo Godoy, cutting him "crimson," as the papers said, the night before we wed. This was in 1940, June, just one year after the Rosenbergs had got married. A lot was happening in the world, but we were oblivious to it—Pat and I were anyway, I can't speak for the Rosenbergs. Of course, Pat was always out of it as far as the news was concerned—the only paper she ever read was the one she helped the kids edit at the high school where she taught.

Contrarily, I've always been a newspaper nut. But not that summer. We got married in the beautiful sentimental Mission Inn just as the Germans marched into Paris, honeymooned in Mexico the summer they killed Leon Trotsky down there, and I finally lost my maidenhead the night Harold "The Boy Wonder" Stassen keynoted the Republican Convention that nominated Wendell "The Barefoot Boy from Wall Street" Willkie for President (we were all boys then) . . . but I hardly noticed any of it. It was like I was living on some other plane. It lasted a whole year, longer even. Hitler was attacking Russia by the time we celebrated our first anniversary, and all I remember from that time is the little apartment we had over a garage in Whittier, going to San Juan Capistrano and Santa Monica beach with Jack and Helene Drown, getting out of bed in the morning with Pat, sharing the bathroom, driving into Los Angeles for the opera and a fancy supper from time to time, running civic clubs in town, thinking idly about my law career, mostly just exploring this new condition which I somehow thought of as unique in the world. On my own, I should say. Pat never liked to talk about it, not with me anyway, she just went her own way as before, which for the most part suited me just fine.

We were a perfect pair. At least it was a perfect pairing for me—Pat was a little restless and uncertain for a while, I could tell by the way she nagged. (Something to do with the mating part maybe, which, looking back on it now, wasn't so good at first. I had to spend a stretch in the Navy before I really got the hang of it. Something a lot of people don't understand about sex: it's something you've got to study just like you study anything else—musical instruments, foreign languages, poker, politics, whatever. I did my homework in the Navy, and Pat was not a little bit surprised when I got out. Happily surprised, I think: we had two kids—*whap bang!*—before she even knew what hit her, and for a couple of years there it was pretty fantastic.) But for me it was like coming home. Pat had simplified my life, brought it all together for me. Not by doing anything. Just by being Pat and being mine. Without having to say a thing, she became my arbiter, my audience, guide, model, and goal. Sometimes she felt she did have to say something, but it was usually better when she kept quiet. She looked good in photographs. I understood myself better when I looked at those photographs. She was the undiscovered heroine whom I could make rich and famous and who would be my constant companion. When I explained myself to Pat, I knew I was explaining myself to what was good in people everywhere. Everything became easier for me. I wondered if it had been somehow like that for Julius Rosenberg? Had he, too, been waiting for someone to come along and make it possible for him to do what he had to do? Or maybe it was the other way around? Ethel was the one, after all, who'd been doing the waiting. Julius was just a kid when she found him.

The Cloakroom was filling up in anticipation of Knowland's big play. Not everybody was happy about it. A lot of them had planned to be well out of the city by noon today. Hendrickson popped in asking for Bill, but nobody knew where he was.

"Do you think he's drunk?"

"Not with this vote on, he hasn't touched a drop."

Somebody said they'd seen him in Joe McCarthy's committee room, and Hendrickson sent a staff member down there to ask Knowland if two o'clock was still the target. I glanced at my own watch: just minutes away. Bob hurried back out on the floor, and the talk shifted to Joe McCarthy's latest act. I stayed out of it. Tail Gunner Joe was dangerous to the peace around here, which it was my job as a kind of double agent —doubled and redoubled—to preserve.

"Jesus, it's a real fucking carnival down there, the whole place wired up with klieg lights and microphones, reporters and photographers everywhere, crawling under the tables, on their knees in front of Joe's table, perched up on windowsills—he's really got something going, all right!"

My main problem was how to keep McCarthy safe inside the Party with all the enormous power he now commanded, here on the Hill and throughout the nation, and at the same time prevent him from getting out of hand and setting the whole house on fire. This wasn't easy, old Joe could wax pretty evil at times, especially when he saw a crowd gathering around a speech of his and lacked a climax to what he was saying—he became increasingly reckless and impulsive then, and could get very dangerous. "Joe," I'd say, "the best tactic in the face of suspicion from a large segment of the press and public is to be certain you can prove every statement you make about Communist activities." But when I said things like that, his eyes would just spread apart and focus on some point way behind the back of my head, far out on the horizon. Ike could say, "I am not going to engage in personalities," and so keep his lily-white fanny clean, but I couldn't. And Joe was a tough sonuvabitch, he had energy to spare, a killer instinct, access to secret files, and a lot of allies. He didn't fit the genial Foghorn image when he came here, and he'd had a hard time at first establishing a power base—so, like me, he'd formed his own club, picking up dissidents and outsiders, going out and working the vineyards, getting his own men—guys like Butler, Welker, Goldwater, Dworshak, Dirksen, and the like—elected. We had other things in common, too, Joe and me: we were both born poor and were shy as kids, both worked in grocery stores, went to Bougainville during the war, came back to make careers in politics off the Communist issue, and both of us had helped make Wheeling, West Virginia, famous. Also we were both Irish, but this was in fact what separated us. And Joe—like all those young beavers around him, Scoop Jackson, Cohn, Kennedy, Schine—lacked my patience, my thoroughness, my iron butt.

"I hear he's got some sonuvabitch down there today who was supposed to be the head of a Phantom goon squad assigned to knock Joe off!"

"Ho ho! No shit! Who says?"

"Some guy from the FBI, used to be a double agent."

"Fantastic! Where the hell does Joe dig up these guys?"

"You gotta admit, it's the best show in town! I mean, he's a legend in his own goddamn lifetime—how many of us can say that?"

Just then, through the Cloakroom doors came the missing Majority Leader, Bill Knowland, puffing in on us like an old World War I armored car, snorting and bellowing: "Okay, goddamn it! muster the troops! the vote's on!" Bill slapped my back as he roared by. "C'mon, Dick! History calls!" And he barreled on out into the Chamber. A few of the Senators trailed out after Knowland, others came pouring in, genial with booze and rumor. I stood at the edge of the activity, moving my lips as though counting heads, just to give them the idea I was acknowledging their presence, and remarking to myself on the essential plainness of this famous "anteroom to history": just a bunch of old sofas strewn with papers and pillows, some tables for signing correspondence, a couple of old typewriters, and upended jugs of Poland Springs bottled water—I remembered the time when, still green and as always overeager, I had made the mistake of going over to one of them to get a drink, breaking one of the innumerable idiotic traditions of this place. Now, not to get caught in another and to avoid the tensions when Joe McCarthy came storming through, I returned to the Chamber.

There weren't that many more people out here than there had been when I'd come through earlier, but the atmosphere had completely changed. It was wonderful how you could feel this, the sense of an impending drama, the agitation, the swelling excitement: "King Cong" aroused. Movements were quicker, expressions less jaded, conversations more intense. Joe McCarthy's Maryland protégé John Marshall Butler and the Democrats' Pat McCarran were on the floor arguing about our new hanging bill—Judge Irving Kaufman's idea—which would restore the wartime death penalty for espionage (McCarran wasn't arguing against the bill, he was just trying to steal it), and the court reporters were hustling about the Chamber with an augmented sense of purpose, tuning in on each Senator as he spoke, working their fifteen-minute shifts before running back to the Reporters' Office to feed their shorthand notes into a dictaphone. The pages were suddenly awake and dashing back and forth with chairs instead of idly goosing each other, the chairs mostly for staff members who now came bursting through the swinging doors at the back—and it *was* filling up now, the tide was rolling in.

I waited for Purtell to order the reading of the conference report by the Chief Clerk, then, while it was being recited, bumped him from his seat as presiding officer. Nobody applauded my arrival. Not that I expected it, but I remembered how warmly old Alben Barkley was always received whenever he came over here while I was in the Senate. Why didn't they greet me that way? I was an ex-colleague, too. Of course, I didn't have Barkley's length of service, nor did I share his fawning admiration for this bunch of rummies. I was always too independent for this place. I'd liked the House, I could operate there, but I could never get used to the Senate, and stayed away as much as possible. Coming here two years ago I had that same lost feeling I had in the war when I first went into the Navy and got shipped out to Ottumwa, Iowa. Since my school days, I've always been allergic to smart-ass private cliques and fraternities, avoiding the tuxedo snobs of the other outfits by forming my own. This place with its almost medieval exclusivity was even worse than most, because, in spite of the surface camaraderie, there was no real interaction here, just obedience to some primitive unchallenged customs and a blind loyalty based on the blood of Party. Each of these clowns lived in a world of his own, like a feudal baron, each one isolated from the other by his retinue of clerks and lawyers, trading favors, garnering wealth and power, loyal only to his own fiefdom. No wonder the Presidents always had trouble with the Senate: Enlightenment or no, we still had our roots in the Dark Ages.

"Mistah President . . ."

"The Senator from Texas is recognized for five, uh, minutes."

Johnson, I could see, for all his surface composure, was hopping mad. Knowland had really pulled a fast one on him today, and Lyndon didn't like to get outdrawn by anybody. It tickled me to see the old operator so discomfited. He had been feeling pretty smug that TIME had been running about the world this week wearing his face, calling him everything from "Rope Dealer" and "Combination Man" to "The General Manager" and "Landslide Lyndon." What TIME didn't talk about was all the tills the General Manager had his hand in; the Depression had been a real goldmine for Lyndon, and he didn't do bad during the war either. Well, hell, why not? he had the smell of magnolias about him, as they say, magnolias and cowshit, no chance ever to be President, he might as well get rich instead. Anyway, I'd had my day with the Poet Laureate as the "Fighting Quaker," and deep in my heart I knew, unlike Johnson, that if I stayed clean and on my toes, I'd have more. I wondered what kind of mail Lyndon was getting. I thought of some other alliterations besides "Landslide" and a good play or two on "Rope Dealer." You could do plenty with "Combination Man," too. Maybe I ought to send him one, I thought. He'd never guess. Take him down a peg.

"Ah submit that if'n the muhjority of the Senate is gunna legislate in thet way," he blustered, lifting one big hammy fist, "it is legislation bah suhprise! it is a patronage grab in the dark, without notice! it is legislation bah *steamroller!*"

While he raged, spicing his argument with raunchy Texan broadsides, which his staff would later patiently excise from the record, the Chamber filled up behind him, the party Whips keeping tabs and waiting for

the right moment to call for a quorum. There was an increasing racket
and both sides were trading a number of more or less friendly insults
without first asking for the right to speak. Like a bunch of bored and
drunken cowboys, aching for a little action to liven up the town saloon.
I tried to maintain a semblance of order for the sake of the visitors up in
the galleries, and watched the doorways (seven, like the holes in a man's
head) to see who was coming and going. Over each of the three principal
doors there was a statue: "Patriotism," "Wisdom," and "Courage."
Perhaps, in time, there would be a statue of me in here, I thought.
Not just a bust like the other Vice Presidents, but a real statue. "The
Fighting Quaker." It fit. The motto over the east entrance translated,
"God Has Favored Our Undertakings," and over the south door: "In
God We Trust." Tailor-made for me, just like the "E Pluribus Unum"
over my head. But the slogan that excited the imagination was the
one attached to "Courage" over the doorway to the West, my part of
the country: *Novus Ordo Seclorum.* Yes, this was what America was all
about, I thought, this was the true revolution of our era—Change Trains
for the Future!—and I was lucky enough to be alive just at the moment
we were, for the first time, really getting up steam. It was our job
now—it would be *my* job—to bring this new order of the ages to the
whole world. My boyhood engineering dreams were coming true! Naturally, it wasn't in the bag, there was already a lot of talk about jettison-
ing the Vice President, I knew I'd have to fight to stay on the ticket in
1956. And friends were few: my legislative power base was gone and I
was a lonely outsider in Eisenhower's administration of hoary-headed
millionaire amateurs—but then I've always been a lonely outsider, that
was my power. Besides, Ike, disliking me, was in fact helping me, constantly labeling me the "politician," the pro, the Party man, and so
identifying me with the real power structure of the actual nominating
conventions. Yes, in reality, the old General was only setting the scene
for me, preparing the way for the New Order that it was my destiny, and
through me the destiny of my generation, to bring to the world! Of
course, you had to be careful—revolution, new order, it was the kind of
language people like the Rosenbergs used, too—but in ignorance, in
darkness: yes, the truth about the Phantom was that he was a *reaction-*
ary, trying to derail the Train of Progress! I was enormously pleased
with this insight. Maybe this was why Uncle Sam got me mixed up in the
Rosenberg case, I thought. Another object lesson in American dynamics
for the heir to the throttle. I took out an index card and made a note.
On the bottom, I wrote: START THE 1954 CAMPAIGN NOW!

"What? What?" I asked. Johnson had just addressed me. He'd been shouting something about "any gahdamn Senator" and "gunna ram it down yore throat!" The Parliamentarian whispered that he'd asked for a quorum call. "Oh . . ."

"Mr. President," Knowland interrupted, "will the Senator withhold his suggestion of the absence of a quorum so as to permit the acting Majority Leader to make a statement?"

"Suttinly, Bill . . ."

Knowland launched a counterattack then, giving his reasons for pulling this surprise vote today, and making it clear he'd given Johnson fair warning, so I was able to settle back again. Knowland and I had known each other since my very first campaign in 1946. You could almost say we were friends, were there such a thing in politics. We'd fought a lot of political battles together, had both had our problems with Honeybear Warren back home, and we'd fought shoulder-to-shoulder out here against the Eastern Establishment. Bill had shown me the ropes when I reached the Senate, had sworn me in as Vice President, and it was his shoulder I wept on in that famous photo after the Fund Crisis. "Everything's gonna be all right, Dick," he'd said, mothering me, and I'd bawled: "Good old Bill!" On the other hand, we'd had our differences, too. I'd more or less stolen Murray Chotiner away from him and with Murray as my strategist had jumped over Bill's head to the Vice Presidency in what looked to him like a sellout to the Eastern internationalists, and now I was fighting him still. During the Fund Crisis, he'd been the man called in to replace me after all, and neither of us could get over that overnight. Well, it's an old truism, just as a nation has neither friends nor enemies, only interests, so there are no enduring loyalties in politics except where they are tied up in personal interests. Uncle Sam taught me that—or maybe I learned it somewhere in grade school. Knowland and I would be real friends again only when we wanted something from each other. Like when I'm President and he and his newspapers are looking for a job in government.

As Knowland carried on, I glanced about the Chamber: it was going to be close. The Whips were scurrying in and out of their respective Cloakrooms, counting adversaries across the aisle, sending staff out in search of missing partisans. I looked down on all this old-man bustle from my marble rostrum, toying with the fragile old gavel—ivory capped with silver and said to have been in use since the first Senate meeting in 1789—and trying to imagine what it felt like to be the Incarnation of Uncle Sam, the physical *feeling* of it as the transformation came over you. Terrible, some said. I had the conviction Uncle Sam preferred Republicans for this process: somehow he never seemed to fit just right in Democrats, and he had left a number of them in pretty bad shape after. We Republicans were closer to America's sacred center than the Democrats, which was what made it easier in a way to be a "good" Republican: the catechism belonged to us. But the people, living their day-to-day profane lives, were closer to the crude worldly pragmatism— the bosses, boodle, buncombe, and blarney—of the Democrats, and so, except on ritual or crisis occasions, tended to vote for them. Who listens to his conscience unless he must?

Bill asked for a quorum call and I said: "The Secretary will call the roll." I realized, as the roll was called, that I was getting keyed up. It was like an election. "A quorum is present," I said, and Knowland moved that the Senate proceed to the consideration of the conference report. The Democrats tried to stall and there was a lot of individual playing to the galleries, but when the vote was called, there were 39 "Yeas" and 39 "Nays." "Under the Constitution," I announced, feeling very good about it, "the President of the Senate, who has the right to vote in the case of a tie, casts his vote in the affirmative; and the motion to proceed to the consideration of the conference report is agreed to!"

Knowland flashed me a thumbs-up victory signal and the Chamber began to empty out again, as Homer Capehart commenced his arguments on behalf of the report. That reference to the Constitution had just given me an idea. I was just about to hand the gavel back to Bill Purtell and write a note to myself when Lyndon Johnson came rushing back in from the Democratic Cloakroom with Russell Long, who cried: "Mr. President! Will the Senator from Indiana yield?"

Oh oh. I sat back down. Knowland stayed his troops and sent Hendrickson hustling into the Republican Cloakroom. "For what purpose does the Senator from Louisiana request that I yield?" Capehart wanted to know.

"I was not able to be in the Chamber at the time of the takin' of the last vote, suh!" said Long. "I understand it was a tie vote, and I should like to move to have the vote reconsiduhed!"

"Well," I said, "does the Senator from Indiana yield for, uh, that purpose?"

"No, damn it, I—Mr. President, I refuse to yield!"

"The Senator from Indiana declines to yield for that purpose," I said, and rapped the gavel smartly. I didn't know if it was a proper occasion for rapping the gavel, but it seemed like a good thing to do: BANG! It was like a gunshot, and Long jumped.

"Yeah, well then, uh, Mr. President," he said, eyeing me suspiciously, "as soon as I kin obtain reckanition, I shall move to have the last vote reconsiduhed."

Capehart conferred briefly with Knowland, then started up his report again, and once more the Chamber began to empty out. I gave the gavel back to Purtell and headed out for the elevators. The day was fast wearing on and I hadn't yet clarified my thinking on the Rosenberg case. It was still possible they'd be burnt tonight, I'd have to be out there front and center, and I had to be ready. Why had Uncle Sam asked me out at Burning Tree about the Clark House Players, for example? Why had he brought up that Ayn Rand play I'd been in? Julius's reading of Horatio Alger, or my duel with Alger Hiss? Kaufman's link with Justice Clark in—? Knowland intercepted me, his big boozy face flushed from all the exertion. "I'm afraid it's not over yet," he said.

"Doesn't look like it, Bill. Where was Joe McCarthy?"

"I dunno, that sonuvabitch—hammin' it up for the newspapers probably. And Dirksen, too! Where'd he disappear to?"

"Last I saw Ev, he was on his way to use the head."

"He was, hunh? Okay, I'll try to round 'em up. Capehart'll be good for an hour or two, but don't go far away."

"I'll be in my office."

"Good boy. And . . . listen, Dick . . ." Knowland wrapped one weighty arm around me like an ape, softening some, glanced around to be sure he wasn't being overheard. "Uh, if you see, you know . . . Uncle Sam . . . tell him I hope I didn't screw things up with this little diversion, I just wanted to get off on the right foot, you understand? Just wanted to set the scene right. Tell him . . . tell him we're pullin' for him and, uh . . . give him my best, will ya, Dick?"

He's going to kick your ass so hard, Knowland, you'll have to take off your bowtie to shit, I said to myself, giving Bill a sincere look. "I'll do that, Bill. You can count on me." I took out an index card and wrote a note. I let him think the note was about him, but what in fact I wrote was: LOOK UP HIGH-SCHOOL SPEECH ON CONSTITUTION FOR POSSIBLE USE ON FIGHTING QUAKER MONUMENT.

"Thanks, Dick, I . . . I hope he's . . . okay. Tell him he's . . . tell him, Dick, he's in our prayers!"

4.

Uncle Sam Strikes Back

Metal and glass are flying everywhere, the scream of tires and crash of cars send the Viennese locals diving into cellars, but the American soldier on the FEAR Military Patrol leaps for the runaway patrol car, whips the door open, grabs the fleeing Russian soldier by the arm—the car careens, tips, smashes into a second patrol car. The four Russians reach for their weapons, but the Yank's pistol is already out: the Rooskies, outdrawn, are disarmed, forced to leave the car at pistol point. Czech refugee Jaroslav Lukas—the man they were trying to kidnap—is still alive. And free. A lean tattered figure crawls slowly out from under the wreckage of the smashed-up patrol cars, stands, brushes himself off: *it's Uncle Sam!* "Yippee!" he mutters, somewhat breathless, "heav'n-rescued again!" He straightens out his crushed plug hat and clamps it firmly on his brow, and on the other side of the world a hundred escaped North Korean prisoners find themselves back inside South Korean stockades. "Our crool and onrelentin' inimy," says the Superhero, bugging his eyes, "has damn near discombobulated us!" GI units shore up, as he tucks his shirttails in and buttons up, the breached ROK defense lines north of the Hwachon Reservoir. A figure gaunt and grand is Uncle Sam, the emptiness of ages in his face, and on his back the burden of the world. He winks and Albert Einstein, no longer with the angels, comes down with the flu. He tugs at his balls and cargo transports airlift the heaviest tonnage of the year. "That pestifferous varmint may have got us in a drefful sityeation," he declares in the old style of Holy Writ, while pinning a Merit Badge on the American soldier of the

FEAR Patrol, "but by Godfrey Daniel, we ain't been knocked outa this ballgame yet—no sir! if them sarpents mean to have 'em a ginewine knife-plyin' skalp-t'arin' punch-up, then, brothers, *let the deevastation commence!*" Flags are fluttering and somewhere a band is playing "Possum Up a Gum Stump." Here, as the Evangelist Ed Markham so fairly put it, was a man to hold against the world, a man to match the mountains and the sea!

His eyes burning fiercely like Mandrake the Magician's, a transfiguring glory in his bosom and a wad of chaw in his jowls, he reaches up and out, seeming to stretch and grow, and with a smile of Christian charity lets fly with the Pow'r that hath made and preserv'd us a Union: "Whoopee-ti-yi-yo! it's yore misfortune, little dogies, and none o' my own!" he booms from above, and—ka-BLAM!—decimates a whole paddyful of contentious gooks. "Come on, boys! The only way to resumption is to resume!" One is reminded of Zack Taylor astraddle Old Whitey running down greasy spics or Andy Jackson routing the heathen Creeks, as the Yankee Peddler, gusty and overcast, like a tempestuous blast, leads the Legion of Superheroes forward on the Korean frontier to recapture Finger Ridge and Christmas Hill. His fighter-bombers strike the Phantom's main highways, destroying bridges and bicycles, making road cuts. Defiance gleams in Sam Slick's eye, a sneer curls Sam Slick's lip—no more Mr. Nice Guy now, he's shooting from the hip! "Fer pleasure or pain, fer weal, fer woe," he roars, walking softly but swinging a big bat, " 'tis the law of our bein', we rips what we sew!" And off he goes to quench fires, still earthquakes, keep planes aloft, confound mischief.

His tattered coattails gallantly streaming, he roars through the Third World, up the Iron Curtain, making it flap in the gale of his wake, and into Times Square—what a mess! He sweeps away the Phantom's debris, reconstructs the Sing Sing stage, wipes the obscene slogans off the walls, chastises the reckless traffic. "Force rules the world still," he thunders, his chinwhiskers aquiver in the fitful upper breeze, "has ruled it, shall rule it—meekness is weakness, strength is triumphint, over the whole dingbusted earth, still is it Thor's Day!" Thus, with the timely aid of the Prophets, Uncle Sam manages to transform even this outrageous disruption by the Phantom into a seeming piece of his own Weltordnung: Thor's Day! He lifts his steel-blue eyes and spies a message scrawled across the billboard high over the Death House mock-up: COMMUNISM IS THE RIDDLE OF HISTORY SOLVED AND IT KNOWS ITSELF TO BE THIS SOLUTION! He contemplates this a moment, with doubt and strange surmise depicted in his troubled look, then spits in disgust. "The dadblame Phantom's gone too far on that one," he snorts dryly, restraining his mounting rage. "I'll be swacked if that nasty mortiferous boogerman don't seem to hanker after these burnings even more'n I do!" Then, his anger bursting its bonds, he rips the billboard down and erects new hoardings in its place: FELLOW CITIZENS! GOD REIGNS AND THE GOVERNMENT AT WASHINGTON STILL LIVES! And with that, the air seems to clear, a furtive presence seems to dissipate and let the sun through, and the electrical sign reading AMERICA THE JOKE OF THE WORLD begins once more to metamorphose, Uncle Sam accomplishing in three clean moves what it took the Phantom to do in sixteen dirty ones:

> AMERICA THE POKE OF THE WORLD
> AMERICA THE POPE OF THE WORLD
> AMERICA THE HOPE OF THE WORLD

Thus does Uncle Sam struggle against this new tide of darkness and perversity, unleashed in effect by one man, Supreme Court Justice William O. Douglas, acting alone in his chambers and against the will and necessities of the entire nation. Uncle Sam himself appointed him to this High Council of Elders as guardian of the sacred laws and interpreter of the Covenant, setting him "as a banner in the vanguard of Righteousness, as one who interprets with knowledge deep, mysterious things, as a touchstone for them that seek the truth, a standard for them that love correction," but now he's fucked it up. Was he innocent in his pernicious decision, or has he fallen prey to the Angel of Darkness, stumbling knowingly into wickedness and falsehood, pride and presumption? This is what he said:

> I have serious doubts whether this death sentence may be imposed for this offense except and unless a jury recommends it. The Rosenbergs should have an opportunity to litigate that issue. . . . It is important that before we allow human lives to be snuffed out we be sure —emphatically sure—that we act within the law. If we are not sure, there will be lingering doubts to plague the conscience after the event. . . .

To be sure, if any conscience is to be plagued it will be his, for thus, with one stroke, he has nullified over two years of careful preparations, over two years of exemplary Anglo-Saxon jurisprudence and liturgy, granting not merely a stay but ordering the case sent back to the District Court, thence to the Court of Appeals, giving the atom spies not respite but life itself, and making Uncle Sam, Judge Kaufman, Edgar Hoover, and the entire U.S. prosecuting team look like a bunch of clowns. And he has done so knowing that the Court is in recess and scattered, the world is in turmoil, an A-bomb attack is imminent, and the legal point raised by these shady interlopers is so flimsy that even the Rosenberg defense attorneys rejected it.

Haven't the Pentagon Patriots already warned us . . . ?

> . . . Now some quack lawyer with a flair
> Shall try to save them from the "chair,"
> But such a shyster (mark him well)
> Is paid with gold that comes from hell.
> So with God's lash, he, too, should share
> Death with this Communistic pair!

> . . . Still, should some court support their prayer
> And save them from death's "waiting chair" . . .
> If such there be, who'd stoop to spare
> Their hides from Sing Sing's "burning chair"
>> We'll brand his brow
>> With marks of guilt,
>> And link his name
>> With traitors
>> In the sewers of shame!

As one voice, the free press of America cries out against the "treason" of Justice Douglas, calling him "arrogant . . . crafty . . . disruptive." FBI agents secreted in the Warden's garage at Sing Sing wire the Boss reassuringly that newsmen "are considerably upset as a result of the stay and it is Denno's opinion they will probably blast Douglas." And blast him they do. Leslie Gould in the *New York Journal-American* brands him "a headline-grabber with political ambitions, a tramp who has reverted to type," and in the *Chicago Tribune* Walter Trohan writes:

Douglas, it must be remembered, has been the darling of the Communists. He dissented from the Court decision upholding the conviction of 11 top Communists. He called for recognition of Red China by United Nations at a time when the Red Chinese were killing American boys in Korea. . . . He compared the Communist uprisings in the Far East to the American Revolution. . . . Douglas aspires to the presidency. Most of his evil might still be before him!

The *Washington Post* laments that "Justice Douglas has plunged this highly controversial and internationally important case into utter chaos!" and the *Philadelphia Inquirer* asks: COULD JUSTICE DOUGLAS HEAR MOS-COW'S CHEERS . . . ?

Justice Douglas has done his country one more monumental disservice . . . after the Court had adjourned until fall, [he] took it upon himself to reverse the whole Supreme Bench by a masterpiece of legal red-hair splitting [and then] hurried quietly away from Washington.

For the moment he is supposed to have gone to Oregon. Some say he will soon head for Moscow, is due there July 1. Many others will wish he would go back to Tibet, climb on a yak—and stay there. . . .

The blackest treason in American history must not be condoned.

This is the man, incredibly, who might have been Franklin Roosevelt's fourth-term Vice President, and thus ultimately the Incarnation of Uncle Sam himself! Uncle Sam must have had his eye on him even then—probably why he dumped the old satyr into all those sex scandals. Maybe he caught something in all that friskiness, a dose of venereal anarchy or something. And if so, what's to prevent the whole damned Bench from coming down with it? "One scabbed sheep infects a whole flock," warns Uncle Sam on the floor of the House of Representatives, and Congressman W. McD. Wheeler of Georgia leaps up as though he's been goosed to introduce a prophylactic resolution "that William O. Douglas, Associate Justice of the Supreme Court of the United States, be impeached of high crimes and misdemeanors in office," whereupon a special subcommittee of five is created instanter to act on the resolution. "Ah see no pahticulah point in sendin' mey-un to Ko-REE-ya to dai, Mistah Cheymun," declaims Congressman Wheeler, "whahl ay-tomic spies are allowed to liy-uv heah at HOME! One Justice yieldin' to the vo-CIF'rous my-NOR-utty preshuh groups of this yere CUNT-tree is indee-FEN-suble! Ah canNOT sit ahdly by heah in this yere layjus-LAY-tuv BAHDY without seekin' to DO somethin' abaout it!" Don Wheeler is warmly cheered by his fellow Georgians, all of whom have been aching for years to see this nigger-loving New Deal cowboy stuffed as deep in hell as a pigeon can fly in a week, and they figure now they've finally got a clean shot at him.

The Rosenbergs themselves, of course, are elated. Their spirits had sunk pretty low of late, Julius burning his eyes out with futile late-night searches through the trial record, Ethel suffering from migraine headaches and sobbing herself to sleep at night. Columnist Leonard Lyons's report recently in the *New York Post* that they were actually anti-Semites at heart who didn't even want a rabbi with them on their Last Walk apparently rattled them, and they've been singing themselves hoarse at the prison services ever since, seemingly in the mad hope that somebody outside the walls would hear them. Julie had to have two teeth pulled out (Warden Denno in his economy-minded way making sure he got temporary plates only), and when his mother, Sophie, visited him while he was still dopey from shock and Novocain, what he said was: "Mama, I don't feel good. Oh Mama, where is my wife? Where are my children? I'm sick, Mama. If only I were home you and Ethel could take care of me." Ethel has evidently stopped writing letters to him altogether. She hasn't wanted to go out in the exercise yard and play boccie-ball any more. Julius has tried to exercise, to keep in shape, but his knees have been like putty. When he's tried to flip cigarette butts at the toilet bowl in his cell, he's not only been missing, he's been burning his fingers as well.

Now all that is changed. Their happy singing, as they call it, is driving the other cons up the wall, and their lawyers are dancing impertinent jigs right out in the streets: it's a real breakthrough! They have until October now at the very least, even if the Appeals Court rejects the new arguments. Time to design hundreds of new questions, dig up more confounding evidence, get more signatures on the clemency appeals. The Korean War could end, the Soviet peace offensive could lead to detente, the whole climate could change. And what is this that Dr. Urey and others are saying about there being no secret to the A-bomb in the first place? Where is that spy ring the FBI has been shouting about? Who the hell is Harry Gold after all, and where did he come from? No, there's *reason* to dance, and what's more, the Appeals Court might even sustain the new argument, hold that they were indeed sentenced under the wrong law—then the whole indictment would be quashed and they'd both be set free! The government would have to obtain a new indictment and get up an entirely new trial! This time there'd be no mistakes, those Greenglass diagrams would be held up to public scrutiny, Gold would be cross-examined, Morty Sobell would testify, the complicated Greenglass finances would be probed, questions would be asked about where that list of prospective jurors came from, and they might even be lucky and get a Presbyterian judge.

But, like Justice Douglas on his way to the woods, they have not reckoned with Uncle Sam's resourcefulness and his old-trouper determination that this show *will* go on—he sends for The Man to Send For, the Clean-Up Man, as TIME calls him, A LEGAL MIND & A POLITICAL BRAIN, Attorney General Herbert J. Brownell. "Get that Court back here, Herb," he says. "I want this thing now!"

"Won't be easy. There's never been a special term of the Supreme Court just to review a stay granted by one of its own members."

"Yeah? Well, new occasions teach new duties, boy!" His beard seems to darken and a wart flowers momentarily on his cheek: "The occasion is piled high with difficulty, and we must rise with the occasion! Find Vinson! *Lean on him!*"

"O-okay, I'll do what I can—but he's not one of ours, I don't know if he'll—"

"What, not a Republican, you mean? Hell, neither are Kaufman and Saypol. So what? These guys are professionals, they know the score. Come on, boy, hop to it! This ain't a political campaign, it is a call to arms!" His teeth flash and a silver cigarette holder seems to sprout from between them—he snatches it away and whips it out the window. "I said, shag ass, mister! Put his feet to the fire! *I want what I want when I want it!*"

"Y-yes-*SIR!*" The Attorney General wheels around in his red-leather swivel chair and grabs up the phone. Chief Justice Vinson is on vacation like the rest of the Court, but he tracks him down. "Hey, Fred, get everybody back here! You gotta vacate Douglas's goddamn stay! Right now! Today, tomorrow—but quick!"

"Vacate a stay? It's never been done!"

"Yeah, well, the occasion is piled high with you-know-what, and it's about to hit the fan! Uncle Sam's breathing hot down my neck, Fred! It's important in the interests of the administration of criminal justice and in the national interests that this case be brought to a final determination as expeditiously as possible!"

Vinson caves in so fast, Brownell figures Uncle Sam must have got to him first. Justice Hugo Black is dragged, protesting, from his hospital bed, others from crap tables and hunting lodges. Justice Douglas is apprehended in Uniontown, Pennsylvania, heading west. He's snapped back to Washington so fast his feet don't even touch the ground. The mothproof dust covers, laid down a day ago for the summer holidays, are hauled off the furniture by emergency cleaning crews, 350 excited members of the public and press are admitted to the big red-draped air-conditioned chamber, and at twelve noon on Thursday, June 18, the Nine Old Men—reportedly "tense and snappish"—file in under a frieze of Truth holding a mirror up to life and take their seats behind the long dark bench. Lawyers crowd in, FBI agents, some of Herb Brownell's lieutenants, members of the original Saypol prosecuting team, tourists, reporters, and sightseeing foreign dignitaries.

It's a dramatic moment, unique in United States history, but Uncle Sam does not have time to see out the formalities. Around the world, the Phantom has Sam Slick's lean back to the wall. The situation in Korea, for example, is still very bleak, riots are breaking out, there's a new threat of invasions, rumors of nuclear warheads moving into the area,

Rhee is as obstreperous as ever, even the Pusan whores are out in the streets bellyaching against the Yanks—biting, as it were, the probang that feeds them—and the Phantom has conjured up a dense fog to hide the North Koreans in their mischief. Undaunted, Uncle Sam sends his forces right into the worst of it. They get cut up, but they hold the line. The hardnosed 187th Airborne Regimental Combat Team, commanded by an up-and-coming tough-as-nails brigadier general named Westmoreland, is flown in from Japan to round up Rhee's rampaging prisoners, put them back in the barbed-wire stockades, and quell the riots. This is the same bunch of cowboys used to break up the Red riots in the Koje Island P.O.W. camp last year, they take no shit from anybody. Uncle Sam wants the truce negotiations to proceed, he's had it with all this yo-yoing, but the Reds say: no roundup, no peace talks. Sam snorts at the cultural ironies and tells them they'd better get their yaller hunkers back to the goddamn table or he's *really* gonna cream 'em, but he's infuriated with Syngman Rhee just the same. WHY'D HE DO IT? the newspapers ask. IT'S A MISTER RHEE! Uncle Sam lines up his boys around the world and they let Rhee have it—the barrage of abuse and repudiation is deafening. Rhee, unabashed, responds with a cablegram to the Ashland, Ohio, *Times:* The United States, he says, is being influenced by European countries that "are too far gone toward Communist ideology." Who the hell does he think is running the world anyway?

In East Berlin the situation is even worse, hopeless in fact, it's a real free-for-all for the Phantom and his T-34 tanks. A few guys throw rocks, West Berlin's Mayor Ernst Reuter declares that it's "the beginning of the end of the East Berlin regime," President Eisenhower announces "with particular satisfaction" an additional fifty million dollars in economic aid to West Berlin, and some trolley wires are pulled down, but there's not much else that Uncle Sam can do, his own tanks are just too damned far away, and his best stuff is tied down in Korea. Willi Goettling, an unemployed West Berlin housepainter with a wife and two small daughters, is caught by the Russians on the wrong side of the city, accused of being a hired gun of Uncle Sam and "one of the active organizers of provocations and riots in the Soviet sector of Berlin, taking part in the banditlike tumults directed against the organs of power," and he is taken out and unceremoniously shot. Uncle Sam charges the Phantom with "irresponsible recourse to military action" and lack of imagination. Who's going to remember Willi Goettling twenty years from now? he asks petulantly, but all he gets in reply is what sounds like a distant fiendish chortle.

Stung, Uncle Sam cranks up the Voice of America wattage to stimulate new riots, organizes a demonstration of two hundred thousand hungry workers in front of the National Palace of the "Red Colonel" in Guatemala, has Herb Brownell arrest fifty-five Chinese for deportation to Red China in retaliation against Chairman Mao's hassling of the Roman Catholic Missions there, keeps things boiling in Lithuania, where the Kremlin bosses have already had to order drastic party and government shake-ups, and helps Generalissimo Francisco Franco inaugurate four new hydroelectric power plants in Spain, which amazingly all seem to work. "Intimates," Sam murmurs, kissing Franco on both plump cheeks and stuffing a hundred million in his field-jacket pockets, "are predestined . . . !" The Radical Party of Argentina cables President Eisenhower, demanding clemency for the Rosenbergs—President Perón, whose own plump cheeks no doubt tingle in anticipation, promptly arrests seven Radical leaders. From one end of the world to the other, all these kissable men: General Sir George Erskine, for example, arriving in Nairobi and announcing his intention to discredit "this Mau Mau business" everywhere and make it "unfashionable" in the eyes of all likely to come into contact with it. It's a kind of disease, and people must be made to understand that it can easily be fatal. To exemplify this, the British Royal Air Force is given the task of making certain prohibited areas "unwholesome." In a trial run, a force of 1200 African Kenya Home Guards, supported by British planes and white mercenaries, attacks Mau Mau hideouts in the Aberdare Mountains, and at least thirty of the savages are exterminated by saturation bombing and strafing alone. Smiles Sir George: "By good discipline and common sense, we shall do our duty, distasteful as it may be!"

In New York, however, the iron curtain around the Statue of Liberty continues to vex the American Superhero. He moves the wage dispute directly to Washington, and there are hints of an operation along the lines of the Berlin Airlift if the boats don't get moving again in time for the gathering of the tribe during the atom-spy burnings. And when is that to be? Crowds have been drifting all day through Times Square, but there seems to have been no sense of conviction—it is still scheduled for eleven o'clock tonight, but there is no jostling for front-row seats. Uncle Sam joins Cecil De Mille and Busby Berkeley briefly on the Astor Roof for a cinematic overview of the rebuilt Times Square arena, and gets the image of isolated thunderheads scudding through the Square but without the final massing up of unbroken storm clouds. And some of those thunderheads, he sees, are hostile, threatening tempests of another sort—he assigns Allen Dulles and Edgar Hoover the task of collecting and collating I.D. data from these gathering pro-Rosenberg clemency demonstrations, and sends the Holy Six out on the streets to propagandize against them, try to break them up. The Six—Rabbi William Rosenblum, Father Joseph Moody, *Christian Herald* editor Daniel Poling, former Presidential adviser Sam Rosenman, Notre Dame law dean and mystic Clarence Manion, and "Electric Charlie" Wilson, ex-president of General Electric—have formed a kind of transcendentalist brotherhood with the aims of discrediting the Rosenberg clemency drive, preserving America's Judeo-Christian heritage intact, and laying their own claim to a piece of the exorcisory action. In newspaper ads across the nation recently, they declared:

> The case of the convicted atom spies, Julius and Ethel Rosenberg, is being exploited by typical Communist trickery to destroy faith in our American institutions. . . . Racial and religious groups as such have no special interest in the Rosenberg case and cannot properly become involved in appeals on their behalf. Those who join in organized campaigns for clemency in this case have knowingly or unwittingly given assistance to Communist propaganda!

This campaign has in fact effectively scared a lot of people, but many others of weak faith are still putting their signatures to clemency appeals and turning up in the streets bearing inflammatory placards. The streets of New York and most other great cities are clogging up with them, and a special Clemency Train has this very day brought hundreds of these people to the very precincts of the Supreme Court—most of them are ganged up around the steps of the Court, but some have actually slipped by into the gallery up on the main floor—where now Chief Justice Fred Vinson is rapping the special term to order.

The government's task is a formidable one, in spite of the known sympathies of most of the Justices—the point is, they don't want to set any precedents for slapping each other down. Uncle Sam's proxy is Acting Solicitor Robert L. Stern, dressed impeccably in striped pants and black cutaway coat. The Rosenbergs are represented (if that is the word) by four noisy belligerent outsiders—John Finerty, Dan Marshall, Fyke Farmer, and Emanuel Bloch—whose clothes look like they're been slept in and who don't seem even to know each other. Bob Stern argues that the Rosenbergs have already been allowed too many appeals, the new point is frivolous, further delays would make a mockery of our judicial system, and the stay should be vacated. "The defendants have been convicted of a most terrible crime," he reminds the Court (two of whom are already starting to doze off), "nothing less than the stealing of the most important weapon in history, and giving it to the Soviet Union. Haven't the Rosenbergs had their full day in court and more? The public's rights and safety are no less precious than the Rosenbergs'. We do not think those rights should be violated any longer!"

The Rosenbergs' lawyers scramble about these points, attempting to blur the sharp edges, cast doubt on the applicability of the various laws, and question the need for such haste and impatience in deciding the issue—at one point, tall loose-jointed Dan Marshall even grabs the counsel stand with both hands and does a fair imitation of a country preacher, though he lacks the radiance of a true Man of God, rocking back and forth and crying out: "I doubt whether even a justice of the peace would call the meanest pimp before the bar on such short notice!'

"Now, now," scolds the Chief Justice, "don't let your temperature rise!"

But it is cranky old jut-jawed John Finerty—whose connections with the Phantom go back to Tom Mooney, and to Sacco and Vanzetti—who really wakes up the nodding Bench and reveals his team's true colors, or color: he denounces the special term as an insult to the Court and the integrity of Justice Douglas, scathingly accuses Brownell and Vinson of a kind of legalistic conspiracy, attacks the Justice Department for perpetrating along with Judge Kaufman a knowing fraud based on rigged testimony and phony evidence, and caps the whole outrage with a blustering assault on Irving Saypol, the original U.S. prosecutor in the case and one of the most admired men in America: "There never was a more crooked district attorney in New York!" he cries. Justice Tom Clark, himself a former Attorney General and a personal friend of Kaufman, Saypol, and Brownell, is offended by this frontal attack and leans forward to put a stop to it. Even Hugo Black grimaces at Finerty's tirade, but this may only be a gas cramp. "If you lift the stay," snaps Finerty, his Irish cheeks aflush, "then God save the United States and this honorable Court!" There are gasps in the courtroom at this old reprobate's vain use of the Lord's name, and many are sure they heard him say "dis-honorable Court."

Argument has been edging toward violence, so Fred Vinson cuts it off and the Nine Old Men retire to their private conference room, where a very hostile atmosphere prevails. Black and Douglas are fit to be tied, and Vinson is not confident he has any of the other three New Dealers with him on this one either. It helps, of course, that they're all browned off at Douglas for playing the devil with their holiday like this, this special term being a disconcerting precedent. On the other hand, the

new impeachment threat against Douglas may provoke a show of solidarity—they don't want any precedents set in that direction either.
Listening to them wrangle like schoolgirls, Vinson figures he's about had
it with this goddamn job. If he doesn't quit soon, it'll kill him. He tells
them all to go home and sleep on it, they'll announce their decision
whether to vacate the stay or not tomorrow at high noon. That's right,
high noon, why the hell not. He makes Burton go out front to pass the
word, since he's been drowsing through most of the arguments and so is
less riled than most.

The public—jammed not only into the courtroom, but into all the
corridors of the building as well, and in the doorways, stairwells, windows, down the steps, out into the street and onto the lawns of the
Methodist Building and the Library of Congress—takes the news with
mixed feelings. Apparently the Rosenberg lawyers have not been per-
suasive enough to convince the Court, or they'd have said so; the delay
is most likely just to give the old fellows time to work up a few eloquent
touches to their decisions, something to be remembered by in *Bartlett's
Quotations*. Also, let's face it, the delay heightens the drama, and as long
as everything turns out well in the end, that's probably a good thing,
makes everybody feel more alive. Okay, but the troubling thing is, it
should have been easier than this. No matter what happens tomorrow,
Uncle Sam has plainly lost this night to the Phantom! Though the day is
warm and the sun though lowering still high in the sky, a faint shudder
passes through the crowd as they drift away from the Court, not together toward Times Square as they'd hoped and planned, but sepa-
rately toward their own private executions, slow, but inexorable;
uncelebrated. Alone in the dark, tonight anyway. With the Phantom
loose in the world. Scary. . . . By the time Uncle Sam staggers, bruised
and bedraggled, into the courtroom, it is empty. The drapes have been
pulled and dust floats sullenly in the beams of afternoon sunlight.

The weary Superhero slumps heavily into a pew at the back of the
room, lifts his feet, stretches his legs out in front of him. "Ah well," he
groans, his voice echoing like a hollow wind through the empty marble
halls, "no gains without pains. Like the man says." There are holes in
the soles of his boots, and a soft caved-in look through his cheeks. "A
wise man," he murmurs, tipping his plug hat forward over his nose,
leaning his head back, "don't try to hurry history . . ." His eyes close.
He yawns, chuckles wryly to himself under the plug hat. "Everything
human," he sighs, "is pathetic . . ."

A husky broad-shouldered man in laced-up walking boots emerges
from the back rooms, pulling a cloth windbreaker on over an old

sweater. "Where ya goin', Bill?" asks Uncle Sam coldly from under his hat.

"Out to walk the canal towpath. Want to come along?"

"Naw. Too bushed. I been working my ass off, you perverse sonuva-bitch. The blisters on my heels are so big it hurts when I bend my elbows, I got tank treads up my spine both front and back, and I'm so dadblame hungry my belly thinks my throat's been cut!"

"Well, come on then. Maybe we can make it up to the little store that sells that home-smoked country sausage before it closes . . ."

"That goddamn towpath of yours—I got half a mind to concrete it over and make a six-lane highway out of it, damn you! I'd go do it tonight, if I wasn't so bodaciously whacked. Why'd you do this to me, Bill?"

"Well, the law . . ."

"To hell with that. You been voting with us in this case all along, I thought maybe you were coming around at last, why'd you go and blow it like this? Eh? Why'd you get us in this mess? Has Hugo been work-ing on you again?"

"No . . ."

"That miserable tote-road shagamaw, he still can't get over his days of whooping it up in the Ku Klux Klan back when they was still hanging coons, he's a incurable overcompensator. Don't let him make a fool out of ya, Bill!"

"Hell, he's got nothing to do with it," says Douglas flatly.

"The eccentric sonuvabitch, he's even trying to boycott the executions by sneaking off to the hospital," grumbles Uncle Sam from under his hat. He feels through his coat pockets for his corncob pipe. "If he ain't careful, he might not come out again!"

"I tell you, Sam, it's a matter of law . . ."

"My ass. You're not gonna get away with it, you know." Douglas sighs and shrugs his shoulders, glances up at the old clock dangling like an antiquated fob watch over the bench. "Like Mr. Dooley says, 'No matther whether th' Constitution follows th' flag or not, th' Supreme Coort follows th' iliction returns.' You may have sunk our show for tonight, but your buddies are gonna have you shovelin' shit tomorrow, boy!"

"Maybe . . ."

"No maybe about it. If they were ever gonna stick by you on prin-ciple, they'd of done it today. No, it's time to pay up and look pretty—they're gonna stomp all over you, Billy."

"If they do, they're wrong. The cold truth is that the death sentence may not be—"

"Ain't no such thing as cold truth, hoss . . ." He finds the pipe, peers squint-eyed into the bowl from under the brim of his plug hat.

"—may not be imposed for what the Rosenbergs did unless a jury so recommends."

"Huh!" Uncle Sam snorts, and sucks on his empty pipe. "Who says?"

"It's a law too elemental for citation of authority, Sam, that where two penal statutes may apply—one carrying death and the other imprisonment—the Court has no choice but to impose the less harsh sentence."

"That ain't *my* Court you're talkin' about—damn it, Billy, you're as ornery as ever you was!"

"Well, I know deep in my heart I am right on the law."

"Deep in your heart, hunh?" Uncle Sam lowers his feet, sits up slowly, pushes his hat back off his nose, squints up at Justice Douglas. "Well, the law and your bleedin' heart be *damned!* Watch out, my friend, morality is a private and costly luxury. Like your pal Felix says, 'Courts ought not to enter this yere political thicket!' "

"Brer Rabbit had an answer to that one, Sam," replies Douglas with a wry grin.

Uncle Sam finds some tobacco and stuffs it in the bowl of his pipe. "Fergit Brer Rabbit and remember the Prophets, my boy: 'There is no good in arguin' with the inevitable. The only argument available with a east wind is to put on your overcoat.' " He scratches behind his ear and withdraws a wooden match. "I'm tellin' you plain, mister," he says, holding the match up like a pointer, "them two traitors is gonna—" He strikes the match down Douglas's pantleg, but it fails to light. He stares at it, dumfounded. "What the hell—!" He strikes it on his own pants: "Are gonna—" This time the head falls off. "Tarnation. Musta got it wet in Wonsan Harbor . . . uh . . . hey, Billy, ya got a light?"

Douglas tosses a packet of safety matches with a Smokey Bear warning on them down to the American Superhero. "Speaking of traitors, that's another thing that's been bothering me: this conspiracy law. I mean, using it to give somebody a harsher penalty than you could give him if you convicted him of the crime itself, or using it to get around—"

"Harsher penalty! Hell, man, this is treason!"

"Yeah, I know, everybody from the Judge and Prosecutor to the FBI and that goofy knuckle-headed Incarnation of yours keeps repeating that—but the Constitution says: 'No person shall be convicted of treason unless on the testimony of two witnesses to the same overt act, or on confession in open court.' No act in this entire case involving the Rosenbergs has been corroborated by a second witness, Sam, and they have *not* confessed!"

"So what? Everybody knows that. That's why we had to use the conspiracy law, we didn't *have* two witnesses to any of this shit, it was in the nature of the case!"

"I understand that, but if you *convict* them on a lesser or broader law, then I don't see how you can *sentence* them on a more serious or precise law. You'd do well to think it over, Sam."

"In two words, chum," says Uncle Sam, dragging on his pipe and blowing smoke, "im-possible!" He jabs the pipe at Douglas menacingly. " 'When the ignorant are taught to doubt,' quoth the Prophet, 'they do not know what they safely may believe!' So let's get this straight, wise guy—"

"Well, *I've* got no doubts," snaps Douglas, turning away to leave the chamber. "I'm sure of the answer, my duty is clear. I'm not sucking ass on this one, Sam, and if you'd stick a pin in that inflated head of yours and stop showing off for five minutes, you'd—"

"*What? What!!*" roars Uncle Sam, rearing up in anger. "Listen, this is *my* circus, you old coot! And I'm gettin' goddamn sick and tired of you pretendin' to know better'n *me* what's right for this country!"

"Yup, well, while I'm at it," replies the Justice, rumbling calmly on, one big hand resting lightly on his canteen as though on a holstered six-shooter, "don't you think it's about time you got down off this Sons of Light and Darkness kick? I've about had it with all this—"

"You've about had it is *right!*" storms the enraged Superchief. "You're in more trouble than you know, boy! This country's after your scalp! You're so smart at giving advice, lemme give *you* some: *Quit!* If you don't, Congress is gonna heave you outa here so fast they won't be able to see your ass for dust! You hear me? You'll be lucky if they don't lynch you in the bargain! You—what the hell are you laughing at!?"

"Hell, Sam, you got about as much respect for those fatuous Dixie gasbags as I've got—they're not gonna get anywhere, and you know it. When you turn Hayden or Aiken or Saltonstall loose on me, I'll start to worry, but for now I think I'll just go for my walk. You coming along or—?"

"*NO!*" Uncle Sam blusters. His face is flushed, his white chinwhiskers are standing on end, his blue eyes blazing. "I—I promise you, mister, we're gonna *get* you! One way or the other, *you are going to be sorry!*"

Justice Douglas stares for a moment at the irate Superhero. "Yes," he sighs, shaking his head, "I suppose I will," and wheels out of the room, nearly bowling over the janitor just coming in to clean up.

"Who you talkin' to, boss?" asks the janitor, peering bug-eyed into the empty Supreme Court chamber. "You talkin' to yo'self?"

"Yeah," says Douglas without turning back. "It looks that way . . ."

5.

With Uncle Sam at Burning Tree

I was sitting on the floor of my inner office, surrounded by every scrap of information I could find on the Rosenberg case, feeling scruffy and tired, dejected, lost in a surfeit of detail and further from a final position on the issue than ever, when the bell on my clock rang twice for a quorum call. It was late, goddamn late, I thought Lyndon Johnson had long since given up. I desperately wanted to get rid of this atom-spy affair and go home—if I left the damned thing now, I'd just have to come back, and then where would it end? Why the devil had Uncle Sam got me into this? Just to convince me of the enormity of their crime? But I was already convinced. How many Americans had died and would die because of what they had done? Would the Reds have dared invade South Korea, rape Czechoslovakia, support the Vietminh and Malayan guerrillas, suppress the freedom-hungry East German workers, if the Rosenbergs had not given them the Bomb? We were headed, truly, into a new Era of Peace after World War II, our possession of the ultimate weapon and our traditional American gift for self-sacrifice would have ensured that—and we might even have helped our friend Chiang return to the Chinese mainland where he belonged, loosened things up a little inside Russia to boot—but the Rosenbergs upset all that. When the Russians tested their first A-bomb in 1949, I was one of the first to hit at Truman's failure to act against Red spies in the United States. And then when they got Fuchs in England in 1950, I called for a full congressional investigation of atomic espionage to find out who may have worked with Fuchs in this country—I moved quickly, caught most Congressmen nap-

79

ping, got most of the headlines. And deserved them. No, Dick Nixon knew what was going on all right, and was quick to say so, that's how I beat that fancypants movie star for Senator that year, and even though finally I didn't have all that much to do with the Rosenberg case itself, I always felt that—indirectly anyway—it was my baby.

All the more so when you considered that it was my successful pursuit of Alger Hiss which had given courage and incentive to the entire nation, made Communism a real issue, restored the dignity and prestige of HUAC, changed the very course of America and the Free World, and ultimately had made these electrocutions possible. In Whittaker Chamber's new best-seller, *Witness,* he wrote: "On a scale personal enough to be felt by all, but big enough to be symbolic, the two irreconcilable faiths of our time—Communism and Freedom—came to grips in the persons of two conscious and resolute men. . . . Both knew, almost from the beginning, that the Great Case could end only in the destruction of one or both of the contending figures, just as the history of our times . . . can end only in the destruction of one or both of the contending forces!" And hadn't I been the catalyst that gave Whittaker and the Free World victory? To hell with your goddamned "McCarthy Era"! *I'm* the one!

I'll never forget the day that Hiss, beaten, walked over to the old davenport in Room 1400 of the Commodore Hotel in New York to examine Chambers's molars: "Would you mind opening your mouth wider? I said, would you open your mouth!" What pathos! If these two were indeed, as Whittaker had suggested, the momentary Incarnations of the contending forces of the universe, there was something profoundly ironic about the Force of Darkness and Evil poking petulantly but almost tearfully among the dental ruins in the soft but firm jowls of the Force of Goodness and Light. I think he hoped that Whittaker would bite him so that he could cry from pain rather than humiliation. I had already guessed the real bond between these two guys, and Alger's desperate scrutiny of the intimate details of Whittaker's mouth, full of so much sadness and decay, began to embarrass me. I finally had to ask him: "Excuse me, before we leave the teeth, Mr. Hiss, do you feel that you, uh, would have to have the dentist tell you just what he did to the teeth before you could tell anything about this man?" From that moment on, Hiss was finished; like that snake that eats its own tail, he just couldn't keep his foot out of his mouth after that. It mas maybe the most fun I ever had in politics, outside of elections, and when it was over I felt like one chosen. Like Whittaker said: "I do not know any way to explain why God's grace touches a man who seems unworthy of it. But neither do I know any other way to explain how a man like myself . . . could prevail so far against the powers of the world arrayed almost solidly against him, to destroy him and defeat his truth." Which was even more true of me, who unlike Chambers must struggle for a lifetime. Not that I'm unworthy. No, that's just it, the powers arrayed against the good man are formidable and indefatigable, there are few who can stay the course. Defeat and disappointment dog every footstep. If old Hiss hadn't been a liar, for example—and an eager one besides—I might have been destroyed before I could ever get started. So thank God at least for that: it gave me the power to prevail, it was a milestone in human history, and marked me once and for all as the greatest of the Early Warning Sentinels.

In short, my conscience was clean—so why had Uncle Sam brought this Rosenberg case up, especially so late in the ballgame? Of course, he'd only mentioned it in passing while washing his balls on the seventh tee, but I had long since learned that with Uncle Sam nothing was mere happenstance, you had to listen to him with every hole in your body. The case itself seemed cut-and-dried: a routine FBI investigation, a sequence of confessions from Fuchs to Gold to Greenglass, leading directly to Julius and Ethel Rosenberg. They denied all accusations, but then so did Hiss—in fact, their reactions were very similar, high and mighty sometimes, hurt and offended others—you could smell the ham in them. And they had a much more telling witness against them than a fat spooky slob like Whittaker Chambers. David Greenglass was also something of a fat slob, true, and a bit spooky as well, but he was more than that: he was also Ethel's own brother. His story of his recruitment by Julie and Ethel, how he drew up the lens-mold sketches and lists of personnel, passed them on to Harry Gold, how he discussed these things with the Rosenbergs, with little details of family life mixed in, how Julie tried to help him escape—it was all very convincing. The only question remaining really was: who else was in the spy ring besides the Rosenbergs, Greenglasses, Gold, and the Russian Yakovlev? Uncle Sam had wanted maximum pressure to be applied to the Rosenbergs to make them talk, which was the reason Judge Kaufman had given them the death penalty, together with a hint that confessions might soften his heart. No one had to tell Kaufman this, he knew what he had to do, though he'd apparently sent Saypol down to Washington just to make sure. There had been a lot of evidence brought forward over the past two years to support some of the Rosenbergs' minor testimony and try to damage David's credibility as a witness, and having studied the case now, I could perceive a lot of backstage scene-rigging and testimony-shaping by the prosecuting team that deprived the courtroom performances of some of their authenticity and power, but there was no shaking off the basic conviction: the Rosenbergs were guilty as hell. So why—?

The "Yeas and Nays" bell rang. I leapt to my feet, hauled on my jacket, and dashed out the door. I took the subway car over to the Capitol, arriving breathlessly in the middle of the roll call. "Jesus, Dick, where the goddamn hell ya been?" whined Knowland through clenched teeth. I rushed forward to relieve Purtell and count the vote: it was another tie, this time 41 to 41. Once again I cast the tie-breaker, but then into the Chamber came Dennis Chavez, Democrat from New Mexico: "Mr. President, ah, due to unavoidable circumstances . . ." That did it. All this effort for nothing, I thought. I felt weak from the run over, sweaty—I realized I'd forgotten to have lunch; mustn't let supper go by, I could make myself sick. Willis Robertson, yellow-dog Democrat from Virginia, announced flatly, almost sadly, that he wished to speak for three minutes on the dubious merits of the issue, and then he would call for a vote on the conference report itself and have it simply voted up, eh, or down . . . that is, unless the distinguished Senator from California wished to postpone a vote on the report until three p.m. Monday, as the Democrats had originally requested.

I watched the collapse set in on Knowland's big florid face. It was like an old fortress turning to putty. There was nothing more that I could do. He rose slowly, heavily, like a tired old walrus, and made one last stand: all right, goddamn it, not till Monday then—but two p.m., not three p.m. Knowland probably thought the Democrats would let him have that point to save his pride on this, his maiden sally as Leader, but if so, he should have known better. Chavez in fact suggested they delay the vote until Tuesday. Knowland, crashing to defeat, agreed to hold the vote no sooner than three p.m. Monday. Johnson, grinning like a possum, nodded, and it was all over. Monday!—it seemed light years away! I was eager now to get back to my office and get some of my thoughts down on index cards before I forgot them—not just about the Rosenbergs and their goddamned fourteenth anniversary either: I remembered that I'd had an important thought about the 1954 campaign tactics that had already slipped my mind, and another about justice and my generation. And then, as I banged the ivory gavel down, terminating the exercise and giving the Democrats their victory, it suddenly occurred to me: ivory was the traditional gift for fourteenth wedding anniversaries! The trouble with me, I thought, is that I'm too attentive, I see things too clearly. One could well envy old boozers like Bill.

I took the elevator down to the subway, jammed in with the others on their way to their offices and homes, but once below decided against riding the subway car—it was crowded and I saw I might have to sit facing the rear of the car, something I always hated to do. It even made me motion-sick sometimes, short a ride as it was. Also, they were squeezing as many as sixteen to eighteen on the damned thing, and I hated to sit that close to anybody, especially perspiring as I was now, so I set out on foot on the walkway beside the monorail, glancing back over my shoulder from time to time, mindful that John Bricker had nearly got assassinated down here five or six years ago. It was windy in the tunnel, it was always windy in here, but it seemed windier than usual today, threatening, almost as bad as it was out at Burning Tree Sunday. The Burning Tree Golf Club was also known on Capitol Hill as the Smouldering Stump, but I now thought of it as the Burning Bush because it was there, during the past few months, where Uncle Sam had most often dropped his mask and talked with me directly about such things as statecraft and incarnation theory, rules for the Community of God, the meaning of the sacred in modern society and the source of the Phantom's magical strength, the uses of rhetoric and ritual, and the hierology of free enterprise, football, revival meetings, five-card stud, motion pictures, war, and the sales pitch. And it was there last Sunday, in the comparative seclusion of the seventh tee, that he slipped out of his duffer's disguise, hit a hole in one, and on the way over to rinse off his balls, asked me what I thought about the Rosenberg case.

In the aftershock of Uncle Sam's transmutation, it is difficult even to hear a question, much less to grasp or answer it. One is struck by a kind of inner thunder, a loss not so much of vision as of the coordinates of vision, and a loosening of all the limbs as though in sympathy with the dissolution of the features of Uncle Sam's current Incarnation. I say he went over to rinse off his balls and asked me about the Rosenbergs—but perhaps he had asked me long before, while watching his drive arc distantly toward the flag on the sixth green, for example, or even during the backswing, somewhere in that timeless era between the first snap and crackle of metamorphosis, Ike's blue eyes flashing me a glance full of fear and trembling as the moment grew in him, and my own slow recovery from the awesome dazzle of this miraculous transubstantiation. My senses only began to pull together and function again, as it happened, while watching his large pale freckled hands plucking the little white balls, gleaming wet, out of the suds and popping them into the gray folds of the towel: at that moment it came to me that Uncle Sam, freshly shazammed out of the fretful old General, had just whipped out a five-iron, smacked the ball four hundred yards to the green, vacated the tee like a priest his altar, and somewhere along the way, asked me my opinion on the atom spies.

I realized he was putting me on the spot, testing me, and I didn't know quite what to answer. Did it have something to do with Korea? Stalin? My Checkers speech? American jurisprudence? Alger Hiss? I raked my mind for some clue to his drift. He was leaning against a bench, tossing the shiny white balls up in the air, juggling them two, three, seven . . . thirteen at a time. His white cuffs flashed in the sunlight like signal flags. Of course, I expected to be tested like this, expected it and welcomed it, knew it to be part of the sacred life, something Uncle Sam had to do to protect his powers. And I trusted him—he'd never used kid gloves on me, but he'd never been unkind to me either, I was pretty sure he liked me—I trusted him and was eager to please him. Maybe he only wants to be reassured, I thought.

I was glad about the way the case turned out, of course, but he knew this already. After all, having gone out on a limb about it back in '49, I couldn't help but be flattered when J. Edgar Hoover actually found a spy ring and busted it. But past that, I had to admit, I didn't know too much about the case. The trouble was, by the time it came up in '51, I had begun to catch fleeting glimpses of Uncle Sam's blue coattails and was busy chasing them, and so I had pretty much stayed out of Hoover's and Saypol's way. Oh, I knew well enough what the Big Issue was, my whole political career had been built on it. And I knew, of course, that the Rosenbergs were part of it, an important part: Edgar had called it "the Crime of the Century" in the *Reader's Digest*, and I'd gone along with that, even if I did think he should have given equal billing to the perjury of Alger Hiss. And even though I didn't follow the details—about all I knew for sure was that Fuchs had led the FBI to his American courier Harry Gold who had led them to Ethel Rosenberg's brother David Greenglass who subsequently had turned state's evidence against the Rosenbergs (Morton Sobell fitted in there somewhere—maybe he was the one who tore the Jell-O box)—I did admire Irving Saypol's dynamic, intransigently hostile prosecution of the case, applauded the breadth of Judge Kaufman's vision and courage, and was properly relieved when the Supreme Court, still dangerously New Deal–tainted, refused to review the case. On the other hand, let me say—and I don't mind being controversial on this subject—I was a little sorry that two people, a father and mother of two little boys, had to die. I'm always sorry when people have to die, my mother taught me this. Especially women and children. But how much of the world's sadness can

any one man handle, no matter how sensitive he is? I had troubles of
my own, and I knew that Uncle Sam would do what was right and
necessary; just stay on the reservation, keep the faith, do your own job
well, get your rhetoric ready, and don't ask too many irrelevant questions: that seemed the best policy.

But maybe it was not. Maybe I had not done enough. I fussed about,
choosing a ball for teeing up, worried about this. Everything was re-
markably green, the sky was deep blue, the balls a blinding white: my
senses were still on edge from the transmutation. Uncle Sam was now
balancing a putter on his sharp thin nose while juggling the golf balls.
The empty tee awaited me: the novice called upon to show what he
knows. I'd built my reputation on the thoroughness with which I'd
pursued the Hiss case, after all, and maybe I'd gone soft on this one, lost
some of my fabled diligence and so part of my image as well, perhaps
this was the thrust of Uncle Sam's question now. He somehow had his
old plug hat up on top of the putter and was twirling it around. His
playfulness could be deceptive. Don't take chances, I thought—stick
with what you know. I wasn't sure whether or not the actual conspiracy
charge had been proven, but let's be frank about it, it was just a technicality anyway—mainly because of the statute of limitation, I supposed,
and the fact that in these espionage cases there were rarely two witnesses to anything. They were being tried in fact for treason, never mind
what the Constitution might say, which was anyway written a long time
ago—and on that charge, J. Edgar Hoover's word was as good as a
conviction.

"Well," I said finally, poking around bravely in my golf bag, "well, I
believe they're, uh, probably guilty."

Uncle Sam blinked in amazement, gathering in the balls with one big
hand, catching the putter and hat as they fell with the other. *"Guilty!"*
he roared, his chinwhiskers bristling. I realized, glancing away, pretending to study the distant green, that Abraham Lincoln, whom I'd always
admired, was probably the most terrifying man of his age. "Well, hell,
yes, they're guilty!"

I knew by his reaction I must be miles off the mark, but my answer
still made sense to me and I resented what seemed like some kind of
entrapment. Instinctively, I counterattacked: "Well, naturally, I haven't
had ample opportunity to study the transcripts carefully, but I, uh, from
what I've seen of them, the case has not been proven—"

"The case!" he snorted incredulously. "Proven! Gawdamighty, you do
take the rag off the bush, boy!"

I stared miserably into my golf bag while he railed at me. Not only was I giving all the wrong goddamn answers, I was also having trouble with my drives. I do not believe that some men are just naturally cool, courageous, and decisive in handling crisis situations, while others are not. I chose a number two wood for a change. I knew this was a mistake and put it back. "There . . . there was no hard evidence," I said, pressing on desperately. "And since the Rosenbergs refused to cooperate, all we had left really was the brother's story!" I wasn't sure this was true. I'd read it somewhere. I thought: there is less than a 50 percent chance that what I'm doing will help me. "And to get *that*, we'd had to make this deal with him and his wife which—"

"So all that courtroom splutteration was a frame-up," he blustered—he was in a ferocious state, "what trial isn't?"

"Wait, that's not what I meant!" I protested. "Irving Saypol's a fine trial lawyer!" I wished I could keep my mouth shut. But I'd always admired Saypol, the greatest of the anti-Communist trial lawyers, though I knew he was mean and ornery with a mind about as broad as a two-by-four, and a Tammany Democrat to boot. I pulled out my driver, swished it around a little. My hands were so sweaty it nearly slipped right out. "I don't think he'd ever—"

"Rig a prosecution?" Uncle Sam laughed sourly. I knew better, of course, I was being a fool. "Hell, *all* courtroom testimony about the past is ipso facto and teetotaciously a baldface lie, ain't that so? Moonshine! Chicanery! The ole gum game! Like history itself—all more or less bunk, as Henry Ford liked to say, as saintly and wise a pup as this nation's seen since the Gold Rush—the fatal slantindicular futility of Fact! Appearances, my boy, appearances! Practical politics consists in ignorin' facts! *Opinion* ultimately governs the world!"

"Yes, but . . . I thought—"

"You *thought!* Cry-eye, look out when the great God lets loose a thinker on this planet, we're all in for it! I'm tellin' you, son, the past is a bucket of cold ashes: rake through it and all you'll get is dirty! A lousy situation, but dese, as the man says, *are de conditions dat prevail!*"

I felt my neck flush, so, to cover up, I stooped and concentrated on teeing up my golf ball, grunting to kill time. My hand was shaking and the ball kept falling off. I seemed to see my father down in the front row at a school debate, flushing with rage as I disgraced myself with a weak rebuttal.

"And so a trial in the midst of all this flux and a slippery past is just one set of bolloxeratin' sophistries agin another—or call 'em mettyfours if you like, approximations, all the same desputt humbuggery—and God shine his everlastin' light on the prettiest ringtailed roarer in the courtroom! Am I right? You remember that Ayn Rand play you were in years ago: a game for actors!"

I didn't know he knew about that. If he knew that, what didn't he know? How could I compete? I felt like a fighter wearing sixteen-ounce gloves and bound by the Marquis of Queensberry rules, up against a bare-knuckle slugger who gouged, kneed, and kicked. But life for everyone is a series of crises, I cautioned myself, it's not just you, and with that I finally got the ball on the tee. I stood, gazed off toward the seventh green, trying to see the flag there. It was red, I knew. I was on to what this golf game was all about, all right, but I still hadn't figured out what Uncle Sam was up to. Did he mean the Rosenbergs might be innocent? Or their crime insignificant? I addressed the ball. My brand-new golf shirt was wet with sweat. I remembered my opening line from that Ayn Rand play: *Gentlemen of the jury—on the sixteenth of January—near midnight—the body of a man came hurtling through space, and crashed —a disfigured mass—at the foot of the Faulkner Building.* That was just how I felt. "But you said—I mean, President Eisenhower said, and J. Edgar Hoover, Judge Kaufman, everybody: a crime that has endangered the lives of millions, maybe even the whole planet—!"

"Damn right!—and much of Madness to boot, and more of Sin, and Horror the soul of the plot, but we're not just talkin' about that little piece of technological cattle-rustlin'! Even though that's more than enough to scrag a man all right—like Sweet Andy Carnegie used to say: upon the sacredness of property civilization itself depends—but still, we all know how he got his: no, a little healthy thievin' never hurt anybody. But real guilt, real evil—listen, son, get that right hand around there on that club, like you're shakin' hands with it, not jerkin' it off!"

I twisted my hand around on the club: the toe turned in and tapped the ball accidentally, knocking it off the tee again.

"God may forgive sins," Uncle Sam observed grimly, "but awkwardness has not forgiveness in heaven or earth—that'll cost you a stroke." He could be as cold as a New England parson sometimes. "No, guilt, real guilt, is like grace: some people got it, some don't. These people got it. Down deep. They wear it like a coyote wears its lonesomeness or a persimmon its pucker. They are suffused with the stuff, it's in their bones, their very acids, it's no doubt a gift of the promptuary, even their organs are guilty, their feet are guilty, their ears and noses—"

"You mean, because . . . because they're Jews?"

"Jews! What in Sam Hill has *that* got to do with it?" I'd missed again. I was completely lost. I couldn't even find my goddamn tee. "Irving Kaufman's a Jew, isn't he? Is *he* guilty? Is Irving Saypol guilty? Roy

Cohn? Hell, I got a touch of kike in me myself, son, not much, just enough for a little color and wile and to whet my appetite for delicatessen—shoot, I might even incarnate myself into one of 'em some day . . ."

I glanced up. He was as stern as ever, but there was a mischievous twinkle in his eye. My mind raced uneasily over the possibilities. I felt sure I had a good head start on all of them. I knew, too, it would help a helluva lot if I hit a decent tee shot for a change. If I could find my tee. "It's under your right foot," Uncle Sam said flatly.

"No, bein' a Jew ain't it, though it probably didn't help them none either. Their kind of depravity is something deeper even than that, something worse. You don't see it so much in the shape of their noses as in the way they twitch and blow them. You see it in how they shuffle and squat, how they bend, snort, and grimace. You see it in their crummy business, their greasy flat, their friends—even their crockery betrays them, their lawyers, their pajamas, their diseases. It's no accident, son, that they've been nailed with such things as Jell-O boxes, console tables, and brown paper wrappers—and it coulda just as easily been the studio couch they slept on, their record player, medicine chest, or underwear—they stink with it, boy, it's on everything they touch!"

I knew now what he meant. It was the feeling I'd had about Alger Hiss. Others, less perceptive, had had that feeling about Whittaker Chambers. In our case, it had been pumpkins, carpets, typewriters, and teeth. Whittaker, who had smelled a little unhealthy himself for a while, had emerged aromatic as a saint. "Perjury wasn't Hiss's crime either," I said. I'd been talking more or less to myself, but as soon as I said it, I knew I was on the right track at last.

"No," Uncle Sam agreed. "That's right." I glanced up. He was watching me closely, fierce as a tiger and cool as a cucumber, as the Gospel says, rolling the balls around in his mighty fist as though he were peddling them to me, a gesture of such iconic depth that I felt suddenly elevated past myself.

"It wasn't . . . it wasn't even espionage or double-dealing!" I was nearly there. . . . "Uh . . ."

"They have walked in the path of the spirit of perversity," whispered Uncle Sam hoarsely, leaning toward me like an eager schoolmaster, urging me on, "violators of the Covenant, defilers of the sanctuary . . ."

"Sons of Darkness!" I cried.

Uncle Sam leaned back and smiled, not a smile of self-contentment or amusement, but a smile of blessing, the smile of a life-insurance salesman who has just successfully put your affairs in order, or of a parent who has come to see you graduate from Duke Law School—or any law school, for that matter—and he set his plug hat back on his head. I knew I'd turned the corner. I began to feel I might actually hit a decent drive after all. "And what's the reward for all them what walk in such ways?" He tossed one of the golf balls up in the air and smashed it with his putter, baseball fashion, out of sight. "A multitude of afflictions at the hands of all the angels of destruction!" *Whack!* "Everlastin' perdition through the angry wrath of an avengin' god!" *Swat!* "Etarnal horror and perpetual *re*-proach!" *Smack!* "Darkness throughout the vicissitudes of life in ever' generation, doleful sorrow, boils on the ass, contumely in the opinions of Christian men, bitter misfortune and darklin' ruin!" *Slam!* "And the disgrace of final annihilation in the . . ." *splat!* ". . . fire!"

He was something to watch, all right—he had a lot of style. A lot of styles, I should say: now that of Larry Doby, next Country Slaughter, then Mel Ott, Hank Greenberg, Johnny Mize, Luke Appling—but though he'd organized baseball's liturgy and had governed its episcopacy (to be sure, there was more of Judge Kenesaw Mountain Landis in his briary nineteenth-century features than of, say, Warren Harding or Herbert Hoover), he'd never actually played it. Golf was his game, the first he'd come to, back in the capacious days of William Howard Taft, and it was still the only one he played regularly. Before that, he'd pretty much limited himself to hunting and fishing, riding, swimming, war, billiards, and the odd cockfight—indeed, the very idea of Uncle Sam wasting his time playing idle games would have been unthinkable fifty years ago. But such was the character of our twentieth-century revolution: gamesplaying was now the very pulse and purpose of the nation. It was Taft's successor, Woody Wilson, who gave it its fateful turn: he was sometimes out on the course as early as five in the morning, even played the game in the dead of winter, using black golf balls to find them in the snow, until that awful day when the transmutation did not quite come off and left only half of Wilson still working. Now golf was part of the Presidential discipline—indeed, why else would I be out here?—and every time Uncle Sam eagled out or blasted his way mightily from a sand trap to the pin, somewhere the Phantom cringed.

I dug up my tee and set my ball on it, took a practice cut at a dandelion. "But how can you, uh, tell for sure?" I asked, and—*whick!*—took the head off the dandelion. Why couldn't I hit a golf ball like that? "I mean, even Foster Dulles trusted Hiss . . ."

"Ah, well, the pact with the Phantom is no less consecratin' in its dire way then gettin' graced by Yours Truly," said Uncle Sam, and imitating

Stan Musial's quirky stance, smacked another golf ball out over the horizon. "Ask that mackerel-snapper Joe McCarthy about the Grace su'ject!" He tossed up his last ball and belted it high in the air—in fact, I lost sight of it completely. I wondered, if it got up high enough would it just stay there? Where does gravity run out? But finally it did come down, about fifty feet from the seventh green, and lodged in the roots of a tree. I supposed he wanted to keep his hand in on approach shots. Or got a kick out of blasting trees—Burning Tree indeed! you'd think it was Ben Franklin's private lightning lab to see the way Uncle Sam's left the vegetation out here. Now he tucked his putter under one arm and withdrew his corncob pipe, knocked it out on the heel of one boot. "The impure, through their presumptulous contact with the sacred, are momentaneously as lit up with this force as are the pure, and it's easy for folks to confound the two," he said, leaning back against the bench, "as much, I might add, to the unwarranted sufferin' of the holy as to the ephemeral quickenin' of the nasty . . ." He gazed at me meaningfully . . . aha! so *that* was why I had been accused of the secret slush fund! why, in spite of everything, I was still so distrusted many people said they wouldn't even buy a used car from me! The Philistines wouldn't have bought a used car from Jesus either, right? Things were becoming clear now. I concentrated on the ball, sitting firm on the tee like truth itself, and took a practice backstroke, trying to keep my elbow straight. "You're gonna top the ball, son," Uncle Sam said gloomily.

I did. I tried my damnedest to lift the ball and I swung so hard I splintered the tea, but the ball only plopped about six feet ahead. Judas, I thought, I really hate this fucking game.

"Ya know, you're about as handy with that durn stick," muttered Uncle Sam irritably, tucking the pipe in his mouth, "as Adlai Stevenson is with a set of dumbbells!"

I was badly stung by this. I would be a good golfer if I had the time to play regularly, but a man can't give himself to everything on this earth. And the innuendos worried me: Stevenson was a loser. I realized it was still touch and go . . .

Uncle Sam sucked on his empty pipe a couple of times, then blew it out, reached into his pantaloon pockets for tobacco. "There's one thing about criminals and kings, priests and pariahs," he said. He packed the tobacco into his pipe with one long bony finger, peering at me as though over spectacles. "They may be as unalike as a eagle to a rattlesnake, but they both got a piece a that dreadful mysterious power that generates the universe!" As he said this, he whipped a long wooden match out from behind his ear. "The difference," he went on, "is what happens when they try to use it. The ones with the real stuff, the good guys, they achieve peace and prosperity with it—these are . . ." he scratched the head of the match with his thumbnail and it popped ablaze: ". . . the Sons of Light!" He cupped it over the pipe bowl and continued: "The other geezers, the (*puff!*) Phantom's boys, well, if you (*puff! puff!*) don't watch out, those squonks can haul off and (*puff!*) exfluncticate the . . ." he looked up and held the match out, still burning, then crushed it in his fist: "*whole durn shootin' match!*"

It's true, I thought, he's not exaggerating, the Rosenbergs no longer belonged to the ordinary world of men, that was obvious, you could see the sort of energy they now possessed, even though stuffed away in Sing Sing prison, in the rising fervor of world dissent—in France, the whole damned government was being shaken. I walked up to my ball, teed it up on a little hump of grass. I felt a little shaky myself. "You mean, we're not executing them . . . just because . . . ?" I poked my toe about, looking for firm footing.

"We ain't goin' up to Times Square just to fulfill the statutorial law, if that's what you mean," Uncle Sam said. He blew a smoke ring, then another and another, each inside the other, ending with a little puff of smoke for the center. "This is to be a consecration, a new charter of the moral and social order of the Western World, the precedint on which the future is to be carn-structed to ensure peace in our time!" He hacked up a gob and spit into his smoke rings, hitting the bull's eye. . . . "We're goin' up there to *wash our feet,* son!" A miniature mushroom cloud welled up from the center, and the concentric rings flattened out and spread like shock waves.

I understood his question now. I turned back to my ball, dug my feet firmly into the turf. Times Square, the circus atmosphere, the special ceremonies: form, *form,* that's what it always comes down to! In statesmanship get the formalities right, never mind the moralities—why did I keep forgetting that? I smiled. "Then, wouldn't it have been better to burn them at our Inauguration?" I commenced my backswing, shifting my weight confidently onto my right foot.

"Tried that," said Uncle Sam, "but we got knocked down with a lame duck. Anyhow, don't matter, now we got the summer-solstice and the anniversary angles—"

"Eh—?" I was so startled my knees buckled and I sliced the ball out of bounds. "The—*what?*"

"Thunder and tarnation, boy! That's four strokes already, and you ain't even off the damn tee yet!" cried Uncle Sam.

"I . . . I'm sorry! I, uh, thought you said . . ."

"The solstice and the anniversary, soap out your ears, son!" he repeated irascibly. He had blown a smoke ring shaped like an outline map of the United States and, as it expanded, was trying to fill in the several states. "The Rosenbergs signed their dierbollical pact fourteen years ago come Thursday the eighteenth," he muttered around puffs and rings. He was trying to squeeze the District of Columbia into his map, but it was getting very cluttered in that area. He seemed about to lose his patience. "I thought you knew that!"

"Ah . . ." So, it was also the Rosenbergs' anniversary! I'd thought for a moment he'd been referring to *my* wedding anniversary! When Kaufman had set the date finally for the week of June 15th, I had seen that it could fall on Pat's and my anniversary—our thirteenth!—on June 21st. And I'd seen that summer-solstice angle, too: after all, we hadn't married on the 21st for nothing. It was the climax to our "Beauty and the Beast" game, time of the roar of Behemoth and all that. Then, when I learned that this year June 21st was also Father's Day, it had suddenly looked like a sure thing. I'd said nothing to anyone about this, but it had worried me: if it was intentional, were they doing it as a favor, giving Pat and me something extra to commemorate? or was somebody out to get me? I'd feared the latter, usually the safest of the two assumptions when you're in politics. But then the marshal had scheduled it officially for the 18th, and I'd forgotten about it . . . until now. I teed the new ball up, twitching my shoulders and wrists, trying to loosen up. I had a better understanding of things now, but it didn't make me feel any easier. Their fourteenth! And what were *we* doing here on the seventh tee? "I . . . I guess I missed that," I admitted frankly.

"It seems to be you missed just about everything!" snapped Uncle Sam. "You don't know no more about this case than a goose knows about rib stockings!" He had given up on the map and with a flick of his finger had drawn the Canadian border up to a straight perpendicular line, the Great Lakes clustering like a knot, turning the whole thing into a kind of gigantic hangman's noose. "Do you know what law the Rosenbergs were actually convicted under? Do you know who the Clark House Players were? Sarah O'Ken? Helen Rosenberg? Catharine Slip? Do you know why they called David Greenglass 'Little Doovey' or what Julius Rosenberg's secret Talmudic name was? Why was Julius born in Harlem? How is it that Roy Cohn was working for Irving Saypol? What were the Rosenbergs doing in Peekskill in 1943 or Irving Kaufman in Washington in 1948? Eh? Did you even know that Ethel Rosenberg played the Major Bowes talent rackets? that Julius read Horatio Alger

and Tom Swift and took to the stumps against the National Biscuit
Company? or that Emanuel Bloch's marriage is on the rocks? And
who's that screamer workin' for anyway?"

"I thought you . . . you said the past was a pot of lies . . ."

"We ain't talkin' about trials now, boy, stay awake, *we're talkin'*
about the sacraments!"

"I . . . I'm sorry," I said, and stepped up to the ball. I felt like I'd
been stepping up to this goddamn ball all afternoon. Roy Cohn once
mentioned that Saypol used to be a really rotten golfer himself, but that
he read almost every book ever written on the subject, and it improved
his game immeasurably. Maybe that was what I ought to do.

Uncle Sam raved on and on about the case; most of the time I had no
idea what he was talking about. I tried to pay attention, I knew it was
important, but the coincidence of anniversaries and my own stupid
panic about it when he brought it up were still troubling me. "And what
about the CCNY Class of '39? Why was J. Parnell Thomas sent to the
same jail as Ring Lardner, Jr., of the Hollywood Ten? What the hell's a
proximity fuse? Should we feed 'em on cheese and barley cakes and
beat 'em with fig branches? Why does that Russian astronomer now say
that the vegetation on Mars is blue? Eh? Eh?" Of course, June, a lot of
people get married that month, Eisenhower's own anniversary was just
another ten days away, wasn't it? It wasn't all that improbable. But it
was all tied up somehow with those generational vibrations which were
exercising such a grip on me these days—how many other parallels
might there be? I was afraid to find out. Maybe it was because I'd just
passed forty, things like this happened to people when they reached
forty, I supposed. Uncle Sam was trying to explain why it was the
Rosenbergs, why the Lower East Side, the Foley Square Courthouse
(another link to the Hiss case! my subcommittee *met* there, it was just
before I finally nailed the bastard!), Sing Sing, and now Times Square,
why Nelson Eddy and Bernard Baruch had to be there, Louella Parsons
and Dr. Kinsey, why an electric chair instead of sending them out to sea
in a leaking boat as in the old days, and why just now, this week. . . .
"I mean, McCarthy's got such a cactus up his cornhole, he's bound to
blow it soon, and now that we've laid the threat of a A-bomb attack on
them heathen Chinks, they gotta fold their hand any day now, and what
with Stalin dead the whole goddamn mood could change—this may be
our last chance to kill these people! And what if the Phantom squeezes
an extra day out somewhere? Have you thought about that? That
hodag's known to have a lotta contacts in the jew-dishiary—then what?

If we had to go through the Fourth without them atom spies burnt or burning, the whole shebang could come unhinged like a hog shed in a Okie twister!"

"That's . . . that's true," I agreed, vaguely aware of the wind commencing to blow across Burning Tree, but unaware at the time how prophetic he'd been—or had he been telling me something I should have picked up on? Should I have got Edgar to put a watch on Douglas right then? I was too distracted to think about it—a few days to play with, a couple of days' delay: then Pat and I could *still* get hit with it!

"This week, son! We gotta *move!*"

"*Yessir!*" I cried, and took a violent swing at the ball, topping it again and sending it skittering this time into the rough about a hundred yards away. Well, shit, at least I was off the tee.

"Damn it all, boy!" thundered Uncle Sam, rearing up off the bench, brandishing his putter like a saber and stomping forward like Ulysses Grant debouching from his field tent. "The brave man inattentive to his duty and who don't keep his eye on the ball is worth little more to his country than the coward who deserts her in the hour of danger! Life is real! Life is earnest! You gotta get on top of this thing! You gotta get your ass in gear!"

"I'm sorry . . . I just can't seem to get the hang—"

"That's just it! We *gotta* get the hang! We gotta exsect these vinimous critters this week or our name is shit with a capital mud! This ain't just another ballgame, johnny, we are gonna have to fight for the reestablishment of our national *character*, and we shall nobly save or meanly lose the last best hope of earth—namely, *me!*"

"*You—?*" I croaked. "But you . . . you're . . . you can't—!"

"Die? Oh, I ain't immortal, son, I'd hate to think I was. Nothin' goes on forever, Amber, not even History itself, so why should I? Sooner or later, the Phantom gets us all!"

I was truly shaken. I caught myself staring at him the way I used to stare at my mother when I first realized that she had to die. Suddenly, everything seemed very fragile and tenuous. Brittle. "But you're so . . . so strong—!"

"Remember the old kings, boy, the times don't change. I'm the force what'll raise up the whole sin-besotten world, see if I don't . . . but I'll get et by it, too!"

"I . . . I don't understand . . . ?"

"I would not live alway, I ask not to stay, loveliest of lovely things are they, on earth what soonest piss away, so long as you get your kicks in in the passin'! That's poetry, boy! Xerxes the Great did die; and so must you and I!"

Yes, I was shaken, but oddly I also felt like I was very near the center of things. There's been a point to all this, after all, I thought. I felt closer to Uncle Sam than I'd ever felt before.

"Oh, probably, after it was over, like Christ, I could come back some day . . ." He sighed wistfully, puffed on his pipe, blew a plume of smoke shaped like a bird—an eagle. "But it wouldn't be the same . . ." He added wings and it flapped off into the sun: I was blinded by the light, but as far as I could see it simply disappeared. When I looked back at Uncle Sam, he was staring at me very strangely, his blue eyes glowing as though lit from behind. "Sometimes," he said softly, "sometimes I almost *want* to die. . . ."

A cold chill rattled through me. My sense of Uncle Sam's presence in front of me dipped briefly, almost imperceptibly, as a candle will gutter in a faint draft—and for that fraction of a second, I seemed to have an intuitive awareness of everything happening in Uncle Sam's head. And then, as quickly, it had passed. My head ached slightly and I felt a momentary emptiness down in the marrow of my bones. Then that, too, filled up.

"Don't worry," Uncle Sam laughed, "it ain't such a grave matter, if you'll pardon the pun, son—in fact, it's a lot more fun this way." He put his arm around me and led me down the fairway toward my ball, his white locks blowing in the cool breeze. He seemed to have shrunk some in the last few minutes. "It's like old Tom Paine useter say, panics in some cases got their uses—we ain't had a party good as this one's gonna be since you were just a little tyke sayin' your breakfast prayers back home on Santa Gertrudes!" I felt swarmed about with fears and absences. Paradox. But I felt protected at the same time. I had a feeling that everything in America was coming together for the first time: an emergence into Destiny. . . . "Oh, I don't reckon we could live like this all year round," he said, "we'd only expunctify ourselves. But we do need us an occasional peak of disorder and danger to keep things from just peterin' out, don't we?" I nodded, remembering my own peaks— the Hiss Case and the Checkers speech, and before that my school highs, debate wins, romances with Ola and Pat, the war, even my brothers' deaths—and I knew how they could light things up, make everything new again: after all, that was what light and darkness, the sacred and the diabolic, death and regeneration were all about! "Well, okay," said Uncle Sam, pocketing his corncob pipe and clapping me on the shoulder, "let us, then, be up and doin', with a heart for any fate; still achievin', still pursuin', and though hard be the task, keep a stiff upper lip!"

"Oh, yes!" I said, flushing with pride and joy and eager to begin, for he'd just singled me out among all men: that fractured echo from the past was a piece of Longfellow's "Psalm of Life," which Grandma Milhous penned by hand under a photo of Abe Lincoln she gave me on my thirteenth—*thirteenth!*—birthday! I kept it on the wall above my bed all through high school and college: *Learn to labor and to wait!* "I will!"

"Good boy!" he said. "I press thee to my heart as Duty's faithful childering! Be prepared for anything, for this is one a them hard contests where men must win at the hazard of their lives and at the risk of all they hold, dear! But be brave, and whatever happens, just remember the sagassitous words of that other Poor Richard long ago: 'Fools make feasts . . . *and wise men eat 'em!'* So whet up that *appetite!*" He hugged me, then gave me his club to swing with, saying: "Now, listen here, a golf ball is propelled forward by the verlocity imparted to it by a clubhead, see—this is physics, now, my boy—and it's kept aloft by underrotation or backspin, which producifies a cushion of air, and this is what gives the ball lift. To get this backspin, the clubhead's gotta travel *downward*, right swat whippety-snap through the *center* of the ball, and this is where you been goin' wrong. You think you gotta lift the ball up, and this is makin' you pull your swing . . ."

"Ah . . ."

"Actually the uplift is projectorated by the spin, and the spin is got by hittin' *down* and *through*, you got it? Now, another problem is movin' your maximum verlocity back to six inches . . ."

Down and through, got it. I took a practice swing, keeping my shoulder down, my eye on the ball—then, because when I looked up I realized that people were staring at me (got to watch it, can't let my guard down like that), swung on up into a friendly wave at a carload of Senators disembarking the subway car. "See ya, Dick!" "Don't miss the show!" "Not for the world!" "Take it easy!" Down and through. And out and up, back to the office, get rid of this goddamn thing. With maximum verlocity.

6.

The Phantom's Hour

The curtain rises upon the Warden's office, a large old unfriendly apartment, with bare floors and staring whitewashed walls, furnished only with the Warden's flat-topped desk and swivel chair, a few straight-backed chairs, and an eight-day clock. On the Warden's desk are a telephone instrument, a row of electric bell-buttons, and a bundle of forty or fifty letters. There are two large windows, crossed with heavy bars, at the back of the room, and doors left and right. The Warden is verging toward sixty, and his responsibilities have printed themselves in italics upon his countenance. With him, staring out the window, is the Prison Chaplain, dressed in slightly shabby clericals. The Chaplain's face, normally calm, intellectual, and inspiring, is presently depressed. The Warden blows a cloud of smoke to the ceiling, drums on the desk, and peers over his shoulder at the Chaplain. He clears his throat and speaks brusquely: "Has it started raining?" "Yes, it has," says the Chaplain, without turning around. The Warden glares at his long thin cigar and impatiently tosses it aside. He is wearing a dark brown suit, open shirt, and black string tie. "It *would* rain tonight," he complains.

In fact, it is not raining tonight at Sing Sing. It is a warm clear evening, a little heavy, and there are rumors of an impending heat wave, maybe as early as Saturday. The prison officials, who have had to proceed today with all the usual death-chair preparations, are dressed in short-sleeved shirts with open collars. Not until Justice Burton's announcement of the Supreme Court recess at 6:29 p.m. has the evening's Death Watch been canceled, the electrician and rabbi sent off duty.

Yesterday on the central radio speaker, during the seventh-inning stretch of the Dodgers' baseball game, the Rosenbergs heard the news of Justice Douglas's stay, and Warden Denno reported that they were "overjoyed," but all that joy was soon dispelled by Attorney General Brownell's rapid countermoves. The Rosenbergs still cling to hopes of further delays, but among the professionals it is generally felt that Douglas has overstepped himself on this one, and the odds are on for a vacated stay and a quick execution. They have their own reasons: all those preparations down in Times Square, the other executions stacking up, the daily expense: Ethel alone is costing the state $38.60 a day, Julius is due for more dental treatment, and there's the burden of keeping 290 prison police and nearly as many New York State Troopers on constant guard, defending the prison against protest marches by the Phantom's Legions of Darkness, even——who knows? (guards in the tower gun emplacements flex their shoulders, scrutinize the prison borderland, now losing definition in the gathering dusk)—a mad attempt at escape.

Not that the Rosenbergs are showing any signs of sudden defiance—if anything, they seem to be mellowing as they near their exterminations. It could be a ruse, the kind of trick Errol Flynn often uses on his way to a last-minute rescue. Or it might be saltpeter in their diets. Most likely, though, they've known for years that the Phantom has intended this role for them, and they've been practicing. Ethel especially: for some time now she has ceased resisting and has taken the part on and made it her own. Julie still seems unable to believe it is all really happening to him, and continues to search frantically for the legalistic dodge that will get him out of here. "Everything seems so unreal and out of focus," he writes, "it seems like we're suspended somewhere, far off . . ." Today is their fourteenth wedding anniversary, and as a present from Sing Sing prison, they were allowed a full ninety minutes together at the dividing screen this evening. Not that they made much use of it—they sat as though tongue-tied half the time. What is there really to talk about on a warm June evening through a fine mesh screen with someone one's been married to for fourteen years, after one's been preparing all day to go to the electric chair? It's all been said. Too many times. They're weary of each other's arguments, illusions, complaints. They're weary of their own. Talking about the children only makes them cry or feel angry or guilty. They love each other, of course, more than ever—love indeed is why they're here—so they could talk about the night they met at the Seamen's ball on New Year's Eve or their Sunday strolls through the Palisades or that first room they had together in Marcus Pogarsky's apartment, but none of that seems real any more—it's somebody else's past, it belongs to those other people whose Death House letters are being read around the world. Anyway, they're boxed in by prison guards and snoopy FBI agents with big ears, why give them a thrill? So they talked about things they've heard on the prison radio. How their suppers have settled down. The demonstrations. What they'll do next if Justice Douglas's stay is upheld. An interesting magazine article about the discovery of the Dead Sea Scrolls. Julius said he read in LIFE that Henry Ford II's personal income in 1951 after taxes was $87,000,000. After taxes! This was on his mind because of his intention to write out their own last will and testament later tonight. Ethel repeated her wish to see Arthur Miller's *The Crucible* playing in New York. She's heard that the audience applauds when a character says toward the end that he'd rather burn in hell than become a stool pigeon. They sat silent a good part of the time, not even looking at each other, as though afraid of what they might see in the other's face, yet like a pair of octogenarians at the fireside, finding familiar solace in each other's company, glancing up from time to time, then away, listening to the trains rattling by along the river, sounds floating up from the town below: music, kids playing softball, trucks grinding up a hill. Now they are separated, Julius struggling with the text of his will, Ethel perhaps dreaming of opening night many years ago of the Clark House Players' production in the settlement house on Rivington Street of *The Valiant,* in which she starred as the sister of the condemned man, who was played by Paul Muni in the movies. . . .

"Was he quiet when you left him?" asks the Warden uneasily. "Yes, yes," says the Chaplain, "he was perfectly calm, and I believe he'll stay so to the very end." The Warden lights a fresh cigar. In the wings, the young girl awaits her cue. "You've got to hand it to him, Father. I never saw such nerve in my life. It isn't bluff, and it isn't a trance, either, like some of 'em have—it's sheer nerve. You've certainly got to hand it to him." He shakes his head in frank admiration. "He still won't give you any hint about who he really is?" "Not the slightest. He doesn't intend to, either. He intends to die as a man of mystery to us."

What is this unnatural intransigence? It is not silence, no, the Rosenbergs are rarely silent. But their declarations are all bombast, impertinence, self-indulgent pique, nothing of substance, nothing Uncle Sam can use. At this very moment, there is a telephone in Warden Denno's office linked directly to the Justice Department in Washington: the

Rosenbergs need only avail themselves of it, agree to a public confession of their own duplicity and exposure of those who have schemed with them (not that the FBI actually needs this information, apparently—newspapers almost daily announce, just as they have done for the past two years, that the FBI has broken the ring and is "closing in" on the rest of the spies), and what is now a time of worldwide risk and disorder might well be converted into an occasion of national victory and joyous in-gathering, and even, if only briefly, a happy family reunion as well. But still, unnatural parents, they remain adamant. "We are confident of the righteousness of our cause," Julius Rosenberg has written, "and we will not allow ourselves to be used as tools against the fight for peace, freedom, and decency."

Ah yes, the fight for peace, freedom, and decency—everybody knows what a Communist means when he uses language like that. Wasn't Uncle Sam struggling right now against a cunning Soviet "peace" offensive? They seem almost eager to die, as though in spite. "I shall not dishonor my marital vows and the felicity and integrity of the relationship we shared to play the role of harlot to political procurers," Ethel has declaimed, her spontaneous use of that metaphor confirming what everyone has long believed about this tough little number off the ghetto streets, handmaid of the Phantom. The world has not forgotten the day twenty years ago when she and more of her kind descended upon those poor truckdrivers like frenzied maenads, ripped off their pants, and lipsticked I AM A SCAB all over their bottoms. And speaking of vows, what about her Pledge of Allegiance to the American Flag? "I should far rather embrace my husband in death than live on ingloriously upon such bounty." Meaning the rumored commutation of her death sentence, while burning Julie, so there'd still be the possibility, eventually, of getting the spy secrets out of her. "How diabolical! A cold fury possesses me and I could retch with horror and revulsion, for these saviours are actually proposing to erect a sepulchre in which I shall live without living, and die without dying. . . . And what of our children! What manner of mercy is it that would slay their adored father and deliver up their devoted mother to everlasting emptiness?" Ronald Colman did it a lot better in *A Tale of Two Cities*. As for the children, everyone from the Judge to the President has observed that they loved their cause more, and indeed sacrificed their children to it. Even now their boys are being dragged around to all the clemency rallies to cozen old ladies with soft hearts and loosen purse strings, and their parents are actually using them as grounds for their contrariness: "As long as we do the right thing by our children and the good people of the world, nothing else matters. . . . The love we bear our two sons and each other demands that we hold fast to these truths, even to the death which may destroy our little family. . . . One thing I feel sure of—that when they are older, they will know that all the way through, we, their parents, were right, and they will be proud." Pride, yes: that's the key to it.

Even were they not guilty of stealing the secret of the A-bomb, such grandstanding, reminiscent of the hyperbole of their student days, together with their open-faced provocation of international unrest—"The world has come to recognize the true nature of our case and the people, the most effective force on earth, are behind us and are demonstrating a thorough awareness that they know how to fight for peace and freedom!"—would alone warrant their present condemnation. For make no mistake: that the world is tonight in crisis, that the Phantom is afoot with rare favor and authority, is largely due to the persistent agitation of Julius and Ethel Rosenberg, who will not talk and who will not be silent. The Rosenbergs have been honing their incendiary rhetoric for twenty years, testing their vitriol on the likes of Andrew Carnegie and John D. Rockefeller, Henry Ford and Standard Oil—they've even propagandized against Nabisco cookies! Ethel launched her oratorical career, after a fling at the stage, as a union whip and street shrieker, Julius as a student agitator, participating in the Stalinist purges of decadent Trotskyites. The FBI has accused them of "premature antifascism." In their flat, they found an empty collection can bearing the label: SAVE A SPANISH REPUBLICAN CHILD, VOLVEREMOS, WE WILL RETURN! And now their training in perversity has come to fruition, their target is the entire American System:

> No need for any pretense—the farce is exposed. / This harsh and cruel decision was sired in madness / part of a pattern of pro-fascist and bellicose actions by those who rule our land— / this is political prosecution, shameless, blatant, cynical. / The executive arm of our government has become a party to murder. / They hide their demagogy under a mask of super-patriotism, wild lies and charges. / The courts have deteriorated to the point that they are mere appendages to an autocratic police force and in political cases the rights of defendants and the protection of the Constitution no longer operate. / Such a situation will only lead to a police state at home and war abroad. / While we are able, we must prevent these evil men from enslaving the mind as a prelude to complete subjugation— / it is imperative to stand up to these fascists and nail them to their own lies! / Progressives are beginning to fight back against McCarthyism—the fuehrer

of American fascism. / At this late hour, I am still confident the good people of our country will make their will felt in Washington and stop the execution!

And indeed, now, tonight, as evening marks the close of day and skies of blue begin to gray, the "good people" emerge, as though on cue, to protest the executions, attack Uncle Sam and his Legion of Superheroes on the frontiers and harass him within, violate human decency, threaten the Free World with terror and disruption, and strike ruthlessly at the very faith that binds it together. It is no real surprise that in the vanguard of the rebellion are agents of the Phantom disguised as ministers of the Holy Gospel—clemency appeals and rabid protests have been pouring in all week from preachers and theologians in Chicago, Philadelphia, Detroit, California, Latin America, the Vatican, France, and the Evangelical Churches of Italy. Nearly 2300 American "clergymen" sign a last-minute appeal for clemency, demand an audience with the President. There is loose talk about "peace" and "justice" and "mercy." One would think the *Daily Worker* had seen the light, so many churchmen appear these days in its pages. "Obvious evidence that the Angels of Darkness are deceiving the very Elect," FBI undercover agent Herbert Philbrick warns, "is the increasing number of Communist-sponsored petitions going out over the imprimatur of ministers of the Gospel and the outsized number of clergy who are signatories! Never is an Angel of Darkness more secure than when he poses as an Angel of Light!" In Washington, the Rosenberg forces move with a cynical snicker into "Inspiration House" on Kalorama Road. Thousands hold a protest vigil in front of the White House, pretending to "pray" that the Rosenbergs be spared. "I saw those ministers in action," G-man Philbrick confides, "ruthless Communist leaders prostituting the Christian ministry to the evil ends of atheism and oppression!"

"The Bible teaches us that we are engaged in a gigantic spiritual warfare," explains the Reverend Billy Graham, "and when God begins to move in a country, as He is now moving mightily in America, *Satan also begins to move!*" And not only in America: around the world, demonstrators gather, chant, sing, metamorphose into dangerous mobs, egged on by the inflammatory letters of the Rosenbergs: "We are confident that the people will raise a mighty cry against this new great danger which threatens to engulf millions by dooming two innocent Americans first!" Protests flow in from Mexico, Quebec, Tel Aviv, Copenhagen. Hundreds of mesmerized workers converge on the U.S. Consulates in Milan and Genoa. In Paris, Jean-Paul Sartre calls the

Rosenbergs victims of "legal lynchings": "Whenever innocent people are killed," he declares, "it is the business of the whole world!"

If you will not hear our voices, hear the voices of the world.
Hear the great and the humble: from Einstein, whose name is legend, to the tyros in the laboratories of Manchester; from struggling students at Grenoble to Oxford professors; from the world-famous movie directors of Rome to the bit players of London; from the dock workers at Liege to the cotton spinners of India; from the peasants of Italy to the philosophers of Israel . . .

Read the tons of petitions, letters, postcards, stacked high in your filing rooms, from the plain and gentle folk of our land. They marched before your door in such numbers as never before, as have their brothers and sisters in London, Paris, Melbourne, Buenos Aires, Ottawa, Rome. They ask you not to orphan our two young boys. They ask brotherhood and peace to spare our lives.

Hear the great and humble for the sake of America.

So cry the Rosenbergs, and in Dublin, two homemade Molotov cocktails crash through the windows of the U.S. Information Agency. British Prime Minister Winston Churchill is set upon by an entire motorcade— they push him to intercede with President Eisenhower, but Winnie does not flag or fail, he braces himself to do his duty: "It is not within my duty or power to intervene." There are threatened boycotts and work stoppages around the world. Egghead leftists in Europe plan a counter-trial of the people who have judged and sentenced the Rosenbergs. Onstage at the Martin Beck over on Forty-fifth Street, Reverend John Hale in Arthur Miller's *The Crucible* is saying: "No man may longer doubt the powers of the dark are gathered in monstrous attack upon this village. There is too much evidence now to deny it!" Nearby, in Times Square, the electric chair lies, uprooted, in the gutter, blocking traffic, while tricked out in nigger colors on the marquee of the Criterion is the strange message, attributed to some frog named Du Bois:

WE ARE THE MURDERERS HURLING MUD!
WE ARE THE WITCHHUNTERS DRINKING BLOOD!

The helmet of night has fallen upon man the word-carrier. *It is the Phantom's hour . . . !*

"I am not much good at saying goodbyes," Julius Rosenberg writes to his lawyer from his cell in the Death House, "because I believe that good accomplishments live on forever but this I can say—my love of life has never been so strong because I've seen how beautiful the future can be. Since I feel that we in some small measure have contributed our share in this direction I think my sons and millions of others will have benefited by it."

"This front of his makes me nervous as the devil," the Warden says. "I feel just as if tonight I was going to do something every bit as criminal as he did. I can't help it. And when I start feeling like that, then I think it's about time I sent in my resignation." Why is it that the most obvious things in the world, she wonders, watching the Warden and Chaplain from the wings, seem to elude the understanding of men like these? It's not that they have failed to learn something, but rather that they have learned too much, have built up ways of looking at the world that block off natural human instincts. It's as though society through its formal demands were bent, not on ennobling people and leading them toward art and truth, but on demeaning them, reducing them to cardboard role-players like the characters in this play, *The Valiant.* And the deeper they get into their roles, the less they remember who they were before they took on the parts. But what is the alternative? Going on with life at all means having to adopt one role or another, even if it's a rebellious one, doesn't it? She is sixteen years old and she doesn't think so. She thinks this is the defeatist argument of old people who have failed, people like her own parents, her teachers, those two men out on the stage. It was the argument one of them tried to use on her when he walked her home the other night from the cast party at the Paramount Cafeteria. She said, no, life is more open-ended than that. Then he jammed her up against a wall in a dark doorway, dragged up her skirts, and pushed his knee into her crotch. Some argument. "His whole attitude has been very remarkable," the Chaplain admits reflectively, winking at her from the stage. "Only a few minutes ago I found myself comparing it with the fortitude that the Christian martyrs carried to their deaths, and yet . . ." "Has he got any religious streak in him at all?" the Warden asks. "I'm afraid he hasn't," the Chaplain sighs. "He listens to me very attentively, but . . ."

Atheism, as J. Edgar Hoover of the FBI has so often reminded us, is the first step toward Communism, the very "cornerstone of Communist philosophy." Marx, Engels, Lenin, they all got started that way. A clue leading to the apprehension of the Rosenbergs was their admitted apostasy. Julie had given up the Talmud in favor of Tom Mooney and premature anti-fascism. Ethel, depressed, had gone to a psychiatrist instead of her rabbi. Phonograph records ridiculing the Kol Nidre chant were found in their flat by the FBI. The Phantom, G-man Hoover has warned, is out to "sap religion's spiritual strength and then destroy it. . . . Communists have always made it clear that Communism is the mortal enemy of Christianity, Judaism, Mohammedanism, and any other religion that believes in a Supreme Being!"

Julius and Ethel Rosenberg have written hundreds of pages to each other and the world, and there's not a word in them about a Supreme Being. They never mention the afterlife, angels, or the Holy Trinity. Peace, bread, and roses, that's all they talk about: their materialist dream. Even Justice Douglas in his eccentric recreancy admits that "we are a religious people whose institutions presuppose a Supreme Being," and if pressed, he might even be able to tell you His name. It's true, of course, Patriot John Adams, in one of his spasms of quirkiness, did pretend that no "persons employed in the formation of the American government had interviews with the gods, or were in any degree under the inspiration of Heaven," but the Prophets have since corrected him— the Lord Himself has declared right out in the *Doctrines and Covenants* of the native-American Latter-Day Saints:

I established the Constitution of this land, by the hands of wise men whom I raised up onto this very purpose!

Nothing could be clearer than that. When Tom Jefferson swore "eternal hostility against every form of tyranny over the mind of man," he swore it "upon the altar of God," that Heavenly Engineer who set the world going, fathered Jesus Christ, and fired the shot heard round the world, and Long Tom himself once asked in a theocratical fit: "Can the liberties of a nation be thought secure when we have removed their only firm basis, a conviction in the minds of the people that these liberties are the gift of God? that they are not to be violated but with His wrath?" This afflated reflection has stirred the hearts and minds of American Super-heroes from General George Washington right down to the current Incarnation, who is much given to visions of God working His wondrous will through the invention of America. His Quaker Vice President, lay evangelist and cleanser of the temple, has often echoed him, and more: "Our beliefs must be combined with a crusading zeal to *change the world!*"

LET THE CHURCH SPEAK UP FOR CAPITALISM!

For there is, as the Christian missionary John Foster Dulles, former Chairman of the Commission on a Just and Durable Peace of the Federal Council of Churches (now U.S. Secretary of State), has said, "no way to solve the great perplexing international problems except by bringing to bear upon them *the force of Christianity!*"

But is there time? A young girl appears. She is fresh and wholesome, and rather pretty, but her manner betrays, as the authors say, a certain spiritual aloofness from the ultramodern world which separates her from the metropolitan class. She is dressed simply and wears a blue tailored suit with deep white cuffs and a starched white sailor-collar, and a small blue hat over her fluffy hair. Her costume hints at the taste and repression of an old-fashioned home, the sort of home perhaps which would have taken to heart Mr. Edgar Hoover's firm advice:

> Since Communists are anti-God, encourage your child to be active in the church. . . . Whether you know it or not, your child is a target. His mind is the fertile plot in which the Communist hopes to implant his Red virus and to secure a deadly culture which will spread to others. When enough are infected the Red Pied Piper hopes to call the tune. He lives for the day when he can draw constantly increasing numbers of American youngsters away from their families and the sound traditions and principles which have guided this Nation thus far along its course and enroll them in the service of the Red masters!

J. Edgar Hoover's advice is to use faith, history, hickory, and old-fashioned prayer on these susceptible young. The girl onstage, however, would seem to need none of them. Incorruptible purity is her essence. She is neither timid nor aggressive; she is self-unconscious, an open-faced contrast to the more devious Warden and Chaplain. Her expression is essentially serious due to the present mission; ordinarily she takes an active joy in the mere pleasure of existence, according to the script. She has just heard the Warden say, with regard to the doomed prisoner: "I don't want any such yelling and screeching tonight as we had over that Greek!" Now, seeing her, he half rises from his chair, much affected by her youth and innocence, and with grave deference offers her a chair. The audience's laughter at the image of the screeching Greek subsides. The young girl regards the Warden trustfully, being a good actress. He says he understands she wishes to see the prisoner. "Yes, sir. I *hope* I'm not . . . too late . . ."

But maybe so. Terrorists creep out of their jungle hiding places and lay waste villages in Indonesia, Malaya, French Indochina. A full company sweeps down on U.N. positions north of the Hwachon Reservoir in Korea and a U.N. effort to retake Christmas Hill is repulsed by the Phantom's hyped-up forces. Two hundred Indian fishermen are reported missing forty miles off Madras in the Bay of Bengal. Officers sift through the ashes of the fire in Whittier, Alaska, named after the

Quaker Poet who once prophesied that "evil breaks the strongest gyves, / and jins like him have charméd lives!" They agree that the important U.S. military port is now totally inoperative. Damages are estimated at $20,000,000. John Greenleaf Whittier also gave his name to the home town of the young Vice President, and some wonder if the Phantom had really been aiming at him but missed? HUAC, clutching their dossiers and taking for the Congressional bomb shelters, issue a warning that roaming the nation's streets unchecked, intent upon committing all manner of sin and transgression against the American government, are 469 heretical organizations, not least of which are all the Rosenberg clemency committees to whom are rallying thousands of people, all displaying "a shocking readiness to join hands with treason!" Hardly have names been named when new demonstrations crop up in London, Chicago, Jakarta, Japan. In Times Square, the stage, unchaired, is dark, torn Jell-O packages flutter through the streets in a cold breeze, and suspicious-looking characters lurk in the doorways. "This is a sharp time, now, a precise time," Deputy Governor Danforth is saying onstage at the Martin Beck, "we live no longer in the dusky afternoon when evil mixed itself with good and befuddled the world. Now, by God's grace, the shining sun is up, and them that fear not light will surely praise it!" Yes, but the sun is not up. The sun is down.

And as the fatal midnight hour, when all evil things have power, closes down on them, the children of Uncle Sam, slipping uneasily into their beds, are beset with nightmare visions of Soviet tanks in Berlin, dead brothers lying scattered across the cold wastes of Korea, spreading pornography and creeping socialism, Phantomized black and yellow people rising up in Africa and Asia in numbers not even Lothrop Stoddard could have foreseen, and the Rosenbergs, grown monstrous, octopuslike as Irving Saypol depicted them, breaking out of their cells, smashing down the walls of Sing Sing with their tentacles, and descending upon the city like the Beast from 20,000 Fathoms. They knock over buildings, crush automobiles under their bodies, swallow policemen whole, get tangled up in a Coney Island roller coaster. Bullets do not stop them. They are joined by Walter Ulbricht the Coffinmaker, wading ashore with his firing squads; the Necrophile John Reginald Halliday Christie, his huge organ bloody and gangrenous; a big black white-eyed giant with SUPER MAU MAU emblazoned on his savage breast; thousands upon thousands of groaning victims, blinded, their flesh eaten away, from Hiroshima and Nagasaki; and Chairman Mao, swirled about by fumes from the dens of vice, like a bloated gold-toothed Fu Manchu. The Rosenbergs pulverize synagogues and cathedrals in their monstrous tentacles. Super Mau Mau smashes the windows of supermarkets and department stores, letting the dark out. With a lash of his tail, Chairman Mao reduces Wall Street to rubble. Christie grabs little girls out of Sunday schools and beauty parlors, smearing whole handfuls of them against his calloused peter and laughing maniacally. As the Red Pied Piper tootles, Nero, Pontius Pilate, Genghis Khan, and juiced-up Red Indians from *Ambush at Tomahawk Gap* smash their way out of movie palaces, crying: *"The weapons with which the bourgeoisie felled feudalism to the ground are now turned against the bourgeoisie itself!"* The people scrunch down in their sheets, shivering in spite of the warm June weather, chilled by the Phantom's echoing laughter, dismayed by the prospect of a never-ending night. How did this happen? Where did all the good times go? Whatever happened to the rendezvous with destiny?

But then they hear, distantly, the cheering thump of Nelson Eddy singing "Stout-Hearted Men," and over that, through the deep darkness, comes the voice of Uncle Sam, firm, resonant, unwavering: "O suffering, sad humanity! O ye afflicted ones, who lie steeped to the lips in misery, *illegitimi non carborundum*, as Vinegar Joe useter say: Don't let the bastards grind ya down! I know the gloomy night before us lies like a black arse in a coal-hole, but jumpin' jig-a-jig! we ain't weak if we make a proper use of those means which the God a Nature has placed in our pockets! So punch, brothers, punch with care! Punch in the presence of the passenjare, so when Jesus comes to claim us all and says it is enough, the diamints will be shinin' but no longer in the buff!"

"But O Uncle Sam," cry the people, making doleful moan and groan, "the Angel of Darkness is loose in the world, and iniquity goes unpunished! They go on contriving the mischief of their hearts, opening their shameless mouths, unleashing their lying tongues like the venom of adders fitfully spurting forth, vipers that cannot be charmed! Confusion and panic beset us, horrendous anguish and pain, like to the throes of travail!"

"Damn my britches!" sighs Uncle Sam, "for the land what is sown with the harvest of despair! I hear ya talkin', piggy-wigs, but is it not wrote in the ancient Scrolls: 'When they engage the Phantom, amid all the combat and carnage of battle, the Sons a Light'll have luck three times in discomfitin' the forces of wickedness; but three times the host of the Phantom shall brace themselves to turn back the tide. But on the seventh occasion the great hand of Uncle Sam shall finally subdue the Phantom, and He will make truth to shine forth, meanin' me, bringin' doom down upon the Sons a Darkness like a tom-tit on a horse-turd!' "

"Yea, six times have they appeared before our Judges, men well versed in the Book of Study and in the fundamentals of the Covenant, and this is the seventh," reply the people. "Thou bringest us cheer, O Uncle Sam, amid the sorrow of mourning, words of peace amid havoc, stoutness of heart in the face of affliction!"

"Well, awright then," thunders Uncle Sam, "straighten up and fry right, friends! Go forth to meet the shadowy Future, without fear, and with a manly heart on, for they are but anathema maranatha, and dirty dogs to boot! Don't fergit that all that has been and is and shall be throughout all time are in my hand, so there may be storms in my path, but I'll wear a smile, cuz in a little while, my path'll be ro-o-*ses!* And so, trustin' in Him who can go with me, and remain with you, and be everywhere for good and anon, let us remember the *Maine*, cock a snook, cover the embers and put out the light—toil comes with the morning, and broil with the night! Hoo hah! God bless you all!"

"Thine is the battle," respond the children of America. "From Thee comes the power; and it is not ours. The base of spirit wilt Thou burn up like a flaming brand in a hayrick, a brand that devours wickedness and that will not turn back until guilt is destroyed!" Then they tune in their radios to an all-night station playing Frankie Laine's "I Believe," and drift off, their minds freed of the Phantom's terrors, dreaming peacefully of baseball, business, and burning hayricks.

For the Rosenbergs, it is not so easy to sleep. Julius has dutifully composed his last will and testament, but Henry Ford II he is not. In fact, he has nothing to leave his two sons but best wishes, three cartons of rather pathetic personal effects which the FBI is bound to paw through, some dead bugs, and his exemplary misfortune. He has good reason to doubt they will possess even his name. "Love them with all your heart and always protect them in order that they grow up to be normal healthy people," he begs his lawyer, Manny Bloch. "Our children are the apple of our eye, our pride and most precious fortune." He last saw his sons two days ago. Unless Justice Douglas's stay is upheld, he will not see them again. They were dragged away, screaming, confused. He can't write to the boys himself. Ethel will do that. He is afraid the boys will be angry. With him. He is afraid their memories will be erased. Or will not be. He is afraid his legs will fail him on his way to the chair and make his boys ashamed. "You Manny are not only considered as one of my family but are our extra special friend. Be strong for us, beloved friend. *Never let them change the truth of our innocence.* For peace, bread and roses, in simple dignity, we face the executioner with courage, confidence and perspective, never losing faith. As ever, *Julie.*"

It is time for the prisoner in the play to die, and the young girl must make her farewells. She endeavors to smile, but her voice catches in her throat and she nearly breaks down. She and her brother used to have a game at bedtime, reciting lines from Shakespeare, and though the prisoner has made it clear he is not after all her brother and doesn't know Shakespeare from Barney Google, she wishes now she could. . . . "What was it?" the prisoner asks. "I . . . I told it to you once, and you said it was silly." "Say it again," the prisoner says softly. The girl swallows, looks up at him. " 'Good-night, good-night!' " She cannot quite control her voice, but struggles on, thinking: at the end, this is all there is. " 'Parting is such sweet sorrow . . . That I shall say good-night till it be morrow.' " She goes toward the anteroom, hesitates, hoping—in vain—that he might yet respond with the matching lines, and then with a choking sob hurries through the door and closes it behind her. For several seconds the prisoner stands rigidly intent upon that door, until at length, without changing his attitude or his expression, watched raptly by the Warden and the Chaplain, he speaks very tenderly and reminiscently:

> "Sleep dwell upon thine eyes, peace in thy breast!
> Would I were sleep and peace, so sweet to rest!"

"P.S.—Ethel wants it made known that we are the first victims of American Fascism."

7.

A Little Morality Play for
Our Generation

The play is over. The girl has made her tearful exit, and her brother, the condemned prisoner, has gone through the act of clutching his throat and quoting Shakespeare on the fear of death, amazing the Warden and the Chaplain. The Jailer has arrived to call the prisoner to his execution, and the prisoner, standing erect like a soldier at attention, regarding them all fixedly and with a voice low and steady, has replied: "All right, let's go." They've gone. The curtain's come down and the audience, if there is any, is now applauding. They take curtain calls. Now the condemned man is smiling and so is the girl in her little sailor dress. All just make-believe. Then, let's see, they . . . uh . . . they scrub off the greasepaint and change out of their stage costumes. Always liked that part, the makeup. A kind of transformation comes over you, a kind of metamorphosis. It was while a girl in my class was putting makeup on me one night that I thought she was in love with me. Maybe she was. Probably I didn't make the right moves. Water under the bridge. Anyway, off with the makeup and costumes. There's a cast party afterwards at the Paramount Cafeteria tonight, they're all going to that and hurrying to get ready. Everybody in the cast is lusting after little sixteen-year-old Ethel Greenglass, the sister in the play, and they all drop by casually to poke their noses in while she's changing, but she's too excited by her own performance to notice. She supposes that middle-aged men winking and blowing congratulatory kisses at her in her underwear is just part of the theatrical life. Anyway, let's face it, she's a tough little broad from the slums, a lot of horny brothers, this isn't exactly Whittier High School, she knows the score. Anuses, dildos, the

111

whole lot. She's probably seen all there is to see right in the hallways of her own tenement house. Whores have often lived there, working their trade in the rooms next to her own bedroom, she's no goddamn innocent. But has she ever . . . had it? Hard to guess. Probably not. Certainly no boyfriends. Not till Julie. Probably too idealistic. Standoffish. Too much familiarity with it has made her shy away. She wants something better out of life. She dreams of escaping the slums. She's young, bright, pretty, talented, she can sing and act and she's got nerve—that's the famous Broadway formula for success, isn't it? Just like in the motion pictures—and it's all just a few blocks away. Each night they do *The Valiant* in this crummy little makeshift dump of a neighborhood theater, she thinks: Tonight I may be discovered! But each night nothing happens. She goes home to her lousy room in that stinking slum tenement, where her wretched old witch of a mother rails at her: "You'll never get ahead, you smart-ass little twit! There's no place in life for arty people!" Maybe she didn't say "you smart-ass little twit," I just made that part up. Quite likely, though. Or something just like it in Russian or Polish or whatever the hell the old lady was. Ethel has had to leave school and go to work. She makes seven dollars a week as a clerk in a shipping company on West Thirty-sixth Street, and gives it all to her mother. She gets two dollars back for carfare and lunches, but she walks to work and often skips lunch to save for voice and piano lessons at the Carnegie Hall Studios. At her job, left-wingers are trying to seduce her into union activities: she's cute and has a lot of personality, she might make a good organizer. She likes the special attention they give her. She could be headed for a life of lawlessness and disorder, strikes, premature anti-fascism, a *Daily Worker* subscription, subversion, treason, and death in the electric chair. Or the theater could be her salvation. If she became another Clara Bow, her life and that of thousands of GIs fighting in Korea could be saved. And she doesn't even have to become another Clara Bow—just so her *dreams* of success are not soured. That's the secret: keep them hoping. But after the party at the Paramount Cafeteria, one of the older guys in the cast, some bum in his mid-forties, offers to take her home. Uh, the Lower East Side streets are dangerous, he'll see her home safely, something like that. I didn't know if the Paramount Cafeteria served beer or not. Probably not, anyway it was still Prohibition. I think. The guy probably had a hip flask. So he says he'll see that she gets home safe, nothing wrong with that. The condemned brother maybe, good irony in that. Probably not, though, because that was the part played by Paul Muni in the movie—a younger guy. So maybe it's the Chaplain, a pious man, maybe Catholic in the play, chastity vows and all that, though in fact he was probably a Jew or an atheist, most theater people are. Or maybe the Warden, keeper of law and order. Anyway, she's grateful. She's still feeling dreamy. Exhilarated. She's glad to have somebody to talk to on the way home. What about? Her hopes, her fantasies. The old guy encourages her, putting an arm around her sympathetically. Like a father. She opens up her young heart to him. In response, he pushes her into a dark doorway, hauls up her skirt, tears his fly open, and tries to push his throbbing cock between her legs. She screams. No, she can't scream, who would she scream for? Besides, uh . . . he's pressing his mouth against hers. What does she do? She bites him maybe. Knees him in the nuts. Something like that. It's a very rough scene for a little starry-eyed sixteen-year-old girl. She runs all the way home, terrified and disheveled, crying, her dreams shattered, thinking: So that's what the theatrical life is like! She becomes a Communist instead and commits espionage.

Maybe. Maybe not. Too pat somehow. And the details were blurred. Where was the Paramount Cafeteria? And what dark doorway was it? Maybe it was her own. Under the peeling gold letters of her father's name. I sighed, sat up, stared at all the notes and data spread around me on the office floor. It was getting late and I was floundering about in midfield, getting nowhere. Pat and the girls had no doubt wondered why I wasn't home for supper. Should have called. Pat was probably still waiting up for me. But I couldn't go home. Not yet. I had to complete this investigation, make sense of it somehow. Douglas's stay of execution, coupled with the sudden rise of tensions throughout the world, had cast a whole new complexion on the case. Uncle Sam had projected me into the heart of this thing and I had to respond. Anyway, Pat would suppose I was in some emergency meeting, that was all right. Or preparing a speech. She was used to my late nights. At the time of the Hiss case, I spent as much as eighteen to twenty hours a day at my office, we hardly saw each other. At such times, I deliberately refuse to take time off for relaxation or "a break," because my experience has been that in preparing to meet a crisis, the more I work the sharper and quicker my mental reactions become. "Taking a break" is actually an escape from the tough grinding discipline that is absolutely necessary for superior performance, and Pat has had to learn to live with this. Many times I've found that my best ideas come when I think I can't work another minute, when I literally have to drive myself to stick at the job. Sleepless nights, to the extent the body can take them, can stimulate creative mental activity, it's happened to me lots of times. Oh, you have to take the machine out of gear once in a while, but it's never wise to turn the engine off and let the motor get completely cold, not when you're on to something. I could write a goddamn manual about it.

This was why my golf game disappointed Uncle Sam so. I couldn't help it. It wasn't just the game, it was the going and coming, the time lost in the clubhouse, all those empty-headed boozers clomping around in golf shoes, a whole day could get shot down. Whenever I was in the middle of a period of intense study or work, leaving the problem for a day on the golf course simply meant I had to spend most of the next day getting myself charged up again—to the point of efficiency I had reached before leaving the task in the first place. That was why I was collecting all this flab around the middle, too. I knew that was something I had to watch—Americans rarely elected fat men President. Old Taft got away with it, but that was because he went to the other extreme. But just fat and sloppy, never. As long as I was down on the floor, I decided to do a few sit-ups. After a couple, though, I felt a little giddy—hungry probably—and so stayed stretched out, my head pillowed in bomb diagrams. I had already studied these sketches, looking for hidden objects, thinking they might be some kind of puzzle pictures, but I hadn't turned up anything. They tended to suggest sex organs, but this was natural with bomb diagrams.

I lay there, just letting my mind wander. Often I got good ideas this way. Felt good, too. I thought about the names of the principals in this case: all the colors. Strange. Green, gold, rose . . . which nation's flag was that? I played with the street names, codenames, names of the lawyers, people at the edge of the drama—Perl, Sidorovich, Glassman, Urey, Condon, Slack, Golos, Bentley. I realized that the initial letters of the names of the four accused—Sobell, Rosenberg, Rosenberg, and Yakovlev—would spell SORRY were it not for the missing O. Was there some other secret agent of the Phantom, as yet unapprehended, with this initial? Oppenheimer? Oatis? No, he was our man, we'd just got him back from the Czechs. O'Brien, the FBI man? What a fantastic idea! Bobo Olson? The OPA maybe. Always hated the OPA. My first political job. I was glad to see it liquidated six weeks ago—fulfillment of my oldest campaign pledge. Those goddamn hucksters. And that awful joke that went around when I got into politics: Dick Nixon of the OPA, maybe that one would die now. "Meet J. Edgar Hoover of the FBI . . . !" Obnoxious. Odious. Or how about the Orthogonians—somebody out of my old fraternity at Whittier? A Square Shooter who was a Double Dealer? It would explain why Uncle Sam had pulled me into this case. But it was hard to believe. Football players mostly, hardly the type. We did wear those big "O's" on our sweaters, though. I remembered those symbolic suppers of beans and spaghetti we used to have. One would taste pretty good right now, and fuck the symbols. Also there was Old Nick, and Ola, and Señor Ortega, a role I had in a play once. No, I was getting pretty far off the track. Then suddenly I recalled that Justice William Douglas's middle name was Orville. Mmm, that fit, that was probably it, all right. He'd sure set us back with that stay of his, which if nothing else was goddamn disrespectful of the wishes and wisdom of the American people. The tramp who'd reverted to type. Just as the Rosenbergs had caused the Korean War, so perhaps had Douglas enabled the Russians to crush our revolt in East Berlin. Why not?

I felt that I was close, hovering as it were (even though in fact I was flat out on my back) over the answer, not quite able to pick it out. Something about judgment. Time. My generation. My lousy drives. The city. The riddle of history, the letter O. Growing up. Balance. Motion. . . . I wondered if I should trace the travels of Harry Gold on a map to see if some kind of picture would emerge. Roughly, in my mind's eye, they seemed to trace out half a cheese sandwich. I remembered that he said somewhere that the Greenglasses asked him where they could find good Jewish delicatessen in New Mexico. Or maybe Gold asked them. I realized the bomb diagrams somewhat resembled cheese blintzes. Deviled eggs. Stuffed cabbages. My stomach rumbled. I realized I should stop thinking about food.

I tried to think instead about the money, the amounts exchanged, what got done with it. Murray Chotiner taught me this rule: When you're attacking an opponent, looking for scandal, ask first about the money. But the sums here were small and the evidence even for these was dubious. In fact, the only people with real money in this story were the Judge and Prosecutor, Attorney General, and FBI Director. The jury members were modestly but comfortably salaried, most of the witnesses were getting by, while the Rosenbergs were the poorest of the lot. Which was maybe the point: O for zero. They ran a small business that lost money, apparently donated their services to the Phantom for nothing—real fanatics. Well, I could understand Julius's business failure: I'd gone that route myself once with frozen orange juice, and my father had entertained us all with a whole lifetime of successive failures. I could even understand their working free for the Phantom—I'd do the same for Uncle Sam, though I was glad he had never asked this of me. How could he? Money is dignity, he's told me that himself. What I couldn't understand, though, was the Rosenbergs *staying* poor. Not that poor. Not in America. They didn't even have a car or a TV. Hell, I was earning money by the time I was eleven years old, picking beans on farms and working in my Dad's store, pumping gas, grinding hamburger, culling rotten apples and tomatoes—Dad didn't give me any abstract lessons in the American Way of Life, he simply turned over the vegetable shelves to me, let me fill them, keep them in order, and take the profits. I learned everything I needed to know about hard work. And its rewards. Now, even the simplest lump could pump gas or grind hamburger, so I figured Julius Rosenberg had to be faking it. Their poverty was just a cover. They no doubt had a secret bank account somewhere— Poland probably, since that country had had the brass to offer them political asylum. There were people who said Julie was throwing money around like water toward the end—I think it was the FBI who said this—he was buying clothes, photographs, eating out at expensive restaurants. I wondered if I should take Pat out to an expensive restaurant on our anniversary. There was a good Mexican place on Connecticut I'd heard about. At one time, I'd been eager to take up Mexican food, because I had so many California constituents who ate the goddamn stuff, and I knew it was something you had to get in practice for. Pat would probably want to eat fish down by the river. Where all the mosquitoes were, very romantic. I'd settle, as always, for a good well-done hamburger. And a pineapple malted. Or even a dish of cottage cheese. I eat a lot of cottage cheese, I can eat it until it runs out my ears. And one thing I do that makes it not too bad is put ketchup on it. I learned it from my grandmother.

My stomach growled. I loosened my belt a notch, belched emptily, ate an antacid. I've been at this too long, I thought. If I wasn't careful, I'd make myself sick again. How did other people get where they were without having to work like this? Since the moment I'd got in off the course Sunday, I'd been going at it. I hadn't even paused to take a shower in the clubhouse (of course, I rarely shower in public places any more—I agree with Ulysses Grant about that, I don't think it's wise to let people see what any Incarnation of Uncle Sam looks like without his clothes on—or even in his shorts or pajamas; I just couldn't understand Eisenhower making his valets help him on with his underpants every morning, it seemed like some kind of unnecessary strategic risk), I'd rushed straight back here and headlong into a full-scale exhaustive study of the Rosenberg case, the trial, the background, personal histories and peripheral issues, appeals, the impact on world affairs, everything. This is my way with every project, scholastic, political, athletic, or romantic: I talk for hours with every person I can find, spend every spare moment studying reports and recommendations, gather up and try to absorb every known bit of information, make hundreds of calls, read whatever philosophy or political science or history I need to accomplish the task. "Iron Butt," they called me in law school. There was always a tradition of hard work in my family, especially on my mother's side, the Quaker side. And it always paid off.

I assumed it would pay off now, though I still wasn't sure just what that payoff was going to be. Of course, I could only think of one thing these days, and that seemed a long ways off, but I knew how important it was to keep your eyes open at all times, miss nothing—one moment of carelessness or distraction, and you could stumble and fall from sight forever. Like that fund they set up for me in California, I hardly thought about it at the time, and I nearly got erased by it. The least detail could make or break you. Or maybe I was making too much of this thing. Maybe it was nothing more than just an exemplary entertainment of sorts. Who could tell what was on Uncle Sam's mind? Certainly it was very theatrical. There was the drama of a brother sending his big sister to the electric chair; the implied tragedy of the Rosenberg children who would be left orphans; the curious spectacle of Jews prosecuting and judging Jews, then accusing each other of tribal disloyalties; an almost Wagnerian scope to the prosecution's presentation, incorporating many of the major issues of our times, whether or not relevant to the crime charged; the sense throughout that this was clearly a struggle between the forces of good and evil . . . and a lot of pretty fair spy stories to the bargain, if the prosecution was to be believed: secret codenames, recognition signals, covert drop sites, escape plans, cover stories, payoffs, cat-and-mouse games with FBI surveillance teams, border intrigues. But there was more to it than that. Not only was everybody in this case from the Judge on down—indeed, just about everyone in the nation, in and out of government, myself included—behaving like actors caught up in a play, but we all seemed moreover to be aware of just what we were doing and at the same time of our inability, committed as we were to some higher purpose, some larger script as it were, to do otherwise. Even the Rosenbergs seemed to be swept up in this sense of an embracing and compelling drama, speaking in their letters of sinister "plots" and worldwide "themes" and "setting the stage" and playing the parts they had been—rightly or wrongly—cast for "with honor and with dignity."

And that was another thing: not just the Rosenbergs, but almost everybody involved in this case was about the same age—*my* age! Judge Kaufman, for example, who in many ways had emerged as the real star and hero of this thing—he must have been going through his own fortieth-birthday crisis at the time of the trial two years ago. The

Boy Judge: I had to admire him. I'd always thought of myself as a fast starter—I've been "the youngest ever" to do a lot of things in my life—but even I was no match for Irving Kaufman. He'd entered Fordham when he was only sixteen, had graduated so young from law school he wasn't even eligible to take the bar exam, and while I was still dusting Tom Bewley's office library back in Whittier and working on drunk cases, divorces, and traffic shit, he'd already been fighting the big ones, right in the heart of New York City, for over five years! He'd become an assistant D.A., helping gangbuster Tom Dewey and winning fame as the "Boy Prosecutor"—the Roy Cohn of his day. No wonder they got on so well. I hardly thought of national politics until I got asked to run for office in 1946, but Kaufman had already been called in personally by F.D.R. to help choose a federal judge way back in 1939 (*fourteen* years ago!), and by the time I'd got to Washington as "the Greenest Congressman in Town," he was a Special Assistant to Attorney General Tom Clark, on a first-name basis with Edgar Hoover, and getting big write-ups in all the newspapers. When Harry Truman made him a federal judge in 1949, he was only thirty-nine years old, the youngest in America. And now he was being touted for the U.S. Supreme Court. His friend Tom Clark, Truman's old hatchet man, was already sitting there, no doubt promoting his cause. Well, if I was ever in a position to nominate and he hadn't made it yet, provided the Jewish seat was open, he'd be a likely candidate. I'd have to get over the resentment I sometimes felt at the fact that while I was fighting seasickness and mosquitoes in the South Pacific, Kaufman was sitting out the war in a private law practice, pulling down $100,000 a year with well-heeled clients like Milton Berle, but I figured if I ever became the true Incarnation, all such feelings would drop away like Clark Kent's spectacles. Certainly he was my kind of judge—and a popular choice with the opposition at the same time: Pope Kaufman, the All-American Christian Orthodox Jew, a Tammany Hall Democrat whose law partner was a prominent Republican leader, hard as nails and heart of gold, "radical one day," as the *New York Post* said of him in a headline story, "reactionary the next," a natural. This judicious balance: it was his special genius. He could appear both strict and generous, scholarly and worldly, intense and serene, innovative and traditional. He'd even produced a set of twin sons. And smoked exactly two cigars a day.

In the Rosenberg trial, this talent helped him make all the right motions with regard to due process and fair play, while in fact keeping tight control over the development of the case. Whenever Irv Saypol seemed in danger of floundering, Kaufman would pop a telling question at the witness and get the Prosecutor back on the track, but he coolly kept his peace when Bloch was making all the obvious blunders on the other side. Whenever Bloch did get onto something at last and begin to peak, the Judge would deflate him with a blunt, sometimes even derisive, interruption, and Bloch would have to start all over. He knew how to heighten a prosecution moment with a brief recess, how even as a Jew to bring the Spirit of Easter into the courtroom, and how to reduce a rebellious defense attorney to abject silence: "Don't give me any course of instruction as to what is usually done in a courtroom! This is the way I am running this courtroom, and I think I understand the way a courtroom should be run! I don't care to hear anything further from you!" Then there was that day when the Rosenbergs were taking the Fifth on the Communist issue. They were looking bad enough without any help, but upstairs in the same building gangsters like Joe Adonis and Frank Costello were also taking the Fifth before the Kefauver crime-investigation committee, and Kaufman evidently couldn't resist. He interrupted the interrogation, cleared the court, asked the jury to stay, and invited down that old New Hampshire windbag, Senator Tobey. "I'm very glad to be here and meet you," Tobey said to all of them as Kaufman scrambled down off the bench to greet him. "We could use people like you upstairs." Who could miss the connection? Another time, when Saypol ran into trouble on a query from Bloch about possible wiretapping, it was Kaufman who got him out of it—"It *is* ridiculous!"—even managing at the same time to remind the jury that whatever the United States Attorney said must, *de fide*, be true, and obscuring the fact that the question was never really answered (of course Bloch was probably right about the wiretap, but nobody wanted this fundamental case to be obscured by a technicality, maybe not even Bloch—besides, Kaufman *liked* wiretaps: thirteen years before, he'd been the first prosecuting attorney in the district ever to use one in a federal case; he'd played it on a small portable phonograph, creating a big stir in the courtroom, even the defendants had crowded around to see how it worked). He was like the director of a play who knows how to boost his actors' egos and give them a sense of participation in the staging and interpretation, while in fact pulling all the strings—a fantastically smooth performance, Bloch himself had to applaud it at the end.

Applause, director, actors, script: yes, it was like—and this thought hit me now like a revelation—*it was like a little morality play for our generation!* During the Hiss case, I had felt like a brash kid among seasoned professionals; now my own generation was coming into its own—and this was (that lecture at Burning Tree was making sense to me at last) our initiation drama, our gateway into History! Or part of it anyway, for the plot was still unfolding. In the larger drama, of which the Rosenberg episode was a single act, I was a principal actor—if not, before the play is ended, *the* principal actor—but within this scene alone, I was more like a kind of stage manager, an assistant director or producer, a presence more felt than seen. This was true even of the trial itself: I felt somehow the author of it—not of the words so much, for these were, in a sense, improvisations, but rather of the *style* of the performances, as though I had through my own public appearances created the audience expectations, set the standards, keyed the rhetoric, crystallized the roles, in order that my generation might witness in dramatic form the fundamental controversy of our time!

Of course, I knew it was foolish to place too much weight on a court record, even as didactic theater, Uncle Sam had already warned me about that. What's missing in the record is the atmosphere of the courtroom: the expressions on faces, gestures, inflections, betrayed emotions —in short, what are elsewhere called acting values. But it could equally well be argued that the court record, like a baseball box score, was even more reliable than the actual trial: some people were better actors than others, and the emotions of a courtroom could often get jurors into such a state they couldn't even hear what was being said. Practiced liars could overwhelm the hardest evidence against them, turn it to their own credit, and reduce a whole courtroom to tears, while simpler folk, accustomed to telling what they thought of as the truth, could get caught in a small exaggeration or personal embarrassment and become so flustered that everything they said afterwards sounded false. Some attorneys blew their best material right at the outset like a premature ejaculation, saving nothing back with which to bring the jury to climax just before they retired for a decision, and so finding themselves getting beaten by an opponent with nothing but nonsense, innuendos, and a superior sense of dramaturgy. Class identifications or hostilities could evoke juror responses completely unrelated to the testimony, well-timed comedy could provoke gratitude or ill-timed comedy shock, and evidence suddenly produced by surprise could obscure the fact, later obvious, that it was worthless. The point of *Night of January 16th*, for example, that Ayn Rand play I was in back in Whittier, was that there was no final conclusion to be drawn, no "right" or "wrong" judgment, the evidence was ambiguous, the testimony contradictory, and each night a jury selected from the audience was invited to render its own verdict. Depending on our various performances, the verdict changed from show to show. I played the part of the District Attorney and prided myself on winning more nights than I lost—one of my most successful roles actually: I was a natural as a prosecutor, could have made a Tom Dewey career out of it. But I would have taken just as much pride in winning for the defense.

The genius of Irving Saypol—himself just forty-five then—was how well he understood all this and used it in the Rosenberg trial. He even stole one of my lines from the play: "I am not going to appeal to your 'souls,' or to those 'deep secret chords of your hearts'—but to your reason alone!" He himself had said somewhere: "A well-turned case is just like a stage play really," meaning by that not merely that convictions depend upon dramatic entertainment, but that justice *is* entertainment. His own performance as Prosecuting Attorney was inspired, his backstage manipulations imaginative and exhaustive. With the help of a cooperative and close-mouthed FBI, he had produced a brilliant working script and then had rehearsed his principal witnesses for weeks—he'd even lodged Harry Gold and David Greenglass together up on the eleventh floor of the Tombs prison (the "singing quarters") for several months so that they could perfect their interlocking testimony—while at the same time, he'd seen to it that the defendants were kept too disturbed even to think properly, disrupting their family life, isolating them from each other and driving them to despair over fears for their two kids, depriving them of their freedom and personal dignity, not to mention an ordinary sex life, terrorizing them with ominous rumors, exposing them to vitriolic press and radio campaigns, dividing their own families against them, keeping them ignorant of his own strategy while maintaining tabs on theirs by intercepting their communications and planting FBI informers in the cells near Julie, holding back from them the vast amount of back-up support and research he was getting from the FBI and other government agencies, forcing them to rely entirely on their own limited resources, knowing that no one would come to their aid since to do so could implicate that person in the "conspiracy." Saypol had even managed to arrange a complete dress rehearsal—sort of like trying the show out in New Haven—in the thematically similar, though less serious, Brothman-Moskowitz trial four months earlier, in which virtually the entire cast—including the Judge and excepting only the accused—was the same. Thus, the Rosenbergs and their lawyers were the only ones not rehearsed, and were in effect having to attempt amateur improvisation theater in the midst of a carefully rehearsed professional drama. Naturally they looked clumsy and unsure of themselves . . . and so, a bit like uneasy liars.

Saypol was terrific in the courtroom, too: shrewd, thorough, quick on his feet, cold-blooded, and powerful enough in his hushed no-messing-around way to make what might later seem like nothing more than a series of overlapping fictions cohere into a convincing semblance of historical continuity and logical truth—at least long enough to wrest a guilty verdict from an impressed jury. True, he accomplished this more with adjectives and style than with verbs and substance, but, given the difficulties, this was all the more to his credit. Knowing he'd have a group of middle-class jurors (most of them were accountants and pro-fessed anti-Communists—and here again, in jury selection, Saypol had done his homework, having complete access to police and FBI dossiers withheld from the Rosenberg team), he saw to it that all his witnesses were properly dressed and carefully schooled in witness-box manner-isms, so as to create the undercurrents of awe, rapport, sympathy, or believability he wanted, and he himself stood tall and stern, like Lou Gehrig or Randolph Scott, speaking softly but wielding a stick as big as Uncle Sam's forearm. Poor old Manny Bloch, contrarily—stocky, stoop-shouldered, and baggy-eyed—looked a little sinister and out at the elbows, and his clients behaved strangely—shrill, pompous, abject, seedy, emotionally unstable—for this jurybox of middle Americans, so like my own constituents. I knew the way Saypol's mind was running: with this jury, dowdiness *was* guilt.

Bloch treated him deferentially and sometimes fawned on him, con-ceding he might be right on this or that minor point, or accepting his word and thanking him for his "courtesies," obviously angling for Say-pol's pity and sense of fair play, but there was no reciprocal gesture from Saypol. He just accepted the compliments as though deserving them and lashed back, never giving an inch. A natural killer. As he himself once said: "As a prosecutor in a criminal case, one in my posi-tion has armament like an iceberg." Every word was calculated to fur-ther the impression that the defendants were tampering with or dodging the truth, and that even their lawyers were embarrassed at having to defend them—a one-track mind, that track leading straight to the elec-tric chair, which Saypol firmly believed in. And those you couldn't eliminate, teach: "I've often wondered," he has said, "whether the whipping lash wouldn't be a greater deterrent than what we have now." Mr. District Attorney. According to Roy Cohn, Saypol loved to play cop, interrogating suspects himself, investigating them—he even carried a gun around in his back pocket like Sam Spade.

Nevertheless, tough as he was, I could have whipped his ass from Foley Square to Jenkins Hill and back again, could have beat the rap for the Rosenbergs—though of course this would have been a miscarriage of justice. Bloch, the Rosenbergs' lawyer, was a dunce, a push-over—in fact, he played so naïvely into Saypol's hands at times that I suspected Uncle Sam must have had something to do with frazzling his mind somehow. Giving him bad dreams so he didn't sleep well or something. He buckled under to the Judge, overpraised the Prosecutor, joined the chorus of admiration for the FBI—who were, though he never seemed to grasp this, his real opponents in this trial: in the final analysis, it was their word against his, and it was his job to destroy their credibility. But this never even occurred to him. He just didn't know what the game was all about. He neglected to bring in friendly witnesses and refused to cross-examine key government witnesses, bungled the Fifth Amendment procedures, seemed not to hear half of what got said. Nor did he challenge any of the physical exhibits, a lot of which were very dubious looking and should have been exposed to public scrutiny— hell, the FBI has a special section which does nothing but produce fake documents, they have to do this, it's a routine part of police work, the kind of thing I might have enjoyed doing if they'd given me that job I asked for when I left Duke—and much of the stuff that Saypol offered up looked like it might well have come from that factory. Of course, what choice did Saypol have? The real evidence was in Russia. You had to credit his ingenuity. Just as you had to fault the defense for chickening out under pressure.

Bloch's crosses were hardly likely to get him into the Hall of Fame either. He failed to ask who if anybody helped Greenglass prepare those new sketches, presumably copies of the originals, for the trial, even leapt up and urged the impounding of the goddamn things in a phony act of patriotic grandstanding that fooled nobody, stamped the drawings as the real McCoy, and drew an awful lot of excitement to the testimony of Greenglass which followed. He neglected to probe into Greenglass's complicated finances, failed to follow up when Greenglass talked spookily of "memories and voices in my mind." He did not demand to know the details of the prosecution's careful rehearsal of David, Ruth, Harry Gold, and the others during the six months preceding. In short, he lacked a win complex. I believe you have to stay on the offensive, wait for windfalls, get what dope you can on your adversary, and then blast him, whether in a courtroom, an election campaign, or a summit meeting. Saypol had built a house of cards and Bloch just didn't blow. "Every man sitting over here is an honest man," Bloch said in his summing-up: "The FBI representatives, Mr. Saypol and his staff, every man of them, they are doing their duty." Saypol must have had a hard time just to keep from laughing.

Bloch's most astounding blunder was to refuse to cross-examine Harry Gold. Gold was the alleged courier-link between Fuchs, Rosenberg, and Greenglass, and if he was lying—or if the jury could be made to think so—then Bloch and the Rosenbergs had it made. Gold, like most spies, even our own boys over in the CIA unfortunately, was an incorrigible fantasist, who in the course of his operations had invented a wife, twin children, an apartment, a house purchase, a polio attack on one of the children, a separation, his brother's death, and even a fictitious list of "contacts" which he gave the Russians, sharing intimate moments from this fantasy life with friends and associates, acting it out for the world in all its bizarre detail, while in fact living at home all the time with his mother, at least until she died. His wife's name in this saga was Sarah O'Ken, a former gun moll of an underworld villain named Nigger Nate; he said he'd met her while courting another girl with one blue eye and one brown eye (his mother had such a pair). John Hamilton, who had once been our National Committee Chairman and who somehow got Gold as a client, told me he sometimes wondered if Gold was even a spy, maybe he was making the whole thing up; he had all the apparatus, all right, but it was all down in his basement, even the stuff he was supposed to have given the Russians, boxes of it, like the raw materials of some novel. He told me Gold was something of a self-destructer, too, a man with no sense of his own being, and as a boy—probably now in prison, still—he played these weird baseball games with decks of cards, inventing a whole league of eight teams with all their players, playing out full seasons, keeping all the box scores and statistics, even taking note of what they looked like! It's a wonder one of his ace pitchers didn't turn up in the trial testimony as a contact or something. Maybe one did. And vice versa.

He was apparently fascinating to watch on the witness stand, a man so used to living in make-believe worlds under one cover or another he couldn't remember rightly the real one any more, yet outwardly very calm and convincing, with an ingenious sense of detail—a man at home within the artifice of a courtroom trial. Maybe Bloch was afraid to probe such talent, no telling what he might come up with. That smug self-confidence reminded me in some ways of Alger Hiss, except that Gold was both creepier and humbler than Hiss and could spin it off with less self-consciousness. He had a round face with a sharp nose and big dark eyes, wore a pinstripe suit with enormous lapels and fat bright ties—he looked like a silent-film comedian doing an imitation of Roy Cohn. Outpost Harry. Must have seemed like a gift from the goddamn gods to the FBI, and maybe that was the best way to think of it. He was the man who supposedly turned up in Albuquerque one day with half a card from the back of a Jell-O box that matched a half that Julius Rosenberg had given David Greenglass, told David "I come from Julius," and then exchanged some money for some atomic-bomb sketches and other material. Thus, he was the master link that brought it all together, made a "spy ring" out of it. Hamilton told me that in his early conferences with Gold, he'd apparently forgotten all of this, but once he'd had a couple of weeks with the FBI agents, it all "came back" to him. That "I come from Julius," for example, maybe the key piece of corroborative testimony: at first glance it was very damaging. But in fact, if true, it was strong evidence that Rosenberg was *not* involved, since these intelligence agents always use made-up names, not real ones, especially in recognition signals. Moreover, Greenglass had felt obliged, after the exchange of money and data, to give Gold Julius Rosenberg's name and phone number as a way of getting in touch when David was in New York on furlough, so in any case both of them must have assumed Gold was referring to some other Julius. Fuchs, for example: one of his middle names was Julius. So for that matter was Herb Brownell's. Hamilton didn't even think this was the real signal used. He said that in his first conversations with Gold there'd been no mention of these signals at all—in fact, no mention of Greenglass or A-bomb sketches either —all this had come later after Gold had had several helpful sessions with the FBI. But even after Gold had begun to "remember" Greenglass, there had *still* been no Jell-O box and no Julius, just "something on the order of Bob sent me or Benny sent me or John sent me or something like that."

Admittedly, Bloch didn't know then what I knew now—and thank God for that, I suppose, God and John Hamilton, who kept his mouth shut—but how the hell are you going to find out if you don't ask? Bloch had surely read the transcript of the earlier Brothman-Moskowitz rehearsal when Gold had spun off that fantasy-family routine—with that alone I could have split that screwed-up schizoid in two, right slap through the void in his middle. He could've walked out of the courtroom afterwards through two separate doors. And one thing about a witness with a penchant for all those cute little supplementary details: keep egging him on and he'll invent one too many, ask any of those famous inspectors from the classic murder cases of literature. Or take that baseball game played with a deck of cards, I can just imagine what I might have done with that one . . .

DEFENSE: Say, by the way, this fella "John," you know, your Russian contact—an older fella, I gather, tall and sort of blond . . .

GOLD: No, he was about five feet nine inches in height, had a medium build, which tended toward the slender, and he was about twenty-eight or thirty years old . . .

DEFENSE: I see. But blond and—

GOLD: No, he had dark or dark brown hair and there was a lock of it that kept falling over his forehead, which he would brush back continually . . .

DEFENSE: Tried to keep it stuffed under his cap, I suppose . . .

GOLD: Yes, and he had a rather long nose and fair complexion, dark eyes. He walked with somewhat of a stoop . . .

DEFENSE: Like a catcher, you mean. Or a rightfielder . . .

GOLD: No, first base was his position actually . . .

DEFENSE: Not too tall, but agile . . .

GOLD: Yes, he had a good reach, and . . . uh . . . ah . . .

DEFENSE: I see. Tell me, Harry, what . . . uh, what team did John play for?

GOLD: (*A slight twitch in the left side of his face. His fingers flutter as though shuffling cards, as his eyes glance to and fro uneasily.* DEFENSE *smiles at the* PROSECUTOR.)

Like taking candy from a baby. Which makes one wonder why Gold caused Bloch such distress. He seemed very eager not to hear more. It may have been simply that Rosenberg didn't want anyone else to get implicated, and just couldn't trust a fabulator like Gold. Gold had said little so far that touched Julius, had admitted he didn't know him at all, but if you kept him talking, who knew what friends or relatives might get dragged in? And maybe Julius knew damned well who Gold was and what he might say. According to Edgar's secret files, Gold, under prompting, had begun to "remember" passing Julius on a street corner in Jackson Heights during an aborted "contact" with an unknown agent back in 1950, Julius suited up in the style of his newspaper photos, scowling and wallowing a cigar like Groucho Marx. A preposterous tale, but who could say? More than once what looked like a complete Gold fantasy had resulted in arrests and confessions, almost as though he were dreaming the world into being. Maybe *he* was the real playwright here. And maybe the Rosenbergs quite reasonably feared some irrevocable casting. Whatever, the net effect was terribly damaging to them.

Most of Bloch's blunders, in fact, implied that he was running scared, that a wrong move could sink them all—implied in short that the Rosenbergs were indeed guilty. As no doubt they were. You only had to look at them. Like Uncle Sam said: They reeked with guilt. Their arrogance, their clumsy lying, their hiding behind the Fifth Amendment, those obvious Communist links they wouldn't admit to, their obsequiousness, their phony complaints about bad health, their frequent failure to "recall" simple facts, all the political grandstanding—from considerable experience in observing witnesses on the stand, I had learned that those who are lying or trying to cover up something generally make a common mistake—*they tend to overact, to overstate their case*. Even the way they took the Fifth was different from the way an innocent man might take it on principle. Like Alger Hiss, they'd hung themselves with their transparent deceitfulness, their pompous denials, their pretensions of injured innocence.

Part of what seemed to give the lie to their testimony, of course, was the phony role they'd cast themselves in: the ordinary middle-class American couple, romantic and hardworking, loving parents, being framed by a deceitful and unnatural brother, backed by a monstrous State bureaucracy, victimized by some ghastly error. Julius wore a business suit. He carefully obeyed every rule. He had never broken a law, though he'd once been fired from an Army job as a suspected Red. Ethel pursed her lips and wore a cloth coat like Pat. Their children had neat haircuts and scrubbed faces. Julius kept his chin up. Ethel smiled at the witnesses. They said they loved their mixed-up brother. They were shocked at Saypol's indecorous puns. They held hands and kissed each other through wire mesh. "All our lives," wrote Ethel for international publication, "we lived decent, constructive lives . . ." They had probably moved automatically, even gratefully, into these middle-class clichés after their arrests—I understood well the solace and protection you could find in them—but they wore them awkwardly. Julius moved like a whey-faced automaton in his stiff blue suit. The jurors called Ethel's courtroom composure "steely" and "stony." They had the wrong kind of friends, which didn't help, noisy old left-wingers from college days whom they'd stayed loyal to—they just couldn't play the bourgeois act straight, knowing those friends would be tuning in, watching for betrayals, contemptuous of anything less than heroics. Every time Julius said "sir," you suspected him of satire. They were very impressive in their open willingness to put themselves in the witness box and in their bold denial of all charges, but their taking of the Fifth on ideological questions undid all that and suggested continuing Party orthodoxy, while deep in their voices like an indelible stain ran irrepressible un-American accents, the sour babble of steerage passengers and backpack peddlers, scarcely concealed, the pedantic precision of bright children whose parents don't speak proper English. The electorate, needless to say, were not fooled.

But then who were the real Rosenbergs behind their role-playing? Probably never know. FBI reports had hinted at a taste for pornography and histrionics. Their apartment was cluttered with cheap junk, and they hung out with friends who lived pretty unconventional lives. People Pat and I wouldn't even know how to talk to. They seemed to live without any structure, without any roots, yet they never went any-where. I'd grown up across the river from the Mexican ghetto of Jim Town, so I knew what one looked like, but I couldn't imagine *living* in a ghetto. I couldn't understand why people didn't just move out and go somewhere else. Lack of imagination or something. Terrible life there, they both got pushed around a lot. Ethel, just sixteen, had gone to apply for a job and had got knocked down by police fire hoses. Her ghetto past had haunted her, frustrated her theatrical career, just as I'd been frus-trated in my hopes for a New York City law career by my small-town California past, only I didn't let it embitter me. Julie had taken a lot of punishment, too, and seen worse. He'd become a left-winger in college, but ghetto Jews were *supposed* to be left-wingers at a time when most right-wingers were Jew-baiters, so in a way he was being just as conven-tional as I was back at Whittier College. He'd seen young Bundist toughs beating up bearded old Jews playing chess in Seward Park, Ne-groes shot in race killings. He'd got stopped one night near Union Square by two brownshirts who'd asked him what CCNY meant. "City College of New York," he'd told them. "Naw!" they'd laughed, shoving him off the sidewalk: "It means Christian College Now Yiddish!" And then, one thing had led to another. They'd stayed loyal to the left-wing friends who'd admired them—their constituency, as it were—and the next thing they'd known, there was a war on, the Communists were amazingly our allies, Julius was working for the Army and Ethel had a brother out on the A-bomb project, other engineering friends were simi-larly dispersed—so suppose the request came through: how could they say no? Get out of the overt activities of college days and withdraw to the very center of the heresy that excited them: why not? After all, I'd become Vice President of the United States of America by a chain of circumstances not all that different, one thing drifting into the next, carried along by a desire, much like theirs, to reach the heart of things, to participate deeply in life.

Maybe Julius, like me, had somehow gotten this quality from his mother. Sophie had come to the United States at the age of fourteen, had worked eleven hours a day, six days a week, for eight dollars a week, and had somehow saved enough out of that to bring her own mother and four brothers over from Poland, then had wed Harry Rosenberg, a fellow worker, at age eighteen. They'd been flamboyant, romantic, in love with the old Polish culture, but terribly poor, living on the top floor of a five-story tenement on Broome Street where the roof leaked and in winter icicles hung from the ceiling and windows. Like my own father, Harry Rosenberg had tried to keep a store going, a dry-cleaning business, but had failed, fallen into abject poverty, and then, through hard work and tenacity, had fought his way back through bread lines and soup kitchens, had finally reached the point where he could afford for his family an apartment with steam heat. Like something out of a Horatio Alger story, except that Harry was a socialist. Phantom-seed brought from the Old World like lice in an old hat brim. Also, Judaism was not the prevailing faith of the Alger heroes, but in this regard one couldn't help but admire the Rosenbergs' orthodoxy and commitment. Little Julius had been very serious about his religion as a boy—we shared this—and moreover he'd been a strict fundamentalist. At the synagogue, they'd called him "Jonah," and he'd been elected vice president of the Young Men's Synagogue Organization. Like me, at Christian Endeavor. He had led lessons and had even considered becoming a rabbi, just as my mother had always thought I might become a Quaker missionary. He was younger than me, about the age of my baby brother, Arthur, who'd died when I was twelve. Julius was a sickly boy with bad eyesight, given to allergies, sudden illnesses—he'd nearly died of a ruptured appendix when he was ten, just a year or so before my bad attack of undulant fever, and he'd suffered from asthma and other psychosomatic problems. Kept him out of World War II and set him up for his spying mission—he became an inspector of electronics products manufactured by private industry for the Army Signal Corps—but his draft deferment pissed me off: didn't he care about all those poor fellow Jews in Germany? Whose war was this anyway? A lot of things he'd said at the trial and in letters had disgusted me, but one of the worst was when he got Reveille mixed up with Taps. Of course, I suffered from hay fever myself, but my problem was strictly physical, and I joined the Navy anyway. His problem was, he was sick. Probably started when he was a little boy and his mother had to go with him to the bathroom at night to hold a lighted candle—it was down an unlit corridor, and he was afraid of the dark. A stinking place used by everybody on the floor. Rats rustling behind the walls, drunks sprawled in the hallways. Maybe one of them asleep on the toilet right now. Or holding a knife. Back in the night of my parents' bedroom, I could hear my father calling me a baby. I was afraid that when I stepped through the door I'd fall down a deep hole. Mother was angry and told me to hurry. Tallow dripped into the stool. It was clogged up. Stuff seemed to be moving down there. I couldn't get started. I thought I could hear my dead brother crying behind the walls. . . .

I reared up with a start. Where was I? I glanced about: the office was empty. Just the documents scattered about. Ah yes, the Rosenbergs. . . . I gazed blearily at all the litter, wondering what Pat might have back home in the icebox. What a mess. What if somebody came in here and saw me like this? I thought. At least I should sit up straight, be seen to be thinking, concentrating. The Spartan look. But I was too tired. My back was stiff and my butt hurt. I wondered if I'd got blisters from sitting too long. Or boils—didn't that happen to somebody famous? My old butt ain't so ironic as it used to be, I mused to myself as I got to my feet and staggered off to take a piss. I grinned at this and said it out loud: "My old butt's not as ironic as it, uh, used to be . . ." It didn't sound as funny out loud. Like Saypol's puns at the trial: "Did you say 'a Russian business' or 'rushing business'?" Even Bloch pretended to enjoy that one, and Judge Kaufman said: "Try to restrain your desire to be another Milton Berle." Which might sound like a scolding, but which in fact was a gentle compliment, drawing an affectionate link between himself, the comic, and Saypol, and serving in its embracing humor to unite Judge, jurors, lawyers, spectators, the outside world—indeed everyone except the two outcast defendants, suddenly more isolated than ever—while at the same time subtly providing a bit of promotion on the side for Uncle Miltie, one of Kaufman's former clients and oldest friends, setting him up as the very paradigm of American wit and humor.

I checked the refrigerator again. For the fortieth time. Nothing there but an empty cigar box, empty cottage cheese carton, half a bottle of ketchup, and a tin of maple syrup, almost empty. I uncapped the syrup, tipped it up—it took forever draining down, and then all I got from it was a long stale lick. I threw the can in a wastebasket, did a few deep knee-bends, trying to stir the dead cells, get alert enough to bring this thing to a close, make conclusions, clean it up. Late. Very quiet. Spooky in fact. I could hear voices very far away, chanting. I knew the National Gallery Orchestra was performing some new work celebrating the Old South this week, but it didn't sound like "All Quiet Along the Potomac

Tonight." Too late for that anyway. The demonstrators probably.
They'd been infiltrating the Capital all week. Clemency vigils tonight at
the Odd Fellows Hall. Could be dangerous out there. I should get home
and get to bed. Cabinet meeting tomorrow morning early. But in fact, to
tell the truth, I *liked* staying up all night. Got in the habit back in high
school when I had the bell tower to go to. I was always more efficient at
night, something about the pressure in the air, and I liked the dark
down around me. So did Kaufman, apparently. He liked to brag he slept
only ninety minutes a night during times of stress. And visited the
synagogue several times a day. For meditative catnaps probably. I
yawned.

Jesus! I realized I was stretched out again, this time on the leather
couch. I scolded myself angrily, did three fast sit-ups there on the cush-
ions, then sprang to my feet and resumed my pacing, throwing short
shadow punches like Rocky Marciano. Unff! Unff! All right, wrap it up,
I said to myself. Something's bugging you, what is it? Something about
the linkages. If you walked forward through all this data, like the journalists, like the FBI invited everybody to do, the story was cohesive and
seemed as simple and true as an epigram. The Soviets tested an A-bomb
in 1949, sudden proof they'd stolen the secret from us. The nuclear
scientist Klaus Fuchs, arrested in England by Scotland Yard, verified
the theft and led the FBI to his courier Harry Gold, who confessed that
his Russian contact was Anatoli Yakovlev. Yakovlev had sailed away to
Russia with his wife, two kids, and all relevant secrets aboard the S.S.
America some time earlier. Journalists tended to find the name of the
ship deeply ironic. Gold also put the finger on David Greenglass, a
machinist at Los Alamos and former Communist, and Greenglass in
turn, his wife Ruth collaborating, turned state's evidence against his
sister Ethel and Ethel's husband Julius Rosenberg, also ex-Commies. Or
maybe not ex. Other witnesses substantiated this charge and widened
the ring to include Morton Sobell, who had fled to Mexico, but who
with the help of Mexican police had been "returned" to the U.S. and captured. There were no doubt others—the Rosenbergs and Sobell seemed
like small-time operators at best—but so far none of these three had
said who the people behind them were. Or, if Hoover was right and
Rosenberg was the Master Spy, who the others in his ring were. Which
was why maximum pressure was being applied, although in fact the FBI
already had plenty of evidence on other members of the conspiracy.
They said.

Okay. So far so good. The Crime of the Century, by J. Edgar Hoover.
But working backwards, like a lawyer, the narrative came unraveled. All

that the minor witnesses really substantiated was (1) that people were indeed spying for the Russians in this country, as everybody knew, and (2) that Julius Rosenberg was a left-winger, probably a Communist or at least a sympathizer. But no links between (1) and (2), no hard evidence that the Rosenbergs themselves were spies. The principal evidence against Sobell was his wild flight to Mexico. This was pretty peculiar, all right, but who knew what he was actually fleeing from? He'd been a Communist, after all, and that by itself was a federal crime. The FBI had not been able to connect him in any way to the theft of the bomb secrets, only to a ring of City College classmates with unhealthy opinions, including Rosenberg. So forget Sobell. Yakovlev had been out of the country for years and wasn't apt to come back to the U.S. to deny the FBI charges, and as for Harry Gold, not only was he a notorious fantasist, but his testimony in any case had nothing to do with the Rosenbergs, only the Greenglasses. Moreover, though I got the impression from the files that Gold seemed to know Yakovlev all right, this FBI legend of Fuchs leading them to Gold and Gold to Greenglass just didn't hold up. Gold had hardly begun to speak vaguely of some "unknown individual in Albuquerque" but what the FBI had Greenglass under questioning. Where did they find him? The files didn't say. But they did show that as soon as Gold—with FBI assistance—"remembered" this contact, the FBI showed him a list of twenty possible names and David's was already on it. And prior to that, the FBI had descended on Gold long before getting any help at all from Fuchs. In fact, Fuchs had told them time and again that Gold was *not* his courier, in spite of Harry's signed confession. But the agents working on him in England were very persistent fellows, and Fuchs may well have gone along with them finally just to get them off his back. So, if anything, it was Greenglass to Gold to Fuchs.

What about the Greenglasses, then? Without their testimony the government had almost nothing left: a few suspect associations, meetings, uncorroborated assertions, the open sesame of "I come from Julius," patently fabricated by the prosecution, a sackful of photo equipment, and the solemn word of the FBI that they knew what they were doing. And maybe they did. Certainly the Greenglass confessions seemed real enough, especially since they involved a brother sending his own sister to her death and himself to the penitentiary, but it was a bit odd that the night the FBI first picked him up for a preliminary interview, David laughingly told them everything. Almost as though it had been rehearsed. All except any references to his sister Eth, who he insisted from the beginning had nothing to do with it. Nailing Julius, though, seemed to please him. By the time of the trial, he had stopped laughing, but he was still grinning. It made him look like Joe McCarthy. His trial testimony, like Ruth's, was smooth and polished—too polished. They seemed to remember odd facts too readily, facts all too similar in type to those used successfully by the Saypol team and approved by Kaufman in the earlier warm-up Brothman-Moskowitz trial. And there was too much that never got said, too much information concealed that might have muddied the argument, too much hanging over the Greenglasses' heads. Not just the thefts either, maybe the FBI was really ignorant of that, but espionage, Communism, and possible perjury as well: their letters through the war showed them to be committed Party zealots, enthusiastically working for a "socialist America" and "raising the Red flag," Ruth helping to organize New York City units, David proselytizing among his fellow soldiers—they even called each other "comrade" and signed their letters "with all the love of Marx and the humanity of Lenin"! Yet the very openness of these letters seemed to militate against any subplot beneath the text, about the only hint of anything out of the ordinary being David's remark in a 1944 letter from Santa Fe that by 1948 "we should have made our contributions to the world, at least one such contribution." Which could mean just about anything.

Then would they just jump into wild charges of atomic spying all by themselves? No, but it could have been the other way around. Maybe the FBI had told David that they already had the goods on Ethel and Julius, knew a lot of things in fact that even David didn't know, they only wanted him and Ruth to "confirm" certain things—the FBI often worked this way, and the Greenglasses were easy marks. And maybe the FBI *did* know about the uranium theft and used that to scare him into "cooperating." After all, the FBI *had* to win this one—their whole reputation depended on it, as well as their budget and a lot of jobs. Including Hoover's: the Democrats had been out to get him for years, and what better opportunity than to be able to turn the "soft on Communism" charge back on the old Master Red-Baiter himself? The British had made a chump out of him with their arrest of Fuchs, now he had to top them to save his neck, and with no other big guns in sight, only a vast network would make it for him. And if some links were lost, maybe others would have to be forged. Or David might simply have been guilty as hell, and jumped at the chance to save his own skin and Ruth's. Certainly, given the apparent commitment of their wartime correspondence, there was something very hard and cynical about their sudden "conversion." Weirdly, it was only by chance that David got sent to Los Alamos in the first place—another guy in his unit was assigned to go there but went AWOL, and David was his last-minute replacement. Who was that AWOL soldier, and did he know what, in effect, he'd done? But for one moment of an unknown GI's weakness, the Balance of Terror might not even exist and the Rosenbergs might be home tonight, celebrating their anniversary and wishing something exciting would happen to them for a change.

As for a brother sending his sister to the chair, maybe too much had been made of this. There was nothing unusual about it, after all, it happened every day. Fathers threw their children out of tenement-house windows, kids kicked their grandmothers down the stairs, brothers and sisters ratted on each other from the moment they could talk. When you're up against it, survival's the thing, I'm not sure I'd trust my own goddamn brothers in the same situation. Besides, it was widely known that there was a lot of bad feeling between the brothers-in-law, largely because of their postwar business venture which had gone sour, and one thing that became transparent during the trial was the wholehearted eagerness with which the Greenglasses laid it on the Rosenbergs. The files suggested that David had even been blackmailing Julius for some time—this was seen as a corroboration of sorts of the charges, the final $4000 at the end being then a last frantic payoff, Julius well aware that if arrested David would spill his guts. Ethel and Ruthie didn't get along either, old jealousies over David, and old lady Greenglass apparently hated Ethel and the whole Rosenberg lot with her. She seemed almost pleased her daughter was getting the hot seat, letting the world know that if Julius and Ethel died in the chair, she wouldn't even go to their funerals. A lovely family. It was even likely, now that I thought about it, that David and Ruth had hoped for the death penalty all along, so they wouldn't have anybody around afterwards to remind them of what they'd done. Gone from the face of the earth. I'd known guys like Greenglass. Not quite bright enough to come to grips with the world or understand what any of it was about, yet not dumb enough to find a conventional place in the herd and stay out of trouble. You could talk them into anything, they were full of emptiness and longed to be filled up. Women wrapped his kind around their little fingers: his mother Tessie, his big sister Eth, his tough unhappy wife. Greenglass had no real connection with actuality. Yesterday it was Ruth and Ethel telling him what to do, now it was Saypol and Cohn—a man disciplined by shrews at home and so obsequious abroad.

What was I saying? That the FBI, convinced maybe that they'd located the spy ring or at least were very close, but lacking hard evidence, had arm-twisted all these people into concocting a bomb-theft plot? It hardly seemed likely, yet all the linkages, walked through backwards like this (in fact I was now down on my hands and knees, crawling through them), did seem to come undone. Supposing Gold really was Fuchs's courier, for example: would the Soviets have been so crazy as to risk compromising this connection by sending Gold to the Greenglass flat? Fuchs to the Russians was like a dream come true—he was, literally, almost everything they needed. Greenglass, by comparison, was just some dumbnuts YCL on-the-make Army kid who through sheer stupidity and overzealousness could spoil everything. Who could be sure? he might even be an FBI plant! And anyway, if Rosenberg *was* in on it, then they hardly needed Gold—anything David had for them, Julie could get. Well, I knew what the pressures were in a place like the FBI. Each division had to justify its budget and salaries, come up with the goods when pressed, and each man had to think of his own advancement: assuming the Rosenbergs were guilty (and perhaps no man at the FBI doubted this from the beginning, one man's beliefs or assumptions supporting the next, just like in religious cults, augmented by the incredible state of paranoia—Fear Bullshit Insecurity, they called themselves—and the blind obeisance to the Director that prevailed over there), then the man who nailed it down stood to win the prize. Rewards and punishments: this was how it worked. On May 31, 1950, just eleven days after the case had been opened, for example, there were Gold's interrogators T. Scott Miller and Richard Brennan getting Bureau commendations for their "imaginative, resourceful, and vigorous" handling of the assignment and being recommended for "meritorious increases in salary." An instant parable for the whole force, all of whom were out there competing for the prizes in this one. The biggest one of all: the Crime of the Century. Hoover, reacting with "shock and anger," had grabbed up the intercom in 1949 and said: "Get that spy ring!" And so, like unquestioning soldiers of Christ, they had gone out and got one. It would have been just the same at the OPA. Of course, we never electrocuted anybody at the OPA.

And then what if, I wondered, there were no spy ring at all? What if all these characters *believed* there was and acted out their parts on this assumption, a whole courtroom full of fantasists? Certainly most of them had a gift for inventing themselves—or, as they'd say in the CIA and KGB, for elaborating their covers—maybe, helplessly, they just dreamed it all up. Whereupon the Rosenbergs, thinking everybody was crazy, nevertheless fell for it, moving ineluctably into the martyr roles they'd been waiting for all along, eager to be admired and pitied, to demonstrate their heroism and their loyalty to the cause of their friends, some of whom, they were certain (the FBI said there was a spy ring, there had to be one), were members of the alleged conspiracy. In 1943 the Rosenbergs were known to have dropped out of all overt Communist activities, canceling their subscription to the *Daily Worker*, refusing to sign any more petitions. Saypol argued that these were signs they were going underground, and maybe that was so. But maybe not: what with the new baby and Julius's well-paying Army job, a brighter-than-ever future, they might merely have been ducking out on their friends, something they'd still feel guilty about eight years later. In the interim, Julie loses his job, Ethel thinks she's having a breakdown, they sink into a drab and scummy life, and then suddenly—BINGO!—the A-bomb trial, a chance to recover their pride and juice up their meaningless existences with real content. Sobell, meanwhile, doesn't know what the hell is happening—is it a fascist takeover?—and in panic flaps off to Mexico. When he hears about the Rosenberg spy ring, he probably believes it. So do the other witnesses: why not? it's possible . . . we *all* believe it . . .

I lay on my face gazing across the wide spread of scattered paper. I was somewhat lost in all these speculations. At sea. It was a little like lying by the irrigation ditch in Yorba Linda and gazing up at the endless sky, watching truths blow by like shifting clouds, only now it was more serious. What was fact, what intent, what was framework, what was essence? Strange, the impact of History, the grip it had on us, yet it was nothing but words. Accidental accretions for the most part, leaving most of the story out. We have not yet begun to explore the true power of the Word, I thought. What if we broke all the rules, played games with the evidence, manipulated language itself, made History a partisan ally? Of course, the Phantom was already onto this, wasn't he? Ahead of us again. What were his dialectical machinations if not the dissolution of the natural limits of language, the conscious invention of a space, a spooky artificial no-man's land, between logical alternatives? I loved to debate both sides of any issue, but thinking about that strange space in between made me sweat. Paradox was the one thing I hated more than psychiatrists and lady journalists. Fortunately, I knew, I'd forget most of this—these errant insights always fled and something more solid, more *legal*, sooner or later took over. I'd find the right question, take a side, and feel on top of things again. Gain perspective. Courage, Confidence, and Perspective: the Rosenberg formula. It was in all their letters. Maybe it had a secret meaning. Something about the Communist Party. "CCCP," I knew, was the way the Russians wrote USSR. I had to admit that it resembled somewhat my 1952 "K_1C_3" campaign slogan: Korea, Communism, Corruption, and Controls. Or Costs—we never got that sorted out. The Great Crusade. Dean Acheson's College of Cowardly Communist Containment. For Peace, Bread, and Roses. Things we'd learned in the thud and blunder of college politics, Julius and I. . . .

Different from me, though. His moustache alone was proof of that. A kind of holyroller in his way. Gullible, emotional. We were more like mirror images of each other, familiar opposites. Left-right, believer-nonbeliever, city-country, accused-accuser, maker-unmaker. I built bridges, he bombed them. A Talmud fanatic at age fourteen, Manifesto zealot at fifteen. He moved to the fringe as I moved to the center. He argued with his Socialist dad, helped kick the Trotskyites out of the Party while he was still just a kid. If he'd been born a Catholic or Lutheran instead of a Jew, he might have been a Nazi. Probably some kind of sexual deviant as well, most of these ghetto types were. Too many people piled up on top of each other, it was easy to imagine a lot of combinations country kids would never think of. When the FBI raided the Rosenberg flat, the one thing they found besides old check stubs chronicling the dismal decline of Julie's failing business was a set of pornographic records and other records ridiculing religious cere-monies, like the Kol Nidre chant. What Eisenhower in his news confer-ence yesterday called "violations of human decency." Saypol thought those records were enough alone to hang them on: "An indication of their state of mind," he liked to say.

Certainly, if what I'd heard about their first reunion inside Sing Sing was true, they didn't care who was watching, they could go at it like dogs in the playground. They'd been separated since the trial, and had been working themselves up for this meeting. When the door opened and they saw each other, they broke away from their guards, rushed together, smothered each other's faces with hot kisses, started pawing at one another wildly, pulling at their clothes, Julius had Ethel's blouse out and her skirt up, she was going for his pants—they'd have been fucking on the floor in front of everybody in five seconds if the guard and matron hadn't recovered from their shock, grabbed them apart, and locked them up. They called it love but it was clearly a lot more danger-ous than that. Warden Denno had issued orders that henceforth they were to be handcuffed, sit at opposite ends of a seven-foot conference table, well guarded, and never be allowed to touch again.

They'd met in 1936 in New York at a New Year's Eve fund-raising ball given by the International Seamen's Union. Probably another front for the Phantom. One of those seamen's unions was on strike right now, tying up ports, putting an iron curtain around the Statue of Liberty. It seemed like everything in the city was a front for something else, made me nervous just to walk the streets up there. Not like that out in Yorba Linda or Whittier. What was it about cities? When I was a boy, I sometimes dreamed of going to the city and leading a double life. Even now, I felt freer there. If that was the word. Ethel had been waiting to go onstage to sing "Ciribiribin." This was her famous number, but she was out of practice. She'd been spending too much time as a labor organizer, her stage career was nearly over . . . just as I had been slowly giving up my secret dreams at that time of being a playwright and actor. Julius had walked up to her, got introduced, and asked: "Why are you nervous?" What a line. Why are you nervous. Just like one I might have thought of. Only I'd probably have said: "Why am I nervous?"

It was possible: I might have been there myself that night. I was in town. I was excited and lost, but pretending to know my way around. I could have stumbled in anywhere. I kept my head down, trying not to gawk at the skyscrapers, walked purposefully, even when I didn't know where I was. To tell the truth, I rather liked New York, but I wasn't all that impressed. There was something run-down about it, and it struck me as being a very cold and ruthless place to live. Not even exactly American—a kind of Hong Kong West. Therefore exciting, though; and challenging. A fast track, faster even than Los Angeles. A man needs that, even if he doesn't like it. Any person tends to vegetate unless he is moving on a fast track. You'd have to bone up, I thought, to keep alive in the competition here, but I felt ready for it. I was about to graduate from Duke Law School, and I was looking for a position with a big law firm. I knew I'd get it. I looked forward to going back on campus and bragging about it. Modestly, of course. Writing home about it. I jotted down details I could use in letters. I enjoyed the prospect of passing the word more than the thought of living here. I was third academically in my class, president of the student bar association, a member of the Order of the Coif, and had worked for the *Law Review* and the *Duke Bar Association Journal*, had written an important article on auto-insurance law and helped Dean Horack research his goddamn book, it was a sure thing. But I didn't get a job. They all looked down their noses at me. I felt like my clothes didn't fit right or my haircut was too fresh or something. Maybe the accent gave me away—I told them I'd won the Harvard Club of California Prize in high school, but it didn't seem to help. The two guys who went up to the city with me got positions, great positions, but I didn't. I felt like a goddamn ass. If I'd gone to the International Seamen's Union Ball that night instead of to Rockefeller Center and Times Square, I might have become a Communist and changed the course of history, I was pissed off enough. Later, when I settled down, I realized I'd been a little too generous in praising left-wing judges, and as president of the student bar had brought a hotshot New Deal trustbuster down to speak at Duke, and I supposed some of my enemies at school had distorted all this to their contacts in New York. That maybe accounted for my striking out with the FBI, too. So, to hell with them, I bought a new blue serge suit and went home to Whittier, did it my own way.

Oddly, though I didn't go to the Seamen's Ball, I seemed to have a very distinct impression of the hall: a vast slick floor, heavily waxed, a Victrola cabinet in one corner, a little stage, kitchen off the far end. Musty smell. Six-piece band. Balloons overhead. Julius and Ethel went to a room backstage so she could practice her song on him. His idea. He was trying to make out. And why not? I didn't think it was a real dressing room. Just an empty room back there, couple of chairs maybe, some scribbling on the cream-colored walls. Might have been a mirror. I could see her smiling balefully up at him, giving it a try. *"Cheery-beery-BIN!"* Thin. But pretty. So open and bright-eyed. It turned out they were neighbors—to Julius, Ethel was literally the girl-next-door, just like in all the movies, even if she was three years older than he was and lived in a part-time whorehouse. "More than a decade ago, at Christmas time, 1936, I met a young lady, fair, sweet, unassuming . . ." So different from all the others. She had no other boyfriends either, never ever had one. Not like Pat. More like me. Afterwards, walking her home, Julie had explained that he was in trouble with his grades at college because of all the student activities. The activities at City College of New York were different from those at Whittier College, but I could see how he would get involved. "I'll help you," she'd said. No one had ever said anything like that to me. "I'll help you." Of course, I'd never been in trouble. With my grades or anything else. "I'll help you. . . ."

I sat up abruptly. I thought I'd heard it, heard her voice. A sheet of paper was stuck to my cheek. I peeled it off. "Light of my life, rose of my heart, you my beloved being kept apart from me, are the thing I hold most dear. When I see your beautiful expressive face I know we are as one." *Was this for me?* Ah no. The Rosenberg letters. Right. I must have imagined the voice. Maybe it was my own. I'd started to doze off. I was very tired. It had been a long day. Crisis conferences, world tensions, chairing the Senate, fear for Uncle Sam, phone calls, the Rosenberg affair. I'd better clean up this mess and go home, I thought. I may be needed tomorrow. Home to Pat, the icebox, the kids. If I could just get organized. Couldn't leave this mess for the girls to see tomorrow. I remembered someone had said that in prison Julius had read Thomas Wolfe's *You Can't Go Home Again*. Maybe he said that himself in one of his letters. Laugh-a-minute Julie. Some home: "The constant battle against rats and vermin still is vivid in my mind." Be fair: that was when he was a kid. I staggered to my feet and stumbled over to my swivel chair, dropped heavily into it. I tried to reconstruct the thoughts I'd just had about the case. I couldn't remember them. Only a vague sense of a dark hallway, the K_1C_3 campaign formula, something about Manny Bloch and the FBI. That he was a secret agent? No, impossible. His ears stuck out too far. You couldn't have ears that stick out like that and get into the FBI. Wrong kind of nose, too. You had to be big, athletic, deep-voiced, look like a young businessman, and wear gabardine coats and snapbrim hats. Also it helped if you were a Republican, Catholic or fundamentalist, an ex–military officer or lawyer, and chewed gum with your mouth closed. I wondered if I had a stick of gum somewhere in my desk. Or maybe a candybar. I rummaged through the drawers. I used to be able to live on candybars. Julius Rosenberg was fond of candy, too. There was this story about him at the age of four on his way to his Grandma's house. He begged a penny off his brother and ran across the street to a candy shop. Crossing back over, he ran into the side of a passing taxi. He was okay, after treatment, but the shock caused his mother to give premature birth to her next baby and it died. America came that close to being delivered of one atom spy and saving its secrets. Because of a sweet tooth.

The episode had made a large impression on me because I, too, had nearly died young when our hired girl let me fall out of her lap and under the iron wheel of our horse-drawn buggy. It ran over my head and split my scalp open. I was rushed twenty-five miles to the nearest hospital in the neighbors' automobile, and it took eleven stitches to sew my head up. I didn't remember falling out of the buggy, remembered nothing of the hospital or my mother's fright, all I remembered was the upholstering on the seats of that automobile. It was owned by people called Quigley and I think it was the only automobile in Yorba Linda. We were all terrifically impressed. I still had the scar—all the way from my forehead to my nape—but you could hardly see it because I parted my hair over it. At the time, everybody thought I was going to die. But then later two of my brothers died instead. What would history have been like, I wondered, if my brothers had lived and I had died? I found I was utterly unable to imagine this. I was also unable to find anything to eat in my desk. "Shit," I grumbled, and slammed the last drawer shut, slumped in my chair. I started to say this again, more earnestly, but I was suddenly afraid Uncle Sam might be watching somewhere. I still had some difficulty getting used to this—and I would have to live with it, I knew, all the rest of my life. People don't appreciate the sacrifices you have to make if you want to be President. There were times I wished I could have been happy just getting rich like Smathers or being an admiral in the Navy or a famous playwright or something.

I could be happy right now, I thought, with an ice cream cone. A hot beef sandwich. A slice of chocolate cake. Even one of those dirty dates off the streets in Whittier. Other kids used to pick them up and eat them, but my mother told me it was filthy to eat things off the ground, and so I never did. They had big seeds, hardly any fruit at all. But I'd eat one now. Probably. Ethel Rosenberg used to buy ten-cent ice cream sodas when she was a little girl, I'd read, in a place called Marchiony's on the Lower East Side. The FBI probably had the place staked out. Or maybe it was gone by now. I imagined a dark place with grimy windows and cockroaches crawling up the wall. Probably lousy sodas, too, not nearly so creamy and rich as the sodas in California. The people out here in the East are very arrogant about food, but they don't know a goddamn thing about it. There's a popular tendency to ridicule my tastes and call me square, but history will show I was one of the few Americans of my time who really knew how to eat.

I grew up with food, after all, what with my father's fruit ranch, and then our family store, delivering groceries, buying produce, talking about food with the customers. And when Harold got sick and Mom took him to Arizona for a couple of years, leaving the rest of us alone in Whittier, I did a lot of the cooking, whipping up terrific suppers of canned chili, spaghetti, pork and beans, soup, even learned to fry eggs and potatoes. I could right now eat a can of pork and beans—cold! Yum. A western with mayonnaise. Jell-O with bananas and whipped cream. A chicken salad on white, roasted marshmallows, a Coke float. But all I had was another antacid, so I ate it.

There was some fuss at the trial, I recalled, about the flavor of that torn Jell-O box used as a recognition signal between Gold and Greenglass: raspberry. Raspberry? Maybe this was just an in-joke down at the FBI: giving them the old raspberry. The flavor had to be red, naturally. I always liked raspberry Jell-O, I hoped they didn't take it off the market now. It was one of the things Pat did very well. She baked good pies, too, like my mother did. While we were going together, she used to help Mom bake pies to sell in the store. Sometimes I had the feeling she was going with Mom more than with me, but I didn't mind. Her own Mom had died young and Pat had had full charge of all the family chores when she was only thirteen, taking care of things until her Dad died, so she was right at home there in the kitchen. It was beautiful watching her make pies with Mom. She reminded me of Tillie the Toiler. And I was faithful Mac. Only a lot smarter.

I'd known a lot of girls, but not well. I'd helped them with their homework, served on committees with them, debated against them. But I'd only had one steady girlfriend before Pat—Ola—and she hadn't appreciated me. Not that I hadn't wanted to make out with almost every girl I ever knew. Oh no, I'd already wanted this when I was eight or nine years old, maybe younger, and there were times as the years went on when I could hardly stop myself from reaching out and grabbing a girl's butt as she bent over a water fountain in the school corridor or brushed by me in a movie theater—but I couldn't even talk to them right, much less grab their butts. I just couldn't bring myself to say all the silly things I knew had to be said before it could be accomplished, this was my problem. Partly, too, it was shyness, of course—I had this Milhous face which made me look too serious and bookish to be any fun, and I didn't know how to get around this. People don't realize it, but I actually have to work harder, physically harder, to smile. They make jokes about my smiling calisthenics, but it's not a joke really. I've always envied people like Dwight Eisenhower who are born grinning. I looked like a preacher the day I was born. Gloomy Gus, they called me. Maybe this was why Foster Dulles and I got on so well. And girls and I so poorly. They admired me for my brains and leadership, but they wouldn't get in the back seat with me. They wouldn't even go into the Sarah B. Duke Gardens with me. Sometimes this angered me, this inability to excite a girl beyond a kind of friendly respect, and I'd become momentarily reckless, but I was always disappointed.

And then came Pat. I'd been living like a monk at Duke and no better back home in Whittier. I hadn't even kissed a girl in years when I met Pat that night at Little Theater tryouts. There she was, just like Jack Drown had promised: "a gorgeous redhead!" She was all the girls I'd ever dreamt of: she'd been an orphan, a student, a New York secretary, a hospital technician, waitress, librarian, movie extra, and salesgirl—and she was beautiful, industrious, popular, and Irish, to boot: it was fate. So that night I met her, the spirit of Christmas and homecoming and the New Year upon me, I proposed. That I did this, many people have found hard to believe and there have been a lot of stupid interpretations of it—even Pat thought I was joking, or else was some kind of nut: "I guess I just looked at him—I couldn't imagine anyone ever saying anything like that so suddenly!" But to me it was just part of the unfolding pattern, my guided life, most natural thing in the world. Pat was looking for a real adventurer like her Dad—a whaler, surveyor, prospector, and world traveler, who had finally married a poor widow in the Dakotas with two kids, and had settled down as a miner in Nevada to have three more, Pat being the last. It took her a while to realize that I was the adventurer she was looking for. She dated around a lot after that night we met, having to find out the slow way, while I waited, patiently playing my part. I didn't put on any backstage rush, as I had with Ola. It wasn't necessary, I knew. I'd read the ending. Sometimes I even drove Pat to her other dates. Didn't matter, not at the time, I knew what had to happen. And eventually, after a couple of years, it did. On June 18, 1940. At first, I think, she'd identified me too much with the part I'd had in the play, but since then I'd—June 21, I mean. I was about to say that since then I'd shown her . . . never mind.

I pivoted in my chair to stare out the open window. It was a warm humid evening, very still, somewhat pregnant as though with rain, yet with a faint trace of the midsummer night's light in the sky. Well, they'd made it, happy anniversary. I felt the leather straps, the electrodes, the hood: I realized that it made me sweat to think about getting electrocuted, anniversary or no anniversary. And how did they celebrate it? Seemed like they ought to be allowed to sleep together on the last night. If it was the last night—I shivered, remembering: the Phantom's out there! That was what gave the night that heavy leaden feeling. What did Uncle Sam mean: "Even the Phantom's having fun, I bet" . . . ? I wondered if I should have driven home while it was still daylight. At least I was lucky I'd brought the car in today, it was too late now to bother my chauffeur. After midnight. I sighed, rubbed the back of my head. Perhaps, I thought, if I am ever electrocuted, my scar will prove to be a nonconductor and save me.

When was the last time a man and wife were executed the same day? French Revolution probably. Given the French sense of humor, they probably let them do it, but through the bars. Of course, there were no appeals then, anything could yet happen with the Rosenbergs—further delays, then a pregnancy, it could get to be a real mess. Still, think of it like the last meal, a final . . . ah, well, that was an idea, no risk of pregnancy either. Something I'd always been curious to try. Not with Pat, though. I could imagine the chewing out I'd get if I even brought it up. The Rosenbergs had no doubt tried everything. Since they were little kids maybe in the ghetto, being Jews and all. Ethel was two years younger than I was, around Don's age, Julius was younger. We all probably went to the same movies, sang the same songs, read some of the same books. We were the Generation of the Great Depression. Now I was the Vice President of the United States of America. They were condemned to burn as traitors. What went wrong? Why was this necessary? Of course, they had had congress with the Phantom, I truly believed this, they had touched the demonic and so were invaded: and their deaths, I knew, would kill a part of the Phantom. What did it feel like, I wondered, to be possessed by the Phantom? Some said it was like swallowing a cold wind, others that it was a kind of fire that ran through the veins. Some believed he invaded through the eyes, like a hard light you could feel, others that he used the genital organs, that he could fuck like a man, but had no semen, leaving his chosen ones feeling all filled up, as though with an immense belch or fart they couldn't release. I lifted one cheek. I was still okay, no difficulties at all. The Farting Quacker. Take that, you villain! Ungh! And that!

I sat there, firing shots at the Phantom, one part of my mind trying to plan out an orderly clean-up of the office so I could go home, the other part floating idly back through time, back beyond the Pink Lady and the Hollywood Ten, the Snack Shack on Green Island and Dick Nixon of the OPA, past all the torts and plays and campaigns and debating contests, to my childhood in California, recalling the lonesome train whistles in the night, the prayers and Bible verses at breakfast, the Rio Hondo near Jim Town, the fishing, the grinding sound of cranking up the old Ford, the smell of produce and plowed earth and hot tar, the nervous excitement of smoking cornsilks where Dad couldn't see, the rusty taste of ice chips off the bed of the iceman's wagon, the odd impression of my little brother's clumsy kiss when I came home after a long time away, my first recital in the eighth grade when I played "Rustle of Spring." But somehow these memories were mixed up with other images, just as vivid, but strange to me. I seemed to remember things that had never happened to me, places I'd never been, friends and relatives I'd never met who spoke a language I didn't know. I recalled narrow streets filled with trucks, lined with crude stalls, stacks of trousers and shirts and underwear, chicken feathers in the gutter. I distinctly remembered a kind of tacked-up wooden cross with work gloves hanging from it, ties draped over it, sweaters and slips heaped and tumbled below, short fat men with glasses and flat-billed caps haggling with women dressed in long shiny black dresses and bell-like bonnets down around their ears. There was a hand-painted sign overhead of the bottom half of a man, with the words PANTS TO MATCH. A white nag hitched to a truck with wooden wheels, scales eight feet tall, barrels of fish, men in overalls shoveling chopped ice from wooden crates. A dingy room with no curtains on the windows, just a shade, some kind of pot, an old woman gabbling in a foreign language, the roar of vans and trains outside.

Hey—where did I get these memories? Me, a farmboy, born in Yorba Linda, California, the first child ever born there—it was so unusual there was an eclipse of the sun the next day. I lived all alone with Mom and Dad and my three brothers in a lemon grove and dreamed of becoming a railroad engineer on the Santa Fe. When I was school-age, we moved in to Whittier where Grandma lived—"Ye Friendly Town," where folks believed in "plain living and high thinking"—just a meadow with scattered houses, chosen by the Quakers as a place to settle because of its remoteness from the blighted urban East: what did *I* know about the stink of sweatshops and fish markets and fifth-floor cold-water flats? Yet, sitting there in my swivel chair, wet with sweat myself and staring numbly out the window into the night, I could smell them, see them, it was very peculiar. And it was also somehow pleasant. I felt richer somehow. Girls with bobbed hair and plain cloth coats, clutching soft handbags to their flat bosoms, seemed to come walking toward me, heels clicking on the hot city sidewalks, ogled by men wearing vests and dusty pants. A fat Gypsy lady in a flowered blouse grabbed up a piece of material, stretched it, and an old man rose feebly to protect his small heap of goods. I saw the kosher live-chicken merchants on Delancey Street under the Williamsburg Bridge holding up their squawking birds, the heads rearing, wings flapping madly, saw doll buggies perched on wooden crates, men leaning over the slatted sides of pick-up trucks, saw huge rolls of newsprint piled on the sidewalk in the shadow of an elevated train on Canal Street, kids chasing each other, heard a window break—I ducked: no, it was still whole. They've found me, I thought. All the way from Sing Sing! My heart was beating wildly. I could hear it thumping in the empty room, the hollow night, the dark silence. I sat rooted to my seat, trying to force my mind back to Whittier, back to Yorba Linda . . . the picnics, the Sunday comics, the palm trees and sandlot ballgames, grinding hamburger in the store, sharpening pencils at school—

And then suddenly I had this stunning vision of little Ethel Greenglass, about six years old, standing naked by a kitchen coalstove, pulling on a pair of white cotton panties, watched furtively by her brothers, her mother nagging at all three of them from the kitchen table where she was laying out some kind of breakfast. It looked like bread. The table was spread with an oilcloth. Her swollen belly was pressed against the lip—

I tried to shake it off. But the stove was still there. There was something like linoleum on the floor. I could smell the breakfast and feel that early-morning tremor of getting ready for school. Then I remembered that my brothers and I always used to get dressed huddled around the kitchen stove like that in Yorba Linda, and I caught this exact look of midwinter grayness out the window, only there were old brick buildings out there, not a lemon grove. And this peculiar sensation that Mama—Mrs. Greenglass, I mean—was pregnant, I could see the very shape of her swollen belly just about eye-level. Was it when my mother—? And Ethel's amazing bottom: we didn't have any sisters. Only the hired girls.

I leapt up, grabbed my jacket, switched off the lights and, praying fervently: "God, get me home safe!", fled the office, afraid even to look back over my shoulder, much less clean the place up. As I ran down the corridor of the old Senate Office Building toward the elevator, my footsteps echoing and reverberating through the empty marble hallways of that dark tower, I seemed to see rats and vermin everywhere, to hear the grinding racket of traffic and feel the violence and dereliction of tenement houses crowding around me, yet at the same time I felt the stomach-churning excitement of a school football game, a piano recital, dance date, my nostrils twitching with a wild murky reminiscence of chlorinated pools, choir robes, girls' hair, pie crusts, and greasepaint. I felt angry with myself for giving way to panic like this, it was like lurching offside in a big football game, I tried to stop myself but couldn't—I heard footsteps just behind or beside my own, somebody breathing, the stairwells were sunk in a swarming darkness, doors seemed to be yawning open. At the elevator I pulled up, tried to catch my breath, my heart was beating wildly, I—*what?* something rustling in the dark space behind the elevator! I wanted to cry out, to run the other way, but I was determined not to lose my cool, not to show fear in the face of the Phantom, not any more than I already had. I knew I had to do something unexpected. I turned and walked directly toward the shadow behind the elevator. "Coward!" I gasped, and gritted my teeth. There was a wall back there and I hit it with my face.

I staggered back, half blinded by the blow, feeling hurt and alone. I found the elevator button and leaned against it, remembering that hired girl who let me fall out of the carriage and get run over, her big lap, big to me, yet not big enough. I could almost smell her as she came to tuck us in, fresh from washing up. To listen to our prayers. Read to us from James Whitcomb Riley: "Listen, boys . . ."—the elevator door gaped: a big mouth—I was frightened of it and took the stairs down, jumping them three at a time—". . . I'm tellin' you . . .

"The Gobble-uns'll git you ef you don't watch out!"

INTERMEZZO

The War Between the Sons of Light
and the Sons of Darkness

The Vision of Dwight David Eisenhower
(from *Public Papers of the Presidents*, January 20–June19, 1953)

Tonight,
as you sit in your homes all across this broad land,
I want to talk to you about an issue
affecting all our lives—the question
that stirs the hearts of all sane men:

How far have we come in man's long pilgrimage
from darkness toward the light?
Are we nearing the light—
a day of freedom and peace for all mankind?
*Or are the shadows of another night
closing in upon us?*

Since the century's beginning,
a time of tempest has seemed to come upon
the continents of the earth—great nations of Europe
have fought their bloodiest wars; thrones
have toppled and vast empires have disappeared.
The shadow of fear has darkly lengthened across the world.
We sense with all our faculties
that forces of Good and Evil are massed and armed and opposed
as rarely before in history.

149

No principle or treasure that we hold,
from the spiritual knowledge of our free schools and churches
to the creative magic of free labor and capital,
nothing lies safely
beyond the reach of this struggle.
    You are even puzzled
as to whether it is wise to say anything,
because anything that one in my position might say
could be used as an excuse to make
these conditions worse.

    But do you cure cancer
by pretending it does not exist?
We must see, clearly and steadily,
just exactly what is the danger before us;
it is more than merely a military threat.
    The forces threatening this continent strike directly
at the faith of our fathers and the lives of our sons,
at the very ideals by which our peoples live!

    Freedom is pitted against slavery;
    lightness against the dark!

    Here, then, is joined no argument
between slightly differing philosophies—
for this whole struggle, in the deepest sense,
is waged neither for land
nor for food nor for power
    —but for the Soul of Man himself!

    We are Christian nations,
deeply conscious that the foundation
of all liberty is religious faith:
we trust in the merciful providence of God,
whose image, within every man,
is the source and substance
of each man's dignity and freedom.
    This faith rules our whole way of life—
we live by it and we intend to practice it.

    I think that is not hard to prove
in the case of America: when we came
to that turning point in history, when we intended
to establish a government for free men

and a Declaration and a Constitution to make it last,
in order to explain such a system we had to say:
    "We hold that all men are endowed by their Creator"
—thus establishing once and for all
that our civilization and our form of government
is deeply imbedded in a religious faith.
    Indeed, those men felt that
unless we recognized that relationship
between our form of government and religious faith,
    that form of government made no sense!

    Now, that is the doctrine of the administration.
It is most certainly the doctrine of the Republican Party
and those Republican leaders in Congress.

    The faith we hold
belongs not to us alone
but the free of all the world.
    This common bond
joins the grower of rice in Burma
and the planter of wheat in Iowa,
the shepherd in southern Italy
and the mountaineer in the Andes,
the French soldier who dies in Indochina,
the British soldier killed in Malaya,
the American life given in Korea.
    We believe.

    The enemies of this faith
know no god but force, no devotion but its use;
they tutor men in treason;
they seek not to eradicate poverty and its causes
but to exploit it and those who suffer it—
they feed upon the hunger of others.
    These forces
seek to bind nations not by trust but by fear—
whatever defies them, they torture,
especially the truth. Against these forces
the widest oceans offer no sure defense.

    We live in a time of peril.
This is one of those times in the affairs of nations
when the gravest choices must be made—a moment
when man's power to achieve good or to inflict evil
surpasses the brightest hopes and the sharpest fears
of all ages.

The worst to be feared
and the best to be expected can be simply stated:
the worst is atomic war . . . the best:
a life of perpetual fear and tension.
We must act from a lesson learned at terrible cost:
to serve our reasoned hope for the best,
we must be ready steadfastly to meet the worst.

These plain and cruel truths
define the peril and point the hope
that come with this spring of 1953 . . .

The world, at least, need be divided no longer
in its clear knowledge of who has condemned
humankind to this fate—we all know something
of the long record of deliberately planned Communist aggression!
It has been coldly calculated by the Soviet leaders,
for by their military threat they have hoped
to force upon America and the free world
an unbearable security burden leading to
economic disaster!
They have plainly said
that free people cannot preserve their way of life
and at the same time provide enormous military establishments
—Communist guns, in this sense,
have been aiming at an economic target
no less than a military target: prolonged inflation
could be as destructive of a truly free economy
as could a chemical attack against an army in the field!

They seek to promote,
among those of us who remain free and unafraid,
the deadliest divisions: class against class,
people against people, nation against nation—
we cannot escape the implication of these attacks,
their complete indifference to human life and to the individual;
it is clearly part of the same calculated assault
that the aggressor is simultaneously pressing
in Indochina and in Malaya,
and of the strategic situation
that manifestly embraces the island of Formosa—
    the destruction of freedom everywhere!

It is, friends, a spiritual struggle.
And at such a time in history, we who are free

must proclaim anew our faith; we are called as a people
to give testimony in the sight of the world
to our faith that the future shall belong to the free!
    History does not long entrust
the care of freedom to the weak or the timid—
we must be ready to dare all for our country!
Human liberty and national liberty
must survive against Communist aggression
which tramples on human dignity;
upon all our peoples and nations
there rests a responsibility to serve worthily
the faith we hold and the freedom we cherish
    —which means essentially a free economy.

    Let none doubt this:
we are free men.

    I don't like the word "compulsory";
I am against the word "socialized";
everything about such words seems to me
to be a step toward the thing
that we are spending so many billions to prevent—
the overwhelming of this country by any force,
power, or idea that leads us to forsake
our traditional system of free enterprise.
Private investment has been the major stimulus
for economic development throughout this hemisphere;
this is the true way of the Americas—the free way—
by which people are bound together for the common good.

    Make no mistake:
the reason we have representatives around the world
is to protect American interests
wherever they may be endangered or in difficulties;
we do everything we can to protect the interests
of the United States everywhere on the globe—
the peace we seek is nothing less than
the practice and fulfillment of our whole faith!
It is on such simple facts as these, ladies and gentlemen,
that your foreign policy is founded
and established and maintained.
    I know these facts, these simple ideals,
are not new; this idea of a just and peaceful world
is not new or strange to us—all of this springs from

the enlightened self-interest
of the United States of America.

  But to be free and stay free,
  we must be strong—and we must stay strong!

  We shall never try to placate an aggressor
by the false and wicked bargain
of trading honor for security!
If we allow any section of the world that is vital to us,
because of what it provides us—say, manganese,
or uranium, or cobalt—anything that we need
—if we allow any of those areas to fall
to a form of government inimical to us,
that wants to see freedom abolished from the earth,
  then we have trouble indeed!

  It is necessary
that we earnestly *seek out and uproot*
any traces of Communism at any place
where it can affect our national life,
that all of us by our combined dedication and devotion
may merit the great blessings
that the Almighty has brought to this land of ours!
It is up to every American to realize
that he has a definite personal responsibility
in the protection of these resources—they belong
to the people who have been created in His image:
they must, at any cost, remain armed, strong,
and ready for the risk of war!
In that way only, can we permanently aspire
to remain a free, independent, and powerful people,
living humbly under our God—
  in the final choice, a soldier's pack
is not so heavy a burden as a prisoner's chains. . . .

  But there is no security for a free nation
  in the sword alone.

  Security must spring
from the hearts and minds of free men—
our defense, our only defense,
is in our own spirit and our own will!

If we ponder this a moment,
we all know that this really means the defense
of those spiritual values and moral ideals
cherished by generations of Americans
—the true treasure of our people;
this treasure of the spirit
must be defended above all
with weapons of the spirit:
    our patriotism,
    our devotion,
    our readiness to sacrifice.
Whatever America hopes to bring to pass in the world
must first come to pass in the heart of America;
the true way to uproot Communism in this country
is to understand what freedom means,
and thus develop such an impregnable wall
that no thought of Communism can enter;
and we must seek
    in our churches,
    our schools,
    our homes and
    our daily lives,
the clearness of mind and strongness of heart
to guard the chance to live in freedom.

I know of nothing I can add
to make plainer the sincere purpose of the United States.

My grateful thanks
go out to each of you for your prayers,
because your prayers for divine guidance on my behalf
are the greatest gift you could possibly bring to me.
Today I think that prayer is just simply a necessity,
there is a need we all have in these days and times
for some help which comes from outside ourselves
as we face the multitude of problems
that are part of this confusing situation—
if we can back off from our problems
and depend on a Power greater than ourselves,
I believe that we begin to draw these problems into focus.

In our quest of understanding,
we beseech God's guidance.

We have begun in our grasp
of that basis of understanding,
which is that all free government is firmly founded
in a deeply felt religious faith;
if we understand, then we won't have Communism.
   That, it seems to me,
is the prayer that all of us have today:
that we shall remain free, never to be proven guilty
of the one capital offense against freedom,
   a lack of staunch faith. . . .

That is the way I see it.
My friends, thank you for being with us. Good night.

God bless you.

PART TWO

FRIDAY MORNING

8.

What a Glorious Morning for America!

reads the sign being erected on the Roof of the Astor Hotel overlooking Times Square. The sun is rising, sending its prophylactic shafts deep into the city canyons, dispersing not only the Phantom and all his legions, but all thought of them as well. Although the Supreme Court will not reconvene for hours, there is already, with the first hazy glimmer of sunlight, a new certainty in the air, a confidence, bookies refuse to take more bets, the electrocutions seem a sure thing, preparations resume. Traffic is once more blocked off, carpenters and electricians busy themselves about the sabotaged stage, the Phantom's filthy litter is swept away by Sanitation Department crews. There is a resurgence of pride, even the taxi drivers leave off their complaints as traffic snarls around the edges. The temperature is already in the seventies and rising, the humidity is falling, it's going to be a beautiful day. It feels good to wake up, get out on the streets.

Except for the Sanitation crews maybe—the Phantom has laid a formidable task on them this morning. The stage is wrecked, the props lie smashed and strewn for blocks around, wires have been ripped out and knotted, the bunting hangs in shreds, and the litter of pornography and propaganda is worse than a midwinter snowfall. Sanitation is no small task in New York City any day of the year: there are about 6000 miles of streets to clean, flush, and service, with more than 24,000 tons of refuse to collect and dispose of every single day, over 12,000,000 pigeon bowel movements to cope with, 5000 tons of daily dogshit, so the clean-up crews are hardly fans of the leafletting and wreckage-strewing Phan-

159

tom. Given the arduous mission, they are joined in Times Square this morning by volunteer teams from the Fire Department and the New York City Transit Authority, as well as a good many of the city's 19,000 cops and most of its 200,000 pigeons.

The area's capacity to absorb these multitudes is but one of its many and renowned magical properties. It is actually *home* for over 50,000 people, and thousands more of transients from all classes sleep here— now stirring, scratching, yawning, blinking out on all this bright activity, watching tow trucks haul away parked cars, overalled workers sweep up the gutter flyers and scrape the clemency snipes off the NO PARKING signs and hooded traffic lights, scrub the graffiti off the tall chalk-white statues on the Bond clothing store. Some 357,750 commuters begin to pour into the center, soon to be followed by tens of thousands of shoppers, sharks, and eager sightseers.

Including the previous Incarnation and his First Lady: Harry and Bess Truman, now what the press calls just another couple of ordinary American tourists, have arisen before dawn this morning back home in Independence, Missouri, birthplace of the Reorganized Church of Jesus Christ of Latter-Day Saints and likely site of the New Jerusalem, and have set out in a brand-new automobile to come to the big city to see the show and visit their daughter Margaret. Just what Harry thinks about these ceremonies he hasn't said, but it was his own Attorney General who pushed for them in the first place, and when Harry had his own chance to act on a clemency appeal from the Rosenbergs last January, he simply passed it on, without comment, to his successor, granting amnesty and full pardon instead to his old crony J. Parnell Thomas, the HUAC Early Warning Sentinel who'd been jailed for taking salary kickbacks from his office staff. Some say he passed the buck on the Rosenberg appeal just to complicate the new President's life. Others that it was an act of modesty and generosity, typical of Harry Truman: let the new man have the headlines. Many, though, believe he'd simply lost touch with Uncle Sam by then and didn't want to take any chances.

As for the new man this morning, he's wandering around the White House in his pajamas in a playful mood, practicing his oral clumsiness and startling his staff with bounding Eisenhoppers—those little plastic grasshoppers with springy metal legs and rubber suction cups on the bellies, given to him by his old friend Louis Marx the Toymaker, not to be confused with his Martian theorist. Reporters christened them "Eisenhoppers" at Christmastime and they've since sold like hotcakes. There is much curiosity, even among insiders, as to how and when Uncle Sam chooses his disguises. The National Poet Laureate has called

Dwight David Eisenhower "The Man of Destiny," and certainly there
have been few Incarnations less obvious (as Harry himself has said:
"Why, this fellow, this fellow don't know any more about politics than a
pig knows about Sunday!") and yet more inevitable than this grinning
aw-shucks farmboy from the wrong side of the tracks who clowned his
way through West Point and the Mexican border troubles, only to find
himself suddenly the Supreme Commander, Allied Expeditionary
Forces, and, without firing a shot, the Number One Hero of World War
II. And yet, it must be admitted, *all* American Superchiefs are "men
of destiny." So few men actually seek the office, it should be easy to get if
they want it, yet there seems to be no evident connection between their
own eagerness to surrender to the hypostasis and the actual takeover—
indeed, it's often just when they're giving up and looking the other way
that suddenly and improbably the famous plug hat falls down around
their ears. How does this happen? Why them? Does Uncle Sam groom
his Incarnations from birth, for example, or does he play it more impulsively, adjusting to the surprises that come along? Does he field a range
of options for himself and drift speculatively among them, or are these
apparent alternatives merely illustrations of discarded possibilities?
And what about the reserves: do the same rules apply to the Vice
President, or is this a kind of wild card that Uncle Sam allows the world
to play just to liven things up every twenty years or so? Finally, when a
candidate does arise (or is conceived), does the actual Incarnation hit
him like a ton of bricks, a sudden brutal invasion of the Presence, or has
it been growing in him all along? Does the voter, entering the polling
booth, exercise his own free will, or is he too the captive of some larger
force—and if the latter, is that power exercised upon him directly by
Uncle Sam, or more subtly through some sort of force field that even the
American Superhero cannot entirely control? Are political parties, in
short, living organisms, abstractions, solvents, catalysts, viable alternatives, or merely the visible form of Paradox in the world?

Well, only Uncle Sam knows why this or that receptacle is chosen to
receive the Host, but one thing is clear: Uncle Sam moved toward
Dwight Eisenhower with more conviction and gusto than toward any
other Incarnation since the Father of the Country himself. The new
President was packaged and sold by BBD&O as "Strictly a No-Deal Man
Clean as a Hound's Tooth Who Will Go to Korea Restore Faith in God
and Country and Carry On a Crusade to Clean Up Creeping Socialism
Five-Percenters the Mess in Washington Crooks Cronies Mink Coats
Deep Freezers and Rising Inflation," but the true source of his power
was summed up more simply in the big badge Uncle Sam wore last fall

on his blue lapel: I LIKE IKE. Uncle Sam seemed to *want* Eisenhower like a child wants happiness. Perhaps it was because he was nostalgic for the old days, the time of his childhood when life was simple and causes were clear, the days of the Minutemen and Bunker Hill, of cracker barrels and hayrides and old-time religion. A "crusade" Eisenhower called his political campaign, and he told stories about his old Uncle Abraham Lincoln Eisenhower galloping his goofy gospel wagon through prairie villages, shouting "This way to heaven!", and he told about selling hot tamales three for a nickel and riding a raft in a flood with his brother Ed while singing "Marching Through Georgia," learning to fire old muzzle-loading guns with powder and shot, about seeing a real cowboy shootout on Texas Street in Abilene. He conjured up the crackle of a campfire, the taste of country fried chicken and thick potato salad at church picnics and the thump and clank of a game of horseshoes, lamented the passing of the old country store, and recalled the time during the Spanish-American War when the whole town ran out in the streets on hearing the rumor: "There's a Spanish airship over Abilene!" —it turned out to be a box kite advertising a sale of straw hats. Straw hats! Box kites! Airships! Wow, it felt so *good* to think about these things again! The early 1950s has been a time of great national prosperity but also a time of great national malaise: things seem to have gone sour somehow. Uncle Sam is running half the world and scaring the pants off the rest, but it's not as easy or as much fun as people had thought it would be. So maybe Uncle Sam just wanted to get inside all those old memories again, experience for himself once more the dusty heat of a lazy summer day on the prairie, the excitement of hearing the C. W. Parker Circus parade coming down Main Street, the romance of a young happy-go-lucky officer in a Mexican border town on a Saturday night, even the old-fashioned sting of a hickory stick on his fanny. It may be so.

"Behind the dingy walls inside cramped rooms," his Man of Destiny is declaiming now, "and airless, ah, there are thousands of homes let me say in which parental love and care burn as brightly as, as intensely . . ." He spies his wife's personal secretary, presses an Eisenhopper down on her desk, pokes his finger in his ear as though absently cleaning it. "As in the homes of, uh, Abilene . . ." She pretends to be startled when it pops up and Eisenhower roars with delight. Mamie, staggering half-blind out of her bedroom, fumbling with trembling hands for a wake-up fag, asks him what the hell's so funny this morning, what's got into him? He grins, that effortless affable grin that has brought him to these premises (what's got into him? well, for one thing,

he woke up a short while ago with the handsomest hard-on in a dog's
age, dreaming of his old Irish WAC girlfriend, they were both stark
naked, running around in France somewhere in the middle of the war,
he wasn't even sure which side of the lines they were on or who was
winning or losing, but they were balling the jack something fantastic,
out in the open fields, in tents and bivouacs, village streets, in the mud
of the trenches, and the only thing spoiling the fun at all was a weird
little runny-nose private—he looked foreign or Jewish or something—
who kept wandering by looking miserable and threatening to tattle on
them . . . but somehow even this was exciting in its way), and says:
"Hey, listen, Mamie, what do you think of this: Hemmed in by masonry
and, uh, by masonry walls confined to thin streets, boys, let me assure
you, in New York even as in Kansas they have found ways to enjoy
themselves without hurt to property or to their elders, the farm boy and
the tenement boy are one, ahem, at heart. That's what I'm trying to get
at." He smiles. His wife stares at him for a moment through squinting
eyes. Then she grunts, shrugs, and shuffles back into her bedroom. "I
should say, or remind you," he calls after her, "that does not mean that
we can forget about the unforgenate, uh, FORTCH-inut circumstances
growing up—which many young per—people grow up in trusting that
good will! Ah, will flower out of evil! At least that is my opinion!" He
has meanwhile pressed down another Eisenhopper, having glimpsed his
own secretary coming in the door behind him: the hopper leaps with a
loud BO-I-I-ING!, the secretary squeals, Ike's laughter booms.

The President's assistant, Sherman (The Abominable No-Man)
Adams, is in the Oval Office laying out the President's agenda for the
day, which includes a Cabinet meeting, a therapy session with the
stricken Bob Taft, and a possible address to the nation after the Supreme Court meets at noon. Adams, hearing all the shrieking and laughter and seeing the President promenading out on Harry's Balcony in his
peejays, wonders if, by coincidence, Eisenhower woke up this morning
in the same state of oddly disturbing excitement that he'd experienced
himself. It's impossible, of course, for Sherm Adams to know, but were a
poll to be taken, he would discover that not only he and the President,
but also most of Congress, the Supreme Court, lesser courts and commissions, the Fourth Estate, Cecil B. De Mille and Cardinal Spellman, the
Holy Six, the Vice President sacked out on his living-room couch, and
the entire Cabinet—even old Ezra Taft Benson of the Council of Twelve
Apostles—have all awakened this morning from the foment of strange
gamy dreams with prodigious erections and enflamed crevices. Some,
like Irving Saypol, have wisecracked about it. Others, like Foster Dulles,

have felt furtive and guilty. It has made Joe McCarthy boisterously reckless, Felix Frankfurter confused, the Boy Judge grumpy, Emily Post gay. Edgar Hoover has taken a cold bath. But none, curiously enough, has used his or her aroused sexuality on a mate, it's as though, somehow, that's not what it was all about, and all are left in a state of suspended agitation, feeling itchy and faintly irreverent, giddy and bemused yet unsatisfied, somehow detached and isolated, but gregarious at the same time, and with an unwonted appetite for risk and profligacy. Which makes them nervous. Hoo-eee! have to take it easy today or things could go haywire. Few, however, can put their finger on what it is that's disquieting them. One who has no such difficulty is the Sing Sing Executioner Joseph Francel. Brushing his teeth in his bathroom in Cairo, New York, Joe winces at himself in the mirror (his is frankly hurting him) and says: "Hmf. (*Spit.*) Better get down to Times Square this morning."

Times Square, the Crossroads of the World: it is said that half the people on Forty-second and Broadway at any given moment are from out of town—and the other half are Armenians. Shabby by day, luminescent by night, it is the most paradoxical place in all America, and thus the holiest. Historians have written that everything that happens in the Western World originates in Times Square and—to judge by the souvenir shops, auction galleries, gutter debris, and panhandlers—dies here as well. The Heart and Cock of the Country, it is called. Sin City U.S.A. The Entertainment Capital of America. The United States is the first electric nation of the world, and this is its luminous navel. The Diamond Stickpin in New York's Shirtfront. The Brightest Ten Blocks in the World. Here pilgrims come to kiss the holy stones, the despised second sons of the world to seek their fortunes, mystics to walk the Great White Way.

There is an ancient tradition for this. Nomadic tribes crisscrossed the island for centuries, and transience is the profoundest element in the American Spirit. Broadway itself, as legend has it, is an old Indian trail—certainly this would explain its erratic polestar course down through the island. It's said the last to use it were the Mana-hatta tribe, who departed by it after nicking gullible old Peter Minuit, first of the tourist yokels, for twenty-four dollars. Many Italians have come here, more than there are Italians in Italy, but the first was a navigator named Verrazano, who claimed the island for the French. Next came an Englishman named Henry Hudson on behalf of the Dutch, who named it Niew Nederland and commenced to settle it. The English wrested it from the Dutch in the name of the Duke of York, then lost it to their

rebellious colonials a century later (even then, the inhabitants of Med-
cef Eden's meadows, eventually to become Times Square, stayed out of
it, played both sides, and raked what profit off the Revolution they
could). By the time it had become the Capital of the United States of
America and seen in its streets the Incarnation of General George Washington as Superchief I, there were more than thirty thousand people,
heterochthonous the lot of them, passing through the borough's precincts, and half that many again in nearby Breuckelen, Bronck's Land,
Queens, and Staaten Eylandt.

Now, a little over a century and a half later, there are seven and a half
million people living in 116 villages around Times Square, these in turn
surrounded by another 574 suburban communities of millions more, and
half of them are foreign-born or one or more of their parents were. The
huddled masses yearning to breathe free, the wretched refuse, getting
processed for destiny now in Uncle Sam's melting pot. Lithuanians,
Thais, Persians, Jamaicans: this is the place of their initiation into
Americanism, the Great White Way. The heaviest migrations come west
from Italy and Russia, but there are thousands upon thousands of Germans and Czechs, too, and Irish, Austrians, Hungarians, English, and
Welsh. And it is these, the tired, poor, and tempest-tost, more American,
as they say, than the Americans, who each year play host to the summer
inswarm of country boobs, come east to Mecca like flies drawn to a pig's
ass.

From planes, cars, trains, ships, and buses, they debouch upon the city
in a breathless rush and scatter, squealing in awe and umbrage, clicking
cameras, streaming through the narrow streets in their patterned sportshirts and J. C. Penney dresses like blind and anxious ants, hot on the
trail of the unknown. There are bright clusters of them at Rockefeller
Plaza, Greenwich Village, Fifth Avenue, crawling all over each other,
going where the others go, seeing what the others see. The Battery. The
United Nations. The Waldorf-Astoria. Scurrying about, chasing tempta-
tions, ogling heights, asking directions, bumping into each other, dropping parcels, taking bus tours, panicking at intersections, getting lost.
Some find themselves on the subway while looking for the men's room.
Some try to leap off the Empire State Building or photograph the burlesque shows, others get off at the wrong stop on the Third Avenue El
and miss everything. They consume staggering quantities of egg rolls,
shish kebab, knishes, French doughnuts, Hungarian goulash, oyster
stew, and pizza pie, lick millions of postage stamps, trample hotel carpets to shreds, and wrinkle, stain, and burn holes in enough sheets to

tent the nation. They get aroused by streetwalkers, maligned by cab-drivers, lectured in Union Square, sunburned at Coney Island, and raped in Central Park.

But wherever they go, sooner or later they will come to Times Square. Today, of course, this is required of them, even the locals will be here tonight, but even without the public electrocutions, they would gather here. Partly because of the sex: this is the home of the G-string, the cut-rate hustler, the dirty book and naughty record, the bedroom comedy and cheap condom, and the American tourist is well-known—and far beyond his own shores—as the horniest creature this side of the Bronx Zoo. Whatever he needs, he can find here, from an orchestra view of famous movie stars onstage in their skivvies to a quick blow job in a subway john, but this is not in the main why he is drawn here. For if sex is dirty, it is also, at its dirtiest, cleansing; if it defiles, it also sanctifies: the principal reason for the traffic into Times Square—this place of feasts, spectacle, and magic—is that it is the ritual center of the Western World.

Is this really the ground the storied ancestors trod? Is this the actual place where Peter Minuit invented the American Way of Life with his twenty-four dollars? Is this hole, now a subway entrance, really the one from which Uncle Sam sprang in all his glory—full-grown, costumed, and goateed—from the belly of Mother Earth? Who knows? It hardly matters. Tradition has hallowed it and investment has certified it. The nation's dramas are enacted here, its truths tested and broadcast, its elections verified, its material virtues publicized—who has not stood in awe before the famous Wrigley chewing-gum sign, the giant smoke rings and waterfalls, the tipped whiskey bottle that never empties? In Saint Augustine's words: *et inhorresco, et inardesco!* It is here where one might have slept with the Yankee Doodle Boy, George M. Cohan, in the Knickerbocker Hotel, got soused on the New Amsterdam Roof with Florenz Ziegfeld, kissed the hand of Sarah Bernhardt, and gone to confession after with Father Duffy, the Fighting Chaplain, at the Holy Cross Church on Forty-second Street—and even today one can still break bread with Milton Berle and Phil Silvers at Lindy's on Tin Pan Alley, sneak a smoke with Rosalind Russell behind the Winter Garden. This is the site of the world's largest New Year's Eve party, where hundreds of thousands gather to watch the ball drop on the Times Tower, exercising its perennial charm against death and entropy. The oracle that "he who circles Times Square will end by falling inside" only inspires greater feelings of awe and desire in the people: "Far from fleeing, we draw nearer . . . !" The American Showcase, Playland

U.S.A., the Electrical Street of Dreams—it was inevitable that Uncle Sam should choose it as the place to burn the atom spies.

Flags are now unfurled from all the hotels and from atop the Times Tower, and huge blow-ups of Uncle Sam strangling a bear and a dragon are mounted under the starry-digited clocks on the Paramount Building, with General Eisenhower's immortal D-Day rouser as a caption:

I CALL UPON ALL WHO LOVE FREEDOM TO STAND WITH US NOW!

Not only is a terrible dignity thereby attached to this momentous occasion (D-Day having been the nearest thing to the Second Coming mankind will probably know until the real thing comes along), but an overwhelming sense of righteousness and ultimate victory as well—some start calling it E-Day, Electrocution Day, the proper sequel, long-awaited; but others prefer D-Day II: a Day of Death, Drama, and Devotions. Not to mention Decency, human Decency. The little man in the Johnnie Walker whiskey spectacular above the Whelan drugstore is today sporting a red-white-and-blue topper, and the sanitation crew-members wear little badges that read THE LARGE THING TO DO IS THE ONLY THING WE CAN DO. A blue-white-and-orange flag—same as that of the Netherlands in 1626—with the seal of New York City in blue on the white stripe is hung out on the façade of the Times Tower, the five stars above the seal indicating that Mayor Vincent Impellitteri is in the Square or soon will be. Still early, but the Square is filling up. Cafeterias are crowded already, and they're standing in line under the Eveready sign at Elpine Drinks. Workers, theater people, young execs, guys in sportshirts with cameras around their necks, women in sleeveless blouses with high collars, long pleated skirts. Carpenters and electricians, too, already in some dismay over the seemingly impossible task that confronts them here this morning. Colored boys are sweeping out the theater lobbies, grinning up at the sun, jigging around their brooms like the late departed Bojangles Robinson, winking at all the passing girls. And off to the north, over Central Park, there are already kites in the skies.

The Police Commissioner, overseeing the Times Square operations alongside the Sanitation Commissioner, is examining the statue of Father Duffy. It has been splashed during the night with a bucket of red paint—now being scraped away by the clean-up crews—but it's not certain whether this was the Phantom's doing, or a citizen's righteous protest against the rising tide of treason among, not only American clerics, but scientists, teachers, and judges as well. To be sure, someone has daubed Omar Bradley's famous line all over the pavement: WE HAVE

GRASPED THE MYSTERY OF THE ATOM AND REJECTED THE SERMON ON THE MOUNT! But on the other hand, right there on Father Duffy's bronze behind are the words THE ABOLITION OF RELIGION AS THE ILLUSORY HAPPINESS OF THE PEOPLE IS REQUIRED FOR THEIR REAL HAPPINESS, so it's a moot point.

"These are the times that try men's souls, George," says the Sanitation Commissioner with a sigh.

"Yes, Andy, an appeal to arms, and to the God of Hosts, is all what is left us."

President Eisenhower, of course, has long insisted that "the church, with its testimony of the existence of an Almighty God is the last thing, that it seems to me, would be preaching, teaching, or tolerating Communism," but even the President is said to be taking a hard second look this morning. For a starter, the Chief has turned over to Edgar Hoover's G-men the names of 2300 clergymen who signed a "special plea for clemency for the Rosenbergs," as well as the list of 104 signatories to a follow-up letter, taken to be the hard-core Comsymp preachers. "The Rosenberg campaign," warns Harold Velde's Early Warning Sentinels, has "afforded the Communist conspiracy a momentous opportunity to remount a long-planned invasion of the churches of America!" FBI undercover mystery man Herbert Philbrick thinks many of the 2300 are dupes, "unsuspecting victims" sucked in by the wily Angels of Darkness at the center, but turncoat Joe Zack Kornfeder, former bigwig in the American Communist Politburo, disagrees:

REP. GORDON SCHERER, OHIO: Among those two thousand ministers were, however, some just idealists and pacifists, were there not?

JOE ZACK KORNFEDER: I do not think so. I think that those two thousand were pretty close to the machine.

Demonstrators, moving past the White House this morning toward the Supreme Court, are actually carrying blown-up posters of the Son of God Himself, with the text:

REWARD

—for information leading to the apprehension of Jesus Christ . . .
    Wanted—for Sedition, Criminal Anarchy, Vagrancy, and Conspiracy to overthrow the established Government . . .
    Dresses poorly . . . has visionary ideas, associates with common working people, the unemployed and bums . . . Alien—believed to be a Jew . . . Red Beard, marks on hands and feet, the result of injuries inflicted by an angry mob led by respectable citizens and legal authorities.

"One of the most sacrilegious propaganda pieces ever used by the Communists!" scream the Early Warning Sentinels, still much agitated by their overnight dreams and eager for some kind of consummating encounter. "The Communists did not need the churches in past years; they had ample other channels of subversion," G-man Philbrick warns, coughing up a little early-morning phlegm: "They *do* need the churches now; *they will fight savagely for your church!"*

And for anything else they can get: Uncle Sam has been whipping about his vast domains all morning, struggling against crooks, Commies, and crawfishing backsliders. He has just been called to Coney Island to investigate a report of a monster said to be tangled in the roller coaster there, but this turns out to be a metaphorical alarm. Not so phantasmal is the corpse of Steve Franse, former owner of the Howdy Club down in the Village, found brutally beaten, face down, on the rear floor of his automobile just south of Times Square, nor the cynical overnight robbery of the Muscular Dystrophy Association on Broadway: at least nine grand missing, only the Phantom could do such a thing. "Just thinkin' about it," quips Uncle Sam, "takes the starch right outa me!" And then a call comes in from further up the street: a thief has just jammed a pistol in the back of a Greystone Hotel secretary and seized a $3600 payroll. Uncle Sam draws himself up, gazing austerely in the direction of this newest outrage, his blue eyes glinting in the morning sunlight, his famous top hat cocked forward on his brow in manly defiance, shoulders squared, lean jaw rippling with suppressed fury, exhibiting all that "rugged strength and radiant beauty" so admired by the great American Prophetess Sarah Hale, ready as ever for his "humble toil and heavenward duty," but clearly pretty pissed off at the same time. He looks like Grover Cleveland confronting the election returns of 1888.

"Do not delay!" the people cry, gathered apprehensively about their Superhero in front of the sacked Muscular Dystrophy offices, "the golden moments fly!"

Uncle Sam turns and gazes compassionately down upon all these common people whom the Lord and careless fucking have made so many of, and gripping his lapels like Abe Lincoln, declares "Yes, friends, the fack can't be no longer disgised that a Krysis is onto us. But, hey, politics ain't beanbag, folks, and repose is not the destiny of man! The ripest peach is often highest on the tree in the boisterous sea of liberty! Yea, the credit belongs to the man who is actually in the arena, whose map is marred with sweat and dust and bloody bung-balls, so shoot if you must this old gray head, for the manners of women are the surest criterion by which to fool all of the people some of the time! If destruction is to be our lot in order to insure domestic tranquillity, a new frontier, and a full dinner pail, we must ourselves be its author and finish the work we are in until every drop of blood shall be sunk in this sea of upturned faces!" It seems like no one can hold back from celebrating the Poets and Prophets this morning, least of all the American Superhero, who speaks by custom with the grandeur of a nation of runesmiths, from Davy Crockett to Longfellow, the Carnegies and Cranes to Hank Williams and the Whittier Poets: "The tree in which the sap is stagnant, my friends, is one percent inspiration and ninety-nine percent perspiration, so like that sweaty old nigger piss-fire Ira Aldridge used to say, 'The bow is bent, the arrow flies, / *The wingèd shaft of fate!*' " And off he flashes—WHOOSH!—up Broadway to the north.

On his way, Uncle Sam stops off in Times Square to inspect the clean-up operations and reconstruction of the Death House set, finds the electricians despondent over the condition of the electric chair, uprooted and half-wrecked, lying in the gutter, draped with the broken Uncle Sam manikin with its Hitler moustache. Workmen are painting over a sign on the south face of the Hotel Claridge that says THE TRADITION OF ALL PAST GENERATIONS WEIGHS LIKE A NIGHTMARE UPON THE BRAIN OF THE LIVING. Uncle Sam strips the manikin of its wig, Uncle Sam suit, and moustache, and what he discovers under all that is not a replica of himself—that stern puritanical visage and lithe powerful frame—but a figure that looks like a cross between Bishop Fulton Sheen, Everett Dirksen, and Our Miss Brooks, and as sexless as Christine Jorgensen. Just a little lump down there, a shiny bulge, like a tumor, and smooth as Ike's bald pate. Uncle Sam turns it over his knee as though to spank it, but actually to inscribe on it Henry Adams's dictum: "*Modern politics is, at bottom, a struggle not of men but of forces,*" and he orders that the manikin, what's left of it, be hung from the nearest flagpole as a kind of old-time Broadway parable on the nature of reality and illusion.

More of a problem is what to do about the electric chair: it's really in bad shape. Wiring all ripped out, legs busted, bolts threaded, leather straps shredded, electrodes swiped. The auxiliary generator has been taken apart and the pieces carried off: nothing left but the concrete base and a protective wire fence. The rheostats and voltmeters are gone, too, and up on the stage, somebody has taken a sledgehammer to the switch panel. Warden Denno, Cecil B. De Mille, Executioner Francel, Electric Charlie Wilson, Rube Goldberg, and others gathered in the Square to put things back together again, are deeply distressed. These electric chairs are relatively rare, no chance to get a new one made this late in the game, and this one seems clearly beyond repair—

But not so! They watch, astounded, as with one fluid movement, Uncle Sam lifts from the gutter the wrecked chair, light as a matchbox for him, squeezes the splintered wood whole again, and bolts it down on the concrete part of the stage with hammer blows of his powerful fists! Wow! A commanding figure, Uncle Sam; crowds have gathered in the Square to ogle him, root for him, worship him even, discovering in their Superhero all that's best in themselves. He now studies, tugging thoughtfully on his white goatee, the ripped-out wiring and sabotaged switch, and one is reminded of Tom Jefferson, rugged and tall, poring over his designs for the White House or struggling with his quirky polygraph machine, or perhaps of Handsome Frank Pierce, puzzling over the metaphysical obscurities in the books of his friend Nat Hawthorne. Just as, yesterday, as he fought back against the Phantom's reckless spree, one saw glimpses of Old Hickory galloping up on Horseshoe Bend, T. R. throwing steers in the Badlands, Abe Lincoln splitting rails, or as now one seems to see George Washington crossing the Delaware or Franklin Roosevelt projecting the Four Freedoms in the simple way in which Uncle Sam instructs the workmen on the repair of the electrical system and sends them off to get the parts they need from Pitt Machine Products Company Incorporated, over by the synagogue on East Houston Street.

"You mean, we just take the stuff, or . . . ?"

He hands them the key, looking like Ulysses Grant handing his manuscript over to his publishers. "It's already took," he says quietly, his voice firm and gentle as Silent Cal's. "That business *used* to belong to Julius Rosenberg."

There is this peculiar quality about Uncle Sam: it's as though his many metamorphoses since his early days as an Inspector of Government Provisions have each left, mysteriously, their mark on him. One discovers Old Tip Harrison's long nose in the middle of his face, little Jemmy Madison's scraggly white hair (or is it Old Zack's or Little Van's? certainly he's got Zack Taylor's craggy cheeks and rough-and-ready ways), Willie (Big Lub) Taft's gold watchchain, old Jim Monroe's bony rump still in its—even then—out-of-date pantaloons. Debilities have been shed, donated to museums, or else never assumed (just part of the real-time cover story)—Washington's rhinoceros teeth and smallpox scars, F.D.R.'s shriveled legs, Cleveland's vulcanized rubber jaw, Abe's warts and Jim Polk's spastic bowels—but virtues and marvels have been laid on, fortified and refortified, many times over: there's the lean virility of Monroe, Jackson, and "Stud" Tyler, steadily augmented by passage through the likes of Long Abe, Doc Wilson, and Ike; there's that willful hard-set jaw, shaped by every Incarnation from "54–40 or Fight" Polk to Reverend Garfield, Ugly Honest Grover Cleveland, and the Roosevelt boys, not to mention the strange subtle influences of such as Hamilton and Burr, Clay and Calhoun, Bill Borah, Harry Hopkins, and even Ed Stettinius; there's the lofty pride of John (His Rotundity) Adams, the shrewdness of the Red Fox of Kinderhook, the Grecian mouth of Millard Fillmore, and a hand calloused by the campaign habits of everyone from Matty Van Buren and Chet Arthur, the Gentleman Boss, to affable Warren Harding, who once shook hands with 6756 people in five hours. When he cocks his head a certain poll-parrot way, he recalls Old Buck Buchanan, who had one nearsighted eye and one farsighted eye—which alone was enough to qualify him as Uncle Sam's Incarnation. And when, as now, tracing leads, fusing wires, unbending panels, putting this electrical system back together again, he scowls in concentration through a pair of antique wire-rimmed spectacles perched halfway down his Yankee nose, one cannot help but remember Citizen Ben Franklin jotting down his scientifical notes by candlelight after successfully sucking electrical fluid down a kite string. Or the old Rough Rider himself, Teddy Roosevelt, squinting to hide his lame left eye. Abe Lincoln trying to read the program in the weak light of Ford's Theater: "Other means may succeed," Uncle Sam says, glancing up at these recognitions, sparks flying between his fingers, "this cannot fail!" *Fsst! Sizzle! POP!* "As America's greatest Prophet once said, 'There is always a best way of doin' everything . . .'" The marquee lights dip, there's a crackling hum on-stage and a faint glow: it is done, the chair is ready! "'. . . *Even if it be to bile an egg!*'"

Huzzahs from the crowd, beaming smiles from the gathered functionaries, who try to get as close to Uncle Sam as possible. The workmen line up and sing "Hail to the Chief," then test out the chair by burning six or seven chimpanzees in it. And high over the Square behind Father Duffy, up where the Chevy sign used to be: the headlines from the *Newton Kansan* of exactly eighty years ago today, June the 19th, 1873:

LET PATRIOTS EVERYWHERE PREPARE TO DO THE CLEAN THING
BY UNCLE SAM AND HIS BALDHEADED EAGLE!

9.

The Vice President's Beard

Shaving that morning, I thought: I was born a hundred years too late. If I could let this damn thing grow, I'd look like Ulysses S. Grant. There'd be no more talk about shyster corporation lawyers and used-car salesmen then. I could say what I pleased, glowering over my beard, and everybody would listen. Black and bushy, like Saint Peter or Henry VIII or Whit What's-his-name. Walt Whitman. My skinned nose and forehead gave me a special ferocity this morning. I growled at myself in the bathroom mirror: *G-r-r-row-w-f-f!* Beauty and the Beast, that game I used to play with Pat before we were married, my secret self. She thought it was funny, she didn't understand. Mess up my hair, roll my eyes, shake my jowls, the good old days. I could always get a laugh then. If I'd worked at it, I might have been another Jack Benny.

I actually started a couple of beards back then, always got embarrassed, shaved them off before anyone started to notice. That drift from the focal center, which was somehow clean-cut and open-eyed—it had to do, I suspected, with the approval of old men. And fear of turning into the grizzly irresponsible red-eyed derelict I looked like after a day or two of stubble. With a beard you were expected to move differently, say different things, become more cynical and detached, I got conscious of my hands, eyebrows, lips. I could let myself look like that bent over law books on a Sunday night, but not in class on Monday morning. Then, before I knew it, I was a prosecuting attorney, had to set a community example, then an OPA civil servant in the war and soon a J.O. in the U.S. Navy, where hairiness was frowned on more even than gonorrhea, unless you wore it on your chest, and I wasn't even out of the Navy before I was running for Congress. With that, my public face was set. Change it, lose votes, I was no longer a free agent. How a candidate looks is a lot more important than what he says, and the most important thing is to look familiar. Even our rare vacations became public appearances, I put it out of my mind. Except occasionally while shaving in the morning. Maybe someday when I'm President. Like Lincoln. Have some little kid write to me and suggest it. That would solve the television makeup problem, too—I can shave thirty seconds before I go on camera and, unless I put some powder on, still have such an obvious beard that people write me letters about it. The five-o'clock phantom. My enemies will stop at nothing.

As I'd feared, I'd had a sleepless night—probably for the best, it could be stimulating at a time like this, I knew, but for the moment it made me groggy, unable to see clearly how close the shave was, I had to go by feel. I'd been pushing too hard, consuming all my reserves, making myself vulnerable. All those disturbing apparitions, those images out of a life not my own. . . . It was as though something had got into me last night, like an alien gene, and I'd lacked the strength to fend it off—all my Early Warning rhetoric about "boring from within": I'd suddenly begun to understand it for the first time. It was pretty stupid, banging my face on the wall like that, but in a way it had been a good thing. It had cleared my head, and by the time I'd reached my car I'd pretty much forgotten about old lady Greenglass's inflated belly and the chickens and traffic on Delancey Street. Soft summer night out, new moon over my shoulder: I'd rolled the windows down, turned on the car radio, tuning in a station playing old songs like "Heartaches" and "Whispering Hope," and had cruised down Independence, taking the long way home so as to calm down some, letting my mind fill up with reassuring pictures from my own past, my boyhood vibrating in me like an old movie: the Anaheim Union ditch in Yorba Linda where I went wading, Easter eggs and May baskets, the adventures of the Gumps, Grandma's big austere house at Christmastime and "Joy to the World" being trumpeted out from our Meeting House steeple, Lindbergh's flight and all the little stuff we collected from it, a book I read told by an abused dog, hanging baskets of smilax ferns on sunny porches, the Four Square Gospel Temple and Ken Maynard rolling off his horse inside the Berry Grand . . . Goddamn! I'd thought: I've lived a wonderful life! I'd remembered playing railroad fireman, learning to salute the flag at school and sing "Old Black Joe," nosing through the Books of Knowledge, memorizing stanzas of "Snowbound" and struggling with "In a Persian

Market Place" on Aunt Jane's piano, sweating in the heat of a Tucson summer, mashing potatoes for Mom. I was good at that like everything else and Mom was always pleased because I never left any lumps, using the whipping motion to make them smooth instead of going up and down like the other boys did. I'd recalled—tooling past the Smithsonian and up around the Washington obelisk—mashing those potatoes, and it was like some kind of epiphany. I'd felt like I felt one morning at Whittier College when I'd been up for nearly three straight days and everything was incredibly beautiful—or that day, not all that long ago, when I was sitting on a dilapidated rocking chair on Whittaker Chambers's front porch in Maryland, the warm sensation sweeping over me that it was all falling into place.

It had felt right, this feeling, I hadn't resisted it. History working things out for me in its inexorable but friendly way: my brother had got sick and my mother, overburdened with work and worry, had sent me to live half a year with Aunt Jane. I had hated this and had felt cheated somehow. This was natural. I didn't even like Aunt Jane. But that was where, feeling lonely, I'd learned the piano, and it had been an important part of my life ever since. Just as when I'd followed my mother over to Arizona. She'd taken Harold to a sanatorium there and was helping to pay the hospital bills by cooking and scrubbing at the sanatorium. I'd felt guilty tagging along without helping, so I'd got a job in the Prescott rodeo, cleaning out the stables. I'd been as thorough at that as I was at everything else, and so they'd asked me to be a barker for their wheel of chance. This was a come-on, I'd discovered, for the dice and poker tables in the back room, but everything out front where they'd put me was legal, the prizes were real hams and bacon, and I'd earned a dollar an hour and praise from the old guys for all the business I brought them. In many ways, in spite of the money, it had been the worst job I'd ever had, I was nervous for hours each day before I started, was scared to death of some of the people in those crowds—a complete waste of time, I'd thought . . . but without that experience, I would never have survived the cruelties of that whistle-stopping campaign tour last autumn when news broke about the so-called secret fund. Destiny. My Dad decided to open a gas station in 1922. He could have had a site in Santa Fe Springs, but he chose the one in East Whittier. The next year they found oil—lots of it—on the Santa Fe Springs property: we would have been millionaires. It gave my father bleeding ulcers, but for me, what was being a millionaire? Being at the center was everything, and this meant having nothing in excess to throw you off balance. Except power. Power, I knew, was something that existed in the universe like electricity. There was no reason to be a conductor. There was no reason not to be.

I'd skirted the Tidal Basin and wheeled around toward the Lincoln Memorial, then had followed the Potomac around to Rock Creek, letting the old tunes on the radio—"Have You Ever Seen a Dream Walking" . . . "Me and My Shadow"—call up all the old feelings, the old scenes, the old dreams. No patterns, just a sweet nostalgic flow . . . the church picnics with homemade ice cream . . . the dense odor of the inside of my violin case . . . Tunney and Dempsey and the Irish Rebellion (how my father raged against it! "But aren't we Irish, too?" I'd asked him; "Not that kind!" he'd bellowed) . . . a beautiful print we had in our house, an advertisement I think for Edison light bulbs, called "Shedding Light," with a boy sitting on a purple rock in a misty rose and green landscape, gazing up at the light bulb glowing in the branches of a summery tree, looking for God up there, I supposed, as I always used to do while watching the clouds go by . . . or maybe it was a girl sitting there, I'd forgotten exactly. Passing the locks, "The Sweetheart of Sigma Chi" fading in and out on the distant station, I'd had sudden total recall of Fredric March's transformation from Dr. Jekyll into Mr. Hyde and back, which was nevertheless mixed up somehow with *The Best Years of Our Lives,* probably the greatest movie I'd ever seen, though I no longer remembered much of it. And so it had gone: the Armistice parade and a circus, Wallet finding a baby on his doorstep in "Gasoline Alley," Grand Canyon through the stereoscope, the fear of Bolshevism, the strange light at Christian Endeavor meetings on Sunday nights, the 1924 World Series on our new radio and then Babe Ruth hitting sixty home runs when I was fourteen years old. But mostly school memories, ballgames, girls, clubs, bike rides, and things at home, Dad's knuckled hands on a gas pump, the way his ears stuck out when he was dressed up, Mom's smile when I brought things home from school, fights with my brother Donald, Harold's vague grin, Dad coming home one day to tell us there was a little doll over at the hospital, a real live doll—poor little Arthur, who'd died so young. I'd once written a school composition about him, a kind of threnody . . . "And so, when I am tired and worried, and am almost ready to quit trying to live as I should, I look up and see the picture of a little boy with sparkling eyes, and curly hair; I remember the child-like prayer—If I should die before I awake, I pray Thee, Lord, my soul to take—I pray that it may prove true for me as it did for my brother Arthur . . ." I got an A for it. A for Arthur. . . .

I'd swung off the deserted Parkway and up onto Massachusetts, better lit but just as empty, my fingers drumming on the wheel, picking out the song on the radio—Count Basie's "One O'Clock Jump," I think—I might have been a great jazz pianist, or a very good one anyway, if I'd had the time. This was the long part of the drive home, up past Washington Cathedral and American University, almost all the way to Maryland. But not quite all the way: we lived in Alexandria when we first came here, but now I wouldn't live outside the District if they'd give me title to all of Montgomery County. I was dangerously close, I'd realized, to Inspiration House, headquarters for the pro-Rosenberg forces, and, wheeling around past the Naval Observatory, I'd flashed again suddenly on Ethel's bare bottom by the kitchen stove, but I'd pushed it away before all the tenement stuff started crowding in, concentrating instead on the broad dirt streets of Yorba Linda, the scattered one-story wooden buildings, distant hills, the hair rolled tight on top of Grandma's head, the elections I'd won, the first time I got to drive the truck alone, things I'd thought about when I was a janitor at the swimming pool. "My Wild Irish Rose." The drunken Mexicans over in Jim Town. Snitching grapes. Throwing passes. Standing under the big lamp on the corner of Greenleaf and Philadelphia, talking with guys late into the night. A full moon one night that seemed to separate itself from the street lamp as I walked out from under it—it's God! I'd thought, it's proof!—and then a girl's window, lit: but she was dressed, and then, unbuttoning her blouse with one hand, she pulled the blind with the other. My eyes had closed a moment, capturing that lowering shade—and I'd almost wrecked the car, two blocks from home, right on Wesley Circle. Easy, boy. Don't let your guard down.

Checkers had greeted me, threatening to wake up everybody in the house. I'd petted him roughly and cracked his nose to shut him up. The most famous dog in the nation since Fala. The goddamn spare room was still full to overflowing with dog collars, handwoven dog blankets, dog kennels and baskets, and enough dog food to feed all of Southeast Asia, sent to us by dog lovers and other lonely people. Some of them had actually thought that my Checkers speech was an appeal for charity! Thus: one more profession, if all else failed. I'd found a rib bone in the refrigerator for Checkers, a bowl of vanilla pudding, three overripe slices of tomato, a french-fried chicken back, a partial tin of Spam, a plate of soft fudge, cole slaw, a Dr. Pepper, some sour gherkins, a peach half in syrup, and a cold hamburger for myself—more or less in that order and eaten as discovered. I was very hungry and it all tasted good. There was actually some red Jell-O in there with canned mixed fruit in it: I wasn't sure of the flavor, but I ate it up anyway, thinking: Who knows? it may be the last of its kind. I'd also cleaned up what was left of a jar of apple sauce, bottle of skimmed milk, bowl of tapioca, and tin can of cold baked beans, followed by caviar and strawberry ice cream, lit up a ceremonial pipeful of Rum and Maple, and sat down in an armchair to digest.

Foo. I'd eaten too quickly. I felt terrible. But one had to be uncomfortable, I knew, to do one's best thinking. I'd tried to think about the case again. Here at home, pull it all together, solve all the problems. What did it mean that they'd found the missing console table, that Schneider the photographer had committed perjury with FBI connivance, that Greenglass had spent six months in the Tombs with Harry Gold preparing their testimony? Nothing. The table could be any table, Schneider's alleged perjury was merely technical, witnesses are always schooled. I'd belched sourly, shifted in the chair, knocked out the pipe (why do I smoke at all? I hate the goddamn stuff), and recalled that in one of the confidential notes stolen from her lawyer's office, Ruth Greenglass had been reported admitting that her husband, David, had "a tendency to hysteria": "Once when he had the grippe he ran nude through the hallway shrieking of 'elephants' and 'lead pants.' " Lead pants? Maybe he'd seen our secret research into anti-shrapnel underwear for Marines. I'd realized I was just pooping around, so I'd chased Checkers off to bed and gone that way myself.

In the bedroom, I'd seen that Pat had got tangled in the sheets, her bottom exposed: was she trying to tell me something, I'd wondered? Such a lean pale spiny rear, yet slack and inviting at the same time. Calvinist but charitable. I'd struggled, grunting, into pajamas, had slipped into bed feeling very heavy. Hot, too—I could afford an air-conditioner now, why hadn't I bought one? Residue of that goddamn campaign. Pat needed a new coat, too, but I still couldn't risk it. Of course, thirteenth wedding anniversary: the proper gift for that was furs and textiles, wasn't it? Might be the occasion. Now that I was lying still, my face had started to sting again where I'd hit it on the wall, and I'd felt a throbbing ache in the small of my back from sitting too long on my office floor. I'd remembered that Ethel Rosenberg had suffered from back pains all her life because of a ricketic curvature of the spine. This was supposed to explain a lot of things. I could see how it could make you cranky, all right. I couldn't get comfortable. I'd tossed about, sweating, conscious of Pat's butt, reminded of the time I'd got nauseous working as a handyman in a packing house and had had to quit. What a miserable job. It had been like some kind of seasickness, all that meat, everything churning and hammering—I'd been too chicken to quit right away and had stuck it out for sixteen weeks, worst time in my life. Too dogged and persevering to quit, I mean. Oh man, why the hell did I eat all that junk? There were awful moments in the Navy, too, and in cars—about the only thing I dreaded about becoming President was having to take the Presidential yacht out from time to time. Pat had complained softly in her sleep, and I'd got up, opened a bottle of beer, and moved to a couch.

I'd thought, stretching out: I must do what I always do, I must consider all the worst alternatives as cold-bloodedly as I can, and reach an analytical conclusion. But instead I'd dozed off and found myself in bed with the guy I slept with at Duke. He had been studying so hard he'd set his ass on fire, and he was trying to show me the burns. Curiously, he had a thin black moustache and wire-rimmed glasses, was wearing a double-breasted suit jacket, white shirt, and tie. "Don't be embarrassed," I said as I pried the cheeks of his butt apart to see what was the matter. We didn't have any electricity in that place and it was dark, but by peering closely I could tell that the whole area was festering and badly inflamed. It was almost like somebody had taken a meat cleaver to it. I felt nauseous and sorry for what I'd done. I wanted to comfort her but I was worried what the lasting impression would be. Dad came in and suggested a poultice of hot mustard. He didn't seem to understand the problem. I shouted: "Summer solstice, not poultice!" He seemed utterly abashed and ashamed of himself. I was ashamed, too, because I knew he'd never finished school. Pat lay naked on the bed, her eyes closed, moaning softly, literally shedding light. I was at the sink. Perhaps I'd been washing the dishes, or else I'd been vomiting. "She's the Sweetheart of Sigma Chi," Dad said solemnly. He was dressed up for church and his ears stuck out. I went outside, thinking: Didn't they know *I* could die, too?

I'd awakened, vaguely recalling a warm sunny scene, very attractive and soothing, as though from some pastoral painting: green hills, a brook, the house receding . . . I'd drifted back trying to recapture it, but found myself instead giving a guided tour of the Coney Island boardwalk to gruff old men in flat straws and red suspenders. There was something before this about shit. Maybe it was something about cleaning the stables at the rodeo in Prescott. Except the shit was from people who were frightened or made sick by the carnival rides. I was still wearing my pajamas and an old woman with cheap spectacles came over to feel the cloth. The fly on the pants gaped and my peter kept flopping out. The old woman was Jewish and had hairs poking out her nostrils. She didn't seem interested in my peter, only the pajamas. Her fingernails were long and scratched at my skin. I was afraid the old men would walk away. I knew everything depended on them. I was trying to sell them a ride on the Whip, and I made some kind of joke about going round and round instead of up and down, which didn't go over at all. They became angry and grumbled in some foreign language. The old woman—my God, I realized, it's Bob Taft!—looked up at me and winked, then shrank away. This was because I was getting bigger. And I realized my face was changing—rough clumps of hair were sprouting on my forehead and nose. I felt crude and ugly. I smelled bad. I seemed to be getting tangled up in the roller coaster. I was afraid of the wires. I woke up and realized that Checkers had crawled up and was sleeping with his head on my belly. I seemed to remember a rifle range, and near it a lady carrying a parasol and a white handbag, girls lying on the beach in candy-striped swimsuits. The pool was closed and I was sweeping out the girls' changing room: smell of chlorine and damp wool. I thought of places I could hide in here to watch the girls dress. I dreamed of discovering secret things while sweeping up, but all I ever found was a pair of wet cotton socks. I peed once in the girls' toilet and was frightened by my own face in a mirror. I woke again. Or had I been sleeping? I had an erection and needed to use the bathroom. Peeing, I realized that the scene in the girls' toilet at the swimming pool was not a dream at all, but a true memory from a job I had in high school. The sweeping, the mirror, the guilt. I'd turned the socks in to "Lost and Found," feeling virtuous. Then what about the rifle range at Coney Island? I looked in the mirror and saw that I'd given my face quite a whack on that wall. I put some cold cream on it. I looked puffy and hairy, I hardly recognized myself, some kind of monster. I seemed to see Uncle Sam's face behind me, his blue eye glinting with amusement. Or fury. I can only do my best, I thought. What more does he want of me? Later, I dreamt of tomatoes with big dark bruises on them. I couldn't find a good one in the lot. This seemed to justify an old proverb: There is no little enemy. I had to struggle to remember this proverb—at first it kept reading: There is no little enema. I thought I could make the best of the situation by making juice out of them, start a business. I took the rotten tomatoes to an electronics shop. The sign over the shop door said: OPTIMO CIGARS. Taxicabs went by with tires mounted in their right fenders. I thought: Somebody could get killed! The man in the cigar store said: "I don't know nothing about pressing tomatoes, mister, I'm in underwear machines." He seemed frightened. There were children huddled around a radiator that was hissing like a snake. "I come from Julius Caesar," I said. A woman was putting bread on a table. The children seemed to resent me. I was wide awake, not dreaming at all.

"David gave me your number," I explained helplessly. I thought I must be going mad.

Now, in the hard light of day, scraping the bristle from my forty-year-old throat, freshly shampooed and showered, the sweat of yesterday's ordeal sent safely down the drain, I could see that many of those associations from last night were more innocent than they'd seemed at the time. I'd pushed too long without rest or nourishment and had momentarily blown a few circuits in the memory-retrieval system, that was all. Opened up the gates and flooded the syntax routes. In fact, it could be fun, if you didn't do it too often. Take that vivid image of Pat lying flat out on the bed, for example. I realized now that she was also somehow my little brother Arthur. And Mother was there all the time, though I don't remember where. There was some kind of satire on the Rosenbergs mixed up in it, too, because at the time I had said to myself, watching Pat thrash about: "For peace, breast, and Moses."

Also, I realized now where some of those New York images might have come from, which last night had seemed so enigmatic. As a boy, for example, working in my folks' store, I used to drive a pickup into the produce markets in Los Angeles in the early morning hours so I could get the fresh fruit and vegetables back in the store and ready for sale when we opened at eight. Not that L.A. was New York, but then neither was my image of New York New York. And for small-town kids like me back then, New York was like some kind of Jerusalem, an El Dorado. There were picture books and photos in the papers, newsreels, stereoscopes, and later, Tru-Vue films, all those movies about the great Empire City—who knows? those skylines in my mind may have been painted a few miles away in a Hollywood studio. The so-called Great White Way: invention of Warner Brothers probably. Washington Square. The Battery. The Chrysler Building and Astor House. And the Lower East Side: the mysterious ghetto with its hives of colorful immigrant populations, the place where the melting pot melted. Yes, we'd all been there. For a kid who loved baseball like I did, it was a real dream town, that was where the Babe and Lou and Burleigh and Red Ruffing lived, John McGraw and Zack Wheat, three great teams all in the same city—when I was a boy either the Yanks or the Giants were in the World Series almost every year, and more often than not, both of them. On street corners, we talked about New York. One of the first tunes I learned to bang out on the piano was "The Sidewalks of New York," and even now I liked to play it and call up that city of my imaginings. I read a lot of books about the city, too, I think there was one by Horatio Alger with New York in the title, something about a poor kid whose real father turns out to be a millionaire, and that was where Wall Street was and the crash and the bread lines we read about. That's right, no need to get upset last night by what seemed at times like telepathic messages from the Sing Sing Death House, I told myself, and pulled my cheek forward over my jawbone to examine the hidden stubble. "Just misses being handsome," TIME had said. Just misses! If I'm ever President, I thought, I'll send that fairy to the boondocks and give the laureateship to *Reader's Digest*, who deserves it anyway.

It had all started, I remembered, with that inexplicable "memory" of the rented hall on Delancey Street where Julius and Ethel had met at a union ball, and I realized now, old piano tunes tinkling in the back of my head, where that vast gleaming waxed floor had come from: the Women's Clubhouse in Whittier, across from the Bailey Street Park. Mom and Dad got married there. I'd been in and out of that place all the time I was growing up—yes, the old Victrola in the corner, the kitchen . . . some of those pastoral images later on might even have come from the park out front. And the kids dressing around the kitchen coalstove: I'd read in one of the FBI reports that that was the only heat Barnet and Tessie Greenglass had had in their Sheriff Street flat—the family used to huddle around it on cold afternoons, get dressed by it in the mornings. In the report, this was to show how poor they were and to make the point that poverty and injustice were "the parents of revolutionary idealism"—in other words, the poor, given their resentments, were not to be trusted, and if there were any trouble, it was smart to look there first. Naturally, this had reminded me of the stove we got dressed around in Yorba Linda, Mom full-bellied at the time with little Arthur. The Sam and Bernie Greenglass I had pictured might in a crowd have been mistaken for my own brothers Harold and Donald, and as for little Ethel's naked bottom, well, to tell the truth, it had looked a lot like my daughter Tricia's.

Had I resented the implication in the FBI report that, because I had also had to dress around a kitchen stove on winter mornings, my life too might be suspect? Perhaps. But it was not the same. We lived in frost-free Yorba Linda, after all, home of the Mother Tree of the Fuerte Avocado in California, we rarely needed heat at all. And even if we weren't rich, we were never resentful. We just got busy and improved ourselves. "Self-respect, self-regulation, self-restraint, and self-attainment!" my mother always admonished us. Strange I even remembered that kitchen coalstove, it was so long ago. No wonder it seemed like something in a dream! To think of the changes that this country had seen in the few years since I was a boy! Just look at that terrific layout

Pat now had in her kitchen: who would want to change something that was working so well? These Communists were crazy. Every time I flicked a switch, adjusted a thermostat, started a car, boarded a plane, walked through automatic doors, flushed a toilet, or watched a record drop on a turntable, I loved America more. And not just for her material progress either, but for her great traditions as well. Like Thanksgiving turkeys and Christmas trees. Church picnics and the Rose Bowl. The annual Congressional baseball game. The bonfire at Whittier College—it may seem frivolous to some that while Julius Rosenberg at the age of fifteen was circulating a petition for Tom Mooney, I nearly six years older was chairmanning the annual bonfire on Fire Hill and establishing a new all-time record by topping it, not with the traditional one-hole privy, but with a real four-hole collector's item—"the hottest thing that ever happened at Whittier," it's been called—but anyone with any understanding at all of the American mainstream will know that in 1933 Tom Mooney was peripheral to it and that shithouse-crowned bonfire was dead center. Now, twenty years later, Julius Rosenberg was still outside, in fact he was colder than ever, while I was playing golf with Uncle Sam. Oh, he was still trying. Identifying himself with the Founding Fathers, black martyrs, and what he liked to call "the people." But even that yellowed newspaper copy of the Declaration of Independence that he kept taped up on his cell wall, presumably to demonstrate his undying patriotism, was just one more sign of his alienation: the Declaration was never part of the mainstream either.

On my office wall, by contrast, I had the Inaugural Prayer of President Eisenhower, framed and under glass: "Give us, we pray, the power to discern clearly right from wrong." As I told the American Legion: "Among the great privileges that we enjoy is the privilege of hearing President Eisenhower pray at the beginning of his Inauguration. That could not happen in half the world today!" It was a treat, all right, listening to him, his voice high-pitched and straining against the cold, against the strangeness, the vast multitudes, somewhat snappish, militant, overeager, sing-songy at times, a bit tongue-tied and struggling to overcome it. "DEAR FRIENDS!" He really cracked that out, made us all jump. Wonder it didn't start us giggling, but we were all new to this, afraid of forgetting our parts or getting assassinated or something. "Uh, BE-fore I begin . . . THE expression . . . of those thoughts . . . that I deem appropriate . . . uh-TO this mo-MENT . . . would you permit me the privlidge of uttering ay little private prayer of my own . . . and I ask that you bow your heads!" This was amazing, because for Dwight David Eisenhower, religion was something organized by the USO for the entertainment of the troops. When he was a kid it was what dragged you out of the crap games at the Herd on Sundays, and once out of Abilene he had rarely let it interfere with his life any longer. Asking no questions, he suffered no answers. For Ike, Jesus was some kind of loser, attractive to old ladies. Bowing your head in prayer was to make you look tougher and taller when you raised it again. Talking about religion, a consolation for the dying, could be bad luck for a soldier—the less said about it, the better. And then, suddenly, standing there before us was the inspired visionary of the Inaugural Address—here, clearly, was a man who had gone to the center and seen the sacred. You could see it in the sweat on his brow, hear it in the constriction in his throat, the crack and thunder of "faith," "freedom," and "good and evil," rolling off his tongue. "All-might-y GAWT!"

He started going regularly to church again. He joined the National Presbyterian Church in Washington. He rejected the side-aisle pews used by Jackson, Pierce, Polk, Buchanan, Grant, and Cleveland, insisted instead on sitting "front and center." He gave us frequent lectures on American history, tracing our lineage directly back to God. Jefferson's phrase "We hold that all men are endowed by their Creator with certain unalienable rights" was like a tic with him, kept coming to his tongue. But it wasn't the unalienable rights that interested him, it was the endowment by a Creator. "Thee Cree-AY-torr!" It was as though he'd never really believed in God until he discovered Him there in the Declaration of Independence. Maybe he'd read it for the first time while boning up for the 1952 campaign. "The Declaration of Independence established once and for all," he liked to say, "that our civilization and our form of government is deeply imbedded in a religious faith. Indeed, those men felt that unless we recognized that relationship between our form of government and religious faith, that form of government made no sense." Well, when an old soldier returns from the profane world to the sacred heart of his people, when he becomes overnight, without even realizing it, the workaday abode for the spirit of the race, we might expect such declarations. Indeed, the conversion of Dwight David Eisenhower was as great a proof of the immanence and immutability of Uncle Sam as the renewed preaching of the Disciples after their Good Friday dismay and dispersion was of the Resurrection of Christ. Even Ethel Rosenberg had come to recognize him as a "sensitive artist and devoutly religious man." Clumsy as he was, you knew he was the one to know.

I had always had this instinct, I always knew who had it, whether at school, in downtown Whittier, or in Washington. I learned right away to talk things over with Dr. Dexter, president of the college, and Dean Horack at Duke, with Herman Perry, manager of the Bank of America in Whittier, with Herbert Hoover and Murray Chotiner, Karl Mundt and Christian Herter, Tom Dewey, Foster Dulles and his brother—there was a certain vibration they had, and I always felt it. And who was Julie Rosenberg hanging out with? Losers like Morton Sobell and Max Elitcher and William Perl and Joel Barr. Collecting money for the Reds in the Spanish Civil War and signatures for the Scottsboro boys. Organizing the Students' Strike for Peace. Instead of telling his deans and teachers how much he admired them, he insulted them. A great deal of time during the trial two years ago had been spent on describing the Rosenbergs' adolescent activities, what was termed their "premature anti-fascism." The defense objected, but this was demonstrably relevant, not to show "motivation," as Judge Kaufman allowed, but to reveal the hidden patterns of developing heresy.

The first thing I did when I went to Whittier College was help found a new fraternity, the Orthogonians (actually, we called ourselves the "Square Shooters"), which was a kind of bridge between the old-line Franklins with their fancy-dress rules and right-wing pride, and the more open but disorganized and apathetic independent students. Athletes mostly, Chief Newman's boys, but we ran the politics and social scene as well. We met once a month down at Sanders's cafe for our traditional symbolic meal, or sometimes I took the whole fraternity to Grandma's house, and she and Mom fixed the beans and spaghetti. I was always generous like this. The Square Shooters was a real fraternity, all right, with all the usual hoopla, horseplay—I'll never forget our christening ceremonies at a Wednesday-morning chapel service when Sheik Homan tried to break a bottle of Old Taylor over my head!—and campus politicking, but we were also innovators. True, we had "secret" symbols—a boar's head and a square with "Beans, Brawn, Brains, and Bowels" as the four corners—and mottoes and special handshakes and I even composed a chapter song: "All hail the mighty boar, Our patron beast is he!" But at the same time, we got rid of the evening dress, fought against exclusivity, even initiated a Negro football star, shocked the whole campus with our risqué vaudeville skits and plays, most of which I wrote, and made a virtue of being a good guy instead of a rich guy. I've been making bridges like that between tradition and innovation ever since. In a very real sense, Julius Rosenberg was going to the electric chair because he went to City College of New York and joined the American Students Union when he was sixteen. If he'd come to Whittier instead and joined my Square Shooters, worn slouch sweaters and open collars with the rest of us, it wouldn't be happening. Simple as that.

Tricia and Julie were running up and down the stairs screaming, and I could hear Pat calling them down to the table. Breakfast was cooking. I had expected an upset stomach this morning, but instead I was simply hungry. I hoped that Pat grasped the fact that I was in a major crisis and was fixing corned beef hash for me with an egg on it. That I hadn't come to bed all night, that I'd slept in my clothes on the living-room sofa, should be enough of a clue. Probably not, though. She could be pretty insensitive.

I discovered, inspecting my face closely, that I'd somehow missed a patch of beard under my chin. Still not as alert as I ought to be. Hard to focus. I hadn't completely shaken off all that happened last night. I had awakened with an erection, for example—luckily, Pat had come down to call me before the girls had seen it—and it still hadn't gone away. I plugged in the razor again, grimacing at my face. Well, TIME's right, I admitted, lifting my "fat cheeks" and staring down past my "duck-bill nose," it's true, I'm no goddamn Millard Fillmore. But then, what the hell, neither was Abe Lincoln. Once, a little girl came up to me with a news-magazine photograph to sign. After I'd autographed it, she thanked me and said: "It's an awfully good picture. It doesn't look like you at all." I wondered afterwards if someone had put her up to it. But people have often registered an odd kind of surprise on first meeting me face-to-face. They tend to stare at my nose as though measuring its breadth, lost there and unable to find my eyes again. So, all right, I've often said that there wasn't much that could be done with my face. In that regard I'm my own severest critic: it isn't perfect; it's never going to be.

Cartoonists had had a heyday with it. Not even Julie Rosenberg, who had a genuinely sinister mug, right down to the weak chin, pointed nose, and pencil-line moustache, had had to take the kind of punishment I'd received every week from Herblock and the others. Picasso had actually made the sonuvabitch look handsome, very Anglo-Saxon, whereas Herblock always showed me as a jowly, wavy-haired, narrow-eyed tough, linked usually with McCarthy and Jenner, and with suggestions of some bad odor about me, like a little boy who'd just filled his pants or something. He hadn't given any of us a day's rest since we came into office back in January, you'd think we were invading Mongol hordes or something, instead of fellow Americans. His cartoon Ike looked a lot like Jiggs from "Bringing Up Father," only daffier, he drew Herb Brownell like a kind of Dracula, and Joe McCarthy was shown as a sweaty, hairy, cleaver-wielding tramp. I don't know about these other guys, but cartoonists had always had fun with my face. Already back at Whittier College, they were happily nailing me with a few harsh lines: a solid black bar for eyebrows (no eyes), a stretched ski-slope S for a nose, a small sour turndown comma for a mouth, encompassed by curly black hair cut square, little parenthetical ears, meat-platter cheeks, and a stiff neck—just three mean marks and a dark frame. I didn't mind. It was one of the consequences of power. If not a condition: maybe politicians needed faces like that to become recognizable. Something to set you apart: people respected the almost magical force emanating from archetypes, no matter what sort, or who put them there. Or maybe the caricature came first and the face followed. . . .

"Dick!" Pat called from the foot of the stairs. The maid had the sweeper going in the living room, and I could smell bacon frying on the stove in the kitchen. So much for corned beef hash. "Your car's here!"

"What—!" I glanced at my watch: holy shit! nearly eight! I was going to be late for the goddamn Cabinet meeting! I scrubbed my face angrily—it smarted where I'd hit the wall last night, but I deserved it for so much lollygagging—and applied talcum and deodorant, hobbled into the bedroom for a fresh white shirt, muttering irritably under by breath. I was ordinarily a very punctual man: down to breakfast every morning by seven, fruit, toast, a cup of coffee with a half teaspoon of sugar and a touch of cream, break up the squabbles between the girls, check the newspapers and thumb through the *Congressional Record*, get picked up by John just before eight, read *The New York Times* on the way in, and be at work in my office before most of my staff turned up. That I was nearly an hour behind this morning was yet another sign of how disturbed I was by this damned thing—*I've got to get to the office*, I thought with some anxiety, rushing stiff-legged down the stairs, knotting my tie on the run, folding a white handkerchief for my breast pocket, tripping over Julie's doll Tiny, and taking the last of the stairs three at a time, *and clean up that mess!*

10.

Pilgrimage to *The New York Times*

The Friday-morning commuters into the center gather, as is their ancient custom, before their great civic monument, *The New York Times,* there to commune with the latest transactions of the Spirit of History as made manifest in all the words and deeds of living and dying men fit to print. On great slabs of stone, lead, and zinc, words and pictures appear and disappear, different ones every day, different yet somehow reassuringly familiar. It is as though—the slabs seem to tell us—a certain constancy of purpose motivates the Spirit, even when perverse, bringing a kind of fragile episodic continuity to the daily debris of human enterprise, a "handle" as they say on the Great White Way, though it's not certain whether this is thanks to the Spirit or to *The New York Times*'s monumental sign language. TURKS URGE GREEKS / TO RUSH BALKAN TIE. PANAMA AND FRANK / SEE KAYE ON FILM. FAVORITISM REFUTED / IN WESTERN PEA SALE. It is a kind of hunting magic, a talisman against the terrible flux: men fear only surprises. HOLY NAME PARADES IN BROOKLYN.

Some have broken fast, some do so now before the monument. Symbolic foods appropriate to the sober occasion are taken: eggs, smoked flesh, the seeds of living things, uroboric bagels and doughnuts, sustenance drawn from swollen teats. SENATE GROUP FOR OLEO IN NAVY. British Girls Advance. PRODUCERS TRAIL MARY MARTIN. There is a ceremonial drone of wheels on rails, clicking turnstiles, respectful murmurings and rustlings, rhythmically accented by sudden hornblasts and whistles, the wheeze of air brakes, the blowing of noses, the clatter of dishes and

188

whump of doors, a man asking for tickets. CHINESE STAB AT 6 U.N. POINTS. The Milkman Is Slipping. RELIGIOUS FREEDOM WEEK BACKED. EXECUTED GERMAN / A JOBLESS PAINTER. The worshipers move methodically among the slabs, breaking bread and sipping hot stimulants, muttering the traditional responses, snorting and farting, momentarily losing themselves, absorbing the positional metaphors that will preserve the earth's gravity one more day and stay their own panic. PLANTS DISPERSED / TO FOIL BOMBINGS. BRONX PASTOR'S SON GETS CALL. Weddings, murders, mergers, wakes. Recipes and riots, batting averages and book reviews. The Cold War between Uncle Sam and his enemies, hot wars in the bushes. Ominously, the world chooses to publish today *The Art of the Checkmate,* and *Frankenstein,* say the slabs, is being reissued. Reissued? VERY RECENTLY, 19 COPIES OF THIS BOOK WERE LITERALLY BURNED. Shadows cloud the pilgrim faces as they learn that the French World War I ace who shot down seventy-five Bosch planes from his old Spad biplane is dead, but the shadows are dispersed a moment later by the revelation that Ruth Hussey has had a daughter after two sons. Martha Raye is obtaining a divorce from Nick Condos on the grounds of extreme cruelty. The communicants try to imagine this cruelty and wonder if they will be able to watch some of it tonight in Times Square.

Or whenever. *If* ever. There is a pervading unease here at the monument this morning: something is wrong, every responsible voice in the nation has been insisting the executions had to take place last night and they didn't, and now even *The New York Times,* ordinarily impervious in its grandeur to common panic, must acknowledge that the nation needs these deaths and needs them soon, for as Arthur Krock announces, deep inside the maze:

> The operation of justice in the United States is subject to inordinate delays, anyhow, and the Communists have already taken full advantage of this in the Rosenbergs' case to injure the reputation of the judicial system here with our friends abroad and otherwise make effective anti-American propaganda. By granting the stay, and on the grounds he gave, Justice Douglas has enabled the enemies of this nation to besmirch it further. . . .

They read that as a consequence of Justice Douglas's action the Supreme Court is today in special emergency session—CASE SEEN IN PERIL—and that before it the associate counsel for the atom spies has said of the New York Supreme Court Justice Irving Saypol that "there never was a more crooked District Attorney in New York than the one who tried the Rosenbergs!" Perhaps, they conclude hopefully from this, the Phantom

has overreached himself. ROSENBERGS MAY FIGHT / INDICTMENT IF
DEATH / SENTENCE IS UPSET. Circumscribing all these speculations: the
picture of a man sweating behind bars in a B. Altman & Co. advertisement ("Are you facing a 90-day sentence?"), a movie review of *Devil's
Plot,* and a floor-level peek up the skirt of a woman strapped into the
seat of a Colonial Airlines plane to Canada. Father's Day ads for sizzling
steaks. "The Mighty Atom" is dead. TONIGHT AT 8:30. "Something to fit
every taste."

Which is to say, information is one thing, *The New York Times* another. One does not assimilate data in a trance. Communion services are
essentially tactile, not cognitive, a confrontation of life with life. What
compels the attention and taps the wellsprings of prophecy on these
pilgrimages is not this announcement that little Arlene Riddett, 15, of
Yonkers, won the girls' championship in the 28th annual marbles tour-
nament in Asbury Park, New Jersey, nor that picture of two East Berlin
demonstrators throwing stones at Russian tanks on Leipzigerplatz, but
the fact that these things touch each other. There are sequences but no
causes, contiguities but no connections. The government of Argentina
orders the price of theater tickets cut by 25% and the President of the
United States is given a large toy model of Smokey Bear. The execution
of an unemployed housepainter in Berlin takes shape beside the report
that a new collection of wall coverings and shower curtains offers a
variety of choices to homemakers who wish to decorate the bathroom:
BATH WALLPAPERS / ARE EASY TO CLEAN. "Panorama" is one of the wall-
paper designs, made up of impressionistic scenes of the country against
a background of abstract motifs reminiscent of ancient calligraphy. Design as a game. Randomness as design. Design ironically revealing randomness. Arbitrariness as a principle, allowing us to laugh at the tragic.
As in dreams, there is an impressive amount of condensation on the one
hand, elaboration on the other. Logical relationships are repressed, but
reappear through displacement. There are pictures of shower curtains
with cats carrying umbrellas in their tails. The housepainter's wife said
her husband had merely left home that rainy morning to collect his
unemployment check. He had a bad cold and planned to come straight
home. *Handy Man of High Degree.* "Shot through with compassion and
humor. . ." Advertisements for airconditioners, summer suits, and
umbrellas provide the setting for the crash of the Globemaster IN FIERY
SPIN NEAR TOKYO. Cool and carefree as a breeze. SOME UNUSUAL WAYS
WITH COLD SOUP. The news that 905 MORE CAPTIVES / ESCAPE FROM CAMP
is paired with an ad for UNITED HUNTS. *Send them off to camp looking
their nicest after a trip to Best's Children's Barber Shop.*

There are those who commune directly with the words, caressing them blearily with their sleepy eyes or swallowing them like antacids, leaning against the slabs for support whenever the earth should rock, but doubting they represent anything more than themselves. Others gamely seek the space between, likening these cryptic hoarstones to clues in the daily crossword puzzle (and look what's *there* today, first clue, 1 Across: *Burning Tree activity*), signals in an ordered maze, a possibly more or less ordered maze. And perhaps that was why—the tenacious faith in the residual magic of language—this monument was erected in the first place: that effort to reconstruct with words and iconography each fleeting day in the hope of discovering some pattern, some coherence, some meaningful dialogue with time. But so enormous a shrine is it, so prodigious a task just to keep the translation of gesture into language flowing, that all consciousness of any intended search for transcendence must long ago have disappeared and been forgotten, leaving all visionary speculations to the passing pilgrim. Yet even this extravagant accretion of data suggests a system, even mere hypotyposis projects a metaphysic. "Objectivity" is in spite of itself a willful program for the stacking of perceptions; facts emerge not from life but from revelation, gnarled as always by ancient disharmonies and charged with libidinous energy. Conscious or not, *The New York Times* statuary functions as a charter of moral and social order, a political force-field maker, defining meaningful actions merely by showing them, conferring a special power on those it touches, creating the stations of life that others might aspire to. And why not? How else struggle against entropy? PACE AT WESTBURY / TO MIGHTY GRATTAN. *N.Y. Life Officers to Be Elevated.* WASHINGTON ANGRY. Fail to Find a Bomb in School. HOUSE PURCHASED / FOR WORKING GIRLS.

They often come here, working girls, prowling in the Classifieds, searching for fairy godmothers, magic carpets, the secret name of that gold-spinning gnome. Bombers poke about, open-faced and friendly, looking for targets. Politicians, too. Pensioners and passing tourists. Uncle Sam also comes from time to time, mostly just to show off. And the Phantom, though he never shows his face, can often be glimpsed in the dark shadows behind the slabs, exposing his hindend and farting damply. Judge Irving Kaufman, like so many, comes here out of duty, essentially oblivious to the Phantom's impieties, seeking what he would think of as a balanced view. One eye on New York, the other on the World. Tammany Hall is his metaphorical link, just as it is Irving Saypol's. Governor Tom Dewey, whose connection is the Republican Eastern Establishment, those same International Bankers who have put

Dwight David Eisenhower in the White House, rushes here daily, shoulders bulled forward, fists clenched, chewing his moustache, ready for a fight, looking down his nose, or up his nose, at panic-stricken creatures like Mayor Vincent Impellitteri or Mother Luce (her son TIME whistles through here like a thief in the night). As for Eisenhower, he snorts in amusement at all this misplaced sanctitude and steers clear—a man could lose hours in such twaddle; but his Vice President, Richard Nixon, does come here often, pretending disdain (all right, so it's the famous organ of the Eastern Establishment, it's not *that* big), yet not without awe and a certain practiced self-effacement. After all, he is something of a stranger here, and he understands and respects the codes for sojourning in alien lands. Not so, Joe McCarthy. He parades through like a peacock, sporting all his medals, and jabbing his stubby fingers in outrage at any signs of pink stains on the face of the monument (some say these odd blotches are the blood of Innocents, others claim that Roy Cohn and David Schine come at night and sling them there, but most are confident that the Senator knows what he's shouting about).

Even the Rosenbergs turn up. Disparagingly, fearfully, yet eagerly. A sign perhaps . . . ? Ethel wanders dreamily through the entertainment section, purses her lips disapprovingly at the fashion ads, falls into a quiet trance before the Letters to the Editor. Julius, more faithful—a regular dues-payer, in fact—presents himself diligently at Page One every morning at ten o'clock, pressing his nose against the great slabs, frowning through his wire-rimmed spectacles at all this irrelevant history, weeping softly to himself to see such monumental dignity conferred on a world so mad. These bitter tears blur his weak vision, and he is left with little more than the vague sense of a great gray threat, remote, impenetrable, yet for that all the more menacing. Often enough, through his tears, he has discovered himself here on these slabs, or someone they said was himself ("the accused," they call him, but the words keep melting and blurring on him, and what he sees there is "the accursed"), but he has not recognized his own image, grown gigantesque, eviscerated, unseeing: it's like looking into some weird funhouse mirror that stretches one's shape so thin you can see right through it. He used to think that if he could just find his way onto these tablets everything would be all right, but now he knows this is impossible: nothing living ever appears here at all, only presumptions, newly fleshed out from day to day, keeping intact that vast, intricate, yet static tableau —*The New York Times*'s finest creation—within which a reasonable and orderly picture of life can unfold. No matter how crazy it is.

Oh, he shouldn't be surprised, he's a Marxist and has nothing but contempt for the bourgeois capitalist press, yet paradoxically he is also somehow an Americanist and a believer in Science and Freedom and History and Reason, and it dismays him to see cruelty politely concealed in data, madness taken for granted and even honored, truth buried away and rotting in all that ex cathedra trivia—my God! something terrible is about to happen, and they have time to editorialize on mustaches, advertise pink cigarettes for weddings, and report on a lost parakeet! Ah, sometimes he just wants to ram the goddamn thing with his head in an all-out frontal attack, wants to destroy all this so-called history so that history can start again. But even if he martyred himself like that, what would it amount to? just another thread in the fabric, another figure in the eternal tableau, one more little exemplary parable for the hucksters to amuse themselves by, sell a few more books and papers. So much for terrible happenings, good intentions. Two years ago, he came here and stole away, on July the Fourth, a copy of the Declaration of Independence. It was very heavy. Perhaps he thought he could beat down his cell walls with it. But though he pressed his whole body against it until it turned yellow with his fear, he was unable to read what it said. He tried to pretend, but he got mixed up. "It is interesting to read these words," he wrote bravely to Ethel, "concerning free speech, freedom of the press and of religion in this setting. These rights our country's patriots died for can't be taken from the people even by Congress or the Courts." Perhaps, he would often think, squinting helplessly at the quirky script, I need new glasses.

Today, in any case, he is not here, they are not here. Their cells have been stripped and so have they, and they have been moved into the Halfway House in anticipation of the Times Square spectacular, and subsequently, though they will presumably miss this, their own climactic hour on the great slabs. Ethel is now clothed in terrycloth slippers and a cheap green dress with white polka dots, a frowzy second cousin to the one the model's wearing on Tablet 25; Julius has been dressed in a loose T-shirt, buff-colored slippers, and fresh khaki pants. Nevertheless, the Rosenbergs have not lost hope; in fact, they feel pretty certain they've won the day, and all these execution warm-up rituals are just one more last-ditch effort by the government to frighten them into confessing. Well, it won't work.

But if the Rosenbergs are absent this morning, they are not missed. No one is missed here. Or recognized either. For curiously, these same slabs which bring pilgrims together each morning in meditation and wonder, creating a fund of common tropes and expectations, also somehow isolate them. The demand made by these tablets on the faithful is quite literally monumental, and they often experience the illusion suffered by mystics throughout the ages: the Spirit, annunciating reality, displaces it, and the tangible world dissolves even as it is being proclaimed. Thus, one may need to read here tomorrow what momentous events were transpiring just behind the slab one stood before today. People press themselves against the Father's Day advertisements and crisis tabulations, fail to notice the people leaping out of buildings, girls being raped on subway platforms, the colliding traffic. They vibrate before the reported joy of the Rosenbergs at news of their stay and the editorial on moustaches (Julie's has been shaved off), but cannot see the crowds gathering outside the Supreme Court building, the writing on the subway walls: OBJECTIFICATION IS THE PRACTICE OF ALIENATION!

Ah, this strange eventful History, witness of the times, the light of truth and a tissue of crimes, the true poetry, distillation of Rumour, mockery of human affairs, chart and compass, this whimsical prophet with his face turned backwards, reciting the manners, the pursuits, the peoples, and the battles of the race. "Aghast I stood," Pope once said, though ignorant of *The New York Times,* "a monument of woe!" RAIL LABOR CHIEFS / ATTACK EMPLOYERS. Greeks Repulse 3,000. MARIE IS REJECTED / AS FRENCH PREMIER. Rhee Rebuffs Eisenhower. PARAKEET ELUDES JAY. POLO GROUNDERS / TRIP REDLEGS. REDS ACCUSE US. Double Jeopardy. F.B.I. ENTERS CASE. *Eternal Son and Patrol Triumph.* DAVID AND GOLIATH: A miracle of fit and flattery. *Remember, too, that in Hitler's Germany it started by burning books in the streets . . . and ended by burning people in the ovens of Buchenwald.* 'Wishful Thinking' Seen. SOVIET GUNS / CALM SECTOR . . .

Then an Atomic Thriller

This is a story about what might have happened if the Russians had planned to set off an atomic bomb at the Coronation Naval Review that took place at Spithead last Monday. . . .

Spithead, Goliath, Frankenstein, Eternal Son: as always, it is names that provide resonance to the experience of the daily pilgrimage. Guilmartin, Frauenglass, Finerty, and Krock. Kirk. Ike. Braque. Bortz, Bricker, and Bobo Olson. If anything on these slabs is sacred, it is these names. It's an ancient maxim of the tribe: If you violate the name, you violate the man. Even if he is dead. In the old days, before *The New York Times,* if you wished to destroy a man, you inscribed his name on a pot and smashed it. Or stuck a clay image with a pin. Now you attach his name to a sin and print it. Such an act is beyond mere insult or information, it is a magical disturbance of History. It is a holy act and an act of defilement at the same time. It may bring peace and prosperity, it may result in madness and disaster. Is Alger Hiss a Communist? Is Joe McCarthy a Fascist? Is Justice Douglas a Traitor? Is Richard Nixon a Farting Quacker who dreamt of selling his pajamas at Coney Island? What matters is: where are such questions being asked? The great experience of the twentieth century has been to accept the objective reality of time and thus of process—history does not repeat, the universe is not changeless, masses dissolve and slide through the fingers, there are no precognitions—and out in that flow all such assertions may be true, false, inconsequential, or all at the same time. Such things are said every day, and no marvels ensue. But *The New York Times* transforms this time-process into something hard and—momentarily anyway—durable: it is as if these slabs, these great stone tablets, were being hurled out into the timestream, causing the river evermore to eddy and swirl around them. And thus the danger. Envoûtements have been known to destroy the priests who practiced them: the keepers of *The New York Times*, though fascinated by the possibilities, are cautious, and they do not stray often into this dreadful domain. Ike's hard-on is not here this morning. Instead, they report that Dutch Schoch is hopeful. Universal-International wants Ruth Roman to share the adventuresome life with James Stewart in "The Far Country." Timothy J. Doody has entered bankruptcy proceedings. The President had breakfast with Bridges, Dirksen, Magnuson, and Dodge. RHEE IS ASSAILED BY HAMMARSKJOLD. They hie to the world where the commonplace unfolds, the place of freedom and property and ease and security, the land of the more or less likely. They celebrate the names—Sinclair Weeks! Virgil Trucks! Bojangles Robinson and Jabbo Jablonski!—but they avoid the sorcery, the terrible center, the edgeless edge. Louis Appelbaum will be buried today. Okay. And Barfield, Bluhm, and Carrie Batt. BERKMAN— Joseph. You are always with us. Jeremiah Troup. Teresa Love, Eva Roller, and Kathryn Ripberger. Sacred stuff, to be sure, but ritualized. QUICK START FOR MISS SWIFT. *Catch Ma Perkins at 1:15.* No breakaway wildness, no terrible conjurations, just the easy knell of names in mild parade. General Withers Burress. Coach Callow. Nero. Ifu-de. MISS BAREA LAMB / BECOMES FIANCEE. Marie Trotzky. Corliss Lamont and Licurgo Costa. Leo Tolstoy. Walt Dropo. Sugarfoot.

Like gongs in the mind, hinting at echoing infinities, names, names and number: Sarah Dougherty sells the 4-story 1-family dwelling at 825 Carroll Street to Mrs. Rudolphine Dick. General Van Fleet kills a 1950-pound Kodiak bear and the 1952 profit ratio for department stores is the 2nd worst in 19 years. *Mangrum Posts 69.* There are big numbers like the $4998732500 foreign aid bill, little numbers like the 5 tons of gravel and dirt that Jimmy Willis is buried under in Lambertsville. The 6-2 record of Vinegar Bend Mizell. *The 500 Fingers of Dr. T* by Dr. Seuss—You've got to see the 480,000-key piano hit an atomic clinker! WITH STEREOPHONIC SOUND! Allison Choate of Apawamis cards a 77, 55 Chinese are ordered out of the country, Eleanor Hortense Almond dies at 103. Volume declines to 1010000 shares on the New York Stock Exchange. The President is visited by 100 schoolchildren, and the Vice President tells Senator Taft: "I broke 100 at Burning Tree Sunday, Bob!" A kind of accountability, but without irrevocable consequence, gently disturbing the timestream on occasions, but never causing it to leap its banks. The Red Sox scored a record 17 runs in one inning, canteloupe is selling at 19 cents for one pound. Even the patterns are usually familiar ones, suggesting cribbage runs, the inflationary spiral, countdowns: Eighth Race: Perón arrests 7 Radicals, a 4-nation chase nets 6 thieves, the French crisis enters its 5th week, Nick Condos was Martha Raye's 4th husband, and Willi Goettling, leaving 3 dependents, is shot between his 2 eyes by the Russians, losing his 1 life. 37 Down: *Zero*. NIL.

Despite all this effort at secularity, some communicants are nevertheless disturbed by these litanies, discovering in them hints of the terrible abysses beyond the tablets. The very enormity of the monument, at first thought comforting, begins to smother and overwhelm them. A few duck out. Others withdraw to a familiar corner, content to follow a recognizable time-line or two and keep their heads intact. But many begin to lose control. They twitch, lurch forward, jerk back, rush ahead, cower, circle back, then panic and race recklessly through the sanctuary as though lost in a circus or a ceremonial abattoir. *Prince Karl Rudolf Marries.* SOME HOPES FOR U.N. / TOO HIGH. Trouble on First Hole. HERE IS WHAT YOU CAN DO ABOUT IT (if you really care . . .): *The Goddess Strapless in fine white* Push-Button Loading. DULLES' REMARKS SHARP: Don't Neglect Slipping FALSE liquid will help you to handle expanding demands as well as to weather adjustments Fair and a little warmer today highest temperature near 23980 entries in McCalls' dress-your-best *Candidate for the worst-dressed woman* scattered with black polka dots RED PLOT! "What's happening? Where am I?" they scream, tearing frantically through the shrine, plowing into other pilgrims, slapping up against the slabs: *"Let me out!"* But Papagos Sees Need for Speed and CLARK KNEW OF RHEE VIEW, *all seams are bound:* PHARMACISTS ELECT Michigan Assassin 'BLIND FATHER OF 1953' Following Crude Advance with that priceless *American Quality*—FRESHNESS! 19 COPIES OF THIS successful businessman keeps abreast of FAILLE LASTEX WANTED IN Mr. Divine's imaginary atomic explosion bathing suit and bra colors * (T-T) TIMES tested! Churchill Voices Shock *STEAK FOR FATHER'S DAY* Wired for sun it'll blast space helmets back to Mars and put all the cowboy hats out to pasture HOGS moderately active. HOW DOES THIS AFFECT YOU? Sabers Down. *Margaret Truman Passes.* "How long has it been . . . ?"

11.

How to Handle a Bloodthirsty Mob

I was getting dizzy trying to read *The New York Times* on the ride in. Actually, I felt very comfortable with a newspaper in my hands, reading them was a lifetime habit of mine, I'd been an enthusiast since I was a little kid, eccentric about it in fact, but I couldn't read *anything* in the back seat of a moving car. And of all the papers, the goddamn *Times* was the worst. Letters too small and uneven, too gray, too much crammed onto a page—what the hell do we want with all this high-minded gossip, anyway? Had to get through it, though; you never knew what you might need in the middle of a Cabinet meeting. I did know what I was likely to need on the way in, however, and so turned to the sports pages: sooner or later my chauffeur was bound to ask me about yesterday's ballgames or tonight's pitchers. Who are you betting on tonight, Mr. Nixon? He was a Negro and so I always tried to have something good to say about Jackie Robinson or Roy Campanella of the Dodgers. Usually this was pretty easy because both those colored boys were having terrific seasons, they were hot and the team was hot, but not yesterday: I was glad to see that they'd both gone hitless and the Cardinals had whipped the Bums' asses, 12 to 4. On the other hand, my own team, the Washington Senators, had lost to the White Sox and dropped back into the second division, overtaken by the Boston Red Sox, who had made a complete mockery of the game by scoring seventeen runs in one inning—the goddamn *seventh*, needless to say—crushing Detroit, 23 to 3. My God, what's baseball coming to? By coincidence, 23 was exactly how many Boston batters had gone to the plate in that seventh-inning outrage. And it was also, it occurred to me, the number of my football jersey back at Whittier College . . . 23. Well, what of it? Nothing.

I leaned my head back a moment, closed my eyes for a little stomach-stroking seventh-inning stretch of my own, then braced myself and turned back to the front pages. Full of the Berlin, Rosenberg, Korean stories, the government crisis in France, the foreign-aid-bill fight in the House, the port strikes. I glanced through for my own name, noticed that Joe McCarthy was still getting a lot of headlines. That FBI agent's hairy tale of the "goon squad" plot to assassinate Joe had made the front pages of all the papers this morning, Joe was also being widely quoted on his anti-Administration support of Rhee's prisoner release in Korea, and there was even a long story on a new member of his staff, yet another "veteran Red-hunter." Certainly, I wasn't getting that kind of press these days, but this was probably for the best. I wouldn't be running for office again for at least three years, and if I was going to create a sense of momentum, I couldn't start from too near the peak. And I hadn't gone hitless, they'd covered my work in the Senate yesterday, even if it was back in the middle pages, and there was even a report on my casual encounter with Bob Taft: "The Eisenhower Administration is improving its collective golf score, whatever luck it is having with its larger problems." At first glance, I was flattered, pleased I'd pulled it off, but I began to wonder if maybe indirectly it was some kind of smear: trying to say we were out playing golf when we should be facing up to our national problems . . . ? I didn't care if they said that about Eisenhower, but it wasn't fair to hit me with that one, I was only doing my goddamn duty. And then the score, too, they were obviously making fun about that: " 'I broke 100 at Burning Tree Sunday,' Nixon declared, then bowed acknowledgement to Senator Taft's congratulations. Taft was on crutches and appeared to have lost considerable weight, but was 'gay' as he exchanged golfing talk with Nixon." Gay? Maybe I'd made a mistake warming up to a dying man. "Bob, I have news for you . . ."

I sighed. News and more news: I read that New York City was installing "Atomic Age" city lights that turned on by radio, that several teachers had been axed in New York City in apparent reprisals against Albert Einstein, and that they were letting Trotsky's killer out of jail—thank God I wasn't paranoid, or I'd begin to worry it was yet another goddamn anniversary gift to Pat and me. At one time in my life, I actually thought I wanted to be a journalist and took some courses in it at college, but I hated it. Only C's I ever got all through school. It was one thing to witness an event, another to go home and make up some story about it. Anyway, if it was worth witnessing, it was worth getting

into—I couldn't just stand stupidly on the sidelines and take notes, I
had to jump in and play a part. Move things around. And then, whenever I did, and chanced to glance back over my shoulder at those cynical
bastards watching me, grinning, jotting it all down, making a fat living
off my spent hide and life-force like some kind of cannibals, even con-
tributing to my suffering with their niggardly reports and mud-slinging
insinuations, how was I expected to respect and admire them? Besides,
it's a fact, while most publishers might be Republicans, most reporters
were Democrats, or worse—look at how they'd smeared me last fall with
that phony manufactured "fund crisis," for example, hurling charges,
ignoring my refutations—trial by press, that's what it was, worse than
trial by ordeal, not even Tass would have dared to do so much to
damage our national prestige at home and abroad—to hell with them.

Pat was luckier, they were kinder to her. Always had been. "Patricia
Ryan as Daphne Martin had a role which called for temperament, and
did she have it? Plenty. She did some fine acting as she wheeled in and
out of the room, always in a semi-rage. Richard Nixon had a small part
but carried his assignment well." No smaller than hers, goddamn it.
That was from the *Whittier News* in its review of that play we were in,
The Dark Tower, the one where we met. It was about actors in the big
city. An evil man's possession of a young girl's mind. Murder. I was the
playwright, Barry Jones, "a faintly collegiate, eager blushing youth of
24," a small-town greenhorn outsider among these snide and pompous
Easterners, a rare part for me since I usually played old men. Pat played
the part of Daphne Martin, "a tall, dark, sullen beauty of 20, wearing a
dress of great chic and an air of permanent resentment," in short, a hot-
pants actress on the make, tough and lethal. In the play we ended up
going off to get married, but it was meant as a kind of cynical joke.
"Jones & Martin, card tricks and sex appeal." It wasn't an altogether
pleasant part to play. All the way through the thing, they made fun of
me, whether I was onstage or not, made fun of my open-faced self-
confidence, my naïveté, my youth, my name, my piano playing, my
writing, my taste, it probably put Pat off me for months. Even as she
and I made our final exit, Pat slipped back onstage to tell the real hero:
"Listen—as soon as he's tucked in his crib I'll call you up!" But they all
forgot one thing. I wrote the play that was the title of this play, the play
within the play—or perhaps the play that embraced the play. *The Dark
Tower* was mine, and they all lived in it. . . .

"Eh? Stole what?"

"Stole second, Mr. Nixon. That's how him and Sammy White scored
when Umphlett singled, see . . ."

"Oh. Yes, I see . . ." I realized John had been talking for some time. Trying to tell me about that mad 17-run inning. "A good move . . ." While John talked, I turned to the entertainment pages, looking for some place to go Sunday on our anniversary. Washington was out, the National was closed, getting ready for *Guys and Dolls*, nothing on but *Man and Superman* and *Show Boat*. Some good boxing matches, but she'd probably never go along with that. Maybe the new *Cinerama* or one of those 3-D movies like *House of Wax*. I'd feel silly wearing those goddamn cardboard glasses, though.

". . . So with the bases loaded, Jim Piersall singled and Dick Gernert homered, so that was seven runs in . . ."

"Izzat so?" I smiled. I'm generally very good at these one-to-one relationships.

"The pitcher come up and singled and they started the whole lineup over again. Sammy White . . ."

There was a new Dr. Seuss movie premiering in New York about a boy who hated piano lessons, but it looked a little childish. Mary Healy looked like she had big boobs, though. And another new one with Sylvana Pampanini in it called *O.K., Nero*—wasn't that the guy who used corpses as torches? A little heavy maybe for the season. To tell the truth, the idea of going to a movie bored the hell out of me, boobs or no boobs. I recalled the days when I was investigating the Hollywood Ten with HUAC, that proximity to the stars—in fact, I was surprised how ordinary they seemed. There were Bogart and Bacall out there, pushovers for the Reds. Cooper was a hopeless dope, I haven't been able to sit through one of his pictures since, even if he was on our side, and guys like Menjou and Disney and McCarey weren't much better. Then came the stoolies, guys like Parks—whoo. . . . Made me angry in a way. Of course, having lived near Hollywood all my life—and even married, as it were, into the industry—I'd never been really star-struck like other people. And besides, there was my father's eccentric habit of naming all his cows after movie stars—after you've milked Lillian Gish and remarked on her swollen blue teats, slapped Greta Garbo on the rump, and cleaned up Mary Pickford's shit, it's hard to be romantic about them.

"No kidding!" I said, since John seemed to have paused in his story.

"Right, so they bring in another pitcher, the third one this inning—and *he* can't get the ball across the plate! He walks one guy, filling the bases, then walks Gernert, forcing a run in! And then the pitcher comes up and gets another single . . . !"

One thing I wanted to do was go in to New York and see Arthur

Miller's *The Crucible* after all I'd heard about it, but we couldn't risk giving it any kind of official sanction, and besides, Edgar was probably photographing the audience for his files. Could go and denounce it publicly, maybe. Should get a headline or two. Protocol-wise, though, the smart thing would be to take her to that film of the British corona-tion ceremonies which was such a surprise box-office smash. England had spent five and a half million dollars to crown the Queen and now they were going to get it all back in film royalties. Make history, make money . . .

"Say, uh, how much longer is this going to go on, John?"

"It's wild, ain't it, Mr. Nixon?" he laughed. I rattled the paper impa-tiently. "Well, so Gene Stephens singles, see, and that's his third hit of the inning, a new all-time record. Umphlett comes up and *he* singles, and Sammy White comes in, scoring his record-breaking third run of the inning. The next guy walks, filling the bases—"

"My God! Listen, I tell you what, John . . ."

"But then finally Kell flies out to retire the side."

"Ah. He probably got bored and did it on purpose."

"How's that, Mr. Nixon?"

"I said, sometimes that's how the ball bounces, John, we all have to live with our victories and defeats, only teams that believe in themselves can rise to their challenges."

"Oh yeah. I see what you mean, Mr. Nixon . . ."

There was a summer ice show, "Scents and Nonsense," on at the Hotel New Yorker, I noticed. Pat might like that, she used to be hot for ice skating before we got married, I busted my head more than once trying to keep up with her, never did get the hang of it. She was a real time-waster, dancing, skating, gadding about, it was a relief to get married and get all that over with. Better skip the ice show, she might get ambitious again. It occurred to me that I had been living with Pat for nearly thirteen years, thirteen years this Sunday, and yet in a real sense she was a complete stranger to me. Only when she was chewing me out did she become somehow real, but the rest of the time . . . well, it was almost as if I'd married some part of myself, and Pat was only the accidental incarnation of that part. Do we all do this? Is this what marriage is all about, finding fleshly embodiments of our ghostly selves, making ourselves whole?

I'd found her very gloomy at breakfast this morning for some reason. Feeling neglected maybe. I remembered the way I'd found her last night. My Wild Irish Potato. People have noted my unusual empathy with despondent people; on the other hand, Pat gets despondent all the time and this only tees me off.

Julie had greeted me at the kitchen door with a sticky strawberry-jam kiss, then had wrinkled up her nose and said: "Oh, Daddy, your *beard!*"

"Don't be silly," I'd said impatiently. "I just shaved it." This had got to be a joke with the girls and I was a little tired of it. I wondered what would happen if Tricia and Julie grew up and met and fell in love with the Rosenberg boys. Maybe that was what was troubling Pat. Looking at her then, standing there at the stove frying bacon in her bathrobe, she had seemed like all those well-washed people from obscure little California towns and suburbs who used to come to see me in July and August when I was their Senator, shake my hand, get an autograph, talk about the weather back home or the condition of the roads or some pet theory about the Red Menace. Plain and simple people, not very bright, not very well informed, nice though, and they were voters. And they were on my side. Pat was a voter. She was on my side. But, no, it was more than that, she was the choice that gave others trust in me, earned their vote. What do the common people care about tidelands disputes or wars in Asia? The important thing to them is who you married, how you live, what kind of kids you've got. I married Pat and revealed to the world something about myself, and so became Vice President of the United States of America.

"Sit down, Dick, and eat your breakfast," she'd said dully, munching toast. "I told John you'd be out in a few minutes. What happened to your face?"

"Eh? Nothing. An accident." I'd dropped irritably into a chair, ducked my head in the *Congressional Record*. Why was it, whenever I was at home, I felt guilty?

"An accident?" One trouble with Pat was that when she chewed you could see the way her jaws worked.

"I, yes, well, I . . . I ran into some . . . demonstrators last night. Near the Supreme Court." Perhaps this is true, I'd thought. After all, history is never literal. If it were, it would have no pattern at all, we'd all be lost. "They, uh . . . one of them hit me with a placard. Nothing, really."

She'd looked at me like my mother used to when I came in from playing touch football in a muddy field. "Oh, Dick!" she'd scolded. I'd realized that it relaxed her to be able to scold me about something.

While I shoveled down my breakfast, conscious of my chauffeur out there waiting for me, we'd discussed where and how we'd meet if they held the Times Square executions tonight. I'd told her about my having to attend that Republican fund-raising dinner over in New Jersey afterwards, had said I was leaving her the car, she'd said she didn't really want to go to the executions, I'd said she had no choice.

"What's a eggsy-cushion, Daddy?" Tricia had asked.

"You'll find out tonight," I'd said crisply, scraping my chair back. Some other time her question might have been cute, but I wasn't in the mood. "Julie, damn it, stop picking your nose at the table!"

Pat had sighed and turned back to the bacon. I knew she didn't like to go to these public ceremonies, I shouldn't have been peeved, but I'd felt like she'd just turned down my plans for our anniversary. Watching her there at the stove while I finished tying my shoes, I'd wondered if her bathrobe was inflammable. Ruth Greenglass had got burned once standing too close to a stove in her nightgown. Nearly killed her. And six months pregnant at the time. We'd just passed a bill about it in the Senate yesterday, the so-called "exploding sweaters" bill, which at least five Senators had voted for thinking it was an anti-pornography law. Ruth had been feverish for weeks, her whole body a mess—like a foretaste of the electric chair. This was shortly before the FBI picked up David. He'd got burned, too, trying to put out Ruth's flames. Lot of goddamn fire in this case. Everything from the Greenglass kitchen stove to talk of an atomic holocaust. Holocaust: burnt whole. Just what the Rosenbergs had to look forward to. "Flaming Reds," the papers called them. "This infernal conspiracy." The day's hot news story. "Gonna put their feet to the fire," Uncle Sam had told me out at Burning Tree: "They've inflamed a lotta passions out in the world, let 'em get their own frizzed a little!" Maybe that was what my dream last night about Pat's burning bush was all about. . . .

"I'll see you tonight!" I'd snapped gruffly, and stamped out of the house into the sun, struggling with my face. We lived in a nosy neighborhood. It ticked me off that she didn't kiss me good-bye in the doorway any more.

And what if she died, I wondered: was I ready for that? Tough, of course. It would hurt. I'd be lost without Pat. It'd win a lot of votes, though. People might even, for once, vote *for* me, instead of against the other guy. Then maybe, later, when I'd got over it, if I ever did, a White House wedding like Grover Cleveland had. In the Blue Room, little Frances Folsom, just twenty-two years old. Tyler'd done well, too, waited two years after his wife had gone and then married a twenty-four-year-old. Woodrow Wilson, there were a lot of precedents. Maybe Uncle Sam even liked it that way, a source of energy and renewal: keep the

Incarnation's pecker up. That was the one thing he was obsessed about: staying young. To him, a closed frontier was like a hardened artery and too much government, too much system, too much political theory, was a kind of senility. It was what made him hate socialists: "a bunch of goddamn zombies," he called them. "Dead before they're born!" Sometimes he frightened me with his vehemence about it. "If those lizards ever get their world revolution, it'll be all over for 'em!" he told me one day out at Burning Tree. It must have been one of the first times I'd played golf with him. "This excitement out on the perimeter is all they've got. Inside, son, there's nothin' but old mold and fungus. They're learnin' the hard way what our Old West was all about, all that tumult and butchery and wild unsartinty. Two pollrumptious screamers shootin' it out on a dusty Main Street over a saddlepack fulla gold: now them two fellers is about as alive as anybody's ever *gonna* be! Socialists are skeered of this, they want everything buttoned down fair and logical and all screwin' up antedeluvian *quiet*, which is to say, they don't want nothin' to *happen!* What's there to live for in a world like that, I ask you—all them sissies runnin' your life for you? No, the earth belongs to the livin', boy, not to cold pickles! You can't tame what don't stand still and nothin' in this universe does! Einstein put his finger on it a long time ago—oh, he's gone off the deep end lately, I know, but listen, he knew what America was all about: don't let the grass grow under your feet! saddle up, keep movin', anything can happen! Ya know, people useter think of time like some kinda movin' knife edge cuttin' acrost the entire universe, but that was on accounta they was locked up in a room in Europe somewhere and not heedin' what was roarin' up over here! America was on the go—not only on horses, but on wheels, on trains, on steamships and automobiles, even into the air. Einstein seen this. And while he was skinnin' his eyes for what this signified, it suddenly come to his attention that a movin' clock appears to run slow set off agin an identical clock sittin' still and the—hope I'm not too fast for you, son . . . ?"

"No! No, I . . ."

"Bodies in motion just don't age as fast, that's what it boils down to. America, by stayin' off its ass, was stayin' young! No surprise Albert come to live here when he got his chance! This here's a country of beginnin's, of projects, of vast designs and expectations! It's got no past; all has an onward and prospective look! The fountain of youth! Lookit me!" he'd cried, and had rolled off a few lively cartwheels, flipped over his golf cart, and done a handstand on a putter, while clicking his boot heels so hard he drew sparks.

"What's that, John?" I asked.

"I said, there's supposed to be twelve thousand of them here today, Mr. Nixon," my chauffeur said.

I realized we'd been slowed to a crawl, and there was a terrific traffic jam up ahead of us around Dupont Circle. I clutched my newspaper. "Twelve thousand what?"

"Demonstrators. You know, the atom spies . . ."

I saw them now, moving down Connecticut toward the White House. "Can't we—can't we do something—?"

"I can try to cut north up toward Howard University, then down Capitol . . ."

Howard was a Negro university and there were a lot of those people in the pro-Rosenberg movement. I felt a sudden twinge of distrust: was John leading me into a trap? "We don't have time to go to the office now," I snapped. "We'd better get straight to the White House!"

"Yessir. I'll try to cut down to the Mall."

But at Washington Circle on Pennsylvania, seven blocks from the White House, there was no movement at all: a solid mass of traffic, people, placards, and photographers. John swerved left, and left again, but all the cars were bumper to bumper, and people were running back and forth in the streets. I was nervous, so I decided to distract myself by working the *Times* crossword puzzle. I found it on a back page, nested among book ads. My eye fell on the first clue, 1 Across: That's easy, I thought with a shudder: GOOF. I suddenly saw the puzzle as a kind of matrix, a field of play which mirrored the structure of the newspaper and thus history itself, the paradigmatic range of "news" and possibility, crossed with real "time-arrow chain-of-events," I felt like Alice lost on her chessboard. I read the clues: why all this business about plays, food, cartoonists, rats, God, women, and cosmetics, I wondered? AHAB was there, SAN ANTONIO, NEGRO, and ROAMERS. 23 Down: HEAT. I dragged my eyes away from the crossword puzzle to the book review: it was about an "atomic thriller," *Atom at Spithead*. Even before I saw it, I knew it would be something like this. Adlai Stevenson's *Campaign Speeches* were being advertised, and a novel called *The Singer Not the Song*: "He could not resist using the girl as one last diabolic weapon. . . ." From all over the page, words jumped out at me: SOCIALISM . . . BUCHENWALD . . . EISENHOWER . . . FRANKENSTEIN . . . BLOOD . . . TENEMENT . . . REVOLUTION . . . CHECKMATE—we were stopped dead. "I'll walk, John!" I cried. I ripped the crossword puzzle out and stuffed it in my pocket, jumped out of the limousine.

Once on foot, I found it much easier to keep moving. Not so many people as it had seemed inside the car. Just enough, together with the sightseers, to bottle up traffic at the intersections and make it seem worse than it was. It also helped that they were mostly moving in the same direction. At first, I supposed they were headed for the White House, and I decided to circle around behind them, past the Treasury and in by the East Wing, but once I reached the back side of Lafayette Square, I could see they were all moving on east. It took me a panicky moment to realize that their objective was not my Senate Office Building, but only the Supreme Court. But though I felt relieved by that, I had to recognize that the worst, nevertheless, was still before me: crossing the park and Pennsylvania Avenue through all this lawless rabble to the White House gates. I began to regret leaping out of the car so impulsively like that.

A mob, you see, does not act intelligently. Those who make up a mob do not think independently. They do not think rationally. They are likely to do irrational things, including even turning on their leaders. Individually, people in a mob are cowardly; only collectively, goaded on by a leader, will a mob appear to act courageously. A mob is bloodthirsty. A taste of blood will whet its appetite for more violence and for more blood. Nothing must be done which will tend to accentuate these characteristics. A mob has lost its temper collectively. An individual dealing with a mob must never lose his or he will be reduced to its level, and become easy prey for it. He must be as cold in his emotions as a mob is hot, as controlled as the mob is uncontrolled, concentrating entirely on the problem which faces him and forgetting about himself, keyed up for battle but not jittery. Since those who make up a mob are basically cowards, one must never show fear in the face of a mob, blocking out any thought of it by a conscious act of will. Since a mob is stupid, it's important to confront it with unexpected maneuvers: take the offensive, don't panic, do the unexpected, but do nothing rash. I knew all this. Nevertheless, I was scared shitless and could hardly think.

Intuitively, I just kept moving. I put the U.S. Chamber of Commerce at my back like a big brother and plunged straight ahead, into the park and toward the White House. I saw it, I knew it immediately: this crowd is all unfriendly—the Phantom has touched them, I thought, he's invaded them, they're all contaminated, we will have to liberate them all, as we've done with the Rosenbergs. I kept my head ducked and bulled hopefully ahead—so far they hadn't noticed me. Just a block, that damned square, but it seemed endless—I felt like I was crossing all of Gettysburg. I prayed to God to get me through safely. I prayed to Uncle Sam, I prayed to Pat. "In the name of Jesus Christ!" I whistled softly between my clenched teeth. What troubled me most was the complete unreasoning hate in their faces: this mob, I recognized, is a killer mob! I suspected some of them were even doped up, and I feared that, if they saw who I was, they'd get out of hand. They carried placards, shouted, and seemed to be picking up things they might throw. It made me almost physically ill to see the fanatical frenzy in the eyes of those teenagers; anyway, something was making me quite ill. I felt absolute hatred for the tough Communist agitators who were driving children to this irrational state, and I wanted to shout at them, or scream, or bite them or something, but somehow I kept a grip on myself, knowing that above all I had to control my emotions and think calmly. The test of leadership is whether one has the ability, as Kipling said, to keep his head while others are losing theirs. By this time, I was virtually running, shoulders hunched like a fullback, snorting desperately.

I slowed. I noticed I was drawing a lot of attention. I worried I might have a heart attack. Or some other kind of seizure, I could hardly breathe. The mob turned toward me and started to close in. It was essential, I knew, that I bust right through: if I turned back now, it would not be simply a case of their bluffing out Richard Nixon, but of the United States itself putting its tail between its legs and running away from a gang of Communist thugs. For an instant, the realization passed through my mind: *I might be killed!*—and then it was gone, mind and all. They were nearly on me. I stopped abruptly. Then I lurched forward. Everybody must have been surprised: as I plunged on, straight at them, amazed at my own impetus, the mob stumbled backwards. In a larger sense, I recognized, this was another round in a contest which has been waged from the beginning of time between those who believe in the right of free expression and those who advocate and practice mob rule to deny that right. I might have calmed myself with such a thought, but there was no time—one of the ringleaders, a typical case-hardened Communist operative, stepped into my path, blocking me off, a look of cold hatred in his eyes. And I realized then, as this was going on, that right here was the ruthlessness and the determination, the fanaticism of the enemy that we faced! That was what I saw in his face. This was Communism as it really is. He opened his mouth—I felt like I was back in the lion's cage with Sheba. *Oh my God—!*

"Excuse me, Mr. Nixon," he said, the rest closing up behind, forcing me to pull up short. "Could I have your autograph?"

"What?" I shouted. This startled them and they fell back a step. I noticed then for the first time that the placards they were carrying read DEATH TO THE JEWISH TRAITORS! and THE HOT SEAT FOR THE ROSENBERGS

—SIZZLE 'EM! It came to me then that this was my own constituency. The range and scope of this crisis began to fall into a pattern. *"Can you have my autograph?"* I yelped, repeating his question to give myself time to think, and also, hopefully, to stop my hands from shaking. I groped for words, for a phrase, something tough and pungent I could exit on. I wanted to do more than simply mouth prepared platitudes, but my mind was completely locked up, like the traffic around Washington Circle. All I could think of was: everyone in politics knows a Vice President cannot chart his own course, it's not my fault! They stared at me, somewhat amazed. A young college boy with a friendly smile was carrying a big picture of the electric chair with the legend HOME COOKING, KOSHER STYLE!, and I saw a priest with a sign that read THE ROSENBERGS ARE MORTAL ENEMIES OF THE ENTIRE HUMAN RACE! I realized it was going to be another hot day. I was sweating like a stoat. "The issue is not whether or not I can give you my autograph," I said at last, leaning toward them as a coach would lean toward his players in a huddle, *"but rather the survival of the nation itself!"* I gazed at them with a very heavy look, and the few who were still smiling went blank, their jaws dropping. For a fraction of a second there, I gave them all a sense of what it felt like to be at the center of things, drew them all in to the High Councils of Power, showed them a glimpse of the brink and its peril. Then I smiled, nodded, clapped a shoulder, waved to someone at the back as though recognizing him, and lunged on through. They parted in astonishment. This has been very successful, I thought.

Except for the mounted U.S. Park Police, some parked buses, and a couple of lonely Red Top cabs that had managed somehow to get through the traffic jam further up the street, Pennsylvania was empty as I crossed it. A long way across, and I felt very self-conscious. Then, off to my right, I saw them: the real demonstrators, marching toward me, seven abreast, down Pennsylvania, headed toward the Supreme Court. What now? I wondered, freezing in my tracks: should I stop and confront them?—and nearly got run down by a trolley car whistling up from behind. Jesus, I thought, picking myself up and scrambling on across the goddamn street, this is going to be one helluva day. At the White House gates, still hurrying forward, I looked back over my shoulder at the crowd in Lafayette Square, thinking: you've got to be careful in a situation like that, you have to think all those things through—and plowed into a child standing there on the sidewalk. I glanced around. Luckily, no photographers had seen this. I set the boy back on his feet, brushed him off, skinny little kid, about the age of my daughters, with big dark eyes and baggy pants. Like the waifs out of those Horatio Alger novels. Very intense and even, somehow, mysterious. I'd given him a thumping whack and he wasn't even crying. He looked up at me as though he were lost, as though looking for a friend or a father, and I thought: he's beautiful, this child! He reminded me of all those March of Dimes posters. I wanted to hug him to my breast, to protect him from all this, to kiss him, I wanted to reach into my pocket and give him something. "Don't be afraid, son," I whispered. His nose was running. I wiped it with my own handkerchief. "It's all right." He gazed up at me with those soulful eyes, parting his small lips—I *know* this child, I thought. As though from a dream, a beautiful dream. I seemed to recall green hills, a rippling brook, a rustic cabin, and inside—and then I realized who it was he looked like. I pushed him away in alarm, wiped my hands nervously on my pants, and, shuddering, hurried on through the White House gates. That haunting face: it belonged to Ethel Rosenberg!

12.

A Roman Scandal of Roaring Spectacle

The special session of the Supreme Court is the tourist sensation of the summer. Thousands stand in line for the 350 available seats to watch the spectacle of the nation's highest court, called back to the bench from golf links and fishing boats, having to decide overnight whether or not to execute without further delay "the principals," as Judge Kaufman has called them, "in this diabolical conspiracy to destroy a God-fearing nation."

It has been a dramatic move. It's obvious that Uncle Sam and his government in Washington are determined, their Fourteenth Wedding Anniversary Celebration having been taken away from them, to exterminate Ethel and Julius Rosenberg now as quickly as possible. And not just out of spite: the anxious haste with which Uncle Sam has summoned the Elders back to National Headquarters suggests he might be fighting for his very life. There's the mounting world pressure of course, the military buildup on both sides, the threat of all-out nuclear exchange, but it's more than that—it's almost as though there is something critical about the electrocutions themselves, something down deep inside, a form, it's as though events have gone too far, as though there's an inner momentum now that can no longer be tampered with, the nation is too deeply committed to this ceremony, barriers have already come down, the ghosts have been sprung and there's a terror loose in the world, an excitement: if the spies don't die and die now, something awful might happen, the world's course might get bent—Look! Out in the world, the frontiers are crumbling—but as the people draw back toward the center to restore their strength, they find an appalling void right where the axis of the earth ought to be, a big black hole inviting them to fall in and be lost forever! There are actually a few who hold that the executions may not have been Uncle Sam's idea in the first place, but rather a devious and calculated maneuver by the Phantom, either to distract Uncle Sam from actions on the frontiers, or maybe . . . maybe to get everybody down to Times Square and then let them have it! Is this what is driving Uncle Sam? Is this why Herbert Brownell has acted so swiftly and with such transparent alarm? No wonder the Courthouse is packed!

Of course, some people scoff at this. They pretend not to see the black hole and they don't respond to the apocalyptic funk. What kind of a rube do these neo-latitudinarians take Sam Slick for? they ask. They even conjecture that the American Superhero may have coaxed Justice Douglas into this brief delay just to heighten the drama and draw a bigger crowd. After all, is Uncle Sam the maker and shaper of world history, or isn't he? Just as he might have engineered the border troubles, goaded the Phantom into exposing himself around the world, provoked the strikes and boycotts, and altered a few marquees and billboards himself just to ignite the occasion with a few titillating "Fee-Fie-Fo-Fums." Some skeptics are dubious about all these anniversary patterns in the first place, and others argue that Uncle Sam simply needed this delay to finish getting the stage built. Or to negotiate an end to that "iron curtain" around the Statue of Liberty. Or to extract confessions from the Rosenbergs by making them live their last hours over and over again.

In any case it's certainly true, no matter whether Uncle Sam and/or the Phantom wanted it this way or not, the Rosenbergs suddenly have a terrific rating—overnight they've shot past every show in the country, and up in the city their executions are already being acclaimed as the biggest thing to hit Broadway since the invention of the electrical spectacular. To be sure, there's not much competition this time of year, it's the off-season for theater and rerun time on TV, but short of a Bowl Game or a return from the other world by Harry Houdini (and where would he appear? the old Hippodrome is gone . . .), it is difficult to imagine any act outdrawing the Rosenbergs. And it's not simply because they're to die, people die every day—look at poor unlamented and uncelebrated Willi Goettling who got executed over in East Berlin: he played to a few pigs and an empty field—no, it's the way they've been linked, like all top box-office draws since the days of the Roman Circus, to archetypes. Irving Saypol and Judge Kaufman have helped them in this. So have Uncle Sam, Congress, the press, the FBI. They have worked hard at it themselves, though they have not achieved exactly the image they sought. And they have become—no less than Valentino and Garbo, Caruso and Bernhardt, the Barrymores and the Bumsteads, Rin Tin Tin and Trigger—true Stars, their performances forever engraved upon the American imagination, their fame assured for generations to come. Sooner will the nation forget Walter Pidgeon and Greer Garson than Julius and Ethel Rosenberg.

Waiting for the Court to arrive, the crowds on the Mall exchange rumors, take snapshots of each other with Baby Brownies, buy pop and ice cream from passing vendors, sun themselves on the grass, listen to the newscasters on their portable radios. The Justice Department is said to be working on back-up moves just in case things go wrong this morning, but there seem to be few doubts which way the Court will vote. Less certain is the outcome, also due today, in another trial out in Hawaii: that of the six longshoremen—the so-called "Aloha Shirt Set"—accused of Communism. The trial has already lasted seven and a half months, during which time eighty-three witnesses have unloaded more than three and a half million words of testimony, and now the jury—all American nationals, but of mixed Chinese, Japanese, Hawaiian, and Caucasian descent, a real goddamn zoo in the minds of most statesiders —has been locked up for over a hundred hours trying to reach a verdict. They're nervous about it, because they're aware that Hawaii's prospective membership in the Union may well rest on the results.

This seems to be the morning's pattern: there are no clear victories. Five thousand Red demonstrators attack a pro-Mossadegh rally in Teheran, but are repulsed—though Mossadegh himself, like Rhee, is a pain in Uncle Sam's fundament. In Quezon City, a security guard and a leader of a Huk rebel outfit trying to sabotage Manila's water supply are shot dead before any damage is done (that's good), but in Indochina, the French Army's biggest fuel dump is ablaze and still erupting after a daring night raid by Vietminh commandos (that's bad). The four-man Vietminh suicide team has run through a wall of French machine-gun fire to hurl firebombs on the steel storage tanks in Haiphong, the tanks exploding just like in all the movies, big orange balls of roiling fire billowing up into the skies, thousands of gallons of burning oil spilling out onto the highway—hundreds of French troops and volunteers are needed just to contain it. Authorities report that ". . . at least one of the raiders was hit." Probably.

In Malaya, Sir Gerald Templer orders house-to-house searches and confiscation of all rice in excess of a week's portion, to keep the villagers from feeding the terrorists ("This is not a punishment! It will enable you to tell the terrorists truthfully that you cannot spare rice for them!"), and progress is reported in the sticky Burma-China talks in Thailand, but while the Legion of Superheroes are fighting it out amongst themselves over what to do with Royal Dutch Shell's rich oil holdings in Sumatra, guerrilla bands sweep down from Galdengoen Mountain hideouts south of Jakarta and murder sixty villagers. As Uncle Sam has often said, muttering through a rubbery jaw, his thumb hooked under a sheriff's badge: "It is a *condition* what confronts us—not a theory!"

WORLD NEWS PUTS DAMPERS ON STOCKS, *The New York Times* has revealed this morning. The instability of the world is frightening people. So are the Soviet "peace offensive" and the threat of a Korean truce. Volume on the Exchange dwindled to a nine-month low yesterday, and is off to an even slower start this morning. The value of such A-bomb stocks as Du Pont is sinking. General Motors, American Telephone, U.S. Steel, General Electric: all down. There's a rash of strikes, new taxes, and rising prices, including hikes in the cost of crude oil, steel, cigarettes, and linoleum. Store sales are down and the profit ratio is at a nineteen-year low. There is frank talk of a coming recession. The American Management Association, ingathering at the Statler, is told that "American industry should prepare now to weather a business recession in order to ward off government intervention, should one occur." Companies are warned to get rid of undesirable personnel now: "Don't discover them when you are trying to cut expenses in a depression!"

In an attempt to offset these fears, Treasury Secretary George Humphrey has let it be known that there is "no reason to fear peace, U.S. military spending is still necessary, armistice in Korea or no." Defense Secretary Charlie Wilson has backed him up on this with talk of the arms race and the need for a lot of new weaponry, and General Gruenther of SHAPE has announced his plans to make use of new atomic weapons in the defense of Europe, few ground troops: a proxy attack by one of Russia's satellites is expected there any day, and a lot of gear is going to get shot up. This morning, in a fresh move, two U.S. admirals—Combs and Oftsie—are sent into the arena: testifying before a Senate Appropriations subcommittee, they urge approval of Ike's request for $115,000,000 in new funds for guided missiles and planes capable of delivering "small" atomic bombs, and lean irascible Admiral Oftsie, pushing for more new supercarriers like the *Forrestal,* says: "Small atomic weapons have created unlimited possibilities for naval aviation," because there are many targets against which the "small bomb is the preferable weapon." Which encourages the First National Bank of Boston to issue this statement:

> The pessimism in some quarters, based on a belief that a Korean truce would have a depressive influence upon business activity, has been substantially modified. . . . It is now clearly indicated that there has been no fundamental change in the Soviet objective and that we must maintain a strong defense program. While savings will be made by the elimination of waste, indications are that no sharp curtailments are expected in our military outlay for some time to come.

And there are other reasons to modify the pessimism down at the Exchange this morning. Television set production is up 70 percent, for example, doing even better than pornography and missiles. Births are still outnumbering deaths nearly two to one, assurances of an expanding market. And there's always American ingenuity: already this year it has come up with such products as plastic carpets, paper snow fences, blind-men's canes that glow in the dark, cockpit listeners, 3-D movies, propane locomotives, chlorophyll cigarettes, and Eisenhoppers. Net sales of General Foods is up from $196 million in 1942 to $701 million today, and mainly, they say, thanks to research and packaging. A packing company has designed a new hide puller, a revolving safety knife, hydraulically operated, that tears a carcass right out of its birthday suit without injuring either suit or meat, a real breakthrough, while out in the nation's meat-packing center a photo of Marilyn Monroe, still in her hide but nothing else, has been uncovered by a horny young cartoonist —and who knows? if he can come up with a magazine to go around it, he may well have the publishing sneak hit of the year with it.

This sensationalist trend in the nation's magazines is worrying to some people, of course. The sex and violence in them have been attacked by everybody from the Phantom's *Daily Worker*—which claims to be offended by "strip cartoons" and "hate campaigns" and "sex reports" and shocked at stories like "Girls in Gangs" and "Love Harvest in Blood"—to Arkansas Congressman Ezekiel C. Gathings, whose House committee, investigating salacious pocket books, comics, and cheesecake girlie mags, finds that the industry has "degenerated into a medium for the dissemination of artful appeals to sensuality, immorality, filth, perversion, and degeneracy." The cheap pornography of the likes of Steinbeck, Farrell, Caldwell, and Moravia is cited by Gathings's committee, along with the depravity of such newsstand successes as *Whisper, Keyhole, Foo, Nifty, Zip,* and *Wham!,* just as the *Worker* goes out after *Flirt, Titter, Wink,* and *Climax, The Saturday Evening Post, G.I. Joe Comics.* But, as Zeke Gathings himself has to admit: "Pornography is big business." And in times like these, one must not, as they say, look a gift horse in his private parts. "Make money," Mother Luce has said, "be proud of it; make more money, be prouder of it! School yourself for the long battle of freedom in this country!" And so, if it works, who can blame the American publishing industry for running pictures of girls in their panties, dead soldiers bubbling blood, or violated virgins, or for keeping up with current events by printing timely stories this week like "The Bride and the Hangman," "The Night Love Turned to Terror," or "We Played and We Paid—the truth about two who took the easy way"?

Likewise the movie-palace managers, struggling against the very TV boom that's cheering others: they're also swinging with the new tits-and-blood trend, what else can they do? and this weekend—at least in the area around Times Square—have booked timely films like *High Treason, A Slight Case of Larceny, Devil's Plot, Three Sinners,* and *The Atomic City,* a flick about G-men hunting down H-bomb spies. They have no illusions, of course, about drawing away any of the nighttime trade from the Times Square burnings themselves. But it's not yet certain just when that show will go on, maybe not for weeks, and meanwhile the streets are filling up with restless undirected masses and the summer sun is climbing in the sky—they can hardly be blamed for trying to lure in a piece of the popcorn action at the very least. If they don't get it, after all, the pickpockets will. Indeed, it's a service to Uncle Sam to keep these potentially inflamed and aimless mobs off the streets and air-conditioned while he's sorting things out at the Supreme Court and the President's Cabinet meeting. So some play the sex angle, others the executions, and many attempt a bit of both at the same time. Rita Hayworth dances for the Baptist's head in *Salome* at the Rivoli, for example, and "Terror Stalks the Screen in 3 Dimensions" at the Paradise in *Man in the Dark.* Three-D "THRILLS that almost TOUCH YOU" can be had all over town today, but the one that's lining them up in the streets is *House of Wax,* which, made by a one-eyed man, is all about reality and illusion and famous people going up in flames. Julius Rosenberg and his boy used to play a kind of baseball game in their ghetto flat using a paddle and a ball on an elastic string, and *House of Wax* pays tribute to this with a stunning bat-and-ball sequence that sends people leaping right out of their seats. "The Year's Shock Drama," *Invasion USA,* is on at the Fox, and *O.K. Nero!,* "A Roman Scandal of Roaring Spectacle," is at the Globe. *Murder Without Crime* at the Beekman shares an imaginative twin bill with *Double Confession,* starring Peter ("the droop-eyed cinemenace," as TIME say) Lorre, whose wife, Karen, is out in Las Vegas this week, suing him for divorce. The Grande puts on an FBI thriller, *Walk East on Beacon,* said to be the story of the original Groun'-Hog Hunt, and at the 6000-seat Roxy, that palatial old queen from the movie heyday of the twenties, *Titanic* gives way to *Pickup on South Street,* "The Double-Barreled Triple-Powered Forty-Five-Calibre Rocker-Socker of the Year: IT'S A BLOW-TORCH!" A veritable paradigm of the times! As TIME, open-eyed, sums it up:

> a pickpocket (richard wid
>   mark) slaps a former road
>   house entertainer (jean
> peters) in the teeth
>   knocks her out with a right
>   to the jaw and revives her by pour
> ing a bottle of beer in her face
>
> the b-girl retaliates
>   by conking him over the head
>   with another beer bottle a communist
> spy (richard kiley) beats up
>   and shoots the girl hits a cop
>   over the head with a pistol
> and kills an eccentric old necktie
>
> peddler (thelma ritter) the pick
>   pocket knocks out the spy by smash
>   ing his head against a wall
> slugs it out with him on a sub
>   way platform and on the tracks
>   in front of an oncoming train
> all this mayhem is brought on when
>
> the pickpocket discovers some micro
>   film containing military
>   secrets in a wallet he has lifted
> from the b-girl's purse by the fadeout
>   the pickpocket and the b-girl have found
>   true love and government agents
> with the pickpocket's help have smashed a
>
>   red
>   spy
>   ring

Yes, there are happy endings, but the world is tough and you have to work for them. No one knows that better than Uncle Sam, who has been flying about the world all morning, coping with the Phantom's overnight malice, sweeping up the Free World streets ravaged by an alien ardor, hurling abuse at Russian tanks in East Berlin, rounding up prisoners in South Korea. All night long, on the battlefront to the north, transport planes on flare sorties have been turning night into day in one of the brightest pyrotechnic displays of the war, dropping million-candlepower flares at short intervals for hours on end, surprising gooks in their nighttime mischief and giving them a kind of preview of the Apocalypse before picking them off. Then, with the dawn's early light, the battle-ship *New Jersey* and cruiser *Bremerton* have led surface ships in an artillery assault on the Korean east coast, and the west coast has been hit by the Polkadot Squadron from the USS *Bairoko*. In the daily air battle, Major Jimmy Jabara, the Wichita Ace, bags his twelfth MIG. In fact, Yanks are reportedly downing fifteen enemy MIG-15s for every Sabre Jet lost . . .

> when the migs offered battle
> in numbers [TIME say] they were being
> knocked down like grouse
> on a scottish moor
>
> one cocky pilot snorted
> that the requirement for ace
> hood ought to be raised
> to ten kills then added:
>
> "ten hell make it fifteen
> or twenty and put a hundred
> pounds of cabbage in our tail
> assemblies as a handicap!"

Wall Streeters might prefer narrower odds, but still, for every fifteen MIGs down, there's another Sabre Jet to be built, and anyway, the replacement demand for some reason seems higher than that.

At home meanwhile, the President's Cabinet has been called into morning session, the Sing Sing prison officials and Times Square pro-gram committees have been put on alert, the Nine Old Men have arrived at the Supreme Court. The Senate, not to miss any of the action, is in recess today, but the House of Representatives is heavily engaged upon major legislation, and the situation there is reported to be "one of anxiety and suspense." Between votes, Congressmen spend a lot of time at their phones. At the White House, queues of visitors are already forming up, waiting for the doors to open, and the guards are jittery: almost ten thousand tourists out here this morning, what if just one of them—? "Simple duty hath no place for the twitters!" Uncle Sam admonishes them in firm Quaker cadences, watching the Vice President squirt across Pennsylvania Avenue from Lafayette Square out of the corner of his eye. "Chins out, chests up, lads, discipline is the soul of a army, and if any strange fruit attempts to haul down the American flag, shoot him on the spot!" He grins thoughtfully to himself as the Veep bowls over a little kid; then he ducks into the White House through a back entrance, meditating on Moe the necktie-peddler's observation in *Pickup on South Street:* "He's as shifty as smoke, but I still love him!"

At the Supreme Court, Chief Justice Fred Vinson takes his seat under the clock in front of the tall Grecian columns and red plush curtains, hastens perfunctorily through the opening rituals, and announces abruptly: "We think the question is not substantial. We think further proceedings to litigate it are unwarranted. Accordingly, we vacate the stay entered by Mr. Justice Douglas on June 17, 1953!"

There's a moment of shocked silence in the packed courtroom—it's come so fast it's caught everyone by surprise, some still haven't taken their seats—then a burst of cheers and boos. The defense attorneys, dark with anger, leap from their chairs, tipping them over, scramble toward the bench—but Justice Robert Jackson objects to the "irregular manner" in which the new lawyers have entered the case, and they are ordered to carry on their unpleasantries elsewhere. Justice Tom Clark notes that the Court has now considered this case seven times, and a moment of awe grips the courtroom—*the seventh occasion!*

But Justice Hugo Black, dissenting from the 6-to-2 majority opinion and doubting the Court even had the right to vacate the stay of a fellow Justice in the first place (". . . so far as I can tell, the Court's action here is unprecedented . . ."), argues crabbily that "it is not amiss to point out that this Court has never affirmed the fairness of the trial!" There he goes again. "What," the people mutter, "is Black and white and Red all over?"

Justice William Douglas, facing possible impeachment, insists bluntly that "the cold truth is that the death sentence may not be imposed for what the Rosenbergs did unless the jury so recommends," but before he's even had a chance to get it all out, Manny Bloch is on his feet, asking for more time to rewrite the clemency appeal, arguing that the doubts of three Justices (Frankfurter has snuck out unnoticed for the time being) is "a matter which is appropriate for consideration on a petition of mercy." He's wearing a brand-new suit, having dumped coffee on his old one this morning: no peace, saith the Lord, unto the wicked.

U.S. Acting Solicitor General Bob Stern snorts at this argument, but Justice Black, cantankerous as ever, points out that clemency from the President is all but pleaded for in the majority opinion itself, which says plainly: "Vacating this stay is not to be construed as endorsing the wisdom or appropriateness to this case of a death sentence." Stern, who is as aware as Black is that this is a mere protective maneuver by the Court to avoid any hint or complaint of error, says flatly that no more time is needed, and the Court, thinking about this for fifteen minutes (the stage is built, after all, and this show is ready to go on), agrees. No more delays. Even Douglas caves in now and votes with the majority, leaving Black alone in his bilious dissent.

The spectators, reporters, court buffs rush from the courtroom, spreading the word to the thousands left outside, all of whom now grab up their children and cameras and race to the White House: *It is nearing High Noon, and now President Dwight D. Eisenhower alone stands between the atom spies and death.*

13.

The Cabinet Meeting

Wrinkling his brow and bulging his blue eyes in mock amazement, the President interrupted Foster Dulles and said: "This thing is so foolish as to be fantastic!"

I jerked my head up. What was he talking about now? The Rosenberg stay, Rhee, Berlin? Double-breasted suits? He was chewing his lip, a bad sign, and doodling on his little white pad: some kind of face with a careless black beard. Guiltily, I touched my own cheeks: already a little bristly, and it wasn't even noon yet. I was still nervous and distracted from having run that gauntlet outside—in fact, I'd barely made it to the White House in time for the opening prayer, slipping through the door just as Jerry Persons was getting ready to shut it—and so was able to tune into the Cabinet meeting with only half my mind, but as usual that was enough, they were never much more than diffuse and errant bull sessions. We sat around the long coffin-shaped table in our high-backed leather chairs, shaking our heads in commiseration, blowing smoke, digesting our breakfasts, struggling to get awake enough to face the inevitable assault of newsmen after the meeting broke up, agreeing with the General whatever he was talking about. Maybe he was only complaining to Foster about waking him up at two in the morning yesterday to tell him about Rhee's release of the prisoners. Dulles made few mistakes, but that was one of them. He wasn't apt to make it again.

Earlier, after the usual opening minute of silent prayer, the old General had raised his head solemnly, taken a drag, and told us all that the last forty-eight hours had been a particularly trying time for him. We all knew this, but we'd listened appreciatively. In South Korea, he'd said, President Syngman Rhee's insubordinate release of 26,000 prisoners of war was wrecking his truce negotiations and had cast serious doubt on the entire Free World chain of command. Then, Supreme Court Justice Douglas's last-minute stay of the Rosenberg executions had made a mockery of all the elaborate preparations this week and brought that whole case to a new crisis—damn it, he'd written his son John a great letter all about the Rosenbergs on Tuesday, had assured Gene Autry on Wednesday that the burnings were all set, and then had gone ahead yesterday right on schedule and issued that cautionary "Statement on the Prevention of Forest Fires," and now he was going to look like a darned fool. And finally, as if these weren't troubles enough, someone had advised him last night that he should stop wearing double-breasted suits! He'd glanced gloomily at the ceiling and then at old Ezra of the Council of Twelve Apostles and said that he couldn't remember a time in his life when he felt more in need of help from Someone much more powerful than he. We'd all nodded our assent, exchanged worried glances, feeling the chill of our adversary's presence, his power and his wile: to derange a trusted ally, penetrate the highest court in the land, and mock the disguise of Uncle Sam: where would he strike next?

Whichever crisis the President had been talking about, Foster now resumed his briefing on the one in Korea, saying that the situation there was the gravest since the day the Communists first invaded the Republic back on June 25, 1950. We all knew this but were somehow reassured by Dulles telling us so. His remarks, however, kept getting interrupted by messengers from Foggy Bottom who came running over with fresh and apparently alarming communiqués. It was hard to know what was in them, but each one made his head jerk and his glasses skid down his nose. John Foster Dulles. The Gray Beagle of Foggy Bottom. Outwardly austere and even obstinate, he was inwardly an emotional and ambivalent man, a masked manic-depressive, lacking conviction and uncertain of his principles, a typical weakness of high-church Protestants. But we sat there listening to him make his agonizing reappraisals and nodded in gloomy assent. Terrible situation. That damned Rhee—who did he think he was? There were even mutterings around the table about the merits of good old-fashioned assassination: Ike himself had often said aloud that he wished the Koreans would overthrow that "monkey," and he had that look on his face today, which we all mimicked—but in fact, down deep, we all appreciated Rhee's act. As Joe McCarthy said yesterday: "Freedom-loving people throughout the world should applaud the action of Syngman Rhee!" And we all loved freedom and a good buffalo hunt as much as the next guy. It was as lawyers we were upset: the scenario we'd been constructing since Ike's trip to Korea last fall had had all the props knocked out by our own client. Ike had led with strength, secretly telling the Reds to negotiate or Pyongyang would be our next H-bomb test site—and now his own shill had called his bluff.

"There's one thing I learned in the five years I served in the Army out there," President Eisenhower said, shaking his head dumfoundedly, "we can never figure out the working of the Oriental mind!"

Foster stared dully at the President over the tops of his spectacles a moment, then turned back to his latest communiqué, while others around the table picked up on this newest theme of Oriental inscrutability. I participated in these discussions as usual, making occasional observations on detail, crisp and to the point, avoiding generalizations and speech-making, and so keeping up a certain reputation, but my mind was on the excitement outside, the demonstrators and counterdemonstrators, the Supreme Court now or soon to be in session, the trial and the executions, and those dreams last night, those memories of an unspent youth which had left me feeling so edgy and reckless. I developed the ability long ago to do this, to say or do one thing while thinking of another. It's a political expediency, like appearing to answer a question emphatically while in fact evading the whole point of the question, or learning to repeat verbatim questions from the floor in order to have time to think of answers. I leaned forward and said that, bad as things were, they nevertheless all but assured the passage of our foreign-aid bill through the House today, but I was thinking: What are all those people doing out there? Why has Uncle Sam let this thing get so out of hand? What are the dirty pictures that they're all joking about? Why is George Humphrey laughing so loudly—are the others feeling what I'm feeling, too? Why is old Foster sitting so hunched over, why is Oveta's throat so flushed, what's Ezra Benson doing with his hands in his lap? Why is the President humming "One Dozen Roses"? "We mustn't forget," I said, "that the principal enemy in Korea is still Communism." The General glanced up sharply. I realized that he had just said this himself. "Like the President says," I said. Around the table, the others nodded solemnly. Charlie Wilson, sitting beside the President, gazed straight at me, his eyes crossing with sleep.

The President reminded us—"bear in mind," he said, wagging a finger at us—that South Korean forces at this moment held two-thirds of the United Nations line in Korea. If Rhee ordered them to attack, what could we do to stop them? How could we prevent this near-truce we'd come to from collapsing into a full-scale resumption of hostilities? We could hold back ammunition, but that would only mean that the attack would flounder and the inevitable Communist counterassault would overrun the remaining U.S. troops. Likewise, if Rhee pulled his forces back altogether, the rest of us could not hold the line. We simply had to get Rhee back in the harness. Much of this was directed at me. I'd had the job all winter of winning over the Asia-first hardliners on this truce idea—they kept calling it a "peace without honor"—and so Rhee had put me in a bind, too.

I pretended a certain personal frustration—everyone knew I'd taken a public stand with those who wanted to liberate the captive nations of Europe, unleash the democratic forces of Chiang Kai-shek on the Chinese mainland, and press for total all-out victory in Korea, hitting them, if necessary, with everything in the bucket—but to tell the truth, I was secretly relieved that being Eisenhower's Vice President put limits on me. I could use a word like "liberation," for example, and get read a thousand ways at once—I'm a rhetorician, not a general, and for me that's power. But today, all those shades of meaning demanded a certain gloominess, my best face in fact, so no one at the table could be surprised I was wearing it.

"It's one of the lessons of politics," I said grimly. "Those one thinks are his best friends often turn out to be the heaviest cross he has to bear." A few heads bobbed up around the table to glance at me suspiciously—I gazed steadily at each of them. Which of them would challenge me, I wondered? Which would stand in my way? I knew that those who reached the top had to develop a certain tough realism as far as friendships and loyalties were concerned—there are no enduring loyalties in politics excepting where they are tied up in personal interests. "What happens any place in the world affects our freedom," I said, "and it might affect the peace of the world. I think that we can keep our freedom, and I think that we can win the struggle against slavery and for freedom throughout the world. I think the way to have peace is to be strong and be prepared to resist those who threaten peace." Amazingly, they all listened to this without batting an eye. I wish I had a friend, I thought. One real friend. I took out my handkerchief and mopped my brow. Then, with a shudder, I realized I'd used it to wipe that little kid's snot, and I stuffed it back in my jacket pocket. I was still very sweaty and shaken from my encounter with that mob—CHAPFALLEN, as it said in the *Times* crossword puzzle: *Weary to an extreme*. The only sensation I could recall like it was when Pat and I had got caught up in the crush of the crowd celebrating V-E Day in Times Square in 1945.

Now, in the Cabinet meeting, in fact, they had started talking about

Times Square. I didn't know how they'd got there, it was just the way these meetings went. Sinclair Weeks was complaining about the shambles up there. I tried to tune into this because I knew that a man was at his best in a crisis when he was thinking not of himself but of the problem at hand. Weeks's problem at hand was that his son was getting married tonight as part of Uncle Sam's in-depth campaign to reaffirm the social order in the face of the Phantom's disruptions, and he was therefore quite naturally distressed about what was going on: could we hold the stage or couldn't we? We'd all complimented Weeks on this marriage tactic right after the prayer this morning, and I'd wished for a moment that I'd had a daughter old enough to give myself. Weeks was bald-headed like a lot of guys around this table. LIFE had said it: "Ike likes them balding." Benson. Brownell. Humphrey—the first time the General saw George, he threw his arm around his shoulder and said: "I see you part your hair the same way I do!" He'd never greeted me that way. I sat between Brownell and Humphrey at the Cabinet table, feeling like the Hairy Ape. I ran my hand through my thick hair, tracing the scar there and wondering: What is it suddenly about baldness? That image of Bob Taft's glowing pate as he turned to walk away from me yesterday in the Capitol flashed to mind. This was something all recent Presidential candidates had in common, I realized, even Adlai. Some personal vanity on Uncle Sam's part? Or did it make the transformation easier somehow? It didn't matter, Uncle Sam surely knew that I'd pluck it all out if it came to that. Weeks's son, of course, was not alone in this endeavor tonight—literally thousands of America's sons and daughters had been pledged to this nationwide ritual of sanctification, including the son of a deceased Republican Congressman, who was marrying the great-granddaughter of John D. Rockefeller himself.

"Thank God for our young people!" I said, and Eisenhower said: "Amen to *that!*"

"Say, Dick, what the hell did you do to your nose?" asked Charlie Wilson, uncrossing his eyes long enough to get me in focus.

"I, uh, some demonstrators outside, they had picket staves, and, it, uh, it's nothing . . ."

Eisenhower took notice then for the first time and I thought I was about to pick up a few points, but then Cabot Lodge leaned forward and said he deplored "the flood of propaganda instead of factual information about this Rosenberg case," complaining that left-wing groups all over the world were distorting the facts and arousing a lot of hostility toward the United States, even building it up into a case of official anti-Semitism. Why weren't we making better use of the Voice of America?

Of course, Lodge was under a lot of pressure about this in the U.N. He was very effective, a little too boyish and simple maybe, but an appealing politician. He'd just been named "Father of the Year," part of a gathering campaign probably. I knew he was one of the favorites around here, and of all the guys around this table, he was the man most likely to challenge me—maybe even three years from now. I knew that was my real task: staying on the ticket in 1956. The chances were good that the General would pass away before 1960, and even if he didn't, it would be an uphill battle for anybody in the Party to unseat me by then. Everybody else in this potbellied timocracy was too antiquated. Lodge used to sit beside me on the Senate floor—I knew just how he breathed, snorted, moved, smelled, fretted. He'd worked hard last fall for Eisenhower, so hard he'd done what no politician should ever do: he'd neglected his own campaign and lost his Senate seat to Jack Kennedy. On the other hand, maybe that was inevitable, and meanwhile he'd scored a lot of points across the country, Ike had provided him a good national forum in the United Nations, and he even had the aura these days of a "what-if" President: had Taft beat Eisenhower out at the Republican Convention, Lodge would have been a logical Party-unifying Vice Presidential candidate, and with Taft dying now, Cabot would be getting ready to take over the country. I worried about the almost complete ambiguity of his past record and the dapper three-piece suits he wore. Those cool narrow ties: you couldn't even buy ties like those out in California!

"We must mount a mighty ideological offensive," I said, "which will prove to peoples everywhere that the hope of the world does not lie in turning toward dictatorship of any type, but that it lies in developing a strong, a free, and an intelligent democracy."

Not everybody was pleased at this. I rarely said anything at these meetings, and then only about tactics. Why was I sounding off like this? If I was trying to speed things up, I wasn't succeeding. I sat back, letting my gaze float out through the tall glass doors and on down the long soft green slope of the White House lawn, determined to say nothing that would prolong this goddamned meeting any further. They were terrible, these Cabinet sessions, the consequence of Ike's "team concept": get all the "best brains in the country" around a table and reach an inspired consensus. They lasted forever and resulted in lowest-common-denominator policy-making and an appalling dilution of power. Or so it always seemed while sitting in one. Just a screen, probably. Our very drowsiness must have given the American people added confidence: faiths fall when the priests get nervous. Thus, when I took over a couple of months ago and spent the whole time harping about the urgent need to get the next campaign started now, I was only rocking the boat.

I sighed, fished the crossword puzzle out of my pocket, as though consulting statistical notes. Down and through, these clues, from *Burning Tree activity* to "—— *in Boots*," like some kind of tortuous labyrinthine sentence. Meaningless, silly even—yet why did it make me think of my dreams again? I found AVER, ASSUAGE, TURN, STOP, and ROAR. Arthur Summerfield was there: his "responsibility"—I glanced up at him uneasily, but he seemed to be sleeping. When I got in trouble last fall, Art was the only major Republican official on the Eisenhower train who was arguing openly and strongly that I should be kept on the ticket, defended, and supported. Of course, we'd all turned up in these puzzles (I wondered in fact if VEEP was not an invention of crossword puzzlers), but why had Art been singled out today? 53 Down: *Player chased in a game.* HERO? HEIR? HEAD? And who was the *Duncecap wearer,* the *Companion of humidity,* who the *Hardy heroine,* the *Candidate for worst-dressed woman?* This last one was a five-letter word, but luckily it began with "F"—but on the other hand, there was 61 Across: *Be superior to,* and for this one I already had some of the letters: E —— EL!

Beside me, Herb Brownell was bringing up the possibility of issuing a "white paper" on the Rosenberg case, but he interrupted himself momentarily to ask dryly if that crossword puzzle I was working was going to be the next order of business?

I'd been deep in thought, trying out "T" and "H" in those blank spaces, and his question startled me. But I was prepared for it. "No, not the puzzle, Herb," I said, then sat forward to look around at the others, "but this advertisement beside it." The others turned to me expectantly, leaving a chagrined Brownell momentarily eclipsed and biting his lip. "It's for a book ostensibly about *Soviet Civilization,*" I said, "but in fact it's a blatant plea for 'co-existence'—and we all know whose kind of talk *that* is! It's published by an outfit up in New York which calls itself the Philosophical Library and they're not only out to peddle this propaganda, they're also trying to whip up another new letter-writing campaign to the President!"

"Oh, no!" groaned the President. "I thought when this Rosenberg thing was over, I'd—what do they think I am, a darned mailbox?" Summerfield woke up at this reference to his own Cabinet post and glanced about in panic as I passed the ad around. "Can't we classify it as obscene mail or something? Nobody reads all this foolishness, nobody could even if they wanted to, the most we can ever do is weigh it and burn it, and the incinerators are all stuffed as full as we can get them as it is!"

Summerfield snorted and coughed, and snatched up the clipping to see what we'd been talking about. He studied it blearily, somewhat amazed. "You mean OAF?" he asked finally.

Our laughter was interrupted by a messenger from the Supreme Court: all nine Justices had arrived and the Court was sitting. The Attorney General glanced coolly at his watch, then said: "In just a few moments, Chief Justice Vinson is expected to announce that the Supreme Court is vacating Douglas's stay. As soon as possible after that, the President must issue a final denial of clemency, which we've already drafted, and then the Justice Department will follow with its announcement that the Rosenbergs will be executed tomorrow night at the latest."

Someone pointed out that that was the Sabbath.

"We're not going to burn them on Sunday!" the President shouted, rearing up from his doodle, his blue eyes flashing.

"No, General, the *Jewish* Sabbath," Herb explained. "These people are Jews."

"Oh, all right, then," said the President.

All of this was just a joke, everybody was just trying to calm down.

The Attorney General pondered the problem a moment, then said: "Well, in that case, we'll finish it tonight. We'll set it up as soon as the Court stops sitting."

"Before sundown," someone said. "It starts at sundown, their Sabbath."

"Right, sundown. Thanks."

Friday. Sunset. The two thieves. Jews condemned by Jews. Some patterns had been dissolved by the overnight delay, it was true, but others were taking shape. Uncle Sam could not be entirely displeased, I thought. But the President only belched grumpily and shifted in his seat. He said he still didn't understand what the issue in the Supreme Court today was, still didn't see why there had been this delay. If they were guilty, they ought to be punished; if not, let them go. The speechwriter Emmett Hughes, once part of the retinue surrounding the National Poet Laureate, scribbled away, his dark brows bobbing, taking notes on all this for posterity—not what he was being paid to do, but you could spot these parasites a mile away. I supposed, no matter how tight a ship you ran, there'd always be one of these guys slipping in. "I must say, I'm impressed by all the honest doubt about this expressed in the letters I've been seeing," the President said. Was this true, was he really unable to understand so simple a point of law, or was this too part of his disguise? The good soldier, forthright and true, the man of arms too honest to grasp the devious men of letters? Sometimes simple people are more mysterious than those of us who are more complex.

Herb explained once more about the 1917 Espionage Act and the 1946 Atomic Energy Act. As soon as he said that the issue was purely technical, I thought: he's just given it all away, he's just told them Douglas was right. Just as, in a purely technical sense, Don Wheeler was also right in calling for Douglas's impeachment. But I also knew Eisenhower would not realize this, or would not seem to. Was he testing us, I wondered? I recalled his offer—his challenge, rather—to reopen this case at any time before the executions if any one of us believed that to do so would serve the best interests of the United States. Thus, each of us was on the spot. . . .

"Well, the proof of admission there's no frameup," I said, "is the complete silence of the Phantom-controlled press in the Soviet Union and elsewhere. It's obvious they're expecting the Rosenbergs to confess and they don't want to look like a bunch of clowns. And I'll tell you something else. Morton Sobell's wife said something very funny recently out in Far Rockaway. She said: 'Julius and Ethel could save their own skins by talking, but Julius and Ethel will never betray their friends!' I mean, it's obvious, isn't it?" Of course, I'd got this from a guy who'd got roughed up at that meeting and so was pretty biased, and a right-wing Jew at that, nervous about the anti-Semitism the Rosenbergs could arouse, but that hardly mattered, I understood the essential truth of it and so did everybody else around the table.

Except perhaps the President. He scowled and unwrapped a cigar. "Well, now," he said, "if the Supreme Court decides by, say, five to four or even six to three, as far as the average man's concerned, there *will* be doubt—not just a legal point in his mind." He was himself that average man he was talking about, of course. This was the secret of his success. He really was average, a cheerful unimaginative boy from Abilene, and yet he was also the man who won World War II, so that just showed what an average man could do. So long as he was an American. Uncle Sam always chose his disguises to fit the times.

"Well, who's going to decide these points," Brownell argued, "pressure groups or the Supreme Court? Surely, our first concern is the strength of our courts. And in terms of national security, the Communists are just out to prove they can bring enough pressure, one way or another, to enable people to get away with espionage. I've always wanted you to look at evidence that wasn't usable in court showing the

Rosenbergs were the head and center of an espionage ring here in *direct* contact with the Russians—the *prime* espionage ring in the country!"

The President stared blankly at Brownell, then lit his cigar. "My only concern is in the area of statecraft," he said. "The *effect* of the action." He understood: it was as though he hadn't even heard Brownell's offer to look at the secret evidence. If there was any. It was strange that no one questioned Brownell on this, even though nobody had ever seen this material, Eisenhower especially. I watched this short-tempered old man, Uncle Sam's new real-time disguise, and thought: the important thing is that there be room for the Incarnation to take place. A man can't be solid and a mask at the same time. Yes, image—I knew all about that. The essence of power is paradox and ambiguity. Learning to live with this was the hardest thing of all—I was still too precise, too self-critical, too anxious to make everything perfectly clear. While I worried and sweated over every phrase, Eisenhower just leaned back and let fly. "The area of statecraft . . . the effect of the action . . ."

I feared I would never be able to deliver these homilies with such ingenuous sincerity. "All I do is belabor the obvious," he said, but with him it looked easy. Take "enlightened self-interest," that maxim he stole from George Washington, and which was still one of his favorites. Uncle Sam once explained this to me. He said that it had long been recognized that self-interest was like some kind of sin, something born of the devil, the source, like money, of all evil—the Greeks knew this, indeed so did the Mana-hatta Indians. Self-interest was irrational and man had long dreamed of the rational utopia, free of self-interest. But reason was also known to be the source of all evil. Enlightenment did not illuminate, but spread a greater darkness. The dream of utopia made men miserable, both through disappointment with their flawed existence and through the horrors they inflicted on each other through pursuit of the rational—and therefore unattainable—ideal. Thus, "enlightenment" and "self-interest" were two sides of the same coin, and if there was evil in the world it was due to our failure to see both sides at once. "Enlightened self-interest" was a stoic formula of acceptance, part of the tragedy of history. But for Eisenhower, it meant: Don't take any wooden nickels.

He'd traveled the world, this man, and now he was running it, and he still hadn't progressed past the simplest kind of home-town table talk. In his cowtown world, he could use words like "instinct" and "freedom" and "sincerity" and "decency," and assume any darn fool would know what he meant by them, and if they pretended not to, they were either cantankerous or nincompoops. Free economy was God's truth, that was

all, plain as the nose on your face, and he figured if you'd just show the
Soviets the facts they'd agree with you, they'd have to. After all, as he
said when he called on the Almighty to watch over the Communists
when Stalin died: "They are the children of the same God who is the
Father of all peoples everywhere." It was easy. "Now let us begin talking to each other," he'd say. "And let us say what we've got to say so
that every person on earth can understand it. Let's talk straight: *no*
doubletalk, *no* sophisticated political formulas, *no* slick propaganda
devices. Let's spell it out." Then he could never understand why this
didn't seem to work: "We are trying to present certain salient facts to
the world, facts for example as to what our purpose is, our intent, that
we are not imperialistic, we are simply trying to help create a world in
which free men can live decently, and they have not understood; we
have tried to be helpful and have earned nothing but vituperation!" In
fact, he even seemed to blame me somehow when things went wrong, as
though I were responsible for corrupting the language of the world so
that it obscured all these self-evident truths. He thought almost any
problem could be solved if America would just keep its heart right into
the job, as he put it, and do the right thing. "Heart, Determination, and
Productivity." He cherished old proverbs about the good life and rags to
riches, thought the first World War even more glorious than the second,
truly *believed* in Manifest Destiny. He *liked* to fish and hunt! *He still
remembered the Alamo!* Businessmen to him were simply people who
knew how to solve problems and save money, so he filled up his Cabinet
with them and admonished them to remember the *little* fellow—my
God, how could you *not* like him? Laborers were like foot soldiers in
the forward march of free enterprise, and he talked about creeping
socialism as if it were some kind of mole eating up the golf course.
"Before I appoint anybody to any important position, I call him in and
ask him about his philosophy," he'd say with a straight face. It's amazing how little some people can understand about the world we live in,
even on the simplest level!

By grunts and nods, we'd seemed to come to some agreement that
there was no need for a white paper, but that we should enlarge some on
the President's clemency denial previously drafted by the Attorney
General, acknowledging the worldwide "concern" over the case, but
answering this Phantom-inspired ruckus with a vivid depiction of the
horrible nature of the Rosenbergs' crime (millions of innocent people
may die, etc.) and a little self-congratulatory canticle on behalf of the
generous and humane system of American justice and due process of
law. I pointed out that the case had had 23 applications to the courts

and 112 judges had reviewed it, but no judge had ever expressed any doubt that the Rosenbergs had in fact spied for the Russians. Of course, I knew as well they'd never asked themselves the question and so had had no cause to answer it, confining themselves to legal technicalities, not questions of fact, scrupulously avoiding any improper opinionating about "guilt" or "innocence," as indeed they had to, but I counted on the General's ignorance of the appellate system, and sure enough he smiled and said: "Put that in, Herb: 'No judge has ever expressed any doubt . . .' "

Conversation shifted now to the ceremonies tonight in Times Square, the seating arrangements, special events, electrocution protocol, and Doug McKay, as Secretary of the Interior, gave a brief report on the problems of security and set reconstruction, apologizing somewhat abashedly for his failure to solve the Statue of Liberty boat strike. The more this dragged on, the more anxious and annoyed I became. My staff would have arrived by now and discovered the Rosenberg mess in my office. I worried about that, worried that they'd see it and gossip around the Senate Office Building about what they saw, or, worse, that they'd try to do me a favor and clean it up. They knew I liked a clean room. My desk is always clean. You can't let your mind get cluttered, I believe that, you have to live like a Spartan, spare and clean, be at your best at all times, be physically and mentally disciplined to make decisions in a balanced way, and people who have messes around them all the time also have messy minds. I have a note to myself somewhere on the subject. But right now, I knew, my office was a goddamn disaster area, the Rosenberg letters strewn everywhere, the trial transcripts, secret FBI reports, my notes, books on the floor—if anybody who knew me well saw it, they'd think old Dick Nixon was losing his mind. Or else that somebody hostile to me, malicious, vindictive, had got in while I was out. But there was nothing I could do about it until this meeting broke up, and at the present rate, I'd be lucky to get over there before it was time to show up in Times Square. I really blew it with that shave this morning, I thought irritably, watching Ike doodle that blackbearded bum. Is he stretching it out on purpose, I wondered—is Uncle Sam just toying with me?

Defense Secretary Charlie Wilson now suggested ringing the area around Times Square an hour before the executions with atomic tanks, which he said he thought he could supply. Joe Dodge, the Budget Director, doubted that this would be economical. Wilson said he just thought he'd throw the idea out to let us kick it around. Watching all these theatrical performances, I thought: Only Uncle Sam is real:

there's no one over his shoulder. An awkward situation, though—he had nothing to believe in except himself. An audience of one. Herb Brownell informed us that the old *Look Ahead, Neighbor Special* was being rigged up for VIP runs to the city, and Commerce Secretary Sinclair Weeks said that the subway system there had been commandeered to assure us all easy and safe access to the center and out again. Oveta Culp Hobby expressed her appreciation of this. Of course, the whole Cabinet out in public and in one place like that—not to mention Congress, the Supreme Court, FBI, Joint Chiefs of Staff, and indeed the better part of America—we were very vulnerable, the Phantom might even throw the big one at us. Foster Dulles gloomily discounted this likelihood, and Lewis Strauss, Chairman of the Atomic Energy Commission, smiled and said there was nothing to worry about.

After that, the President, apologizing, read through the speech he planned to deliver at the electrocutions tonight for our approval. It was okay, his usual bumbling incoherent but plainly sincere style, and when he was finished I clapped along with all the rest. I was wondering, though, how to get the discussion shifted back to my injuries. "I read it far more for your blue pencils," he said, as though genuinely embarrassed, "than I did for your applause." Why is it, I wondered, that people think of *me* as the cagy and devious one? "Because at first, in our attempt to state a philosophy of government, we were not close enough down to our daily living. One reason I wanted to read it now is so that you can think it over and be ready to tear it to pieces."

"I think it is wonderful," said Charlie Wilson. "I am in favor of flying the flag pretty high."

"I am, too," boomed Eisenhower, clapping his left hand to Wilson's shoulder. Art Summerfield awoke with such a start he nearly fell over backwards in his chair. "I would get out and shout it out loud but you have also got to bring basic principles down to living because here is this thing going out to probably one of the greatest audiences that has ever heard a speech. It is going in the papers, here are thousands out in front of us. You want every person there to carry home with him a conviction that he can do something."

"A free society stimulates the efficiency of millions," Wilson said. Engine Charlie smelled the end of this meeting, and his eyes had come uncrossed. So did I, and I leaned forward to gather up my papers. "We should urge that we accomplish more with the same effort for the good of all!"

"It is on a high plane and for the occasion it is very good," said Ezra Benson, understanding Wilson's remarks as a criticism. It would be

Ezra's role to deliver the invocation tonight and to ask God to forgive the Rosenbergs for their sins, a touch of charity we all approved of. "I think it is wonderful."

"We want to keep it largely on a high spiritual plane with exhortation, but at the same time," said Ike, gesturing broadly, "trying to relate it to our everyday living."

"I did not see anything I would want to change," Wilson said.

I got ready to stand up, but then Cabot Lodge objected to a reference to Moscow as having been formerly the center of autocracy and as being now the center of revolution. He said he thought that implied that the Russian government was no longer autocratic—and as for revolution, well, that was a word that appealed to a lot of downtrodden people in the world.

"Despotism?" suggested Ike. "You are right." He seemed pleased at Lodge's suggestion, and cast a brief curious glance at me. In my resolve to keep quiet, I realized, I'd let Lodge steal a line from me there.

"If you gave us a flip from autocracy to despotism," Wilson chimed in, "it would be better." Now that he was awake, Charlie couldn't seem to stop talking.

It suddenly came to me what my problem was: I'd spent too much time on reviewing the trial, not enough on everything else. Hadn't Uncle Sam warned me about this? Nothing had been or could be proven. I could have challenged Brownell on that suppressed evidence, for example, but I'd sensed somehow it wasn't relevant—it might have been a week ago, or even yesterday, but it wasn't any more. Why had I been so slow to see this? Why had I waited so long to get into this case at all? I wasn't just a Congressman from Southern California any longer, I was a heartbeat away from the Incarnation! Everything mattered! This was the central problem as one rose higher in the echelons of national power: how could one continue to isolate and define the essential debate, keep it clean from diffuseness and mind-numbing paradox? I've only begun, I thought. There'll never be time enough! I had to reread the letters, the biographies, search out the hidden themes, somehow reach a panoramic view of the event, and *write a speech!* That was the point: I had to go before the people tonight and unleash a real philippic, communicate the facts, publicize the truth, help them all stand taller and feel proud to be Americans! *That* was what Uncle Sam was expecting of me! That was what language was for: to transcend the confusions, restore the spirit, recreate the society! Ahead of me, I knew, was a day of almost superhuman effort.

"I personally am a little bit reluctant ever to talk," said the President, "in terms that look like we are running a school. I do believe in this particular one—Lincoln himself didn't say, 'Eighty-seven years ago.' He said, 'Fourscore and seven years ago.' He, instantly on the opening of that speech, established a certain stateliness, he didn't use the language that he knew better than anybody else—if you will read some of the stories that he told. I am open to argument on this, but in this speech I deliberately tried to stay in the level of talk that would make as good reading as possible at the Quai d'Orsay or Number Ten Downing but I particularly tried to make the words that would sound good to the fellow digging the ditch."

Wilson, beaming (we were all beaming) : "You flew the flag! It was wonderful!"

"Uh, my nose . . ." I began.

But just then in burst Sherman Adams with the news: The Court has met! The stay has been vacated! The crowds on the Hill and in the Mall are on the move—*and they're headed this way!*

14.

High Noon

Here they come, streaming up the Mall toward the White House, and leading them it's TIME himself, America's laureate balladeer, carrying a blow-up of Gary Cooper crashing through a door with the legend "BLOOD, SWEAT AND TENSION," and singing his own words to the famous tune:

> high noon united artists creeping
> on hadleyville pop four oh oh
> one hot sunday morning is the
> moment of crisis
> of crisis for the
> the little western cow-ow town

> desperado fra-hank miller
> whose jail sentence has been commuted
> through a political deal is coming
> on - the - noon - train

> the marshal is no hero he is
> g cooper leaving with his wife
> grace kelly to open a general sto-hore
> but he turns ba-hack
> there is a jo-hob
> law and order-her are at stake

the solid citizens of hadleyvi-hille
are laying odds that the marshal is dea-head
five minutes after miller gets off
          off - the - noon - train

left high and dry in a town para
lyzed by fear and morally
bankrupt the sweating marshal has to
          face miller and three
          three of his fellow
fellow desperadoes alone

the picture builds to its high noon climax
in a crescendo of ticking clo-hocks
railroad tracks stretching long and level
          hushed - deser - ted - streets

throughout the action dmitri tiomkin's
plaintive high noon ballad sounds
a recurring note of impending doo-oom
          as the heat and drama
          mount relentlessly to
to the crisi-hiss of high noon . . .

The poet shows none of Lloyd Bridges' shameful funk, but moves jauntily, a proud and eager Deputy, grinning like Jack Palance and shaking
his hips to Tiomkin's thumping music like Smiley Burnette, and the
people follow. The law has prevailed. The law and the spirit. Judge
Fred Vinson's court, its subversive heavies Douglas and Black shot
down, the Jew Judge Frankfurter locked up in uncertainties, has spoken
for the last time. The lives of the A-bomb rustlers are now in the hands
of that gangly wire-tough old general, Ike (Swede) Eisenhower, who's
seen a lot of border action himself in his day, in Eisenhower's hands and
the hands of the old clock on the wall. In the House of Representatives,
Democrat Frank Chelf of Kentucky rears up like Tom Mix on Tony to
interrupt the debate on the foreign aid bill with the excited announcement that "the Supreme Court has just voted to set aside the stay of
execution in the Rosenberg case. *Praise God from Whom all blessings
flow! We thank the Supreme Court!*"

Not that it's all over. No, already the Phantom's desperate last-ditch
mob action is mounting. A steady trickle of unwholesome-looking extras
leaks out of Inspiration House on Kalorama Road, moving toward Pennsylvania, like Miller and his gang debouching from the noon train.

Pickets appear: WE ARE INNOCENT! WE WILL NOT TRADE DECENCY & TRUTH FOR LIFE! DON'T LET THE ROSENBERGS DIE ON THE WORD OF A LIAR! The air, as in Hadleyville, is oppressive, weighted with the stagnant threat of time and swarthiness. Something is not yet clean. "Ah nevuh believed ah would li-yuv to see whut ah have seen in WAW-shinton in the past few days!" The people streaming from the Court to the White House pause to listen to the elegant old cadences of Congressman E. L. Forrester, Democrat from Georgia's Third District, pouring out at this instant from the Capitol, as though through the swinging doors of the town saloon . . .

> Last Sunday I saw six or seven thousand mongrels picketing the White House, parading with banners, charging that our Government had bribed witnesses, and with banners demanding that two particular children not be made orphans. Not one of that crowd was concerned over the widows and orphans of our fine young men who died fighting communism in Korea. Yesterday the Capitol Grounds were alive with hundreds of people who have no interest whatsoever in our country except to destroy it, even to take our country over. Today as I came down to the office, I saw that riff-raff picketing the President of the United States! . . . Mr. Chairman, I despise communism! And the people I represent despise communism! . . . I want you to know that the section, which I come from—*the section where there is no communism*—will gladly make every sacrifice and risk every danger and fight until this scourge is completely removed as a menace!

Fighting words, worthy of Johnny Mack Brown and Tim McCoy before him, even the lazy old Chief Doorkeeper Fishbait Miller is on his feet: time to strap on your shootin' irons, boys, give the Sheriff a hand! But even here, here in the town meeting hall, there is cowardice and indecision, maybe even treachery—else the enraged Georgian wouldn't be laying all this heated-up rhetoric on them. There are those who aren't even here, ducking out just when it's time to stand up and be counted. Moreover, the foreign-aid bill under debate this morning includes payoffs to Communist outlaws like Tito of Yugoslavia, and Wisconsin Congressman Alvin O'Konski is jumping up and down, trying to get the floor to raise hell about that: *whoa! what kind of a Congress is this anyway?* Congressman Forrester eventually yields to him, but not before laying the blame for all the street fights looming up today squarely on Justice Douglas and the "civil rights Congress": "Too many have gawn CRAY-zy ovuh so-cawled SS-EVIL rahhts, a CUM-yunist propaganda FAY-vrit, and this heah class a PEE-pul is most ri-SPAWN-subble fer this heah FOO-lishnuss!" O'Konski's target this morning is those "Communist devils" who were sent to instigate and "engineer a civil war in Spain," and in particular the "unwanted Communist horror and terror" of the priest- and nun-killer Josef Tito, who's in for a piece of cash from the foreign-aid bill, and as the crowds rush anxiously on toward the White House, uncertain even of the loyalty and backbone of the town's leading citizens, they can hear Alvin's angry words ringing in their ears . . .

I am wondering how it feels to aid and abet Communism and help kill freedom-loving people? I am wondering if this Congress has any heart or conscience?

And so, as they gather on the White House lawn, mingling with the last of the sightseers just emerging from their guided tour, there is a tremendous excitement, a sensation of being overswept by something larger than oneself, something divine and magnificent, beyond history even, roaring this way like the noon train. The people glance at each other, nervously, excitedly, smile at each other in recognition, their hearts beating in pride and anxiety to some half-heard drumroll, the clickety-clack of train wheels, galloping hooves—yes, it's as though the frontier is doubling back on the center, bringing wildness and danger, the threat and tumult of the wide open spaces, disrupting system with luck, law with the wild card. As they shuffle about under the White House balcony, they feel like they're back in *Arizona* with Wesley Ruggles, joining up with Roy Rogers's posse in *Bells of Rosarita*, marching down western streets with Barbara Pepper and Patsy Montana to vote for Sheriff Autry, riding *The Big Trail* with John Wayne. Something great is happening. Yes, they all feel it. It's like being with Sam Houston at the San Jacinto or with old Rough-and-Ready at Resaca de la Palma. Drinking buffalo blood with the free trappers along the Snake, fighting with Sam Brannon's vigilantes, massacring Comanches at Plum Creek, Kiowas in Palo Duro Canyon, Pueblos in the mission church at Taos. A great day for America, something out of the past to revive the future, fired with risk and destiny. But then again, perhaps a terrible day . . .
It's all up to Ike.
And what about the President? Is he still the man they say he is, or has he too been Phantomized like the rest of them, Truman and Acheson and Alger Hiss, all those people the Vice President himself has described as supporters and defenders of the Communist conspiracy? Senator Joe McCarthy has said: "Freedom-loving people throughout the world should applaud the action of Syngman Rhee!" Then why isn't the President applauding it? Why does he want to give money to that spic Tito? On the other hand, can one finally trust two characters as dark

and grizzly as Joe McCarthy and Dick Nixon? Do they give you the feeling of being around Buck Jones or Sunset Carson? Hardly. The President is no mere Marine rowdy, after all, no Navy shyster—this is a foot soldier, a gunslinger, a tall, handsome, blue-eyed Westerner who looks a lot like Bill Boyd. Harry Carey. Randolph Scott in *The Frontier Marshall.* This is the man who said in Indianapolis: "No American can stand to one side while his country becomes the prey of fear-mongers, quack doctors, and barefaced looters! He doesn't twiddle his thumbs while his garden is wrecked by a crowd of vandals and his house is invaded by a gang of robbers! He goes into action!" You can hear those swinging doors slap and flutter. "Neither a wise man nor a brave man," he told them in Cincinnati, "lies down on the tracks of history to wait for the train of the future to run over him!"

He is the Man Who Won the War, but he is also a man of the people, born and reared on the lonesome prairie, a man who knows what it's like to sleep out under the stars, listening to the howling of coyotes and the lowing of little dogies, a man who can ride and shoot and use his fists, a man who's walked through acres of dead men and kept his chin up to fight another day. "We live," he was saying just last week in Minneapolis, "not in an instant of peril but in an age of peril—a time of tension and of watchfulness," and his answer to the Phantom is strength: "The hand of the aggressor is stayed by strength—and strength alone!" As a boy, he learned how to lick the bullies of Abilene, saw a shootout in the dusty streets of that cowtown, got a pistol in his own ribs in St. Louis. An old trapper-guide named Bob Davis, whiskery as Chill Wills, taught him how to shoot two ducks at once with a double-barreled shotgun, feather a flatboat paddle, win at poker, trap a muskrat . . .

"Eh bub, how do ye catch a muskrat?"

"I don't know, Bob . . ."

"Well, I'll tell ye, ye go and look fer his slides, and then ye put yer trap on a short chain, see, so's he'll drown . . ."

"Gee, Bob . . ."

He packed up his one good suit and went off to West Point, where he got assigned to the Awkward Squad and Beast Barracks, clumsy as old Coop himself. He clowned around, got in trouble, gawky fun-loving Western boy amid fancypants Southern dudes. His injured knee was ruined in monkey drill, his grades fell off, he took to rolling Bull Durham and sowing wild oats for miles around, he got busted from sergeant to private and would have been dismissed had it not been for Major Poopy Bell's timely intervention, not unlike the good works of Wallace

Beery on his better days. He was getting as reckless as Doc Holliday and might have gone that handsome scoundrel's route had they booted him out of there. He was already laying plans to go ride herd on the Argentine pampas, when his commission in the Infantry came through after all and he got sent out to join General Pershing and the Carranzistas on the Mexican border in Superchief Wilson's "Punitive Expedition," a little moral exercise to keep everybody busy until a real war came along.

Well, he was a full-grown man by then, but you wouldn't know it, he was still the same old irrepressible Ike, a cocky shavetail with the proverbial wild hair up his ass, hungry for any kind of excitement and screw the consequences—but then, in ole San Antone, he met Mamie Doud, in those days still as saucy and sober a Belle as the West had seen since Blanche Sweet. No more crap games, no more restless whoring, no more barroom brawls, it was like the conversions of badguy Bill Hart as he first gazed on Eva Novak or Clara Williams or Bessie Love: "One who is evil," the captions would read as the lovesick villain melted saintward, "looking for the first time on that which is good." Not that either Bill Hart or Ike Eisenhower were ever really evil, of course—no, you might as well say that America itself was evil. What they both experienced was rather that exemplary transcendence, through action and beauty, of the strong man's wild streak, which, in effect, is what the West is all about. On Valentine Day in 1916 Ike gave Mamie his class ring and a year later he got struck by lightning.

Now, over loudspeakers, as the clock ticks inexorably toward twelve noon, comes the friendly rumbling but worried quaver of Tex Ritter, the Texas Cowboy:

> I do not know what fate awaits me,
> I only know I must be brave,
> And I must face a man who hates me
>> Or lie a coward,
>> A craven coward,
> Or lie a coward in my grave . . . !

There's a strange unsettling drumbeat in the song, maybe that's what they've been hearing all along. The crowd shifts about uneasily, like a movie audience deep in the third reel. Men feel their cheeks for signs of bristle, pat their hips as though reaching for six-shooters. Women hug their children to their skirts. It's not the same, of course. They're not like those yellow-livered cabbageheads in the Hadleyville town saloon, not at all. The President, unlike Gary Cooper, is not alone—no, the nation is ready for this, the whole damn town will be marching down

Main Street tonight behind Uncle Sam and Ike and Dick and Edgar and Joe and Irving and all the rest, no one's forsaking anybody, oh my darling, we're all in on this one, everybody from the Supreme Court, Congress, and the Cabinet, down to your average housewife, ditchdigger, man in the street, give or take a skunk or two. Who will be dealt with. HUAC has already launched an investigation of all those protesting the executions, noting that "nowhere has the craven hypocrisy of Communism been exposed so tellingly as in the monstrous campaign organized in behalf of atomic espionage agents Julius and Ethel Rosenberg!" Why, it's as bad as Billy the Kid protesting against "mob law" when he got sentenced to be hung for twenty-one murders. The essence of the Phantom's campaign, says HUAC, alerting the Internal Revenue Service, is deception and fraud, "fraud with sinister purpose and spectacular profit, [seeking] to blacken the name of America throughout the world, and [milking] the American people of some half million dollars while it did so!" Not that they've loosened the bonds on these two copperheads. On the contrary! As *The Commonweal* has noted:

> They have maneuvered the President into a position where if he did grant a stay it would be widely interpreted as succumbing to Communist pressure in this country and the pressure of Communist propaganda abroad—which is precisely what the United States cannot afford at this time. . . .

No, it cannot. The American press is unanimous: "The switch must be pulled!" The people, a poll shows, agree. "The will to execute them," in the words of the Catholic weekly *America,* is "an affirmation by America, as the voice of humanity, of its will to survive. . . . Such conspirators against humanity must either die or relent if humanity is to live!" Eisenhower knows this. He's in complete agreement, he has said so. Then, why this strange titillation, this odd anxiety, this recurring note of impending doo-oom that makes one want to giggle and clutch his balls? Of course, there are precedents for last-minute clemency. During the Civil War, for example, General William Tecumseh Sherman, never one to fuck around about such things, arrested one of Horace Greeley's newspaper correspondents, charged him with spying, and was about to shoot the man, when Abraham Lincoln stepped in and saved the reporter's life. Of course, Abe himself got shot after that, the lessons should be clear. No, it's something . . . ah! the woman perhaps! And the children, the two boys . . .

> The Rosenberg case focuses attention once again on the fact that Communism is a profound spiritual and psychological evil as well as a

conspiratorial and military force. . . . "He that loves a son or daughter more than Me is not worthy of Me." Communism has proven to be a vicious caricature of Christianity. The Rosenbergs, who were willing to betray their people, their country, and humanity itself, stand ready now to leave their own two children orphans. . . .

Yes, *The Commonweal* is right, something so malignant here as to fall beyond a decent man's understanding: who can account for a Spirit so perverse that it turns Jesus on His head and tears perniciously at the roots of parenthood all at once, mocks sainthood and the social contract at a stroke? These two boys, so cheaply exhibited these past few weeks, yet so pathetic . . . and the President himself is a father, is he not, a grandfather, an affectionate man who tragically lost his first little boy; only a day or so ago there was that touching scene with Smokey Bear, and now Father's Day coming up Sunday—who in all this crowd can truthfully say he or she would deny these boys their parents, this family their longed-for reunion? And who is not, at the same time, flushed with awe and excitement at watching this real-life drama, its tragic end foretold, unfold inexorably before their very eyes? And listen, not only must the President orphan these two small boys, he must—this gallant lover from the border wars—kill a woman in cold blood. Could Bill Hart have strung up little Eva—or even the town trollop? Could old Lafe McKee or Bill Farnum bring such a judgment down on a lady, even were she Belle Starr herself? Of course, a lot of women died in the West, not all in their beds, but more often than not it was an accident, a stray bullet, or a whore's impulsive sacrifice. Not even villains like Walter Miller or Arthur Kennedy ever dragged them out to the tree and slapped the horse's rump. There's only one woman who's ever been put to death by federal authorities in American history before, and that was Mary Suratt for helping to murder a President. True, like the Judge says, a "crime worse than murder" . . . yet there is a softness here, deep in the heart of the American soul, that is being probed, pinched, palpated . . .

> Oh to be torn 'twixt love and duty!
> Supposin' I'd lose mah fair-haired beauty!
> Look at that big hand move along,
>   Nearin' high noon . . . !

And then he appears: the President of the United States of America. High up on the White House balcony, surrounded by family and friends. Tall, gentle, handsome, shy, his blue eyes twinkling.

The crowd is at first silent, momentarily awed, train wheels pounding through their heads—then they shake off the strange spell and break into thunderous cheers.

"WE LIKE IKE! WE LIKE IKE!"

Already, distantly, bells are tolling.

"Put your trap on a short chain, Ike!"

"Change trains for the future!"

"Whoo! Whoo!"

The President smiles, lifts his arms. "Friends . . ."

The crowd falls silent. Expectant.

TIME say: "At the focus of pressure, / Dwight Eisenhower did not flinch. . . ."

INTERMEZZO

The Clemency Appeals

A Dramatic Dialogue by Ethel Rosenberg and Dwight Eisenhower

Bare stage. Dim figure of Justice in the background. Low distant hum of the world's ceaseless traffic. At no time during the dialogue does the PRESIDENT address the PRISONER, or even acknowledge her presence on the same stage. The PRISONER, aware of this, sometimes speaks to him directly, but more often seems to be trying to reach him by bouncing echoes off the Audience:

PRIS: (*liturgically*)   Petitioner respectfully
prays that she be granted
a pardon or commutation
for the following reasons:
FIRST . . .

PRES: (*clearing his throat*) I have given earnest consideration . . .

PRIS: (*insistently*) FIRST: that we are innocent.

PRES: I have made a careful examination . . .

PRIS: Innocent, as we have proclaimed and maintained from the time of our arrest.

PRES: . . . into this . . . case . . .

PRIS: Innocent. This is the whole truth.

PRES: And am satisfied . . .

PRIS: Do not dishonor America, Mr. President, by considering as a condition of our right to survive the delivery of a confession of guilt of a crime we did not commit.

247

PRES: I am convinced . . .

PRIS: We told you the truth: we are innocent. The truth does not change.

PRES: There is no question in my mind . . .

PRIS: We have been told again and again, until we have become sick at heart . . .

PRES: No judge has ever expressed any doubt . . .

PRIS: . . . that our proud defense of our innocence is arrogant, not proud, and motivated . . .

PRES: The only conclusion to be drawn . . .

PRIS: . . . not by a desire to maintain our integrity, but to achieve the questionable "glory" of some undefined "martyrdom."

PRES: . . . is that the Rosenbergs have received the benefit of every safeguard . . .

PRIS: This is not so.

PRES: . . . which American justice can provide.

PRIS: We are not martyrs or heroes, nor do we wish to be.

PRES: Every safeguard . . .

PRIS: We do not want to die. We are young, too young, for death.

PRES: Every opportunity . . .

PRIS: We wish to live. Yes, we wish to live . . .

PRES: The fullest measure of justice and due process of law . . .

PRIS: . . . but in the simple dignity that clothes only those who have been honest with themselves and their fellow men. Therefore, in honesty, we can only say that . . .

PRES: . . . their full measure of justice . . .

PRIS: . . . we are *innocent* of this crime.

PRES: . . . in the time-honored tradition of American justice.

PRIS: SECOND: We understand, however, that the President considers himself bound by the verdict of guilt, although, on the evidence, a contrary conclusion may be admissible.

PRES: Now, when . . .

PRIS: But many times before there has been too unhesitating reliance on the verdict of the moment and regret for the death that closed the door to remedy when the truth, as it will, has risen.

PRES: (*firmly*) Now, when in their most solemn judgment the tribunals of the United States have adjudged them guilty and the sentence just, I will not intervene in this matter.

PRIS: You may not believe us, but the passage of even the few short months since last we appealed to you is confirming our prediction that, in the inexorable operation of time and conscience, the truth of our innocence would emerge.

PRES: (*flatly*) I will not intervene.

PRIS: (*after a moment's hesitation*) THIRD . . .

PRES: And I have determined that it is my duty . . .

PRIS: (*mustering strength*) THIRD: The Government's case . . .

PRES: My duty in the interest of the people of the United States . . .

PRIS: (*weakening, turning toward the* PRESIDENT) The Government's case . . .

PRES: . . . not to set aside the verdict of their representatives.

PRIS: (*softly, to the* PRESIDENT) It is chiefly the death sentence I would entreat you to ponder.

PRES: (*as though to himself*) I must say that it goes against the grain to avoid interfering in the case where a woman is to receive capital punishment.

PRIS: (*gently*) At various intervals during the two long and bitter years I have spent in the Death House at Sing Sing, I have had the impulse to address myself to the President of the United States.

PRES: (*more firmly again*) Over against this, however, must be placed one or two facts that have great significance. The first of these . . .

PRIS: (*dreamily*) And Dwight D. Eisenhower was "Liberator" to millions before he was ever "President."

PRES: The first of these is that in this instance it is the woman who is the strong and recalcitrant character . . .

PRIS: Always, in the end, a certain innate shyness . . .

PRES: The man is the weak one.

PRIS: . . . an embarrassment almost, comparable to that which the ordinary person feels in the presence of the great and the famous . . .

PRES: She has obviously been the leader in everything they did in the spy ring.

PRIS: (*sighing, turning away*) True, to date, you have not seen fit to spare our lives.

PRES: The second thing is that if there would be any commuting of the woman's sentence without the man's then from here on the Soviets would simply recruit their spies from among women.

PRIS: (*to the* PRESIDENT, *more firmly*) Be that as it may, it is my humble belief that the burdens of your office and the exigencies of the times have allowed of no genuine opportunity, as yet, for your more personal consideration.

PRES: The execution of two human beings is a grave matter.

PRIS: But now I ask this man, whose name is one with glory . . .

PRES: A grave matter . . .

PRIS: . . . What glory there is that is greater than an offering to God of a simple act of compassion!

PRES: But even graver is the thought of the millions of dead whose deaths may be directly attributable to what these spies have done.

PRIS: (*angrily*) No one, other than the trial judge, has even pretended that the atom-bomb material allegedly transmitted in the course of the instant conspiracy was of any substantial value to the Soviet Union!

PRES: The nature of the crime for which they have been found guilty and sentenced far exceeds that of the taking of the life of another citizen; it involves the deliberate betrayal of the entire nation and could very well result in the death of many, many thousands of innocent citizens.

PRIS: Specifically, in relation to this case, the Government itself, after the trial, conceded that: "Greenglass's diagrams have a theatrical quality," and because he was not a scientist, "must have counted for little."

PRES: By immeasurably increasing the chances of atomic war, the Rosenbergs may have condemned to death tens of millions of innocent people all over the world.

PRIS: It is perfectly clear that such valueless information could have had little effectiveness "in putting into the hands of the Russians the A-bomb," even had they not possessed the "secret."

PRES: By their act these two individuals have in fact betrayed the cause of freedom for which free men are fighting and dying at this very hour.

PRIS: (*a bit desperately*) We submitted documentary evidence to show that David Greenglass, trapped by his own misdeeds, hysterical with fear for his own life and that of Ruth, his wife, fell back on his lifelong habit of lying, exploited by his shrewd-minded and equally guilty wife, to fabricate, bit by bit, a *monstrous* tale that has sent us, *his own flesh and blood,* down a long and terrible path toward death!

PRES: (*oblivious to this outburst*) When democracy's enemies . . .

PRIS: We ask you, Mr. President, the civilized head of a civilized nation, to judge our plea with reason and humanity—and remember! *we are a father and a mother!*

PRES: (*pressing on*) When democracy's enemies have been judged guilty of a crime as horrible as that of which the Rosenbergs were con-victed . . .

PRIS: (*rising to full power*) Our sentences violate truth and the instincts of civilized humanity! The compassion of men sees us as victims caught in the terrible interplay of clashing ideologies and feverish international enmities. As Commander-in-Chief of the European theater, you had am-ple opportunity to witness the wanton and hideous tortures that such a policy of vengeance had wreaked upon vast multitudes of guiltless vic-tims. Today, while these ghastly mass butchers, these obscene racists, are graciously receiving the benefits of mercy and in many instances being reinstated in public office, the great democratic United States is proposing the savage destruction of a small unoffending Jewish family, whose guilt is seriously doubted throughout the length and breadth of the civilized world! We appeal to your mind and conscience, Mr. Pres-ident, to take counsel with the reasons of others and with the deepest human feelings that treasure life and shun its taking. *The facts of our case have touched the conscience of civilization!*

PRES: (*momentarily weakening*) My only concern is in the . . . area of statecraft. The *effect* of the action . . .

PRIS: (*seizing on this*) If you will not hear our voices, hear the voices of the world! Hear the great and humble for the sake of America!

VOICES: (*rolling in behind the* PRISONER's *last speech, overlapping each other, slowly augmenting in volume, then diminishing when the* PRESIDENT *interrupts*) We the undersigned rabbis and religious leaders of the Holy Land . . . Our committee is today comprised of men who you know, Mr. President, to be of the highest character . . . Will you express in my name the deep revulsion . . . I, an Orthodox rabbi . . . I had the honor to fight with the American Army . . . spiritual and executive leaders in their respective denominations . . . Is it customary for spies to be paid in wristwatches and console tables? . . . utterly disproportionate to the offense for this couple with two young children to be put to . . . sinister threat of fascism and a new world war . . . Mr. President, all of us, as pastors . . . aggressive pressure of the anti-Semites, Negro-haters . . . hope thus to honor and render justice to the memory of my brother Bartolomeo Vanzetti, who before dying said . . . indeed regrettable . . . profoundly moved by the death sentence pronounced on Ethel and . . . the extreme severity . . . a tragic event for all lovers of the . . . when conducted in a climate of fear and suspicion which breeds reckless and irresponsible action . . . I cannot but deplore . . . My conscience compels me . . . without precedent in the West . . . I pray the Lord and hope the cruel sentence passed . . . contemplate with horror . . . obtained during a period of mounting hysteria . . . never before imposed . . . Together with nearly twenty-three hundred other clergymen . . . cruel, inhuman and barbaric in the extreme . . . in the name of God and the quality of mercy . . . your deep religious feeling and your awareness of the spirit of good within you . . . in the very name of our common ideal of justice and generosity which we derive from the Bible . . . political murder . . . to use the power which the Constitution of the United States gives you . . . urge you to commute . . . in the spirit of love which casts out fear . . . your prerogative of clemency . . . to reconsider your refusal . . . this savage verdict . . . would it not be embarrassing if, after the execution of the Rosenbergs, it could be shown that . . .

PRES: (*interrupting fiercely,* VOICES *fading*) I am not unmindful of the fact that this case has aroused grave concern both here and abroad in the minds of serious people.

PRIS: (*to the* PRESIDENT, *trying to hang on to the momentum*) The guilt in this case, if we die, will be America's! The shame, if we die, will dishonor this generation!

PRES: (*as though calling out to the vanished* VOICES) But what you did *not* suggest was the need for considering the known convictions of Communist leaders that free governments—and especially the American government—are notoriously weak and fearful . . .

PRIS: Mr. President—

PRES: . . . and that consequently subversive and other kinds of activities can be conducted against them with no real fear of dire punishment on the part of the perpetrator.

PRIS: (*urgently, almost amorously*) Take counsel with your good wife; of statesmen there are enough and to spare.

PRES: It is, of course, important to the Communists to have this contention sustained and justified.

PRIS: Take counsel with the mother of your only son; her heart which understands my grief so well and my longing to see my sons grown to manhood like her own . . .

PRES: In the present case, they have even stooped to dragging in young and innocent children in order to serve their own purpose!

PRIS: . . . with loving husband at my side even as you are at hers!

PRES: The action of these people has exposed to greater danger literally millions of our citizens.

PRIS: Her heart must plead my cause with grace and with felicity!

PRES: Within the last two days, the Supreme Court, convened in a special session, has again reviewed a further point which one of the Justices felt the Rosenbergs should have an opportunity to present.

PRIS: (*on her knees, pleading*) I approach you solely on the basis of mercy . . .

PRES: (*edging away*) This morning the Supreme Court ruled that there was no substance to this point.

PRIS: . . . and earnestly beseech you to let this quality sway you rather than any narrow judicial concern, which is after all the province of the courts.

PRES: The legal processes of democracy have been marshaled to their maximum strength to protect the lives of convicted spies.

PRIS: It is rather the province of the affectionate grandfather . . .

PRES: Accordingly . . .

PRIS: . . . the sensitive artist, the devoutly religious man . . .

PRES: Accordingly, only the most extraordinary circumstances . . .

PRIS: . . . that I would enter. I ask this man . . .

PRES: Only the most extraordinary circumstances would warrant executive intervention in the case.

PRIS: I ask this man, himself no stranger to the humanities, what man there is that history has acclaimed great, whose greatness has not been measured in terms of his goodness? Truly . . .

PRES: If any other different situation arises that makes it look like a question of policy, of state policy, they can bring it back to me. As of now . . .

PRIS: Truly, the stories of Christ, of Moses, of Gandhi hold more sheer wonderment and spiritual treasure than all the conquests of Napoleon!

PRES: As of now, my decision was made purely on the basis of what the courts had found in all this long discussion.

PRIS: We do not want to die!

PRES: We are a nation under law and our affairs are governed by the just exercise of these laws.

PRIS: We are young, too young, for death. We wish to live!

PRES: The courts have done for these people everything possible.

PRIS: We told you the truth! We are innocent of this crime!

PRES: Have adjudged them guilty and the sentence just.

PRIS: *Innocent!*

PRES: Given them every right.

PRIS: Please—!

PRES: I will not intervene in this matter.

PRIS: *We do not want to die!*

PRES: I will not intervene.

PART THREE

FRIDAY AFTERNOON

15.

Iron Butt Gets Smeared Again

I left the President out on Harry's Balcony, delivering to the sunburnt and straw-hatted crowds below his "Statement Declining to Intervene on Behalf of Julius and Ethel Rosenberg," to return to my office, taking as circuitous a route out of the White House as I thought I could get away with—when was the General ever going to show me around this place, I wondered? What I'd been allowed to see of the White House, I'd liked: it was roomy and comfortable, if maybe too public, and it had a lot of interesting corners. I especially liked the Lincoln Sitting Room. There was an old chair I had that would look good in there. I'd never been up to the Solarium where Ike held his stag parties, but I hoped it was like my bell tower back in Whittier, only fancier.

On the way out, I passed Eisenhower's valet polishing up the Presidential golf clubs for an afternoon on the course. Or maybe to pot around on the White House lawn when the mobs had left. Familiar sight this spring: the Man of Destiny out there in his white sport shirt, tan cap, and gray slacks, whopping golf balls around the grounds like popcorn, like snow-white Eisenhoppers, while his faithful old Army sergeant, now his valet, chased about after them with a yellow bag, reminding old-timers of Woodrow Wilson's shepherd out on the White House pasture gathering up sacksful of scattered wool tufts and dung for the vegetable garden. His valet did everything for him: helped him on with his clothes, put paste on his toothbrush, buttoned his fly, ironed his shoe strings, probably even wiped his ass when he shat, if he even did that for himself.

A tremendous cheer exploded out on the White House lawn. He'd got to the main part. This, I thought, was what made Eisenhower great, this was why he was our President: he knew how to kill. He knew how to deal with valets and orderlies, and he knew how to kill. "My only concern is in the area of statecraft . . ." Just close the switches, smile like a monkey, then go out and swat a few. Of course, it was easy for him, growing up in a town that had had Wild Bill Hickok for its sheriff, he probably had it in his blood. I had naturally put myself in his position: could *I* have refused them clemency? I wasn't sure. I knew what the national consensus was and I rarely bucked it, but I could see Grandma Milhous shaking her dark head solemnly from her rocking chair, Mom watching me wistfully from a distant room, softening my heart. But then, as I held out my hand to them in reconciliation, there was Dad, rearing up red-faced in front of me with the strap in his hand. Certainly, no matter what choice I made, I would have been troubled and depressed by the decision long before and long after. Eisenhower merely weighed the effects their deaths would likely have out in the world (mainly positive, he supposed: show them we mean business), affably declined to intervene, and departed for the golf links. Nothing more complicated than sizing up the distance of an approach shot and choosing the right iron. And everybody loved him for this. Even Ethel Rosenberg, about to be wired up and wiped out by the callous sonuvabitch, saw him as "an affectionate grandfather" and "sensitive artist." The Supreme Court had just warned him, I'd read it myself: "Vacating this stay is not to be construed as endorsing the wisdom or appropriateness to this case of a death sentence"—all but a plea for mercy, but the sensitive artist, with a blank happy smile, ignored it. He probably never even read it. Well, he'd been hit by lightning himself, after all, maybe he underestimated the effects.

I first met the General at the Bohemian Grove near San Francisco in 1950, shortly after I'd won the Republican nomination in California for the Senate, and instinctively, with that first handshake, I'd known him: the most popular boy in school, star of the team, reluctant grinning stud, the easygoing joker who was always getting into the kind of fun-loving trouble I shied from but envied, pulling shenanigans that made the old folks grin and shake their heads, making out with everybody, the natural leader. Oh, I was a leader, too, of course. If there was an election, I ran, and often as not, because I worked my butt off, I won. But a vote isn't love, an election is not an embrace. The girls looked up to me, but if I grinned or kidded with them like the other guys, they'd get puzzled and upset, push my hands away. It was like we were in some

kind of play, like they knew already how things had to come out and I
was threatening them with a disturbing change in the plot. Growing up
was difficult for me. Of course, I soon discovered that Eisenhower and I
had a lot in common, too—we both came from small towns out west and
families of brothers, both dreamed of becoming railroad engineers or
seeking adventure in Latin America, both loved football, suffered from
nervous stomachs, became military officers, played poker, and had had
genuine Horatio Alger careers. But there was always a difference. I
dreamed of becoming a railroad engineer because I knew I *ought* to—
Eisenhower actually would have been happy throwing his life away on a
goddamn train. Or punching cows in Argentina. The only reason I
wanted to go to Cuba was to make money and become respectable in
Washington and New York. Also I was in trouble with a judge and getting
my ass sued off by an irate client in Whittier for fucking up my first big
law case, and I figured I might want to go where the rules were less
suffocating. And quickly. This could never have happened to Eisenhower, he was too dumb. As for the football team, I sat on the bench
and cheered till my lungs hurt, and sometimes they told me they
couldn't have won without me there, but just the same my name wasn't
in the newspapers next day, and nobody carried me off the field on their
shoulders, like they did Ike. The only action I ever saw was in practice
when they used me as cannon fodder, a tackling dummy with legs. They
wouldn't even give me a school letter, the fucking tight bastards. And so
there I was that day in San Francisco, on the very threshold of such
fame and glory rarely even dreamed of by one so young, and yet utterly
subdued, held in total wonder by that loose-witted old man—*He's been
chosen!* I thought, though at the time I wasn't thinking so much of the
Presidency.

We were luncheon guests that day of former President Herbert
Hoover, who, though shrunken, still emanated vestiges of that ancient
power. Like a shadow behind the eyes. He liked me, as most old men
did, we were both California Quakers, after all, and believers in the
Four Selfs. I'd actually had direct correspondence with his wife some
years before when I was student body president at Whittier College, her
alma mater, and when I'd first had a chance to meet him, I'd boned up
before on all his writings in order to quote back at him some of his pet
phrases about "rugged individualism" and "economic liberty," winning
the old boy's everlasting support, only hoping all the time it wouldn't
some day prove an embarrassment. We'd even got so close he'd confessed to me what it felt like, that awful day in 1932, when he first felt
the power going out of him. The strange hollowness, the painful defla-

tion as his body closed in upon the void, the headaches, back trouble. . . . Naturally, I'd wanted to know everything, what the Incarnation felt like, how you knew when it had begun, the possibilities . . .

"How did it happen, Mr. Hoover . . . the first time?"

He'd given me a strange look then, pity maybe, or envy, I didn't know what it was, but it had seemed somehow unbecoming for a former President of the United States. "I'd, uh . . . I'd rather not say, son," he'd said.

Anyway, he was pleased to make the introductions that day at the Bohemian Grove, and had even tossed a few familiar superlatives about me Eisenhower's way, saying my election to the Senate would be "the greatest good that can come to our country"—but I don't think the General even saw me during that handshake. A bright friendly twinkle in his blue eyes, but they were restless, took in everything at once, and nothing. What was he looking for? Comradeship? A way out? He laughed so easily. Everything he said was dumb, yet somehow attractive. And he seemed completely in awe of politicians, held his expletives in check as though among priests, made fun of his own political ignorance. "What does an old soldier know about such things?" he grinned. He'd be hell to beat in a poker game, I thought.

Actually, I'd seen him before—but from a distance—five years earlier, and then my impression of him had been that of every other American: he was not only a great hero, but also a real good guy in the best tradition of the American heartland. It was just after V-E Day and I was still celebrating my own survival: I couldn't complain, in spite of the exile I'd had a fairly soft tour—even enjoyable at times and wildly free from the restraints of home—and now, sane and whole and with a pocket full of poker winnings, there I was, just thirty-two years old, about to become a father for the first time, and the whole wide world spread out before me. I was finishing out my Naval duty by negotiating settlements of terminated war contracts in the Bureau of Aeronautics office in New York City, and from a twentieth-floor window of that dreary building I'd watched General Eisenhower go motoring by, standing up in the back of his car, both arms raised high over his head. Instinctively, I'd raised my own: it had felt good. That's a terrific gesture, I'd thought then. Churchill raises two stubby fingers, a Texan raises both his arms. But even from that distance, I could see that this man was no intellectual giant. No man who thought seriously about things could smile like that.

For the past year and a half now, since my historic trip to his SHAPE headquarters in Paris, I'd got to know him a lot better. After all, we'd

suffered the rigors of a tough campaign together, had won an election
and now ran the country together, we were a team. Yet that San Francisco luncheon seemed to have set the tone and conditions of our relationship ever since: he was the General, I was the deferential junior
officer; I was the professional lawyer and politician, he was the reluctant
amateur, acknowledging my know-how but skeptical of its source; he
was the Old Man, I the son he was surprised by once a week at Sunday
dinners. He had his cronies, old and new, people like General Clay and
George Humphrey, and he laughed and snorted with them, but not with
me. Whenever I drew near, they stifled their laughter, interrupted their
conversations, broke their back-slapping huddle, turned to give me their
attention, scarcely concealing their impatience and disapproval. He
liked people around him who were confident and cheerful, and I could
never be both at the same time. The trouble was, most of those smug
pals of his didn't know shit from Shinola around here—politics is a
science and a skill like any other, and I was one of the best professionals
in the business, but he never seemed to give a damn about my opinions,
only asking me for them because he'd been brought up in the military to
do that, consult your juniors so they don't get too restless. Everyone
always admired how hard I worked, but Eisenhower seemed to accept
this like he accepted everything else: he measured my capacity and then
took it for granted, as a fact he could work with. Typically overeager,
though, I'd tried to take on the world during those early days and so
had set a standard for myself I could never live up to and survive. When
overstretched, I needed praise or pity to keep going, but I learned very
early not to seek it from the Old Man—nothing turned him off faster. I
had to go to Bill Rogers or Bert Andrews or Pat instead. I learned to
move at the periphery of his vision, in profile as it were: self-assured,
intense, preoccupied, businesslike. He watched me as though from another room, somewhat amused.

Maybe, taking a few chances, I might have cracked through this con-
descension and made out with him on some deeper, more intimate level
—but I couldn't take those chances, I couldn't take *any* chances, not
now: I was waiting for the big one, and I couldn't risk blowing it. There
are people who do not wish to surrender to the Incarnation, who do not
wish to be possessed by Uncle Sam, be used by him, moved by him, who
do not wish to feel his presence pushing out from behind their own
features, distorting them, printing them on the blank face of the world,
people who fear the forces leaking out their fingertips, the pressure in
the skull, the cramp in the groin. Let me say right here that I was never
one of them. It's true, sometimes I envied these people: they were free

of constraints I too had once been free of, they could blaspheme and grow beards, trade wives and mink coats, go on a bender, be emphatically inconsistent—the paradox of power: to lead a nation of free men is to be the least free among them. Jefferson once said that when a man assumes a public trust, he should consider himself as public property. Property! Jefferson knew how to choose his words. To lead a land of free-enterprise entrepreneurs was to be their communal socialized possession. But this was what I wanted and so to that extent I was free: if these were chains, I chose them.

Eisenhower, who thought himself free, was in fact the real captive, much more the victim than I would ever be in his place. Because—and this was the central truth about Dwight David Eisenhower and that by which his whole role in world history must be judged, far more important than his deviousness, his lack of sophistication, his gregariousness, his selfishness, his bumbling style or calculating ambition—he was unconscious. Oh, alert, yes, and he wasn't stupid—our best historian and mathematician, his classmates at Abilene High had called him back in 1909, bad as his grades had been—but in any larger sense, he was simply unconscious. He didn't know what was going on. And maybe in fact this was why we all liked him. He really supposed he'd done his duty to God, country, and Abilene, won the war in Europe for all the good guys, treated his juniors and Mamie fairly and squarely, and now led his people as their President by holding these weekly bull sessions in the Cabinet Room, their team captain and cheerleader. He even thought that people were listening to him and doing the things he suggested they do! He sat in the Oval Office, signed bills, received ministers, set the barometer, and kept his desk clean, and he didn't even grasp what it was he was doing, people had to explain it to him. Whenever Uncle Sam shazammed himself back into the General, the General would blink, glance around in amazement, then shrug and say something like: "I keep telling you fellows I don't like to do this sort of thing."

I'd been a witness to an occasional transformation as that stern old steel-fisted top-hatted Superhero submerged himself into Dwight D. Eisenhower: there was always a certain broadening of the nose, softening of the mouth, hair falling out, elongation of the ears, slumping of the shoulders. And then back again the same way. It looked easy, and as far as I could tell, Eisenhower didn't suffer at all, though there was a perceptible aging each time. I'd tried it myself, at home, alone—except for Checkers, who, it seemed to me, was closer than I was to making it—but nothing had ever happened. Ever since the Checkers speech, I'd had the feeling I could do it if I tried hard enough, and I'd crouch in front of the bathroom mirror and grunt and push, but all that ever came of it was that I'd get Checkers overexcited, and he'd start barking his damned head off, wake the whole house up. "What are you doing to that dog, Dick?" Pat would scold sleepily from the bedroom. I often wondered if it was bad luck to live on a street named after Sam Tilden. The neighborhood had jinxed Kefauver and Sparkman, after all . . . I'd have to think about this.

Outside, the grounds and streets around the White House were jammed with noisy people, tourists mostly, probably friendly, and on an ordinary day I'd enjoy emerging from an important meeting, still wreathed in authoritative sources, informed circles, those close to the center, and moving boldly into their midst, shaking hands, exchanging small talk. I have a strong emotional feeling for the problems of what I'd call ordinary people. I've known unemployed people, for example, and I know what their problems are. As to shaking hands, I like to do that—it brightens people's lives to meet a celebrity, and besides, I'm rather good at it. I'm able to treat each person as an individual. As a matter of fact, I have even shaken hands with some Communists. But today I was in a hurry: my own skull was tingling with the imminence of the electrocutions and I knew I'd have to work fast to get everything sorted out. Besides, I'd had enough scary encounters with mobs for one day. There are tricks in dealing with crowds, and if they begin to press too hard, I look around for a thin spot and move back through it toward a car. I didn't see my own car anywhere, John apparently hadn't got through, so I slipped through a gap in the mob created by the mounted Park Police, between the ass ends of a couple of horses, past the farmers posing for snapshots and the guys in checkered caps hustling bus tours, and grabbed a battered old Coastline cab, just clattering by. Perfect! I was buoyed up by all the excitement, I had a very "up" feeling, very positive, it was as though the day were getting under way at last, an important day: this one might mean the Presidency for me or no! "Senate Office Building," I ordered, leaping in, "and, uh, step on it!" Just like in the old George Raft movies, I felt pleased by my luck and aplomb, the perfect timing, all I needed now was a fat black cigar, everything was clicking, I might even pick up something from the cabdriver, touch the pulse of the nation, so to speak—eight hours to go, and by God I was going to make the most of them, I was already making the most of them. The only thing that spoiled this great feeling was the pile of horseturds I'd apparently stepped in on my way past the mounted cops.

"Step on *what*, mac?" growled the cabdriver, rolling around to glare sourly at me. Ugly man, hard, looked foreign. Pimply, unshaven, thick dirty glasses, fat lips.

I glared back at him, keeping my cool, then hauled the door shut, but it was loose on its hinges and it just whumped up heavily against the frame and swung open again. People had turned to stare at us, some seemed to recognize me, they were moving toward the cab. I grabbed the door with both hands and yanked it hard—it slammed to with a crumping smashing noise, and the window dropped three inches, a crack branching through it like a pencil drawing of a tree.

"Nice goin', big shot," said the driver drily. "Ya broke it. That'll cost ya five bucks." He stuck out his hand at me, grubby, short-fingered. "Right now, or we don't go *no*where."

I sighed irritably. Trick window, I supposed, I was just getting taken, but what could I do about it? This was the only cab in sight and I did not want to get out there with those people again. I reached into my pocket for my billfold, pulled out a five-dollar bill. The Raft movie was over and I was into something more familiar.

He snatched the bill out of my hand with a grin, started to swing around, then turned back, wrinkled his nose, sniffed, winced at me: "Is that you makin' that smell, chief?"

"I . . . I stepped in . . . something," I explained.

"Yeah? Well, that'll be another five bucks," he said, and whipped another bill out of my wallet—it looked like a ten.

"Hey, wait a minute," I said, but he had already pitched around, shifted gears, gunned the motor, honked the horn, and was moving aggressively into the crowd. To hell with it. Cut your losses. I could probably get it back out of my office expense fund.

"Say, what's the high muckey-mucks doin' in there," he asked, scowling and shaking his fist at the crowds that clotted the streets, "givin' away free nookie?"

"The atom spies," I replied stiffly. "The, uh, President is delivering his—"

"You mean Eisenhower?" he shouted back over his shoulder. "Hey, I hear Mamie's askin' for a divorce!"

"A divorce—? No, I—"

"Yeah, she says she's gettin' sick 'n' tired of him doin' to the country all the time what he oughta be doin' to her! Haw haw haw!"

Ah, screw the pulse of the nation, I thought, sitting back, scraping the horseshit off my shoe on the back of the seat in front. The cab was edging slowly around past the Ellipse, General Sherman rearing up on my left like his pants were on fire, lumpen pioneers and the Washington obelisk holding the right. Washington had got the obelisk, Jefferson the dome and circle, Lincoln the cube, what was there left for me? I wondered. The pyramid maybe. Something modern and Western would be more appropriate, but all I could think of were the false fronts in the old cowtowns.

"Hey, speakin' a horse manure," the driver hollered, lurching and braking through the milling crowds, "Harry Truman got in trouble with his daughter about that! Margaret come to her old lady and complained that Harry had disgraced the family by sayin' 'manure' insteada 'fertilizer' when he come to present the prizes at her Ladies' Horticultural Club. 'Hell,' says Bess, 'that's okay, it's took me thirty years to get him to say manure!' "

I humph-humphed ambivalently. A stupid joke, but it was enough to remind me that I had my own speech to think about: should I take the high road or the low road? I ran over some phrases in my mind: uh, peace in the world . . . reduce the danger . . . I cannot and will not, uh, I have determined that, reached the conclusion . . . uh, with the help of a mobilized public opinion . . . what I am suggesting, just running it out hypothetically, is that, uh, some very strong medicine . . . getting down frankly into the arena . . . moving upward strongly . . .

"Bess, ya know, has decided to become a model! Yeah, now that Harry's out of a job, she's gonna be a model for dowager styles, see? A friend asked her: 'But whaddaya gonna do about that big ass o' yours, Bess?' And she says: 'Oh, he'll stay home on the farm!' Hoo hah!"

Ah, some of our good partisans . . . many decent, uh, decent Americans . . . gathered here . . . something about, let's see, we must, uh, we must seize the moment, yes, not just cosmetics, but . . . ah, on the brink, yes, I think we would be less than candid were we not to admit . . .

"I got three little girls, ya know—well, they ain't so little any more, in fact they just got married the other day. All on the same day, a cute idea!"

"Oh? Yes . . . yes, it is . . ." I could get a lot fancier, of course. But people have known me too long for me to come on all of a sudden talking like Adlai Stevenson. If I'm to convince people, it'll be in simple declarative sentences, by the force of facts.

"Yeah, and they all spent their first night in my house, see? When they come down to breakfast the next morning, I ask 'em, I says: 'Honey, whaddaya think o' married life?' Well, the first one, she says: 'Daddy, with my husband it was just like Winston Churchill, all blood, sweat, and tears!' And the second one, she says: 'My old man was like

Roosevelt, I thought I'd never get him out—four times, before he finally died on me!' "

Roosevelt had a lot of style, all right, I thought as the cabbie jerked and wormed through the crowds. I wondered if there was something of his I could borrow for tonight. Maybe a variation on that four-freedoms idea—the freedom of the modern housewife, for example, or the freedom to hear Ike pray at the Inauguration, the freedom of television, and so on. Work the Rosenbergs in somewhere maybe. The main thing, though, was: keep it short and blunt, sound a warning note or two, and tell 'em what they want to hear. My greatest weakness was getting over-intellectual in my speeches. I'm known as an activist and an organizer, but some people have said I'm sort of an egghead in the Republican Party. It's true, I'm more on the thought side than the action side—I'm like Wilson in that regard, except that he always overdid it. I know how to avoid that, I can tame and coddle the intellectual Dillingers as easily as I can outsmart the double domes. . . .

"So I asked the third one, 'Well, what about you, honey?' And she says, 'Well, mine was just like Harry Truman, Daddy. He wanted out before he'd ever got in, then when he did get in, he didn't know what to do there. Finally, he just rolled over and quit, and when I asked him why, he says: "Lady, the fuck stops here!" ' Haw haw haw!"

Well, at least it wasn't about me, I thought. My shoe seemed to be caught under the front seat. Shoestring snagged or something. As I twisted it back and forth, trying to get it free, it suddenly came to me that the roller coaster in my dream last night had not been a roller coaster at all, but one of those rides they call an Octopus, and it had had a sign on it that said MOSAIC OF HISTORY. Funny how dreams kept developing after you'd dreamt them . . . I seemed to remember that little Ethel was wearing an "A" on her chest, too. And that she looked a lot like my first girlfriend back in Whittier. Maybe because of Sheriff Street . . . my girlfriend's old man was the local chief of police . . .

The cabbie, leaning on the horn, bulled his way around a bus, through an onrush of latecomers pouring over from the Hill, and suddenly we were free, shooting up toward the old Willard Hotel. "Hey, pal!" he shouted back over his shoulder: "Am I steppin'? Am I steppin'?"

I let myself smile. I wondered if I was going to have to take my foot out to get the shoe free.

"Say, I heard a good one about the Vice President," he shouted back. "What—!?"

"Back in the war, see, when he was tryin' to dodge the draft, he went to work for the OPA. And while he was there, he picked up this chick and took her out by the old quarry and parked with her. He says, 'I hope ya don't mind if we park here a little while—it's okay, cuz I *am* Dick Nixon of the OPA!' And she says, 'Well, I don't usually do this sorta thing, but I guess it's all right, so long as you're Dick Nixon of the OPA . . . !' "

"Uh, listen . . ."

"So he puts his arm around her, see, and he says, 'I hope ya don't mind my puttin' my arm around ya like this, it's really okay, on accounta I *am* Dick Nixon of the OPA!' And she says, 'Well, I usually don't allow—' "

"Yeah, listen, I've heard that—"

"Wait a minute! It gets better! He puts his other hand on her knee, see, and—"

"*I said I've heard it!*" God, I hated this small talk. "*Don't you know who I am?*"

"All right, all right, don't get sore! Just tryin' to cheer ya up. Jesus . . . !" He was grimacing at me through the rear-view mirror, not watching the street. There were people wandering back and forth in our path and I was afraid he was going to kill somebody. Mrs. Fillmore, I remembered, died in the Willard Hotel. Uncle Sam was through with her by then, though.

Suddenly, the cabbie spotted a pair of copulating dogs in the street—"*Whoopee!*" he cried, took aim, and roared forward. I was thrown back, anchored by my stuck foot, into the hard rusty springs of the old ruptured rear seat. The cab had no shocks left at all. It was like a jeep ride I'd had through a shelling near Bougainville, only the jeep had been in better condition. The dogs saw us coming, wound about frantically trying to get separated, finally lurched in a six-footed panic across the wide avenue toward the distant curb, hopelessly hung up on each other. I noticed, as the cabdriver, yowling like a wild Indian, reeled cross-traffic after the dogs, that we were near the FBI building, and I hoped I wouldn't be recognized.

I cried out something, I don't remember what, didn't matter, I couldn't even hear myself over the cabbie's hallooing. I was hanging onto the door with one hand, the seat with the other, and I saw as I glanced up at the rear-view mirror that I was grinning madly. Oddly, the cabdriver was looking back at me, not out at the street. Buses and automobiles swung in and out of our path like the crazy cars in the old Keystone Kops movies, the dogs blundering through the screeching wheels, yelping with pain and dismay, scrambling miserably for a foothold. Some people ride in taxis all the time. They say they like it. They like to make contact with the man in the street, they say. They must be crazy.

We were closing in on the dogs. The one on top was half twisted away now, both front paws down on the pavement to one side of the bottom dog, but his left hind leg stuck straight up in the air. They seemed to be trying to go in two different directions, and each time the top dog kicked, the bottom dog's back legs splayed out. I watched aghast as we bore down on them. I no longer even knew which direction we were headed. I was afraid I might get carsick. We crossed paths with a trolleybus, sideswiped an open police car, and caught the dogs just as they reached the curb, clipping the top one in the butt and sending them both skidding, still locked up, spraddle-legged and yipping wildly, right into the doorway of the National Theater. Closed, I saw. *Guys and Dolls* coming June 29. Cast Intact. Interrupting Its Sensational New York Run. *"Goal!"* the cabbie cried.

The cab had spun sharply and stopped dead. I sat back in a cold sweat. I was too weak to open the door and get out. *"Hoo-eee!"* the driver crowed happily, leaning back over the seat and slapping me on the leg. "That's one piece o' ass them old houndawgs won't soon fergit!" I winced at the contact. I'm no shrinking violet, I'm a political animal, after all, I know what it is to be down in the arena—but I can't go out and grab people and hug them and carry on, and I don't like them grabbing me. Especially on the leg. It doesn't come natural to me to be a buddy-buddy boy, with cabdrivers least of all. He winked and squeezed my knee. Reflexively, I jerked my foot right out of its trapped shoe. "Yeah, I know who ya are, Nick," he said.

"Nick . . . ?" I squeaked. Nobody had called me that in eight or nine years. Not since the Navy, the South Pacific . . .

"Green Island, remember?" he grinned. He turned back to restart the motor. "I guess it's *Commander* Nick now, ain't it? Haw haw! Just read about your promotion!"

I stared numbly at him in the mirror, trying to place him. Some guy I'd cleaned out in a poker game out there? Was that it, had he been lying in wait for me all these years? I tried, feebly, to smile. "Do I, uh . . . ?"

He pushed his way brusquely back through oncoming traffic to the right side of the road. "Ho ho, Nixon's by God Hamburger Stand, remember that? You sure had it made out there, Nick! Green fuckin' Island, no shit—you musta hated to see the war end!"

"What do you mean?" There was a tightness in my chest. I felt a little like that guy wrestling a horse in front of the Archives Building we'd just passed. "It wasn't . . . there wasn't—"

"Everything from cunts and whiskey to captured Jap rifles, cupcakes and influence, you spread an amazin' menu, Nick! A livin' legend! They say ya socked away a cool hunderd grand on that tour!"

"*Ten* thousand, that's all," I protested, but he seemed to laugh harder than ever at this. "Besides, that . . . that was from poker."

"*Sure* it was, Nick! *Sure* it was! Haw haw! And where'd all that famous chopped meat come from you was boondogglin'? Most of it was headed for those poor dumb cocksuckers out to sea and off in the battle zones, wasn't it, Nick? Booze for the enlisted goddamn men, am I right? Eh, Commander?"

"Well, if I hadn't . . . somebody else . . ."

"Haw haw! Right! I *believe* you, Nick! I'm *with* ya! The only fuckin' goddamn legitimate American hero in the *war,* Nick, I *mean* that! Hairy Dick, the Hamburger King a the South Pacific! The Big Bug a Green Island, the Sultan of SCAT—they shoulda give you a *medal,* Nick!"

"It wasn't like that at all—!" Why was I arguing with him? I knew no one could keep pace with a concerted smear campaign. The man in political life must come to expect the smear and to know that, generally, the best thing to do about it is to ignore it—and hope it will fade away. "I was only doing my—"

"Duty! Right? I know, and you couldn't *stop* doin' it! We hadn't even got around to makin' them Jap warlords cry cockles, and you was already down there in Los fuckin' Angeles, all duded out in your gold-braid monkey suit and good-conduct ribbon, runnin' for a suck at the public teat, tellin' the yokels back home how it was in the fuckin' *fox*holes! 'The clean forthright young American what fought in defense of his country in the stinkin' mud and jungles of the Solomons!' *Hoo hah!*—Nick, ya break me up! Fuckin' genius, *you* are, a real bull-whacker—you shoulda been in *show* business!"

"Now, see here—!"

"Aw, Commander, don't—haw haw!—don't gimme that look! Save it for your dumb fuckin' mutt!" He seemed to remember something and broke into more guffaws. The two dogs we ran down probably. I recalled there was a drugstore back there across from the Willard Hotel, and I needed more antacids. Not the time to go back, though. Do it later. I was furious, but I knew I couldn't let myself be seen to lose my equanimity. The burdens of life sometimes outweigh the pleasures, you can't let it get you down, makes a bad impression on the public. After all (I told myself) I believe in the battle, it's always there wherever I go. I perhaps carry it more than others because that's my way. Besides, this would soon be over, we were coming onto Constitution now. Lot of activity up there, toward the Capitol. . . . "And now, by the sweet cock o' Uncle Jesus, you're the Vice fuckin' General Manager of the whole—WHOA!"

He swerved suddenly over to the curb where a lady was handing out pamphlets. She looked like a Jehovah's Witness type. This was my chance to get out. I reached down and tugged at my shoe. But he rolled on by, grabbing one of her pamphlets on the run, dragging her along a few clumsy steps, then roared ahead. "What . . . what is it?" I asked.

He peered at it, turned his nose down. "Ahh, it ain't nothin'," he grumped. He handed it back over the seat to me. It was Ethel Rosenberg's final appeal for clemency, with two sketches above, one of her and the other of Julius, signed by Picasso. I'd seen them before. Picasso was a notorious Red, the Rosenbergs were just hurting their own cause with blatant associations like this, but it was nothing they hadn't been doing all along. "You shoulda seen the ones they was handin' out last night! Haw! There was some cute ones of you, Nick! You'd be prouda the dong they hung on ya!" He winked at me in the rear-view mirror and spread his hands out like he was measuring some big fish. "Of course, I can't say it was gettin' put to the best *use! R-raw*-haw-haw-haw-haw!"

"Now, that's uh, just about—!"

"Easy, Nick, haw haw, don't let it go to your head! I mean, there was a lot of 'em showin' you with your face smeared with shit, too. Or eatin' it—I gotta admit the shit looked good there, Nick, you'd make a terrific President! Yaw-haw-haw!" He was crumpled up over the wheel with laughter. "Hey, ya know? I seen that lady back there before! She was up at the White House tryin' to get in!"

"The White House—!"

"Yeah, she said she wanted to have an intercourse with the President!"

"You mean, interview . . ."

"Yeah, that's what the guard said, but *she* says, 'Naw, I mean intercourse! I wanna see the nuts that're runnin' this country!' *Waw-haw-haw!*"

We'd stopped behind a sightseeing bus and I meant to jump out, but I couldn't get my goddamn shoe loose from under the seat. He reached around suddenly and nearly poked me in the face with a big cigar. "Woops! Excuse me, Nick! Whaddaya doin' down there on the floor? Here, no hard feelin's, have a cigar! I remember how you loved to blow through these things out on Green Island, I been savin' it for ya!"

"Oh, well, thanks, but I don't—"

The bus started up. The cabbie thrust the cigar in my hand, swung around to get moving again.

I sat back, I had to think, I had to keep my head. It would have been stupid to have jumped out there anyway, the place was full of demonstrators. No mistake about it this time: they carried pictures of the Rosenbergs with pleas for mercy printed on them. All along, I'd been noticing something peculiar about these pro-Rosenberg people, I hadn't been able to put my finger on it, but suddenly it came to me: *they were all middle-aged!* There was hardly a kid among them, the young ones were all over on the other side, *my* side, these Rosenberg people were all . . . well . . . my age. . . .

"Hey, you may not believe this, Nick," the cabdriver said, "but I know that broad on all them posters there."

"Who, you mean—?"

"Yeah, Rosenblatt, the atom spy. I went to fuckin' school with her!"

"You mean, uh, Rosenberg—?"

"Yeah, she lived around the corner from me there on Whatchamacallit Street . . ."

"Sheriff?"

"That's it! Sheriff Street! Ain't that a laugh, Nick? Just goes to show that truth is stranger than fiction, don't it? Sheriff Street! Jumpin' Jesus, lemme tell ya, she had a sweet ass on her, Nick! We useta sneak into the back lot there and peep in her window—"

"But she slept on the second floor, didn't she? I think I read—"

"We used ladders, Nick! We climbed trees! There was a fire escape. I had a buddy in the building behind—shit, we saw *everything!*"

"The other rooms, too?"

"What other rooms, Nick?"

"They say that sometimes, uh, prostitutes rented out—"

"Right, Nick! It was a kinda whorehouse! Did I forget to mention that? That's probably where she learnt her game, right? Listen, by the time she was fifteen years old, buddy, she could do more things with a banana than you and me could ever dream a' doin' with our dingdongs in a lifetime! She sure showed all us boys a trick or two—I mean, I'm lucky to have a cock left at all, Nick, she subverted the goddamn thing to ribbons!"

"Really? But they always said she never even had a boyfriend until—"

"Don't you believe it, Nick! She was one hot little twat—all them Commies are, you know that! It's part of their religion! Sweet Betsy, she couldn't keep her pants on! I mean, it turned into a real act, she got famous, she went all over the fuckin' town doin' it in the moviehouses!"

"You mean the Major, uh, Bowes Amateur Nights—?"

"Haw haw! Amateur, my ass! Amateur, my *ass*, Nick!"

"I . . . I thought she always sang 'Ciribiribin'—"

"She didn't *sing* it, Nick—she *did* it! God in ass-fuckin' star-spangled heaven, she was a sensation! They finally had to move her into the burlesque circuit to accommodate the mobs, it was worsen back there at the White House! We useta catch her act ever Saturday night. We was pretty dumb, don't hold it against us, Nick, but we thought it was *innocent*—ya know, just dirty sex, twirlin' her tits, suckin' up quarters with her cunt, things like that. We didn't realize she was suckin' up a lot more than quarters, and then flushin' it all straight to Russia! You read about it, Nick: she had A-bombs up there, Jell-O boxes, Red herrings, passport photos, Klaus Fucks, the Fifth Amendment—shit, she could probably get a whole fuckin' P-38 up her snatch and have room for Yucca Flat and the Sixth Fleet to boot! They say there was a ray gun in her navel, a walkie-talkie hid in her G-string, and a camera stuffed up her ass—when she spread her cheeks at us, we always heard this click and thought she was blowin' kisses at us out her rectum! What fuckin' innocents we was, Nick! Never again, hunh? I mean, we've grown up, ain't we, Nick? We're through suckin' Russky hind tit like babies, ain't we? We ain't on Green Island no more—!"

"I don't think this, uh, has any—"

"You tell 'em, Nick! By God, you tell 'em! You remember that persecuter—what's his name?"

"Saypol?"

"That's it! Saypol! 'Imagine a wheel,' he says. Remember that? 'In the center o' the wheel, Rosenblatt, reachin' out like the tentacles of a octopus—'"

"Uh, Rosenberg . . ."

"Right! Well, that sonuvabitch knew what he was talkin' about, Nick, he musta caught the act! She was like Plastic Man, I shit you not! Her hair wriggled out at ya like snakes, wrappin' ya up, ticklin' your ear, creepin' down your shirt, her toes jigged in all the aisles at once, she'd clip your foreskin with fingernails willowy as reeds, sock ya in the snoot with her clit!" I used to go to the burlesque in Los Angeles with my cousin. We must have gone to the wrong shows. "What an act! Her tits popped out at ya and lit up like beacons: one if by land, two if by sea—and lemme tell ya, those weren't the only two fuckin' options Julie had, Nick, not with *them* bazooms! She'd do the Dirty Crab on her back, slappin' out Morse-code spy messages with the cheeks of her ass and then—"

"Did you say, uh, Julie . . . ?"

"Yeah, right, Juliet. Juliet Rosen—"

"*His* name is Julie. Her name, uh, is *Ethel*."

"Oh . . . ?" He looked confused, crestfallen; but there was a sly grin twitching at the corners of his mouth. "Musta been a different Juliet Rosenblatt . . ." I realized we'd been stopped in front of the Senate Office Building for some time. I reached into my pocket for some money, noticing too late that my hand was smeared with horsedung. "Forget it, Commander. It's on the house. For old time's sake. Anchors aweigh, Nick. Lest we forget . . ."

"Oh. Well . . ." Some vague suspicion troubled me. Then, as I reached down to work my shoe free, I noticed for the first time the label on the cigar he'd given me: OPTIMO! I glanced up in alarm. He was gazing at me, the grin gone, his eyes dark with a kind of weariness, a kind of resignation, as though . . . as though he knew too much. I've got to keep calm, I cautioned myself. And I've got to get the hell out of here.

"Look," he said, his voice mellowing, losing its hard twang, "can't we get past all these worn-out rituals, these stupid fuckin' reflexes?" It wouldn't do any good to grab him, I knew. The ungraspable Phantom. He was made of nothing solid, your hand would just slip right through, probably turn leprous forever. "They got nothin' to do with life, you know that, life's always new and changing, so why fuck it up with all this shit about scapegoats, sacrifices, initiations, saturnalias—?"

"I know who you are," I rasped. I could hardly hear myself. "The game's up!"

I braced myself. I expected him to flash back in fury, I expected demonic sparks to fly from his eyes, fire from his parted lips, something violent and amazing. I was ready to die. But he only sighed. "Yeah," he said, "I'm only a lousy cabdriver. Shit, I don't know everything. But I think you're on the wrong track. Easter Trials, Burning Tree, morality plays, cowtown vendettas—life's too big, you can't wrap it up like that!"

Where the battle against the Phantom is concerned, victories are never final so long as he is still able to fight. There is never a time when it is safe to relax or let down. How had I let myself lose my shoe under his seat like this?

"I seen that mess you rigged up in Times Square. It's frivolous, Nick! You oughta burn Connie Mack and Sonja Henie up there. Or Native Dancer and Elsa Maxwell . . ."

I should carry a gun in my hip pocket like Irving Saypol, I thought. But you couldn't shoot him either, bullets just go through him. I fought to tear my shoe free—was he holding onto it somehow?

"Listen, it ain't too late, Nick, there's still time to turn back—forget this dumb circus, get on to something more—"

The shoe came loose! I threw my shoulder against the door and tumbled out. "You'll never get away with this!" I cried, shaking my shoe at him. I didn't know exactly what I meant by this, but I needed a line for the other people on the street and this was the first one that came to me. I jumped up and brushed myself off. Chief Newman would have been proud of my form. He always said I played every scrimmage as though the championship were at stake—and now, literally, it was. My shoulder hurt like hell, though.

He was shouting at me, something about the war, or the whore, or maybe he was hollering at me to shut the door, but I scrambled to my feet and made for the Senate Office Building—and crashed into a crowd of newsguys just coming out: Drew Pearson, Westbrook Pegler, Walter Winchell, Elmer Davis, Bob Considine, Gabriel Heatter, the whole god-damn Fourth Estate.

"Whoa, what's up, Dick?" Pearson asked.

"The Phantom!" I cried. "He tried to get me!"

"What Phantom, Dick?" Pegler asked. "Where?"

"That driver, watch out—!" But the cab was gone. I swallowed, tried to stop gulping air. Couldn't let these bastards get the wrong impression. "There was a cab . . ."

"What'd he try to do," Pearson asked, "steal your shoe?" He was stifling a grin, bugging his eyes. Making fun. Was this the thanks I got for saving his life when Joe McCarthy tried to kill him?

"Hmmm," said Winchell, taking it from my hand and sniffing it. "Seems like he tried to take a crap in it."

"That's pretty serious, all right," said Elmer Davis, mock-solemnly. "Maybe we oughta tell Louella about it." They all yuff-huff-huffed.

"You newsguys are all the same," I said, snatching back my shoe. I was disgusted by their cheap cynical laughter. It wasn't me I was thinking about, it was the nation. Didn't they understand that the Vice President of the United States of America had just been locked in a one-on-one battle with the Phantom? That the security of the whole country and the cause of free men everywhere were at stake? They were sick with their own self-importance—I knew I had to blitz them, I had to shame them. "You think you're such big public heroes, but ultimately you're all dupes of the Phantom!" I cried. "What do you know about the truth? It's all sensationalism, cheap scandals, a lot of irresponsible rumor-mongering in the name of a free press!" I took out on them all of the fury and frustration that had been building up within me on the ride over. "That's just the kind of loose fellow-traveling attitude that got us into the mess we were in in the forties! Well, just wait! The people of this country are getting fed up with hucksters like you! There's going to be a day of reckoning—!"

"Whoa there, Dick," said Pegler. "If you're gonna fling your hand around like that, use your clean one!"

This wisecrack brought a few guilty titters, but the audience gathering around us now were there, I knew, to hear *me*. Opinion makers, people in all walks of life. . . . "The Pentagon Patriots have got you bums pegged," I declared. "Preachers of lies, prophets of deceit, garblers of truth—"

"Say," said Winchell, sniffing, "did anyone ever consider that the Phantom might be a horse?"

"Dick the Horse?"

"Alan (the Horse) Ameche?"

"Horace Greeley?"

"Some donkey, more likely," said Heatter wryly. "One of the Phantom's more famous disguises . . ."

"Can't you SOBs take anything seriously?" I demanded. "I'm telling you, the Phantom is out to destroy this thing today! The heat is on! Look what's happening around the world! Germany, Korea, Africa— you saw what he did up in Times Square last night! This place may be next! He'll do anything to stop us! We have the fight of our lives on our hands! I was lucky to get away from him just now—and it's not just me he's after! He's after us all! He . . . he even wanted to get Sonja Henie!"

"Gee, that's terrible, Dick," said Pearson, winking at the others.

"Maybe he wants to take a crap in her ice-skate," said Winchell.

"Ah, go to hell!" I muttered, and brushed on past them. I moved quickly, planning my next move. I was tensed up, I admit, and my shoulder was nagging me, but I still had control of my temper. The kind of treatment I was getting was pretty hard to take, but I knew the greatest mistake I could make would be to lose my head. I'd suffered these smear attacks before, I'd suffer them again. But the people on the street, I knew, were with me. Some of them applauded as I jogged away, rocking somewhat with only one shoe on, but feeling sure of myself, confident of my timing, pleased with the points I'd made. Maybe I should throw a line from Lincoln at them, I thought.

But before I could come up with a good one, Bob Considine forced the issue: "Hey, Mr. Vice President!" he called from behind me. "Give us a hint! Who's behind the Rosenbergs?"

I spun around at the doorway. "I don't know," I said gravely, "but I do, uh, know this: you guys are so lost in your Fourth Estate fantasyland," a good line, I thought, a damned good line, "that if he were standing right here in front of you as obvious as King Kong, you wouldn't recognize him!"

"Is that a clue, Dick?" asked Winchell.

"Straight from the horse's mouth," said Gabriel Heatter.

"Anyway, it explains King Kong's five-o'clock shadow," said Pearson.

With that I really blew my stack. I just couldn't take any more. Those vicious mudslinging irresponsible Commie-stooge idiot bastards! But even as the circuits popped and sizzled in my head, I hung onto myself, clung to the old debate discipline, bit my tongue, kept my movements in check. As best I could—I kept flashing from smiles to scowls and back faster than I would have liked. I jabbed a finger at Pearson through the ugly laughter, even though it hurt my shoulder, and cried: "All right, gentlemen, you've had a lot of fun with all this jackassery, but when it comes to the manure hitting the fan, let me just say this, you can give me the shaft, I expect a lot of blood to be spilled and you have a right to call it as you see it, but make no mistake, you're not just giving *me* the shaft, you're sticking it in the butt of the whole American Way of Life!" I tried to smile, scowled, found myself smiling again. "I won't say you're traitors to your country, but I will say I'm not known for being rough on rats for nothing, and when you go out to shoot rats, just remember, if an egg is bad, *then let's call for the hatchet!*"

I let that sink in a second, not quite sure just what I'd been saying, but trusting my reflexes, then brought my hand down to my side, chopping off any rejoinder they might have thrown back (but in fact they seemed speechless—well, they asked for it and they got it), turned sharply on my stockinged foot, and made my exit. Entrance, rather. Yet another ordeal. Fortunately, I thrive on them.

16.
Third Dementia

It is on. The Rosenbergs are to die at last. Television networks interrupt scheduled programs with the announcement: "President Eisenhower and the Supreme Court of the United States of America have refused to spare the lives of atomic spies Julius and Ethel Rosenberg." At the Bernard Bach home in Toms River, New Jersey, a small ten-year-old boy is watching the baseball game between the New York Yankees and the Detroit Tigers on Channel 11 when the announcement is made. The score is 0-0, but Yankee first-baseman Joe Collins has just beat out a drag bunt in the bottom of the fourth. It is a sunny day and the boy is thinking about going out to play baseball with friends in the neighborhood. That's what Sonia Bach wants him to do. But he's fascinated by the television and can't pry himself away from it. The announcer says the executions are scheduled to take place tonight. He looks very intent and serious. The boy tries to see past him to the ballgame again, but the announcer won't go away. "My Mommy and Daddy," the boy whispers, feeling that someone or something is watching him. But he doesn't know what to add. A prayer? A seventh-inning stretch? At the ballgame, nobody seems even to have noticed that the announcement has been made. Yankee outfielder Gene Woodling has come to the plate during the interruption, and he now watches a ball go by. There's something very magical about TV, everything seems to happen at once on it, the near and the far, the funny and the sad, the real and the unreal. Tonight! Collins, taking a big lead off first base, is not thinking about this. He doesn't care. The boy hates Collins for his cheap hit. Just like the Yankees. His Mom and Dad like the Brooklyn Dodgers; the New York Yankees are Judge Kaufman's team. Judge Kaufman is rich and lives on Park Avenue and takes his sons to see them play. The boy feels that awful lump growing in his stomach again. His little brother is out on the front porch with Leo painting a homemade Father's Day card with watercolors. Father's Day is Sunday, a long time away. "That was their last chance," the boy tells himself, trying to picture this new finality in the same way he sees the Tiger pitcher stretch, study Collins at first, then whip the ball toward the plate: *ball two!* Are the other guys in the neighborhood watching the game, did they hear the announcement? His Mom and Dad have told him it's not manly to be afraid, but he is afraid, he can't help it. He feels like there are two of himself loose in the world, one who likes to play baseball with friends and come home to Mom and Dad and sometimes push his little brother around, and another one on television and in the newspapers who is threatening to eat the other one up. Both of them, the one eating and the one getting eaten, are frightened, because they both believe the world is not crazy, how could it be? and yet why is it doing these maniac things? why is it killing his Mom and Dad like this, and why is everybody so excited about it, and what is it they want with him, a plain ten-year-old boy who's still learning his fractions and doesn't even know how to fix a television or throw a curve ball yet. "Why don't you go play catch with Steve?" says Sonia gently. She is being too nice to him. Like everybody else of late, even Mr. Bloch. Sometimes he feels like shouting at them: damn you all! Woodling slams a one-strike, two-balls pitch clean out of the ballpark, and the Yankees lead, 2-0. The television camera shows people cheering and waving and having a terrific time. If people really loved one another, he wonders, would the world be like this? His poor Mom! What is she thinking? How does it feel? What *is* love in a world where people behave like this as if it were normal? Woodling circles the bases. His little brother comes in, wearing his Brooklyn Dodgers T-shirt all smeared with paint, and asks Sonia for a glass of milk. "That's it. That's it," the boy says. "Good-bye. Good-bye." Nobody's listening.

His folks' lawyer Manny Bloch is having the same experience: he and his defense team are flinging themselves frenetically at any judge they can find at home or in chambers, but they all seem to have either vanished or gone deaf. A stone wall. Manny fires off a telegram to President Eisenhower, raising the Hugo Black point that the case has never been reviewed by the Supreme Court, but this wire is short-circuited by Special Counsel Bernie Shanley and "transmitted to the Justice Department"; Eisenhower never sees it. Bloch, who has fallen unprofessionally in love with this entire family, is beginning to lose his forensic cool and is having flashes of self-destructive temper, as the doors slam shut in his face. He and others plead for a stay of the eleven-p.m. executions tonight because of the Jewish Sabbath which begins at sundown. Kaufman, playing it close to the chest, says he has already spoken with Attorney General Brownell about that: the executions will not be carried out during the Sabbath. The lawyers take this to mean a delay is in the offing, past the weekend at least, and relax a moment: at Justice, they exchange knowing winks.

The Rosenbergs themselves, locked away in the stillness of the Sing Sing Death House, are remote from all this noisy maneuvering, but they are not unaware of it. One thing they know: they are not alone in this world. Julius even clings yet to the mad hope that justice will be done, that they will both be vindicated, these walls will come crashing down, and they will ride out of here on the shoulders of their friends, the people, but Ethel, though never more strong and serene, shares her son's mood of grim resignation: that's it, good-bye, good-bye. She sits with Julie, separated from him by a wire-mesh screen, composing a farewell letter to the two boys. What she wants above all is to save them from cynicism and despair, and so she speaks of the fellowship of grief and struggle and the price that must be paid to create a life on earth worth living. Julie, watching her, nods in agreement, awed by her radiant tranquillity . . .

. . . Your Daddy who is with me in the last momentous hours, sends his heart and all the love that is in it for his dearest boys. Always remember that we were innocent and could not wrong our conscience. We press you close and kiss you with all our strength.

Lovingly,

Daddy and Mommy
Julie   Ethel

Julius's mother, Sophie Rosenberg, turns up meanwhile at the gates of the White House asking to see the President, but they don't let her even get close—her emotional behavior is notorious, and besides, she's not in good health, and people near the end are capable of anything—so she has to do her scene in the streets. Much is happening out there. Demonstrations are building up in Washington, New York, around the world. Riots are expected and police everywhere are put on special alert. Bloch blames Judge Kaufman for stirring up all this trouble through his merciless intransigence: "Tens upon tens of millions of people in this country, in Europe, in Asia, know about this case!" The Boy Judge is not taken in: "I have been frankly hounded, pounded by vilification and by pressurists—I think that it is not a mere accident that some people have been aroused in these countries. *I think it has been by design!*" On a crepe-paper banner strung out above the Republic Chop Suey eatery in Times Square, Senator Frank Brandegee's immortal rejoinder to Woody Wilson:

I AM NOT GOING TO BE BUNCOED BY ANY OLEAGINOUS LINGO
ABOUT "HUMANITY" OR "MEN EVERYWHERE"

Things are heating up here in the Square: in the 80s now and still climbing. The masses moving into the area are no longer scudding through, but pressing toward the center. There's a certain unwonted recklessness in the air, something left over from a restless night, and many merchants close shop early, fearing that American business and consumer ethics might not be taken as seriously this afternoon as they ought. Most of those arriving now are young, their elders having to finish out their workday before coming—boys in jeans and crew cuts, girls with ponytails and Woolworth pearls: the youth of America, cracking gum between their strong white teeth, jostling each other aggressively, scratching their crotches, trying to keep their bra straps from peeking out under their white summer blouses. They carry portable radios on which Nat (King) Cole sings "I'm Never Satisfied," interrupted by newscasters who report that American Sabre Jets in Korea have bagged six more MIGs, the atom spies still refuse to talk, and B-29 Superforts have bombed Pyongyang. The boys laugh at this and elbow each other knowingly, because they think the announcer said "poontang."

Up by the Times Tower, workmen are putting the final touches to the Death House set, refurbishing the executioner's alcove, straightening and oiling the gurney wheels, polishing the brass studs in the leather seat of the electric chair. The props committee has come up with an old mahogany table with turned legs and center drawer to fill the empty space against the wall upstage right, just like the one at the real Death House in Sing Sing, though most people in the Square mistakenly assume this is the notorious Rosenberg console table and meant to be used for kindling. The set has no ceiling, of course, but since one of the principal features of the Sing Sing electrocution chamber is the greasy skylight above the chair, this has been ingeniously suggested by a floating glass bell, suspended on wires, which also contains, out of sight, the stage spotlights. This mock skylight will actually trap, ironically, those same fumes that the real one at Sing Sing is designed to let out, though the illusion after nightfall will be the opposite. And this, after all, is what counts, as Cecil B. De Mille explains patiently to a disturbed Warden Denno, a practical-minded man, unaccustomed to the magical razzamatazz of showbizz. "See, life and the real stuff of life aren't always the same thing, Warden—like, one don't always give you the other, you follow? So sometimes, to get your story across, you gotta work a different angle or two, use a few tricks, zap it up with a bit of spectacle—I mean, what's spectacle? it's a kind of *vision,* am I right?" It's like the character Matty Burke is saying in the 3-D movie *House of Wax* over at the Trans-Lux. He's the business partner of the wax-museum artist Professor Jarrod, and he doesn't like Jarrod's style. Too tame, too cute. He wants a Chamber of Horrors. Jarrod, who's played by Vincent Price, argues effetely: "There are people in the world who love Beauty." "Yeah," snaps Burke, "but more who want sensation!"

Up and down the streets leading into Times Square, there are makeshift sideshows catering to these sensation-seekers and visionaries—a tentful of freaks from Hiroshima, the Rosenberg prison cockroach collection, the iconography of J. Edgar Hoover—even the old-time flea circus at Hubert's Museum is enjoying a revival. The fleas have all been temporarily renamed after characters in the Rosenberg drama, and there's a courtroom scene of the sentencing that has everybody in stitches. In one of the sideshow tents near the stage, amid Russian T-34 tank models from East Berlin, burnt and pissed-on posters from Czechoslovakia, and the ripped-off ears of a Red Brandenburg judge, a body is displayed, said to be that of the West Berlin vagrant Willi Goettling, shot by the Russians for allegedly provoking the East Berlin riots, though skepticism about the genuineness of this body is expressed by some visitors to the exhibit: something shabby and ordinary about the corpse, they say. Something, well, profane. . . . Skeptics everywhere. There are those who doubt the authenticity of bearded ladies and wild men from Borneo, after all, and who think levitation is done with mirrors.

The genius behind the sideshows and vendors' gimmicks is the Grand Master of the Spin-Off, Walt Disney, and needless to say, he and his Disney Imagineers have reserved a number of key corner locations for their own Mouse Factory specials: a rocking model of Steamboat Willie's tub, the Dwarfs' cottage, the belly of the Whale, and an adults-only show of the girl centaurs from *Fantasia* with their nippleless breasts and oddly disquieting horse-rumps. Not that the spin-off is original with Walt: he learned the trick from the great granddaddy of them all, J. Edgar Hoover of the FBI. But Disney, a semiliterate cartoonist who can't draw a straight line and color it brown, seized on the G-man's invention with all the desperation of a drowning wood-carver and turned it overnight into one of the monumental fortunes of the Western World—already back in the Depression he was admitting to gross sales of over $300,000,000 in Disney products, and there were reported to be tribes in Africa who wouldn't even accept free bars of soap from missionary doctors if they didn't bear the Mickey Mouse imprint. Here in Times Square today, his beautiful-beasts exhibits run from pure political drama like "The Three Little Pigs" to good old-fashioned Americanist celebrations, as in the tent where Donald Duck keeps playing "Turkey in the Straw" while Mickey Mouse is trying to conduct everybody else in a performance of the *William Tell* Overture. He has also built a scale model of Sing Sing prison, using all the little braying schoolboy truants from *Pinocchio* for the prisoners, and an imaginative simulation, using life-size models with moving eyeballs, of Harry Gold's complicated fantasy love life. A little far out maybe, but as Professor Jarrod says: "A man has to be a little nuts to be a good showman." Some say he's just a quick-buck hustler, but that only means Walt Disney is a man in tune with himself. Hucksterism after all is part of the human constitution: repress it (as that old Yankee Peddler Uncle Sam himself always says, explaining what's sick about socialists), you get the same results as repressing sex.

While Walt sits in the Whale's mouth, studying the Death House set and dreaming up further novelties, and Matty Burke burns down Professor Jarrod's wax museum to collect the fire insurance ("All you have to do is strike a match and the thing is done!" he chortles), New York State Troopers deploy themselves in a concentric series of barricades and roadblocks to defend the Square against protest marches. Commissioner George Monaghan puts his city cops on alert, and all precinct captains and detective squads are ordered to remain on duty through midnight. Newsreel cameramen move cameras and klieg lights into position, and TV generator trucks are brought in before the thickening crowds make it impossible. A concert is arranged up in Central Park— the Goldman Band opening their thirty-sixth season with Honegger's "March on the Bastille"—to take up part of the overflow; indeed, the crowds are already pushing north into the Park, east and west toward the rivers, south to Macy's, which is jammed to the walls this afternoon with shoppers seeking those novel "Dr. T Caps" with five rubbery fingers sticking up on top, inspired by the new Dr. Seuss movie premiering this afternoon at the Criterion. These caps are the occasion among the boys for a lot of wisecracks and naughty monkey business, all of which causes the girls to groan and shake their ponytails and snigger conspiratorially amongst themselves, fanning themselves with movie magazines and shaking their skirts out: my, but it's hot! The boys agree, but that's how they like it. They don't know exactly what's going to happen tonight, but all squeezed up like this, they can hardly wait. They've got knuckledusters and cherry bombs in their pockets, carry signs that read TWO FRIED ROSENBERGERS COMING RIGHT UP! and IF YOU CAN'T STAND THE HEAT, GET OUT OF THE KITCHEN!

Which is just what the *House of Wax* heroine Sue Allen (Phyllis Kirk) would like to do . . . but not a chance. She has been stripped naked by Professor Jarrod and is about to be plunged into a bath of boiling wax: *"There is a pain beyond pain, my dear, an agony so intense it shocks the mind!"* Jarrod knows what he's talking about. When his partner set fire to the wax museum, he tried to save his beautiful creations and was horribly mutilated in the conflagration: his flesh was literally melted. So much for idealism. Unable to use his hands after, he conceived the idea of murdering his models and fixing them in a wax bath, and it's now his heart's desire to metamorphose Sue into Marie Antoinette. Her boyfriend, unwaxed, is out cold with his head in a guillotine and is about to get sliced like Globaloney by the Professor's mad-freak assistant. The cops arrive and break it up, but not before enjoying a stupendous brawl in Natural Vision 3-D in which everything but Sue's pudicity gets thrown out at the audience. It's as though, without this moment of unmitigated whoopee in the last reel, it would all be for nothing. Finally, of course, Sue and her boyfriend are rescued as they must be, Professor Jarrod himself perishes in his tub of hot wax, and his crazy assistant gets busted. Lieutenant Brennan (Frank Lovejoy) picks up a sculpted head of Jarrod's assistant and remarks with a wry grin to a fellow cop: "Ya know, Shane, by the time that guy gets outa Sing Sing, this head will grow a long beard!"

The movie lets out and the people pour out onto the street, moving as one aroused body toward Times Square. The sun's at its hottest, and they gasp for air after the refrigerated atmosphere of the Trans-Lux. One man, still somewhat possessed by the images of famous historical persons going up in flames, their waxy faces melting horrifically, their stiffened bodies crashing forward into his lap, is disoriented by this new swirl of pictures out in the street. Sometimes he staggers forward, sometimes he gets turned around and pushed backwards. It doesn't help that he has forgotten to remove his 3-D glasses with the cardboard frames, and so sees everything through the eye-straining H-Polarizer haze of alcohol and iodine. He gets swept along in the rush, spinning and stumbling, feeling like Vincent Price lurching about out of his wheelchair. He has had no difficulty in bringing the two film images together in the theater, and in fact he still has an ache in his forehead and the back of his neck from trying not to flinch when the fellow with the bat and ball started whacking the thing right between his eyes, but now, tumbling along out here on the street, he seems to see two separate and unassimilable pictures, each curiously colored. Everything is flat, distances are deceptive, and he keeps crashing into people, getting angry wary stares in reply. An elbow, while remaining very plainly at least eight theater rows out in front of him, nevertheless hits him in the nose. He feels like he's grown a beard from his forehead down. Somewhere Julius LaRosa is singing "Anywhere I Wander," and he wonders if it's possible after all that the world is turned by some malevolent design.

The scene to the right now seems to show a street with laughing shouting people, and the sound track confirms this; the scene to the left, a long row of buildings with large doors and display windows full of flashing reflections. He leans to the left—but he is again deceived: he stumbles off an unexpected curb into the mob's path: now I'm John Wilkes Booth slumping forward on melting ankles, he thinks, attracting more attention for some reason than usual and worried about his inability to get his own extremities and the feet pounding over them into the same picture. He crawls hand over hand through the stampede, recalling that moment, early in the picture, when the wax museum is ablaze, waxen heads are melting and tilting bizarrely onto collapsing shoulders, glass eyeballs are bulging and falling out, fingernails are dripping, and Vincent Price is dragging himself painfully across the floor in all the fiery havoc, past a little sign that reads MOTHER LOVE. And then the whole room explodes, strewing the audience with burning debris. He reaches, his clothes smoking, feeling like one molten in the furnace, hit by the wingéd shaft of fate, and run over on the tracks of history, a curb: he pulls himself up over it and presses on until he smacks up against a building which wasn't in either of his lenses, but which now appears in the right one. He slumps there briefly, thinking: God has not favored my undertakings, my condition is not fundamentally sound.

He stands when he's able, and, leaning to the left, brushing the wall with his shoulder so as not to fall back into the crowd again, moves on down the street. He assumes a very serious and meditative expression so that people will not think him drunk, and does his best to walk along like any normal self-confident American, while still keeping contact with the buildings by way of his left shoulder. Thumping along like that, shredding the padding from the shoulder of his New Look sport jacket and thinking about the heroine in the movie out on the foggy streets, pursued by the artist-monster, he stumbles upon a shop selling fresh fruit and vegetables. Since he seems to be inside the shop, he buys six golden oranges, remarking in a friendly manner that they are as big as grapefruit. The fruiterer stares at him curiously, perhaps in part because he now seems to be standing in a box of ripe tomatoes, and says: "Those *are* grapefruit, Mac!" People stare at him as though his brow were branded with marks of guilt. He is reminded of the guillotine in *House of Wax*—CRASH!—and concludes, as he pays for the grapefruit and tomatoes, I must be the nice guy who always finishes last.

He's about to exit by way of a plate-glass window when the fruiterer collars him and pushes him brusquely out what is probably the door, plunging him reeling back into the heart of the maelstrom, past a news-stand where, grasping for support, he acquires some newspapers and magazines, and then, though this is not exactly his intention, on into a subway entrance. He tumbles, clutching newspapers and grapefruit, down the stairs, one lens showing him an advertisement of *Dangerous When Wet* with Esther Williams in a swimsuit, a moustache under her nose and a Ulysses S. Grant beard between her legs, the other a time-lapse overview of traffic patterns on the subway platform. At the bottom, pausing to wonder if "the Balance of Terror" is a communicable disease which he's somehow caught, he tries to locate himself—without suc-cess—in a gum-machine mirror. All he sees there is Abraham Lincoln with his beard on fire. A train pulls in, arriving from separate directions in the two lenses, and he allows himself to be swept aboard by the crowd. Or perhaps he wishes to take the train, he can't be sure. He finds an empty seat, but when he sits down it isn't there. The bottom of his paper bag splits open and the grapefruit roll about on the floor. He tries to pick them up but they're never just where or what they seem to be. Sometimes they change color before his very eyes, turn into people's feet which kick him or step on his hands, roll out opening doors at one stop and back in the next. What am I doing down here on the floor of this subway train, he asks himself, chasing grapefruit? I don't even *like* grapefruit! He stands and proceeds nonchalantly to read his newspapers and magazines, disowning the grapefruit, as the train rocks along. Through one eye he learns that President Eisenhower has encouraged the reading of Marx and Stalin and a mad artist-professor in Rome has discovered the tomb of Saint Peter, and through the other reads about a plot to liquidate Senator McCarthy. Liquidate! Perhaps they hoped to use his body as a model for Joan of Arc. There are articles, severally, about electrocutions, creeping socialism, frozen bull semen, and "The

Night Love Turned to Error." "Terror," rather. He cannot seem to focus on the atom-spy news, but keeps getting a composite picture of the two spies: a small dark woman with gold-rimmed spectacles, moustache, and fake fur collar, who for some odd reason reminds him of Marie Antoinette in a black string tie, going up in oily smoke. It must be the circles around the eyes, the gold rims. The coat, he observes, is a good Republican cloth coat, the Brooklyn Dodgers T-shirt underneath notwithstanding.

The doors slide open, he gets shoved out of the subway car, slips on a revenging grapefruit, slams into an I-beam that bears the legend TRACK 3, and then staggers on up the stairs into what turns out to be the exercise yard of a federal prison, if his left eye is to be trusted, or else the New Jerusalem. Police are protecting some construction or other from the souvenir-hunting zeal of summer tourists. What is it? It appears to be a stage with an electric chair. Or else a movie lobby with sawdust on the floor. Above him, a billboard seems to read I TELL YOU, FOLKS, ALL POLITICS IS APPLESAUCE, but he no longer trusts what his eyes tell him. I've walked through that 3-D movie, he thinks, and I've come out the other side. He doesn't really believe this, it's just a joke to lighten a little his sinking heart. Sinking because it's all coming together—the stampeding masses, the creeping socialism and exploding waxworks, the tracks of history and time-lapse overviews—into the one image that has been pursuing him through all his sleepless nights, the billowing succubus he's been nurturing for nine months now, ever since the new hydrogen-bomb tests at Eniwetok: yes, the final spectacle, the one and only atomic holocaust, he's giving birth to it at last. Like the mad artist, we're all going to die horrible fiery deaths, and there's nothing we can do to stop it, nothing we can do to stop ourselves, it's in the script, in the frozen semen, the waxen MOTHER LOVE. What does it mean that Shakespeare wrote *Julius Caesar* or that Edison invented the light bulb? Nothing, it's all over, the human race is shutting itself off, it has a craving for emptiness and futility, we've grown too much brains and we can't cope, it's all wasted, my life is wasted! Thus, he laments the waste of his life and Shakespeare's. The theater marquee above him reads A GOOD MANY THINGS GO AROUND IN THE DARK BESIDES SANTA CLAUS.

In the lobby, he feels safer. It's not as bright in here, things are not so clear. He finds display blow-ups of what he takes to be pages from the Books of Knowledge but turn out to be transcripts of the record of the Easter Trial. He concentrates on them, thinking: At last I'm going to do something with my life! On page 493, someone called THE WITNESS is saying: "He said there was fissionable material at one end of a cube and at the other end of the cube there was a sliding member that was also of fissionable material and when they brought these two together under great pressure, that would be . . ." He cannot find page 494. But he knows, he knows; he feels his body full of cubes and sliding members. THE COURT is asking about Jell-O boxes. Imitation raspberry! There is testimony about smallpox inoculations, implosion lenses, and flushing money down the toilet. The statue of Columbus. *Stop Me If You Have Heard This.* Doris Day is singing "I Didn't Slip, I Wasn't Pushed, I Fell." Somehow, this all makes sense. THE COURT says: "It is so difficult to make people realize that this country is engaged in a life and death struggle with a completely different system!" He blinks. He realizes he has come upon some radical truth. In one eye, anyway. But then THE COURT says: "Yet they made a choice of devoting themselves to the Russian ideology of denial of God, denial of the sanctity of the individual and aggression against free men everywhere instead of serving the cause of liberty and freedom." This he doesn't understand at all. The fault of the cubes and sliding members maybe. He is feeling light-headed. The walls seem to be full of groundhog holes. The theater air-conditioning is off and the lobby is stuffy. He staggers out into the street again, gulping for air, pursued by a recurring note of impending doo-oom.

The area is full of people who shove and push. Perhaps they are actors pretending to be prisoners in the prison yard. Peddlers are hawking Cherry-Oonilla ice cream and miniature A-bombs that produce edible mushroom clouds. He samples the ice cream, but as he bites into it, his right eye tells him it's Marie Antoinette's left pap from the wax museum—no telling which eye to trust, it tastes milky and waxy at the same time. People are carrying signs that his right eye tells him read SAVE THE ROSENBERGS! and HEIL EISENHOWER!, his left BOMB CHINA NOW! and ETHEL ROSENBERG BEWITCHED MY BABY! He is no longer surprised by these ocular reversals, in fact he is very clear-headed, which is the main cause of his panic. It strikes him that he is perhaps the only sane man left on the face of the earth. The faces of the earth, because he still sees two of them. He plunges forward through the Community of God, crawls over a barrier that says DIG WE MUST FOR A GROWING NEW YORK, is struck down by the Preamble to the United States Constitution. *"I did it!"* he cries, rearing up, his face smeared with the bloody remains of his Cherry-Oonilla ice cream cone. *"A crime worse than murder! I've altered the course of history!"* He knows this is true, knows he's done it, because he has imagined it: sanity is murder. *"I've brought on the holocaust!"* He staggers to his feet, slams into the stage, clambers up on it. One eye shows him a distant policeman, his limbs outflung, caught in a web of concentric circles, intersected by pointer lines indicating the relationship of the planets to the human microcosmos; in the other eye, the electric chair, identified by a small brass National Parks sign as THE LIBERTY TREE, comes bounding toward him, then recedes, like a ball strung to a bat with elastic. He realizes he has grown a moustache and a fake-fur collar, a pair of spectacles. *"Don't be afraid!"* he shouts, staggering about, searching for the chair. *"The Court is innocent! Doris Day is innocent! Go home to your children!"* For all his bravado, he feels like a dreaded outcast, the last pariah, a scabbed sheep, the target of a punitive expedition, the victim of Martian theory, chapfallen, weary to an extreme, his human decency violated, his human dignity trampled on—only Beauty sends him reeling so earnestly around the rocking Death House. *"I shall do my duty, distasteful as it may be! I will save you all!"* The chair hits him behind the knees and he falls into it as into a vat of boiling wax, a miracle of fit and flattery. I am the coward who dies many deaths, he weeps, as police with flailing nightsticks crash forward on melting ankles, trailing stars and planets like small balloons. *"The President said it: 'The one capital offense is a lack of staunch faith!' THROW THE SWITCH!"*

But they drag him out of there, whacking and prodding with their sticks, push him into a long white car. *"BEWARE THE MAD ARTIST!"* he wails, but they're all laughing.

"Jesus, that's the thirty-second nut we've had in the chair today," a policeman is saying, tipping his cap back.

"Hope we don't see no more. That's the last loony wagon we'll be able to get in here through that pack-up!"

"They're cleaning out the Whale's belly for us, and once the show starts, we can stow 'em there."

"Whew! Didja check those weird cardboard specs, Chief?" says another. "He looks like that silly little character with the big glasses who's always turning up in those Herblock cartoons, asking stupid questions!"

"Yeah, I know. He probably thinks he's Albert Einstein. The last one claimed to be John Wilkes Booth in drag and wanted to set himself on fire, and the one before that had horns, a tail, and the face of Leon Trotsky painted on his ass. Okay, boys, take him away!"

They punch him in the arm with a needle and he passes out, thinking: Well, that does it. I've done everything I can, and what's come of it? A few bruises. A few laughs for the condemned. A misspent Friday, a curious episode on the way to Armageddon, nothing more.

17.
The Eye in the Sky

I had to stop in a washroom on my way to the office to clean up, couldn't let my staff see me like this. I slapped through the swinging doors, still keyed up, ready for battle, but the place was empty. Those goddamn organ grinders out there pissed me off, Pearson especially—Winchell wasn't so bad, he'd never got past the sixth grade, after all, never read a book, probably couldn't, you had to make allowances. Understood his role, too: an entertainer; you could work with that. Apparently we were in the same class of reserve Lieutenant Commanders, he also was up for promotion. Shit, maybe I ought to quit politics and go back in, the Korean War's nearly over, shouldn't be too dangerous, and it sure as hell would be easier than this. I recalled those days in the Navy with a lot of affection, I'd grown up there, tried everything I'd been scared to try till then—I hated to think how square I'd been before, a silly little Sunday-school bigot, ranting about the disgusting evils of tobacco and alcohol and gambling, never saying anything worse than "hell" or "damn," shying from women, hadn't even gone with a whore—well, all that'd be different now. Commander Nixon of the USN. I was still young enough to cut the mustard, so why not? Well, for one thing, the seasickness . . . and having to kill all that time, kiss the asses of a lot of clowns who kissed mine now—no, it was a drop in rank, I was better off here, in the thick of it, no matter how rough it got: once you get used to the fast track, once you've hit the big leagues like I have, you can't resign yourself to just puttering around. Anyway, I'm at my best when the going is hardest—that's when you find out who has what it takes. I

once wrote a note to myself, I made it up myself, I still have it somewhere: "Live so that you can look any man in the face and tell him to go
to hell!" I looked up at myself in the mirror. "Go to hell!" I shouted.

I realized I was still very wrought up. Something of a mess, too. My
shirt was limp with sweat, face and hands streaked with horseshit, some
on my suit, my jacket shoulder scuffed and splitting at the seam, jowls
already darkening with bristle, hair mussed, face bruised, Jesus. I've
always been very particular about my physical appearance, even as a
little boy. Something deep in my character. I used to get up at least half
an hour early on school mornings so I'd have plenty of time, my mother
always remarked on this. I brushed each tooth, using all the right motions, gargled ritually, made Mom smell my breath to make sure I
wouldn't offend anybody on the bus. I was always afraid this might be
part of my problem with girls. I never could get used to kissing them on
the mouth—I thought I could smell my own and worried that they did,
too. Even at Duke, where we had no running water in our cramped
room, and where a certain unkemptness was fashionable, presumably
bespeaking a student too involved in his studies to take proper care of
himself, I maintained my tidiness. The other guys thought, when I
snuck out of bed early every morning, lit their fire for them, and disappeared, that I was off cracking the books somewhere, but in reality I was
in the gym using the showers. Had the whole place to myself then, I
liked the feeling of it, stalking around in the dawn light like a wild
animal, it set me up for my day in the law library. In fact it was in
there, in front of the gymnasium mirrors in the morning grayness, where
I first tested out some of the great trial-lawyer gestures that became my
hallmark as a politician.

I washed up as best I could, combed my hair, straightened my tie,
brushed my clothes off with toilet paper. I found my handkerchief
stuffed in a jacket pocket, remembered where it had been that day, and
flushed it down a stool. Weirdly, as it got sucked down the hole, I
seemed to hear a child cry—I realized my imagination was working
overtime, like I still hadn't come out the other end of those goddamn
dreams. Have to take a vacation when this thing is over. I cleaned my
shoe with soap and water. The lace was crusted with the stuff and had
got broken when I tore the shoe out from under the cabbie's seat, so I
threw it away. To get at the crud in between the sole and top of the
shoe, I wrapped toilet paper around a pencil point, an old trick I
learned long ago on those long hot evenings after cleaning out the
stables at the Prescott rodeo. Sooner or later, my enemies in the press
would try to use that rodeo job against me, too—he got his start in life

with both feet in the shit, they'll say. Just as they'll claim that I learned all I knew about politics when the bosses took notice of my good work and promoted me out front to bark for the Wheel of Fortune. Well, that's fair game, you've got to be able to take it in politics, but they'll be wrong about it, as usual. The stables taught me discipline and silence— the best test of a man is not how well he does the things he likes but how well he does the things he doesn't like—while the Wheel of Fortune gave me an appreciation of risk and the rudiments of mob psychology. I learned out there how to make my mark among total strangers, people whose lives were totally different from my own, and how to keep quiet about it after. The whole Frontier Days Rodeo scene gave me a special ceremonial perspective on the legend of the American West, too, and it ended once and for all whatever squeamishness I might have had toward the cruder side of life. I can be around blood, shit, dead bodies, beatings, tragedy, any kind of garbage or ugliness, and not be bothered like most. In a concentration camp, I not only would survive, I would probably even prosper. And it was why Uncle Sam, I knew, could count on me tonight at the electrocutions, where others might lose their color, if not their courage and suppers as well. Tonight! Whew, it hardly seemed possible that it was really going to happen, after all, just a few hours from now! I didn't know if I was pleased or not. I felt like I used to feel when an exam was rushing up on me I wasn't prepared for. Hey! I had to get that speech written!

I hustled out of there and on up to my office. The girls greeted me as usual, but they were less than natural about it, something in the way they ducked their heads, glanced at each other, fussed with the pamphlets and brochures stacked out for tourists. Had they spotted so quickly my laceless shoe? Caught a whiff? Or—ah! I'd forgotten to lock the door to my inner office last night, they'd witnessed the mess in there. Encountering so much disorder in an office kept as neat as mine must have been as shocking to them as finding Foster Dulles' office filled with empty gin bottles or Cardinal Spellman's quarters littered with lace panties. I should get them out of there, I thought. I didn't have much time left, and they were no help at a time like this. A nuisance, in fact.

I checked the mail, signed some letters, remarked favorably on a peculiar-looking beanie with five fingers sticking up that one of them had bought for a nephew, asked for a cup of coffee, looked over the advance copy of a special feature article on me for this Sunday's *Washington Post*, apologized laughingly for the confusion in the other room, glanced at the appointments calendar. "I was working late last night on a report for the President, and let me say frankly, I, uh, didn't get a chance to straighten up after," I said with a loose chuckle. For some reason, I didn't recognize a single name on the appointments calendar. "This Rosenberg thing, you know—the President wanted all the, uh, facts before making any final, I've been working sixteen hours a day on this thing, any final judgment on their petition for clemency."

"What's going to happen, Mr. Nixon? Has it been postponed again? We heard all the shouting—"

"No, the Court has held the line and the President has refused clemency. Everything's all right. It is my understanding that they will be executed tonight, sometime around eight, if all, uh, goes well." It was cold in here, the girls had the airconditioner on, and my shirt was sticking damply to my skin. I hoped I had a fresh shirt somewhere in my office. I realized I was reluctant to go back in there. One glance brought back everything from last night and my butt even began to ache again. I sat down on one of the tall black leather chairs out where the girls were.

"A pity," one of the girls said. "Those two little boys . . ."

"Well, let's not deceive ourselves, they should have thought more about those little boys when they started working for the Phantom," I said with a smile. I leaned forward earnestly. "We're fortunate that we have a President of the United States who isn't a sucker and who isn't going to be made one. I think the only man that can save America is Dwight, uh, Eisenhower."

"Well, maybe," the girl said, handing me a cup of hot coffee, "but it seems like it should be enough if they just electrocuted the man and let the woman go take care of the kids, maybe just cut off one of her arms or her tongue or something—I mean, it was probably mostly his fault anyway, women always do what men tell them to. *I* certainly do!"

I laughed jovially. "That's funny," I said, standing up. "I always had, uh, the idea it was just the opposite!"

The girls laughed. "Oh, you men!" one of them said.

I felt pleased with myself. I sat down again. I wasn't usually so successful with this kind of banter. Maybe that encounter with the Phantom and the reporters had loosened me up: a good fight stirs the blood. And other things, too. Certainly, everybody was in a jocular—almost holiday—mood now, and whatever uneasiness there might have been when I entered had apparently been forgotten. "Well," I grinned affably, "if the dry rot of corruption and Communism, which has eaten deep into our body, uh, politic during the past seven years, can only be chopped out with a hatchet—then let's call for a hatchet!"

This was less successful. "My goodness!" said one of the girls, breaking the silence. "Eight o'clock, did you say? That's only about seven hours from now!" I stood and looked at my watch. "And people are probably going there right now to get the best places!"

"All right," I laughed in a yielding manner, "I can take a hint! Go ahead and cancel all my afternoon appointments and take the rest, uh, of the day off." Things were working out better than I might have hoped. I felt freer now—I'd be alone, and alone I could work this thing out, bring it all to some kind of summation, find the words I'd need tonight at the ceremonies. I sat down. But I didn't mean to. I got up again. I chuckled. I tried on the beanie with the five fingers and then handed it back. I strode cheerfully, chin high, into the maelstrom of my office, threw open the heavy red drapes, turned upon the debris as a manager might turn upon his ballplayers—trailing, exhausted, dispirited, but not yet defeated—in the bottom of the seventh. All right, boys, they're all watching us now, let's pick it up and put it together.

While the girls bustled about in the other rooms, tidying up their desks, freshening their makeup, making the necessary phone calls, I pretended to clean up my own office, snatching up the papers disinterestedly from the floor and chairs, stacking them more or less by date, dumping part of them as though carelessly into the wastebasket. "Early hath Life's mighty question thrilled within the heart of youth," I mused, recalling that Whittier quotation from over the mantel outside the President's office back at college, "with a deep and strong beseeching . . . what and where is—?"

"Shall I empty that wastebasket for you, sir, before I go?"

"What? *No!* Er, I mean, no, thank you, Rose, that's very kind, but I'll take care of it." I gave her a fatherly look. "You can run along and, uh, enjoy yourself."

"Well, if you're sure . . ."

"Of course, I'm sure." I forced a smile and gestured casually—wrong arm, it was the shoulder I'd struck the cab door with. I winced.

"Oh, Mr. Nixon," she sighed, "you're just going to make yourself sick again!"

"If you believe in certain principles of government," I said in all seriousness—I remembered having said this to my mother once, "you have to be willing to sacrifice yourself if necessary."

She looked at me. The coffee tasted sour, but I sipped at it nervously. In the outer office there were drawers opening and closing, filing cabinets clicking shut, low hushed titters. "And, uh, anyway . . ." But she was gone from the room. Well, let them giggle. We all have our liabilities, I thought, I know I won't win any personality contests, each man has his strong points and his weak points. Public-relations experts have advised me to take speaking lessons, to get in more quips and so forth, but like Lincoln I'm at my best when I'm using the language of the people. Only the people aren't the same as in his day, they've all been to college for one thing, and I don't have his appetite for building up to climaxes, I hate all those heroics, those fancy rhythms. Anyway, when you really have a crunch, when it is really tough, when the decision to be made may determine the future of war and peace, not just now but for generations to come, people are going to make the choice in terms of an individual who is totally cool, detached, and with some experience, like me, and not some breezy Adlai Stevenson type or his gag writer. And that goes for my goddamn secretaries as much as anybody else.

Charisma, basically, I think most sophisticates say, is style, and mine is robust, intelligent, determined, articulate, aggressive, clinical, thorough, industrious, conscientious, courageous, and cool. This is not merely my opinion, others have said this of me—I have a rule that I've always followed in political life, never to attempt to rate myself. That sort of juvenile self-analysis is something I've never done. I think that's the responsibility of others. That feature article planned as a wedding-anniversary gift for Pat and me in the Sunday *Post*, for example: I could see that it focused on my long workweeks, my coolness under pressure, my popularity as a public speaker, my modesty, and my trouble-shooting talents on behalf of Ike's amateurs: "catching foul balls and line drives for the administration on the Hill, so quickly that few knew he was in the Capitol outfield." But especially the workweeks, the discipline: there's no public-relations gimmick, in school, politics, or just growing up, that will take the place of hard work. In order to pass an exam or make a decision, one must sit on his rear end and dig into the books. In this respect, I was like Stevenson: he was an intellectual and he needed time to contemplate. People liked that "old shoe" image of his—the sole with a hole in it—because it reminded them of a butt worn raw by a lot of laborious and conscientious sitting. But there was no iron there, beneath the hard leather surface Stevenson had a butt of cork, a butt of soft rubber, of warm oatmeal, he was all veneer and no substance, a man plagued with indecision who could speak beautifully but could not act decisively. I could do both, and if my style wasn't as euphonious as Stevenson's, it wasn't as phony either: and it got the votes. I'd won oratorical contests, debates, and extemporaneous speaking contests from grade school to law school, and I was, in effect, still winning them.

This was not to be sneered at. I learned a lot from those debates and contests, the plays I was in, too. You're not born with "character," you create this as you go along, and acting parts in plays helps you recognize some of the alternative options—most people don't realize this, and that's why they end up with such shabby characters. We're all conscious of the audience from an early age—but we're not always aware of the footlights between us. The extempore contests taught me agility, coolness in crisis situations, and how to manipulate ambiguities when you don't have the facts and aren't even sure what the subject matter is. I learned in debates that the topic didn't count for shit, the important thing was strategy, strategy and preparation: to marshal your facts, an army of facts, present them in pyramidal fashion to overwhelm your enemy, undercut his pyramid with slashing attacks on his facts or reasoning, pull off a climactic surprise if possible, and then, win or lose, forget everything and start over again the next morning. Voorhis and Douglas didn't stand a chance against me. Neither did the Republicans, for that matter, when I got invited to give the main speech at their fundraising dinner at the Waldorf-Astoria a year ago. *Our* dinner, I should say. I knew what was at stake. I knew Dewey had his eye on me. I devoted a full week to preparing that speech, and it turned out to be one of my more successful efforts. When I concluded, the audience gave me a standing ovation. As I sat down, the old kingmaker Tom Dewey grasped my hand and said: "That was a terrific speech. Make me a promise: don't get fat; don't lose your zeal. And you can be President some day."

Me, lose my zeal? Zeal *is* my charisma! Coolidge liked to say that "four-fifths of all our troubles in this life would disappear if we would only *sit down* and keep still"—but I could never understand why anybody would *want* them to disappear. I'm like Teddy Roosevelt, I like to be down in the arena. They used to say of Roosevelt that "when Theodore attends a wedding he wants to be a bride; when he attends a funeral he wants to be the corpse." I'm like that. And what's most important, I have the faith: I believe in the American dream, I believe in it because I have seen it come true in my own life. TIME has said that I've had "a Horatio Alger–like career," but not even Horatio Alger could have dreamed up a life so American—in the best sense—as mine.

Boy, just thinking about this got me all fired up. As soon as the girls had vacated the place, I locked the door, switched off the airconditioner, threw open the windows, emptied the pockets of my jacket and hung it neatly up, put the cigar in the fridge, loosened my tie, removed my cufflinks and folded up my shirtsleeves, unbuckled my belt, retrieved the notes and letters from the wastebasket, spread everything around me again, and sat back to contemplate it all. Outside, I knew, the tensions were building. The streets were filling up fast, Inspiration House was leaking demonstrators like some kind of insidious spore, the city was becoming a thicket of angry placards, a forest of diatribe—reaching the center today had been like negotiating some terrible free-fire zone, and my own home out in Spring Valley now seemed far away across an impassable no-man's-land. Vengeance Valley. The Badlands. Which existed, I knew, not here in the Capital alone, but wound its serpentine way through the whole world, coiling about our periphery, dripping poison as it slithered through the more vulnerable points in the Free World, threatening now to strike at the very heart. Uncle Sam's countermoves had been dramatic and effective, momentous even, but the Phantom was still dangerous—maybe, backed up like this, more dangerous than ever. This was bigger than anyone had anticipated, perhaps even a tactical mistake, but we were committed now, there was no turning back. It was exactly the kind of desperate situation I was best suited for. I began to understand that Uncle Sam had until the last few weeks protected me from this case so as to maneuver me first into this key role, but that now he needed me, needed my skills and talents, my rhetoric—there was something he wanted from me up there tonight that only I could provide.

A cold chill passed through me: was Eisenhower's life in danger? Was the Incarnation to come to me even sooner than I had expected? I sat there for a moment in a kind of mindless shock, staring blankly into space, unable to think of anything but the Inauguration ceremonies, Pat at my side, Mom in the front row, my hand on the family Bible, the blinding light . . . and then slowly I calmed down. I realized that this was not the best way to get started. I recalled that I was fatalistic about politics, I made myself remember that. I brought my attention carefully back to the Rosenberg papers, my speech for the ceremonies. I picked up a letter from Julius to Ethel. I read: "Somewhere in the long ago I had a normal life with a sweet wife and two fine children and now all is gone and we're facing death. . . ."

I stood, stretched, went to gaze out the open window, get my thoughts in order. I knew better than to try to psyche out Uncle Sam. The important thing was to do my duty here, be prepared, know the facts, find the phrases. I recalled my high-school paper on the Constitution: "There are those who, under the pretense of freedom of speech and freedom of the press, have incited riots, assailed our patriotism, and denounced the Constitution. . . ." Yes, I should look that up, get back to the origins—

and I should read the Rosenberg letters again, more seriously this time, also the FBI dossiers, the news clippings. Some mosaic out of all that, a succinct rebuttal, something on brainwashing maybe (I was watching the demonstrators down below), "the deadly danger of the propaganda that warps the mind . . . destroys the will of a people to resist tyranny. . . ." Needed to rethink the trial through from some fresh angle, too, assimilate more of the background material, examine the Death House years, get an overview. Why, for example, was the campaign to save the Rosenbergs so designed by the Phantom's agents as virtually to ensure their deaths? What was the Phantom up to? Was this some kind of trap?

The people down below seemed to be having a picnic, listening to popular songs on their portable radios, eating ice cream and box lunches, playing checkers, sunbathing. Some of them had placards protesting the executions. Were they all dupes? And the Rosenbergs? Who was behind them? Were they really as transparent as they seemed? Or were there strange patterns of depravity concealed behind the middle-class clichés of their trial testimony, secret messages buried in the banalities of their Death House letters? How had their son managed to get elected president of his fifth-grade class in the middle of all this, and what did this signify? Was he on his way to a Horatio Alger–like career, too? All these questions: why did I feel I had to ask them? Why did I have to keep going back over this material, starting over, driving myself? I felt caught up in some endless quest, a martyr to duty . . . but duty to what? My self perhaps, its creation and improvement, the need to show I had what it takes, that I *deserved*, no matter what I got. . . .

This dogged sense of purpose, this conviction that easy wins are tainted, lay behind most of my difficulties with girls, I realized. The problem was, all the girls I met when I was young seemed to be living lives that were out of mesh with my own. Out of sync, I think they say in the movies. They seemed to be on some other plane, moving at some other angle. Not that I understood much about where I was going, I admit. I never thought about national politics, for example, didn't even vote when I was old enough, in spite of all the preaching I used to do in high-school essays about it, had no idea I'd be where I am today, nor even had any specific ambition to be here. Yet I knew instinctively that those girls weren't going where I was going. I was driving toward the center, they were spinning around on some merry-go-round out at the edges. And because of that, I was afraid of too much intimacy with them, more afraid than they were, afraid of getting lost in some maze of emotions, of surrendering my self-control, afraid of . . . afraid of exile.

From myself. Even though I craved that surrender, ached for release from my inordinate sense of mission. Those long lonely nights up in the bell tower, dreams deep and dangerous . . .

My weakness, I knew, was an extreme susceptibility to love, to passion. This is not obvious, but it is true. A politician cannot display his emotions in public, this is part of the job. Nor can you enjoy the luxury of intimate personal friendships. You can't confide absolutely in anyone. You can't talk too much about your personal plans, your personal feelings. I believe in keeping my own counsel. It's something like wearing clothing—if you let your hair down, you feel too naked. Yet, I longed for this nakedness. My testing ground was Ola, the only steady girlfriend I had before Pat. She was pretty, lively, exciting, she brought out my more reckless side, in fact I loved her, but she wouldn't get off the merry-go-round, and I couldn't get on it. It took me six years to realize that— we went together, off and on, all through my senior year in high school, four years of college, and my first year at Duke—or maybe I realized it all the time, maybe the six years was for something else. . . .

Ola was the daughter of the local police chief, and maybe that was why I started going with her. However far we went, I thought, it would be somehow legal. Under the arm of the law. At the same time, it seemed dangerous, dating a cop's kid like that, a challenge worthy of the class president and wingading honors man. Sometimes I walked around school feeling a little bit like Douglas Fairbanks slipping into the caliph's harem. I admit, I knew nothing about girls, I had only brothers, I didn't even know what their underside looked like or what you were supposed to do when you got there. "Menstruation" was a distant rumor. I expected holes of some kind, but I wasn't sure how many—at the burlesque shows, all you saw were tits and bottoms, and even then we were too nervous to sit down in the front rows. I didn't know what a clitoris was until years after I was married. In fact, I'm still not sure I'd know one if I saw one. Ola had no brothers, perhaps we started even, but I supposed at the time she knew everything, she was cute and popular and very self-confident. And a Democrat besides, which suggested a lot to me at the time. Also, she liked all the dangerous things— which in those days were the movies with their "jazz babies" and "red-hot mamas," beach parties, and dancing—I was clumsy as hell at dancing, but it always made me hot, I could see why the wild people liked it.

We got off to a terrific start, playing the romantic leads in a high-school Latin Club production of *Aeneas and Dido*. There were omens in this: Dido was abandoned by Aeneas and killed herself. Not that Ola had it in her to kill herself, far from it—but she did marry a guy who locked her into that small town forever, a kind of suicide, and I've always thought she did it to spite me. On the other hand, to be accurate, it was really she who abandoned me. But that was years later; the end came slowly. At the time, the play gave me a vocabulary different from my own that I was able to use for a while with great success. And those white togas, they were like flimsy nightshirts, like bedsheets—I had to wear a jockstrap so as not to make a spectacle of myself. Those goddamn Greeks and Romans, they must have been at it all the time. I got a handful myself every time I threw myself on Queen Dido's bier at the end, best part I ever had. Everything was great—but only so long as the play lasted. Then she fell into the same clichés about me as all the other girls. Maybe they'd been talking to her too much. I fought against this, acted silly or loud or flirtatious or belligerent. I hated myself at these times. I assumed an air of possession wherever we went, looking old and already half-married, hoping she would fall into the same patterns and find herself past the barrier without remembering when she'd crossed it. She looked up to me, more than any other girl, even Pat, she went with me everywhere, said I was a man of the world and she felt so stupid around me, sometimes even almost afraid, but she wouldn't give in, stop being frivolous, and just be mine. She was even more goddamn stubborn than I was.

We had arguments. About religion, politics, friends, what to do. But we didn't argue about what was really the problem. We didn't even mention it. I tried everything. When my brother Harold died, I even suggested I might get TB too, might be dead soon . . . This was even less successful than the political arguments. Each day the opportunity receded. I had black moods and unhealthy imaginings—I felt she knew what was wrong and was only taunting me. And it wasn't her virginity I wanted, no, I was frightened in fact by the prospect—what I wanted was her surrender. I wanted her to *give* herself to me, utterly, abjectly, deliriously. That was all. She had nothing to fear. And perhaps much to gain. Our political arguments were surface manifestations of this deeper struggle. I thought if I could so break her self-assurance as to make a Republican of her, the rest would follow. She did not understand the importance of these arguments. She would get flippant about them, make fun of my seriousness. I would become ill-tempered and bark at her. She'd start to cry. But I wasn't being doctrinaire—all of us Quakers were for Hoover in 1932, that was natural, but I hardly noticed when Roosevelt smashed him that fall. We were in the middle of final rehearsals for *Bird-in-Hand* and I gave the greatest performance of my life on opening night, just two days after the elections (admittedly, I got a certain perverse pleasure out of the line about what kind of Conservative I was: "Governing folks as isn't fit to govern themselves!"). And then a week later I entertained my entire fraternity in Grandma Milhous's home, the whole football team was in the fraternity and the party was to celebrate the Poets' victory over Loyola, forty guys were there—Christ, what the hell did we care about politics? Couldn't Ola see this?

In the spring we even had the romantic leads in a revolutionary play about the sordid life of Scottish coal miners, a thing called *The Price of Coal.* It was mostly my idea, in fact I thought we might recapture the spirit of Aeneas and Dido, but somehow we got lost in the dialect. Also the lighting was fucked up something awful, it was a disaster. As usual, we put it on in Founders Hall. There was something wrong with that building, my whole romance was tied up in it and there were thousands of places to hide, but somehow nothing ever seemed to happen, we always ended up out in the corridors or on the benches built into the stair landings—already mine was a public life. I was running everything, arranging picnics, staging plays, bringing bands to campus, winning debates and scholarship honors, holding the fraternity together, participating in clubs, running for offices, literally working my ass off, and somehow this only made Ola laugh gaily and go off and date some other guy. I remembered walking around on that tight little stage on the second floor—it was Friday-morning chapel and everybody out front was still half asleep and bored shitless—thinking: Goddamn it, she has no sense of *value:* Jock the Miner or Aeneas the Father of the Romans, it was all the same to her, let's face it, she's too flighty, I could never marry her. But I still wished to break her down, prove to her she needed me. And then, probably, I would marry her. Back in the wings, sweating under the greasepaint smudges, aroused by the musty odors of the costume racks, I'd give her long deep looks. She'd sigh and complain about the electricians. Or glance over my shoulder and wave at a friend.

And then we got into a fight one night at a dance. I walked out on her. I expected her to follow me. She didn't. She called her folks to pick her up. That should have been the end but I kept trying. I don't give up easily. Then we suddenly had the best night we ever had together. It was the night I found out about winning the scholarship to Duke. I felt so terrific I wasn't even trying to make out—and then I almost did. I'd bought an old 1930 Ford and we rode around in it all night. I think she was really in love with me that night. But I was so in love with myself I didn't notice until it was too late. By then we'd celebrated too long and she was sleepy, wanted to go home. I didn't want to spoil anything, we were both so happy, there was always tomorrow . . . but there wasn't.

When I went away to Duke Law School, I wrote her every week, went home on holidays to see her. Clear across country. She was going with other guys. I was desperate and tried to ignore this. But when she wouldn't even let me come see her, I lost my temper and broke it off. As I slammed the phone down, I thought I heard her giggling. Yet I was relieved. I'd been saved. I realized I'd been pursuing my passion like a career—I'd even considered throwing over law school and going back to Whittier for good!—but now I used my stifled passions as energy in my pursuit of a career in law. Oh, I never doubted I would marry, keep a woman beside me, have children, I was normal—but the law degree, I knew, was like a potent aphrodisiac, obtainable through abstinence. I remembered that history book that Aunt Edith gave me when I was ten years old: lawyers ran the world. And could have, I assumed, whomever they pleased. Even there, in that dismal unlit room in Whippoorwill Manor without toilet or running water, burning crumpled newspapers in the old sheet-metal stove to stay warm, sharing a double bed with old Bill "Boop-Boop" Perdue, listening to Brownie and On-the-Brink Freddie over in the other bed spinning off their horny tales of coquetry and conquest, worrying about the next round of exams, cold, miserable, and poorer even than Jock the Miner, I knew this mating must happen to me. And it did. In *The Dark Tower*. Not Ola, of course, but I didn't forget her. Years later, out on Green Island, I wrote a note to myself: "There's a kind of love for permanence. There's another kind that's just champagne bubbles and moonlight. It isn't meant to last but it can be something to have and look back on all your life. . . ."

I yawned. I was drifting. It was a beautiful day out, lush and warm, the kind of day to get out the old glove and toss the ball around. Probably be good for my sore shoulder, get the kink out. Stupid as hell to hit the door like that. Yes, go out and shag a few, the Capitol outfielder. Julius and Ethel Rosenberg often did that: went up on the Death House roof to toss a ball around. Not both at the same time, of course—give them half a chance and they went at each other like animals. Maybe one of them was up there now . . . warming up in the bullpen, as it were, loosening up for the big one. "At lunch," Ethel once wrote, "the up and coming athletic star of this jail went up on the roof and hit three home runs. It is wonderful to punch a ball and run and enjoy wind and sun." I supposed a home run was when you knocked the ball off the roof. Dangerous place to chase a fly, there were probably a lot of homers. In fact, the matrons playing with her were probably a little peed off that the aggressive little twat kept knocking the damned ball away. "Come on, Mrs. Rosenberg, play nice."

The Rosenbergs were Brooklyn Dodger fans. Or pretended to be. They talked about it in their letters. Of course, I understood the emotional and political motives, it was rhetorically sound, I'd used much the same techniques myself—but what was wrong with the Rosenbergs' appeal was that it was obvious they didn't know the first thing about baseball, had no feel for the game at all. The Dodgers had won three pennants in the last six years and were a close second so far this year, and the only thing that excited the Rosenbergs was the fact that Brooklyn had broken the color barrier when they brought up Jackie Robinson and Roy Campanella. As Ethel wrote, after allegedly "chewing her nails" over a boring 10-0 rout: "It is chiefly in their outstanding contribution to the eradication of racial prejudice that they have covered themselves with glory." Now, I ask you, what kind of baseball talk is that? Maybe they called it "beizbol" now that the Russians had laid claim to inventing it. This, after all, was part of their defense. The *National Guardian* had argued that, just as the Russians had invented everything first, including baseball, they also knew all along how to build atomic weapons, but humanistic considerations had deterred them from doing so.

True, some of our own eggheads were contending much the same thing, Harold Urey for example: that there was no secret to the A-bomb, and that the Russians could have got more out of a Flash Gordon comic strip than out of Greenglass's famous diagrams. It was Urey's argument, and that of other offbeat scientists like him, that anyone could figure out how to build the Bomb, the important thing being to have the wherewithal to put what you knew into hardware. The Russians were presumably slow in developing the A-bomb because their industrial establishment had been wiped out by World War II. Well, Urey was a Nobel Prize winner and all that, but he had heavy water on the brain. Even if he was telling the truth, it was interesting that he had waited until now to spring it on us—he and his buddies had built up a profitable and very private sinecure for themselves on the assumption all this time that there *was* a secret. Even their goddamn budgets were so highly classified that in Congress we rarely had any idea what we were giving them money for. For all we knew, we were buying them retirement homes in Odessa. And anyway, it wasn't likely Urey was telling the truth. J. Edgar Hoover had said there was a secret, and so had Truman and Eisenhower, it was on the record. Even the Rosenbergs and their lawyer obviously believed there was such a secret, this much they'd effectively confessed to. I remembered from my days at HUAC that Urey had had a long association with fronts for the Phantom, had even helped to launch a few. Maybe he was even one of the mystery spies behind the Rosenbergs. Along with Dashiell Hammett and Albert Einstein. Paul Robeson. The Hollywood Ten. I gazed down at the demonstrators parading in the sun. Only a few years ago, there were 1,157,172 people in this country willing to vote for Henry Wallace. Who were those people? Where were they now? Why hadn't we done something about them? Old Wallace . . . might have been President. But he didn't have it. Got too near the sacred fire and went berserk. Risks of the game . . .

I turned away from the window. I was running like a dry creek. Very sleepy. My personal desire was to sack out, but it was not a question of what I personally wanted to do, but what was best for the Party and the nation as well. I stood and gazed down on all the documents and records scattered about the room, trying to get an overview. What a mess. I didn't even know where to begin. Even so, I had to keep moving. Confidence in crisis depended in great part, I knew, on adequacy of preparation—where preparation was possible. The Boy Scouts were right about this. And it had been my experience that once the final period of intense preparation for battle began, it was not wise to break it. It always took me a certain period of time to "warm up" to the point where my mind was working, and it was important to keep the juices flowing. The natural tendency was to procrastinate, because the body and the mind rebel at being driven at a faster pace than usual over any long period of time, like now, for example. But there was never a period when it was safe to let up in the battle with our Communist opponents. They were out to win, and one of the tactics they used was to keep the pressure on. They tried to wear us out. To keep them from winning and to win ourselves, we had to have more stamina and more determination than they had. I squeezed my mouth shut around a yawn and leaned my head back. I realized I was sunk down in my chair again.

I dragged myself to my feet, jangled around a little, shaking myself awake. I had less than seven hours, the day was racing past, I had to keep my mind on this thing, what was the matter with me anyhow? I thought about the Hiss case, how I broke it. What had I done then that I was forgetting about now? Well, for one thing, the lines had seemed less blurred: Chambers was an honest Quaker, Hiss an Ivy League smart-ass, I knew what I was doing. Greenglass was as fat as Chambers and even less stable, and Rosenberg was skinny like Hiss, but Greenglass lacked Whittaker's wit and vocabulary—Checkers was probably brighter—and Rosenberg was poor, like me, thick-tongued, and dressed ten years behind the times. Hiss had been the millionaire gone sour in the Horatio

Alger novels, the evil nephew trying to con his rich uncle out of his cousin's inheritance, the wily traitor in a plain respectable man's troubled business. Rosenberg, on the other hand, had been born into a true Horatio Alger family, poor but honest, he should have made a fortune. He'd even sold penny candy on the streets during the Depression, earning as much as eighty cents a day. But somehow something went wrong. The boat did not come in. The rich patron with the sweet tooth did not materialize. There was no happy ending.

So where was I to find my bearings? And Ethel Rosenberg, how did she fit in, what was I to do with her? It was Eisenhower's contention that she was the prime mover, but according to the testimony, she was mainly guilty of typing up notes. Irving Saypol had made as much of this as he could: "This description of the atom bomb, destined for delivery to the Soviet Union, was typed up by the defendant Ethel Rosenberg that afternoon at her apartment at 10 Monroe Street. Just so had she on countless other occasions sat at the typewriter and struck the keys, blow by blow, against her own country in the interests of the Soviets." Blow by blow. The whole argument reminded me a little too much of my high-school debate: "Resolved: Girls are no good." But maybe Saypol and the President knew something I didn't.

She *was* pretty goddamn tough, all right. Once, when she was only nineteen years old, she led 150 fellow women workers in a strike that closed down National Shipping. This was during the Depression and the company was fighting for its life, so naturally they hired a new staff and tried to keep operating. But Ethel led the girls in an illegal riot that terrorized the non-union girls and shut the plant down again, in spite of the protective efforts of the whole New York City police force. When a delivery truck tried to crash the picket line, Ethel and the girls hauled the driver from his cab, stripped him bare, and lipsticked his butt with I AM A SCAB. My own butt tingled with the thought of it. When more trucks came, they blocked up the streets, threw themselves down in front of the wheels, slashed up the trucks' cargo, and pitched it all out in the gutters. Later, in the war, she got a job at the Census Bureau in Washington, the same time I was there in the OPA. We might have met. Julius was back in New York. "It's all right, miss—after all, I *am* Dick Nixon of the OPA. . . ." I grinned to myself. Yet I supposed she was a lot like the people I hated so much in that place—all those ruthless, self-serving, supercilious, cynical wheeler-dealers. That old violent big-city New Deal crowd—we were still trying to get rid of the sonsabitches. Everybody maneuvering for advancement, managing to make a little

work look like a lot so as to build their little pyramids—I discovered I
could have done the work of the entire OPA all by myself and still take
long weekends, but when I tried to introduce a little efficiency, they
ostracized me. If anything turned me into a conservative, it was that six
months in the OPA. Maybe Ethel was the one most like Hiss. . . . On
the other hand, she didn't last long there either, maybe she was as
unhappy as I was. Now she sobbed herself to sleep at nights, hugged her
pillow so tightly she got cramps, was frightened by mice, needed cold
compresses to soothe her migraines. Poor Ethel . . .

I stared gloomily at the paper strewn across my office floor. Which was
real, I wondered, the paper or the people? In a few hours, Julius and
Ethel Rosenberg would be dead, their poor remains worth less than that
horseshit I'd stepped in, and the paper too could be burnt, but what was
on it would survive. Or could survive, it was a matter of luck. Luck and
human need: the zeal for pattern. For story. And they'd been seduced
by this. If they could say to hell with History, they'd be home free. The
poor damned fools. Maybe this was yet another consequence of growing
up in the city. One of the first shocks a country boy gets when he leaves
home is the discovery that no one has been logging all that terrific
history he's been living through. Until he thrusts himself into the urban
fracas, he might as well never have lived at all, as far as History was
concerned. In fact, part of the fun of becoming famous was to bend the
light back on the old home town and stun them with their own previously unnoticed actuality, make guys like Gail Jobe and Tom Bewley
jump and stutter. Yet, I knew what the Rosenbergs felt, because I had
felt it, too.

The Rosenbergs' self-destructive suspicion that they were being
watched by some superhuman presence came early, perhaps years ago,
back in college, or when Julius got fired maybe, but certainly—and with
force—almost immediately after their arrests. In many ways their first
letters were the best of the lot: quiet, unassuming, written in haste,
often dropping their pronoun subjects and abbreviating, full of ordinary sentences that touched the heart: "Just got through hanging the
clothes as Mike didn't get to sleep until 11:30 . . ."

But then came the death sentence, and what was striking about all
their letters after that was the almost total absence in them of concrete
reality, of real-life involvement—it was all hyperbole, indignation,
political cliché, abstraction. Oh, there was some impressive political
rhetoric in them, and though I was no judge, Ethel's poem was probably
a classic of a sort. And now and then they did make a half-hearted effort

to describe something of their lives in prison, the boredom of it, the killing of cockroaches, Jewish services, playing chess or boccie-ball, but frankly it was as though they were responding reluctantly to editorial suggestions from their lawyer or the Party: "Dearest Ethel, Shall I describe my prison cell? It is three paces wide, four paces long, and seven feet high . . ." And Julius occasionally worked hard at inventing a sympathetic past for himself: "I was a good student, but more, I absorbed quite naturally the culture of my people, their struggle for freedom from slavery in Egypt. As an American Jew with this background, it was natural that I should follow in the footsteps laid down by my heritage and seek to better the lot of the common man . . ." That was admirable, I might have come up with the same phrases myself ("follow in the footsteps laid down by my heritage": I made a note), but all these half starts quickly collapsed, and more often than not into maudlin self-pity: "Ethel, My Darling, You are truly a great, dignified and sweet woman. Tears fill my eyes as I try to put sentiments to paper. . . . Our upbringing, the full meaning of our lives, based on a true amalgamation of our American and Jewish heritage, which to us means freedom, culture and human decency, has made us the people we are. All the filth, lies and slander of this grotesque frame-up will not in any way deter us, but rather spur us on until we are completely . . ." et cetera et cetera. Culpable of deceit, he accuses others of the same thing! With such grandstanding, who would not find them guilty? Who or what did he think History was—some kind of nincompoop? A little unimaginative maybe, and yes, eccentric, straitlaced, captious, and rude—but feebleminded? Hardly.

Maybe Julius had had intimations that something or someone was watching him as long ago as his famous encounter with the street-corner Tom Mooney pamphleteer, in the same way that I'd been touched by Aunt Edith's history book—but intimations are one thing, real awareness is another. Intimations reach you like a subtle change of temperature; real awareness hits you like a bolt of lightning. I'd seen this awareness crash on others before it fell on me, most dramatically during my HUAC investigation of Alger Hiss, and it was a pretty awesome experience. It was as though the whole world had slowly shifted gears and pivoted to stare down upon the incredible duel of Hiss and Chambers, and when they looked up and saw that Eye there, it nearly drove both of them mad. Poor old Whittaker even tried to kill himself. Though I had basked in the peripheral glow of this gaze and was granted my first close-up glimpse of Uncle Sam, I wasn't touched directly, I wasn't burned. It wasn't until the fund scandal broke last fall that I really for the first time in my life felt the full force of it. Julius and Ethel Rosenberg receiving the death penalty was minor-league stuff compared to it.

I was on my campaign train, the Nixon Special, whistle-stopping north from Pomona, California, toward Oregon and Washington— *Change Trains for the Future!*—when the gears started to shift for me. SECRET NIXON FUND. I tried to ignore it, concentrated instead on technical problems like microphones and schedules, boning up on local color, dealing with the small-time politicos who got on at one stop and off at the next. I had this weird illusion that if we'd just get up a little more steam we could outrun it—instead, we seemed to draw closer and closer to the hot center. RICH MEN'S TRUST FUND KEEPS NIXON IN STYLE FAR BEYOND HIS SALARY. I tried to skirt it. I joked about it. I shouted at it and ran. But it did no good. The fund issue was becoming a national sensation. Willy-nilly, I was entering the arena.

I decided to counterattack, the only possible defense against a smear, especially when it's largely true. "I was warned," I cried out from the back of my campaign train, "that if I continued to attack the Communists and crooks in this government, they would try to smear me! Ever since I have done that work of investigating Communists in the United States, the left-wingers have been fighting me with every smear that they have been able to!" But they only laughed and everywhere we went there were more and more hecklers. SSH! ANYONE WHO MENTIONS $16,000 IS A COMMUNIST! The fat was in the fire. Not only Democrats, but Republicans, too, were demanding my scalp. Eisenhower turned his back on me. It was because of him I was in trouble. I'd had to double-cross Earl Warren and his gang at the Convention to break up the California delegation and swing the nomination to Eisenhower, and it was some of those soreheads, I knew, who had spilled the beans on the fund—and now he turned his back on me! He said he didn't know me well and if I was honest, I'd have to prove it. "Of what avail is it for us to carry on this crusade against this business as of what has been going on in Washington if we, ourselves, aren't clean as a hound's tooth?" He made me feel like the little boy caught with jam on his face. Stassen and Dewey told me to get off the ticket. Friends were not at home when I called them on the phone. Knowland was summoned by Sherman Adams all the way from Hawaii to take my place. Out on the trail, the people wanted blood. I felt like I'd been hit by a real blockbuster, much of the fight had gone out of me, and I was beginning to wonder how much more of this beating I was going to be able to take. Was the whole nation in the Phantom's power? I got hit by pennies in Portland. NO MINK COATS FOR NIXON, JUST COLD CASH!

I knew the time had come. Either I had to turn and face it, or else I had to quit. In meeting any crisis, one must fight or run away, but one must do something. Not knowing how to act or not being able to act is what tears your insides out. I began to notice the inevitable symptoms of tension. I was mean to live with, quick-tempered with the members of my staff. I lost interest in eating and skipped meals without even being aware of it. I was preparing, I knew, for battle. It wasn't just a question of who was on the right side, it was a question of determination, of will, of stamina, of willingness to risk all for victory. I tossed through sleepless nights, elbowing and kneeing Pat until she cried, struggling with myself. Of course, I had no intention of quitting. But I didn't want to get pulped, either. Back in July, I'd had to lock Pat up in a Chicago hotel room one whole night with Murray Chotiner, who had a helluva job pressuring her out of threatening to leave me if I ran for the Vice Presidency—he said afterwards she was a real tiger—so now I got no pity at all from her. She became thin and haggard and even my breakfasts were lousy. But Jack Drown told me not to worry, Bert Andrews talked to me like a Dutch uncle, and some of my old schoolteachers wished me well. I felt better. "You are the lightning rod," Chotiner told me, "and if you get off this ticket, Eisenhower won't have the chance of a snowball in hell in November." The lightning rod. I knew then that what I did would affect not just me alone, but the future of my country and the cause of peace and freedom for the entire world. It was a crisis of unbelievably massive proportions. I wanted to disbelieve in the Eye. I wanted to ridicule it. But I also wanted to lick the Phantom. And I wanted like hell to be Vice President. If Eisenhower wasn't going to help me, I'd have to help myself. The soul-searching was over. "General," I said to him when he called me on the phone from his *Look Ahead, Neighbor Special:* "there comes a time when you either have to shit or get off the pot!"

Just saying that released me. I knew now what I had to do. I determined to face the Eye in its nakedest form: the television camera. This was no eye-in-the-sky pipe dream: you could see it there, hard and shiny, black, heartless, unblinking. I would go before it. I would bare my soul and my bankbook before the nation. Actually I only wanted to bare my soul, but Ike insisted on baring the bankbook as well, so since he was paying for it, I agreed. I had learned from my experience in the Hiss case that what determines success or failure in handling a crisis is the ability to keep coldly objective when emotions are running high. That experience stood me in good stead now. I found myself almost automatically thinking and making decisions quickly, rationally, and unemotionally. When my advisers excitedly urged me to go on the air after the "I Love Lucy" show on Monday night, I coolly vetoed the idea. "No," I said. "Tuesday night." Tuesday—? "That's right. After Milton Berle."

On my way to Hollywood to make the speech, I jotted down notes on picture postcards I found on the plane in the seatback in front of me. I was thinking of course of the legend of Abe Lincoln scribbling on a train on his way to Gettysburg. Actually, the notes were useless, I had to throw them away, but the legend—my own now—lives on. This ploy reminded me that Lincoln had said something about the common man, and I got one of my old Whittier profs to look it up for me. Roosevelt had made good use of Fala, I decided to work Checkers in somehow. Use Pat's cloth coat against the Truman mink-coat scandal. Lay out all the monies I'd ever earned: this gave me the opportunity of using a lot of attractive boyhood images. How poor we were, and all of that. I was glad I hadn't let Smathers and his old high-school buddy Bebe Rebozo talk me into their real-estate schemes. I decided to demand that everybody in the campaign publish his finances just like me, Eisenhower included. I knew it would piss him off, I did it to needle him, let the disloyal cocksucker find out what it felt like—Jesus, I was mad at him! Him and all those naïve amateurs around him, I was eager to watch them squirm— and by God I was *not* going to go to him like a little boy to be hauled off to the woodshed, properly punished, and then taken back into the family, I'd had enough of that shit with my old man! I was going to win this one! I wondered if I could bring George Washington, Nathan Hale, Lou Gehrig, Little Orphan Annie, and Sergeant York into it somehow. This broadcast had to be a smash hit—one that really moved people, inspired them to enthusiastic, positive support, left even the Uncle Miltie fans gasping.

I should have sent the Rosenbergs a copy of that speech. It was just four days before Ethel's birthday—maybe she heard it on the prison radio. Not likely though; she would have mentioned it in her letters. Too bad. It might at least have helped them prepare their last words. Our purposes, after all, were much the same; to convince a stubbornly suspicious American public—our judges—of our innocence. And we *were* innocent. The Rosenbergs, in their internationalist confusions, did not see themselves as traitors any more than Hiss, Acheson, or Stevenson did. And the press was wrong about the fund—what I wanted was not the money, but the guys who gave it, a nickel was enough, I wanted their names, their commitments. What did money mean to me? Oh, of course, like all American boys, like Julius Rosenberg out selling penny candy no doubt, I used to dream of rescuing a generous millionaire from being robbed and murdered by a thug and receiving a thousand-dollar reward that propelled me into fame and fortune, being named in the rich man's will and perhaps even marrying his daughter, who was disguised as a poor girl selling apples on the street corner, but all this was behind me now. Not that I hadn't made good use of the money, it was what had made it possible for us to buy our Spring Valley home, but to tell the truth, I rarely thought of money any more except when there were bills to be paid. People have accused me of a lack of taste, but it isn't that, it's a simple lack of desires. If I were rich, the only thing I could possibly want to buy would be the Presidency.

And so we had presented to the public the facts of our case, the Rosenbergs and I, using the medium we found to hand—but where the Rosenbergs had fallen back on exaggerated postures of self-righteousness and abused innocence, I had remained humble and sincere. And objective. Where they had lathered their Death House letters with sententious generalities and vague romantic intimations of lives together that had been all sweetness and light ("Twelve glorious years we've spent together, always sharing, seeking together life's joy . . ."), I had named names and places and times, reported specific conversations and moments of doubt and difficulty, laid bare everything I owned and owed—not just a car, but a *1950 Oldsmobile,* not a bank debt, but *a $4500 debt to the Riggs National Bank of Washington*—it moved people to hear me pronounce that name: *The Riggs National Bank of Washington.* I mentioned Tricia's age, the Hiss case, Abraham Lincoln and the common people, Pat's maiden name and her respectable Republican cloth coat—she sat over there and modeled it for me, she looked great, even her terrible skinniness, the circles under her eyes, were a plus for me—and when I got to Checkers, I even told exactly how the dog had arrived in a crate at Union Station in Baltimore—I said that: *Union Station in Baltimore.* "And you know, the kids, like all kids, loved the dog, and I just want to say this, right now, that regardless of what they say about it, we are going to keep it!" Now, that was very goddamn moving, it could still make me choke up a little, and it made me one of the most famous Vice Presidential candidates in American political history—it was virtually a kangaroo ticket after that, old war hero at the top or no.

Darryl Zanuck the movie mogul called me up afterwards to tell me it was "the most tremendous performance I've ever seen!" I'd asked for letters in my support, and over 300,000 of them came to the Washington Republican Party headquarters—they were stored for posterity in Whittier now in a box labeled "The Dead Sea Scrolls." Ike caved in and called me "a brave man." We created the Order of the Hound's Tooth, my own cufflinks gang, and threw a party. Later, in Wheeling, the General embraced me and called me "my boy" and let me walk on his right side. I felt like love and death were all around me, and I remembered that moment so long ago, coming home and being kissed by little Arthur, soon to die—I couldn't help but cry. "Good old Bill!" I'd wept, falling on Knowland's shoulder, but what I'd really meant was: "Mom! It's your good dog Richard! I'm home!" Clean as a hound's tooth. Thanks to Checkers. Thirty years since I wrote that letter to Mom, pretending to be an abused dog—not that things come full circle in this world, but that in a random universe, ironical patterns are thrown up, and sometimes, as pattern, they turn and operate on the world . . .

My Dear Master:

The two boys that you left me with are very bad to me. Their dog, Jim, is very old and he will never talk or play with me.

One Saturday the boys went hunting. Jim and myself went with them. While going through the woods one of the boys triped and fell on me. I lost my temper and bit him. He kiked me in the side and we started on. While we were walking I saw a black round thing in a tree. I hit it with my paw. A swarm of black thing came out of it. I felt a pain all over. I started to run and as both of my eys were swelled shut I fell into a pond. When I got home I was very sore. I wish you would come home right now.

Your good dog
Richard

Even today that letter broke my heart—why hadn't the Rosenbergs been able to get that kind of feeling in their correspondence? That "swarm of black thing" was more terrifying than anything they'd said in over two years of self-pitying anticipation of the electric chair. "It is incredible," Ethel wrote to Julius on the occasion of their twelfth wedding anniversary and their first spent in prison, "that after 12 years of the kind of principled, constructive, wholesome living together that we did, that I should sit in a cell in Sing Sing awaiting my own legal murder." What was more incredible to me was that she apparently could not recall a single day, a single event, from those twelve principled et cetera years worth mentioning. In all her letters, there was only one image that came to her mind from the past: that her younger boy used to call a certain kind of ice cream "Cherry-Oonilla." The very loneliness of that image made it all the more touching. As for Julius, his recollections of the past read like the obituaries in small-town newspapers. There was not even any mention of their idyllic 1943 holiday in a rented cabin in Peekskill, where they presumably swam and hiked, chopped wood, made love in a hammock in front of their friends. Of course, it was right after this that they dropped out of overt radical activities, maybe in fact this was where they took their spy-training program, the love-play just a cover. . . .

Nevertheless, pedantic and other-directed as they were, these letters seemed to be the most meaningful contact Julius and Ethel had with each other. Perhaps the prison setting estranged them. Maybe they feared what each knew about the other. People had claimed early on to have seen them kissing each other through the wire mesh, but this must have lost its charm pretty quick, and maybe it had been a lie. After they had meetings together or with the boys, their letters were full of apologies for their tears, bad tempers, or sullen silence. They found it easier to write to each other than to speak to each other. And behind all the rhetoric, something real did trickle through: in Julie's case, an eagerness to please, to be admired, not only by the world, but by Ethel, too; in Ethel's, her loneliness and her love. "Dearest Julie, I hold your dear face between my hands as I used to do so long ago and kiss you with all my heart. . . . I talk with you every night before I fall asleep and cry because you can't hear me. . . . I see your pale drawn face, your pleading eyes, your slender boyish body and your evident suffering. . . . Oh, what shall I do? Hold me close to you tonight, I'm so lonely. . . ."

Well, I knew from my own experience how love, awkward in the flesh, could blossom through the mails. Even now, I often wrote Pat letters at night for her to read in the morning. It was a way of working things out for yourself, exploring your own—then suddenly it occurred to me, what should have been obvious all along: she didn't love him. She never had. She needed him, but she never loved him. "Daddy, I never saw you and Mommy kiss." She had loved, yes, she was a lover, but she had no proper object for her love. I understood this. She was using his slender boyish body as I had used Pat's cloth coat: to cop a plea. She had married Julius to fulfill something in herself, the old story, something maybe that got into her that day long ago when she got knocked down by the police fire hoses on Bleecker Street, but it was a portion of her will she had wed, not a lover: "Julie dear, I have such utter respect and regard for you; how well you know the score! Hold me close and impart to me some of your noble spirit!" Yes, a perfect marriage, and he had not disappointed her, this young activist, not up till now anyway; but she could recall nothing—or would not—of their past together, was given to confusion and tantrums when they met, even forgot their anniversary last year, though in prison she had almost nothing else to think about, and for the last few months had apparently stopped writing to Julius altogether, as though he no longer had ears to hear, or never did. And thus the deep longing in these letters mailed to the world: "Sweetheart, I draw you close into loving arms and warm you with my warmth." She could as well have been speaking to me.

I sighed, leaned back in my chair. The letters, transcripts, notes, records littered the room, but I was no longer disturbed by this, I even perceived a certain order in it—like an image of time, I thought, not knowing quite what I meant, except that by tomorrow the office would be clean again, and so, no doubt, would I. There was a special fragrance in this soft summer day blowing in through the open window that reminded me of California, the old California which was in the middle of the world, not today's remote, statistical, old-man California over on the other side of the voting continent, and I could hear a song wafting up from the streets below, one I recognized: "Among My Souvenirs"—it was one of the few that the Rosenbergs had mentioned in their letters. Something like the memories of last night rolled over me again, but now not so much as separate strung-out recollections, but rather as a kind of concentrated mass of feeling and abstract imagery that kept swelling and receding like a sort of slow heartbeat. I wanted to hold it constant, examine it, lose myself in it—it seemed to me that the resolution to this whole problem lay concealed in it, my speech, everything, as though on the tip of my tongue, at the edge of my vision—but it kept slipping away. Then I'd sit back and it would sweep over me again. It was very strange, very sweet, I could almost taste it, smell it, feel it filling my lungs, spreading through my limbs, it was warm and dusty and dense, like the heart of a garden, the heart of a city, concrete and leafy all at once. A kind of dusty summer ballpark of the spirit. It seemed almost too beautiful, too heroic, to be a real memory, it was more like . . . like the memory of a daydream, and not even of the dream, but of the sensation of dreaming.

On my desk lay Picasso's doodles of the Rosenbergs. Julie resembled Ronald Colman, only more scholarly, while Ethel had a kind of Little Annie Rooney look—the lost waif. She looked like someone you could talk to. In spite of all our obvious differences, I realized, we had a lot in common. We were both second children in our families, we both had an older brother, younger brothers, both had old-fashioned kitchen-bound mothers and hard-working failure fathers, were both shy and often poor in health, I admit it, both preferred to be by ourselves except when we were showing off publicly on a stage, both found escape in books and schoolwork and music, both were honor students, activists and organizers, loved rhetoric and drama, worked hard for our parents, had few friends, never dated much and mated late, had dreams. Ethel dreamed of some glorious future as an artist or musician, a singer maybe, or actress. She entered an amateur-night competition at Loew's Delancey Street theater one night and won second prize singing "Ciribiribin." She was spotted by a Major Bowes talent scout, who put her on the professional amateur-night-competition circuit, and by the time she was seventeen she was all but making a living at it. She took voice and piano lessons from some lady at Carnegie Hall, paying for them out of her lunch money, and she bought a used piano and dragged it home—her finances were even better than mine, she supported herself and her family and still knew how to invest. She always kept a rigid schedule, writing it out every day, charting her consistency, always woke up at six, practiced an hour, went off to work, studied scores at lunch break, took lessons in the evening—like me plotting out my college activities program or preparing for a political campaign.

She auditioned for the Schola Cantorum at the Metropolitan Opera House and was accepted, the youngest voice the choir had ever had, it looked like her dreams were coming true. But she couldn't go on tour with them because she couldn't leave her job, so they dropped her. Her mother said: "If God wanted you to have lessons, God would have made them possible." She was like the heroines in all those musicals who starve and suffer unnoticed, until one night the star gets a sore throat and can't go on, and against the better judgment of the fat cigar-chewing manager, the heroine takes over, wins the hearts of millions. Only Ethel never took over. She wasn't there when the star got a sore throat. She married Julius Rosenberg, typed up spy notes, and got sentenced to the electric chair instead. What happens to us in life seems, in retrospect, inevitable. And much of it is, the main patterns anyway. And yet we are full of potential, there are many patterns in us, and there are significant moments in life when we can choose among those parts of ourselves we might fulfill. What if I had met her years ago? I could have recommended her for a scholarship at Whittier, she might have studied music like Ola, they might've even been friends, we could have acted in plays together. She was just a year behind me, having skipped a year, she was very bright, and I was virtually running Whittier College from my freshman year on, it would have been easy—Dr. Dexter would have admired the suggestion, bringing a poor girl from the Eastern ghettos out to the clean air and warm sunshine of Southern California, I'd have probably got special mention in the yearbook for arranging it. We could have taken walks and talked about all my student activities: the fraternity, football, debate and theater, politics—she might have helped me with my studies. I didn't really need help, but I was always getting depressed about them, and she could have kept me going.

I breathed the June air deeply, feeling the campus palm trees swaying gently overhead, and wondered if Ethel, too, a dreamer like myself breathing this same air, was being similarly moved, similarly drawn back into this trance of timelessness, on this, her last day on earth, falling in love all over again with life itself, or at least a dream of life? "Now I kneel down to a crevice in the concrete, filled with earth painstakingly accumulated from the underpart of moss, small velvety crumbs of which cling to the damp cool parts of the yard where the sun's rays rarely penetrate. In this crevice an apple seed which I planted, and have watered patiently, is sprouting bravely. All my love, darling." Just the thing to take root and crack up the concrete, I thought, the prison people must love it.

In the Horatio Alger novels, in spite of everything, the heroines were always saved at last by rich uncles. Ethel didn't have a rich uncle. Neither did I, growing up—except for Grandpa Milhous's money which put me through school, we were as poor as any other middle-class family —but later I got adopted. By teachers, businessmen, Herbert Hoover, eventually Uncle Sam himself. I was successful with old men, she wasn't. Was this it, then? Was this the reason that that serious little curly-headed girl watering an apple seed in a prison exercise yard was going to get 2000 volts bolted through her brain tonight? A missing character, a lost "closing scene"? Or had the story taken a wrong turn somewhere, putting her beyond the reach of rich uncles? That night she got attacked by that old guy from *The Valiant* cast, for example, or the day they knocked her down with fire hoses on Bleecker Street.

What would I have done, I wondered—what would have become of me if they'd knocked me down with those hoses? Ethel was just sixteen years old, a sensitive little girl with a pretty voice and big dark eyes, trusting, innocent, bright and lively. She didn't want to change the world, she wanted to love it, to sing to it, to give herself to it. Just like me. But it was 1931, the unemployed were marching on Washington, her family was wretchedly poor, and there was a job to be had: as clerk in a paper-box factory on Bleecker Street. "You'll never get ahead!" her mother had screamed at her, pushing her out the door. "There's no place in life for arty people!" But all right, she would get a job, share her money with the family, and still somehow save aside enough to take music lessons, maybe even go to the university, enter theater—it happened in the movies every day. But when she got to the factory, there were already a thousand people there ahead of her, trying to get the same job. I knew how she felt, I'd been through this, too, that Christmas in New York, trying to land a job with a law firm. But in her case, there was no private interview, there was a riot. The police were called and the crowds were broken up with fire hoses. Ethel was knocked down twice.

I tried to imagine this scene, but it was confusing. I thought of the street as narrow with little restaurants and movie houses, but I knew that further east, near Lafayette Street and the Bowery, it didn't look like this. Rows of plain dirty brick buildings, I thought, five or six stories high, a lot of fire escapes, balconies, drainpipes, green paint. The street would be clotted with trucks, not to mention the rampaging mob, yet I felt the trees around, blue sky, room to run. I could see the police springing down out of their patrol wagons, faces alert, turned up, catching the sun, hands on their sticks or at their belts, tense yet exultant, like footballers taking the field, could see the hoses uncoiling from fire trucks, connected to fire hydrants that looked like stubby circumcised peckers, could feel the hoses suddenly fattening with surging water, could sense the excitement of the crowd, men mostly, tough and angry, and big women—where was Ethel? I saw her, small, all but lost in the huge crowd, an uncertain child, wanting to run, yet drawn obediently toward the job she'd been sent to ask for, thus moving neither with the crowd nor against it, and so isolated, a tempting target, framed in the solid arched doorway of a dingy yellow brick building, a kind of warehouse or something—and the guy with the hose, blasting away at the big broads, the clumsy old men, spies her standing there, legs spread, eyes wide open, clutching a handbag to her small breasts, and slowly he bends that big gray snake of his—I run toward her: "Ethel! Look out!" She looks up—but too late, the spray hits her full in the face and down she goes, kicking against the current, the jet blasts up her skirt, driving her, skidding on her backside, to the wall—I throw myself in front of her, absorbing the brunt of the spray. It slams hard against my butt, my head, I'm thrown against her, we tumble together in the driving shower, she clutches me to hang on, I fall between her legs, but I keep my back to the spray and she manages, protected, to scramble to her feet. "Run!" I say. "Get away while you can!" She grabs my hand. "Come!" she cries. Her voice is small, almost strident. Somehow, we're out of the spray and running free, past the milling angry crowds, wheeling vehicles—then suddenly it hits us again, from a different direction maybe, knocks our feet out from under us, she's down and hurt, skirt up around her waist, I pick her up, plunge forward through the driving spray, duck behind a car, then around a corner: safe!

I set her down, lower her wet skirt. We stare at each other a moment, our faces blank with shock and exertion: and then we laugh. She pushes her curly hair out of her eyes, notices that my hair is curly too. We look down at our wet clothes, pasted to our bodies. She takes my hand: "My brother Sam's got some clothes that will fit you," she says. Her voice is gentle now, and musical. We walk south on the Bowery, past locked-up doorways, windows with junk piled high in them or cardboarded up, there in the sunshine, talking about our lives. It does not seem far. I feel at home here with her: she seems so at ease in the city. It excites me to watch her move, so self-assured. I tell her about my play, *The Little Accident,* and she laughs gaily, squeezes my hand. My fraternity, the Square Shooters, had just put it on in April, a "real shocker" they called it at Whittier—it was about a football star who gets benched for bringing his girl back to the dorm after eight o'clock. It had a lot of daring scenes like Coach Newman kissing his star goodnight when he tucks him in. The unique thing was that all the characters were real people, and the plot, though outlandish, was nearly true. Ethel says that's very experimental. I tell her how I played the part of Joe Sweeney, my debating partner in real life. The *Whittier News* said it was "one of the cleverest skits of the year." She is greatly amused when I tell her that the climax of the play is when the star of the team is allowed to enter the game at last, but in a final wild effort to win the game, falls on his face on the three-yard line. "Really! Well, don't worry," she says laughing, and pulls me along. She tells me about the settlement-house theater groups and says I should write something for them. Why not? I think. This may be my big break! She leans against me. Water is running down through the drains in the streets from the melee now far behind us. When we get near the place she lives, she makes me wait. "It's okay," she says when she comes back. "My mother's out shopping, my father's busy in the shop, and the boys are gone."

There's a big plate-glass window with her father's name on it in peeling gold leaf: BARNET GREENGLASS. Two doors: one goes into the sewing-machine repair shop; we take the other and climb a steep flight of stairs. Her wet body is silhouetted against the dim daylight at the top as though it were naked. Her room is separate from the rest and opens off the hallway. It is plain but clean, a bed and a chest of drawers, some pamphlets and books, musical scores, ashtrays, a wooden chair. Right away, I want to buy her something for it, flowers maybe, or a soft doll. "Get your clothes off," she says, "and I'll go get you a towel." I remember a movie in which Clark Gable and Claudette Colbert spent a rainy night together in a hotel room with a blanket up between them like the walls of Jericho. I try to strip the cool way Clark Gable did, but I feel more like Claudette Colbert. My shirt and pants are heavy, and I see there's a puddle where I've been standing. I lay them across the windowsill.

She comes back with a towel and some clothes. A warm bath would feel good, but the only tub, I recall, is a large primitive enamel affair with a heavy wooden lid down in the kitchen by the stove. Water for it is heated on the stove, like for the big metal bath Millard Fillmore installed in the White House a century ago. She has unbuttoned her blouse and pulled it out, and now she kicks off her shoes. I'm standing near the window in my underwear, my hands crossed in front of me, but unable to hold back the bulge of my excitement. She lays her brother's clothes out on the bed, turns toward me questioningly with the towel. I pull my undershirt over my head, feeling vulnerable. She watches as though admiring me. She rubs my back and chest hard with the towel. I know that Jewish girls have no religious restrictions against having . . . doing . . . going all the way. She peels my underpants down, kneeling as it were to the crevice—my penis, released, falls stiffly forward, brushing her cheek. "Let me get you out of those wet clothes," I say hoarsely, pitching my voice down like Clark Gable's. Her fingers are trembling as she unlocks the stay on her skirt. Her brassiere slips forward off her narrow shoulders. "Richard," she whispers, "I've never . . . never . . ." "Neither have I," I say softly. We stare at each other in the bare room. A warm summery breeze is blowing in through the window, a song from some radio. We kiss. I slide her wet panties down over her cool damp bottom, getting a glimpse of her black round thing, my heart beating wildly. She strokes me gently. "I draw you close into loving arms and warm you with my warmth." She pulls—

"Well, I see that the old flagpole still stands," somebody said. It wasn't Douglas MacArthur, it was Uncle Sam, who had just flown in through my open window. "You know, son, you'll go blind playing with yourself like that," he said. "It can make your hair fall out and your brain rot, too!"

18.

The National Poet Laureate Meditates
on the Art of Revelation

The boatmen's strike is over. The Iron Curtain around the Statue of Liberty is down, the sightseer ferries are running again. The jam at the south end of Times Square collapses momentarily as crowds stream away to the Battery to make the traditional birth voyage in the sunshine-yellow ferries across to Bedloe's Island, there to enter into the Mighty Lady and reach the fount of Liberty: "Oh Mother of Exiles, merciful and mild, refuge of the tempest-tost and comfort of the wretched refuse, conceived without the stain of sin, full of grace and reinforced copper, noble couch of the three branches of government and perfect holocaust of Divine Love whose flame is the imprisoned lightning, watch over us!" But the Square soon fills up again as thousands of newcomers arrive and press toward the center, where now the Entertainment Committee is making a special announcement: to beat the Sabbath and any further postponements, the executions have been moved up from eleven p.m. to eight o'clock—the Federal Express is not only on time, she's three hours early! The Rosenberg defense lawyers, already wild with frustration, explode in a fit of incoherent anguish and suicidally charge the Square —they're allowed to pass through, one time, end to end, like fraternity pledges running the gauntlet, pelted with laughter and good-natured abuse as they go shrieking by, into the center and out, zooming along like their tails are on fire, into well-deserved oblivion. Or so everyone hopes.

Smiling wryly at all the hidden ironies, the National Poet Laureate watches them go, then wanders unobtrusively through the area, collecting images, experimenting with various forms and meters, searching for the metaphoric frame by which to contain and re-create tonight's main ceremony (". . . the last scene . . . the seventh decision . . . dance to his violent tune . . . shouts of anathema . . . as the clock ticked on . . .") and cause it, by his own manifesto, "to happen in people's heads." This is what his art is all about, this is what it means, as his mother says, to be "called to be the servant of truth." It is not enough to present facts—something has to *happen* in time and space, observed through the imagination and the heart, something accessible and yet illuminating to that reader he writes for, the Gentleman from Indiana. Raw data is paralyzing, a nightmare, there's too much of it and man's mind is quickly engulfed by it. Poetry is the art of subordinating facts to the imagination, of giving them shape and visibility, keeping them *personal*. It is, as Mother Luce has said, "fakery in allegiance to the truth," a kind of interpretive reenactment of the overabundant flow of events, "an effective mosaic" assembled from "the fragmentary documents" of life, quickened with audacious imagery and a distinct and original prosody: "Noses for news lie betwixt ears for music." Some would say that such deep personal involvement, such metaphoric compressions and reliance on inner vision and imaginary "sources," must make objectivity impossible, and TIME would agree with them, but he would find simply illiterate anyone who concluded from this that he was not serving Truth. More: he would argue that objectivity is an impossible illusion, a "fantastic claim" ("gnostic" is the word on his tongue these days), and as an ideal perhaps even immoral, that *only* through the frankly biased and distorting lens of art is any real grasp of the facts—not to mention Ultimate Truth—even remotely possible.

Thus, debating uneasily with himself, less self-assured than his readers might suspect or hope, he threads his way through the masses in Times Square, alert to his task, but reflective in mood, worried that he's got off the track somehow, fearful of his powers even as he fears their diminishment, and conscious, a young man at the pinnacle of success and in the full bloom of life, of his own mortality—didn't Mother Luce predict his death as long ago as 1936? He and his brothers must surely die, she said then: "I don't suppose we can establish the date for the euthanasia . . . But one way to look at them, at this date, might be to say that they have twenty more years of life. . . ." He was only thirteen years old when she said that, and it had frightened him to think that, like Jesus Christ, he might have only thirty-three years to walk this earth. And it was possible, it was all too possible. Not only were the actuarial tables dismal enough for poets like himself, but hadn't his own father died prematurely at the age of thirty-one? A sudden and sordid death on the night of young TIME's sixth birthday, he's never quite got over it. Almost like his Dad was trying to tell him something. The hard way. Though TIME loves his mother and is often inspired by her, it's the ghost of his unhappy father, he knows, that he carries in his poet's heart. And now thirty of his allotted thirty-three years have washed away, he has just three of them left, three short years to sort things out, find some way of rejuvenating himself, of overmastering the world's entropic attack on him before it's too late. And in this, he knows, his fate and America's are linked: he and America both seem to have lost, as his mother says, "that feeling for the future, the confidence in the bigger and the better, the spirit of you-ain't-seen-nothin'-yet"—but perhaps tonight . . . ?

Twice before, he thought he'd found the secret: once, just before World War II, with his dream of "The American Century" ("We must undertake now to be the Good Samaritan of the entire world . . . the dynamic leader of world trade . . . the powerhouse from which the ideals [of Western Civilization] spread throughout the world . . ."), and again three years ago, at the outbreak of hostilities in Korea, with his vision of perpetual War: "One of the great perennial themes along with Love and Death." His mother's vision, actually, but as always he had been inspired by her: "In the next few years Americans will have to live with War as they have not since the days of the settler and the Minute Man. . . . War always has been, is and always will be part of man's fate until Kingdom come. . . . In any case, *we* are not going to end War without practicing it some more—and living with it. . . . If 'coexistence' with the present Soviet Communist system is impossible, is total War 'inevitable'? Maybe so, maybe not, but what no man has a right to say is that we can live peaceably and happily *with* this prodigious evil. . . . The Soviet Empire will continue to expand unless it is opposed with all our strength and that includes the steady, calm and constant acceptance of the risk of all-out War. . . . *The truth will be made plain by wrath if not by reason!*"

But both dreams have soured. The other Free Nations, misunderstanding his charitable intentions, took unnecessary offense at his laying claim to all of the Twentieth Century, and even his fellow Americans seemed to lack the imagination to "accept the thrust of destiny," to go out and take over the world and "create the first great American Century." Didn't they care? What has gone wrong? "I think this country, far from having a George-Washingtonian belief in the rightness of its cause at home and abroad, is actually very uncertain of itself, very divided and confused in its 'soul,' and almost totally lacking in basic realistic notions as to its 'objectives' in the world situation!" The War in Korea looked more promising, as War always does, especially when, largely through TIME's inspired advocacy, General Eisenhower was elected Commander-in-Chief—it brought back the halcyon days of World War II (the naming of wars like kings was TIME's own conceit), which saw, almost overnight, the transformation of this young *enfant terrible* and adolescent American hustler into a powerful and serious poet and—even before the War had ended—the Poet Laureate of the Nation. How could he not love War? Indeed, he even loved the Japanese for making it possible. As Mother Luce wrote to his brother LIFE following the attack on Pearl Harbor: "This is the day of wrath. It is also the day of hope. . . . For this hour America was made!" He felt suddenly ashamed of his "pusillanimous" youth, which he identified with that of his country: "It is not even possible to call these years tragic, for tragedy implies at least the dignity of fate. And there was no dignity in these years, and nothing of fate that we did not bring upon ourselves. The epoch that is closing was much less tragic than it was shameful. . . ." He felt like Paul struck down on the road to Damascus, like Dwight Eisenhower hit by a bolt of lightning in Texas: he was a new man, a new poet, purged of his supercilious past. Of course, his readers might not notice the difference, but inside, he knew it was true. An era ended for TIME in 1941 and a new one began. Then, three years ago, he felt like the same thing was happening all over again, a resurgence of the old hope and joy, the glorious struggle—he might even become Poet Laureate of the World! Calling for "an unambiguous defeat" of the Reds, forecasting the imminent advent of World War III, and whooping it up like a drunken cowboy, he rushed off to the Korean front, pen in hand.

But now, what? it's all come to nothing. A meaningless stalemate. And every sign of a disastrous truce about to be consummated. He had loved and defended General MacArthur, remains even tonight absolutely convinced of the need to carry the War to the Chinese mainland, and has these past months been struggling to keep General Van Fleet's "total victory" appeals before the people, but he knows it's a lost cause. He can feel it. He can't even get a decent poem out of it any more. His "Night on Old Harry" last week with its "ugly sausage / shaped ridge," its "littered slopes" and "crumbling trenches," is about the best he's done since the earliest lyrics of the War, and that's probably because all it's about is holding on desperately to something useless, his present unhappy condition. Might better have called it "Night *in* Old Harry" . . .

> . . . one by one the bunkers
> > collapsed covering
> american and chinese
> > bodies with sand and dust
> king was reinforced
> > the reds attacked again
> during the night
> > twenty thousand shells
> exploded in an area
> > smaller than times square
> but the hill remained
> > in u.s. hands
> the hill remained

And though it's all right, even that one's a far cry from, say, his account of the assault on No Name Ridge, or the taking of Pyongyang (". . . the end of the war loomed as plain / as the moustache on Stalin's face . . ."), or his classic cables of World War II. Ah, where's it all gone? he wonders, pushing through the Square, pressed in upon all sides by people from whom he feels increasingly alienated. The Gentleman from Indiana, he laments, is dead. For thirty years he has shared his dreams with him, and now the old boy has taken them with him to the grave. And yet, at some deep unexamined level, though they've failed him, he still has faith in both dreams. He still believes that "America alone can provide the pattern for the future . . . [and] must be the elder brother of the nations in the brotherhood of men." And he still believes in War.

This great poetic affinity for War is perhaps inborn, a consequence of his having been conceived in a World War I Army camp back in 1918 by two underaged but passionately eager shavetails named Brit and Luce, a pair of Yale romantics who longed, as Luce said, "to be officers of the Army of the United States, go to the front and fire at the enemy." Though she never had that pleasure, she did manage a kind of vicarious experience of the War, and if not exactly heroic, it was at least a contribution. As it happened, she came on a group of enlisted men one night who were having some doubts about just what the devil they were fighting for, and, in what she called "one of the greatest successes of my life," she roused them to high patriotic fervor with her account of the sinking of the *Lusitania*, marched them off to the railroad station singing "Over There," and saw them off with a "Good-bye and good luck!"; the train took them, cheering wildly, to the docks, where they boarded the transport, the *Ticonderoga*, and halfway across the Atlantic got sunk by a German torpedo. Brit shared Luce's zeal. As he wrote his Mom: "I long to be sent overseas as a Battery Commander or Major General or something, and there to take part in the great 1919 drive, the one that will end the war and smash Kaiser Will!" Instead they both got sent back to Yale. But not before one "sickeningly hot" night out behind the barracks, which TIME's mother recalled many years later at her son's twentieth-birthday party: "One night Brit and I were walking back to our barracks through the vast, sprawling camp. At each step, our feet sank ankle-deep in mud. I think it was in that walk that TIME began. At the center of our lives, at that point, everything we had belonged to each other. We ploughed on for hours . . ."

Inception was prolonged—nearly five years. But this is not uncommon among geniuses. After a stormy but loving on-again off-again romance, Brit playing the restless Odysseus, Luce the patient but busy-fingered Penelope, both parents were at last reunited, and pregnancy, if doubted before, was now assured. TIME was born in an old remodeled house of vaguely Italianate style not far from here at 141 East Seventeenth Street. As midwife Culbreth Sudler once described it: "You thumped one step down from the street into the windowless dining room on the ground floor and then mounted to the living room which ran across the front of the house. The paint on the woodwork was so thick it was like cheese. Here we set up loft-type tables." And it was on those tables, one wintry February night just after midnight in 1923, that Mother Luce, drenched in a cold sweat, stretched out and spread her thighs and—with the father assisting in his green eyeshade—gave birth to baby TIME (so named because his mother had been frightened by an advertising headline: "Time to Retire"—or was it "Time for a Change"? she never could remember after, the riddle perplexes her still). He was thin, pale, unhealthy, attractive like all babies, but less appealing than his parents had hoped. Folks said he looked a lot like Uncle Joe Cannon. Few thought he'd last long.

But, though poor and sickly, TIME was born with a great will to survive, and by the time he was four, after a couple of convalescent years out in Cleveland (which nearly killed his fun-loving father and threatened to break up the marriage), he began to get a little color in his cheeks. Though his early verse was often cocky, strained, flippant and superficial, derivative, and of course childish, he was already showing signs of that prodigious talent that would one day set him above all his rivals, even the powerful Franklinesque *Saturday Evening Post*, Poet Laureate of the day. . . .

Hearing a slight scratching
In the ceiling above her,
She raised her eyes in time to see
A pointed grey face
Peer at her from
A hole in the plaster. The hole

Widened, the thin mortar
Crumbled and an enormous
Black rat fell into the water with her,
· Splashed about,
Caressed her with its
Clammy paws and insolently ogled her . . .

The seeming discrepancy of a black rat with a grey face created considerable literary controversy, needless to say, and raised the hackles on the backs of academic purists, but the controversy itself attested to the spreading recognition that here was a young poet to be reckoned with. His verse was fresh, penetrating, epigrammatic, candid even to the point of insult, sometimes startling, always provocative. No poet ever became great by being, in his young days, overly polite: his father taught him that. And he rarely was. Anything too physical or too spiritual alike aroused his wrath. Zealots as well as shirkers suffered from his "one-finger type, two-finger brain, / six sneers and one suggestion." He hated pomposity and timidity, yesterday's ideas and tomorrow's fashions, partyboys and doomcriers, Babbitry and Bolshevism. And he struck them down with style. When Leon Trotsky fell ill, he wrote gleefully:

criticism to the left of him
enmity to the right of him
jealousy in front of him
the Red Army behind him
a high fever within him
all tried to blight him

he resolved to take a trip to the Caucasus . . .

Yes, a frankly acknowledged above-the-board package of prejudices, essential to his genius. As his mother recently warned the hired help with regard to the "Aloha Shirt Set," who just this afternoon have at last been found guilty of Communist plotting to overthrow the Government under the Smith Act:

This is to state as a matter of policy that . . . TIME is 100% in favor of the property owners, capitalists, and corporations of Hawaii and 100%

against Harry Bridges and anyone who is in any way allied with him. (If there are any worse names for property owners and capitalists such as "reactionaries" we are for them, too.)

"Business," his mother always liked to say, "is, essentially, our civilization." She called it "the smartest, most universal of all American occupations . . . the largest of the planets which make up our system." In the past, TIME's business bias has been bruisingly attacked, but few would dare challenge it today. They still call him an opportunistic thief, a pastepot-poet who steals from everybody, but that only means he's squarely in the mainstream of American poets, most of whom have been great eclectics, gatherers and enhancers of the detritus from the passing flux, collage-shapers—and as for being opportunistic, so what? As he himself wrote when T. S. Eliot's *Waste Land* was being "revealed" as a hoax: it's immaterial, "literature being concerned not with intentions but results." And who can doubt his own results? TIME's number one, "not only at the box office but . . . in the opinions of a large part of mankind."

His mother's words. She loved the adulation, the wealth, the power. His father loved the poet's life more than its rewards, loved controversy, loved style. True genius, he once told his young son, is to be faithful to one style, while exploring intransigently all that it contains—like making love all your life to one woman. Maybe he learned that from Ernest Hemingway. Or vice versa. TIME in any case has kept his father's counsel, pursuing those stylistic infatuations that bedizened his earliest work and have been ever since the only passion he's ever known: the puns and quips, inverted sentences, occupational titles, Homeric epithets and rhythms, compound words, cryptic captions, middle names and parenthetical nicknames, ruthless emphasis on physical details, especially when somewhat obnoxious, extended metaphors ("slowly the ribbon of his voice unrolled / with here and there a knot . . ."), alliteration, rugged verbs and mocking modifiers, and TIME's own personal idioglossary of word-coinages, inventions like "kudos" and "pundits" and "tycoons" and hundreds more which have passed into the national lexicon. He called footballer Red Grange an "eel-hipped runagade" and G. K. Chesterton a "paradoxhund" before most children his age could even spell "cat." A Charlie Chaplin movie was "a gorgeously funny example of custard-piety," and when the Queen Mother of Spain died, he looked up the true meaning of "the Escorial," where she was buried, and blithely penned: "They took her to the Dump." Well, he was a youngster, he could do such things and get away with them, even the

Queen Mother might have smiled. And if sometimes he strove too hard to be clever and overshot the mark ("A ghastly ghoul prowled around a cemetery not far from Paris. Into family chapels went he, robbery of the dead intent upon . . ."), if sometimes the coinages proliferated into self-parody and "backward ran sentences until reeled the mind," it was understood that such excess was a necessary flaw in any great poet: you have to take your pratfalls while you're still young—the old man who suddenly lurches into audacity late in life is a fool.

TIME was close to his father and deeply mourned his sudden passing—more perhaps than Mother Luce did, though she was pregnant again and so had worries of her own—and though he kept his feelings largely to himself, one could sense in him ever after a restless unconscious search for his missing father. Perhaps—he forced himself to admit this—perhaps he needed his father's death, needed the search, the inexpressible longing, in order to achieve the emotional depth and maturity essential to a Master (and let's face it, there was always something sophomoric and nihilistic about his father's influence, loving and protective as he was, something of the restless jock and compulsive boozer), perhaps in all great poets' lives there had to be these early tragedies, and this was his. His mother, though increasingly occupied with other children, took over his development for a while, and though his most important formative years were behind him, she did instill in him a stricter discipline, a wider-ranging urbanity, and a greater appreciation of intimate detail. The growing cynicism and detachment, however, were his own.

His sister FORTUNE was born the week of his seventh birthday, a beautiful child, well-endowed, ultimately more brilliant and sophisticated than he, tutored by songsmiths and loved by the rich, but though she sometimes teased him and once even called him a "fascist" (admittedly he was flirting at the time with the far right, supporting Franco in Spain and Mussolini in Italy, picturing Haile Selassie as "squealing for protection" for his "squalling Abyssinia," and smearing Jews and Socialists—but all that only went to show he was a lot smarter than Julius and Ethel Rosenberg, who'd been growing up with him), FORTUNE always looked up to him as her big brother, and depended upon him, a father surrogate of sorts, for guidance and protection. As did his baby brother LIFE, even though he'd enjoyed a success in the art world the equal of TIME's in literature, radio, and film. There were other children along the way, some adopted, some stillborn, others neglected and allowed to die, even a bastard called HIGH TIME, apparently engendered in a nightmare by the Phantom and quickly done away with when the truth was known; but the pride of Mother Luce, and indeed of the nation, were her three remarkable and close-knit sibling prodigies, TIME, LIFE, and FORTUNE. . . . Or at least up till now. The old lady's been getting skittish again of late, seems to be losing interest in the arts, flushes like a schoolgirl at ballgames and boxing matches. There was a big party just a few days ago, everybody high as a kite and letting themselves go, he's pretty sure she's been knocked up again.

He's not jealous—why should he be? Oh, some people say she's trying to breed his successor since she fears for his life, but he doubts this: one Poet Laureate is all any mother can hope for. What does upset him, though, is that she's being drawn away from him, just like when his father died. He feels his self-confidence draining away. Tonight's events, for example: how will he cope with them? What can he hope to achieve? MOTHERLESS CHILDREN HAS A HARD TIME WHEN THE MOTHER'S DEAD—he saw somebody a while ago carrying a picket with that written on it, and when he should have laughed, he shuddered. Has he lost the way? This spectacle, even as it fascinates him, frightens him with its challenges to the imagination, its dangers, its hints of hidden appositions, confrontations with the Shape-Shifting Absolute, webworks of treacherous abstractions that make his verse somehow irrelevant, unequal to the occasion, silly even. Everybody else seems to be rejuvenated by coming here, he feels years older. His instinct is to flee, forget it—it's not his mission "to exorcise the Doubt which is conquering the Western World," his mother's already told him that, his job is to stay alive—but he is a poet (he reminds himself) and he can do no other than to stay. Art is not an idle affectation, it is a solemn calling, a penance, a manly devotion to something behind the profane world of baseball games and movie reviews. The poet is not merely an entertainer, though this would be the easy way out, not merely a celebrator of his age—he is also a prophet of religious truth, the recreator of deep tribal realities, committed "desperately, whimsically, absurdly, cockeyedly, whole-souledly" to Revelation. "TIME will reveal everything," Euripides prophesied. "He is a babbler, and speaks even when not asked."

And so, though circuses and theater generally fail to move him, though he distrusts mobs and is dubious about the selection of Times Square for the executions (as Mother Luce has said: "New York is in the bloodstream of America and America flows hot through New York. But New York is not America, son . . . New York is the fascination of America—where vices easily become virtues and virtues vices . . ."), here is where he must be tonight. It is, as his mother would say, his "manifest duty." And he is not without defenses. If worse comes to worst, he will do what he has always done. If he bursts through the scrim of phenomena and grasps the whole of tonight's events, he will celebrate them; if they overwhelm him, he will belittle them. He's a professional, after all.

19.

All Aboard the *Look Ahead,*
Neighbor Special

"I been busy as a one-armed paperhanger with the nettle-rash," stormed
Uncle Sam, "copin' with riots and wars, payroll robberies, murders, and
onscrofulous sabotage! Them parleyvoos, who can't even get a damn
guvvamint together, are tearin' up our Embassy, the Bolsheviks are
massin' for a riot in Munich, I'm exposed to all the dangers of invasion
from without and convulsions from within stirrin' a 'ruption in me equal
to a small arthquake, time is fast runnin' out, I need ever' able hand at
my command at full strength and manly firmness—and Holy Foley! what
do I find *you* doin'?!"

I stood with my back to him at the marble fireplace, flushed with
shame, afraid even to look up at my own face in the mirror, trying to
unjam the zipper on my fly—he'd startled me so, I'd leapt out of my
swivel chair like an Eisenhopper, nearly castrating myself on the edge of
the desk as I'd slammed past, and, trying desperately to yank shut my
fly, had trapped my shirttail deep into the zipper.

"Remember, you shall have joy, or you shall have power," admonished Uncle Sam, "but you cain't have both with the same hand! These
repeated abuses and usurpations ain't such as to render it at once an
example and fit instrument for flyin' the flag! You cain't Tippecanoe
and till her, too!"

I struggled desperately with the snagged zipper, not even trying to
puzzle out whose voices were leaking through him now, in fact I could
hardly hear him, all my senses seemed blocked off somehow—yet I knew
he was there, omnipresently there, jamming up all the corners. I longed

330

for the privacy of the old bell tower over our store in Whittier, where things like this never happened. My trouble, I thought, is that I'm an introvert in an extrovert profession.

"So what's the matter, son? Pat pregnant again?"

"No! No, I . . . I don't know," I whispered hoarsely. "It's like . . . like I've been going backward . . . I'm sorry . . . it's silly—backward in time! It's hard to explain . . ."

"Aha," mused Uncle Sam, "backward in time, is it?" I caught a furtive glimpse of him in the mirror over my shoulder. His face was in shadows, his back to the window. He might have been giving me a look of utter disgust. Or he might have been laughing. Either way, I knew, the fat was in the fire. I'd recognized from the time I became a member of HUAC, and particularly after my participation in the Hiss case, that it was essential for me to maintain a standard of personal conduct that was above criticism, and now—ah, I had faced some problems in my life perhaps more difficult than this one, but none could approach it in terms of personal embarrassment and chagrin. "Sounds like the fortieth-birthday blues to me," he said.

"Uh . . ." Was this an excuse? It didn't sound like one. "That was five, uh, five months ago, I don't think—"

"You were busy then, Inauguration and all, it usually doesn't hit you until a few months go by. . . . Say, boy, you want me to give a jerk on that thing for you?"

"No!" I cried. "No, I . . . I have it now . . . I almost have it . . . !" But I didn't. I couldn't even see the damned thing, everything was blurred, and my hands were shaking. Heart whamming away like ninety. This crisis is worse even than the fund, I thought. "It's not my . . . it's just my shirttail . . ."

"No doubt," snorted Uncle Sam. Hands in pockets, he kicked heedlessly across the room through the clutter of notes and documents. "Well, lemme tell you, hoss, backward in time is one place Americans don't never go, grand climacteric or no! Herbert Hoover was born a penniless orphan, but he didn't look back, and at the age of forty he was worth four million smackeroos—and he wasn't even President yet! In fact, later on, bein' a mite skittyish, he finally did look back—and got royally creamed for it, too! You know what Henry Ford done when he turned forty? He gave up small-time mechanics and went out and founded him the goddamn Ford Motor Company, that's what! Forty, yes, he was forty! Now his boy, who ain't even as old as you, is pullin' in upwards of a hundred million bucks a year, not bad for a kid, and even payin' taxes on some of it, just to show his heart's in the right place!"

He picked up one of the Greenglass sketches, turned it one way, then the other, finally shrugged and tossed it back on the floor. " 'At twenty years of age, the will reigns; at thirty, the wit; at forty, the judgment'— old Ben Franklin wrote that, and passin' forty hisself, sold off his press and bought up Dr. Spence's do-it-yourself electrical kit—if he hadn't a flown that kite, we wouldn't be here today! When Paul Revere was forty, he spread the alarm through every Middlesexed village and farm, and Ulysses Grant used *his* fortieth year to put the squeeze on Vicksburg and that ain't just another name for your old John Thomas! Now, what woulda happened if *them* snorters had opened their pants, got bird in hand, and looked backward in time? *Eh?* No, my friend, remember the Prophets: Look not mournfully into the Past, it comes not back agin!"

"It wasn't . . . exactly my own past exactly . . . more like . . ." Never mind. Just make matters worse. I struggled to recall that line from Shakespeare about hearts and hell that I copied down years ago when I was in the Navy, I knew it would be useful. When I was away from Pat for a while. . . . But it wouldn't come to me. Instead, what I did remember suddenly was the name of that old Clark Gable movie: *It Happened One Night.* This scene, however, was not in it.

"I will say to your credit, though, you're more natural at that than you are at golf or politics—if you loosened up like that out in public, might make all the difference! You'd probably be floggin' a lot fewer problems at home, too. . . ."

"I'm not having problems!" I protested. Did he know about Pat and me? Politicians lived in glass houses, I knew, but surely there were decent limits . . . maybe not, though—I'd only really come under the gaze about nine months ago, I was still mapping this out. "It's . . . it's got nothing to do with that . . ."

"No?" Uncle Sam, his white locks curling down around his shoulders, was peering at me as though over the top of Ben Franklin's reading glasses. "Maybe not. But remember just the same, lad, a little wife well tilled, willed, I mean—in a word, don't keep it to yourself, boy, stand beside her and guide her, a used key is always bright along the Wabash!" His voice had softened to a throaty rumble—like that of Raymond Massey playing Abraham Lincoln. His playful fade had calmed me somewhat, and I'd managed to work a tooth or two of the zipper free from the cloth, but the rest wouldn't budge. "Listen, you're fightin' the problem, son," he said, leaning toward me as though he might come to help.

"I've got it!" I cried, and in a panic gave a great yank on the zipper:

it parted and my shirttail was free at last! My fly, however, would never close again. My shoulders relaxed—I began to feel the tension going out. I felt defeated and liberated at the same time. "The most virtuous hearts have a touch of hell's own fire in them." That was the line. Probably not Shakespeare, though. Or useful either.

"What's *that* got to do with it?" demanded Uncle Sam.

I hadn't realized I was talking out loud. I was very tired. And depressed. Shit, I thought. What a mess. Maybe I ought to get sick. "Just . . . just something I—"

"Cock's body," swore Uncle Sam, kicking through the papers on the floor, "I ain't seen so much shit piled around in one place since we cleaned out Harry Gold's basement! You know, I think your problem is, you been spendin' too much time indoors. I know how much your famous Iron Butt means to you, and I reckanize it gets you more votes than your face does, but you don't wanta get musclebound in one joint while the rest just withers away! You probably ain't eatin', drinkin', eliminatin', bathin', whoopeein', and sleepin' like you ought neither— you get aholda Dr. Calver's Ten Commandments, fella! You look worse'n John Brown's molderin' body!"

Maybe Napoleon said it, I thought. Or else Mark Twain. I wondered how I was going to get home in time to change into a new pair of pants before tonight—have to buy a whole new suit maybe . . .

Uncle Sam picked up one of my large lined yellow legal pads, and, peering down his long white nose at it, commenced to read: " 'I can't speak for the lives of other men, but my own has always seemed to me to have purpose, and so events which might have seemed like accidents or casual decisions to others'—what the hell is this?"

"It's a . . . a position paper . . ."

"Yeah, some position all right—it's all flat and sprawled and bends ever' which way! I ain't seen such wretched penmanship in high places since the days of the early railroad barons! Gotta give you credit, them 't's' are real killers, but the rest is all stingy and crabbed and outa balance! And why is it, boy, when I set you to cogitatin' a problem like this case, you think only about *yourself?*"

"Not . . . not *only*—"

"What are you jerkin' around like that for? You got the Saint Vitus Dance? And look at *me* when I'm talkin' to you!"

"I . . . I can't—!"

"No, you're in bad shape, mister! The *solid* earth, that's what you need!" What I needed right now was to lie down, but he was blocking my access to the sofa. A man ought to be judged by the decisions he made or didn't make, I thought light-headedly, not by how he dots an "i" or crosses a "t." "The *actual* world! the *common sense! Contact! Contact!* There are times when in the course of human events, you gotta let the dead Past bury its dead, and act—act in the livin' presence! No more time-outs, son, it's out-under-the-open-sky-root-hog-or-die time!"

I turned and stared dismally out the window on the balmy June day. Perhaps he's right, I thought. I could go on a speaking tour, see America. Anything would be better than this. On a patch of grass, far away, I could see a group of people. They seemed to be playing croquet. Or else taking snapshots of the Capitol. Or carrying pickets. Ah, why did nothing in America keep its shape, I wondered? Everything was so fluid, nothing stayed the same, not even Uncle Sam. Of course, this *was* what stayed the same. . . . "Aren't we making too much of all this?" I asked, trying to keep my voice from breaking. Foolhardy maybe, but I knew the rules: stay on the attack, find your opponent's weakness and lean on him, and if he attacks you, don't answer, don't go on the defensive. I was scared, though. I didn't know where I was with him any more. I tried to recall the arguments the Phantom had used on me, but all I could remember was Ethel Rosenberg doing the Dirty Crab, slapping the stage with the cheeks of her ass, and the bit about Native Dancer and Sonja Henie. I gritted my teeth. "All these old, uh, acts . . . we've made our point . . ."

"Where the battle against the Phantom is concerned," said Uncle Sam ominously, "victories are never final so long as he is still able to fight!" This was familiar. I'd heard it somewhere before. I turned to face him: he was staring at me darkly. I knew what was coming next, it was as though we were in some play, I felt like I'd fallen into a river and was getting swept helplessly along: There is never a time. . . . "There is never a time when it is safe to relax or let down!"

"No," I said, groping for my lines, my place. "No . . . but what can the Phantom *do?* Like you said, this one's in our home, uh, ball-park . . ."

"Yeah, well, so was Grant's second Ordination and look what that onry galoot done to *that!*" replied Uncle Sam.

"Grant?" I gasped in disbelief. I didn't know whether I was on dry land again, or going down for the third time. "You mean the . . . the *Phantom?* Way back—?"

"You durn tootin'! Cast such a outdacious petterfactin' shadow that all the thermometers went bust in the freeze, coldest goddamn Investiture in national history, Grant never got over it! Oh, that sarpint had us all on the skids in that one, I never felt such a awesome chill—except for the time I tried to incarnate myself back into Warren Harding, not noticin' he was dead! And whoopee! what a wind! It come rippin' hell's bells outa the north big as all outdoors and gettin' blacker by the minute—seemed like it was tryin' to push all the District real estate clean over into Prince Georges County! It whistled bucklety-whet through the parade like shit through a tin horn, whippin' away decorations, clothing, wives, horses, and even Old Glory—blasted Grant's daughter Nellie all the way to England and broke his goddamn heart! It sure tore up jack! And cold? The champagne at the Ball froze solid as the rock a Prudential, not to mention the poor little singin' canaries and emancipated jigaboo servants! I swear to Jesse, if we hadn'ta got one helluva dance revved up, he mighta turned the whole Tabernacle to ice crystals, shattered it with his twister, and blowed it clean off the face of the earth! No, son, you don't fuck about none with the Phantom!"

"But . . . you mean—? but it's the middle of June—!"

"Of course it's the middle of June!" roared Uncle Sam. "My God, it ain't hard to see why you bombed out as a used-car salesman and orange-juice czar, you haven't got the *brains* for anything faster than politics! I'm warnin' you, mister, you had better set yourself for a mighty carnage, a evil hour of darkness and adversity and bodacious peril, a most horrible contwisted embranglement that'll tar up the earth all round like that Worcester tornado and look dreadful kankarifferous!" He strode violently through the room, lean and long-legged, kicking through my paperwork as through a snowdrift, a pile of dead leaves, hands clutching his blue lapels, whirling on me from time to time and riveting me with a fiery glance—terrible those eyes: you could see the lightning coiled behind them, ready to flash out, that incredible power . . . that could be mine . . . if only . . . "On accounta we are up against the archenemy of the whole human race, sir, the meanest son of a misbegotten wildcat on the skin of the goldurn globe, all hot sulphur but the head and *that's* aquafortis!"

"Aquafortis—?"

"Heavy water, boy! Pure sorcery and dangerous as a Massassip alla-gator with a tapeworm! They call him Sudden Death and General Deso-lation, half cousin to the cholera and godfather of the Apocalypse! He's all what most maddens and torments, all what stirs up the lees a things, all what cracks the sinews and cakes the brain, all the subtle vinimus demonism of life and thought, that mysterious fearsome force which from time immemorious has menaced the peace and security of mankind and buggered the hopes of the holy, the Creator of—"

"But, but I thought, uh, heavy water was—"

"Hold your tongue, mister, whilst I'm recitin'!" Uncle Sam bellowed, spinning on me fiercely, *"or you shall smell brimstone through a nail hole!"* I thought he was going to draw a six-shooter like Andy Jackson and gun me down. It occurred to me I ought to leap out the window to save myself, but I couldn't even move. "I say, he's the Creator of Ambiguities, out to conquer the world, refashion it in his own craven image, enslave it to his own utopian ends! A warlock, a wizard is he, and lord a the wind and the sea, half wild horse and half cockeyed catamount, and the rest of him is crooked snags and red-hot snappin' turkle! You hear me? The massacree of isolated communities is the pastime of his idyll moments, the destruction of nationalities the serious business of his life! Why aren't the Rosenbergs talkin'? Who's sewn 'em up? Why's the whole world goin' crazy? Who made you get a grip on your old whangdoodle insteada the problem at hand? It's the *Phantom*, boy, our natural and habitual enemy, a rantankerous mean shape—"

"But—"

"Shut up, boy, and lissen! If you don't say nuthin', you won't be called on to repeat it! I'm tellin' you, true as preachin', he's a rantankerous mean shape a the brumal rain, and the darkness fearful and formless, lean, hongry, savage, anti-everything, the maker a deserts and the wall-eyed harbinger a deevastation whose known rule a warfare is an undistinguished destruction of all ages, sexes, and conditions! the Hog-Eye Man! the arch-degenerate! alien to us in ever' way—habits, hopes, blood even—and he infects everything, our litterchur, art, religion, games, deemocratic system and free enterprise, with the pizen—you remember all this, son, you can use it yourself some day—with the pizen of his evil sinister influence! Why, even our decision to burn them two lefties in Times Square mought not be ours at all, but his! A trap! That sassy rascal, he's capable of anything!"

"You . . . you think there's a chance," I gasped, "that the Phantom can actually break, uh, this thing up?"

"Yea, I tell you, mister, we are at the precipice, it is a bloody desput condition what confronts us, and if we don't mind our P's and Q's, we shall all be fissionated quicker'n a allagator can chew a puppy!"

"You mean—!?"

"I mean what I say!" Uncle Sam glared ominously at me through the storm of notes and documents now fluttering slowly to the floor, then turned on his heel and went in to use my john.

I was struck dumb. Was this it, then? Of course, I knew it could happen, we all knew it could happen any day, we talked about it all the time, Rockefeller had his bomb-shelter business in high gear, we were already counting out the holy remnant—but now, so close, so sudden? Was this the bloody condition, the perilous fight, the evil hour? Had Uncle Sam not announced, long ago, an uproarious tumult, a time of tribulation but a redemption which shall last forever? Was this more than a mere symbolic expiation? Were the Rosenbergs in fact the very trigger—living high-explosive lenses, as it were—for the ultimate holocaust? And was *this* what Uncle Sam wanted me to share in? The crashing roar of his urine drowned out my thoughts—he'd smashed up more than one solid-marble toilet bowl in this building with that mighty Niagara of his, and I always worried when he used mine. Like those fire hoses on Bleecker Street, I thought, oh fuck my luck. "Whew," he groaned from in there, "this is the most magnificent movement of all!" It was said that he could generate enough power with his flow to light up all Latin America, so long as they didn't mind the odor, and that once, to prove he could stop time, had pissed Old Faithful back down its hole, and thereby had created the Hot Springs of Arkansas. Something to look forward to during the Incarnation . . . if I survived. . . .

Uncle Sam emerged, looking pleased with himself, buttoning up his pantaloons. "I promised you a veritable day of havoc, my friend, and it ain't over yet! Nosirree, bob, I know what I'm explanigatin' about, there'll be a hot tamale in the old town tonight, so you better get a grip on your braces, boy—when Jesus comes to claim us all, it's gonna be no place for skonks and cookie pushers! We're in for a turrible grumble and rumble and roar, a most strenuous and fearful concatenation of orful circumstances, so stay with the procession or you'll never catch up!" Maybe the pissing had done him good, he seemed more relaxed and playful again. I felt hopeful. But then he poked his nose into my refrigerator and his face fell. Nothing in there, I knew, but an empty cottage-cheese carton and a bottle of moldy ketchup. "Damn it, you spread a wuss table even than that Yankee pinch-fart Coolidge—only thing I ever got outa him was his wife's apple pie, which was like eatin' raw shrapnel, but even that was more wholesome than—hullo! what's this! Say, I ain't smoked an Optimo since before the last Depression!" He sniffed it, peeled the cellophane, bit off the end. "Do you mind?"

"Well, no, but—"

"But me no buts, son, you gotta learn to *give* a little!" he scolded, tucking the cigar in his cheek. "No, like I'm noratin', this is no local matter up in Times Square tonight, are you listenin'? The whole pesky world's in on this one, always has been. It is, and I shit you not, it is a irrepressible conflict betwixt opposin' and endurin' forces! Why, it's said that when the very angels fell—now, this was a long time ago, son, before your time, even before Grant's time—it's said their fall was on accounta unnatural lust and the betrayal of 'etarnal secrets which were presarved in Heaven.' You see? Even then! And you know what them secrets were?" He fumbled behind his ear, took off his plug hat and searched the inside band, slapped at his pockets. He swept the stacks of paper off my desk, finally found buried there a lighter Pat had once given me on some anniversary. "Well, come on, boy, I asked you a question, don't stand there dumb as a dead nigger in a mudhole! You know what the secrets them angels betrayed were?"

"N-no, sir!" I replied with a start.

"They taught men *how to make weapons!*" said Uncle Sam solemnly.

"Ah . . . !"

"Whereupon, God stretched forth his little finger . . ." He flicked the lighter importantly, but nothing happened. "What the hell . . . ?" He thumbed it several times, but it wouldn't light. I knew this would happen, it had never worked since she gave it to me. "Goddamn world's goin' to the dogs!" he muttered irritably, "it's them poxtaked Japs, the shiftless cusses," and he struck it like a match on the seat of his pants. "Right . . . stretched forth his little pinky, then, and them traitor angels was consumed . . ."—he drew the flame slowly toward the cigar—"by (*puff! puff!*) . . ."—glancing up as smoke began to curl out between his lips, tossing the lighter out the window: ". . . *FIRE!*" The cigar exploded in his face.

I couldn't breathe. I stared at him in disbelief. His eyes were bugged out and crossed over his nose with astonishment, his face tarred with soot, his white eyebrows bobbing like a minstrel comic's, the peeled-back cigar butt still quivering in his puckered lips like a blackened daisy. I've lost it, I wept. I'll never be President!

"*BY GOD!*" he roared. The few papers left on my desk lifted and settled again, and Ike's framed prayer crashed from the wall. "*WHAT IN TARNATION IS GOIN' ON HERE!?!*"

"I'm—I'm sorry!" I cried. "I didn't—!"

"*OHH! DUMB BE PASSION'S STORMY RAGE, WHEN HE WHO MIGHTA LIGHTED UP AND LED HIS AGE, FALLS BACK IN NIGHT!*" he bellowed—the chandelier splintered and crashed, and the refrigerator door blew open and fell off its hinges. He was in a truly awesome rage, his face puffy and almost ugly, like a choleric John Adams or Teddy Roosevelt, and now black as Rochester's to boot. I was clutching my breast in absolute terror. It is not a pleasant picture to see a whole brilliant career destroyed before your eyes, I thought, tears

streaming down my cheeks, especially when it is your own! My knees
had turned to Jell-O—jelly, I mean—and my—

Suddenly his index finger sprang forward and waggled in front of my
nose—it was just like those new 3-D movies, he didn't seem to move an
inch, just flashed that pointing finger out at me—I jumped right out of
my shoes, even the one with the lace in it, and fell back against the wall.
"LISTEN TO ME, MISTER!" he thundered, cracking the mirror over
the fireplace and pinning me back against the wall with a look that not
even the worst of the Democrats or the most vicious of the Phantom's
blackhearted agents ever gave me. I felt the wall behind me tremble—or
perhaps it was only my own terror. *"YOU'VE GOT JUST SIX HOURS
TO GET YOURSELF STRAIGHTENED OUT OR ELSE!"*

"Oh, please!" I gasped. He towered high above me—oh, he was a
mighty and terrible sight to see! I knew just how those poor criminals
must have felt when Grover Cleveland came to hang them! He hurled
the shattered cigar past my left ear and out the window—it whined by
like a falling mortar shell and something deep inside my head seemed to
blast open. "I can explain—!"

*"FUCK EXPLAIN! THE NECESSITY OF BEIN' READY IN-
CREASES! LOOK TO IT!"*

"I—I was only trying to do what you—!"

But he was gone. I was alone in my office. Terribly alone: Uncle Sam
had always before left something behind when he departed, something
like static, a kind of energy that I could take into myself and use until it
ceased to hum, but not this time. The emptiness was so profound it was
nearly a vacuum. He seemed even to have sucked the room's gravity
away with him: papers, the disturbed red drapes, fragments of the
exploded cigar and splintered chandelier, all hovered without settling. I
moved, afloat, in stocking feet, swimming through all my guilt and
shame, to my chair and fell dully toward it. Debris hung about everywhere, mirroring the awful muddle in my head. Then, slowly, the gravity came back. The drapes sank, the papers fell, I crashed into the chair.
I could hardly move. I felt depleted, threatened with insignificance,
abandoned. My chin sank to my chest, and I stared, sick at heart, at my
gaping fly. I hadn't felt so miserable since Mom went away to Arizona.
How could it have come to this? I've thrown it all away! All I've worked
for since I was ten years old! The odor of gunpowder clung to my
nostrils, faintly acrid, faintly sweet . . . like semen. A last rebuff.

I blew my nose.

I had to move on, I knew. I couldn't stay here.

Go forth, he'd said. Under the open sky. Times Square, he meant. With all the rest of the nation. I dreaded it, all those goddamn people . . .

I swiveled about and dragged my shoes over with one foot. He probably won't even let me sit up front. I was just another throttlebottom, after all, like all the rest. Here today, gone tomorrow. Miserably, I stuffed my foot back into the laced-up shoe, breaking down the back of the heel but not caring, pulled the other one on and strung it up with some yellow packing string from my wastebasket. I stared wetly out on the mad clutter, wondering: Why did Uncle Sam do this to me? Why was I always the whipping boy? Who turned him against me?

I heaved myself up out of the chair, hauled on my jacket, and slumped out of my wrecked office, crunching splintered glass underfoot. Should change suits for tonight, but what did it matter? I found a safety pin in one of Rose's drawers for my fly. Ah, poor Rose, what would she do now? I felt sorry for all my secretaries and assistants. I felt sorry for all the people who had voted for me. And for my poor little girls. I felt sorry for the whole country. It didn't seem fair. I pricked my thumb on the safety pin and was almost pleased. I sucked my thumb and demanded to know: How much must I give? What more can he possibly want from me? I've done everything a man can be expected to do without groveling on his knees, I just can't take any more! I have found that leaders are subject to all the human frailties: they lose their tempers, become depressed, experience the other symptoms of tension. Sometimes even strong men will cry. Like me: I was bawling my goddamn eyes out. Jettisoned! Sandbagged! It was all over! I'd suffered it all: the unwanted child, the unwanted boyfriend, the unwanted husband, the unwanted lawyer, the unwanted Vice Presidential candidate, the unwanted Republican leader—and now the unwanted Incarnation!

After a while, after I'd stopped crying, I thought: maybe it was just as well. After all, look how many of the poor misused bastards had been physically destroyed by the travail of transmutation: one Roosevelt had been brought to his knees, the other blinded, Grant and Cleveland had got their insides eaten out, they'd nearly all got shot at and some hadn't made it through at all, while others—Jackson, for example, Coolidge— had been left a little batty when it was all over. I'd seen Hoover up close, and there was something in his eyes that worried me, too. So what the hell, I told myself, take it as it comes, don't go off half-cocked. I was no quitter after all, I had to ride it out to the end, maybe when these executions were over, things would look different. I wiped my face on my sleeve, put on sunglasses to hide the red eyes—things were bad enough, I didn't want those news shits to start calling me "the Weep" again. And what was the dress tonight? Homburgs probably, since they'd gone down so well before. I found mine finally on a wooden chair back of the hat stand near the secretaries' coffee mess. It was covered with eraser dust and spilt coffee, and somebody had apparently sat on it. By now I expected as much. Brusquely, I popped it out with my fist, swatted it against my pantleg to beat the dust off, and left the office.

It was a warm June day out, bright even with my sunglasses on—too comfortable really, seemed like there ought to be rain, thunder and lightning, high winds, on such a day as this. Was there a clue in the sunshine? No, there were no clues, *no* clues. On the short walk through the park to Union Station, I thought: there's something peculiar about Uncle Sam. He's our Superchief in the Age of Flux, and yet here he is, worrying about something beyond it all—call it consistency, the game plan, the script, what you will . . . he's still hungering after some kind of shape to things, I thought. Or else he's putting me on, not telling me everything. . . .

Up to my left, scattered groups of sullen demonstrators wandered around with placards that read THEY MUST NOT DIE! and FIRST VICTIMS OF AMERICAN FASCISM!, while past me on the right moved knots of cheerful young men whose signs said DEATH TO LEFT WINGERS! and HELP CLEAN THE SCUM-MUNISTS OUT OF OUR CITY! and HANG 'EM AND SHIP THE BODIES TO RUSSIA C.O.D.! These latter were crudely lettered compared to the handsomely printed pro-Rosenberg signs, but at least they bespoke a genuine sentiment. The professionally manufactured pro-Rosenberg propaganda just reinforced the suspicion of conspiracy. I walked up the middle between them, where the children played, thinking: in a way, the Rosenbergs are lucky—at least they know what they have to do. It's not knowing what to do that tears your insides out.

As I neared the station, I saw I was not alone, there were a lot of people arriving with me. Cabs and buses were swinging up, pouring out passengers, and the streets were jammed with illegally parked cars. The whole city seemed to be emptying out, moving toward Times Square. I avoided people I knew, which was easier than usual for some reason. The sunglasses maybe. Or else the homburg—no one else had one. But then a limousine full of *Washington Post* reporters pulled up and unloaded—I ducked around the Columbus fountain, pretended to study the legend up on the west side of the station. It was about fire. And electricity . . .

CARRIER OF LIGHT & POWER. DEVOURER OF TIME & SPACE. BEARER
OF HUMAN SPEECH OVER LAND & SEA. GREATEST SERVANT OF MAN.

ITSELF UNKNOWN.

. . . .

THOU HAST PUT ALL THINGS UNDER HIS FEET

What was one to do with such gratuitous messages? Nothing. The world
was full of them. Union Station itself was a veritable Bartlett's in stone.
THE TRUTH SHALL MAKE YOU FREE, it said elsewhere. THE DESERT SHALL
REJOICE AND BLOSSOM AS THE ROSE. Forget it. Like RID THE U.S. OF RATS!
and SAVE THE ROSENBERGS FROM MCCARTHYISM! If you took such things
seriously you were lost.

I waited until the *Post* reporters had disappeared through the arches,
then ducked my head and bulled my way through the crowd into Union
Station. It was packed in there with people trying to make connections,
get seats, bribe reporters. Lots of extra trains running to New York, so
most would eventually make it, but there was a nervous, almost desperate feeling in the air—as though this were something one dared not
miss, not merely because one had to be up there to say he'd lived
through his own age, but more than that: *because Times Square might
be the only safe place in the world tonight!* Well, I shared their anxiety,
but I wasn't afraid. Right now, the Bomb seemed like a happy entertainment, compared to what I was going through. I followed the signs
for the *Look Ahead, Neighbor Special,* flashed my identification at the
military barrier, received a salute, and was let through—though not
without a suspicious double take at my disheveled state. I worried I
might run into somebody like General Persons or Sherm Adams, but I
was lucky: there was another run of this train later on, and apparently
all the real bigwigs were going on that one. Nothing but second-stringers
on this one, shit, I was demeaning myself again. I did pass Jack Kennedy, standing there on the platform with a leggy brunette—where did
he get these broads? It wasn't just his so-called Irish charm, I was as
Irish as he was. His money probably. God knows that sonuvabitch would
never get accused of a secret fund—his old man was all the funds he'd
ever need, and it was no secret. His girlfriend was apparently going to
take pictures of the executions. She looked familiar. A little like one of
those female reporters who used to hang around outside the Senate
toilet in the President's Room. Maybe she'd bagged Kennedy out there.
They were surrounded by a group of people, all smiling and radiant,
and as I ducked by and slipped into the nearest open car, I heard

Kennedy laugh lightly and remark: "Well, just let me say this about socialism, as Uncle Sam said once—ahh—said to me: At least it's better than the goddamn Phantom!"

This was disturbing. Not the part about the Phantom, but the part about Uncle Sam. Kennedy, I knew, was a skeptic, a freethinker, didn't even believe in Uncle Sam, much less have congress with him—he'd told me so on a long trainride together six years ago. He'd laughed cynically then at my simpleminded fundamentalism and called me a gullible Hollywood primitive. And now—! Well, it was clearly worse than I'd supposed—and Kennedy might not be the only one. It occurred to me that a lot of guys had been showing newfound flash of late—my fair-haired-boy days with Sam Slick were over. But Kennedy? What was happening to Uncle Sam? Maybe we needed to revive the Know-Nothings and the American Protective Association, put a stop to the contamination, I thought sourly. Close the door, fuck the oppressed of every nation, get the Old Man back in the pink again. Distantly, I heard something about "the OPA." Kennedy laughed. The girl tittered. The sonuvabitch. I hoped at least he sat in a different car this time.

That other time was in the spring of 1947, we were both fresh out of our Naval Officer uniforms (I outranked him) and newly elected to the House of Representatives, both on the same Education and Labor committee, and Frank Buchanan had invited the two of us up to McKeesport, outside Pittsburgh, to debate the merits of what was then the hot issue in Congress, the Taft-Hartley Act. I was for the bill. Kennedy was against it. I won. Kennedy was a pushover in fact. Of course, the entire audience was made up of employers, I couldn't help but win, but I could have beat him anywhere. Maybe this had pissed Kennedy off and made him unusually sarcastic. After the meeting, we'd ridden a sleeper from Pittsburgh back to the capital. During the long rocky ride, we'd talked about foreign affairs, the handling of the Communist threat at home and abroad, and religion: where America was going, what it all meant. I didn't recall the details—except that he kept wanting to talk about getting ass and at one point, when I tried quoting Alf Landon on the "new frontier," complained that I had the imagination of a fucking peasant—but of one thing I was absolutely certain: Only I had the true faith. Not that I'd had any concrete proof yet myself, I'd had as much contact with Uncle Sam as I'd had with Jesus, but as usual, my instincts were right about this and Kennedy's were wrong.

At the time, I'd thought: it's probably his Catholicism standing in the way. But he didn't seem to be much of a Catholic either—not like Charlie Kersten, for example, who was on the committee with us, or

Monsignor Sheen or my friend Father Cronin—hell, in a way, *I* was
more of a Catholic than he was! I eventually realized it was mainly his
money and good looks that had agnosticized him: he didn't have to fight
for anything, didn't have to ask hard questions. Probably got a soft push
downhill at Harvard, too. The only reason he'd beat Lodge out of his
Senate seat was because his old man had bought off the pro-Lodge
Boston Post with half a million dollars. At the time I'd seen this as yet
another stroke of historical luck for me, getting rid of Lodge like that,
but now I couldn't be sure. Uncle Sam had a lot of respect for money, I
knew that—hadn't he just lectured me on it? But Kennedy was too
frivolous, too cocky, a pampered arrogant snot who wasn't interested in
anything unless he could get into its pants—he wasn't called "Shafty" in
the Navy for nothing—and if my butt was made of iron, his was made of
peanut brittle. Like my brother Harold, he had a certain reckless charm,
but no discipline, no staying power. I'd never taken him seriously, and
assumed Uncle Sam hadn't either—Uncle Sam was born an Episcopalian,
ate a whole side of cornfed Nebraska beef every Friday night and would
rather whip a papist paddywhack than a nigger any day. Negro, I mean.
Not a single one of his Presidential Incarnations had even mentioned
Jesus by name in an Inaugural Address, much less his R.C.-idolatrized
Mother. The only occasion I'd ever heard Uncle Sam mention the Virgin
was the night he'd interrupted my Caribbean cruise back in 1948—just
the second time I'd ever seen Uncle Sam that close—to fly me back to
Whittaker Chambers's pumpkin patch. He still didn't know me well then,
and, while working the rowing machine in the S.S. *Panama*'s gym, which
we'd snuck away to, he'd asked me a little about my life. I'd begun at
the beginning, as I always do, with the day of my birth, but he'd interrupted to ask me when I'd lost my cherry. I'd stammered something
clumsy about honeymooning with Pat in Mexico, and he'd laughed that
rattling disconcerting peddler's laugh of his and, keeping rhythm with
his strokes, had chanted:

> The Virgin Mary stumped her toe
> On the way to Mexico!
> On the way back she broke her back
> Sliding on the railroad track!
> Queevy, quavy, Irish Mary,
> Stingalum, stangalum, *buck!*

He said the Indians had taught it to him.

Not that Uncle Sam was a secularist—how could he be? He was Uncle

Sam, after all. Faith was essential to the Incarnation, it wouldn't come off without it—"any deeply felt religious faith," as Eisenhower liked to put it, "and I don't care which it is." True, by the letter of the Covenant, any would serve, but on the other hand, Uncle Sam clearly was not partial to Jews, Muslims, Hindus, Buddhists, Voodooists, or Romanists. If he had any favorites at all, they were among people like Ezra Benson's Mormons, the eccentric, evangelical, and fundamentalist sects nurtured here on this soil and here primarily, Adventists, Shakers, Jehovah's Witnesses, Christian Scientists, Hardshell Baptists, Church of Christers, Four Square Gospelers . . . yes, *and* Quakers. And so I hadn't been surprised at Jack Kennedy's blindness, his blasphemies, and as always I'd held my peace when confronted by them: some men are born to greatness and some are not, no point in helping those who are slow to catch on. Especially a rich fucking Ivy League Brahmin like Kennedy—I hated all those guys, not personally, but because they didn't play fair, they corrupted the American Dream with their bankrolled head starts: goddamn it, if they couldn't sell penny candy and rescue millionaires like the rest of us, they could go to hell. I always thought that was how Uncle Sam saw it, too, that enthusiasm he had for the log-cabin starting line, but now suddenly there was this conversion: it could only mean one thing. I shrank miserably into my seat as the train pulled out, huddled in my rumpled clothes, smelling the acids of my fathers rise in an ancient indignation: the only good papist is a dead papist. Poo. I needed a fresh shirt and a deodorant, I stank worse than Sheba, but fuck it, I was past caring.

The car had filled up with festive exuberant people singing songs, uncorking hip flasks, drawing out mouth-harps and decks of cards, lighting up cigars . . . but no one had come to sit by me. Not that I gave a shit, that passion for anonymity was no joke with me, in school buses, at choir practice, on the bench at football games, at family picnics, I'd always had a place apart, I was the original Lone Ranger and wanted it that way, but still I didn't like the implications—it was as though I'd been set up as a humpty dumpty and everybody smelled this on me, knew better than to get contaminated themselves. It was that same total isolation I'd been feeling since the fund crisis, like maybe Checkers had given me rabies or something, it was as though the last dozen years had not happened and I was back in Washington in the OPA, getting crapped on by the big-city Jews and Yalie New Dealers. Could I kill, I wondered? If it came to that, could I kill? Not something easy like the Rosenbergs, but this crowd in here . . . if they got in my way . . . ? Why not? Killing was as meaningless as anything else. The only question was whether you risked getting killed yourself—and even that might be just another reason to go ahead and have a try. Not that I'm suicidal, I'd been scared all my life of dying and I was scared still. Yet I needed to confront it constantly. "That swarm of black thing." I drew energy from it, only provided I didn't name it. Though the threat of it paralyzed me, I was never so alive as when it threatened me. It made mere survival the central principle of my life. It molded my face. It made me reckless. I wanted to plunge into it and out the other side over and over again. It taught me that Self, though nothing, was everything. And it was what dragged me down the aisle that night in Los Angeles, when Dad took us boys in to Dr. Rader's revival meeting. What a night! This was not the Friends Meeting House in tranquil reasonable Whittier. This was the goddamn truth. Awesome and fundamental. No play-acting piety here, no "Joy to the World," there was a terrible choice to be made, and there were no third alternatives. Dr. Rader made one thing perfectly clear: the truth did not make you comfortable. I was wide open and ready for this—I had just started high school the day before and I *wanted* to bleed! We joined hundreds of others that night in making our personal commitments to Christ and Christian service. Or perhaps this was a formula for some transformation deeper than commitment. I remember the crying. How vulnerable my father looked. Jesus was like some kind of radiant loving cloud one walked through out of Death toward Progress. Toward true freedom. I *believed*. I thought: *only in America could this happen!*

We pulled out of the suburbs of Baltimore, picking up speed, and as I felt the train propelling me toward New York, I reminded myself, thinking back on that night in Los Angeles: whatever happens, there's not much I can do about it now—start down the aisle, there's no turning back. This is always true, the stream of events has a terrific force and momentum of its own. Once a man gets into an important position of leadership—mine, for example—he can set off a lot of big waves, but he can't turn the river around completely. All about me, people were singing "Go Get the Axe" and "Tea for Two" and, changing the words somewhat to suggest the electric chair, "On Top of Old Smokey." I didn't join in, I felt less and less a part of them. I sat by myself, huddled up against the window in my homburg and sunglasses, reminded of the Inauguration: looking out over the stone banister at all those strange people. After the General's pontifications, they had all erupted in whistling: wolf-whistles, they'd sounded like, as though it had been Eisenhower's legs they'd liked, not his speech. Some applause, too, but the shrill brutish whistling was what you'd been able to hear best out there in that cold wind. Most people, I've found, are complete fools—

that's why it was so easy to get ahead, there just wasn't any serious competition out there. . . .

We were now ripping along through open country, and the excitement seemed to build as we drew toward New York. The air was heavy with smoke, singing, intense talk, and the smell of booze, which was beginning to make me nauseous. Nobody offered me any of the liquor getting passed around, but just as well. I loosened my collar, leaned my head back. Jesus, that was all I needed now, to get sick. Nothing to throw up, I knew. "Hollow, hollow—like the case against the Rosenbergs." I'd missed lunch again, hadn't had anything to eat since breakfast, and though I couldn't remember what I'd had then, I was sure it wasn't much. No goddamn corned-beef hash, nothing that would have *helped*. All I could recall about breakfast was scolding the girls and barking at Pat, which I regretted, even if she did deserve it. She didn't understand me any more, damn it. I had this big thing to do and she wasn't paying any attention. She'd lost interest. She said she didn't like politics—but it was *me* she didn't like! I could never count on her when I was really down. Take election day two years ago against Helen Douglas: I was sure I'd lost, I knew my whole political career was ended, but I didn't want to show this, I had to make it look like it didn't matter. So I decided we'd all go to the beach. The children, too, I made everybody go. It was a terrible day, I admit, cold and gray, with a bitter offshore wind beating in—it seemed to confirm my worst suspicions and I reveled in its punishment. The girls cried and wanted to go home. I wanted to hit them. Instead, I smiled and told them to go dig in the goddamn sand and shut up. But the worst thing was that Pat didn't understand either. She sat there on the sand wrapped up in a blanket, sulking and nagging, until I finally gave up and took them all home. I was so disgusted I just pulled up to the curb and dumped them out, then went off to a movie by myself. And now, Christ, she was even complaining publicly about my thrashing around in bed, about my jumping up in the middle of the night to take notes, waking her up with my sudden fears or enthusiasms —I'd made her the Number Two lady in the nation, did she think you got something like that for nothing? Some woman had wandered into the car and by request had sat down on the armrest of the empty seat beside me to sing "I'd Rather Die Young" for everybody, which was apparently a big new hit. I stared at the way her bottom plumped out over the armrest, thinking: I was the only goddamn faithful husband in national politics, and where had it got me? Stranded here on the Whip with a carload of boozy loonies, the cockeyed Community of God. Cast Intact.

"Hey, how about 'Down the Trail of Achin' Hearts!' "
" 'Doggie in the Window!' "
" 'Changin' Partners!' "

I sat there in all that smoke and ruckus, feeling sour and overburdened, slumped over my broken fly as over the law books in Durham, wishing the whole thing would get called off somehow. The real crisis of America today, I thought sullenly, is the crisis of the spirit. I'd failed to button my shirt cuffs and the sleeves were bunched up inside my jacket. I knew I should stand and take the jacket off, but I didn't want to draw attention to myself. Besides, I was too nauseous. The thick smoke, the noise, the dust from the old seats were getting to me. I was afraid I might have a hay-fever attack. I leaned my head back again and from under the brim of my homburg read the blow-ups of letters written to the Rosenberg Clemency Committees, mounted over the windows and at each end of the car like advertisements . . .

> To whom it may concern. All I say is why have they been wasting so much time when the government Knows how guilty they are! . . . Its traiters like these human snakes that cause wars. I say Kill them before our silly government turns them loose to cause further *hell* and treachery and torture to our Sons. Just because they are Jews like yourselves you selfishly want them released. You have taken over nearly all the U.S.A. you ungrateful Dogs. If your friends are released I'm no longer an American.

The distraction helped, but not much. I kept seeing Uncle Sam's finger shooting out and trembling in front of my nose. Somewhere a glass smashed and a woman squealed.

> Build a strong wailing wall with four sides, and put dear little Mammala and Papala Rosenberg in the big middle of this wailing wall in Sing Sing, and let them wail and wail and wail. What do the Jew$ do in return [for being] permitted to live in the U.S.? He is without exception the spy, the Saboteur, "Commies," Left Wingers, Infiltrators, hate mongers and all around trouble-makers, to say nothing of their intense Zionism which makes Hitler look like an amateur.

> These *2 Rats* should of been hung long ago & so should you.
>   A good American

There were more, they were plastered all over the goddamn car, but I was getting too train-sick to keep on reading them. Jesus, we seemed to be picking up speed—racing through piled-up industry now, must be in New Jersey already, the slums and factories were racing past so fast you could hardly see them, flashing by like the flipping of pages in a picture book! Somewhere a whistle screamed, the wheels clacked and banged, I whacked my head on the window and my homburg fell off! I grabbed it up and pulled it down over my ears. The drunks in the car were now singing train-wreck songs at the top of their lungs, but they were completely drowned out by the thunderous ruckety-pucketa of the wildly careening *Look Ahead, Neighbor Special.* I like campaign trains, I'm no front porcher, but this was too goddamn much! I once read in a dictionary of quotations that politicians were said by someone to be "monsters of self-possession." Well, we may show this veneer on the outside, but inside the turmoil could become almost unbearable, and that was how it was with me now, I wasn't even doing so good on the outside! I was perspiring heavily, feeling very clammy, clinging to the seat with both hands. It had always been my lifelong conviction that a man should give battle to his physical ailments, fight to stay out of the sickbed, and learn to live with and be stimulated by tension—in fact, I once said these very words to Bob Taft to cheer him up when he first fell ill with cancer —but now, eyes squeezed shut against the impending disaster, mouth dry, stomach knotted up, and smelling very funky, all I could think of was: I quit! Just let me out of here!

20.

Yippee, the Divine Concursus

The sun is settling on the tips of the skyscrapers, the temperature crests at 85 degrees and out on the periphery begins to drop, the humidity begins to rise: out at the edges, one can feel the chill spread of shadows —the people, now arriving by the tens of thousands, press forward, into Times Square, into the center where it's still warming up. Loudspeakers are turned on and tested out, and a bop-talking disk jockey from California is invited to emcee an hour or so of pop records: Rosemary Clooney, Johnny Ray, Harry Belafonte . . . "Hey, zorch, man!" his hepcat fans holler—which is fuzzbeard lingo for the "colossal!" of their folks' generation—and their bodies start to swing and bounce, sending massive ripples through the tightening crowd like the wind blowing across Kansas wheat fields. Some weirdos turn up, Frisco fans of the deejay, with green hair and purple lipstick; they get absorbed (this place can absorb anything) but not imitated.

In between numbers, the disk jockey goes down into the mob with his "raving microphone" to interview dignitaries, zanies, and ordinary mortals against a background of teen-age screams, and to conduct a straw poll on which of the two spies should be burned first. Of the first thousand votes cast, 438 are for Julius, 417 for Ethel, but there are also a number of votes for Mayor Impellitteri, the Dragon Lady, Jackie Robinson, Alger Hiss, Kilroy, Syngman Rhee, Justice Douglas, and Clifton Fadiman, among others, and including one vote each for Mr. and Mrs. Richard Nixon and two for Harold Stassen. Bobo Olson and Paddy

Young, who follow the Rosenbergs on the program tonight with a fifteen-round middleweight-championship fight, are intercepted ducking into Jack Dempsey's Restaurant for some pre-bout sirloins: they vote sportingly for each other.

Out back, poking around in Dempsey's garbage, is an old panhandler who has been working this area since it was Indian territory, long enough certainly to know that though the meat's better over at Al and Dick's Steak House, it's also picked closer to the bone—lot easier to get a full meal back of Dempsey's. This old man is, in his way, as good as a Ford or a Rockefeller at picking up the country's loose change, though he's been slipping a bit since the turn of the century. Now, as he makes his addled way down Broadway, gumming a T-bone, he encounters a gathering of millions. He blinks, casts a bleary eye at the clock over the Square, mops his brow in disbelief, then shrugs, pockets the bone, and hobbles hastily back to his cellar digs for his cap and overcoat.

Below the streets meanwhile in the Times Square subway station, now closed off to ordinary traffic and guarded by G-men, T-men, and city vice-squad detectives, the first trainloads of VIPs are beginning to pull in. The earliest to arrive are first-term Congressmen and their wives, minor administration officials, federal judges from outlying districts, pro-statehood delegations from Hawaii, Puerto Rico, Formosa, and Alaska, and (in the line of duty) the Advisory Board on Historic Sites, Buildings, and Monuments, but others of higher rank are not far behind. Hand-shaking and elbow-tugging, they circulate through the vast undergound complex, doing their best to impress each other and learn a few more names. Special bars have been set up for them, and they dip in cautiously, trying not to let the heat beneath the street and the gathering excitement make them soak it up too fast.

Some slip topside to peek out from backstage at the crowds rapidly filling the Square—still hours to go, and already the crush and jostle is terrific! They'd like to sneak out a minute and visit some of Walt's sideshows, but they're afraid they might not be able to make it back through the jam to their special reserved seats in the VIP section in time for the main proceedings. It's going to be a big show all right—there are bands, choirs, preachers milling about backstage, the Pentagon Patriots have arrived and are unpacking their instruments, Gene Autry is tuning up and Nelson Eddy is gargling with lemon water—but what they all see when they look out is that bare twilit stage and the antique Rube Goldberg contraption bolted to the middle of it. The chair. Two people will sit there tonight and die. Without them, none of this would be possible. Those two are to the program what the soul is to the body: the inner mechanism that sums it up and gives it meaning. In the middle of the middle of the Western World stands this empty chair: and only the Rosenbergs can fill this emptiness. Not the Nazi war criminals, not the disloyal union agitators or the Reader's Digest Murderers, not even the grisly necrophile John Reginald Halliday Christie can sit that seat tonight. For the Rosenbergs have done what none, not even these, may dream to do. They have denied Uncle Sam, defied the entire Legion of Superheroes, embraced the Phantom, cast his nefarious spell upon the innocent, and for him have wrested from the Sons of Light their most sacred secret: the transmutation of the elements. This is no mere theft, no common betrayal, and "plain, deliberate, contemplated murder," as young Judge Kaufman has said, "is dwarfed in magnitude" beside their crime—for they have sought nothing less than the ultimate impotency of Uncle Sam!

Yet if one is filled with dread and loathing, he is also filled with awe. They have done something that has changed the world. Which of these petty politicians peeking out from backstage, listening to Georgia Gibbs sing "Kiss of Fire" over the p.a. system, has not dreamed of doing as much? But feared the price? The Rosenbergs have done it. They have propelled themselves toward the center with such ferocity that now not even Uncle Sam could prevent their immolation, and by doing so they seem for a moment to have brought History itself alive—perhaps by the very threat of ending it! Even their beggarly childhood on the Lower East Side, their clumsy romance, their abandoned children, their depressing withdrawn lives in the enemy's service, acquire suddenly monstrous proportions, as if, by their treachery, new and appalling archetypes have been called into existence to replace the comforting commonplaces of "Stella Dallas" and "Young Widder Brown" being broadcast this afternoon across the nation on NBC radio. Everything they have touched seems suffused now with a strange dark power: this book or habit, that console table, this wristwatch. For years they kept on a shelf a coin-collection can labeled SAVE A SPANISH REPUBLICAN CHILD. Which child is that, and saved for whom? Replicas of this can are being sold by the dozens out there in the Square this afternoon, but there's no magic in them—where is the original, they all wonder, what its force? Even Julius's Talmudic name "Jonah," Ethel's mysterious "Madame" at the Carnegie Hall Studios, the inverted links with America's historic heritage in the location—Monroe Street, Knickerbocker Village—of their one-bedroom flat on the Lower East Side seem to hint at uncracked codes, unpenetrated conspiracies.

The disk jockey breaks for the five-o'clock news: Still no confessions. The Rosenbergs are playing it right down to the wire. The Phantom is said to be active in Milan and Genoa, Paris, London, and Teheran, but all this is coming to seem very remote. No breakthroughs in Korea or Berlin—if anything, the situations are worsening—and in Fort Sill, Oklahoma, a housewife has been injured by a stray shell from an atomic cannon while lying at home in her own bed. Zap. Disquieting, but these frenzied last-gasp activities of the Phantom are to be expected as the hour of the executions draws near. Up in Queens, a forty-year-old window cleaner drops out of his safety belt to his death, there are floods in Bombay, somebody gets shot in Chicago. Weather forecast: a heat wave is predicted. No doubt.

As far as the old panhandler can tell, it has already arrived. He has made it back into the Square, dressed now in his winter overcoat and stocking cap, newspapers stuffed round his feet in his old brogans. He works his way sweatily down a long line of tourists, who are evidently waiting to get into some picture show or something. They all want to take his picture, but that's all right, he's used to that—many's the time he has poked in a wastebasket or curled up on a park bench under newspapers out of sheer narcissism—and anyway it tends to loosen the bigger coins. Dumb tourists are all underdressed, he notes, mopping his face with the frayed ends of his tattered muffler. Not all of them are friendly either: some are parading around gloomily, shouting for justice and shouldering provocative placards. Not only do these types never give him a nickel, they have a way of souring the trade. But luckily they are being shunted out of the area by police and pushed to the south. The old panhandler nearly gets swept up in this net when somebody on the run thrusts a sign in his hand, but fortunately the sign reads CHRIST SAVE US FROM A DEATH LIKE THIS, and the police assume the old man's a walking advertisement for Alcoholics Anonymous. "Hottest goddamn New Year's Eve in living memory!" he's heard to mutter as he bulks along in his thick wraps. One thing about it, though: people are generous this afternoon. Part of the ancient year-end superstition about wasting your goods to ensure a fat year. His pockets are heavy with jangling coins; he hopes he lives long enough to spend them.

The disk jockey, cooling his bop patter and moving toward the center, has slipped sentimentally into his hayseed act, giving a recipe for crawfish pie, telling a joke about a girl who got run over on the tracks of history ("The track was juicy, the juice was Lucy!"), and loading up his turntable with hillbilly hits by the late and great Hank Williams, tunes appropriate to the occasion like "I'll Never Get Out of This World Alive" and "I'm a Long Gone Daddy" and "Sundown and Sorrow" and

> Hey, good lookin'!
> Whatcha got cookin'?
> How's about cookin' somethin' up with me?

Williams, just twenty-nine, died mysteriously on New Year's Day, about the time the Rosenbergs were granted their stay of execution for the Clemency Appeals, and many wondered at the time whether or not his death in the back seat of one of Uncle Sam's convertible Cadillac super-mobiles might not have been a long-planned Phantom counterattack which had somehow gone off prematurely. "Ever since the coming to this world of the Prince of Peace, there has been peace in the valley!" the Montgomery Baptist Church preacher said at the funeral, standing beside the huge white floral piece that carried the legend I SAW THE LIGHT, and most folks assumed he was talking about Hank Williams. After all, he'd died even younger than Jesus. His small ghostly voice now flows thinly, sweetly, from a hundred amplifiers, filling the warm streets, singing the sun down, drawing the Square and indeed all of midtown America into a kind of hypnotic trance with its doleful messages from the other side . . . "There'll be no teardrops tonight," he sings. "Rootie tootie . . . !"

The trance is broken by the sudden arrival of the city mayor Vincent Impellitteri with a burst of glad tidings: he has just signed into law a bill permitting the sale of liquor in public theaters, and, the whole Times Square area being proclaimed one, *booze is on the way!* Amid the wild cheering, makeshift bars are thrown up by the boys from City Hall, bottles are broken out, orders taken. Tension has been mounting all day, and most everyone can do with a few snorts right now. It is impossible to get within two miles of Times Square by car or van, so ice and paper cups are dropped in by helicopter. The whiskey is replenished by a kind of bucket brigade from the periphery, and in the jubilant and prodigal mood of the moment, there's no need to watchdog the supplies: what some people take for nothing, others gladly pay twice for. The old panhandler can't believe his luck. Not only is he beginning to feel like the Bank of America, but people are setting him up faster than he can toss them down. "Thank ye, son! Need a little somethin' to (*burp!*) warm the ole innards, tain't easy sleepin' out nights in a blizzard, not at my age! *God bless!*" But this is just the old litany, blizzards be damned, he's in fact sweating like a stoat, his coat weighs a ton and scratches his poor hide, and he's beginning to wonder if somebody is finally out to get him for good, cutting the years in half. He starts to lift a tourist's watch, then decides to ask what time it is first, lift it after. "Howzat? Just past five? Well, well, thank ye, sir! Long life!" That's it, then, another six hours and then some before the ball drops—if he doesn't get soused and blow it all, he could leave here a rich man. The watch is gold, but very lightweight—don't make them like they used to. The tourist buys him a whiskey. "Here's spit in your eye, son!" he chortles with a sideways wink at the bartender (one born every day, ain't it the truth!), and tips back his cup. There's a crush around the bar, and a kid behind him buys him a refill. The bartender scratches about for another fifth. "Hey, ye still got almost seven hours to go, johnny!" the old man says cheerily. "Y'ain't gonna have enougha that (*wurp!*) sneaky pete to last!"

The bartender glances at his fob watch. "Naw, just three hours now, old-timer, and it'll be all over."

"*Wha—?!*" Now he's sure they're finishing him off. Sonuvabitch, just when he was striking a real seam at last! He throws down the drink, stuffs the paper cup in his pocket, and decides to work his way out in the general direction of his digs, so he can at least die in his own bed like a proper gent. If he can get through—whew! his pockets are so heavy he can barely move, and he wonders confusedly if he's being treated to some unpleasant moral on the accumulation of capital. This is the worst he's ever seen it!

It's true, they're really piling in now, everybody jamming up together, old and young, great and small, of all creeds, colors, and sexes, shoulder to shoulder and butt to butt, missionaries squeezed up with mafiosos, hepcats with hottentots, pollyannas with press agents and plumbers and panty raiders—it's an ingathering of monumental proportions, which only the miracle of Times Square could contain! And more arriving every minute: workers in dungarees, millionaires in tuxedos, pilots, ballplayers, sailors, and bellboys in uniform, brokers in bowlers, bakers in white aprons tied over bare bellies. Certainly this is the place to be, and anyone who's anyone is here: all the top box-office draws and Oscar winners, all the Most Valuable Players, national champions and record holders, Heisman Trophy and Pulitzer Prize winners, blue ribbon and gold medal takers, Purple Hearts and Silver Stars, Imperial High Wizards, Hit Paraders, Hall of Famers, Homecoming Queens, and Honor Listees. The winners of small-town centennial beard-growing contests have all come, the year's commencement speakers, class valedictorians, and quiz-show winners, the entire Social Register, the secretariat of Rotary International. The Sweetheart of Sigma Chi. Yehudi Menuhin, Punjab, Dick Button, who isn't here? Gary Cooper hoves into view up in the Claridge, wagging his shiny new Oscar from *High Noon* and doing his much-loved toe-stubbing aw-shucks Montana grin for all his admirers, both on the House Un-American Activities Committee and off—he's been one of the top ten box-office draws for thirteen years running now—only Bing Crosby has been loved so long so well. Uncle Sam has provided Coop a special position tonight in a third-floor window of the Claridge where he can both see and be seen, along with other Hollywood stars friendly these past years to HUAC's efforts to shrive and scour Movieland—good Americanists like Jack Warner, Elia Kazan, Bob Taylor, Ronnie Reagan and Larry Parks, Budd Schulberg, Ginger Rogers, George Murphy, Adolphe Menjou. Others, more suspect, like Bogie and Bacall, Lionel Stander, Zero Mostel, and Edward G. Robinson (his true identity, after all, is Emanuel Goldenberg of Bucharest!), are shunted off to the periphery, where they'll be lucky, standing on tiptoes, to see a few distant sparks fly.

Harry James arrives, snaking his band through the thickening mob toward the Hotel Astor, where they've got a gig up on the Roof—their rendition of "Ciribiribin" will be featured tonight during the execution of Ethel Rosenberg. Paulette Goddard's in the crowd, José Iturbi and Consuelo Vanderbilt, John L. Lewis and George Mikan. Esther Williams turns up in her tanksuit, hand-in-hand with the Oscar-winning cat-and-mouse team, Tom and Jerry—and old Mickey Mouse himself is there, too, celebrating his twenty-fifth birthday and elbowing his way through the crowd with Minnie, Goofy, Horace, and the rest of the aging Rat Pack. It's also Eastern Airlines' twenty-fifth birthday tonight, and Captain Eddie Rickenbacker has brought four thousand of his employees to the Square to celebrate it. The deejay, from his prominence, catches a glimpse of the famous bald pate of John Reginald Halliday Christie, the polite bespectacled necrophile, brought over here from London to model for wax museums before his hanging (the Mother Country is still catching on to electricity) next month, and in his honor plays Hank Williams's "Lovesick Blues" and "I Can't Help It." It is said that Christie—who murdered at least seven women, including his wife Ethel, and copulated with their corpses, sent an innocent man to the gallows and earned two commendations as a member of the Police War Reserve for "efficient detection in crime"—was wounded in World War I, just like tonight's Official Executioner Joseph Francel, by mustard gas. Patterns everywhere. Little Reggie, led through the Square by a brace of English bobbies, gazes gently at all the women, leaving a wake of frothy excitement. Some women are frightened, some smile, some faint, some come to orgasm. It's supposed that Dr. Alfred Kinsey, invited here to-night to pursue his celebrated studies into the effects of electrocution upon the erogenous zones, cannot be far behind.

In such a pack-up there's a natural rush on anything cold and wet. Some of the bars near the center are running out of liquor—the bottle brigades are drying up before they get all the way in, so heavy is the demand further out—and there's talk of getting Eddie Rickenbacker to fly supplies in. Ice cream vendors are being mobbed, and nobody cares any more whether it's Cherry-Oonilla or not. Fights break out, ice cream is shoved in faces, bottles shatter, people jab each other with their I LIKE KIKES buttons. Marquees read WE ARE SWINGING ROUND THE CIRCLE and THE FIERY TRIAL THROUGH WHICH WE PASS WILL LIGHT US DOWN IN HONOR OR DISHONOR TO THE LAST GENERATION, while around the Times Tower in electric lights circle the oracles of the American Prophet Gil Imlay . . .

EVERYTHING HERE GIVES DELIGHT * * * SOFT ZEPHYRS GENTLY BREATHE ON SWEETS AND THE INHALED AIR GIVES A VOLUPTUOUS GLOW OF HEALTH AND VIGOR THAT SEEM TO RAVISH THE INTOXICATED SENSES * * * FAR FROM BEING DISGUSTED WITH MAN FOR HIS TURPITUDE OR DEPRAVITY, WE FEEL THAT DIGNITY WHICH NATURE BESTOWED UPON US AT THE TIME OF CREATION * * *

Backstage, Uncle Sam, fresh arrived from his containment exercises out in the receding world, is watching all this ravishment and dignity through a peephole cut in the set for the purpose, the profane muscles of his face in tune for laughter and a merry twinkle in his steel-blue eyes. "Great balls of fire!" he whoops. "This may be the biggest thing since we struck oil at Titusville!" With him are some of the night's key performers, due to go onstage any moment for the early part of the show, as well as a few of the heavyweights up from the VIP subway shelter for a sneak peek at the congregation. Which in its glow and vigor is getting a bit unruly. They seem to have been invaded by a certain anxiety out there, a certain exultation now that the sun has slipped behind the skyscrapers, a giddy sense of being at the edge of something terrific—like a striptease or the end of gravity or an invasion from Mars. There are whoops and screams and loud laughter. People are pressing into the sideshows not so much to see as to join them. Teetotalers elbow frantically toward the bars, shy clerks pinch bottoms and make naughty remarks, tourists forget their cameras, businessmen toss off their jackets, empty their pockets. The police are still managing to keep a semblance of order, but they can't help being a little excited themselves—no matter which way they turn, or how quickly they whirl about, there's always somebody behind them they can't see, goosing them with electric shockers.

The Secretary of Agriculture, up for a glimpse of the festivities, objects piously to all this sensuality. "Pshaw! We need it, Ez—sex'll cause the flame to grow," retorts Uncle Sam. "You gotta plow up a field before you can grow something in it—what in tarnation did you think agriculture was all about, my friend?"

Messengers arrive from the subway station below with roll-call lists: most of the Supreme Court has arrived, as well as hundreds of Congressional leaders and State governors, the members of HUAC and the Senate Internal Security Subcommittee, the Rosenberg prosecution team and jury, J. Edgar Hoover and his boys, the Executioner and Guest Speakers. "Sir, before God and his chilluns, I believe the hour is come," grins Uncle Sam, glancing over the rolls, "to hot up the brandin' arns, open up the gates, and get this ro-*day*-oh under way! Yessirree bob! my judgment approves this measure, and my whole heart is flat in it! *I summon all honest men, all patriotic, all forward-lookin' varmints to my side!*"

There's an excited backstage hustle and bustle, rippling all the way down into the station below. Ties are straightened, pants hitched, drinks drained, hair primped, crotches fiddled, lips licked, brows wiped nervously. This is it.

"Hey, wait a minute!" someone calls out. "Where's Dick Nixon?"

21.

Something Truly Dangerous

The sun was slipping off toward the western horizon, dipping down over the Catskills, as I stepped off the empty train and into the streets of Ossining. I felt a little like one of those beardy desperadoes arriving at a dusty Hollywood cowtown for the final showdown. On the other hand, it was like coming home. Not to Sing Sing, of course, hunkering up on the bluff to my right like some impenetrable medieval fortress, ringed round with its high turreted ramparts (or else like a cluster of friendly red-brick schoolhouses sitting in a sunlit playground—everything seemed double-edged like that since my sudden decision to come here, full of promise and danger at the same time), but to this familiar suburban Main Street with its squat three-story buildings, its scattered fleet of dented Fords and Chevies, its shops and billboards promoting all the recognizable brand names. I didn't know whether I was going to be met by the Sheriff or by Mom and Dad. Or which was the more threatening prospect. The very familiarity of this place could be a kind of bait, I recognized. An elaborate trap. Maybe Mom *was* the Sheriff. Not literally, of course, but she was the one I'd turned away from back there in Penn Station, and if I was walking with either of them now, it was the rebellious and hot-blooded old man, not her. The people streaming past me into the station, rushing for tickets on the southbound trains, might well have been found on the streets of Whittier, all right: middle-aged men in shirtsleeves and suspenders, ladies in unfashionable summer dresses, low-hemmed and sleeves to the elbows, a lone Negro—a trusty maybe—idly sweeping out the station. We had a Negro in Whit-

359

tier, too. What we didn't have out there, though, were all these cops—
they were all over the place, it was like a goddamn military occupation.
All this protection was a relief in a way. But also unnerving, given the
reason for my being here. They might not all agree I was on their side.
Some boys were playing marbles down by the tracks. That was what
Tyler was doing, I recalled, when the Incarnation hit him: playing
marbles. Yes, anything could happen. Or nothing. Very scary, but there
was no turning back. Courage and confidence, I told myself. The valiant
never etc. The choice has been made: now live with it.

I hadn't reached this decision in the calmest of circumstances. In fact
it was just when the horseplay aboard the *Look Ahead, Neighbor
Special* had really started to peak that it had come to me what it was I
had to do. But this was to be expected: in a critical situation it wasn't
supposed to be easy, and I often got my best ideas just when the going
was toughest. We hadn't crashed, as I'd feared, but we hadn't slowed
either—if anything, we'd started screaming along faster than ever, and
the closer we'd drawn to New York, the sicker I'd become and the
wilder the scene around me. The songs had got dirtier, the laughter
louder, people were wandering around a lot, exchanging flasks and getting very playful with each other. A couple of young legal assistants up
at the other end of the car had got into a scuffle that no one had seemed
to want to break up. Girls were squealing giddily. A plump prissy clerk
from the General Accounting Office, strutting fruitily up and down the
aisle in crushed field hat, sunglasses, and corncob pipe, and singing "Old
Soldiers Never Die, They Just Fly Away!", had slipped on some spilt
booze and crashed into the arms of TIME's showman kid brother LIFE,
launching what had showed every sign of becoming an outrageous
romance. Anything to keep LIFE busy. The sonuvabitch had been snapping a lot of pictures, probably for one of those anthropological features, "LIFE Goes to a Party," and the popping flashgun had been
making me very goddamned edgy. The few drunks with any voice left
were singing "Roll Your Leg Over" . . .

> "If all little girls were atomical spies,
> And I were the hot seat, I'd juice up their thighs!
> Oh roll your leg over, oh roll your leg over,
> Oh roll your leg over, the man in the moon!"

What was I to do? I had to think! I knew, if I was to avoid a no-win
policy, I had to launch a counterattack—but how? and against whom?
What I needed was an issue, just one good issue—when you're in trouble
like that, you've got to find an issue and concentrate on *it,* not yourself

—I was back on my own one-yard line, it was time to throw a long one! time to punt and pray! Maybe that was it, maybe I *ought* to pray! My Quaker upbringing and religious experience in the Society of Friends had got me out of tough jams in the past, maybe they'd work for me now! But it had been too goddamn noisy. I couldn't even think.

Young women had gone bouncing around the car as though being tossed by the violent rocking of the train, waggling their boobs and falling into guys' laps, grabbing on to whatever they'd found there. Somehow they'd missed me. They hadn't missed me with the food they were throwing around, though—nor with the bottles of pop they were shaking up and firing off at each other like . . . fire hoses. . . . Oh shit, *I'm sorry about what I've done*, I'd thought, feeling the tears spring on cue to my eyes. That was the play I'd learned to cry in, *Bird-in-Hand*. I'd played the old innkeeper—those lines had come rolling back to me now like an ancient judgment: *I shall be sorry for it till the end of my life!* Ah, that poor old fellow! I knew that coolness—or perhaps the better word for it was serenity—in battle was a product of faith, but this was more than I could take! And all because I believed in the American ideal of trying to do my best, trying harder, wanting to do good in the world, to build a structure of peace! *Oh, I've behaved so as I ought to be ashamed, I know,* I'd wept unprompted as an egg salad sandwich hit the window beside me and splattered into my lap—*but this business 'as pretty near broke me 'eart . . . !*

> "This Communist spy had showbizz aspirations,
> Tonight she will be Broadway's hottest sensation!
> Oh roll your leg over, oh roll your leg over . . . !"

But wait a minute, wait a minute—what *about* all these plays, I'd wondered? We'd all been in them, even Eisenhower in high school at the turn of the century—he'd played the sheeny buffoon in a parody of *The Merchant of Venice* and stolen the show: "Dwight Eisenhower as Launcelot Gobbo, servant to Shylock," the town newspaper had reported, "was the best amateur humorous character seen on the Abilene stage in this generation!" It was as though we'd all been given parts to play decades ago and were still acting them out on ever-widening stages. Tragic lover, young author, athlete, host, father, and businessman—I'd played them all and was playing them still . . .

> "I wish little girls were all Jews from the slums,
> And I were the Judge, I'd blister their bums!
> Oh roll your leg over . . . !"

Yes, and a bum, too, one of my best roles, in George M. Cohan's *Tavern,*
our senior play—and a prosecuting attorney: when I laid my case before
the American people and asked them to judge me, yea or nay, during
the fund crisis last fall, I was in effect presenting them with the climax
of *Night of January 16th.* But the important one—right now, anyway—
was my lead in *Bird-in-Hand!* That play was about the conflict between
political parties, and how love bridged the gap between ideologies. I
hadn't played the lover, of course, that role was long behind me, I'd
been old Thomas Greenleaf, the girl's father who stood in the way: *"But
look here, my girl, class is class, we've always known who was who and
which hat fitted which head!"* But as the villain, I was also the hero, the
bridging took place in me, and I had ever since been the healer of rifts,
the party unifier, the fundamentalist who could perceive the Flux, the
hardliner who knew how to cry . . .

> "I wish little girls were all free-loving Commies,
> And I were Joe Stalin, I'd make them all mommies!
> Oh roll your leg over, oh roll your leg over,
> Oh roll your leg over, the man in the moon!"

And then I'd realized what it was that had been bothering me: that
sense that everything happening was somehow inevitable, as though it
had all been scripted out in advance. But bullshit! There were no
scripts, no necessary patterns, no final scenes, there was just *action,* and
then *more action!* Maybe in Russia History had a plot because one was
being laid on, but not here—*that was what freedom was all about!* It
was what Uncle Sam had been trying to tell me: *Act—act in the living
present!* I'd been sitting around waiting for the sudden inspiration, the
stroke of luck, the chance encounter, forgetting everything that life had
taught me! Like that night I gave myself to Jesus in Los Angeles, I had
to get up off my ass and *move,* I had to walk down that aisle—not this
aisle, of course (I cautioned myself and sat back down), it was too full
of crazy people—but the point was I had to make a commitment and *act*
on it! Deeds, not words: that was Ike's hewgag, but now, unless I wanted
to break my back on the railroad track, I had to make it mine!

This, then, was my crisis: to accept what I already knew. That there
was no author, no director, and the audience had no memories—they got
reinvented every day! I'd thought: perhaps there is not even a War
between the Sons of Light and the Sons of Darkness! Perhaps we are all
pretending! I'd been rather amazed at myself, having thoughts like
these. Years of debate and adversary politics had schooled me toward a

faith in denouement, and so in cause and consequence. The case history, the unfolding pattern, the rewards and punishments, the directed life. Yet what was History to me? I was never one to keep diaries or save old letters, school notes, or even old legal briefs, and I had won both sides of a debating question too often not to know what emptiness lay behind the so-called issues. It all served to confirm an old belief of mine: that all men contain all views, right and left, theistic and atheistic, legalistic and anarchical, monadic and pluralistic; and only an artificial—call it political—commitment to consistency makes them hold steadfast to singular positions. Yet why be consistent if the universe wasn't? In a lawless universe, there was a certain power in consistency, of course— *but there was also power in disruption!* I'd let go of the armrests and, farting liberally, had begun to feel a lot better—though troubled at the same time with the uneasy feeling of having learned something truly dangerous, like the secret of the atom bomb—which was not a physical diagram or a chemical formula, but something like a hole in the spirit. The motive vacuum. And I'd understood at last the real meaning of the struggle against the Phantom: *it was a war against the lie of purpose!*

A secretary had staggered through the aisle on her way to the toilet, and three guys and a woman, shouting, *"PANTY RAID!"*, had tackled her and commenced to rip her skirt off. She'd tumbled hard into the empty seat next to me, giving me a jarring thump, but I'd hardly noticed—I could have been hurt, but I'd given little thought to the possibility of personal injury to myself, not because I was "being brave" but because such considerations just were not important in view of the larger issues involved. The whole nation is falling on its ass, I'd thought, my own career is atrophying, only a wild and utterly unprecedented action will save it, will save them, get things going again! But what?

And then, as they'd dragged the dazed woman out of the seat and spread-eagled her down at one end of the car, it had suddenly come to me what I had to do! I had to step in and change the script! It was dangerous, I knew, politically it could be the kiss of death, but it was an opportunity as well as a risk, and my philosophy had always been: don't lean with the wind, don't do what is politically expedient, do what your instinct tells you is right! As Uncle Sam had once lectured me, if the single man plant himself indomitably on his instincts and there abide, the huge world will come round to him—and my instincts now told me, as down at the far end the secretary screamed, the crowd roared, and the *Look Ahead, Neighbor Special* shot underground and began to decelerate: You must go on up to Sing Sing! You've got to reach them! Promise them anything—first-class passage to Moscow, free time on TV, box seats at Ebbetts Field, a Cabinet post, anything! But get those confessions! Stop these executions! Don't let that show go on tonight! *Hurry!*

In Penn Station, the others—hastily combing their hair, wiping away the blood and vomit—had jumped down off the train and rushed to follow the signs to the Times Square subway trains, but I'd ducked away, found a phone booth, called the Warden up at Sing Sing Prison: "Hello, Warden? This is Vice President, uh, Richard Nixon calling. Are the, the atom spies still up there?"

"Yes, sir. We're keeping them here under guard until the last possible moment."

"Good. I will, ah, be coming up to talk to them."

"You will—?"

"I'm catching the next train."

"I see . . . uh . . . is it clemency, Mr. Nixon?" he'd asked hopefully.

"A new offer," I'd said.

"Boy, you fellows are really keeping the pressure on them, aren't you?"

"Pressure?"

"Well, I mean, since you sent Bennett here a couple of weeks ago, you've hardly let up."

"Bennett—?"

"The Bureau of Prisons Director—"

"Ah." I didn't know about this. "Well, we've, uh, got some new information. Listen, will it be difficult for me to get in?"

"It's all cordoned off, but you should have no trouble passing through."

"No, that's true, but, uh, it's important that I draw as little attention to myself as possible. You know, in case it, ah, all falls through . . ."

"Oh yes . . ."

"Could you arrange to pass me through under some other name?"

"Yes, I could do that. What . . . ?"

"Eh . . . Greenleaf. Thomas Greenleaf."

"Greenleaf. Like the poet . . ."

"That's it."

"Yes, sir, I'll arrange it."

On my way across the glass-domed concourse, I'd spotted a novelty shop, and it had occurred to me that maybe I ought to have a disguise, a beard maybe, like Greenleaf had in *Bird-in-Hand*. No beards in the shop, though—the best I'd been able to find was a cheap handlebar moustache. At the New York Central ticket window, the guy had asked me: "Sure you want on that train, bud? Just runnin' it north to pick up the Albany crowd, wasn't plannin' to stop." That'd be Tom Dewey and his lot—Jesus, what if I failed and had to suffer another one of these goddamn trainrides, and this time with Dewey's bullyboys? Probably have that man-eating Great Dane with him, too. "Yes, hurry it up, I don't want to miss it!" I sure as hell hoped I could pull this thing off.

Hustling toward the train, running all alone against the tide, I'd sniffed hastily at my armpits and wished this place was actually one of those Roman baths it'd been modeled after. It was hot and I'd felt sticky and ugly with sweat. Why do I always perspire so much? "Oh, you work hard at stirring up a good stew," Uncle Sam once told me, "but people *see* you work, they see the sweat drop in the soup." Well, couldn't be helped, a man had to live with his liabilities. I needed a shave, too, a clean suit—I'd be playing out this hand looking more like Beetle Bailey than Steve Canyon, but it would have to do. Hadn't eaten since breakfast, I'd realized. My stomach was churning, my mouth was dry, but I'd recognized these symptoms as the natural and healthy signs that my system was keyed up for battle. When a man has been through even a minor crisis, he learns not to worry when his muscles tense up, his breathing comes faster, his nerves tingle, his temper becomes short—in fact, far from worrying when this happens, he should worry when it does not. And I was also feeling an exhilaration, a sense of release and excitement. The worst, I'd reassured myself, was over. Making the decision to meet a crisis is far more difficult than the test itself. And I had made mine: I was changing trains for the future! I didn't know exactly what I was going to do, but I'd felt I'd found my form again. I understood the Rosenbergs as no one else in the world could understand them—not their families, their children, their co-conspirators, the FBI, not even each other. And out of that understanding I could provoke a truth for the world at large to gape at: namely, that nothing is predictable, anything can happen.

I'd reached the train and had stepped aboard, but I'd suddenly been shaken by a cold chill and had stepped back down: was I making a mistake? The train was completely empty, I'd be all alone. I could see others jumping down off the incoming trains and racing eagerly for the subways uptown, and I'd nearly lost heart. The American people are very volatile. They can be caught up emotionally with a big move, but if it fails, they can turn away just as fast. I always felt guilty whenever I deviated from the majority, and now I was bolting the executive party to boot. But what was the alternative? It was Hobson's choice: certain failure, if perhaps less spectacular and final, up at Times Square—or a possible long-shot breakthrough up at Sing Sing, however hazardous. Maybe I should call Pat, I'd thought, maybe she could help me decide. But what would I say? Anyway, she'd probably left home already—for all I knew, she and the girls might be somewhere here in Penn Station right this minute! Couldn't let her catch me like this, she'd never understand. Saint or no, she could be a real bitch at chewing people out, and right now I couldn't take it, not in public anyway. She was like the good fairy who was all right in her place but wouldn't leave you alone. Besides, the choice, the decision, I'd reminded myself, had already been taken. Had it not? *Had it not?* The whistle had screamed and I'd leapt aboard the empty train, thinking: Oh my God! they've left me alone to do it all!

Once we'd pulled out and started to roll north out of the city, I'd begun to feel better. It always helped to move. Connected me with time somehow, made me feel like things were in mesh. Like that time I came flying back from the Caribbean to find all those microfilms in Whittaker Chambers's pumpkin patch. Or my wedding day when Pat and I struck off for Mexico City, the whole fantastic world out in front of us, time-less, borderless, ripe and golden as the unspecified fortune sought by all of the poor but honest boys of the fairy tales. Motion—even random movements—made me feel closer to reality, closer to God. Not that I ever thought much about God—but I knew what I was talking about. Ask the man in the street and he'll tell you that God is a "Supreme Being." But "being" is only the common side of God—his transcendent side is *motion.* Monks on hilltops know nothing about contemplation, all that's just idle daydreaming. I knew a lot about that, too, I'd spent a lot of time flat out in the back yard staring off into infinity, but I knew you had to keep moving if you wanted to find out who you really were and what the world was all about. It was the real reason I'd always loved trains—not to escape west or east or any other direction like that, but to pull back from the illusions of fixed places so as to make the vital contact. If I'd had time for theology, I might have revolutionized the goddamn field.

It had felt spooky being all alone on the train—the echoey emptiness had seemed to emphasize the essential loneliness of all critical decision-making, to set me apart in some awful way—but I'd been grateful for the chance to relax, take off my hat and sunglasses, my shoes, unbutton and stretch out a little, without having to worry about what other people might think. I'd tried the moustache on. It had felt funny. Stiff. Ticklish. I'd stuffed it in my pocket. It's not enough to break the play open with one face, I'd thought, saving the other one to use later in case it didn't work. If I was going to do this thing at all, I had to do it as Richard Nixon—and not even as Richard Nixon, which was already, even in my own mind, something other than myself, but as just . . . me. I'd realized that in some obscure way, through my contact with the Rosenbergs, even as remote and unintentional as it was, I had somehow become tainted myself—as though I'd had some ancient curse laid on me (though I didn't believe in curses, I was getting carried away by those stories from my childhood, the ones our hired girl used to tell, and by this train, its lonesome whistle, the daydreaming—contemplation, I mean) : in short, I was in a lot of trouble and I'd stay in trouble unless I could somehow absorb this contact, intensify it, and turn it finally to my own advantage. In a sense I was no more free than the Rosenbergs were, we'd both been drawn into dramas above and beyond those of ordinary mortals, the only real difference between us being the Rosenbergs' rashness and general poor judgment—but then wait: if that was so, was my breaking out a part of the script, too? Oh shit! but then—I hadn't wanted to think about this, I'd pushed it out of my mind, forcing myself to concentrate on the Rosenbergs instead, how I was going to approach them, what kind of strategy I might best use, what in the end I wanted out of them.

Julius was the weak one, I knew. I'd start with him, and if he cracked, Ethel would have no choice. This was the great thing about conspiracies: you punch a little hole and a whole flood of accusations and counter-accusations comes pouring out. It would probably break up their marriage, but that'd be their problem. They might be looking for a good excuse anyway. And at least they'd still be alive. When things had died down, they'd probably thank me for it. Not that it would be easy. Weak or no, Rosenberg had had two years to shore up his defenses—all those public declamations: he'd thrown up a real stone wall. Mere reason was useless in the face of it, as were threats or cajolery. He'd repel all frontal attacks, I had to sneak over that wall somehow, catch him by surprise from behind.

So what was the angle? To agree with them maybe about the entrapment, the frame-up? I could tell them I'd been the victim of smear jobs, too, I knew what they were up against. But if we were going to make it work, they had to trust me, they had to tell me everything. Of course, if they really were who the FBI said they were, then we were back to square one again. Or if they were really as innocent as they claimed to be: same problem—I had to have *something* to take down to Times Square tonight. But I was convinced the truth lay somewhere in the middle: the Rosenbergs were guilty of something, all right, but not as charged. And if the Rosenbergs could deliver their half, I could probably deliver mine. The FBI had let the word out in a thousand ways that they had the goods on the Rosenbergs locked away in their files, but their repeated declarations on this subject were themselves cause for suspicion—like the Rosenbergs dropping their *Daily Worker* subscription, it could be read two ways. Those guys over there still hadn't grown out of their gangbusting days and the Junior G-Men Clubs, they'd built up a fantastic image for themselves in that Golden Age, and now it scared them that somebody might catch them in a fuck-up. I'd met a lot of them, depended on them in fact for my inside dope over the years, but I had to say that most of them are pretty far removed from reality. Putting on disguises and snooping about after other people makes them think everybody else is doing the same thing only better, even their fellow agents, they get very paranoid, and that filing system of theirs with all those tedious and intertangled dossiers has got them more cloistered than a bunch of goddamn medieval monks. And in spite of all their files and snoopers and crime labs and privileged access, they still crack most of their cases because some guy rats on another, in effect using the FBI as his own trigger, or because some agent plays a lucky hunch. Maybe just because a guy *looks* like a crook. Or a Commie. This is true. They still believe they can identify criminal tendencies by the bones in the face—they run a regular goddamn seminar down there over John Dillinger's death mask! And Julius Rosenberg had a very unlucky face. He looked like the stoolies, the finks, the unsympathetic first-reel victims of all those old gangster movies—once they saw him, they probably didn't think twice. After which, the dossier grew and grew. Like Pinocchio's nose.

Certainly, through all this, one thing became clear. At the heart of this worldwide conflict and crisis lay a simple choice: Who was telling the truth, the Federal Bureau of Investigation or two admitted Reds? At the trial, in the press, in the appeal courts, there was no contest: for what chance did the Rosenbergs have? Kaufman knew this in advance: every juror at the Easter Trial had had to swear under oath that he'd give the same weight to testimony of either an FBI agent or a member of the Communist Party. Of course this was just bullshit, you couldn't *find* twelve decent Americans who'd believe a Commie as easily as a G-man, it was simply Kaufman's way of protecting himself from a mistrial and assuring the prosecutor of a jury willing to fudge a little, but it showed Kaufman knew what the case would ultimately rest on.

Saypol, free from such scruples, could throw the whole weight of the FBI legend against these ghetto outcasts: "There came a day, however, that a vigilant Federal Bureau of Investigation broke through the darkness of this insidious business . . ." He heaped praises on the FBI. So did Kaufman. So did the President, the press and radio, the Attorney General, the nation's civic clubs and leading politicians . . . and me, too, for that matter. So did the FBI itself in its own frequent and popular press releases. Not even the Rosenbergs' own lawyer could stop himself! What did Kaufman and Saypol really believe? Probably that the Rosenbergs were indeed guilty. Why? Because the FBI said so. Hoover himself had flatly announced the Rosenbergs' guilt in the nation's press, who was going to say it wasn't so? Maybe Edgar believed it all himself, locked away in his inner sanctum, reading all those eager-beaver reports from ambitious agents, fluttering through all those inventories and interviews, surveillance reports and signed confessions. Sometimes the entire FBI file on the case read like a strange remote dialogue between Gold and Hoover—a speaker, reaching for the truth, a hearer, avidly sanctifying the revelations: a sinner and his distant God. At the time of the trial, the newspapers were full of front-page stories announcing that "meantime, the Federal Bureau of Investigation is following other leads on wartime espionage." Saypol hinted that there was a lot of FBI material he wasn't free to use because of these continuing investigations (presumably protecting, for example, some new Herbert Philbrick down in the ranks), but if he could, the stuff would nail the Rosenbergs to the wall, and who in the courtroom or all America doubted this? There probably wasn't one American in a thousand who had even paused to think about it. No, if Irving Saypol held up a handful of FBI reports and told them to imagine Julius Rosenberg "reaching out like the tentacles of an octopus," then an octopus is what everyone willingly saw, surprised only that it had a moustache and wore double-breasted suits.

But maybe they were all wrong. Maybe the case constructed against the Rosenbergs had been a complete fabrication, beginning to end, maybe Greenglass *was* the Herbert Philbrick of this investigation and he'd simply fucked it up, had had to agree to the invented meeting with Gold in order to validate many years of otherwise fruitless effort, save the Old Man's job. Or worse: maybe even the FBI didn't know what had happened. Maybe the whole trial had been just an elaborate smoke screen thrown up by the Phantom to conceal the real ring. Perhaps Gold, wilier than anyone had thought, had surrendered to throw the FBI off the track, and the Rosenbergs, innocent of the spying but in on the cover-up, had constructed their tenacious defense to waste Uncle Sam's energies and draw the FBI into a blind alley. Maybe they were even supposed to have pleaded guilty but chickened out at the last moment—certainly this would explain why until a few months ago they'd been completely disowned by the Communist press and abandoned by their old left-wing friends. So was that it, a calculated deflection? A bit crackpot maybe—or as TIME would say, psychoceramic—but even those clowns over at the FBI had noticed Rosenberg's "quixotic behavior," once they'd shown themselves and let him know they were on his tail: they'd reported that he'd continued to traffic with the very characters who later got arrested with him, had made ludicrously elaborate preparations for other people to escape while lingering on himself, had made all manner of furtive and suspicious moves while at the same time bragging openly to complete strangers about his undercover exploits. The FBI planted informers in jail with him after he was arrested and following his conviction, and even there he kept right on blabbing away. In effect, in order to satisfy themselves he was indeed the man they wanted, they'd had to conclude he was a nut. Maybe he was. That story he allegedly told the passport photographer about Ethel inheriting an estate in France was pretty far out after all, nearly as good as Harry Gold's invented family. Providing Rosenberg had ever actually said such a thing: there were a lot of lively imaginations in the FBI, too. But to me all that "quixotic behavior" looked more like a snow job by a couple of con artists, two experienced actors diverting the overeager G-men's (and later the whole nation's) attention away from the real thing.

In short, they seemed to be taking the rap for somebody else. Yes, I was convinced of this now. Maybe they knew who this somebody else was, maybe they didn't, but this was what I had to find out. I could only guess. Maybe Sobell and Greenglass had talked them into it. Maybe even their supposed antipathy toward David had been feigned, David getting the tragic part, as it were. Maybe *they'd* been conned into thinking such a ring existed and were taking the rap for nobody. Pawns in a Cold War maneuver that only Uncle Sam and/or the Phantom knew about. Maybe their own lawyer was setting them up—Bloch, I knew, was close to a lot of hardline Commie causes and had helped to orchestrate the publicity on the case in the Red press, maybe *he'd* masterminded the whole thing. Whatever the case, they'd convinced me of two things: they weren't who or what the FBI said they were, but they did know something, even if they'd only got it, like me, from a backstage glimpse.

And so that was my handle. Exposure of the FBI in exchange for confessions, a partnership in iconoclasm. I had a lot of contacts over at the Bureau, and I knew what kind of crazy and dangerous place it was—Hoover was in many ways a complete loony, arbitrary in his power and pampered like a Caesar, and if he dreamed up a spy network one day, then by God it *existed*. Doubt was out. It was an agent's job to increase the Bureau's "statistical accomplishments" and "personally ramrod field investigations of 'major cases' to successful conclusions," and never to question the remote wisdom of the Director, and I assumed if we moved fast enough, before they had time to tidy up after all the desperate excitement, we could probably find enough deception and confusion over there to blow this case wide open. The Rosenbergs would have to consider it, I was their last best hope. Might get a lot of their friends in trouble, but it'd be, from their viewpoint, for a higher cause, and so justified. And if it worked, if they talked, and if we went after the FBI and the Justice Department, what then? Could the American people take it? The incorruptibility of U.S. agencies and institutions— above all, the FBI—was an article of faith in this country: could the people brook an attack on that faith? Would they even listen? Well, it'd be risky like all great power plays, might even drive the whole nation into dangerous paranoia, but if it worked I'd have them in the palm of my hand. They'd have to believe in something, and I'd be all they had left, not even Joe McCarthy with his assaults on the Army and the State Department could match it. Even Uncle Sam would have to toe the goddamned line! And it wasn't for myself I'd be doing this, and not even just for the nation. Let's face it, the survival of the whole fucking world depended on us, and I was the only guy in the country who could make it work. And I would, too, I'd give everything I had to it. The government would function, truly function, for the first time since the eighteenth century. Then who could stop us? We could do good wher- ever good needed to be done!

This was not idle dreaming: I knew I could do it. I felt my strength reach out to embrace the globe. I saw statues of myself in Berlin, in Seoul, in Prague, Peking, and Peoria. A universal veneration for the hardnosed but warmhearted Man of Peace, the Fighting Quaker. On horseback maybe (I seemed to feel a horse under me)—or better yet, standing, arms outstretched in a great V, in the back seat of a limousine. All done in black marble. Prizes, medals, titles, special investitures, all that shit—meaningless of course, but the people needed ceremony like they needed proteins, and I'd do my duty in this regard as in all others, even as I understood, better than any other man of my generation could, what children they were. Honorary degrees, too, from Oxford and the Sorbonne, Harvard and Heidelberg—and screw those constipated candy- asses from Duke. I would make war and rebellion physically impossible, and world commerce would flourish with an energy and elegance not

seen since the first trade routes were opened up to China. Naturally I'd
be loved. Priceless treasures would be heaped on me but politely refused: what did I care for the world's wealth in my selfless dedication to
its welfare? Well, a special palace perhaps, not for me of course, but for
Mom and Dad, a gift from the peoples of many nations. I could see it far
ahead, standing high on a bluff over a sleepy river, turreted and bejeweled in the sunlight. It was something like the Mission Inn in River-
side (we'd get the best architects), only more beautiful. I seemed indeed
to be riding a horse, decked out in silver armor, some kind of special
ceremony no doubt, yes, I was coming home, there was a festival in my
honor, bands playing, the people were pouring out into the streets,
singing my praises—but, oddly, the trophy I was bringing them was a
gigantic rubber cigar (or was it the pommel on the saddle?) and high
above me I saw as I rode under it, a mysterious dark tower, long soft
tresses streaming from it wet with blood—

I'd come to with a start: it was Sing Sing Prison I'd been staring up
at! My God, where had the time gone? Must have been dozing! I'd
caught just a glimpse of the place as we'd rolled under it, standing up
there in the afternoon sunshine, much closer and more ordinary than I'd
expected, its heavily manned guntowers looking like little yellow and
green toy castles armed with thick stubby cannons (not cannons of
course, but spotlights)—and then we'd shot below through a tunnel and
a kind of trench and reeled with a wheeze and a screech of steel wheels
on rails into Ossining Station. No time to wash up or piss as I'd planned
—in fact I'd barely had time to shove my feet into my shoes, grab up my
other things, hang on to my pants, and leap down before the empty
train had gone lurching on out of there toward the north. I'd caught my
breath, buckled my belt (this was when that Western desperado feeling
had swept over me), tugged my homburg down around my ears, settled
the sunglasses on my nose, and, pressing through the inrushing crowds,
had stepped out into what—flattening it all out a bit and tossing in a
few pepper, camphor, and loquat trees—might have passed for Whittier, California.

I stood outside the station a moment, getting my bearings, gazing up
what I guessed to be the Main Street. Slightly run-down, quiet, sleepily
cheerful—were it not for all the cops, it would have been a very pleasant place, just the kind of village, updated by a century or so, that old
Rip might have come home to. It was no longer a village, though, not
even a town, but already something new: you could almost feel the place
getting pulled toward the south, sucked into the Manhattan orbit. I
understood such places. The same thing had happened to Whittier: I

went into the Navy from "Ye Friendly Town" and came home three years later to a piece of Los Angeles. People all over America who had lived whole lives in such towns and villages, each with its own character and integrity, were suddenly finding themselves being annexed to once-distant urban centers, tied to the fortunes of the expanding city with all its vice and corruption and foreign faces. And its riches: it was hard to resist. We'd lived through a revolution, my generation had, and here at the middle of our lives we found ourselves uneasily adrift between the poles of some ancient dispute belonging to a generation not our own. Ike's gang. Ike and I had both grown up in small communities, known the smell of pastures and cowdung, the feeling of leaving home to go "out into the world," the hostility and perversity of the cities, but his Abilene was a simple old-fashioned village of prairie peasants, the "Cow Capital of the World," with its legendary cowboy shootouts and its Sunday booze-ups and crapshooting joints at the edge of town, just emptiness beyond. For Eisenhower, everything rural was natural, every-thing urban unnatural, but my generation, however much temporary nostalgia we might feel for such simplicities, recognized that there was something wrong with this black-and-white view, just as with the con-trary idea held by the big-city Brahmins and ghetto provincials that only the cities were civilized, the rest of the country untamed and bar-barous. What was missing was the middle ingredient, the place in be-tween where all the real motion took place now that the old frontier was gone: the suburbs, waystop for transients, and thus the true America. My America. Dwight Eisenhower and Julius Rosenberg would never understand each other, but I could understand—and contain—both. Was this to be my role? To urbanize the countryside and bring the wilderness back to the cities? To lead the New Revolution? To bring the suburb to all America?

I pondered this as I walked up into the town, looking for the best approach to the prison. There were wooden barricades up everywhere, even along the New York Central right-of-way, all entrances manned by Ossining City Police and New York State Troopers. All looking tough, especially the locals, Chief Purdy's boys. I hoped that Warden Denno had spread the word. Spencer Purdy was a guy you didn't fool with. When eight hundred New Yorkers came up here last Christmas to sing carols to the Rosenbergs, Purdy had barricaded all streets leading to the prison, had refused to allow the carolers to leave the area of the railroad station, had secreted five hundred cops, deputy sheriffs, and state troopers in an abandoned wire factory nearby with a fleet of buses assembled to convoy them to any trouble, and as much as possible had kept the demonstrators out in the open, under a bitter icy rain. He'd finally let six of them deposit in the prison parking lot a basket of flowers with a legend reading GREETINGS TO JULIE AND ETHEL FROM THE PEOPLE, but as soon as they'd gone he'd had it carted off by a garbage truck to the city dump. All of which was just a quiet little practice run compared to today's operation. The place was like an armed camp. There were patrol cars everywhere, hundreds of sweating unhappy cops, Coast Guard helicopters rattling overhead. I couldn't see them, but I supposed there were National Guard troops up in the hills as well, PT boats in the river. All of which made me feel very goddamn nervous. I decided to wear the moustache, after all, even if it was in pretty shoddy shape after the ride in my pocket—one side of it kept bending out away from my face.

For a while, I just walked the streets, considering alternatives, angles, practicing my Thomas Greenleaf lines for passing through the barriers (if they asked, I'd tell them I was a salesman, a traveling salesman— which was true after all: our greatest salesman against socialism, isn't that what the party regulars called me?), nervously trying to recall the strategy I'd planned to use on Rosenberg. Something about the FBI, a confrontation. . . . The local residents watched me wander by. I hoped they'd take me for a cop or a reporter. Those not running for the trains were all standing outside their houses in the June heat, listening to car radios. Something about the Rosenbergs. I tried to pick it up: ". . . the Rosenbergs confessed. In Congress, heavily engaged upon major legislative work, the day has been one of anxiety and suspense . . ."

What—? Had they talked? Was it all over? This ruins everything, I thought. Forget it. Turn back now, and you'll still have time to make it to Times Square for the ceremonies. I jerked around and started to run back down the hill. But then I reasoned: if they had confessed, what were all these cops doing here? The Phantom would have no use for the two of them now. I tried to reconstruct the sentence. Lot of possibilities: *if* the Rosenbergs confessed, *had* the Rosenbergs confessed, *whenever* the Rosenbergs confessed—I spun around on my heel again and started back up the street. The moustache blew off and I had to press it on again. People were staring at me now. I tried to cool it. I knew this was the most difficult period in a crisis situation, the period of indecision: whether to fight or run away. It was important not to commit yourself irrevocably to a course of action until you absolutely have to do so. Otherwise you're just shooting from the hip, you can miss the target and lose the battle out of sheer recklessness. On the other hand, I'd already passed through this period, hadn't I? Back at the office? On the *Look*

Ahead, Neighbor Special? In Penn Station? Which period was I in, then? I was very edgy and short-tempered, and I was afraid I might blow my stack and throw a tantrum or something. I thought of my old man, doing everything wrong, raging futilely against the world: I'm no better than him! I tried to tell myself that if I didn't feel keyed up like this, it would mean I wasn't ready, mentally and emotionally, for the conflict ahead, but I was too upset to listen to such bullshit. My stomach was boiling, my nose was running with hay fever, and my need for a toilet was getting desperate.

Back on Main Street, I spied a drugstore and crossed over to it. Get some antacids. Find a john maybe. But when I peeked inside, I saw that the place was full of troopers lounging about in their snappy but grim black and gray uniforms. I ducked my nose into a revolving rack of postcards outside the door: tinted pictures of the Calvary Baptist Church, Jug Tavern, the Half Moon, and a tombstone pierced by a cannonball in Sparta Cemetery. I was trying to think, but my mind was a blank. "Ossining is a Sint Sinck Indian word meaning 'stone upon stone,'" said a card depicting the first prisoners setting up the original old marble cell block, said to be still standing. Maybe that was where they were. No, here was the new Death House. There were postcard portraits of famous local Revolutionary War heroes and Death House victims, complete with their last words. Cartoons, too—crude jokes about the electric chair, last meals, and manacled prisoners fantasizing, pissing on their jailers, being tortured with near-naked girls: "Okay, Miss Ladoo, that'll be enough for today!" A prisoner pulling his pants off on one side of a screen, a visitor lifting her skirts on the other, and a cop dashing up, shouting: "Hold it, Diddlemore!"

Inside, the troopers were sucking milk shakes and horsing around with a young high-school girl behind the soda fountain, elbowing each other slyly, looking bored and horny at the same time. I recognized them. The first team. All suited up. A little kidding around, a little grab-assing, ball-tugging, just loosening up for the big game, no harm meant, no rapes intended. One of them was playing a pinball machine that said HOT STUFF along the top, and on the jukebox somebody was singing "I Dreamed About Mama Last Night." Maybe I should risk it, I thought. They won't even notice me come and go. A caramel milk shake might be just the thing I needed, better even than antacids. Or maybe pineapple. I adjusted my moustache and started forward, feeling uneasy, on the wrong side of things somehow—like that day long ago when I entered a strange drugstore to purchase my first packet of prophylactics and found myself face to face with a man who looked like my grandmother.

That time, in panic, I'd bought a lotion for athlete's foot instead. Today it was an old woman who looked like Herb Brownell. She met me in the doorway and said: "What'll it be, mister?"

"Uh . . . this one!" I croaked, reaching blindly behind me and grabbing a card. I fished for a nickel. "And . . . uh . . . could you tell me, please, the best way up to the, uh, prison?"

"Sure, bud," she said eyeing me suspiciously. She pointed: "Right over, uh, there: uh, Hunter Street." Was she mocking me? Behind her, the cops had stopped joshing the little soda jerk and were staring dully out at me. I pocketed the postcard, thrust a coin at the old lady, and fled, nearly crashing into the side of a passing taxi. Behind me, I heard hard belly laughter, and it made my stomach knot up and my knees quake. But I was on the way at last.

At the entrance to Hunter Street, however, I was stopped cold: "Sorry, mac, visiting hours are over." He was a big potbellied gray-haired cop in a short-sleeved blue shirt, wet in the armpits.

"The Warden's expecting me," I said as gruffly and matter-of-factly as I could. "Greenleaf . . . uh, Thomas—"

"Sure he is, sure he is," said the cop sourly, staring vaguely over the top of my head, as though I were too insignificant to be seen. He had a thick hairy nose and small pale eyes: a German, I supposed.

"Listen," I said, "believe me—"

But the cop was busy with two guys who had come up behind me, wearing straw hats down over their noses, unknotted ties, and carrying big Speed Graphics. They flashed some kind of pass, press cards probably, and the cop let them through. I didn't have one. The next guy did have one, though, and he still didn't get through. "I'm sorry, bud, but we're just too crowded." The man shrugged, we exchanged commiserating smiles.

"Hey, you know that guy?" snapped the fat cop, squinting darkly at me, one hand on his pistol butt.

"Wha—? N-no!" I gasped. I felt like I used to feel around Ola's old man: shabby, obsequious, guilty.

"Who was it?" asked another cop, wandering by with a walkie-talkie.

"Fuckin' *Daily Worker* reporter. He had a lotta fuckin' nerve."

"Judas, I'll be glad when this thing is over," sighed the cop with the walkie-talkie.

The fat cop shrugged heavily and mopped his brow. "A job's a job."

"Yeah, so long as the damned you-know-who don't show up," said the other one.

"The Phantom? Shit, I wish he fuckin' would," snarled the fat cop, hiking his gunbelt. "I'd love to tangle asses with that greasy cocksucker. I bet he ain't half what he's fuckin' cracked up to be!"

"Half's enough," the other one said, giving me a long inquisitive stare. "Who's the dude in the handlebars and funny bags?"

"A crasher. Says his name is Nature Boy."

"Greenleaf," I corrected, but I knew it was hopeless. I could see the prison up the hill at the top of the street, so close and yet so far.

"Thomas Greenleaf?" asked the cop with the walkie-talkie. "It's all right, Frank. The Chief said to let him through. The Warden's waiting for him."

Frank shrugged and waved me by, moving to stop some other guy coming up behind me. Made it after all! I braced my shoulders and strode by them—but then the cop with the walkie-talkie grabbed me as I passed: "Hold on there a minute, pal!"

"Eh? What—?! You said I—"

"It's your moustache," he said, leaning down to whisper in my ear: "You got it on upside down!"

"Oh! Uh, right . . . !" Just as well. It was beginning to itch, and changing it around gave me a chance to scratch. The cops' laughter, though, I could have done without.

It got more congested the further up the hill I went. There were other checkpoints, but they were easier to get through than the first: the weakness of all security systems. Once you cracked the periphery, the rest got easier. But not all that easy. At the prison parking lot, I found at least a hundred and fifty reporters and cameramen, some of whom I recognized, and nearly that many more police, among them the Sheriff of Westchester County, apparently a guest of honor in the cavalcade that would soon transport the Rosenbergs to Times Square. "Anything stirring below, Sheriff?" a state trooper asked him.

"Nope, all quiet," he said. "Nothing but Republicans down there." Everybody laughed. Even I was laughing, it was like someone was pulling my face and shaking it.

"They say there's trouble brewing up in the city," a reporter said.

Somehow I had to find a way past all these guys without being recognized. Access was through a gate in a wire fence behind all these people. There were more guards there, then another heavier gate in a thick wall, the prison beyond that. I'd expected gray blocks of marble—stone upon stone—like an old castle, but most of the walls and buildings in fact were made of brick. Brick and concrete. It was large, but it had seemed larger from below. Impregnable, just the same. And archetypal: probably those familiar hexagonal watchtowers with the peaked roofs gave you this feeling. Just like in the Raft and Cagney movies. You could get nostalgic about this place if you hung around long enough. The guards in the towers were armed and wore dark sunglasses. They seemed very relaxed. They reminded me of the captains of some ships I'd been on. There was some kind of walk up through the chopped granite hillside by the north wall: maybe there was a way in through the back. But one of those towers hovered over the place where the walk began, with a lot of smiling cops gazing down. Not a chance.

I stood for a few uncertain moments in the sun at the edge of the parking lot, near a bank of telephones hanging exposed on a fence there. I reasoned: if somebody comes up to me suddenly, I could duck my head over a phone and give someone a call. I realized I'd probably call Pat. I was sweating heavily and my moustache kept slipping. The sun was dropping over the river: time running out. It was now or never. A couple of reporters turned my way, apparently coming to use the phones. I stepped brusquely out into the parking lot as though heading for my car, then turned on my heel and walked straight toward the gate. My moustache fell off: I grabbed it, clutched it in my fist. My heart was pounding away a mile a minute, but I remained outwardly cool. Courage —or, putting it more accurately, lack of fear—is a result of discipline. Any man who claims never to have known fear is either lying or else he is stupid. I was afraid, all right, I knew a lot was at stake, but I'd made up my mind to do this, and now I had to carry through. I was famous for this, this stubborn carry-through, everyone from my mother to Uncle Sam had noticed it, I probably couldn't do otherwise. But I felt like I'd felt getting into that cage with Sheba. There was a sign at the gate:

DEAD
STOP
END

I felt a rush of activity around me as I bulled forward. People turning to stare. Reporters lifting their cameras. Guards rushing toward the gate. Christ, I thought, afraid to look up at the towers, they might even try to shoot me! I couldn't remember who I was supposed to be. All I could think of was Greenglass, but that wasn't it. I glanced up and saw that on the other side of the fence some guy was barreling straight at me with a magazine held up in front of his face like a mask. In my panic I thought it might be me! That I was charging straight at a mirror! That I'd been inside all the time and was rushing out! But that there *was* no "out"! If life is all free flow, I wondered, bracing myself for this astounding collision, then how do such things happen? And if it is not, then what the hell am I doing here?

INTERMEZZO

Their lips have remained sealed and they prefer the glory which they believe will be theirs by the martyrdom which will be bestowed upon them by those who enlisted them in this diabolical conspiracy, and who, indeed, desire them to remain silent.

—Judge Irving R. Kaufman

We shall never try to placate an aggressor by the false and wicked bargain of trading honor for security.

—Dwight David Eisenhower,
Inauguration Address, January 20, 1953

Human Dignity Is Not for Sale

A Last-Act Sing Sing Opera by Julius and Ethel Rosenberg

Julius Rosenberg, prisoner (tenor)
Ethel Rosenberg, prisoner (soprano)
James V. Bennett, Federal Director of the Bureau of Prisons
   (baritone)
The Warden (bass)
The Turnkey
A Matron

Choral effects, courtesy of *Congressional Records*
   under the direction of
   The Hon. Hale Boggs, Paul Shafer, Edward
   Martin, Overton Brooks, Frank Bow, Clarence
   Kilburn, Morgan Moulder, et al.

SCENE 1

The Sing Sing counsel room at 11 a.m., Tuesday, June 2, 1953. JAMES *is standing near the back wall under a huge diagram, much larger than life, of an electric chair with its various auxiliary elements: a dynamo, excitor, rheostat, volt and ampere meters, switches, attachment sockets, and so on, all of it wired up, labeled, and complete with instructions.* JULIUS *is brought into the room by the* TURNKEY, *who then retires, closing the door behind him.* JULIUS *glances curiously after the* TURNKEY's *departure, since this is the first time he has ever been alone with anyone without an officer or Sing*

Sing official present. JAMES *allows* JULIUS *to do a few anxious turns onstage,
then steps forward to commence the Overture:*

JAMES

(Overture:)   Mr. Brownell, the Attorney General, sent me to see you
  and he wants you to know
  that if you want to cooperate with the Government
  you can do so through me.
  Furthermore, if you, Julius,
  can convince the officials
  that you have fully cooperated with the Government,
  they have a basis to recommend clemency!

JULIUS

(*visibly shocked but struggling to maintain his temper and self-control*)
  In the first place,
  we are innocent!
  That is the whole truth,
  and therefore we know nothing
  that would come under the meaning
  of the word "cooperate!"

	JULIUS	JAMES
(*Duetto*	It isn't necessary	Why, do you know
angoscioso:)	to beat me with clubs,	that I didn't sleep last night
	but such a proposal	when I knew I had to see you
	is like what took place	and Ethel the next day
	during the middle ages!	and talk to you
	It is equivalent	about this matter?
	to the screw and rack!	I was terribly worried!

JULIUS

How do you think we feel, sitting here waiting for death for over two years
when we are innocent?

(Aria:)   My family has gone through great suffering!
  My sister had a breakdown!
  My aged, ailing mother is tormented!
  Our children have known much emotional and mental agony!
  Then you talk to us about this?
  Remember, Mr. Bennett, we love our country!
  It is our home, the land of my children and my family!
  We do not want its good name to be shamed
  and in justice and common decency,
  we should be allowed to live
  to prove our innocence!

JAMES

No—not a new trial. Only by cooperating will there be a basis for commutation. Look here, Julius, you didn't deny that you do not know anything about the espionage.

JULIUS

I certainly did, and furthermore, did you read the trial record, sir?

JAMES

No, I did not, but you had dealings with Elizabeth Bentley.

JULIUS

I never did, and if you read the record, she said on the witness stand that she did not know me and never met me.

JAMES

But you had dealings with Gold, didn't you?

JULIUS

Of course I didn't. Gold also said on the stand he never met me or knew me. You should have read the record to be familiar with the facts!

JAMES

Oh, I read the newspaper accounts of it.

JULIUS

(aside to the audience)
It is interesting to note
how they become convinced
of their own lies
and will not stick
to the trial record of the case!

JAMES

Listen, Julius, I was just sent here, but if you agree, I will bring someone to see you who is thoroughly familiar with the case and you will try to convince him you have cooperated with the Government. . . .

JULIUS	JAMES
(Duet:) What do you want to do?	Look, Julius, Gordon Dean,
Have him convince me	the head of the Atomic
I am guilty when I am not!	Energy Commission,
You want him to put	is a very good friend of mine
ideas in my head!	and if he is convinced
You will only be satisfied	that you have cooperated fully
when I say the things	and told all you know
you want me to say,	about espionage
but I will not lie	he will see the President
about this matter!	and recommend clemency!

JULIUS

(*Aria:*)   Our country has a reputation
to maintain in the world
and many of its friends are outraged
at the barbaric sentence
and the lack of justice
in this case!

JAMES

I know there has been a lot of publicity in the case, but that is not ger-
mane. . . .

JULIUS

(*Aria:*)   You yourself, Mr. Bennett, as head of the Prison Bureau,
You know
     that Greenglass and Gold were together in the Tombs
     for nine months discussing the case,
     studying notes from a big looseleaf book,
     rehearsing testimony,
     talking to FBI agents, the prosecution, and their attorney!
You know this
     because the records of the Tombs will show it,
     and yet your department refused to give us
     an opportunity to subpoena these records to prove this!
You know
     that Greenglass was coached on the A-bomb—sketch testimony,
     both verbally and from notes!
You know
     that the prosecution has exculpating evidence
     that they are withholding from the court!
     In short, we did not get a fair trial and we were framed!
Now you want us
     to admit that this big lie is the truth!
     That we can never do!

The history of our country in freeing war criminals, Nazi and Fascist, in not
putting to death traitors and spies, and yet, for the first time, making the
Rosenbergs the worst criminals in all our history—you know this is not right!

JAMES

But, Julius, I am giving you the opportunity to cooperate!

JULIUS

Sure! Judge Kaufman made a terrible blunder with the outrageous sentence
and he has the bull by the tail and he can't let go!

JAMES

(*as the* CHORUS *enters behind him*)

That's right, Julius! He needs you to help him change this sentence and you can do this by telling all you know!

CHORUS

Judge Irving Kaufman has served with dignity and propriety!

Judge Irving Kaufman is a Jew by birth, by affiliation, and by religious beliefs and practices!

Yet, in this amazing society of ours, a judge of the Jewish faith sentences two spies of Jewish origin for treason!

Americanism triumphed!

Not even the most vindictive anti-Semite can ignore the heartbreak of the judge in this case!

Yet he has, in his own words, been "hounded and pounded!"

Never before has a judge in an American court been subjected to such organized mass pressure!

Even the life of that wise and courageous jurist has been threatened!

Judge Kaufman's life and the lives of his wife and children!

He received so large a volume of vituperative mail that he had to stop reading it!

He was called on the telephone day and night until he stopped answering calls even from personal friends!

And from the left he has been subjected constantly to the bitterest abuse and vilification!

All of whom seemed to view Judge Irving Kaufman as an ogre—

JULIUS

(*interrupting the* CHORUS *with vehemence*)

I cannot bail him out of his mistake, for we never should have been brought to trial!

JULIUS	**JAMES**
(*Duet:*) This pressure on us	The *only* way is for you
is cruel and unconscionable!	to cooperate and convince
The only decent thing to do	the officials in Washington!
is to tell Mr. Brownell	Then, they will have a basis
to recommend clemency—	to ask for clemency—

(*They are abruptly interrupted by the prison bells signaling twelve noon.* JAMES *departs abruptly. The* TURNKEY *enters and leads* JULIUS *out.*)

CHORUS

Instead of trying to save their lives by making a clean breast of their crimes, the Rosenbergs prefer to make a plea for their lives by asking for tolerance!

Why is it that we, who are loyal Americans,
are always being asked to prove that we are tolerant?
Why all this agitation over the Rosenberg case?
Too many violent demonstrations against American justice are being
     tolerated!
The time for suppressing this vicious attitude is long overdue!
National self-protection demands that other saboteurs should not gain
     the impression
that spying is relatively safe or that Communist intimidation can gain them
     immunity!
Any nation has the inalienable right to protect itself and its people from its
     forcible overthrow!
Those who join conspiracies must expect to die by them!

There will be no compromise with treason!

SCENE 2

*Twelve noon, the same day, same scene as before, though a sign explains
that it is now part of the women's wing.* ETHEL *is wandering around with
a tin plate of food in her hand, calmly studying the blown-up diagram of
the electric chair, as* JAMES *enters and announces himself. The* TURNKEY,
who has ushered him in, and a MATRON *present with* ETHEL *slip away,
stationing themselves discreetly at the outer barred gate to the corridor.*
JAMES *repeats the theme of the Overture:*

JAMES
Let me come right to the point, Mrs. Rosenberg!
Attorney General Herbert Brownell, Jr., has directed me to inform you
that he could make available to you any official to whom you might care
to divulge any espionage information you have hitherto withheld!
If you cooperate in this fashion,
the Government stands ready to invalidate the death penalty!
I've been visiting with Julie for an hour,
and now I am anxious to have your viewpoint!

ETHEL
(*Aria, short and sweet:*)   I am innocent,
                    my husband is innocent,
                    and neither of us knows
                    anything about espionage!
                    And if the Attorney General
                    were to send a highly

placed authority to see me,
I should simply reiterate
what I have just stated
and urge that clemency
be recommended to remedy
a shocking situation!

JAMES
(gently, coaxingly)
Let me urge you to cooperate!
It is the only way you can help yourself!
Surely you must know something!

ETHEL
Well, now, how could I when I did not participate in any way? In order to cooperate as you desire, I should have to deliberately concoct a pack of lies and bear false witness against unoffending individuals!

	ETHEL	JAMES
	(evenly)	*(properly horrified)*
(Duet:)	Is that what the authorities	Oh, dear, no!
	want me to do	Of course we don't
	—to lie?	want you to lie!
	Is that what the authorities, etc. . . .	Oh, dear, no, etc. . . .

CHORUS
(intruding angrily upon the scene)
This is the story of two kinds of justice—Russian and American!
In Russia, in any Iron Curtain land, these defendants would have been shot long ago!
In Soviet Russia the Rosenbergs would have been put to death as soon as their crime was discovered!
And as soon as they had been forced by subtle torture to name all their accomplices!
To illustrate the Russian justice, let's look at what happened to Willi Goettling of Berlin!
When will Willi Goettling be tried?
And may he appeal if found guilty?
And ask for a rehearing or a stay of execution?
      Don't be silly!
      They sent Willi
before a firing squad and shot him!
That's Soviet justice in action!
Were the Rosenbergs taken out and shot, as they would have been in Russia?
You know that they weren't!

And yet there isn't a shadow of a doubt as to the guilt of the Rosenbergs!
Justice may be hard but in the nearly three years since they were indicted
the Rosenbergs received far more of it than totalitarianism affords!
Doesn't this make one wonder how an American citizen,
possessing all the rights and privileges we hold dear,
can embrace this doctrine of Communism?

(ETHEL, *disdainful of the* CHORUS, *has been casually eating her meal from
the tin plate. Now, with magisterial aplomb, she presents the plate to the*
MATRON, *then steps downstage and in a clear ringing voice repeats her aria
coloratura as though giving an encore.*)

JAMES
(*interrupting the aria*)
Ethel, the Government claims to have in its possession documents and
statements that would dispute that; so if only you were willing to cooperate,
there might be a basis for a commutation!

ETHEL
(*entirely unimpressed*)
If what they have is so damaging, why do they need me to confirm it, at this
late stage? I will tell you this very bluntly:

(Aria aspro:)   The most powerful Government on earth
has sent its representative
to approach us with a disgraceful proposition,
because it is fully aware
that the convictions were illegally procured,
the sentences vindictive!
And rather than risk exposing
their participation in a rotten frame-up,
and with a double execution
they are anxious not to carry out
only days away,
they have the effrontery to try
to forcibly wring from us a false confession,
by dangling our lives before us
like bait before hapless fish!
> Pay the price we demand,
> or forfeit your lives!

JAMES
(*hastening to stem the rising tide of her indignation*)
Come, come, I have not said anything of the sort, you are misinterpreting
me!

ETHEL
On the contrary, I have understood you far too well. So here is our answer:

(Aria nobile:)   We will not be intimidated
by the threat of electrocution
into saving their faces!
Nor will we encourage the growing use
of undemocratic police-state methods
by accepting a shabby,
contemptible little deal
in lieu of the justice
that is due us as citizens!
That is for Hitler Germany,
not for the Land of Liberty!
A truly great, truly honorable nation
has the obligation to redress grievances,
not to demand tribute
of those who have been wronged
for grudgingly sparing their lives
—lives that should never have been
placed in jeopardy at all!

(JAMES *is beginning to flounder in earnest now, the mask of nonchalant authority slipping, revealing his very real discomfiture.*)

JAMES

But we are trying to help you by seeking your cooperation!

ETHEL
(*unmoved*)
Say what you will,
camouflage it,
glamorize it,
whitewash it,
in any way you choose,
but this is coercion,
this is pressure,
this is torture!

(*She points to the clock cheerfully ticking away her life.*)

Let me say to you in all sobriety you will come to me at ten minutes of eleven p.m. on Thursday, June 18, and the fact of my innocence will not have changed in the slightest!

JAMES	**ETHEL**
(Asides:) She must be crazy	I feel sorry for him!
to reject life	Just another cog in a wheel,
when it is there for the	doing a lousy thankless job!

taking!
Ar-r-humph!
—for a price, of course!
Nevertheless
one has to respect
her stand!

Wanting so desperately
to convince me that he is impartial
and finding it increasingly difficult
to maintain an untenable position
against a virile and dedicated
honesty!

JAMES
(*throwing up his hands in despair, calling for the* TURNKEY)
Bring Mr. Rosenberg in, please!

CHORUS
(*while awaiting* JULIUS's *entrance*)
All this has taken place in no atmosphere of hysteria or ferocity!
It has been a cold judicial search for the right course!
The first issue was whether wartime treason was to be condoned!
The Rosenbergs betrayed their country in the most vicious possible manner!
Their crime was one of the most heinous in American history!
Mrs. Rosenberg asked that her life be spared
so that she might see her sons grow to manhood!
This plea was made in the face of the fact that by her actions
Mrs. Rosenberg has sent sons of many American mothers to their deaths
    in Korea
before they could reach the full flower of manhood!
In Korea there are 24,214 American dead, who died largely because of
    the Rosenbergs!
Without American atomic secrets the Communists would never have dared
    risk war in the Far East!
There is always the possibility
that Soviet Russia may unleash
a surprise atomic attack on the United States
to wipe out hundreds of thousands of lives
and destroy military potential!
The Rosenbergs committed an enormous crime
against the 150 million people of the United States!
—Indeed against all free peoples!
We are sorry for the young sons of Julius and Ethel Rosenberg!
But we can find no tears for their parents!
They should have died months ago!

(*The time is 12:30 p.m. when the* TURNKEY *ushers* JULIUS *in. The Overture
is struck one more time, as though through an echo chamber* . . .)

JAMES
Now let me entreat you once more to cooperate!
I even promise to enlist the aid of my good friend,
Gordon Dean, Chairman of the Atomic Energy Commission!

JULIUS
(wonderfully poised and forthright)

(*Aria:*) How can America stoop to such tactics
and hope to command the continued respect
and affection and support of our friends!
It is simply unthinkable!
How can this nation afford to let
such villainy go unchallenged
and be indelibly recorded
to the everlasting shame
of incoming generations!
Just imagine!
Even if it were true and it is not,
my wife is awaiting a horrible end
for having typed a few notes!
A heinous crime "worse than murder," no doubt!
and deserving of the extreme penalty!
while the most atrocious and wanton killers
known to civilization,
the Nazi war criminals,
are being freed daily!

(*Ensemble:*)

JAMES	ETHEL	JULIUS
What you're saying is not germane. Please, if you would only agree to cooperate, something could be worked out! There just won't be any other way! (*Repeat*)	Of course, a hearing based on new evidence is not germane! After all, we might actually be able to prove our claims! But it is germane for the Government of a great nation to victimize two helpless people just because a world controversy has developed as to their guilt, and to tell them in effect "to knuckle under or die!"	Wouldn't it be more advantageous to the United States to let us live? Doesn't your coming here at the behest of the Attorney General indicate that the handling of this case has cost us a good deal of prestige on the other side? Obviously, it would be much less costly to give us the opportunity to prove our innocence!

(JAMES *turns away wearily as the* WARDEN *enters. It is 1:00 p.m.*)

WARDEN
What is this all about?

JULIUS

Mr. Brownell sent Mr. Bennett to tell us if we cooperated with the Government he would recommend clemency to the President.

(*Aside to audience:*)　You will note that
the Warden was not present
when the offer was made!

JAMES
(*to the Warden*)

Please expedite any messages they might care to send me!

(*Aria:*)　Good-bye, Julius!
Good-bye, Mrs. Rosenberg!
(*He turns to go.*)

ETHEL

(*Aria da capo:*)　Grant us our day in court, Mr. Bennett!
Let us live that we may prove our innocence!
That's the decent way, the American way!

(JULIUS *is led some distance away.* JAMES *watches* ETHEL *a moment, then follows* JULIUS *until they are out of earshot of* ETHEL.)

JAMES
(*in a stage whisper*)

Your only hope, Julius, lies in cooperation! Let me bring some people who are familiar with the case and you can submit to answering questions of what you know about this!

JULIUS

Why, this would be like "brainwashing," Mr. Bennett!

JAMES
(*timidly*)

Well, could I—would you like me to come back another time?

JULIUS
(*pointedly*)

Yes, if you can bring me some good news!

(JAMES *exits.* JULIUS *crosses to* ETHEL *for their final duet sequence, the* WARDEN, *the* TURNKEY, *and the* MATRON *forming a silent trio in the background.*)

JULIUS

Our very lives and most cherished principles are at stake here,
and I am glad we met the test well!
I feel strongly that it is our sacred duty
to expose the police-state methods that are being practiced!
Because we are fighting for a just cause our spirits are high,

but at the same time our lives are in very great jeopardy!
Of course the storm is getting greater
but I know we'll ride through this storm in good shape!

JULIUS

Therefore, my sweet,
I can't help admiring you
and telling you over and over again
that you are a great noble woman
—which in fact you are—
and certainly a very charming person at that!
I guess it will not be amiss
if I say I love you most dearly!
Therefore, my sweet, *etc.*

ETHEL

Darling, my darling!
How truly I love you!
And how much
I long to possess
the remarkable qualities
you attribute to me,
and to be worthy of all
that you are yourself!
Darling, my darling, *etc.*

JULIUS

(*Recit.:*) There is great danger in our land if this Fascist stuff is not stopped now! The great difficulty is, that by their control of the mass media of information, they are continuously in small doses "brainwashing" the readers and listeners about our case and the public is misinformed!

ETHEL

The lame attempts
of the Justice Department
to "brainwash" the public on
  an issue
that has been the main burden
of a sickening refrain
for over two long years,
brings to mind
Iago's cynical assertion:

  "Bravery's plain face
  is never seen till used!"

JULIUS

How big can the lie get
and how much deceit are they
  capable of?
Events are happening
at an increasing tempo
and we must continue
to look to each other
to find the strength and courage
to stand up to the terror!

  United in love and spirit
  we will be successful!

ETHEL

You must tell them, Julie: we are the first victims of American Fascism!

JULIUS
(*addressing the audience*)

(*Appassionato:*) The courts are mere appendages
to an autocratic police force!
The rights of defendants
and the protection of the Constitution
no longer operate!
These are the plain facts!
It is happening here!

Yesterday, the U.S. Marshals were up to serve us with papers setting down our executions for our fourteenth wedding anniversary, June 18, eleven p.m.

JULIUS	ETHEL
My wife and I are to be	Seriously,
horribly united in death	this is political prosecution,
on the very day	shameless, blatant, cynical!
of our greatest happiness,	But it must not be
our wedding day!	a cause for pessimism!
When, oh when	It is the relentless struggle
will our agony be over	to live life
and how soon will we see some	that defeats death!
daylight?	

JULIUS
(tenderly)
Honey dear, the Sunday issue of The New York Times
  had an excellent editorial on the essence of June,
  with particular emphasis on the physical beauty
  of the lush green around us! This month was ours!
  Because then we were united as husband and wife
  and found the boundless joy of a flourishing beautiful relationship!
  Precious noble woman, even to the end,
  I am completely devoted to you!

ETHEL
My darling husband—!

(They move to embrace, but are separated by the prison officials. There is an anguished pause.)

JULIUS
(to the audience, with sudden intensity)
WHAT WILL BE THE ANSWER OF AMERICA TO ALL THIS?

(JULIUS and ETHEL are led out through separate exits by the TURNKEY and the MATRON, respectively. The WARDEN studies the diagram a moment, then checks his watch by the clock on the wall. He exits, in fading lights, through a door with a sign above it. A lone spotlight lingers momentarily on this sign, which reads: SILENCE.)

CURTAIN

PART FOUR

FRIDAY NIGHT

22.

Singalong with the Pentagon Patriots

"Between the dark and the daylight,
When the night is beginning to lower,
Comes a pause in the day's occupations,
That is known as the Children's Hour . . ."

sing the multitudes massed in Times Square—they are enjoying an old-fashioned singalong, led by Oliver Allstorm and His Pentagon Patriots, a bit of commemorative showbiz hoopla to honor the setting and get the night's entertainment under way. "I hear America singing, the varied carols I hear," cries Uncle Sam, peering out on the Sons of Light from backstage. " 'Tis grand! 'tis solemn! 'tis an education of itself to look upon!" The Patriots are decked out in bright star-spangled Yankee Doodle outfits, complete with macaroni and bloody bandages, reminiscent of the uniforms worn by Nelson Eddy in *The Chocolate Soldier,* by George Washington in the French and Indian Wars, and by Bojangles Robinson when he danced with Shirley Temple. A bit far out maybe, like the Patriots themselves, not the sort of gear the nation is accustomed to seeing in its nightclubs and churches—you'd never catch Percy Faith and His Orchestra rigged out with so much pomp and flash—but the crowd seems to enjoy it, seems to like the excitement the Patriots generate, and they all sing along with open-faced enthusiasm, full throated and glad hearted . . .

"There's a building in Noo Yawk
That's sixteen stories high,

And every story in that house
Is full of chicken pie . . . !"

The starred, barred, and booted Patriots bounce merrily about the electrocution-chamber mock-up with their fifes and drums like court minstrels for a king who's not yet come to sit his throne, leading the jubilant citizenry through the good old songs of yesteryear, songs their mothers taught them, the hands of mem'ry weaving the blissful dreams of long ago. They recall heroes and hangings, grief and grace, traitors and liars and bloody battles, city lights and purple shadows. They are ecstatic, somewhat drunk as well. They haven't forgotten the Phantom— indeed, rumors circulate even now of riots and uprisings around the world—but somehow the rest of the world is growing more distant, there's the feeling that it's all happening here, here in the street where the whole world meets, on the avenue I'm takin' you to, Forty-second Street . . .

"In the middle,
In the heart of little old New York,
You'll find the crowds all there!
In the middle,
It's a part of little old New York,
Runs into old Times Square . . . !"

The sun has hunkered down behind the Paramount Building on its way to Hoboken, but though elsewhere shadows fall and trees whisper day is ending, here the day seems to reverse itself and brighten again toward high noon, so starry bright is the Great White Way. It's a real Old Glory blowout! The stage where the Patriots work (they've drawn together now, barbershop-fashion, and along with all the others are crooning a set of gentle oldies . . . "Now Is The Hour" . . . "The Farmer Comes to Town" . . . "Let the Rest of the World Go By" . . .) is spotlit; the VIP area, empty still, is bright as a ballpark; newsmen's flashguns pop like Fourth of July fireworks; multicolored electric arrows dart relentlessly at floodlit theaters and hotels; and vast neon spectaculars hawk everything from Planters Peanuts to patriotism, campaign quips to Kleenex: all direct and glaring evidence of the sheer *power* of Uncle Sam and his Legions of Light. The name of the Square itself is picked out in lights atop the Times Tower twice, once in Old English for the origins of the nation and once for its progress in modern sans-serif, and up and down all the streets as far as the eye can see, marquees and billboards glow with apothegms from the Prophets and the Fathers . . .

CHEER UP, THE WORST IS YET TO COME!

WHAT THE PURITANS GAVE THE WORLD WAS NOT THOUGHT, BUT ACTION

SIC SEMPER TYRANNIS!

THIS WORLD IS BUT CANVAS TO OUR IMAGINATIONS!

The Paramount Building has spread an all-electric United States flag across its broad façade, incorporating its starry-digited clock in the blue field like a bittle bit of heaven, reminding oldtimers of the moonclock Al Jolson sat in with Ruby Keeler to sing to her "About a Quarter to Nine," while over the Elpine Drinks counter on Forty-sixth Street, a gigantic flashlight, powered with Evereadies—"the battery with Nine Lives"—shines on a Kodak ad that says: "You press the button, we do the rest!"

EVERYTHING IS FUNNY AS LONG AS IT IS HAPPENING TO SOMEBODY ELSE!

The U.S. map between the two four-story-tall bodies atop the Bond store (tonight figleafed with flags: a Dixie diaper for the woman, and "Don't Tread On Me!" coiled around the man's joint) is bejeweled coast-to-coast with flickering red-white-and-blue bulbs, giving the appearance of an entire nation boiling over with excitement. There are no dark corners. The singing celebrants, their minds full of old revival meetings, busrides, campfires, and beer blasts of the past, stand in pools of luminous shadows, as though steadfastly afloat in a river of light, while overhead, searchlights sweep the fading sky as beacons to the gathering tribe, traditional signals of a Broadway opening, a casting out of demons, a World Premier, a Tent Chautauqua, a Night among the Stars . . .

> "Bring the good old bugle, boys, we'll sing another song;
> Sing it with a spirit that will start the world along,
> Sing it as we used to sing it—fifty thousand strong,
> While we were marching through Georgia . . . !"

They're all whooping their hearts out as they plunge headlong, hand-in-hand with Oliver and the Patriots, down memory lane—which is, itself, from sea to shining sea a marvelous and unending labyrinth: through the streets of Laredo, across the wide Missouri and up Springfield Mountain, over the Old Chisholm Trail on the sunny side of a winter wonderland, in and out of Chattanooga, Detroit City, honkytonk heaven and the Durant jail, up the Brazos, along the E-ri-e, and down by the old mill stream, just travelin' along, singin' a song, side by side . . .

> "Some folks might say that I'm no good,
> That I wouldn't settle down if I could,
> But when that open road starts to callin' me,
> There's somethin' o'er the hill that I gotta see!
> Sometimes it's hard but you gotta understand:
> When the Lord made me, He made a ramblin' man . . . !"

So hand me down my walkin' cane and let us go then, you and I, beyond the sunset, the river, and the blue, down to that crawdad hole above Cayuga's waters, travelin' on down the line from out the wide Pacific to the broad Atlantic shore, over hill, over dale, up a lazy river and down the road feelin' bad, dashing through the snow on a bicycle built for two to catch the night train to Memphis, comin' round the mountain on a wing and a prayer and tramp! tramp! tramp! leaving the Red River valley white with foam to walk in the King's Highway down Moonlight Bay, prospecting and digging for gold . . .

> "Thro' many dangers, toils and snares,
> I have already come!
> 'Tis grace hath bro't me safe thus far,
> And grace will lead me home . . ."

. . where the buffalo roam and the whangdoodle sings way down upon de Swanee Ribber with the greatest of ease, then a turn to the right (every road has a turning), a little white light, and it's off for Montan' on the driftin' banks of the Sacramento, up Sourwood Mountain, over the rainbow, round the rosie and Hitler's grave mid pleasures and palaces, down to St. James' Infirmary on the trail of the lonesome pine, and back to ole Virginny in the State of Arkansas, that toddlin' town where sunshine turns the blue to gold in the shade of the old apple tree—then whoa, buck! open up that Golden Gate 'cause it's back in the saddle again and glide 'cross the floor while the dew is still on the roses, struttin' with some barbecue up Blueberry Hill on the lone pray-ree, bound for the promised land . . .

> "I've been to the East, I've been to the West,
> I've traveled this wide world around,
> I've been to the river and I've been baptized,
> And now I'm on the hangin' ground, oh boy!
> Now I'm on the hangin' ground . . . !"

And here on that ground they stand, all these natural-born ramblin'
men, traveling salesmen, driftin' cowboys, these knights of the road and
brave engineers, rovin' gamblers, easy riders, and wayfarin' strangers in
paradise, slap up against each other as thick as hasty pudding, jiggling
about in unison (they all got rhythm), elbow to elbow and belly to butt,
to the beat of the Pentagon Patriots. They watch the clocks tick away the
last of the Rosenbergs' time on this earth, and, voices raised on high, feel
the heat rise, the light brighten, their own pulses quicken. The political
bigwigs have not come out yet, but celebrities, preachers, warriors, and
millionaires are popping up all over, picked out in the roaming spots of
the camera crews, and they're greeted with tumultuous democratic
cheers: he too! even he is here tonight! Dale Carnegie! Ty Cobb! Gordon Dean! Admiral Bill Halsey and Hank DuPont! Ezio Pinza, Connie
Mack, Cole Porter—and America's answer to Michelangelo, James
Montgomery Flagg! Some duck shyly away when discovered, some wave,
others take a turn onstage with the Patriots, now swinging into one of
their Electrocution Night specials, Lu Ann Simms's current smash hit,
"It's the End of the Line"—"It's all over but the blues!" they groan,
and the place goes wild.

Underground meanwhile, in the closed-off Times Square subway
station, Uncle Sam is busily sorting out the official celebrants and lining
them up for the procession to come: first the legislative branch, which
passed the operant laws, then the judiciary, which has brought the
convictions, and finally the executive branch, whose task it is tonight to
pull the switch: not even during the frenzy of such a grand national
festival as this one does Uncle Sam miss the opportunity for a little
civics lesson. He glances about impatiently for the missing Vice President. "Hark! For his voice I listen and yearn; it is growing late and my
boy does not return!"

"My sources indicate he was on the afternoon train," reports J. Edgar
Hoover of the FBI, and Allen Dulles of the CIA concurs: "Maybe the
rube got lost on the subways."

"C-r-e-a-t-i-o-n!" growls Uncle Sam. "Nature never makes any blunders, when she makes a fool she means it!" He is irate, but oddly there
is a frosty twinkle in his eye. Tipping his plug hat threateningly down
over his eyebrows like a Marine corporal's, he turns on the Boss of the
FBI to snap: "Goddamn it, Speed, what're ya just standin' around here
for? You better *find* that rapscallious young giddyfish and haul him
back here in three double quick time, or cuss me if I don't wool blue
lightnin' outa your nancy-pantsy fanny! I can drag my boots and hold
the earth back a notch or two, but it's got a slick axle and I can't grip it

to a standstill! So get that snoot in the dirt, houn'-dog! If we don't pull that switch before the sun goes down, I wouldn't risk a huckleberry to a persimmon that we'll *none* of us see it whistle up again!"

"I hate to see that evenin' sun go down when day is done and all de worl' am sad and dreary," sing the multitudes up in the Square as though in antiphonal response, but sad and dreary nothing, they're all atremble with joy and anticipation, awaiting the climax of the ceremonies with such fierce eagerness—goldurn! it's a big night, Maude!—that the minutes seem to crawl by like hours. The jam-up makes it hard to shift about now so the boys from City Hall are working the crowd like church ushers, passing community bottles up and down the lines. Eisenhoppers are bounding and squeaking, toy chairs smoking, Fourth of July firecrackers popping. "As John Brown once said," says Uncle Sam, come up from below to watch the proceedings, "this *is* a beautiful country! *Ubi libido ibi patria!*" He signals and Oliver Allstorm and His Pentagon Patriots, illuminated now by weird red, white, and blue flashing lights and supported by the Radio City Rockettes, fan out across the stage to lead the people in their last big number of the night, the hit that has made the Patriots famous and assured their immortality: "Julius and Ethel Rosenberg, Traitors to the U.S.A., Must Die" . . .

> "This man and wife, this guilty pair
> Must die in the Electric Chair,
> So rang the Judge's fervent Cry
> These traitors are condemned to die!
> And burn for treason, guilt and shame,
> So let us note each traitor's name—
>   Julius Rosenberg
>   And Ethel Rosenberg
>   Both tried to sell
>   America to
>   A Russian hell . . ."

Threading her way now through the dignitaries, comedians, musicians, evangelists, and police detachments backstage, dressed in a dark suit with lace frills, a crisp white handkerchief in her breast pocket and her graying hair neatly but not severely combed back, comes General Mills's famous daughter Betty Crocker, hostess for the VIP processional to follow. Uncle Sam greets her with an ebullient wave of his star-spangled plug hat—"Let Grandmaw through there!" he shouts—and invites her to share his peephole.

She bends over stiffly to peer out, and what she sees out there is a terrible excitement, an impressive agitation: thousands upon thousands of people, singing at the top of their lungs, most of them well beyond either sobriety or modesty, led by a noisy group of musicians, even more rambunctious and ostentatious than Rudy Vallee and his Connecticut Yankees, and though they're singing about "cooking" and "frying," she certainly doesn't recognize it as a recipe from *her* cookbook! Goodness! Fights are breaking out here and there in the heat of the packed masses, hard liquor is being passed about freely, girls are kicking their bare legs high in the sky, and there's a lot of rude behavior—but there's a *positive* excitement out there, too. She sees flags being unfurled everywhere, patriotic lighting displays, fireworks, Red Cross teams rushing through the crowds with bromides, film crews hovering from derricks and lifts, capturing it all for posterity, which Betty, like all Americans, believes in. Every window of every building looking out on the Square is packed with happy cheering people, even the rooftops, and the billboards and theater marquees bear impassioned messages like NEW YORK, THY NAME'S DELIRIUM! and LET NO GUILTY MAN ESCAPE! and WHAT A SWELL PARTY THIS IS! "My sakes," she remarks, squinting out through the peephole, "it's getting a bit wild, isn't it?"

"Yes, honey," laughs Uncle Sam, "there yam a dignity, a majesty, a sublimity, in this last act of the Patriots, what I greatly admire! We ain't had so much as a skumpy lynching in this land o' hope and glory for a year and a half, there's a real bodacious belly-wringin' appetite up! You feel it, too? O, it sets my heart a-clickin' like the tickin' of a clock . . . !"

> ". . . Now should this pair outwit the law
> And wriggle from death's bloody maw;
> An outraged nation with a yell
> Shall drag them from their prison cell
>   And hang them high
>   Beyond life's hope,
>   To swing and die
>   And dangle from
>   The Hangman's Rope . . . !"

"But aren't they a little bit . . . well . . . extreme?"

"Don't worry," smiles Uncle Sam, stroking her pastry-fattened thighs. "This is their big moment, but they won't last the night out."

> ". . . Then, while the buzzards make a feast
> On their Red flesh as on a beast;
> Our natives shall rejoice and sing

And shout while these two traitors swing,
And freedom's cry shall soar and swell
With songs that echo—'All is . . .' ' "

"Well," quoth Uncle Sam as the Pentagon Patriots swing into their final chorus, "the ole Doomsday Clock on the wall tells me it is the hour of fate and the last full measure of devotions, so step up, all you screamers—it's outa the strain of the Doing, and inta the peace of the Done!" Besides all the preachers, comics, and politicians crowding backstage with Uncle Sam, there are also scores of actors, dressed up as American Patriots and Presidents, Pilgrims and Pioneers, famous Warriors, Broncbusters, Prophets, Prospectors, and Railroad Barons, all part of the pageant to come. "You are about to embark upon a great crusade, my children, toward which we have strove these many months, so make sure your fly's buttoned up and your seams are straight! I wanna see a lotta hustle tonight—when your name is called up there I want you to *move!* Let the catamount of the inner varmint loose and prepare the engines of vengeance, *for the long looked-for day has come!*"

". . . So when the Rosenbergs lie dead
Wrapped in a shroud of Kremlin-red;
All future traitors should beware
They, too, will burn within the 'chair . . . !' "

23.

The Warden's Guided Tour

The Warden led me down a path through a garden by a house. His apparently, very nice. The sun was dipping low over the Hudson; not so hot now, and there was a breeze off the river. The gun towers were momentarily out of sight, and looking down through the trees toward the river, what I saw was a baseball diamond. Next to it, a tall stack was belching smoke into the pale blue sky. The trees were full of birds. There was even a prison bird-watching society, the Warden told me. Hilly and Dilly Hiss would have enjoyed themselves here, Whittaker, John McDowell, all those ornithological nuts.

"Ever see a prothonotary warbler?" I asked.

"A what?"

My stomach was still tight as a knot, but I didn't feel all that displaced here, now that I'd made it inside. All in all, it wasn't as hostile a place as I'd anticipated. Pleasant even, in its way. I'd always liked cells, whether it was bell towers, library cubicles, or private inner offices. A sweaty animal odor seemed to pervade the place, but you could probably get used to it after a while. Might even get to like it. Like the Whittier locker rooms, the Duke gym. I had the sensation in here of having escaped something wild and unpredictable outside, of having found a peaceful corner in a wound-up and turbulent world. On the other hand, I'd shifted rather heavily back into being the Vice President again, and was therefore beginning to have serious second thoughts about this whole project. Did I really want an out-and-out confrontation with the FBI? What did they know over there about *me?*

"Yes, made from marble quarried right here at the prison . . ."

"Ah . . ."

As we went along, the Warden told me about the age and peculiar architectural features of the different buildings, the improvements made, prisoner capacity, the recreational and religious facilities, famous landmarks and prisoners of the past, basic prison industries, hospital services, ideas for the future. I took it all in, smiling or scowling as seemed appropriate, asking occasional questions, but all the time working out my strategy for breaking the Rosenbergs while protecting myself. "This is a much bigger place than I'd imagined," I said, just as a back-up plan occurred to me: if all else failed, I could attach myself to the police cavalcade south to Times Square, and thus be seen to be bringing the Rosenbergs to justice myself, as it were.

There were guards everywhere—around the gates, up in the towers, along the stone embankment that climbed the mountain to the east, on patrol here in the compound. Most of them in short-sleeved shirts, ties but no jackets, less spiffed up than Purdy's boys or the state troopers, but just as unfriendly. The Phantom would need one hell of a disguise to get through this army, I thought. In fact, I'd nearly lost my nerve again at the gate, I'd been half afraid one of them might get trigger-happy and let me have it, but instead I'd been whisked right through to the Warden. Doors clanking open and shut like applause. Easy as pie. Just a few gestures, the right word, a nod—there was a kind of sub-language working here, just under the surface, shared by keepers and kept alike, and if you knew the code, life was relatively easy. I'd even lucked out and escaped the attention of the newsguys. A lot of them out there knew me, but they'd been distracted by that guy coming at me as I was coming in, the one with the magazine up in front of his fedora: it had turned out that that was David Rosenberg, Julie's brother. He'd come up for a last farewell, but too late: visiting hours were over, they hadn't let him in. And as he'd been ushered out, the reporters and photographers had swarmed around him, missing me. It's moments like that that convince me I lead a charmed life, even though I don't believe in such things.

"Well, I'm afraid the Rosenbergs haven't given you the press in their letters that you deserve," I said as we crossed over the railroad tracks I'd just come up on from the city. We were walking toward the river, the Death House was down there, almost on the edge. Why hadn't the Rosenbergs mentioned the river in their letters? The sounds, the smells, the images of freedom it offered up? "I suppose you'll be glad to get rid of them."

"Not this way," said the Warden simply but firmly, and I felt the back of my neck flush. He could be very direct when he wanted to. Like Grandma Milhous.

"I mean, the nuisance, the, uh, constant pressures . . ."

"We can't complain. They've been cooperative for the most part and in their own way they've tried to add to the life of the prison. They seem to be people who above all want to be liked and who have a very strong sense of community values. They don't exactly fit in, but they work hard at it. They've kept their cells clean, almost homelike, and have been almost overeager to please. Their one real problem has been . . . well, something we've not had much experience in dealing with."

"The argumentation. The bookishness . . ."

"How's that? Bookishness? No, I don't know what they write in their letters about that, but they don't read very much. Less than most of our prisoners, to tell the truth. We've provided them with plenty of books and magazines, but they don't seem to do much reading. In fact they don't do much of anything for any length of time, but then this is typical of a lot of our condemned prisoners." We seemed to be in some kind of courtyard or exercise yard, surrounded by tall buildings. There were trees, flowers, rose trellises, a huge birdbath, prisoners walking around in double file, chatting with each other, laughing, looking bored. Most of them were Negroes. J. Edgar Hoover's crime statistics flashed to mind. "No," sighed the Warden softly, "the problem has been their habit of behaving in what they probably think of as, well, symbolic ways—you know, acting like they're establishing historical models or precedents or something. Very strange sometimes. It's thrown us off more than once and we haven't always reacted the way we should. We don't think much about history and ideological conflicts and long-range notions about the destiny of man in a place like this. We're just ordinary working people, it's about all we can do to get from one day to the next. So they tended to get in a certain amount of trouble at first, more than they deserved probably, doing things we just didn't understand. But we've caught on to most of it now, and it's not so bothersome. In fact, it's almost predictable . . ."

"Yes, I know . . ." That's the difference between us and the Socialists, I thought. Our central idea is to look for what works in an essentially open-ended situation; theirs is what's necessary in some kind of universal and inevitable history. Free individual enterprise versus the predestined structure, social engineering. Surely the Rosenbergs could be talked out of such crap. I tried to remember the arguments Uncle

Sam had used on me. The purification of politics, he'd said, is an iridescent dream. *Government is*— "Eh? How's that—!?"

"I said, like they're on stage or something."

"Oh."

"I mean, the way they act, the things they say—or rather how they say it . . ."

"Yeah. Yeah, I was, uh, thinking the same thing myself . . ."

"I remember when they first came here. We always ask prisoners when they arrive what led them to commit their crimes. Most of them just shrug or tell us to screw off—pardon the expression—or grunt something about being brought here on a bum rap. But the Rosenbergs made very formal and peculiar replies, almost like they were speaking to a vast audience, though in fact there were only eight or nine of us standing around, and not paying much attention at that. Mrs. Rosenberg was the first. They said she was very cheerful on the ride up, chatting about the spring weather and what not. She was wearing a pink blouse and a plaid skirt, a light coat with a kind of furry collar, a black hat— she looked like most any lady here on the streets of Ossining. But when she reached the Administration Building, her whole style changed. That's when I first got the feeling about her being on a stage—when she stepped out of the car it was like seeing someone come out from behind the, you know—what do you call them?"

"The wings."

"Yes. We asked her the question and she clasped her hands and with just the faintest trace of a smile said: 'I deny guilt.' Funny, that smile. I can still remember it. She seemed to be trying to say she forgave us for what we were unjustly doing to her. She seemed proud and sure of herself, yet frightened at the same time, squinting as though she'd just been brought out of light into darkness."

"She's got a lot of talent."

"Mr. Rosenberg came up later. He looked more costumed. I remember a red tie he had on, one with some kind of leafy pattern in it, and he had a clean white handkerchief folded crisply in the breast pocket of his suit. A new suit, I think. We asked him: 'To what do you attribute your criminal act?' And he stood very stiffly like a soldier at attention, yet somehow disrespectful at the same time—you couldn't keep your eye off that absurd white handkerchief in his breast pocket: 'Neither I nor my wife is guilty,' he said. Just like that."

"Their lawyer probably prompted them."

"Unh-hunh. Well, if he did, he did a good job of it. I've seen a lot of prisoners come here, but I don't think I remember the arrival of any of them more clearly than these two."

"Maybe you were keyed up, waiting for it, all the publicity . . ."

"Could be. I don't remember. But I do know I didn't feel it until they actually came through the gates. It was as though they were bringing some outside presence in with them. And it was true, you know—they were. I'm not the only one who remembers what they said. It's been repeated everywhere, it's part of history now." He sighed, gazing off toward the river, which was now right in front of us. A sheen on it put down by the sun. We were facing into it, and it made the distant Catskills hazy and miragelike. There was a big greenhouse down there on the river bank on the other side of a heavy wire fence, a gun tower half-concealed behind it as though playing hide-and-seek. The greenhouse reminded me that I'd been meaning to bone up on farming methods for my Midwestern campaign visits. "It's funny, isn't it, Mr. Nixon?"

"What's that?"

"How billions and billions of words get spoken every day, like all these we've been speaking on the way down here, for example, and for some reason—or for maybe no reason at all—a few of them stick, and they're all we've got afterwards of everything that's happened. Of course, you're more used to that than I am, you're probably always thinking of what the lasting impression is going to be . . ."

"What? I mean, yes!" A direct quote. Was he mocking me? "Part of the public life, Mr. Denno. You get used to it."

"I don't think I ever could. I can't imagine ever saying anything that would be remembered. Or that I'd want to be remembered. The Rosenbergs have been just the opposite. Talking and acting like characters out of Aesop's Fables or something."

"Knowing that Aesop is around to write it down, you mean."

"Yes," laughed the Warden. "Right . . ."

We angled left. "Tell me, is there anything . . . uh, between them?"

"And kind of real intimacy, you mean?"

"Yes, well. Like that. I sometimes get the feeling that all of that, uh, heartthrob stuff has just been part of the, you know, the same show. Public-relations gimmick, you might say . . ."

"Probably. Most of it. Why do you ask?"

"Uh . . . oh, just looking for an angle . . ."

"Mm." He pondered that. I got the idea he was becoming habituated to the idea of reading sentences more ways than one. "There *is* something between them, though. I don't know what you'd call it. Despair, I guess. Even their best hopes seem colored with it. It doesn't make them very happy, but it does create a kind of bond between them. Maybe they don't want to be happy, I don't know. Mrs. Rosenberg seems to feel it worse than her husband. He's got a lot of resources finally, but she . . . well, she's sort of given up. She's become . . . very withdrawn."

"I see. Uh . . . psycho?"

"No, not exactly. Just . . . well, you'll see for yourself . . ."

I took it by his tone that we'd reached the Death House and I glanced up. Ah. Yes, this was it all right. Unlike any other building on campus. In the prison, I mean. We'd been strolling down the bluff past really massive cell-block buildings, at least five stories high with huge dark window areas, everything on a superhuman scale. By contrast, this small clean brick structure was all too human in its dimensions. There was a pretty semicircular garden in front of the main entrance with trimmed hedges, shaped trees, and patches of flowers, but the two-story red brick walls, aglow in the afternoon sun, were windowless. I paused at the edge of the paved walk that led up to the heavily barred front door. It reminded me of the yellow brick road in *The Wizard of Oz*. "So this is it," I said. Already, I'd forgotten all the arguments I'd been rehearsing. Well, I was better at ad-libbing it anyway.

"Yes," said the Warden. "This is it. Come. I'll take you around by the back door."

We walked along the paved pathway between the Death House and the river, the warm June sun beating down on us. At the corner there was a patch of green lawn with a birdbath in the middle of it. No birds though. "These are the, uh, Death House cell blocks . . . ?"

"Yes, that's right, Mr. Nixon. Twenty-four cells for men, three for women. But the Rosenbergs aren't in there any more. They were moved this morning into the special Death Cells."

"The Death Cells?"

"In the middle of the complex. A kind of halfway house, away from the other condemned prisoners. It's where we get them ready."

"Ah, I see . . . get them ready . . ." High above us loomed a gun tower, the guards in it smiling down at us. The Warden waved and they nodded, cradling their weapons. Past them, it was a clean dash to the river, only fifty steps or so. But a long swim. "Is there a . . . a bath-room—?"

"Here we are," said the Warden, and he led me through a door on the south side of the complex and into a plain room with drab tan walls, a few chairs, a table. It was gloomy and sour, stifling hot. I thought I must be in the very heart of the prison, the solitary-confinement area or something, but the Warden said it was actually a meeting room for reporters and execution witnesses. "It will be filling up soon when we get ready to move the Rosenbergs. It's probably not the best place."

"The best place?"

"You said you wanted some place where you wouldn't be bothered, where they wouldn't feel watched."

"Oh yes, right," I said, wiping my forehead with my sleeve (where had I left my handkerchief?). I glanced up at the clock on the wall: after 6:30 already! How much time did I have? Fifteen minutes? Thirty?

"That clock's eight minutes fast," the Warden explained with an apologetic smile.

"Oh, I see . . ." But what did I see? There was a calendar on the wall that read SATURDAY JUNE 20. Like everybody was in a hurry here. "I hope it's not suppertime or anything, is it?" I asked irritably.

"That's all right," the Warden said. "It's only scrambled eggs."

"Scrambled eggs?"

"We didn't have time to fix a proper last supper, I'm afraid. All this has come on us so fast . . ."

"That's not your fault," I said. Actually, scrambled eggs didn't sound all that bad to me. I remembered I hadn't eaten since breakfast. "Where does that door lead to?" I asked, wondering if maybe it was a men's washroom.

"The death chamber." The Warden went to open the door. I was sorry I had asked.

"That's all right," I said, and while he wasn't watching ran the end of my tie around my neck, under the collar. I realized I was still wearing my sunglasses. I pocketed them.

"I'm sorry we don't have any air-conditioning in here," he said. He flicked a switch by the door and the room beyond exploded with light. The walls were whitewashed, which probably intensified the glare, but the lights were bright by themselves. Must be one hell of a shock to walk out of a dark cell into that. But as Uncle Sam would say: That's what it's all about, isn't it? "Here, you can see the setup we have. Can't stay there in the press room anyway, not if you want privacy—it'll soon be filling up with people."

"Ah. Well." I followed him hesitantly into the death chamber. As I moved toward the door, it reminded me somehow of the doorway into the downstairs bedroom off the living room in my folks' house back in Whittier. "I, uh, don't have much time . . ." Because of my brothers, I thought. Where they were laid out.

"New York was a pioneer in the use of the electric chair, you know," the Warden was saying. "The first one was a man named William Kemmler up in Auburn Prison back in 1890. That one was pretty crude and, uh, shocked a lot of people, if you'll pardon the expression . . ." The Warden chuckled loosely at his joke and I smiled weakly, staring at the cherry-colored oak chair with its leather straps and wires, amazed at all the empty space around it. I guess I'd expected a small room, private, glassed off, like the gas chambers we had out in California. There was something weird about all this space. "But we've made a lot of refinements over the years, and it's not so gruesome any more. For the victim, electrolethe, as we used to call it, is probably the best way to be taken off—much faster than gassing, garroting, or hanging, surer than shooting. As far as we know, it destroys them instantaneously—the current melts the brain so fast that the nervous system probably doesn't even have time to register any pain." It's not the shock itself that hurts, I thought, goddamn it, my own brain tingling, it's the anticipation. "Of course," smiled the Warden, "we can't be sure, since nobody's ever come back to tell us what it's really like."

"You mean, it's that . . . it always . . ."

"Not even the guillotine has a better record, Mr. Nixon." It looked like an ordinary high-backed dining-room armchair with leather upholstery, brass-studded, something you might find in an antique shop or up in the attic. Except for the special headrest, the thick cables, and a broad middle leg that stuck out in front like a kind of deck-chair footrest. The burning tree. Maybe that crossword puzzle answer wasn't GOLF after all. . . . "The only near-failure we ever had was just sixty years ago this summer up at Auburn when the chair broke during the first jolt. Took over an hour to repair it, and meanwhile the prisoner, who was still semiconscious, had to be kept doped up with chloroform and morphine. The poor bugger. One wonders what dreams he was having. But here at Sing Sing we're still batting a thousand."

There was a large skylight overhead, the panes sooty. From the inside? The lamps in the ceiling were shaped like flowers. "Is this the first woman you've had to . . . you've had to put to . . ."

"To sleep?" The Warden seemed amused at the expression. "Oh no, she'll be the ninth. If the sentence is carried out." He paused. "The first one we had here was a woman named Martha Place. That was back when Teddy Roosevelt was governor. She appealed to him for clemency, and when he refused her, what she said was: 'That soldier-man likes killing things and he is going to kill me!' She was right enough about that . . ." What was the Warden trying to get at? If he wanted to accuse us of something, why didn't he just come right out with it? "You can buy souvenir postcards of her down in the town."

The Warden stepped into an alcove to the left of the chair and turned on a big barn-door spotlight. "This is where the electrician works," he said. The switch was a long handle with a big knob on the end, like a gearshift lever on an old Ford. It was in full view of the chair, lit up like a special exhibit. The victim was denied nothing.

"Must be hard to find anybody to take the job," I said.

"Last time there was an opening," said the Warden, "there were over seven hundred applicants. That was when we hired Mr. Francel." This seemed to prove something to me that I'd always believed, though I couldn't remember exactly what it was. The Warden stood in the alcove, talking about volts and cycles and amperes, rheostats and dynamos, but I was thinking: the old legends about Death were closer to the truth than the ones we had now—it was a substantial reality, a kind of person, an active intervention in the endless process of life. "The current enters the body through a metal electrode lined with a wet sponge and placed on top of the head, toward the back, the hair having been shaved from this area to provide a good contact."

"I see . . ."

"It leaves the body through a similar electrode strapped to the calf of the left leg. The flesh's resistance to such a current generates a great heat and the body's temperature shoots up as high as a hundred and forty degrees—which is enough in itself to render most of the vital organs inoperative." The cables coiled out from under the chair like snakes, like thick turds, then disappeared into the floor somehow. There were elegantly paneled benches for the witnesses, and near them, oddly, a lavatory. For washing up? But who—? No, I thought: for throwing up in. "The body in the chair struggles convulsively against the straps—it can be pretty appalling to watch, but it's believed to be just involuntary muscle spasms induced by the current."

"Aha . . ." That's what they said about little Arthur when he went into his meningitis death throes. I wondered if the Warden planned to remain throughout the interview. He was probably hanging around trying to find out what the fresh information was I'd mentioned earlier as an excuse for coming here. "Where does that door—?"

"That's the corridor that leads to the Death Cells," said the Warden. There was a sign tacked up over the door that read SILENCE. "We could isolate it for you."

"All . . . all right . . ."

"Do you want to see both of them at the same time?"

"No! Uh . . . no, just one . . ." I think that when a third person is present, one is distracted, wondering what *his* reaction is. Or people sometimes show off to the third man. But if there are just two of you—

"Which . . . ?"

"Either one. Uh, the woman."

While I thought about that, the suddenness of my decision, the Warden led me out into the corridor and asked a guard posted there to have "C.C. 110,510" brought down. I realized that I'd been planning to talk to her first all along, since back aboard the *Look Ahead, Neighbor Special*, maybe before. There were black blinds on all the windows, giving the whitewashed corridor the appearance of being somehow lit from within. Aglow. Empty except for the old steam radiators. The Last Mile. I was reminded of the Ambassador Hotel corridor in Los Angeles, the night of my Checkers speech. "It's so, uh . . . polished . . ."

"The convicts here call it the Dance Hall," smiled the Warden around his long cigar.

"The what—!?"

The Warden watched me a moment as though to ask me: Why are you nervous?—then said: "I think they're coming." And he walked away from me down the corridor to let them in.

He'd left the door into the death chamber open, but there was no time to close it now. I stared in at the electric chair, the coiled cables, the white hospital cart, the long black switch, thinking: So this is it, then. I felt suddenly like running, but my feet seemed stuck to the floor. I looked down on myself and saw the Vice President of the United States of America standing, rooted in panic, in the Sing Sing Dance Hall, awaiting the arrival of the notorious Spy Queen, Mrs. Ethel Rosenberg, and I felt just like I'd felt before the Checkers speech: I just don't think I can go through with this one, I'd said to Pat. Of course you can, she'd said firmly, confidently. Of course you can . . .

I squared my shoulders and turned to face the door at the other end of the Last Mile (it is a challenging world, yes! I told myself, trying to stop my knees from shaking—but what an exciting time to be alive!) just as Ethel Rosenberg, flanked by a pair of matrons, stepped through. I nodded at the Warden and the two matrons, and they left us, pulling the door shut. We were alone.

"It's . . . it's all right," I said. "Don't be afraid. It's just me, Richard Nixon."

24.

Introducing: The Sam Slick Show!

"And now, oh God of our fathers, we will bless Thy name forever, for we are the people of thine inheritance! With our fathers, eight score and seventeen years ago, didst Thou make a Covenant, and Thou hast confirmed and amended it with their seed throughout all Enlightened Time! Thou hast made us unto Thee an eternal people, and hast cast our lot in the portion of light, that we may evince Thy truth, and from old hast Thou charged our Angel of Light, Uncle Sam, to help us. In his hand are all works of righteousness, and all spirits of truth are under his sway. But for corruption Thou hast made the Phantom, an angel of hostility. All his dominion is in darkness, and his purpose is to bring about wickedness and guilt. All the spirits that are associated with him are but angels of destruction. But we—we are in the portion of Thy truth!"

It's knee-bending, God-hollering, crying-in-the-chapel time in Times Square for the sons and daughters of Sam Slick the Yankee Peddler. The restless razzle-dazzle of the Pentagon Patriots and the Radio City Rockettes has been displaced on the Death House stage by the Singing Saints of the Mormon Tabernacle Choir, whose eyes have seen the glory, and a spirit of communion, like half time at a big football game, has settled on the gathered masses. There's been a moment of silent prayer (as silent as one can hope for amid so much bubbling excitement) in memory of the late U.S. Army Master Sergeant John C. Woods, the world-famous Nuremberg hangman; the Reverend Bob Jones, Sr., has unleashed his new sermon, "Shoving Jesus Christ Around," and the

415

Notre Dame Law Dean Clarence Manion of the Holy Six has blistered ·
the so-called intellectuals of the nation for their heretical "allergy to
absolutes," their reluctance to accept the basic facts of the existence of
God and the divine origin of American rights and duties:

> ". . . For the sake of pure political hypothesis, it makes little differ-
> ence whether man is a creature of God or the hind end of a happen-
> stance. But for the sake of American freedom in its life and death
> struggle with Communism, it makes all the difference in the world!"

His fellow Holy Sixers—Rabbi Bill Rosenblum, Editor Dan Poling,
Father Joe Moody, Presidential Aide Sam Rosenman, and Businessman
Electric Charlie Wilson—join him onstage and together they reaffirm
their righteous fury against the reckless Rosenberg Committee clemency
seekers, who "have knowingly or unwittingly given assistance to Communist propaganda . . ."

> . . . Crafty men are they;
> they think base thoughts,
> seek Thee with heart divided,
> stand not firm in Thy truth!
> With stammering tongue
> and with barbarous lips
> they speak unto Thy people,
> seeking guilefully
> to turn their deeds to delusion!

I SAY THE REAL AND PERMANENT GRANDEUR OF THESE STATES MUST BE
THEIR RELIGION! says the Wrigley Chewing Gum sign, and around the
Times Tower on the electric bulletin runs Reverend Phillips Brooks's
evangel: ". . . In thy dark streets shineth the everlasting Light; the
hopes and fears of all the years are met in thee tonight!"

If the hymns—even when rendered majestically by the Singing Saints
and recognizably old American favorites like "It Is No Secret," "The
Christian Warfare," and "No One Ever Cared for Me Like Jesus"—tend
to sound like party songs tonight, if Christ's blood tastes a little like Old
Grandad and crotches are more fingered than crosses, that doesn't
signify there's been a weakening of the faith, a drift into the dominion
of darkness—on the contrary, it's as though it's all coming together here
tonight in a magical fusion, the world of the sacred locking onto the
world of the profane like the two images at a 3-D movie, and all these
provocative confluences are not only possible, but necessary. One visits
the Hiroshima freak show and the belly of the Whale as one would walk
the Fourteen Stations of the Cross, treasures stolen panties like relics of

the True Cross, exchanges dirty jokes like recitations of the Seder Haggadah, knowing that every act is holy because, only so long as God be praised, it cannot be otherwise, and that, like the President says, "THE ALMIGHTY WATCHES OVER PEOPLE OF ALL NATIONS." And takes His pick.

Kate Smith comes out and sings "God Bless America," and then out on stage comes Sister Emma Bennett Fowler, the pride of Perryton, Texas. She squares her frail shoulders, rears back, and lets fly: "God bless America has come ringin' down the corridors of time ever since the *Mayflower* landed on our shores! It was in this faith that our forefathers begun to build, feelin' their way and searchin' for religious truth! Isaac Watts invented the steam injin, revolutionizin' travel and much industry!" She feels her way over to the electric chair. "Eli Whitney invented the cotton gin that done the work of fifty men! And Seth Thomas and his podner Eli Terry seen that by mass production they could cut the costs on *clocks*, enablin' more people to buy and makin' more money for theirselves!"

"They seen the light!"

"The Spirit was up-*on* 'em!"

"Tell 'em about it, Emma!"

"And so it has been through all the ages! Americans have invented thousands of machines, savin' men and labor, enrichin' theirselves and the Nation! And so's it might be *known* to be of God," cries Emma, " 'In God We Trust' was lettered on our coin, and printed on our dollar bills a 'Pyramid under the all-seein' Eye a God.' "

"Oh yes, he's laid us down in the green pastures, Emma!"

"The Eye of God!"

"Shine on!"

"*But!*" she shouts, and her demeanor suddenly changes. A hush falls. Here comes the good part. "After the First World War, Communists begun infestin' our guvvamint, schools, and churches! They got a weird creed which they spread by bein' fanatically inspired by Satan, whose disciples they are! It is with a missionary zeal they spread this pizen all over the world—!"

The people groan and gnash their teeth; women scream, children cry. Everybody is having a terrific time.

"We have refused to live under God's control, and now live under guvvamint control!" cries Emma over the uproar. The sound-system engineers crank the decibels up to give Emma the power she needs to carry above the racket. "The food for which we refused to give thanks has rose to exorbitant prices! The tithes we refused God we must now pay in taxes! Besides traitors in our own guvvamint everywhere, our allies is trickin' us and sellin' goods and weapons to the inimy, and are beginnin' to ridicule us in the eyes a the whole world!"

"It's a cryin' shame!"

"Don't let 'em get away with it, God!"

"Throw the rascals out!"

"We cannot ignore the fact that it is our boys who have suffered all the atrocities only Satan can conceive," Emma shrieks, "and that there are millions a Reds swarmin' all over the world!"

"Get us outa this, God! Give 'em hell, fer Chrissake!"

"Our world is now divided into two groups," cries Emma: "Communism with hammer and sickle, and America and Christians with cross of Christ! But we have placed ourselves where we cannot grow spiritually! God stands outside the door knockin' with His nail-pierced hand!"

"Oh Lord, I hear him!"

"I hear him knockin'!"

Indeed, someone is knocking. It is Uncle Sam, behind the set, rapping at Emma to get on with it.

She spreads her arms out to the people. "May God's richest blessings be upon us and our Nation! Amen!"

"*Amen!*" the people respond, checking their watches. "*Amen!*"

"I'll second that!" affirms Uncle Sam, striding out onto the Death House stage, tipping his top hat, jabbing his finger at the multitudes in that gesture of his beloved by all Americans, draftees sometimes excepted. The people crammed into Times Square roar their welcome. "Thank you, friends and neighbors! Thank you very—!"

"The Lord lift up His countenance unto thee," the people cry, their hands raised in praise and supplication, like bank tellers caught in a raid by audacious and handsome bandidos, "and accept the sweet savor of thy sacrifices!"

"Thanks! I'm sure He—"

"The Lord lift up His banner—"

"All right, that's enough now, the shades of night 're—"

". . . and do battle for thee at the head of thy thousands against this iniquitous generation! The Lord lift up His—"

"SHUT PAN AND SING DUMB, YOU BEAUTIES, BEFORE I REAR BACK AND WHOP AN INIQUITOUS BELCH OUTA YA SHARP ENOUGH TO STICK A PIG WITH!" Uncle Sam's steely blue eyes are flashing, his red bow tie is standing on end, and his teeth are showing white as hoarfrost in a powerful mean grin. "WHEE-EE-O! I don't care how much a man talks, if he only says it in a few words! It's like the monkey remarked tryin' to stuff the cork back in the elephant's asshole: *A little shit goes a long way!* LISTEN TO ME! Do you know that all the great work of the world is done through me? Size me up and shudder, you scalawags! The power to tax involves the power to *destroy*, and don't you forget it! I am the Thunderer, Justice the Avenger, kin to the whoopin' cough on my mother's side and half brother to the Abominable Snowman, a wonder, a grandeur, and a *woe!* WHOO-OOP! I am in earnest! I will not equivocate—I will not excuse—I will not retreat a single inch; and *I will be heard!*"

There is a moment of awed silence—then the crowd bursts into a tumultuous frenzy of applause, whistling, wild cheering.

Uncle Sam grins, stuffs his hands in his back pockets, and rocks back and forth on the stage, acknowledging the cheers and winking at folks he recognizes. "All right, then," he bellows, stilling the roar, "get a muzzle on your passions there, you cockabillies! I know, nothin' great was ever achieved without enthusiasm, like the Prophet says, but now the day is done, and the darkness falls from the wings o' Night, as a feather is wafted downward from a eagle in his fright—flight, I mean— so we gotta get crackin', children! We gotta beat the drum slowly and play the fife lowly, we gotta ring down the curtain, men's hearts wait upon us, men's lives hang in the balance—you *hear?* We gotta bring the flamin' Jubilee before the hills conceal the setting sun and stars begin a-peepin' one by one!" Uncle Sam clamps his corncob pipe in his jaws, withdraws a match from behind his ear, and holds it halfway between the two electrodes on the electric chair—sparks fly and ignite the match, which he cups over the bowl of his pipe. "The law," he hollers, blowing blue smoke: "it has honored us; may we honor it!"

"*Ya-HOO!*"

"*That's tellin' 'em, Uncle Sam!*"

"*Hit 'em where they ain't!*"

"Hey, it's really wonderful to see so many of you here tonight!" beams Uncle Sam. "It's the biggest crowd since the hangin' at Mount Holly in Aught-Thirty-three! And lemme say right here and now, it's you ordinary folks who've made this show possible tonight! If I might quote our elusive Vice President, where'er the hairy li'l tyke might be—" a ripple of consternation passes through the crowd at this news, if news is what it was—" 'God musta loved the common people, he made so many of 'em!' And I might add, He did a tolerable fine job of it, too!"

The people applaud themselves enthusiastically, Uncle Sam joining in. His handclaps crack and pop like rifle fire through the city streets.

"And I see a heap o' folks *not* so common, too! Yes, there's Vince Astor out there! And Charley Merrill! Jack Rockefeller—hullo, Junior! Give the folks a wave there—can you put a spot on him? We wouldn't be here without him! Jack Rockefeller, everybody!" Uncle Sam pauses for a burst of cheering, waves at others he recognizes, tips his top hat to the ladies (underneath his hat he's wearing one of those Dr. T beanies from the Dr. Seuss movie, and when he tips his hat, the yellow rubber fingers make naughty gestures to the ladies): "H'lo, Dinah! Duke! Dottie! Glad you could come! And there's Jonny Wainwright and Old Man Tosc and Artie Sulzberger—and whoa! I see Billy Faulkner, our Nobel Prize-winning mythomaniac! Howdy, Bill!"

"How do you do, suh!"

"How about a few dozen immortal words for us tonight, you old blatherskite?"

"Mah pleasure, suh! What about? Drinkin' or huntin' or—?"

"About God, Billy! About God and the Phantom and the chosen people!"

"Waal . . . In the beginnin', uh . . . God created the earth . . ."

"That's pretty good . . ."

"Then He created man completely equipped to cope with the earth. . . . Then God stopped."

"He stopped?"

"Yuh see, God didn't merely believe in man, He *knew* man. He knew thet man was competent fer a soul cuz he was capable of savin' thet soul—and not only his soul but hisself . . ."

"Himself?"

"Yes, *suh!* He knew thet man was capable of teachin' hisself to be civilized. It ain't only man's high destiny, but proof of his immortality, too, thet his is the choice between endin' the world . . . and completin' it!"

"Aha! A lofty bit of talknophical assumnancy there, Billy—but what about the Phantom?"

"The dark incorrigible one, yuh mean, who possessed the arrogance and pride to demand with, and the temerity to object with, and the ambition to substitute with . . . and the long roster of ruthless avatars —Genghis and Caesar and Stalin and Bonaparte and Huey Long—"

This mention of the Kingfish gets a big cheer. "That's whom I mean, okay," says Uncle Sam, stoking up his corncob pipe. "But what do we do about him, Billy? What do we do about the goddamn Phantom?"

"The answer's very simple, suh," says Faulkner, stroking his moustache. "Ah don't mean easy, but simple . . . It begins et home."

"At home?" Uncle Sam blows a smoke ring that floats out to hover over the Nobel laureate like a halo.

"Yup. Let us think fust of savin' the integer we call home: not whur *Ah* live, but whur *we* live: a thousand then tens of thousands of little integers scattered and fixed firmer and more impregnable and more solid then rocks or citadels about the earth, so thet the ruthless and ambitious split-offs of the ancient Dark Spirit shall look and say, 'There is nothin' fer us here . . . Man—simple, unfrightened, invincible men and women—has beaten us!' "

"Sweet Genevieve, Bill! that's pretty highfalutin' sesquipedalian advice! When I think on this majestic jazz, mine eyes dazzle! And that word 'integer' was a jimdandy, too! Let's give him a hand, folks, he's a good ole boy! And pass him a bottle a redeye! That's right, on the house, nothin' too good for an old Massassip screamer—that boy can head-rassle with the worst of 'em! All them little integers swarmin' around—WHOOPEE! you gotta be born and reared up in the swamps to think 'em up like that!" He gives a puff and the smoke halo over Faulkner's head disintegrates with a little tinkle into a sprinkle of gold dust.

While out front, Uncle Sam picks out more celebrities in the roving spots and hands out foot-long panatellas in appreciation to all those who've helped make tonight's show possible, backstage consternation over the missing Vice President is growing. Some think he might have been assassinated. Others that he's been kidnapped, or else overslept. Or got picked up as a derelict—those who saw him on the train report that he was looking pretty scruffy. Or maybe the Phantom's got him! Even as, from back in the wings and down in the subway station, they join Uncle Sam, the Singing Saints, and all the citizens out in the Square in singing a special Happy Birthday on this 19th of June to the Duchess of Dreamland, Bessie Wallis Warfield of Blue Ridge Summit, Pennsylvania, they are thinking: Somebody may have to take his place. Maybe it's me.

Uncle Sam hugs the birthday girl, feet dangling, high off the boards (the Duchess struggles, smiling gamely, to keep her skirt from rucking up over her knees, while out in the crowd, the Duke squirms uncomfortably among his whooping and hollering in-laws), then sets her down, roughs up her hair playfully, and presents her with one of Betty Crocker's giant angelfood birthday cakes. Amid the huzzahs and many happy returns, Uncle Sam spots the British Prime Minister, Sir Winston Churchill—he coaxes Winnie, who is often confused in the American imagination with W. C. Fields, into coming up on the stage to belt out a few boomers from the Golden Age of the Finest Hour. The P.M. squares his shoulders, winks puckishly, ducks his fat chin in his chest, snorts like a bull, paws the ground with his spatted hooves, jumps up once and cracks his heels together, and with the dignity of pink-cheeked greatness about him commences to bellow like a bona fide blueblood: "Cor blimey! the crisis is upon us, an iron curtain has descended on the broad sunlit uplands, and like the Mississippi, it just keeps rolling along beyond the soft underbelly of space and time! In the past we have a light which flickered, in the present"—here he raps the chair with his walking stick and whips out a new cigar—"we have a light that flames, so do not let us speak of darker days, death and sorrow, the quivering, precarious sinews of peace, blood, toil, tears, and bloody 'ell, God save the Queen, *upon this battle depends the survival of Christian civilization!* DREAD NOUGHT! When you have to kill a man it costs nothing to be polite, short words are best! Now this is not the end, everyone has his day and some days last longer than others, it is not even the beginning of the end . . ."

But while he's blustering like that, Uncle Sam is filling the stage behind him and secret corners of the VIP section with Minutemen and Green Mountain Boys—suddenly they leap out and point their muskets at Winnie: "We hold these truths to be self-evident," they cry, spitting tobacco juice and flourishing buckets of tar and feathers, "that all men are created equal, that they are endowed by their Creator with certain unalienable Rights, that among these are Life, Liberty and the pursuit of Happiness—That to secure these rights, Governments are instituted among Men, deriving their just powers from the consent of the governed —That whenever any Form of Government becomes destructive of these ends, it is the Right of the People to alter or to abolish it, *and to institute new Government!*"

"What? What?" roars Churchill. He puts two fingers in his mouth and lets rip a deafening whistle. People hear troops marching, singing "Yankee Doodle"—they open up to let them pass through—but wait! they're not Americans after all, they're Redcoats! A Patriot comes loping up ahead of them, slapping his thigh, hippety-hopping as though galloping in on an imaginary horse: it's Paul Revere! He warns the Minutemen, and they fall into defensive formations against the attackers. "Stand your ground! Don't fire unless fired upon, but if they mean to have a war let it begin here!" There's musket fire! Screams! Eight Minutemen drop dead! The Redcoats march on into the center, led by the likes of Hair-Buyer Hamilton, Gentleman Johnny Burgoyne, and Lord Cornwallis, strutting like peacocks! George Washington organizes his forces and a full-scale free-for-all breaks out! Rhetoric is flying through the air like musket fire: "The die is now cast," bellows Churchill, popping his buttons with excitement and looking for all the world like John Bull himself, "the Colonies must either submit or triumph!"

"There's something absurd in supposin' a Continent to be perpetually governed by an island!" snorts Uncle Sam. "Come on, boys! From the East to the West blow the trumpet to treason and make the most of it! Now is the seedtime of Continental union, faith and the clash of resounding arms, the original Merrycunt Revilusion! I know not what chorus others may take, but as for me, stick a feather in your girl and call her Maggie Rooney! Whee-oo! I must fight somethin' or I'll ketch the dry rot—burnt brandy won't save me! C'mon, you varmints, the harder the conflict, the more glorious the massacree! Laxation without intoxification is tyranny, so give me Molly Stark or liberty sleeps a widder!"

Blood is splattering everywhere. Washington's tattered troops shrink to a shivering handful. But the old vestryman of Truro Parish gathers them into a make-believe ark and, invoking Divine Providence, they paddle across one of the aisles in the VIP section and take the wassailing intruders by surprise. "A race of convicts—a pack of rascals, sir!" storms Churchill. "They are a set of tatterdemalions, there is hardly a whole pair of breeches in an entire regiment! Bugger the lot!" But it's not to be: the swamp foxes and backwoodsmen scatter through the forest of VIP seats and pick off the Redcoats like sleeping coons, teaching Burgoyne and Cornwallis with buckshot to their retreating rears the fundamentals of guerrilla warfare. "All right, then," says the P.M., reaching inside his siren suit to scratch his distinguished ballocks, "we have been subdued."

Cheers erupt through the Square and beyond as Uncle Sam unveils the stone tablets of the Constitution, said to be the same ones that George Washington brought down off Bunkum Hill. All the "dead" soldiers get up and sing "Yankee Doodle" together, then step back to help guard the perimeter of the VIP area. Winston Churchill and Uncle Sam pick each other's pockets clean, and Winnie is sent off, amid wild cheering, Uncle Sam's Dr. T beanie on his head, its yellow rubber fingers flashing his famous V-for-Victory sign.

Then George Washington, the American Fabius, so-called, brushes himself off and leads out all the other Presidents: His Rotundity the Machiavelli of Massachusetts, Long Tom the Sage of Monticello, Withered Little Apple-John, the Last of the Cocked Hats, Old Man

Eloquent, King Andrew, Little Van the Red Fox of Kinderhook, Old Tippecanoe and Turncoat Tyler, too, Young Hickory the Sly, Old Rough and Ready, the American Louis Philippe, Yankee Purse, Old Buck the Bachelor, the Illinois Baboon, Sir Veto, the Butcher, the Fraud of '77 and his wife Lemonade Lucy, the Evangelist, the Gentleman Boss, the Stuffed Prophet, Cold Ben, Prosperity's Advance Agent, Tiddy the Bull Moose, High-Tariffs Fats, Dr. God-on-the-Mountain, the Mainstreeter with the Soft Heart, the American Primitive, the Great Humanitarian, Old Again and Again and Again, and Give 'Em Hell Harry. As they emerge, wearing their shiny papier-mâché heads modeled from official portraits, they're accompanied by iconic figures from the epochs they represent: Pilgrims, Pirates, Planters and Pioneers, Boston Merchants, Virginia Orators, Inventors, Southern Gentlemen and their Darkies, Canal Boatmen, Land Speculators, Powder Monkeys and Brave Engineers, Pony Express Riders, Bible Belters, Village Blacksmiths and Forty-Niners, Raftsmen and Dirt Farmers, Roving Gamblers, Lumberjacks, Johnny Rebs and Damyankees, Sheepherders and Cattle Kings, River Boat Captains, Desert Rats, Millionaires, Whalers, Cowboys and Indians and the U.S. Cavalry, Carpetbaggers and Ku Klux Klansmen, Country Fiddlers, Coalminers, Oil Barons and Outlaws, Bluebloods and Rednecks, Wall Streeters, Suffragettes, Rough Riders, Motorists, Movie Stars and Moonshiners, Stockbrokers, Shortstops and Traveling Salesmen, Gangbusters, Quarterbacks, Songwriters, Private Eyes, Self-Made Men, and more, all doing skits, singing songs, dancing in chorus lines, miming the high drama of building a nation and taking over the world. A lot of the performers are as stiff-kneed and self-conscious as those of any home-town centennial pageant—many of them are Secret Service agents in disguise and ambitious amateurs with influential relatives— but the acts flow in and over one another so fast there's no time to notice, all watched over by a ceaselessly inventive and unpredictable Uncle Sam, who's out there stirring up a veritable feast of Train Robberies, Famous Debates, Lynchings, Brawls, and Dust Storms, and carrying on his running patter of Yankee proverbs and prophecies, the Singing Saints humming gospel songs in the background.

"Hoo boy!" gasps Uncle Sam, ducking backstage for a second during the Battle of Gettysburg, "what I like mostes' is *showin' off!*" He mops his broad brow with a red-white-and-blue bandanna and conducts a hasty roll call. Some of the Senators and judges are by now too drunk to recognize their own names, but that's hardly noticed. What does rile the old Superhero, though, is the continued absence of his Number Two Gun. "As I'm a cockeyed Christian," he barks, "that craven, chicken-bred, toad-hoppin', duck-nosed mother's son of a unbroke sea-horse is gonna make me slip my cable and unloose more than my matchless magnanimity around here!" He glances at his fob watch. Sundown's at 8:31 tonight, still a couple of hours to go, but the Jewish Sabbath starts eighteen minutes before that, the period of "anticipation," as they call it. It'll take him five or six minutes each to fry the two thieves, so the most leeway he can allow the young maverick is, say, twelve minutes. "Awright, you bandy-shanked double-jawed desperaydos! Zero Hour is one minute after eight—he's got better'n a hour to make it! So hustle up them epistolary numbers! We'll stall till the last minnit with the contest, but if that monkey ain't here by 20:01 we're goin' on without him!"

This epistolary-contest announcement stirs a fresh backstage jostle: Uncle Sam will be awarding silver-dollar jackpots and new top ratings to the funniest, saddest, most terrifying, etc., skits and readings from the Rosenbergs' Death House Letters, and so all the actors in town are suddenly pressing excitedly into the wings, eager to go on for a crack at the winnings, not to mention a chance to play before this fantastic house. This audience is a *dream!*

Pretty dismal material, of course, these prison letters, but real professionals are never daunted by poor scripts. Fred Astaire and Ginger Rogers, for example, are working up a dance routine around a single line from one letter of each of them . . .

JULIE: Honey, I sat so reserved and pent up looking at you through the screen, and all the time I wanted to take you in my arms, smother you with kisses and tell you in more than words of my consuming love for you!

ETHEL: How utterly shameless were my thoughts as I gazed at your glowing face through the double barrier of screen and bar!

. . . in which they hold up a wire-mesh screen between them and fantasize a tender and loving future for themselves, even as they are dancing toward the chair. Bud Abbott and Lou Costello have a cruder act on roughly the same theme, building their gags around the argument of who goes first. Fibber McGee and Molly are incorporating the letters into one of their familiar domestic situations (when McGee's closet is opened a whining cacophony of Rosenberg complaints will come clattering out, and Molly's famous line—" 'Tain't funny, McGee!"—will take on an unsuspected moral force), while Andy Devine and Marjorie Main are going for straight drama, focusing on the erotic bits. Archie of Duffy's Tavern intends to solo with a telephone, as does Red Skelton with a handful of hats. Ozzie and Harriet, contrarily, are bringing the entire Nelson family into their act by picking up on the periodic visits of the Rosenberg boys to the prison, and One Man's Family is even going them yet one better by pushing for a complex fragment of the disturbing Greenglass-Rosenberg family saga.

Standing waist-high among all these characters and looking very down in the mouth is the Boy Judge, Irving Kaufman: he and Irving Saypol have been asked to reenact, as a kind of curtain raiser to the contest, some of their routines from the trial, and although he and Saypol work well together, he seems unsure of himself. He's taken a great risk in setting up tonight's show and preventing it from falling through— maybe too much—and the strain is beginning to tell. Discovering him like that, his old friend and former client Milton Berle, backstage with the rest of the contestants, cautions him: "Be careful, Irving, or you'll drop the world!"

Kaufman smiles foolishly, displaying the gap between his two front teeth, then sighs profoundly. "It's such a terrible responsibility," is what he says, but what's really troubling his mind is that sometimes, like now (Supreme Court Justice William Douglas has just been dragged onstage for a "spontaneous" public spanking—"Only thing not Red about this rapscallion," Uncle Sam has shouted, "is his *bottom!*"and there's a great clamor: everyone, it seems, wants to get his hands or other weapons on Judge Douglas's posteriors, and this, Irving supposes, under other cir-cumstances could happen to *him!*), he gets the feeling he's just being used, that he's as much a victim as the Rosenbergs. Even if now he is a National Hero . . .

Congressman Don Wheeler, brushing past him, rushes out onstage to announce that he's still pressing for Douglas's impeachment and a one-way visa to Russia—then rears back like Babe Ruth going for the fences and lands such a blow on him that it seems he might be trying to belt him over into Phantom country single-handedly. Others come out and holler about the Judge's "arrogance" and "treason" and "villainous ambition" as they whop him, and some even fulminate against his sex life. "Last May twenty-first at a meeting of the American Law Institute," cries Walt Trohan of the *Chicago Tribune*, laying into him, "Douglas said America had lost its position of moral leadership—*this from a man who went vacationing for some weeks with another man's wife!*" There's a lot of hooting and whistling out in the crowd, a tremendous agitation building up. "And from a man who some years ago stooped from the High Court to string obscenities into verses which shocked a select group of Americans, which has numbered two Presidents, a Chief Justice, admirals of the fleet, generals of the Army, Senators, governors, and lesser characters including myself! *I was there when this would-be liberal spouted his filth!*"

Douglas, patiently taking his licking amid all the uproar, remarks to Uncle Sam, over whose knees he's been turned, that as a Superhero he's really degenerating fast. "Not my fault," says Uncle Sam with a coy wink, "I gave you a chance to save me, Billy, but you turned me down!"

"Whew!" complains the Attorney General, out for a retributive barehanded whack at Justice Douglas's nefarious backside, "hitting this guy is like slapping an old weathered board!"

"Presidential timber, Herb," grins Uncle Sam.

Judge Kaufman understands, of course, that every judgment is a kind of marriage, that he and the Rosenbergs needed each other to fulfill themselves, need each other still—judge and judged: two sides of the same coin . . . but what coin was that? He remembers the great up feeling he'd had when they were drawn together—inexorably, it had seemed then—toward that classic Passover Trial of just two years ago, the sense of being Chosen (and he was, yes, he was a Great Man now) and of being *ready*, the magisterial power and artistry with which he'd conducted the trial, the seemingly inevitable convictions and the Maximum Penalty drama that hovered over them . . . and yet, he'd not imagined that it would end this way. And how inevitable had it been really? He felt deep in his heart he had done the right and necessary thing—but could he trust his heart? Had they not been Jews would he have done the same? There were those who thanked him for putting the heat on them—but who has put the heat on whom? he wonders now, as he watches Bob, Bing, and Dottie practicing a sketch called "The Road to Radiance." In the sketch, apparently, Crosby plays a priest who, with a lighthearted wink, sings "Goin' My Way?" as he leads Bob and Dottie to the electric chair, while Hope, trying frantically to hide in Dottie's sarong, gets lost (Lamour loses Hope!), only to come popping out like a champagne cork when they pull the switch on Dottie and go bounding— *boing! boing! boing!*—around the stage, singing "Thanks for the Memory." He thinks: maybe those old priests at Fordham were right about invincible ignorance, after all. At the time, Irving had argued fiercely with them, supposing they were only trying to excuse his Judaism for him (it needed no excuses!), but now it's suddenly come to him, thinking about that indivisible two-sided coin, that the one thing you could never understand was the thing you were intimately a part of; identity, they'd taught him (tried to), made modal and virtual distinctions impossible. Something like that. If he weren't who he was on the face of that coin, if he were just a common citizen out there in the faceless crowd, he might have a better overview of the whole, but—

"Hey, Irving," sings Uncle Miltie softly in the Judge's ear, chucking him under his plump chin and wrapping his arm around him, *"life is just a bowl of cher-ries . . . . !"*

He nods. What, after all, could he do about it? He can only be what he is: vocation is a prevenient grace. Willy-nilly, he's bound up in a mystery. He wraps his own stubby arm around Uncle Miltie's waist and, hoping it will get easier when he makes it to the Supreme Court, croons along with the comic: *"Don't make it serious, life's too mysterious . . . !"*

Certainly he has nothing to fear from this crowd: when he appears, introduced by George Sokolsky of the *Washington Times-Herald* (". . . To the galaxy of America's great judges can now be added the name of Irving Kaufman, servant of the law!"), the ensuing ovation ruptures the applause meter. This technical breakdown momentarily unsettles the audience (measurement is what it's all about!), but it's soon forgotten in all the thrills, tears, and laughter of the acts that follow: everybody from Veronica Lake and the Duke of Paducah to Yogi Berra and the Dragon Lady. Boris Karloff and Elsa Lanchester work a Frankenstein act with all the electrical paraphernalia, then Dean (Ethel) Martin drags Jerry (Julie) Lewis around the Death House set by his lower jaw while singing "One Fine Day" from *Madame Butterfly* in a drunken falsetto. Amos 'n' Andy turn it all into a blackface minstrel show, with Kingfish doing the lawyer's part, very wily, but bungling things up as usual, and then Jimmy Durante and Garry Moore come out and play it for pathos, using the letters to the children. Out front the people glance up at the Paramount clock, their eyes filling with tears of laughter and unabashed sentiment, as Jimmy and Garry climax their skit with Jimmy sitting in the electric chair in a curly wig, playing the piano, and singing: "Oh, *who* will be wit' chew when h'I'm: *far* h'way, when h'I'm: *far* h'away from *H-YOU?*"

25.

A Taste of the City

"I know," Ethel Rosenberg said calmly as the door closed behind her down at the other end of the Last Mile. She stood with her hands at her sides, utterly self-composed, unbroken. A strong woman, and brave, but there was a hardness as well, a kind of cunning: she struck me as something of an operator, like those brittle tough-talking chain-smoking girls I'd met at the OPA. "I've been expecting you."

I was taken aback by this. Expecting me? I stared at her, not knowing what to say. Had she really understood who I was? Or was she already in some other world? She looked a little strange, as though she'd already left her body halfway behind. A little deranged maybe. Well, I could understand this, I'd only been living with the idea of it for a few days and had become pretty giddy myself. "It's all right, Mrs. Rosenberg," I said, "I just . . . I only want to talk."

"Of course," she said, smiling faintly, as though to say she forgave me, and stepped toward me down the glowing white corridor. She was shorter than I'd imagined, dumpier. Older, too. She was dressed in a simple cotton dress of no particular color, a little ragged at the seams, the skirt torn or slit on the left side. Her thighs, which I tried not to notice, were bare and rather thick. Her hair was unkempt, frazzled, as though she'd been trying to tear it out by the roots, and her face seemed shapeless, blank. But maybe it was just the distance, the strange light in this black-blinded whitewashed passageway, because as she came toward me, moving coldly, disdainfully, yet dreamily, as though remote from all this, padding along in her felt slippers and reflected in the waxed floor not as body but as shifting shimmering light, she seemed to grow in stature and her years dropped away. She walked like a good politician, simulating dignity, self-assurance, humility. Already practicing probably for the last walk to follow. But even as this thought crossed my mind, I felt a flush of guilt about it—I understood the depths of my own sincerity and integrity, so undervalued by the world at large, why did I doubt it in others? "But it's no use, Mr. Nixon. There's nothing more to be said."

Her gaze drifted past my shoulder and she stopped dead in her tracks. "This . . . this is a very strange joke to play . . . !" she whispered.

"What—?" I glanced apprehensively over my shoulder, but it was only the chair she'd seen. "Oh, I, uh, I'm sorry about that," I said. "It's not my fault, the Warden left it open. Would you like me to—?"

"There's no need for any pretense, Mr. Nixon. The farce is exposed. The executive arm of our government—with you as its spokesman—has become a party to murder! And now you are desperate to bury us quickly before the entire lid is blown off this stinking plot!"

"Now wait a minute," I insisted, secretly pleased at her nomination, "let's be fair about this!"

"Fair!" she snorted. "Do you call this fair? This is blackmail! Nazi barbarism!"

I could feel my blood rising, but I knew, if I was going to pull anything out of this goddamned hat, I had to keep my cool. Thinking of which, I removed my homburg and, clutching it by the brim by my left thigh, moved my right foot forward slightly and tilted my head as though expecting to be photographed. Or rather, expecting nothing of the sort, but recalling from other photographs that such a pose suggested alertness and vitality and clarity of vision. (She was not a photographer, she was a typist—why was I thinking of cameras? That stripper story that damned cabbie told me, probably.) "Believe me, Mrs. Rosenberg, I can understand your feelings," I said, modulating my voice in the manner of Reverend Peale and trying to forget about the Dirty Crab, "I've suffered a lot of smear attacks myself, you know!"

She snorted again. It was not a very attractive gesture. I felt her contempt of me and was stung by it: was it nothing to her that the Vice President of the United States had taken a personal interest in her case? How could she recognize my power and ignore it at the same time? "I told Mr. Bennett that if the Attorney General were to send a highly placed authority to see me, even if you came just ten minutes before my execution, the plain fact of my innocence would not have changed in the slightest." She was trying to keep her voice from pitching upwards in excitement. "But I didn't believe, even then, you'd be cruel enough to do just that!"

"I've got nothing to do with Mr. Bennett! I'm here on my own! I've come to offer you—"

"We will not be intimidated by your fascist methods, Mr. Nixon!" she snapped. Her words were harsh, but she couldn't hide her desperation. "We have done nothing wrong and if we must die for that, then we shall die for it!"

"If you die at all, it will be because you and your husband *want* to! You've been given a fair chance and it's still open! You're just doing this for your own goddamn glory!"

"Oh no! We do *not* wish to be martyrs or heroes, Mr. Nixon! We do not want to die!" she cried, her voice thin and defensive. "But we won't lie to live!"

"Who's asking you to lie? Listen, I've got a new—!"

"We are not the first victims of tyranny!" she ranted. I could see tears springing to the corners of her dark eyes, and her lip was trembling. I knew if I could keep attacking and counterattacking, I could break her, but it wasn't going to be easy. Hadn't her own lawyer said it? "She is a better lawyer than I am, no doubt!" Relatively, the Pink Lady was a pushover. "Six million of our coreligionists and millions of other victims of fascism went to the death chambers before us!"

"All this crap about fascism is a lotta hooey, and you know it!" I shouted, jabbing my homburg at her. "The only mass executions these days are on the other side of the Iron Curtain!"

"That's not true!"

"Oh yeah? What about Stalin's purges? The death camps in Siberia? The massacres in Poland? What about Rudolph Slansky just last fall in Prague? Eh? He and about ten more of your coreligionists, as you like to call them! Or the Doctors' Plot—that was a good one! And just yesterday over in East Berlin, poor Willi Goettling, not even any goddamn trial, just dragged out and shot! And more being massacred right now!"

"Spies!" she shrieked, trying to drown me out.

"Oh," I said calmly, dropping the homburg to my side. "That makes it okay, does it?" She flushed, trapped. I zeroed in: "And meanwhile, all century long, this country has opened its doors—its doors and its heart—to the people running away from all these tyrannies, no matter what their color, your own parents among them!"

"Yes, that's right," she replied, having recovered more quickly than I had expected, "until *you* came along—you and all those other super-patriotic demagogues and bigots who are taking this country over!"

"Now, wait a minute, don't call *me* a bigot!" I stormed. "I've got plenty of Jewish friends! More than you have, I bet! Catholics, too, and Negroes—listen, when I was in college I helped initiate a Negro into our fraternity!" She seemed nonplussed by this—I took advantage of the point made and pressed on: "I'm a progressive, too, you know—don't believe everything you see in Herblock's cartoons! My ancestors fought with Cromwell in Ireland and George Washington in New Jersey, struggled against the Indians, spied on the British, operated an Underground Railroad station on the north bank of the Ohio, and got buried at Gettysburg! I've always believed in freedom! I personally opened up Whittier College to on-campus dances and championed the end of compulsory chapel! You don't believe me, I'll show you in the yearbook! I lived in a commune once and worked for the New Deal and the OPA and fought against the Axis in the South Pacific! I was at Bougainville! *I might have got killed!*" Christ, I realized I was getting very wrought up. She watched me somewhat agape. I didn't know whether I was getting to her or just astonishing her. She was still very pale. Doe-eyed. Vulnerable: I could see how she must have knocked them out in that role of the condemned man's sister. She looked like Ella Cinders. Her soft dark eyes began to narrow. I could see the shape of the argument forming up behind them, so I beat her to it: "Oh, I know what people say about me, trying to make me out like the heavy in some goddamn cowboy movie, calling me every name in the book—but it's not my fault! It's only because of the campaigns I've had to run and the legislation I've had to sponsor and support. I'm not any happier about a lot of it than you are, but that's politics—a campaign diet of dishwater and milk toast doesn't get you elected to office and you don't achieve a national reputation by putting your name on nothing but blue-sky laws! A lot of blood gets spilled on the way to the top—where at last maybe you can *do* something about the world—and inevitably a lot of it is your own! Blood and mud: I've been accused of everything—bigamy, forgery, drunkenness, insanity, thievery, anti-Semitism, perjury, the whole gamut of misconduct in public office, ranging from unethical to downright criminal activities—but *nobody* knows yet who I really am! *You* should understand this, Mrs. Rosenberg, you've caught some of it yourself! A fanatic, they've called you, an anti-Semite, a lousy mother, even something of a nut case—well, if you think you've suffered, just imagine how it's been for *me!*"

She might have snorted again at this, but she didn't. She was watching me in a new way, studying me curiously. She looks a little bit like Claudette Colbert at that, I thought. Only softer, more like one of those Italian actresses. Her dress hung loosely on her and gave you the impression it was all she had on. She poked absently into her skirt pocket for a pack of cigarettes, gazing thoughtfully at me all the while. She didn't flip a cigarette from the pack, but reached in carefully with her fingertips, plucked one out, and fitted it between her lips. Her hand was trembling faintly as she lit it.

"It's . . . uh, it's not allowed," I said uneasily, glancing up at the NO SMOKING sign on the wall.

"No? What do you think they'll do to me, Mr. Nixon?" she asked drily, and exhaled a lungful of smoke. She seemed almost to be pitying me. I did not object to this. I was no longer sure just what I was doing here, but it had to be for good reasons, and I knew that somehow, difficult as it might be, I would succeed. She stood close to me now, small, delicate, even fragile. I realized that I really didn't want her to die.

"Mrs. Rosenberg," I said as gently as I could, attempting a smile but feeling it twitch away as soon as I'd tried it, "Mrs. Rosenberg, we want to, uh, help, I want to help, Pat and I—"

"You're wasting your time," she said simply. "I am innocent. My husband is innocent. We know nothing about any espionage." She kept her head up but she seemed close to tears. There was a tremor in her voice. How much time did she have left to live—seventy minutes? eighty? She took another deep drag on the cigarette, then dropped it on the floor and squashed it out with her slipper, creating an ugly black smudge in the middle of all that gleaming wax polish. She exhaled slowly, then gazed up at me again. I was touched by her great reserves of strength and serenity. "We understand these desperate moves," she said. "You've made a mistake and now you're trying to get out of it!"

"But, Mrs. Rosenberg—Ethel! You don't understand!" She seemed surprised I'd used her first name, and with such feeling. Dumfounded even. I was surprised myself. "I tell you, Ethel, this has nothing to do with the government—I've run away from the government—believe me, it's *you* I care about, can't you see that?" She seemed startled, confused, disbelieving. I could hardly believe it either, it was sheer madness, but I couldn't stop now, I'd turned some corner and there was no going back. Besides, my instincts told me I was right. "I've come to save you, I don't know how, but I've got to get you out of this, I've got to get you out of here!" What did I mean? That I was going to pick her up and make a run for it? Trade clothes with her like they did in the movies? Maybe it

was the utter impossibility of it all that drove me on—it couldn't happen, so I could be all the fiercer in my insistence that it would. It
reminded me of my greatest moments with Ola. "I don't want your
confession, Ethel! I don't care about the past, it's now I care about!"

"You . . . you can't be serious!" she whispered.

"But I am!" Not serious! To question my seriousness was like questioning Ike's smile. "I believe in you! I've made a careful study—I . . .
I *don't want you to die!*"

Even though she was shorter than I was, I'd felt all the while she had
been gazing down on me. Now we seemed to be on the same footing, face
to face. We were very close. My heart was beating wildly. I thought:
there's just the two of us left! I felt her eyes, dark with anguish and
uncertainty, searching my own. I struggled, with my eyes, against her
distrust. I felt I had not known such intensity since I was a boy in high
school. I wanted to weep so that she would believe me and I tried to
remember those lines from *Bird-in-Hand: I've never had but one child—
that's 'er* . . . Then suddenly she seemed almost to collapse, her knees
seemed to buckle—I reached forward, gripped her arm. She did not
resist. "All right," she said weakly. "All right. Where's Julie?"

"Julie—?"

She drew back, one hand in front of her face as though to ward off
bad breath. "Did you mean you were going to save me and leave Julie to
die—?!"

"But . . . but, Ethel—!" Why did women always expect this of me?

"So that's it! My life is to be bargained off against his! I need only
grasp the line chivalrously held out to me and leave him to drown
without a backward glance!"

The metaphor betrayed her. "You're just pretending, Ethel," I said
coldly. "You're faking it!"

"How diabolical! Oh, I could retch with horror and revulsion! You
are proposing to erect a sepulcher in which I shall live without living,
and die without dying!" All of this sounded familiar. Like lines from
some soap opera. I kept thinking of *Aeneas and Dido*, but that was
absurd. Some Horatio Alger novel probably. "Over and over again, I
shall sob out the last heartbroken wracking good-byes and reel—"

"Damn it, Ethel, cut that out!"

"And what of our children!" I'd forgot about the children. Yes, and it
came back to me now what had happened to my handkerchief, too. . . .
"What manner of mercy is it that would slay their adored father and
deliver up their devoted mother to everlasting emptiness?"

Perhaps, I was thinking, I should just walk out of here while there was still time. But *was* there still time? The state she was in, she'd probably shout it all out at the top of her voice in Times Square tonight, right in front of the whole goddamned world. And how would I explain *that* at Monday morning's Cabinet meeting? I could just see old Foster staring down his nose at me, Ike peering over his spectacles, Lodge licking his chops. I wondered what Abraham Lincoln would do in this situation . . .

"I should far rather embrace my husband in death than live on ingloriously upon such bounty!" Ethel cried, still carrying on. "I shall not dishonor my marital vows and the felicity and integrity of the relationship we shared to play the role of harlot to political procurers!"

Political procurers—! That pissed me off. *"Crap! You don't love him, goddamn it, and you never have!"* Her eyes blazed with fury, the veins in her neck throbbed, she clenched and unclenched her hands. I thought she might lash out at me, claw at my eyes, start shrieking or something, but I was no longer afraid—I was no longer afraid of *anything!* The worst of the crisis, I knew, was past. This was the creative phase now! "It's all been just an act, Ethel, and you know it! Part of the strategy!"

"What . . . what are you saying—!"

"Who do you think you're fooling? You even forgot your anniversary last year!"

She was trembling. I was towering over her. "You're . . . you're saying this to divide us! It's not enough we have to die—"

"Admit it, Ethel! You've dreamed of love all your life! You dream of it now! I know, because I dream of it, too! But you've never known it, you've never given yourself to him, you've never given yourself to anybody!" My God! I was amazing!

"I . . . I don't believe in bourgeois romance," she said hoarsely, but there was no conviction in it. "That kind of love is sick, it's selfish, we mustn't—"

"Damn it, you know better than that! You're an artist, Ethel, a poet! You know what love is, what it might be! All the rest is just lies!"

Her resistance crumbled. I was amazed to watch it. She turned away, lowering her head. Almost inaudibly, she whispered: "I respect him so . . ."

"Yes, and you needed him, I know that—when you met him you felt abused and alone, and he was kind and sympathetic. I know all this, all about the illnesses and bad luck. I know about the bastard who tried to force himself on you, know how your own family frustrated your best hopes, how they failed to understand you, and then the Depression— what a lousy future you had to look forward to! And you thought Julie could save you from it, you thought—do you know what you thought back then?"

"Please . . . stop . . ."

"You thought he could save you from a meaningless martyrdom!"

She let out a soft anguished cry. I thought she would fall. I gripped her shoulders, turned her to face me. "We've both been victims of the same lie, Ethel! There *is* no purpose, there *are* no causes, all that's just stuff we make up to hold the goddamn world together—all we've really got is what we have right here and now: being alive! *Don't throw it away, Ethel!"* Her lips parted. When she looked up at me, I saw a big soft tear welling up in her eye. "Ethel! Oh my God! I . . . I . . ." I kissed her.

She was taken unawares. So was I. I had not planned this. She tried to cry out, but I muffled her mouth with my own, keeping my eye on the door at the far end. She twisted in my grip, fought, pounded at me with her fists, but I held on. In a flush of weakness, I felt guilty about overpowering her like this, even started to release her and apologize— but no, goddamn it, that had been my trouble all my life, I didn't know what I was doing but I did know I was through being polite, I was through being Mr. Nice Guy, I was all done with trying to outargue women, or men either, Uncle Sam included, to hell with respect and consideration, I knew better. If I'd learned anything from seven years of politics, it was that you didn't get anything you wanted by dealing politely from weakness! The meek inherited nothing but regrets and failure in this world! And I was fighting for my political life, wasn't I? And more! God knows what all I was fighting for! I kept my lips glued to hers, partly out of a fierce determination to succeed, partly in fear of what she might do if I let her go, and partly just for the sensation of it, not having tasted such wildness since back when I'd dated the police chief's daughter. And this was different, very different, there was nothing frivolous and jazz-babyish about this kiss—there was blood in it, ferocity, danger! Sheba the lion's gaping maw was one of Aunt Jane's henpecks by comparison! There was rejection in it, too, oh yes, I could taste her scorn, her disgust, her big-city derision, but for the first time in my life I no longer felt inadequate, no longer felt embarrassed and bumpkinish, I was on top of this, I was enjoying it, it felt good, it tasted good! Not sweet—no, it was acrid even, bitter, there was the sour taste of grinding traffic in it, musty corridors and overladen elevators, sweat, steam, asphalt playgrounds, loneliness, gutter fights and sudden death— but I liked it! In fact it was terrific! I pushed my tongue between her lips as she jerked and twisted helplessly in my arms—I was glad I hadn't shaved, I was glad it was rough for her! I felt mean and bulky like a bear (partly no doubt because my shirtsleeves were still bunched up inside my jacket) but erotically powerful at the same time. I'll be god-damned! I thought. This *was* what I'd been planning to do all along! Fuck all the phony excuses I'd made to myself, *this* was what I'd come all the way up here for, I'd been bent upon this clinch since I'd fled the Capital, maybe before, maybe since last night already, or out at Burning Tree—this brink, this body, this mouth! And oh, this was a cold mouth to kiss, a ruthless mouth, an exciting mouth, nothing like this back in Whittier, California—I felt I had to hold on just to stay alive! At moments I felt almost swallowed up, lost, disoriented, pursued even—and frightened: what was going to happen to me now? where was this road going? what was I going to tell Pat? how high were the stakes? But I held her all the more tightly, pushing my tongue along her teeth, prying, probing, battering at the gates of her buried soul! And slowly her mouth opened, her struggling subsided, her muffled plaint faded to soft groans, her tongue touched mine, her hand reached for my shoulder, then slid upwards to grip my neck, her body pressed softly against my own, her tongue slithered past my lips, between my teeth—and now there was a new taste, a far richer taste, the fear was gone, the repulsion, the contempt, her lips became sweeter, her mouth widened and new flavors flowed forth. exotic and strange, an incredible variety, all competing with each other, many alien, yet none disagreeable, all beautiful in their diversity. The tart bite of danger was still there, the bitterness of loneliness and ruthlessness, but they were blended now with the delicacy of innocence, the tang of the unexpected, the nutty savor of playfulness, the subtlety of first encounter—in each corner of her mouth I discovered something new, under her tongue, behind each tooth, there seemed no exhausting the possibilities and I relished them all! I roamed the avenues and alleyways of her mouth, tunneled below her tongue, scaled her alveolar ridge, slipped through secret passage-ways, taxied down her palate, delirious with the joy of it! In my excite-ment, I felt somewhat like I'd felt when I came down with undulant fever back in high school. Her own tongue now searched wildly through my mouth: I opened myself to her as to no other woman in my life. One of her hands clutched at my neck, scratching at the short bristle above the nape; the other crawled inside my suit jacket, tugged at my shirt—I felt like my very roots were being pulled up! I dropped the homburg and explored her back, her breasts, her hips (I'd been right about the underwear—was this one of the rules for electrocutions?), searched for the slit on the left side of her skirt. I was breathless, desperate to inhale deeply, I pulled back, but now it was she who clung to me, her tongue darting and flashing through my mouth, her lips sucking on mine. I snuffled, snorted in her hair, lovely smell, freshly shampooed—she'd shampooed her hair for her electrocution!—and past her head (how had we got turned around?) saw the electric chair, empty, waiting, built for men twice her size, garishly lit in its bright white room. I seemed to see sparks flying already from the electrodes, but this might have been her hair which was wild and fluttery and getting in my eyes. And the time—? I couldn't see, but I had the sensation that somehow I was holding it back by holding her. I closed my eyes: my mind seemed to expand, it was as though her hand were kneading it, stretching it, her tongue lapping its edges, her other hand now digging for its root far below. Oh what a mind! I hardly recognized it! It was full of hidden memories, astonishing thoughts, I'd never seen it like this before, a vast moving darkness and brilliant flickering pictures, new and strange, called forth by the charged explorations of our mouths and hands. Some were frightening: girls knocked down by fire hoses, men gassed in trenches and run down by police on galloping horses, villagers buried in bomb-rubble, lives blighted by disease and poverty, children monstrously deformed by radiation or eaten up by vermin—yet it was all somehow exciting, I reveled in all this experience and knew it to be good. I grasped Ethel's bottom and saw the face of a child. He seemed to live in a great city. I couldn't tell if he was black or white, Mexican, Italian, or Polish, but it didn't matter. I shared his dreams: he was a poet, a scientist, a great teacher, a proud craftsman. He was America itself, everything we've ever hoped to be, everything we've dared to dream to be. But he awoke—we both awoke—to the nightmare of poverty, neglect, and despair. He failed in school. He ended up on welfare. He was drafted and died in Korea. I saw all this as my tongue roamed behind Ethel's incisors. I was weeping, but it was as if with joy, because I also saw Grandma Milhous and she was smiling. Why are you nervous? she seemed to be saying. Ethel was clawing through the hair on my chest. The child was reborn. There was peace. My peace and Grandma's. I was trying to get both of Ethel's breasts into one hand. I saw the villages rebuilt and the demeaned lives uplifted. I smelled Mom's hot pies, felt my fingers moving brilliantly on the organ keys, playing "My Rosary," heard the magical call of faraway train whistles in the night, and it was the sweetest music I'd ever heard. I saw the shackles of work gangs fall away, walls between peoples come tumbling down (I had them both in my hand for a moment, soft and firm and full—One if by land, I thought, two if by sea—then let them slip away, reaching up for her face), slum tenements emptying their multitudes into sunny green meadows. I licked feverishly at Ethel's bruised lips and tasted fresh hot bread, stroked her throat and smelled the fragrance of roses, explored the cleft between her buttocks and felt a peace and warmth and brotherhood I had not known since those mornings we all huddled around the kitchen stove in Yorba Linda and we were still all alive. I felt I'd reached some new plateau of awareness, of consciousness, things would never be the same again, for me or for anyone else—how glad I was I'd come here! I jerked her hard into my body, trapping her hand between us: I wished to squeeze her heart and soul up into her mouth where I could get my tongue into them. I could no longer see her, I could not even open my eyes, but she had become extraordinarily beautiful, a vision almost medieval in its wholeness and purity—even her dress, wrinkling under my grip, had become soft and flowing like a Greek tunic. I couldn't even remember the woman who had entered the corridor. The real Ethel Greenglass, childlike and exquisitely lovely— like Audrey Hepburn, I thought, whom I'd just seen on the cover of some magazine, though Ethel's bottom was softer—had come to the surface and absorbed all other emanations (was this what the dialectics of history was all about? I wondered), and it was I who had called her out, I, Richard Milhous Nixon, who had produced this miracle, my God, I was out of my mind with the ecstasy of it! My head was full of poems and justice and unbelievable end runs. I saw millions of people running to embrace me. I thought: *I am making history this evening, not for myself alone, but for all the ages!*

We broke at last, gasping, groaning, sucking our battered lips, clutching each other desperately. She buried her head on my shoulder, nibbling frantically at my neck. "Oh, Richard!" she moaned. "You're so strong, so powerful!" She tangled her fingers in the matted hair on my chest. "I feel so weak!"

I could hardly breathe for the need to, I was afraid I might have an attack of hay fever (girls' hair often set me off), but all in all I was feeling very good, I won't say I'd never felt better in my life, because I was already beginning to have worries about how the hell I was going to get out of here and hopefully get her out as well, but I was feeling very good. That she had called me Richard and not Dick moved me deeply. I thought: if I'd taken this direct approach more often, I might have had a lot more fun in life!

My mouth was near her ear. I realized she was waiting for me to say something. All I could think of were some lines from a play I was once in long ago: *Gentlemen of the Jury! In a few moments you will be called upon to decide the fate of a woman! Is it in you to understand her? Is it in you to understand the man she loved? Who is on trial in this case?* And they weren't even my lines! "I always . . . I always used to admire Judge Brandeis!" I gasped. Jesus, where the hell had such a thought come from, I wondered? "And Justice, uh, Cardozo!"

"Oh, Richard!" she cried, and kissed me again. Apparently, I could do nothing wrong. Again our hands roamed, again our tongues played. I was beginning to feel at home in there, beginning to discover some tastes for the second time, and I found I enjoyed this even more than the first. She was panting hotly down my collar, clawing at my shirt and pants, ripping away buttons and safety pins, shredding what was not already shredded. I'd found the slit in the dress. Even in a struggle as clear-cut as that between tyranny and freedom, I thought, there are gray areas. "Oh, Richard! You don't know what it's been like for me, these two years here . . . and . . . and the years before . . ."

"I know, Ethel. Believe me, I know . . ."

She gripped me tightly, rubbing her body rhythmically against mine, as though to bring to life that cabbie's story of her Morse-code bumps and grinds. "I'm not like this! You won't believe me, but I've never kissed any man but Julie in my life! Not seriously!"

"I believe you," I whispered. "I . . . I haven't either!" I pulled her close to me. "Kissed a woman, I mean."

"Oh, Richard! What's happening to us?"

I remembered crossing upstage a step, then again facing the jury. This was not *The Trysting Place* or *The Dark Tower*. It was not *The Little Accident*. This was the *Night of January 16th* and I was the Prosecuting Attorney, kindly in appearance but shrewd in manner. Backstage, Pat was watching me. *A few months ago, that well-known figure stood with kingdoms and nations in one hand and a whip in the other. Then why should he commit suicide?*

"It's so strange . . . waiting to die," Ethel said softly. It was incredible this rapport, this perfectly reflected image, it made shivers run up and down my spine. Or maybe that was her fingernail. *But there was another, one whom fate had sent him for his salvation. . . .* "I never dreamed . . . anything like this . . ."

"Listen, Ethel, maybe we can still—"

"Did you think you'd be Vice President of the United States one day?"

"What?"

"When you were a little boy, what did you think you'd be when you grew up?"

"Uh . . . a railroad engineer. But, Ethel—"

"I thought I was going to be a singer. A famous singer. I really believed that!"

"Yes, I know," I said.

"You know?"

"Yes. Later I wanted to be a lawyer in New York and I was in New York the night you met Julie. I was looking for a job. We might have found each other that night. Things might have been different."

"I wouldn't want you to be anything but what you are, Richard! I envy you your power. Your majesty. You are a great man, and I . . ."

"But I always wanted to be free. I wanted to be a bum."

"I wanted to be a great actress. I dreamed of going to Hollywood. I would have had to struggle, work in soda fountains, take bit parts—but in the end everybody would have loved me. We might have met there. I might have got a job in your home town."

"I . . . I gave a speech in Hollywood once. Darryl Zanuck said it was the most tremendous performance he'd ever seen."

"Yes, I know," she said.

"You know?"

"I was accepted for the Schola Cantorum. I was the youngest voice the choir had ever had. But I couldn't go on tour because I couldn't leave my job, my mother wouldn't—" Suddenly, she burst into tears, began weeping helplessly on my shoulder.

"Ethel! My God! *What is it?*"

"Somebody . . . somebody came . . ." She could hardly get it out, she was breaking my heart with the struggle: ". . . to measure me today!"

"What? To measure—?"

"They said . . . *they said it was for a wax museum! Oh, Richard!*" She was sobbing uncontrollably now, trembling violently all over.

"Ethel . . . that's . . . that's terrible!" And I began to cry as well. Real tears!

"I don't want . . . *I don't want to die!*"

"I don't want you to die either, Ethel!" I sobbed. It was like a damburst, all falling out of me. We were clutching each other desperately, completely dissolved in tears. I don't know how we stayed on our feet. "It's terrible! I can't stand thinking about it!"

She squeezed me more tightly than ever. "You won't die, Richard! Don't be afraid!"

"Two of my brothers died!" I bawled. "I always thought . . . I would be *next!*"

"Oohh!" she wailed. "Brothers! Don't talk about brothers!"

"It nearly killed my mother, trying to keep my brother alive! And then he died anyway!"

"*My* mother made fun of me! She said there was no place in life for arty people! She sent me out to work!"

"She was cruel to you!"

"She took my money! She hated me!"

"*My* mother sent me away to live with my aunt! She—she didn't want me!"

"Oh, Richard!"

"Once I went all the way to Arizona to—to clean the horsepoop out of stables just to be with her and she didn't appreciate it!"

"My mother wouldn't let me take music lessons!"

" I nearly died of pneumonia!"

"I have terrible backaches!"

"I get hay fever in September!" We looked into each other's faces. Tears were streaming down our cheeks. "Oh, Ethel! You're so—so understanding!"

"Hold me close, Richard! I feel cold! Warm me with your warmth!"

We kissed again. This time languorously, purposefully, intently. The sweet salt of tears mingled with the now-familiar taste of our lips. I thought: all strength lies in giving, not taking. I wanted to serve. We held each other's hands. In this long chaste embrace, I felt an incredible new power, a new freedom. Where did it come from? Uncle Sam? The Phantom? Both at once? From neither, I supposed. There was nothing overhead any more, I had escaped them both! I was outside guarded time! I was my own man at last! I felt like shouting for joy!

We separated. We stared at each other through our tears. We laughed. We hugged each other, stared, laughed again. We pecked playfully at each other's lips. We patted each other's bottoms. We rubbed noses. It was a bit prominent her nose. Of course. I liked it though: so different from Pat's.

She cocked her head to one side and grinned. "You've got a funny nose," she said. We laughed and laughed.

"I've never been able to let my hair down with anyone before," I said. I licked her lips, kissed her eyes, her cheeks, her throat, caressed her breasts. "I've always been afraid of seeming square. But with you it's not like that—I feel I can talk about anything with you!"

"Yes," she said, and squeezed me happily. "I've always been afraid of seeming weak. Why can't people let other people just be what they are?"

"People are always sweating about their image instead of about loving other people. Why can't we all talk to each other, just say what we feel?"

She kissed my throat, nibbled my earlobe. "You're so serious-minded, so sincere, Richard, I could eat you in sheer extremity of feeling!" she whispered huskily.

We kissed again. Passionately this time, and now that train was passing through Yorba Linda again, or was still passing, was forever passing and whistling, it was beautiful, I had a very warm and heartaching feeling about it, I was waving at it, the engineer was smiling and waving back, it was Herbert Hoover, I was also the engineer, smiling and waving, guiding my train through lands new, exotic, verdant, vast, my hand sure on the throttle. Everywhere I went people cheered and waved. I could actually *hear* them cheering! Aunt Edith. Tom Dewey. Chief Newman. Foster and Allen and Moneybags Wunder: I saw them as we went hooting past! Clickety-clock! clickety—all this motion . . . What was I—? "Ethel!" I gasped, breaking away, nuzzling behind her ear, trying to catch my breath. "We have to get out of here somehow! We have to think of something to tell the Warden!"

She gave me a tremulous hug, shook her head. "No," she said breathlessly. "They'd never let me go now. Just hold me for a few more minutes. I've been so lonely. I don't feel lonely any more."

"But, Ethel, we could make something up, you could tell them you were drugged or brainwashed or your children would be murdered if you didn't—"

"Did you like my letters?" she asked dreamily.

"What? What?"

"Didn't you read—?"

"Yes! Yes, they were beautiful, Ethel! Like everything about you!" Should we use the Warden as a hostage? Or just tell him she'd confessed and walk right out? Hide somewhere until it all blows over? I glanced about but everything was bare and exposed. "And, uh . . . your poetry! I liked your poetry, too!"

"Do you like poetry?" she whispered, holding me close.

"I've . . . I've always had a feeling for literature," I said. I knew I had to keep thinking, but it was hard to think with her tongue in my ear. "Plays especially. I've written some. Uh . . . one or two—I just had a new idea for one last night! It was—"

"You could write the plays and I could act in them! I could even sing!"

"Yes! Yes, it's not too late!" I cried. "We're still young, Ethel!" A vast new panorama seemed to be opening up before my eyes. We could go away! to Mexico!—the South Pacific! Why not? We looked at each other, our faces began to twist up—and we burst into tears again. Now we were both sobbing frantically, hanging on to each other for dear life. "Oh, Ethel!" I wept. "We've got to—we've got to *do* something!"

"It's no use!" she bawled.

I knew deep in my heart she was right, but I didn't want to seem to believe it. "There's . . . there's still time . . . !"

She was weeping as if she could never stop, her tears running down my neck in a flood. Her hand was under my shirt and trying to squeeze down behind past my belt. I was sobbing in her hair, clutching at it with one hand (a bald spot! no, *shaved!* for the electrode! oh my God!), clinging to her bottom with the other. I felt like Aeneas, throwing himself on Dido's bier. I sucked in my stomach so she could push her hand down another inch or so.

"Oh, Ethel! I'd do anything for you!" I sobbed. "If we could only—!"

"Richard!" she gasped, pulling back, her dark eyes flashing through the tears. "Richard, please! You *can* do something! You *must!*"

"Yes! Yes, I—!"

"You must take me! Here!"

"Ye—what?"

"Now! Before I die! Give me a chance! It's the one thing you can do for me!"

"But . . . but—*here*—?"

"Quickly! We only have a few minutes!"

"But what if the Warden—"

"We've still got time! He said thirty minutes!"

"He did?"

"Hurry!" she gasped. "Now!" She was tearing at my belt. "*I'll help you!*" she whispered, and it sent fresh shivers up and down my spine. I tried to help, too, not knowing what else to do. Certainly I was ready if it came to it and if I could be quick enough . . . I usually was . . . nobody would ever know . . . "Two whole years, Richard! Two whole years!"

Our fingers were hopelessly engangled at the buckle. "Try . . . try to rush things . . . ," I wheezed.

It fell out through my broken fly then, as big as I'd ever seen it, throbbing like the breast of a wounded bird. I hardly recognized it. She slapped my hands away from the buckle playfully and unhooked it, whipped the belt apart, snapped my pants down to my ankles. She tried to pull them off my feet, but they were getting tangled. "We haven't a minute to lose!" she cried, glancing anxiously over her shoulder. "Hurry! Get them off!"

"But, but—!"

"You're not going fast enough, Richard! Get them off!"

"Th-they're caught on my shoes!" I cried. Damn it, I was doing my best! I seemed to hear my mother getting me ready for school. You're going to be late!

Ethel tried to help, but the pants were getting hopelessly knotted up. We were staggering about, slapping up against the walls and radiators (fortunately they were turned off), but the goddamn pants would not come off.

I sat down. The bare waxed floor felt cold and hostile to my bum. But I was still terribly excited. I wanted her to do again what she'd been doing just before. "Give a pull!" I shouted.

"We'll never make it!" she whimpered, hauling frantically on my pants, pulling them inside out and bouncing me around the corridor on my rump in a screeching rubbery skid.

"Hey! Ethel! Ow!" I felt like I was on some kind of awful carnival ride. I was afraid of getting blisters. "You're hurting me—!"

She caught her breath suddenly, spun toward the door. "We're too late!" she gasped.

"Oh no!" I cried. "What is it?"

"Can't you hear it?" It sounded like distant chains rattling. "It's the other prisoners banging their tin cups on their bars! They're coming! They're coming to take me away!"

I scrambled clumsily to my feet—they'd got crossed somehow in the tangle of pants and I kept tipping over. "Help me, Ethel! *What am I going to do?!*"

"Quick!" she whispered. "It doesn't matter about me! You must save yourself!" She clutched my arm, looked about wildly, spied the open door. "In there!" she cried, and pushed me toward the execution chamber. "It's your only chance!"

I didn't argue, I could hear the rattling getting louder, I hobbled and stumbled toward the door with her, hauling at my pants. "Well, it is . . . it is important for the nation . . . !" I stammered. She seemed to be rubbing something on my behind. "What are you—!?"

"Your bottom's all filthy," she explained breathlessly. "I'm just cleaning it off—now hurry! I'll try to stall them!" She grabbed up my battered homburg and clapped it down around my ears. She must have been standing on it. The sign over the door into the electrocution chamber, I saw, said: ENTER TO GROW IN WISDOM. DEPART BETTER TO SERVE THY COUNTRY AND MANKIND.

The lights dipped. "Oh my God! What—!?"

"They're testing the dynamos!" she cried. She spun me around, threw her arms about me, held me tight. "Don't . . . don't forget me, Richard!" she gasped.

"Ethel! I don't know what to . . ." I could hardly think, the noises had got louder and I could hear footsteps now, marching up toward the far door. "You've been . . . it's been great—meeting you, I mean!"

She took my face in her hands, kissed it. I was trying not to panic. "You will be a great man," she said softly, speaking as though she had all the time in the world. "I have faith in you. You will unite the nation and bring peace to mankind. But above all they shall say of you: Richard Nixon was a great lover!" She kissed me again, long and passionately. "You need a shave," she said with a shy smile, and tweaked my peter gently. There was a tear in her eye.

"Ethel!" I was afraid I was going to start crying again. I was trying to remember the lines of that play she was in. "Ethel, remember, the valiant die many—I mean, the valiant, uh, taste of death—damn it, I've forgotten it!" I could hear keys being shoved into the locks of the door at the other end of the corridor. The autopsy room, I thought! I can hide in there!

"Cowards die many times before their deaths," she said, "the valiant never taste of death but once." Was there something caustic in her tone? It came to me as though through an echo chamber. I felt terrible that I'd muffed the line.

"Ethel, forgive me!" I pleaded, backing away. I was cold and hot all at once and there was a roaring in my ears. I had the strange sensation of a body lying on the floor of the execution chamber, but I couldn't bring myself to look. Behind Ethel, the door was opening!

I was afraid she might reach out, pull me back, try to kiss me again—she just couldn't seem to get enough! But instead she only grinned sheepishly and winked. "I'll be thinking of you, Richard," she said. They were coming in behind her. I ducked back out of sight, reflecting that a man who has never lost himself in a cause bigger than himself has missed one of life's mountaintop experiences: only in losing himself does he find himself.

26.

Spreading the Table of Glory

JACK: Now let's see, there must be something here in these letters I can use for the contest . . .

(*Welcoming applause.*)

JACK: A thousand dollars for first prize! I've got to choose something that—ah! here's what I'm looking for: "An eternity of time is crawling along and it seems we're in a bottomless pit with no connection to reality . . ." Hmmm . . .

DENNIS: Hello, Mr. Benny! Did you get stuck down in your vault again?

JACK: Oh, hello, Dennis . . .

(*Laughter and welcoming applause.*)

JACK: No, I did not get stuck in my vault, I was just practicing my lines for—Dennis! Why on earth are you dressed up like a cowboy? And what are you doing with that silly hat on your head?

DENNIS: Hat?

JACK: Yes, with that . . . that cherry on top!

(*Laughter.*)

DENNIS: Oh, that's not a hat, Mr. Benny, that's a pie crust! I'm going to enter a contest!

JACK: *What* contest?

447

DENNIS: A Tom Mix Pie contest!

(*Laughter.*)

JACK: A Tom Mix Pie contest! Well, I never—!

DENNIS: Bang, bang, yummy, yummy, Mr. Benny!

(*Laughter, whistles, enthusiastic applause.*)

DENNIS: Are you going to the contest, Mr. Benny?

JACK: Well, yes . . . yes, I am, Dennis. But I'm going to do a more *dramatic* reading, something on the order of John Barrymore . . .

DENNIS: Playing it for laughs, hunh?

(*Laughter and applause.*)

JACK: Now, stop that, Dennis, that's quite enough—!

DENNIS: Well, I gotta go now, Mr. Benny! Betty Crocker's waiting for me . . .

JACK: Betty Crocker—!

DENNIS: Yes, she's gonna help me with my crusts, Mr. Benny. My top crust's light and flaky, but my bottom's a bit soggy—

JACK: Dennis—!

(*Laughter, whistles, prolonged applause.*)

DENNIS: So long, Mr. Benny! I'll see you at the contest!

(*Farewell applause.*)

JACK: That boy! A Tom Mix Pie—that's the silliest thing I ever heard of! It *was* a cute costume though . . .

(*Light laughter.*)

Probably *I* ought to have something . . . hmmm . . . what do spies wear, I wonder . . . ? Oh, Rochester! Where is that—? *Rochester!*

ROCHESTER: Heah, boss!

(*Welcoming applause.*)

JACK: Rochester . . . Rochester, go get me those old wire-rimmed glasses, and my black gloves and . . . let's see . . . a black eyepatch, and my old trench coat!

ROCHESTER: Trench coat? You ain't got no trench coat, boss!

JACK: Of course I have! The one I wore in the war!

ROCHESTER: They didn't have no trench coats in the Spanish-American War, boss!

(*Laughter.*)

JACK: Now cut that out, Rochester, and go get my trench coat! The Spanish-American War—!

MARY: What coat is that, Jack?

JACK: Oh, hello, Mary . . .

(*Welcoming applause.*)

You know, Mary, the one I wore in the war . . .

MARY: With the gold buttons and fancy shoulder boards?

JACK: That's right. You see, Rochester? Mary remembers the coat! Now, you—

MARY: The one that had 'Remember the Maine!' stitched on the collar . . .

(*Laughter.*)

JACK: Yes, it—what?

MARY: Oh, Jack, I gave that coat away to a poor old man during the last Depression!

JACK: You . . . *gave* it away?

(*Laughter.*)

MARY: Yes—in fact, look out there: isn't that your coat that old pan-handler is wearing?

JACK: Hmmm . . . yes. Well, it *does* look like my coat at that . . .

(*Laughter.*)

Oh, Rochester!

ROCHESTER: Yeah, boss?

JACK: Rochester, go give that man a dime and make him give you my coat back!

ROCHESTER: A whole dime, boss? Ain't you gittin' a little loose wit' your change?

(*Laughter.*)

JACK: It's worth it, Rochester—if I wear that coat, I'm *sure* to win the thousand dollars!

ROCHESTER: Well, okay, boss . . .

JACK: And Rochester . . . Rochester, tell the man that if I win the prize I'll give him . . . well, I'll . . . I'll let him have the coat back!

(*Laughter.*)

ROCHESTER: Yassuh, boss!

JACK: Providing . . .

ROCHESTER: Yeah, boss?

JACK: Providing he gives me my dime back!

Out front, a hundred million mouths open wide, a hundred million sets of teeth spring apart like dental exhibits, a hundred million bellies quake, and a hundred million throats constrict and spasm, gasp and wheeze, as America laughs. At much the same things everybody laughs at everywhere: sex, death, danger, the enemy, the inevitable, all the things that hurt about growing up, something that Americans especially, suddenly caught with the whole world in their hands, are loath to do. What makes them laugh hardest, though, are jokes about sexual inadequacy—a failure of power—and the cruder the better, for crudity recalls their childhood for them: the Golden Age. Grandpa Jones delivering lines to Cousin Minnie Pearl about dammed-up passions cracks them up. So does Stan Laurel telling Oliver Hardy (sitting deadly serious in the electric chair with his suit and derby on and one of Ethel's skirts stretched around his fat belly, split ludicrously down one side) in his soft singsong voice: "Your smile, Bunny, your warm kiss, your sweet voice and your understanding mind are my greatest treasure and pleasure!" (Oliver winces and glances irritably at Stan on hearing this last phrase, cocks his head thoughtfully, repeating the words under his breath, then resumes his pose . . .) Or the brash little puppet Charlie McCarthy, nothing but a small polished knurl between his wooden legs, fantasizing doing a Rosenbergs sketch with Marilyn Monroe, in which he slips into her cell at night disguised as the prison chaplain (Mortimer Snerd, the sucker, plays the husband, of course) . . .

BERGEN: I can't see one little reason why we should ask Marilyn Monroe to be in this skit with us, Charlie . . .

CHARLIE: I can see two pretty big ones, Bergen!

BERGEN: (*through the laughter*) Now, Charlie . . . !

CHARLIE: Say, Bergen . . . ?

BERGEN: Yes, Charlie?

CHARLIE: That chair works by electricity, doesn't it?

BERGEN: Yes.

CHARLIE: Well, what'll happen if it doesn't kill 'em? They're only singers, you know, not conductors . . .

(*Laughter and light applause.*)

BERGEN: (*chuckling loosely*) Well, I don't think you have to worry about that, Charlie. Even if they did survive the chair, there are other ways . . .

CHARLIE: You mean, there's more than one way to cook a crook—I mean, juice a goose . . . !

(*Laughter and appreciative applause.*)

BERGEN: Yes, Charlie, only twenty-six states use electrocution. Thirteen prefer hanging, and eight use lethal gas.

CHARLIE: I get it, Bergen: you either yoke 'em, choke 'em, or coke 'em!

(*Prolonged laughter and applause.*)

BERGEN: Yes, that's the idea, Charlie. But I confess I find it rather depressing to talk about it. Somehow, ever since I passed my fortieth birthday, I—

CHARLIE: Fortieth! The last time you passed forty, Bergen, they were still using Roman numerals!

BERGEN: (*through the laughter*) Now, Charlie . . . !

CHARLIE: Well, chin up, Bergen, we all have to go some time.

BERGEN: Yes, I suppose so . . .

CHARLIE: Earth to earth, ashes to ashes, sawdust to sawdust . . .

BERGEN: (*through the loose laughter*) Yes, well . . .

CHARLIE: When it comes my turn, Bergen, I hope they give me a choice. If I gotta croak, I don't wanna be smoked, broke, soaked, *or* choked to death!

BERGEN: No? Then how—?

CHARLIE: I wanna be *stroked* to death, Bergen—by Marilyn Monroe!

BERGEN: (*through the uproar*) Charlie—!

The naughty boy who gets away with it, the old man who needn't try, the dumb broad who doesn't know what's happened when it's happened, plus a little danger, a little violence, anticipation and surprise: these are the things that open the Whale's mouth. As when Buster Keaton, sitting deadpan in the electric chair, calmly turns and throws a custard pie at the Executioner just as he's about to throw the switch: SPLAT! Some have contended that it was America's love of pie-throwing that led the nation to develop the atomic bomb. This may or may not be true, but certainly it does help explain the country's current panic over the possible proliferation of the bombs to unfriendly nations: it's a cardinal rule of the act that one custard pie leads to another, and he who throws one must sooner or later face one coming from the other direction. Which is what's happening to Buster Keaton right now, though he seems unaware of it. The Executioner, forgetting his office, has grabbed up another pie and is rearing back to hurl it at Keaton, who has meanwhile settled back in the chair to await, stonily, his electrocution. One foot, however, is loose from its strap, and after thinking about this foot for a moment, Keaton leans forward to buckle it in—just that split second before the pie would have hit him: it hits the prison chaplain instead. Buster, apparently oblivious to what's happening at either side of him, satisfies himself that his foot is securely buckled to the chair, then sits back once more like a patient bridegroom to await the shock. But now the chaplain has a pie . . .

While this is going on, the countdown has begun—55 minutes to Zero Hour . . . 54 . . . 53—and backstage there is a frenzied shuffling about as Betty Crocker, wielding a soup ladle, lines up all the bigwigs for their Grand Processional. All the major officials who are assigned, according to the Dead Sea statutes, "to attend to the burnt-offerings and the sacrifices, to set out the incense of 'pleasant savor' for God's acceptance, to perform rites of atonement in behalf of His congregation, and constantly to clear away the fat ashes which lie before Him on the 'table of glory,' " must now be introduced and guided to their respective places, and who better to set this table than America's matron saint of the kitchen? Sprung full-formed and all buttoned up from the fat fertile head of General Mills in 1936, Betty is everything one would want in a Holy Mother: sober, efficient, old-fashioned, unblemished, bountiful, and the only undoubted virgin in all America (indeed, it's been said she hasn't even changed her corset since '36), as protective as Athena, as merciful and mild as Mary, as resourceful as the pioneer women who settled America—she is, it could be said, their reincarnation. Her name, which sounds like bullfrogs burping on soft prairie nights, suggests crockery, Crockett, rocking chairs, rockets. "Betty" is a down-home version of traditional majesty, a country nickname for the Mother Country's greatest monarch and now her newest one. A pie, flung from the stage into the wings, slaps the wall inches from her face, causing Cabinet members and their wives to shriek and duck, but Betty, unruffled, only gazes at it with her cool imperturbable blue eyes, sticks a finger in it and tastes the filling: mm, as she suspected, too much cornstarch.

Virtually every significant political figure in the nation is back here tonight, ready to go on, ready to demonstrate their wholehearted enthusiasm for Uncle Sam's purification-by-fire spectacular . . . all but a few like Supreme Court Justice Hugo Black and Vice President Richard M. Nixon. Black, boycotting the show from his hospital bed, is a lousy loser, just about everybody's given up on him long ago, but the absence of that old rocking socking Phantom-fighter and Early Warning Sentinel Dick Nixon is a more disturbing matter. Uncle Sam himself, backstage briefly during the Mickey Rooney–Judy Garland act, is heard to mutter: "Maybe a boxcar of pussyfooters woulda been better after all!" Which is all Harold Stassen needs: "I say, let's dump the sonuvabitch! Nobody likes him anyway, he just drags us all down! I don't want anything for myself, of course—I'm only thinking of what's good for the country . . ." This provokes a lot of harsh nervous laughter, and the next time a pie comes flying into the wings, everybody ducks and lets Stassen take it on the snoot.

Out front meanwhile, a lot of famous people have had a go at the prize money, but the performers who steal the show (and anything else they can get their hands on) are the fabulous Marx Brothers. Partly it's their act, catching the mood of the night; partly it's the deep affection felt toward these local boys, downtrodden city Jews like the Rosenbergs, but without their crybaby ways; and partly it's simply the astonishing cartoon resemblance Groucho and Harpo bear to Julius and Ethel—so real that people gasp when they first appear onstage, Harpo (Ethel) sitting in the electric chair and writing desperate letters to Groucho (Julius), which Chico (the Executioner) reads aloud in his Jewish-Italian accent as Groucho goes stalking restlessly about the set in his famous bent-kneed crouch, puffing a cigar and bobbing his eyebrows . . .

CHICO: "Canna we ever forget da turbulence and struggle, da joy and beauty uvva da early years of our relationship whenna you courted me?"

GROUCHO: I dunno, but we can *try* . . .

CHICO: "Togedder we hunted down da answers to alla da seemingly insoluble riddles w'ich a complex and callous society presented."

GROUCHO: The answer's a cracked egg.

CHICO: "It'sa because we did'n' hesitate to blazon fort' dose answers datta we sit wit'in da wallsa Sing Sing!"

GROUCHO: Loudmouth . . .

CHICO: "It'sa incredible dat I should sit in a cell inna Sing Sing awaitin' my own legal murder, after da twelf' yearsa da kinda principled, connastructive, wholesome livin' dat we did!"

GROUCHO: It ain't incredible—that's the reason!

CHICO: "Incidentally, da clinic doctor he examine my back lasta week and sent a report to da head doctor."

GROUCHO: Yeah, that's what you need all right, a *head* doctor!

The plot of their sketch—if anything the Marx Brothers do can be said to have a plot—turns around the American Government's offer to commute their death sentences in exchange for information about the spy ring. Harpo *can't* talk, of course, being mute, and so is strapped into the electric chair, but Groucho snaps up the offer:

GROUCHO: I'll name anybody! My mother, my agent, even my mistress!

CHICO: Whatta you sayin'? You ain' got a misteriss! You ain' even got a cockyerbine!

GROUCHO: I'll name her, too!

CHICO: Whatta you gonna name her?

GROUCHO: (*singing and rolling his eyes*) I think I'll name her "Jasmine" . . .

CHICO: Jas' yours?

GROUCHO: (*continuing*) . . . Cuz she's mighty lak' a rose!

CHICO: Oh, a Pinko, eh? We're gettin' to da bottomma dis!

GROUCHO: You been there, too, hunh?

CHICO: She'sa da one what's stole-a da bum', eh?

GROUCHO: She didn't steal it, she was born with it!

CHICO: And she gave it to da Russians?

GROUCHO: She gave it to everybody!

CHICO: Dat'sa terrible! Murder is dwarfed by comparitson!

GROUCHO: Yeah, she gave it to dwarfs, too!

CHICO: She's gonna get da hot seat for dis!

GROUCHO: That's no good.

CHICO: No good?

GROUCHO: She's already got it.

CHICO: Hey, you know somet'in'? I t'ink you gotta somet'in' to hide!

GROUCHO: Yeah, well, it ain't nothing to brag about, I admit.

CHICO: Iffa you don' talk, Mr. Roastenbug, we gonna givva you da chair!

GROUCHO: Okay, don't bother to wrap it, I've got my car.

CHICO: I mean-a you gotta sit in dat chair and face-a da music!

GROUCHO: Face the music! That's why you call it Sing Sing, hunh?

CHICO: Dat'sa what I say: you gotta face-a da music music!

Harpo meanwhile has been listening to all of this with goggle-eyed astonishment, and now this talk about music has aroused his curiosity. He searches about the chair and finds two loose wires. He holds one of them expectantly up to his ear: he hears nothing. He tries the other: still nothing. He frowns and rolls his eyes. He holds the two wires a few inches apart and sparks fly. He thinks about this a minute, then, smiling idiotically, sticks both wires in his ears at the same time. There's a buzzing crackling noise and Harpo's smile spreads. His eyes roll round and round and his lashes flutter. He seems slowly to levitate from the chair, his body aglow. Chico, the Executioner, looks up in alarm. "Hey, whatcha doin'!" he cries, and rushes to the switch to turn off the current. Harpo drops back into the chair. Groucho and Chico lift him out and stand him on his feet. He's still grinning blissfully, his head lolling about, his eyes crossing and rolling as though unassociated with each other, his feet barely touching the floor. He makes little fluttering motions with his hands to suggest he's been hearing music. Chico puts his ear to Harpo's chest to listen to his heart: "It'sa Duh-four-shocksa New Worlt Sinfunny!" he cries in amazement. "It is, hunh?" says Groucho. "Well, put another nickel in, maybe the old one's on the other side!" He leans his head in under Chico's to have a listen, but Harpo keels over: his legs and arms twitch and shake, then collapse. "It musta been-a da las' movement," says Chico. "Looked more like Madame Butterfly to me!" says Groucho, bobbing his eyebrows.

CHICO: No, I mean-a he kick-a da bucket!

GROUCHO: Bucket? What bucket?

CHICO: (*looking around*) Ain't dere a bucket?

GROUCHO: No! Let's get outa here before they think we stole that, too!

43 . . . 42 . . . Uncle Sam comes hurrying out, bobbing his stern white brows and imitating Groucho's famous stiff-backed ass-to-the-ground stride, to garner the last burst of laughter and applause and shower crisp greenbacks like confetti on the many prize-winners, reminding all present with his freehanded beneficence of America's greatest asset: her bottomless kitty. Then he rears up straight and tall and hollers out: "Now is the hour, fellers and citizens! Enough of this monkey business! *We stand at Armageddon and we battle for the Lord!*" And with a grand wave of his red-white-and-blue plug hat, he brings on a Texas high-school marching band, batons flying, legs kicking, drums rolling, plumes fluttering, to play "The Star-Spangled Banner." The people bellow forth, drunk enough now to try the high notes, rapturous tears springing to their eyes, their hearts beating faster . . . it's coming now . . . 40 . . .

During the suspenseful "say, does that star-spangled banner yet wave" line, Uncle Sam suddenly whips his top hat high into the air, far out of sight, then dashes backstage, crying out to Betty Crocker: "Okay, get your sweet buns out there, dumplin', and preparest a table before me in the presents a mine inimies!" He whacks her lovingly on her corseted butt as he flies by, popping all her stays and reminding old-timers in the wings of the slap Teddy Roosevelt laid on his favorite niece, Eleanor, as he gave her away in holy wedlock to the Great I Am, or of crusty Zack Taylor smacking Old Whitey on the rump as he sent him out to pasture on the White House lawn. And then the next time he's seen is when he comes riding up from behind the crowd, out of the Disney menagerie tent, astride the gigantic GOP elephant, its red-white-and-blue crown studded with spangles that spell out Long Tom Jefferson's article of faith: WE ARE ALL REPUBLICANS!

Just as the people sing, "What is that which the breeze . . . half conceals, half discloses," Uncle Sam reaches far up into the darkening sky and snatches his plug hat as it comes spinning down . . .

> " 'Tis the star-spangled banner: O, long may it wave
> O'er the land of the free and the home of the brave!"

Uncle Sam pops his hat back on his head, but it doesn't sit there—it keeps hopping up and down and seems to have little feet sticking out. He takes it off and peers inside, and with a surprised look on his face plucks out: a dove! the dove of peace! He lets it go—no, not a dove after all, it's the famous floo-floo bird: there it goes, winging its way backwards over the crowd, squawking raucously and crumpling its tail-feathers on billboards and skyscrapers. The people cheer the bird and shout misdirections at it, fight for the coins spilling out of the pantaloon pockets of Uncle Sam, who's now doing a handstand on the elephant's head. The Democrats' mascot donkey comes trailing behind, evidently excited by all this patriotic brouhaha and so bearing—besides the familiar legend YOU NEVER HAD IT SO GOOD! stitched on its saddle blanket —a hard-on the size of Mickey Mantle's baseball bat. As they near the stage, it nearly gets dumped on by the Republican elephant, which chooses just the moment it's down front to unloose its considerable bowels, making such windy plopping noises you can hardly hear the marching band now playing "The Stars and Stripes Forever."

> ALL HAIL, THOU WESTERN WORLD! BY HEAVEN DESIGN'D
> TH' EXAMPLE BRIGHT, TO RENOVATE MANKIND!

reads the Loew's State marquee, and down the street the Roxy announces:

> A BOUNDLESS VISION GROWS UPON US . . .

Uncle Sam posts the elephant and donkey at either side of the Sing Sing stage and signals for the Disney Rat Pack. Mickey and Minnie, Goofy, Horace, and the rest take up prearranged aisle positions in support of the Secret Service (still in their papier-mâché heads) and to help direct the VIPs; other pageant figures line up around the periphery of the VIP section; the film crews pan their cameras around to focus on the main entrance, stage left, zooming in, and the band plays Mess Call. Which is the cue for Betty Crocker: she emerges, prim and matronly, wiping her hands on her apron, to introduce, like the ingredients for one of her famous stuffed turkeys, all the Very Important People who have come here tonight to witness the public burning of Julius and Ethel Rosenberg.

And while Uncle Sam, using his corncob pipe as a baton, conducts the band in playing "When the Saints Go Marchin' In," out they come, not marching, but jogging on like tensed-up ballplayers, everybody who's anybody in the above-board American Power Structure, each one introduced by Betty in her somewhat tremulous old-lady voice (though if anything, it must be said she's getting younger every day) and welcomed with a rousing "He's our man!" cheer led by the Indiana University cheerleaders. The first few to lope out pull up momentarily before that unfortunate mound of elephant dung, but since there's no way around it and no way back, they flash their vote-getting smiles, square their shoulders, and slog on through, and once a path is laid there are no further hesitations. There's an old panhandler out there, stuffed into a thick wool overcoat like an antique shopwindow dummy from the Great Depression and seemingly rooted to the spot, who's something of an obstacle, too, but the VIP's jogging by merely assume he's some kind of turnstile (couldn't be real, after all, not in prosperous postwar America) and stuff quarters in as they pass.

The VIP area has been divided into three sections, one each for the three branches of government who together have made these executions possible, with pride of place tonight given to the judiciary, the legislative branch seated to their left and the executive to their right. A special section of box seats, decorated with flags and bunting and exhibits from the trial, has been set aside just in front of the stage for those directly associated with the Rosenberg case: the FBI director and agents who broke the case, the Judge, jury, prosecution team and witnesses, the Attorney General, and a ringside front-and-center seat for President Eisenhower, who's never been one to settle for a side-aisle pew. The back rows of the three sections are reserved for state and local officials from around the country—legislators, judges, administrators, mayors,

National Guard officers, tax collectors, Lieutenant-Governors, sheriffs, and the like—and these are the first to come out, followed by all the auxiliary personnel who serve the three federal branches, all the agencies, bureaus, departments, commissions, institutes, foundations, boards, councils, societies, administrations, appeal and claims courts, funds, organizations, banks, services, systems, committees, national centers, offices, and authorities, and all their staff, counsel, secretaries, chiefs, directors, clerks, treasurers, personnel officers, confidential assistants, managers, commissioners, auditors, recorders, consultants, editors, superintendents, chairmen, military aides, receptionists, curators, and parliamentarians. Next come all the key personnel from the major executive departments attached to Cabinet officers, the federal district judges and senior circuit judges in the appeals courts, and all 435 members of the U.S. House of Representatives. It's a colorful lot, and even plain-spoken self-possessed Betty Crocker gets a certain itchy pleasure out of calling out their names: Laurie Battle! Porque Patten! Zeke Gathings! Rubie Scudder! Jimmy Utt! J. Edgar Chenoweth! Prince H. Preston, Jr.! Gracie Pfost! Hamer Budge! Runt Bishop! Shepard Crumpacker! Errett P. Scrivner! Hale Boggs! Tip O'Neill! Richard B. Wigglesworth! Thaddeus M. Machrowicz! Kit Clardy! Elford A. Cederberg! Dewey Short! Morgan M. Moulder! Norris Cotton! T. Millet Hand! Jack Dempsey! Stuyvesant Wainwright! Franklin D. Roosevelt, Jr.! Jake Javits! Usher Burdick! James G. Polk! Page Belcher! Sam Coon! Homer D. Angell! Wally Mumma! L. Mendel Rivers and Gerry Ford! Percy Priest! Olin E. Teague! Homer Thornberry! Winston Prouty! Thor C. Tollefson! Harley Staggers! Melvin Laird! Clem Zablocki!

> "Gubser! Gubser! he's our man!
> If he can't do it, Hillings can!
> Hillings! Hillings! he's our man!
> If he can't do it, Yorty can!
> Yorty! Yorty . . ."

"Whoopee-ti-yi-yo!" laughs Uncle Sam, herding them in, "the whole dingbusted United States guvvamint is corraled in here tonight, I see, everybody from the guinea pigs at Disease Control to the coffee steward at the Pentagon! It's a real smorgasbord! Here muster, not the forces of party, but the forces of humanity, and a appetizin' lot they are, too!" Then he suddenly starts and glances up at the sky, lost beyond the bright lights and hovering smog of Times Square. "God *damn* that tarnacious Phantom if he lets one fly tonight!" he mutters, and a collective gasp shakes the Square. Could it happen? "What am I sayin'? Anything he can do I can do better! I yam strong as the breezes w'ich blows down big treeses, so c'mon, get on with it, punkin, dish 'em up! In skatin' over thin ice our safety is in our speed!"

Nobody knows better than Betty Crocker the importance of proper timing in laying a good table, so she rushes on, bringing out the ninety-six Senators now and all their spouses and children: Lister Hill and John Sparkman of Alabama, Carl Hayden and Barry Goldwater of Arizona, John McClellan and J. William Fulbright of Arkansas, William Knowland and Thomas Kuchel of California, Edwin Johnson and Eugene Millikin of Colorado, Prescott Bush and William Purtell of Connecticut, John J. Williams and J. Allen Frear of Delaware, Spessard Holland and George Smathers of Florida, Walter George and Richard B. Russell of Georgia, Henry Dworshak and Herman Welker of Idaho, Paul Douglas and Everett McKinley Dirksen of Illinois, Homer Capehart and William Jenner of Indiana, Bourke Hickenlooper and Guy Gillette of Iowa, Andrew Schoeppel and Frank Carlson of Kansas, Earle Clements and John Sherman Cooper of Kentucky, Allen Ellender and Russell B. Long of Louisiana, Margaret Chase Smith and Frederick Payne of Maine, John Butler and J. Glenn Beall of Maryland, Leverett Saltonstall and John F. Kennedy of Massachusetts, Homer Ferguson and Charles Potter of Michigan, Edward J. Thye and Hubert H. Humphrey of Minnesota, James Eastland and John Stennis of Mississippi, Thomas Hennings and Stuart Symington of Missouri, James Murray and Mike Mansfield of Montana, Hugh Butler and Dwight Griswold of Nebraska, Pat McCarran and George Malone of Nevada, Styles Bridges and Charles Tobey of New Hampshire, H. Alexander Smith and Robert Hendrickson of New Jersey, Dennis Chavez and Clinton Anderson of New Mexico, Irving Ives and Herbert Lehman of New York, Clyde Hoey and Willis Smith of North Carolina, William Langer and Milton Young of North Dakota, Robert Taft and John Bricker of Ohio, Robert Kerr and Mike Monroney of Oklahoma, Guy Cordon and Wayne Morse of Oregon, Edward Martin and James Duff of Pennsylvania, Theodore Francis Green and John Pastore of Rhode Island, Burnet Maybank and Olin Johnston of South Carolina, Karl Mundt and Francis Case of South Dakota, Estes Kefauver and Albert Gore of Tennessee, Lyndon B. Johnson and Price Daniel of Texas, Arthur Watkins and Wallace Bennett of Utah, George Aiken and Ralph Flanders of Vermont, Harry Byrd and Willis Robertson of Virginia, Warren Magnuson and Henry (Scoop) Jackson of Washington, Harley Kilgore and Matthew Neely of

West Virginia, Alexander Wiley and Joseph McCarthy of Wisconsin, and Lester Hunt and Frank Barrett of Wyoming.

"Oh, when the saints go marchin' in,
When the saints go marchin' in,
Oh, I want to be in that number,
When the saints go marchin' in . . . . !"

Naturally, with the entire American constituency out there as an eager audience, each one of these handsome screamers aches for a shot at the microphones as he goes galumphing grandly across the stage, past the electric chair, and down—*thunk! splot!*—into the elephant patties, but Styles Bridges, the President Pro Tempore and a respecter of hallowed traditions, limits the privilege to a few heroic whoopees from the Majority and Minority Leaders and Whips and a blown kiss and a blessing from the Senate Elders: George, Hayden, Russell, Byrd, and McCarran. Not that this stops the precocious junior Senator from Wisconsin—Joe McCarthy doesn't give a shit for protocol, but grabs the mike out of Bridges' hand (some say they saw Bridges hand it to him) and lets rip with a rampagious spate of old-fashioned, breast-beating, salt-boiler drolleries: "No one can push me out of anything!" he cries, and Bridges winks as though to say: You better believe it! "I'm not retiring from the field of exposing left-wingers, New Dealers, radicals and pinkos, egg-sucking phony liberals, Communists and queers! That fight can't abate on my part or yours until we've won the war, or our civilization has died!" Promising the revelation of "a conspiracy of infamy so black that, when it is finally exposed, its principals shall be forever deserving of the maledictions of all honest men," he announces hundreds of investigations that he plans to launch before the year is out into the State Department with its "prancing mimics of the Moscow party line," the information- and teacher-exchange programs, East-West trade, the Government Printing Office, the defense industry, the Army Signal Corps (the Rosenberg spy-ring story isn't over yet! he hints darkly), and even the Army itself: "I am going to kick the brains out of anyone who protects Communists!" The other Senators are made green with envy and flushed with embarrassment at the same time by all this public hyperbole, but the crowds love it, and even Uncle Sam seems reluctant to shut him up. Finally Joe himself remarks on all the time-wasting here tonight and demands that they get on with it: "It's a dirty, foul, unpleasant, smelly job, but it has to be done! A rough fight is the only fight Communists understand!" He leaps gleefully down into the shit, getting a tremendous ovation—it's a real pick-up, without him the show had begun to stall.

But time, inexorably, has been ticking away: there's less than half an hour now to 8:01. The remaining speeches have to be scrapped and, except for the box-seat guests of honor, the rest of the VIPs—including all the senior magistrates, top military brass, forty-eight State Governors, and the official, unofficial, kitchen, golf, poker, and bedroom Cabinets, and all their families and dogs—have to come barreling out on the double, Betty Crocker, reeling off the names, sounding like one of those new slow-speed records on an ordinary turntable. Only Foster Dulles is given a brief moment at the microphone to release a few lugubrious epigrams from the doctrines of Massive Retaliation, Liberation of Captive Peoples, and Faith in Christ Jesus and the Future of Human Freedom, just to remind the citizens what these executions tonight are all about and to give Uncle Sam time to slip off and shazam himself into the President, but the rest go whipping by like tracer bullets. Betty Crocker's voice now is just a shrieking whir of sound, like an electric beater churning through a fast-thickening pastry dough, as they come streaking out en masse, slipping and sliding, elbowing and punching, thundering right over poor Betty, scrambling frantically for their seats like they're afraid somebody's going to take them away from them. Most of them are well winded by the exercise, they're not used to moving this fast, the judges especially, who are additionally handicapped by their long robes, ripping them on the doorjambs as they shoot out from the wings, tripping and falling over them, having to lift them like skirts to tippytoe at full gallop through the elephant droppings. By the time old Fred Vinson, the Supreme Court Chief Justice, hits the shit, it's much heated up by the frenetic parade and slick as a greased skillet: woops! down he goes! He picks himself up hastily and—*zzzipp! whap!*—he's down again. He proceeds more methodically the next time, placing first one foot under him, then the other, rising slowly . . . his feet slowly slide apart, he gropes for balance and pulls them together again, they spread fore and aft, he tips, rights himself, he's running in place, clawing for air, he's on one foot, the other, neither—*SPLAT!* His old crony Justice Tom Clark rushes to his aid, only to find himself skidding, slithering, pitching out of control, and landing with a mighty—*look out, Fred!—ker-FLAP!* on the Chief Justice's hoary head, just as the old fellow was lifting himself on his hands and knees out of the muck. "That damn fool from Texas," laughs Harry Truman. With the very honor and dignity of the United States Supreme Court at stake, Justices Robert Jackson and Sherman Minton come bounding to the rescue, as Clark and Vinson, leaning on each other, heads together as though in an embrace, butts out for balance, slowly straighten up—cautiously, hanging on, they turn to look toward their seats and what do they see but Jackson and Minton, faces white with panic and feet back-peddling frantically, bearing down on them—*CRASH!* they're all down, wheeling around in the mire like the spinners of children's board games, piling up in a heap finally under the Death House stage. They glance blearily at each other, count themselves, blanch, and duck—and sure enough, here they come: Stanley Reed and Harold Burton, feet flying, robes fluttering, arms outflung and grabbing at space—WHACK! SPLAT! *Ker-SMASH!* When the shit clears, the six Justices are seen, exhausted and blinded by the muck, floundering aimlessly on their hands and knees. Dwight Eisenhower, peeping out from the wings, utters a short cry—"Christ on the mountain! what are those monkeys doing?"—and disappears again.

Standing there backstage with his wife and sons, waiting for the three ritual knocks that will announce his second (formal) entrance as a special guest of honor, Judge Irving Kaufman has been pondering the rewards of virtue and high office, and the essentially—indeed, necessarily—divine origin of the concept of Law, and it occurs to him now, looking out on this scene and listening to one of the prison doctors beside him practicing his lines for later in the show ("I pronounce this man dead . . . I pronounce this woman dead . . . I pronounce . . ."), that it might behoove him to play a part in this rescue, for even if he failed and joined the rest of them down there in the dreck, it might not be the worst thing that ever happened to him. But just as he steps out, unannounced, onto the stage, he hears somebody, far off in the mob, shout his name. *Eh—?!* The man comes tearing through the jam-up, past the Rat Pack and pageant figures guarding the perimeter (it's a piece of the Wild West he breaks through), and right into the VIP section. The man —it's that damned interloping defense lawyer Dan Marshall from Nashville, up to his tricks again!—charges straight down the aisle and up to the foot of the stage: *"A writ of habeas corpus!"* he cries. *"Hear my plea!"*

The Boy Judge, unsure whose body is about to be had, turns back in retreat toward the wings, but sees there Attorney General Herb Brownell gesturing frantically, glancing nervously over his shoulder, urging Kaufman to stall until Uncle Sam gets back. "All right," says Kaufman, trying to keep his knees from knocking together, "get along with your argument, there isn't much time!"

"Please, try to delay the execution until I complete my argument," cries Marshall. "It'd be terrible if I could convince Your Honor that you should grant the application and it would be too late!"

Kaufman sees through the crude tactics: a delay past sundown and the executions are not merely postponed until Monday but will have to be completely rescheduled. Which would give them time to fabricate more appeals, and who knows? the state the Supreme Court's in right now, they might be too lame to sit for a year! "It is unfair to put that kind of burden on a judge," he complains. "I'm aware of the tragedy involved. Now get on with it."

While he beats off Marshall's desperate rhetoric, he sees other defense lawyers pouring through the hole in the line at the boundaries of the VIP section—"We are counsel for the Rosenbergs! We must get through! It is an emergency!"—and squeezing into the VIP seats, grabbing at circuit judges from the U.S. Court of Appeals. Emanuel Bloch has spied Herb Brownell peeking out from the wings—he tries to scramble up onto the stage to reach him, but he's too clumsy and all he's getting is slivers for his pains. Brownell, insulted once too often by Bloch, refuses even to acknowledge his presence, strolling out onstage once to look out over his head and step on his fingers. Some pro-Rosenberg demonstrators have leaked through, too—Judge Kaufman's one abiding passion has been his hatred of quasilegal pressure groups, some of his best work had been his investigation of lobbying for Tom Clark when Clark was Attorney General, and now he feels that anger welling up in him again. They're running about through the VIP section, dodging Secret Service agents and Rat Packers, distributing "fact" sheets and clemency petitions, accusing Uncle Sam of premeditated murder, and shouting disruptive slogans like *No Secret to the A-Bomb!* and *They were convicted by the atmosphere and not by the evidence!*

Which latter is Supreme Court Justice Felix Frankfurter's notorious opinion on the Sacco and Vanzetti case, and Frankfurter, perhaps flattered by this recognition, steps back from the edge of the elephant turds where he'd been about to tiptoe in and offer a helping hand to the other six, and now joins, however belatedly, Justices Douglas and Black in dissenting against yesterday's majority opinion on the stay of execution: "Can it be said," he asks, "that there was time to go through the process by which cases are customarily decided here?" A rhetorical question, but anyway it saves him a nasty fall. Back in the VIP seats for the House of Representatives, Pennsylvania Democrat Francis Walter remarks idly to a couple of his colleagues that he thinks the Supreme Court erred yesterday, having taken jurisdiction when "nothing was before it." Justice Douglas's act was legal and under the law the whole case now had to be returned to the lower courts, whence it must come back to the full Supreme Court via District and Appeals Courts. Walter assumes he is off-mike, but by a quirk in the acoustical system, his voice carries out over the masses and all the way up to Central Park: "There is absolutely nothing in the act of 1925 that gives the Supreme Court authority to review the action of one of its Justices acting under the statutes!"

The people are getting edgy. They'd thought at first this was part of the show and had laughed at the lawyers, supposing they were clowns in disguise, but now it's clear that something is wrong. Where is the President? Where is Uncle Sam? The Vice President? J. Edgar Hoover or Cecil B. DeMille? Nothing but confusion up there—even Judge Kaufman (what's he *doing* out there on the stage?) seems unsure of himself. More demonstrators are pushing into the VIP section and others are circulating out among the common people—how did they penetrate the defenses so easily? wasn't Monaghan supposed to contain these elements down in the ghetto somewhere? where's the Army? where's the National Guard? why is Betty Crocker out flat on her ass? "This is the hour of our country's shame!" some guy is yelling. "No government has such a record of legal murders and legal lynchings as the Government of the United States in the past seven years!" There are rumors of FBI forgeries in the atom-spy trial and stacked decks, perjured witnesses. "We are here to proclaim that if the Rosenbergs die, it will be the most brutal murder ever committed in America!" they scream, seizing the microphones. "They are not traitors! It is those who want to kill them who are traitors to America!"

Distantly, out at the edge, there's a strange clackety noise, starting softly, getting louder: what is it? The prisoners banging their tin cups on their bars! rattling the gates of their cages in protest! To the frightened crowds in the Square, huddling toward the center, it sounds like the Phantom himself shaking his death chains! The Phantom's spectral image seems to appear, not only on door knockers like old Morley's in *A Christmas Carol,* but everywhere they look: in skyscraper windows, in the shadows behind the bright lights, under the stage, in the bottles they drink from! The angry clatter is punctuated by remote but heavy *whumps!*—foreign A-bomb tests! Spreading over the earth like smallpox! News reports ratatat against the periphery of the crowd like the firing of Sten guns: riots in Liverpool, Toronto, and Turin! the American Embassies besieged in Rome and Paris and Ottawa! a port strike in Genoa in protest against the executions! firing squads in East Berlin!

prayer vigils for the Rosenbergs in Iceland and Israel! plane crashes and battle casualties! ten thousand Communists are massing up to riot in Munich! screams of *"Murder!"* from rioters running amok through the streets of Melbourne and London! Copenhagen and Birmingham! there are reports of Mau Maus, Vietminh, Gooks, Arabs trying to break through at the rim, to get in! to get what we've got! "You are afraid of the shadow of your own bomb!" cries a French voice above all the rest. It is Jean-Paul Sartre! "Magic, witch hunts, autos-da-fé, sacrifices: your country is sick with fear! Do not be astonished if we cry out from one end of Europe to the other: Watch out! America has the rabies! Cut all ties which bind us to her, otherwise we will in turn be bitten and run mad!" The French indeed seem to be going berserk: crackly on-the-scene radio reports say they're running wildly through the streets of Paris, carrying big posters of Eisenhower flashing his famous smile but with each tooth an electric chair! "We are in the midst of a cold war," remarks Bernard Baruch dryly to a couple of the Presidents sitting beside him, his hand in his pocket, resting on his billfold as on the butt of a six-shooter, "which is getting warmer . . ."

A new figure, ragged and wild-eyed, now bursts into the VIP section, leaps up on a concrete balustrade, and commences to rant: *"If you are happy about the Rosenbergs, then you are rotten to the core!"* It's that Russian-born Red vagrant from L.A. who caused the day's delay, I. I. Edelman! People laugh at him and throw empty bottles, but they're frightened, too!

Julius Rosenberg's bespectacled old mother, Sophie, is pitching about in a fit of incoherent anguish! Other women are falling to their knees and sobbing and praying and beating their breasts!

The people glance up in anxiety at the clock on the Paramount Building: 19:41! Just 20 minutes to Zero Hour!

The pageant actors try to do something about all this, but fall into arguments as to which of them are Secret Service agents and which not! Some of the iconic Buckskin Militiamen, Sharecroppers, and Prohibitionists are getting hard to handle!

In the confusion, the National Rosenberg Committee has somehow managed to push an entire Clemency Float through the mobs and into the VIP aisles—or maybe they've smuggled the pieces in and assembled it here! It rolls toward the stage, carrying blow-ups of suppressed evidence, banners declaring the innocence of the Rosenbergs, pictures of the soon-to-be-orphaned sons, and signs that read FRAME-UP! and CLEMENCY MISTER PRESIDENT! People close their eyes, look the other way, scream for the police, or take a stiff blinding jolt from the bottles of booze still being passed around, trying to ignore the disruptions.

General Douglas MacArthur, all spit-and-polish in his full battle dress, molded hat, sun goggles, and medals, decides that enough is enough and marches forward to take over and bring some order to this society, but he hesitates at the edge of the elephant dung: the Justices are still wallowing about in there, up to their thighs and elbows in the muck, unable to see which way they're going, bumping into each other like pigs around the feeding trough, it is not an attractive sight. The General stands there, at the water's edge, so to speak, smoking his corncob pipe and musing on the inelegance of democracies. Harry Truman watches him and laughs, which makes the General's neck go red.

Behind him, crowned with laurel leaves and gliding like statues on wheels, come the renegade scientists Albert Einstein and Harold Urey, exploding the "secret weapon" issue and casting doubt on the trial verdict. The Red Parson, Dr. Bernard Loomer, leaps through the disintegrating defenses with a clemency petition, shouting: "The death sentence in this instance is an indication of our national weakness rather than our national strength! It is a reflection of our own growing hysteria, fear and insecurity!" He's clobbered with a dead cat by a Salem Witch and stuffed down an open manhole by a gang of soused-up examiners from the Patent Office, but no sooner is he popped down than Reverend Henry Hitt Crain, the fellow-traveling Methodist preacher from Detroit, pops up: "It implies an altogether unworthy capitulation to the hysterical temper of the times and reveals a recreant willingness to resort to 'scapegoat' devices to appease the homicidal urges of crowd compulsion!" For Christ's sake, the people cry, who let these dingdongs in here? What's Herbert Philbrick doing? Where is Norman Vincent Peale, now that we need him?

18 minutes to go! General MacArthur sighs wistfully, knocks the ashes out of his corncob pipebowl, turns, and fades away, kicking Truman on the shins as he passes. "Dumb son of a bitch!" yelps Harry.

The defense lawyer Manny Bloch has collared the Assistant White House Press Secretary Murray Snyder: "Has the Court's last decision or Ethel's letter been read *personally* by the President?" he demands.

"It's . . . it's not my function to ascertain this," stammers Snyder.

"Damn it!" roars Bloch in a red-faced rage, "people are going to *die!*" 17 . . . ! "*Make* it your function!"

Through the Square, the electric lights dip ominously!

The drum majorettes in the Texas marching band squeal with fright and leap into the arms of the boys in the band, hug them close!

Snyder falls back in alarm!

Whiskey bottles drop and crash!

The packed-up mob flinches, squeezing out of itself an airy moaning wheeze, compounded of gasps, groans, farts, curses, shrieks, belches, and woeful wails.

Judge Kaufman's knees go soft as warm Jell-O—fortunately he's wearing his judicial robes, and all that anybody notices is that he seems to dip with the lights. He glances backstage—*at last! Here comes Uncle Sam!*

The Boy Judge stretches up to his full five foot six and, glimpsing the hands on the Paramount clock just celebrating the quarter hour, flatly denies Dan Marshall's motion, then withdraws to the wings to get his wind back. He wants to fall into somebody's arms, but his wife, Helen, is peering down her nose into a compact mirror, and besides, he's got an audience back here of lawyers, jurors, witnesses, and G-men. They gaze at him, standing apart. *They'll never let me let go of this thing,* he thinks, staring back at them, envying their anonymity. *The trial's over, I shouldn't even be here, it's against every principle of American jurisprudence—but they'll keep me here till the day I die.*

Uncle Sam roars out onto the Death House set, whooping and snorting like a wild stallion with a bee up its rectum. "I have returned! And by the grace of Almighty God, I'm gonna tar up the arth and wreak a outdacious deevastation around here if I don't see more deddycated presarvation of the sacred fire of the Liberty Tree and less petterfacted sunshine patriotism! Great Jeminy! Could I not be gone a minute, but some mischief must be doin'? We've had to pump lead into a kid in Paris and throw hunderds a damfools in the hoosegow all over the world —and we'll trim the heels of a few onduly restless whippersnappers here, too, if things don't settle out a mite less epileptic!"

The people in the Square hoot and whistle and shout out their praises to Uncle Sam. The Singing Saints regroup to sing "O Zion, Haste Thy Mission High Fulfilling," which in turn inspires the security forces to make a coherent charge on the Phantom's agents at last. Lumberjacks smash up the Clemency Float with axes, and the Rat Pack reorganizes its perimeter defense lines. The Ku Klux Klan, Invisible Empire of the South, announces they've paid a visit to Nashville, and children are chasing Dan Marshall toward the Whale's mouth, screaming the Ladybug Taunt at him:

> "Shyster, shyster! fly away home!
> A cross is on fire in your front lawn!"

The Supreme Court Justices are still in a lot of trouble, but Bill Douglas, who has been watching them slop about helplessly in the muck, finally shakes off his wry amusement and, being the only one who's had the foresight to wear heavy boots and leggings, goes now to their rescue, leading them back to their seats, where Oveta Culp Hobby, whose business is health and welfare, is waiting for them with a damp rag to wash off their faces. While lawyers' writs and briefs are grabbed, folded into paper airplanes, and sent flying, the lawyers themselves, along with the Rosenberg Committee operatives, are being rounded up, one by one, straitjacketed or simply conked, and dragged over toward Walt Disney's giant Whale, whose belly has earlier been closed to the public and used until now to incarcerate zanies, sick drunks, and pickpockets.

"Well," laughs Uncle Sam, "it's a frolic scene, where work and mirth and play unite their charms to cheer the hours away!" 7:46 . . . "This was the Phantom's last shot, boys!" he shouts, stooping to attend to his kayoed Mistress of Ceremonies. "You got the bloody Barbarite by the short hairs, nothin' more can happen now—!"

But just then Times Square breaks into an uproar!

A man is backing bareass out onto the stage from the prisoners' entrance, his pants in a tangled puddle at his feet, a crumpled homburg down around his ears, "I AM A SCAMP" lipsticked on his butt. The man turns, hopping on one foot, blinks in amazement—why, it's—!

27.

Letting Out the Dark:
The Prodigal Son Returns

Is it possible to be rational at all in crisis situations? Do crises seem to have many elements in common? Does the participant seem to learn from one crisis to another? All interesting questions which I might well have asked myself, but at the moment, finding myself unexpectedly onstage in the middle of Times Square, staring out on an amazing sea of upturned faces staring back, my shirttails bunched up in my armpits and my pants in a tangle around my ankles, my poor butt on fire from its Dance Hall skid, my shoulder aching, face stinging, stomach rumbling, sweating hands clutching my still-enflamed though fast-shriveling pecker, Uncle Sam rearing up in monstrous astonishment on my left, some woman out cold as a mackerel at my feet, and the electric chair—for some reason splattered with what looked like custard pies since I'd last seen it—standing spotlit and hot with its own latent energies on my right, flashguns popping and cameras with huge glimmering lenses dollying in at me, a band somewhere playing "Happy Days Are Here Again," accompanied by what could only have been the goddamn Mormon Tabernacle Choir, and a pervasive odor of excrement in the air which I was afraid might be my own, all I could think of to say was: *"Oh my God! LET US PRAY!"* Which, when I'd added, dragging my voice down out of its falsetto shriek, *"Let me, uh, say, uh, my fellow Americans, uh, bow our heads—let us bow our heads in a minute of silent prayer cast in terms of all our, uh, fighting boys in, uh, wherever they are and for faith, uh, in—and for our President, in a sense— and also for the victims of Communism around the world,"* was pretty

470

goddamn brilliant: it shut them all up and gave me sixty precious seconds to get my pants up while they had their heads down. Maybe, I thought, in all the excitement they haven't even noticed . . .

While I struggled, sweating furiously in the hot lights, with the birdsnest of trouser legs around my feet—Judas Priest, what a mess, I couldn't even find the cuffs, and the belt seemed to be looped into some kind of cat's cradle!—I tried to collect my thoughts for the statement I had to make, the one I'd been working on such long hours this week, but which just now I'd thought I'd somehow got out of. But I was too confused—all those dreams, Ethel's mouth, the train wheels rolling underneath me—I could smell still the heady fragrance of newfound freedom, new beginnings (what was it? ah! the shampoo in her hair—suddenly I felt double-crossed in every direction at once!)—Christ! I thought in a moment of numbing terror: *I can't even remember my name!* I fought to recover that name, that self, even as I grappled with my trousers, hobbling about in a tight miserable circle, fought to drag myself back to myself, my old safe self, which was—who knows?—maybe not even a self at all, my frazzled mind reaching out for the old catchwords, the functional code words of the profession, but drawing a blank. I ought to quit, I knew, but I couldn't. I didn't know how. I only knew how to plunge forward: no matter what the consequences—in college football, it was always the off-side penalty; now, I thought, God only knows what I'm in for! Which reminded me that I was supposed to be praying and the minute of grace was fast running out. Uh . . . fiscal integrity! Paramount question! Yes . . . ah . . . make no mistake about it! What this country needs is . . . eh . . . no more pussyfooting! a new departure! ragged individualism—rugged, I mean ("Tell the truth, son," I could just hear Uncle Sam saying, "or trump—but get the trick!")—yes, it was time to piss or cut bait, time to basically hunker down, hold the line, take off the gloves and bind up the nation's wounds —but the gloves *were* off (what *wasn't* off?) and if my own wounds got bound up any tighter than they were already, I wouldn't be able to breathe (I *wasn't* able to breathe!)!

I was also feeling suddenly very airy and exposed, almost like a bad wind had got up between my legs, like a French kiss in the wrong place—I glanced up and discovered that everybody in goddamn Times Square was still watching me, not a reverent sonuvabitch in the lot, they'd been watching me all the time, all except Pat, I spotted her now, she was the only one with her head down—even my daughters were gaping at me with stupid smirks on their faces. It looked as though everybody were laughing, but I couldn't hear anything over the whumping thunder of my heart beating in my ears (my God, I can't even let my *hair* down in public, much less my pants! this was worse even than the time I got diarrhea in that jeep in Bougainville!). What crazy things we do, I thought, as I lurched, grunting, wheezing, half-blind from panic and glare, squatting and bobbing about the stage in one last desperate effort to pull my pants up—it was always best, I knew, to do the unexpected if you could get away with it, but this time, damn it, I'd overreached myself. I'd forgotten all the things my Mom had taught me: Don't make a fool of yourself, Richard, don't stick your neck out, don't give yourself away, don't expose yourself! What was it led me up there, led me up here? I remembered the ticket seller's caution: "Sure you want on that train, bud?" The cops at the Hunter Street barricades, the dissuasive phalanx of newsguys, the Warden's curious lecture on history and the convulsive struggle: all warnings I had failed to heed—and yet I was sure I'd been right. "To be great," Ethel had said (I think it was Ethel—was it Ethel?), "is to be misunderstood." She was back there, I knew, standing in the wings somewhere, her head shaved for the electrodes, her own heart beating so wildly in her little breast that you could see it through that sad ragged dress she wore, and I had a sudden impulse to dash back there, grab her up, and make a run for it. But I restrained myself, or my pants did, reminding myself (I was much encouraged by the return of this thought) that I had to think of the effect of my decision on the next generation, and on the future of peace and freedom in America, and in the world. Ethel would want it that way. Courage, confidence, and perspective. Which meant that I had to carry through to the finish, whatever the personal agony it would involve—I had to fight back! No crawfishing, no whining, whimpering, or groveling—if you're always on the defensive, take it from me, you always lose in the end—no, they were asking for it and they were going to get it! I'm a pessimist, but if I figure I've got a chance, I'll fight for it, and I *always* figure I've got a chance—I think that has been a hallmark of my political career. In that respect I'm an optimo. *Optimist*, I mean! (Jesus.) But how was I going to do it? Well, I'm a poker player, one of the best, and a good poker player knows it's important to get good cards, but also that most big pots are won by a bluff. Yes, I had to let fly with everything in the arsenal, throw up a real smoke screen and let out, as Uncle Sam would say, the dark ("Cuttlefish it, boy! If you can't convince 'em, confuse 'em!")—whereupon, having intended something entirely different by such determinations, I stumbled over that old lady's body (Judas, it was Betty Crocker!), touched my toes to keep from falling over on my head, and cracked a stupendous fart. *"AMEN,*

BROTHER!" some dingbat bellowed, and then I *did* hear them—Jesus Christ, they were all howling their asses off!

What was to be done? I stared gloomily at the bespattered electric chair, the famous Sing Sing hot seat, and—my own butt on fire from shame and floor burns—listened to the mob in Times Square behind my back. The door to the Dance Hall was now closed and above it was a sign that said SILENCE. I wondered if it was a message to me. I knew that the only defense I had was offense, that I had to somehow talk my way around this humiliation without admitting to any mistakes, but if I couldn't get my pants up past my ankles, how was I to begin? There was a white hospital cart behind the chair and it looked very comfortable, very restful. I realized I was close to breaking—a man can only take so much!—and that it was now or never. But if now, what? I didn't know whether to point with pride, view with alarm, or just let my ass go on speaking for me. The stage itself offered no clues, only soberingly lethal realities. I was afraid to look at Uncle Sam. I tried to wargame my situation, to reduce it to some set of constants I could work with, but all I could think of was the time my old man caught me swimming in the Anaheim irrigation ditch. On that occasion, he'd picked me up and thrown me back into the ditch—that's right: fire with fire, ditches with ditches!

"All right now!" I cried, turning on the mob at last. I was finding my way again. *"You may wonder what I am doing up here with my, uh, trousers down! Well, let me just say this! We in America, we in the Free World, all of us here tonight—and let me be quite blunt about this—we have ALL been caught with our trousers down!"* An inspired rhetorical ploy which had worked miracles in hundreds of debates, not to mention my famous crisis speech last fall, and which should have worked here, but it didn't—on the contrary, they got rowdier than ever. They were all out there, I recognized them, jammed around the stage, pressing forward, lit up by the flashing lights of Broadway: Congressmen and judges, governors and celebrities, Republicans and Democrats, all sorts of weird characters dressed up in funny costumes and large papier-mâché heads, little kids, old ladies, all whooping it up and laughing to beat hell. *"But this is no laughing matter!"* I shouted over the racket (I saw Harold Stassen snorting and pointing, Cabot Lodge looking pleased as punch, Bill Knowland and Lyndon Johnson rolling all over each other in the aisles—even Bob Taft was splitting his crippled sides with laughter), *"this is a struggle for the souls of men!"* Now what the hell was so funny about *that?* What was the matter with these people? Were they crazy? I thought they must be nuts! *"This is one of those critical*

*moments in history that can change the world, and we need your help,
and so I came here like this tonight—and incidentally this is unprecedented in the history of American politics—I came here like this to
dramatize what the danger is, a mortal danger that we all face!"*

"YOU TELL 'EM, STICKY DICK!" they shouted back at me, "YOU
GOT THE BALLS!"

"I tell you, we are on the brink!" I screamed—I *had* to scream: the
uproar in the Square was deafening, and on top of it radios were blaring
away, bands playing, generators humming, and police helicopters were
rattling overhead, taking pictures and dropping booze parcels. *"Look at
Korea!"* I cried. *"Look at China! Eastern Europe! Our own State Department! Even the Supreme Court! We're exposed on all sides by this
insidious evil! this sinister conspiracy! this deadly infection! Let me
assure you, the Phantom isn't changing! He isn't sleeping! He is, as
always, plotting, screaming, working, fighting! Scheming, I should say!"*
I tried to recall that lecture Uncle Sam had given me about the wall-
eyed harbinger who thirsted for Christian blood, but I was too over-
wrought and afraid I'd fuck it up—I was having trouble enough working my own bromides. *"We owe a solemn duty, not only to our own
people but to free peoples everywhere on both sides of the Iron Curtain,
to roll back the Red Tide which to date has swept everything before it!
We cannot allow another Munich!"* That wasn't bad, a touch of the old
Dick Nixon—I seemed to be getting off the dime at last! They were still
laughing, all right, but they seemed more attentive. *"It's . . . it's not
easy for me to take this position,"* I went on, choking up a little to show
them that I was vulnerable, too, that I was as human as the next guy, or
perhaps because I couldn't help it, *"—it happens that I am a Quaker!"*
Which for some reason set them all off again, snorting and wheezing,
falling off their chairs—Foster Dulles looked like somebody had got
ahold of his old Presbyterian face, which just wasn't made for laughing
with, and was wringing it out like an old dishrag: Christ! what if I
killed him! *"But as Abraham Lincoln once said: 'Uh, other means may
succeed: this could not fail!' "* I felt good about that, coming up with
that quote all by myself—Lincoln was always helpful in a tight spot,
better even than Jesus or Dale Carnegie, and I'd thought he would
rescue me from this one, but I might as well have been quoting Gracie
Allen. Even Douglas MacArthur was chuffing away, his sun goggles
tipped down over his nose, and Oveta Hobby was reared back in her
chair and laughing so hard she was showing her khaki drawers. *"He
. . . he also said that the world will, uh, little remember nor long, uh,
remember what we talk about here,"* I pressed on desperately, *"but just*

*let me say that I think the world will never forget what, uh, the achieve-
ments of this administration here tonight!"*

But they weren't even listening. I stuffed my hand absently in my
jacket pocket, reminded by the Lincoln quotes of my successful Checkers ploy (". . . here it is—I jotted it down—let me read the notes
. . ."), and felt a postcard there. It was the drowning-man syndrome
all over again, but I fished it out just the same, trying to look as mysterious as I could. It was the postcard I'd grabbed off that rack in Ossining. It said HELLO FROM SING SING! across the top and showed two
cartoon cops standing beside an electric chair with a privy hole and a
raised toilet lid, one of them explaining to the other: "He fell through."
I stared gloomily down that black hole, thinking: the hell with it, it
isn't worth it. All this jackassery: I'd Had Enough, Stassen could have
it. Pat was no longer praying, I noticed, if that was what she had been
doing before. She wasn't laughing like all the others either, but I wasn't
necessarily encouraged by that. She was just looking in my direction,
her eyes crinkled up sadly and gazing as though at some point just
behind my left ear, her thin white hands twitching nervously in her lap,
picking at each other. I remembered how Ethel's big dark eyes had
peered so deeply, so directly, so trustingly into mine—almost as though
probing my very soul; you could almost say, rediscovering it—as she'd
said: "I envy you your power, Richard. Your majesty. You are a great
man!" I felt myself being drawn back into her impassioned life-giving
embrace, where everything seemed possible once more, and everything
possible seemed good. "I have faith in you, Richard! You will unite the
nation and bring peace to mankind . . . !" Yes, faith—not loyalty, but
faith! That's what I needed! Not a dutiful peck on the cheeks, but full
firm committed lips pressed on mine, not tight jittery haunches, but a
soft yielding bottom, not thin secretive stone-cold fingers, but a warm
hand tearing at my hair, kneading my—

I shook it off. Christ, I was getting excited again. I pulled my shirttail
down in front and raised my arms (this did not quite work), looking for
something meanwhile to cover myself with. What I saw was Uncle Sam
looking like he'd just swallowed his corncob pipe and was trying to
cough it up again. He was pointing frantically up at the Times Tower,
where under the time and weather clock, which told me it was nearly
ten minutes to eight and eighty degrees (whoo! it felt like twice that at
least!), the news getting flashed to the world was: LET US STRIVE ON TO
FINISH THE WORK WE ARE IN . . . ! Well, I thought, I can't be too far off
the track. *"The issue at stake,"* I cried, turning back to the mob in the
Square, adopting a scowl of deadly earnestness, and recalling for some

reason the night I mounted a table at the Senior Beer Bust at Duke and
gave a deadpan parody of a talk on Social Insecurity (what had I said?
was there something I could use?)—*"The issue at stake, to put it
starkly, is this: whose hand—"* and here I thrust out my hand in a
gesture I knew was very effective, *"—whose hand will write the next
several chapters of human history?"* And then I saw for the first time
the blood on my hand: my God, there was blood all over it! from my
ass! it was coming from my ass! Oh Jesus! *"Let's—let's not deceive
ourselves!"* I gasped, really frightened now: what was happening to me?
*"The heat is on! We have the fight of our lives on our hands! We
already have seen bloodletting and . . . and there'll be some more
blood sp-spilled before it's over!"* No, not blood: lipstick! Oh shit, I
thought, as I mopped the sweat from my brow and plunged helplessly
on: *"I know that this is not the last of the smears!"* Needless to say, I
had just—as though compulsively—wiped the sweat from my face with
my lipsticked hand, a fucking mess, but I couldn't stop myself . . . *"I
was warned that if I continued to attack the Communists and crooks in
this country they would continue to smear me, and in spite of my expla-
nation tonight, other smears will be made!"* Ah, it isn't what the facts
are but what they appear to be that counts when you are under fire, I
thought, as the laughter cascaded around me. Some puffy-eyed clown
was trying to crawl up on the stage in front of me . . . familiar, but I
couldn't place him. Out of some gangster movie maybe. Like this whole
goddamned mob. I realized that out in all that roiling hysteria there was
one static point of reference that my eye kept coming back to: an old
bearded bum standing motionless in one of the VIP aisles in a floppy hat
and tattered old overcoat, his arms out at his sides like a cheap stuffed
doll. A teddy bear. His pinprick eyes, not quite real, and shiny beet-red
cheeks gave the impression that he'd been crying. He stood there as
though planted, old boots driven into the pavement, like a fat scarecrow
. . . or a message. The turmoil in the square raged around him, but the
old bum was untouched by it. I knew him. I'd seen him in my own
mirror. I felt myself being pulled back aboard the *Look Ahead, Neighbor
Special,* rocketing north toward all those grand discoveries—about life,
about myself—intimations of freedom from the Death House of politics
and propriety, the possibility of a fresh start, a new life of love and adventure, instead of all this pretending . . . and I thought for a moment
that maybe I was only dreaming, that in a minute I'd wake up again on
the VIP train (and this time I'd join in, I thought, I wouldn't hold
back), or back in my office, at home, even back at Dress-Up Day at
Whittier High School with Ola—but then something—*whick!*—stung

me on my left ball, and as I clutched my nuts and doubled away in pain, only to take another one—*swack!*—on my poor overabused butt, I knew I was where I'd always been: front and center on the stage of human history, never mind how silly or brutalizing, a victim of my own genius and God-given resources, and nowhere to go but on . . . and on and on . . .

Well, by God, I could and I would. I think of history in terms of tragedy—but not my own. I saw Uncle Sam, his pipe coughed up at last, the stem turned into a peashooter, striding forward to cut me off, but I didn't give him a chance. Taking my cue from the flag-leafed Bond clothing store statues I'd just glimpsed rearing chalkily above me, a bronze shield between them with the legend EXCELSIOR, I coldly turned my other cheek and, hopping to the other side of the stage, snatched the first piece of bunting I could reach (which turned out to be a flag actually, the first one, circle of thirteen stars), wrapped myself in it, and then whirled with a vengeance (which was not as easy as it sounds, hobbled as I was: I had to face them cross-legged in the end, nearly lost it again before I'd even got started) on this mindless boozed-up but malleable rabble: *"My fellow Americans!"* Uncle Sam stopped short, eyeing me curiously. Herb Brownell, slipping out from behind the wings with his program notes, blinked and stepped back in again, elbowing Judge Kaufman in the right eye. The Warden was back there, too, I noticed, muttering something in the ear of the skullcapped Prison Chaplain and chewing bemusedly on his long black cigar—and now out front I discovered my old man, sitting on the edge of his chair, glowering intently, just as he used to do at all my school debates—my biggest thrill in those years was to see the light in his eyes when I destroyed my opponents, and by God I was not going to let him down now. Or Mom either, seated quietly beside him, hands folded in her lap, a goddamn saint. *"We live in an age of anarchy!"* The mob, which had been applauding itself drunkenly, now broke into laughter again, but there were cheers and whistles as well. Let them laugh, I thought. This is a generation that wants to laugh, a generation that wants to be entertained, thanks to the movies, TV—a sea of passivity, but so much the better for us swimmers. I stared boldly out at them, mob and cameras alike, feeling very much in control of things once more, wiser than I knew. . . . *"We see mindless attacks on all the great institutions which have been created by free civilizations in the last five hundred years!"*

They were listening now, even as they continued to whoop it up. People have noticed that "peculiar sales executive charm" I have, and I poured it on, smiling, scowling, clutching the flag tight around me with one hand (though it was all hand-stitched and the seams chafed me sorely), hammering home my points with the other—not for nothing had Dick Nixon won the Reader's Digest Southern Conference Extemporaneous Speaking Contest so many years before! I started out by laying on them a real eye-opening, tub-thumping, hackle-raising sermon on world history (I've always been basically a history buff): the rise, development, and—as some would argue—partial decay of the philosophy called "liberalism"; the parallel emergence of a liberal heresy called Communism; the assumption of world leadership by two superpowers, America and Russia, each wedded to a competing faith; and finally, the present confrontation of these two faiths and these two superpowers in every part of the world. *"America today stands almost alone between Communism and the Free Nations of the world!"* I told them, and now I was addressing myself to all the people leaning out of hotel and business block windows and the anonymous masses crammed into the distant streets and avenues all the way up to Central Park as well, Jesus, I was in good voice. *"If you could lift the United States bodily off today's globe, the rest of the world would live in sheer terror!"* This was my big play, and, egged on by my father's grins and grimaces, I swung into it with all my might. I told them we had to roll back the Phantom's power, had to give up the negative, futile, and immoral policy of containment which abandoned countless human beings to a despotism and godless terrorism, and set out immediately to liberate the captive peoples. *"All that is needed is the will to win—and the courage to use our power— ALL our power—NOW!"* The mussed-up clown trying to crawl over the lip of the stage gasped and slipped back, clinging to the edge by his fingertips. Conscious of the cameras on me, I flashed a smile and demanded that the Russians dismantle the Iron Curtain, free the satellites, and unite Germany under free elections. I called for all-out victory in Korea: *"The only way to end the war in Korea is to win it on the battlefield!"*—and made it clear that we should warn the Chinese Communists that *"unless they cease their aggression against Korea by a certain date, our commanders in the field will be given the authority to bomb Manchurian bases! History tells us we are on the right side! Man needs God, and Communism is atheistic, so what we must do is to act like Americans and not put our tails between our legs and run every time some Communist bully tries to bluff us!"* Hoo boy, I was really wound up! I thought of things I hadn't even thought of yet! I argued for a naval blockade of Red China, a massive invasion of Southeast Asia, and if necessary, a preventative attack against mainland China itself: *"All we have to do is take a look at the map and we can see that if*

Formosa falls, the next frontier is the coast of California!" I bounded forward, coins and belt buckle jangling against the stage floor, and shouted that we should not be afraid to use—wherever and whenever— all the massive, mobile, retaliatory power at our disposal! *"Remember, it's a cause bigger than yourself! It's the cause of making this the greatest nation in the world—the leader in the world—because without our leadership the world will know nothing but war, possibly starvation or worse in the years ahead! With our leadership it will know peace, it will know plenty—"*

"What a shifty-eyed goddamn liar," complained somebody in the front pew. I recognized that sour country whine. "I can't figure out why people listen to him!"

This set off more derisive laughter from the horde, but I welcomed the challenge and wheeled to meet it: *"I am not going to engage in personalities,"* I cried, *"but I charge that Mr. Truman is a traitor to the high principles of his own Party! I charge that the buried record will show that he and his associates, either through stupidity or political expedience, were primarily responsible for the unimpeded growth of the Communist conspiracy within the United States—the one that has led us here to this historic occasion tonight!"* The crowd cheered at this and Truman took a mocking bow, but I forged on, confident now, back on the tracks once more and returning to the fold, so feeling the power wax in me. Dad was still scowling, but he seemed pleased. I caught Darryl Zanuck's eye and he threw me a thumbs-up sign. Truman was maybe not as discomfited as I might have wished, but then I bore him no grudge, and in fact I was grateful to him for throwing me a cue. *"If the Russians had been running our State Department during the seven years of Trumanism, they couldn't have developed a better Asiatic foreign policy from the Soviet viewpoint! I say we must deal sharply but fairly with internal Communism as an idea, but with its agents as DOUBLE-DYED TRAITORS!"* Some goddamn donkey had started braying in the middle of this and a lot of the crowd were heehawing along with it, including (I could hardly believe it!) my old man, but I shouted them all down: *"When our administration came to Washington on January twentieth, we found in the files a blueprint for socializing America! This dangerous well-oiled scheme called for socialized medicine, socialized housing, socialized agriculture, socialized water and power, and perhaps most disturbing of all, socialization of America's greatest source of power, atomic energy! For the first time in American history, the security of the nation was directly and imminently threatened!"* Uncle Sam was still jumping up and down and pointing frantically up at the clock, but I wasn't about to quit now. I was coming home, I could feel it, running up the walk from that long exile up at my aunt's to be kissed at the front door by little Arthur just a few months before he died, stepping down from the war in my Navy whites onto U.S. soil and into Pat's arms and Mom's, returning to the fold of the Party and Ike's grandfatherly embrace in Wheeling—for *me*, I thought, this whole thing: *it's all been for me!* And as my mind cleared at last, the mad dreams fading like spent fireworks, the old familiar phrases came rolling back to me about the competitive spirit and moral values and history will be the final judge and shooting Reds like rats. *"When an egg is rotten you throw it out!"* I recalled Tom Paine's times that try men's souls and Harding's God-given destiny of our Republic, remembered Teddy Roosevelt's counterattack on the professional pacifists seeking to Chinafy this country and Calvin Coolidge's American legions armed with the cross, Wilson's summons to all honest men—and our own Great Crusade, Ike's and mine . . . *"The American people will be eternally grateful for the achievements of the Eisenhower administration which is kicking Communists, fellow travelers, and sex perverts out of the federal government by the thousands! The Communists conspiracy to which Julius and Ethel Rosenberg devoted themselves with such blind fanaticism is being smashed to bits by this administration!"* I slapped the electric chair with my free hand for emphasis (luckily it wasn't live) and glanced toward Uncle Sam for approval: surely now—but he was in a furious temper, his blue eyes blazing, his elbows and coattails starchily akimbo, stamping his feet and holding up eight fingers, all atremble with rage . . . and what was amazing was that he seemed to be holding all of them up on one hand!

What was wrong? What was he trying to say? The Paramount clock said 7:53, but all I could think of at the moment were the eight minutes on the Doomsday Clock, and I broke out in a cold sweat—though it wasn't any goddamn international apocalpyse, which I only half believed in anyway, that I was thinking of, but my own: I was at the cliff's edge! This was sink or swim, do or die! *"Fellow citizens!"* I gasped, trying to calm myself, keep the words (something about liberty, the incomparable Constitution, and shrinking violets) from disintegrating in my mouth. Would he strike me? *"We must seize the moment! Complacency is dangerous! So, uh, we must stir our stumps and go to work. I remember our mother used to get up at five o'clock every morning to bake pies, and . . . and . . . what I am saying is that America is what made hard work great! Or rather . . ."* I could feel it all breaking down inside, like wires fusing, burning at the ends, bulbs blowing: why did this always happen to me? Why could I never please him, no matter what I did? *"That and a certain inner drive, and the power of prayer, and moral fiber, and, uh, moral—dignity! No, decency!"* Was that right?

My head was fizzing and popping. Out front, people were shouting: "SPEAK UP! CAN'T HEAR!" A fight had broken out in the VIP section between some business types (lawyers?) and some larger-than-life Suffragettes who seemed to be trying to drag the poor bastards off to a beached whale a couple of blocks away, Harold Stassen was grimacing openly and poking Bob Bliss meaningfully in the ribs, and back in the wings Brownell, Kaufman, Saypol, and the rest were all whey-faced with some sudden terror, which so far as I could tell had something to do with the baggy-eyed character who was still trying to crawl up onto the stage in front of me—he had one elbow over the top now and was groping about for something to grab ahold of with his other hand.

"We must communicate the facts and save the American dream because it is related to the innermost striving of the whole world!" I cried desperately. *"And I can promise you that we will usher in an era unbelievably prosperous with three television sets in every garage—I mean, automobiles! No . . ."* What the hell was I talking about? What was the *issue?* Where was Rose—why wasn't she getting me out of this?

"These people have *stones* for hearts," the guy trying to clamber over the edge of the stage complained huskily, pausing a moment to get his wind back and peer up at me. "They have the souls of *murderers!*"

Aha. I understood now who he was. The Rosenbergs' shyster Manny Bloch! I hopped forward to kick him in the face. But my feet and pants got tangled up in the flag and I went sprawling there in the puddle of stars, stripes, and inseams, engulfed yet again in belly laughs, and wondering if I could ever, like Truth, rise again. Just like the old potato-sack races at the Friends' Sunday School picnics, I thought: my head always ahead of my feet. I'd given all I had to give, and all for nothing, it was too little and too late and now—and then it came to me what I had to do! Despite the lack of sleep or even of rest over the past six days, despite the abuse to which I had subjected my nerves and body—some way, somehow in a moment of great crisis a man calls up resources of physical, mental, and emotional power he never realized he had. This I was now able to do, because the hours and days of preparation had been for this one moment, and as I picked myself up and rose naked once more to yet another occasion (or was it the same occasion, infinite in its challenge, that I was forever rising to?), I put into it everything I had. I knew what I wanted to say, and I said it from the heart: *"Now,*

*my friends, I am going to suggest a course of conduct—and I am going to
ask you to help! This is a war and we are all in it together! So I would
suggest that under the circumstances, everybody here tonight should
come before the American people and bare himself as I have done!"*
There was a moment of stunned silence. It was apparent they didn't
entirely understand me. I was frightened, of course; but basically I am
fatalistic about politics. The worst may happen but it may not. Don't
worry, I counseled myself, hang in there. It'll play. Just bring 'em down
that aisle! *"I want to make my position perfectly clear! We have nothing to hide! And we have a lot to be proud of! We say that no one of the
167 million Americans is a little man! The only question is whether we
face up to our world responsibilities, whether we have the faith, the
patriotism, the willingness to lead in his critical period! I say it is time
for a new sense of dedication in this country! I ask for your support in
helping to develop the national spirit, the faith that we need in order to
meet our responsibilities in the world! It is a great goal! And to achieve
it, I am asking everyone tonight to step forward—right now!—and drop
his pants for America!"*

That last pitch—the mounting rhythms, the repetitions, the "right
now!" evangelical challenge—all that was straight out of Dr. Rader's
memorable Los Angeles sermon, and I looked about now for friends of
the cloth—Billy Graham, Dr. Peale, Father Sheen, Ezra Benson—seeking their support and encouragement: maybe I could even get one of
them up here with me! But the person who caught my eye out there in
the mob was my own father: he looked like somebody had just hit him
between the eyes. He blinked twice, looked around in amazement, then
leapt out of his chair and, thumbing off his elastic braces, cried: *"That's
tellin' 'em, sonny!"* Down went his baggy britches, underneath which he
was wearing his old white longjohns (good old-fashioned homespun
appeal in that flannel underwear, I told myself hopefully, though in fact
I felt myself turning fifteen colors of the rainbow, as embarrassed for
him as I was for myself), and while he fumbled with the big white
buttons, others began to follow suit—or unsuit: first, friends like Bill
Rogers and Bert Andrews, Mundt and O'Konski, then Bill Jenner, Tom
Dewey, my brothers Donald and Edward, Homer Capehart, Strom Thur-
mond, George Smathers, and with that some of the Democrats, too, guys
like Stennis and Rivers, Don Wheeler, Jimmy Byrnes . . .

"IT'S A SHOWDOWN!" they cried.

"PANTS DOWN FOR GOD AND COUNTRY!"

"PANTS DOWN FOR JESUS CHRIST!"

"WHOOPEE!"

"FOR THE COMMON MAN!"
"DEEDS NOT WORDS!"
"PANTS DOWN FOR DICK!"

It was spreading now, spreading fast, some of those larger-than-life Cowboys were dropping their chaps, the Pilgrims, Riverboat Gamblers, and Doughboys, governors and judges, secretaries and bureaucrats, and on out into the masses beyond: I saw old Joe Kennedy's pants come down in a twinkling, Herbert Philbrick's, too, Yehudi Menuhin's and Hopalong Cassidy's, Rocky Marciano's, Sumner Pike's—and it was even catching on among some of the left-wing radicals—Humphrey Bogart, Dean Acheson, Walter Lippmann and Herbert Lehman, Ralph Bunche, John L. Lewis—the din of crashing belt buckles and ripping zips was deafening! And women as well—Elsa Maxwell, Teresa Wright, Bess Truman, all the ladies in the Mormon Tabernacle Choir—all hiking their skirts and pulling down their drawers, corsets, girdles, whatever they had up there! A few of the more fastidious types were pulling their pants all the way off, but most of them just left them in a heap around their feet, staggering about in tight little circles to cheer the others on and see what their neighbors had. There were scattered screeches of protest from the timid, a few ugly assaults by the lunatic fringe, small riots breaking out in the vicinity of Mickey Mantle, Marilyn Monroe, Captain Video, and Eleanor Roosevelt, and a major stir when Christine Jorgensen's drawers came down, but essentially it was a great success, a real vote of confidence! Not that it wasn't a pretty traumatic experience to see Mom with her underwear ballooning down around her feet, Dad in a ferocious Black Irish fit, still tied up in his longjohns, or Pat, the strain showing on her thin sad face from trying to hold back the tears, stoically raising her printed cotton skirt and fumbling with her garters, but I knew that, whatever the cost, I'd won the day, the victory was mine!

"I have a profound conviction," I cried, *"that with that kind of patriotism, that kind of love of country, we shall never lose sight of the American dream! And with that spirit, we shall make that dream come true! I pledge to you tonight that I shall meet—"*

"Hey, dat's ma boy, over dere, doing dat!" laughed Uncle Sam coldly, striding forward to cut me off at last. Behind him, I saw Herb Brownell and Irving Kaufman, their pants half-lowered, not knowing which way to jump. "Lo, how he urges and urges, leavin' the masses no rest nor britches neither! Hoo boy! it takes a long cumbustificashun to throw dust in the eyes a commonal sense!" He looked outwardly cheerful, but under the forced laughter it was plain to see he was really smoldering—

and for good reason: after all, if I was right about his having rigged this entire humiliation ceremony for my dubious benefit, I had turned the tables on the old coot and fucked up his timetable to boot!

I glanced coolly up at the clock: *Wha—?!* It still said seven minutes to eight! *"Just . . . just let me say this last word!"* I stammered. *"Regardless of what happens, I—I am going to continue this fight! I am going to—!"*

"Great Beltashashur!" stormed Uncle Sam, lifting me up in the air by my collar, the dead weight of flag and pants dragging down my dangling feet. "One more last word outa you, mister, and I *tell* you what you're gonna do: you're gonna find your damfool sittin'-piece on 'tuther side a the Great Divide! The thrill is gone, boy, every rainmaker becomes a bore at last, so zip your lip! In times like the presence, men shouldn't utter nothin' for which they wouldn't willingly be responsible from here to eternity and back—you ain't the only pebble on the beach! We got a couple *burnin'* issues on the docket tonight, we gotta 'sist a coupla *flamin'* Reds, *firebrands* a the *infernal* Phantom, to see the *light,* and we don't need no more of your hissin' and blowin' and generally discombobulatin' *splutterations!"*

Well, I might have taken his warning to heart—true luck consists, after all, not in the cards, but in knowing just when to rise and go home, Green Island had taught me that and Uncle Sam himself had put it into words for me—if only he hadn't blown at my shirttails ("What is that which the breeze," he wondered aloud, "as it fitfully blows, half conceals, half discloses?"), clucked his tongue ruefully, and with all the cameras dollying in, remarked wistfully to the mob at large: *"Ah, vanished is the ancient splendor!"*

"Wait a minute!" I hollered through the freshly unleashed crash of derisive laughter. *"Wait just a goddamn minute!"* The laughter subsided for a moment, and there was a moment of grinning silence, waiting to be filled. Even though I was still dangling by the scruff of my neck, I plunged right into it: *"MY pants are down! YOUR pants are down! EVERYBODY'S pants in AMERICA are down! Everybody's—EXCEPT HIS!"* This stunned the Square. A deadly hush fell over everybody. That, I thought, is what you call putting a cap on it. . . .

"You fool!" rasped Uncle Sam, dropping me back down on the stage. He glanced apprehensively up at the night sky, dark and starless. *"You're going too far!"*

I was frightened (how had it got so dark so soon?), but I had passed the point of no return—it was like lurching offside in a football game and seeing the flag go down, yet having to complete the play just the same, no matter how punishing and futile: *"The chips are down! If you're not with us, you're against us!"* I cried. *"And until the facts are in, a doubt will be raised!"*

I had shocked everybody with my sudden challenge, but now, slowly, steadily, a chant sprang up and began to sweep through the Square: "PANTS DOWN! PANTS DOWN! PANTS DOWN!" Louder and louder it grew, spreading, swelling, more and more insistent, led now by some cheerleaders with big red "I's" on their white sweaters (they moved slowly, dreamlike, as though in great awe of the occasion), while behind them drummers from some band thrummed a heavy augmenting beat. *"PANTS DOWN! PANTS DOWN!"*

"What mad project of national sooey-cide *is* this?" complained Uncle Sam, clearly taken aback by the spontaneous uprising—there was nothing more terrifying, I knew, than the aroused voice of the people. As they shouted, he looked slowly about him, as though at the threshold of some door or other, his blue gaze falling finally on me. A gentleness seemed to settle over him, a kind of sadness—I felt sorry for what I had done, and I wanted to take it back, but my heart was in my throat and I couldn't speak—and then he seemed almost to grin. "Okay, son," he said, or seemed to say, as he settled back on his heels: "Experience keeps a dear school, but fools as they say'll learn in no other."

I stood rooted to the stage floor, petrified with terror and anticipation, my eyes glued helplessly on his strong pale hands as they pushed back his sky blue swallowtail coat, unhooked his braces and unbuttoned his fly, gripped the waistband of his red-and-white striped pantaloons, and pushed them down.

There was a blinding flash of light, a simultaneous crack of ear-splitting thunder, and then—

BLACKOUT!!

28.

Freedom's Holy Light: The Burning of Julius and Ethel Rosenberg

There is panic and some scream: *"UNCLE SAM IS DEAD!"*

"DEAD!" comes the echoing scream, and terror rips through the hooded Square like black wildfire, a seething conflagration of anti-light, enucleating the body politic: *"LEMME OUT A HERE!"*

Out! the people want out!—but where is out? The emptiness at the edge has inundated the heart, the center is gone, the power cut, there's no way in *or* out!

"IT'S THE END OF THE WORLD!"

"THE VICE PRESIDENT'S DONE IT NOW!"

"HOWLY JAYZUSS!"

It is utter madness to try to break out, worse madness to stand still— the communicants, following in the footsteps laid down by their heritage and so seized as ever by the American go-go-go mania, lurch violently in all directions at once, shackled by dread and drawers, flailing their arms about wildly, and so being wildly flailed by what, in this unnatural darkness, this nighttime of the people, seems like some mindless hundred-armed monster! like a black forest of disconnected centipede legs! OH MERCY!

"UNCLE SAM IS DEAD!"

"WHO CAN SAVE US NOW?"

And in the nighttime of the people, there is a great wailing and gnashing of teeth, just like in the old days, a million-mouthed moan more horrible than the roar of Behemoth! People cry out to God, to Christ, Ike, Con Ed, the Pope, to anyone who might listen, who might

486

help, to the Forefathers, to the FBI, Bernard Baruch, loved ones here and gone, fearing even those they call upon, Wyatt Earp, the Statue of Liberty . . .

"MADRE MIA, WHOSE THIS IS THE SWEET LAND O'—HA-A-ALP!"

In the nighttime of the people, everything is moving and there is nothing to grab hold of. The very pavements seem to dissolve into an undulating quagmire, vortical and treacherous, dragging the screaming citizens by their bundled ankles into the deepest bowels of the earth! Or perhaps it is the violent restlessness of the bundled ankles that is disemboweling the earth—who, since none can see, can say?

"WHY IS IT SO DARK?"

"THEY'VE TURNED OFF THE WHOLE UNIVERSE!"

"WE SHOULD NEVER HAVE BROKE THE SOUND BARRIER!"

Imbalances are unchecked and human dignity is trampled upon in the nighttime of the people. Pageant figures crash into each other, their big heads bursting like ripe melons! Anxieties scurry like vermin, manhole covers rattle underfoot, plate-glass windows explode and splinter, and behind the shouts and moans and crashes and the dreadful ticking of what can only be the Doomsday Clock can be heard the hollow evil laughter of Uncle Sam's worst nemesis since Nimrod Wildfire. . . .

"OH NO!"

"IT'S THE PHANTOM!"

"THE PHANTOM'S KILLT UNCLE SAM!"

"HE'S STOLE THE LIGHT!"

"HE'S FREED THE SPIES!"

"AND NOW—!"

"—HE'S AFTER US!"

Fears, in the nighttime of the people, seem almost to materialize, to rise like palpable fog from the stricken hearts of the multitude and coil into unseen but damply felt shapes, nebulous, capricious, but no less manifest than destiny itself was in a sunnier time: fears of the Russian Bolsheviks, the Chinese Reds, of cabalists and parlor pinks, Gooks, Nips, Huns and Huks, fears of Hottentots and Snollygosters, MIGs and Mau Maus, existentialists, cancer, Pusan whores and tortured truths!

"YIKES! ONE OF 'EM'S GOT ME!"

"TAKE THAT, YOU SONUVABITCH!"

"I CAN'T BREATHE!"

"AA-AR-RGH!"

In the nighttime, thus, the people wrestle with their fears and with each other, not knowing whether what they've got hold of is a diseased idea of the Marxist Virus, Nigger Nate's scrotum, the mess in Washington, or their own grandmother! Principally it is their own sudden and unprecedented impotence that terrorizes them, but sometimes this fear feels like the dry rot of corruption and Communism, other times it's got the texture of a boxcar of pussyfooters or the Beast from 20,000 Fathoms!

"YECC-CH! IT STINKS!"

"IT'S ALL HAIRY!"

"IT'S GOT A MOUSTACHE!"

They feel themselves swarmed about by mousy little engineers, scabbed sheep, dirty books, and goon squads, but when they lash out, try to get a handle on what's tormenting them, the emanations dissolve and mutate, leaving them with nothing more than a numinous armload of the March of Time, heavy water up the snoot, and a fistful of torn Jell-O boxes and sweaty pubic hair. . . .

"MY GOD! IT'S A CREEPING SOCIALIST!"

"A FIVE PERCENTER!"

"THE FIFTH COLUMN!"

"YEE-EEEE-K!"

"THE VOICE FROM THE SEWER!"

"IT MUST BE ALGER HISS!"

"THE ANTICHRIST!"

"HOLY SMOKE!"

"BRING BACK THE LIGHT, LORD!"

"LIGHT!"

But the light does not return, and in the ever deepening nighttime of the people, the shapes of their fear are drawn from ever deepening wells, roiling visions of the imminent imbalance of terror commingling now with shades of half-forgotten nightmares from all their childhoods: V-2s and gas ovens and kamikazes, the hurricane that tore through Overlord, the holocaust at the Cocoanut Grove, gremlins and goosesteppers, malaria, unfaithful wives, starvation at Guadalcanal, U-boat wolfpacks and Jap snipers and warplanes over Pearl Harbor, vampires and striking workers, hoboes, infantile paralysis, bread lines, bank failures, mortgage foreclosures and dust storms, King Kong and Scarface Al, Wobblies, werewolves, anarchists, Bolsheviks and bootleggers, Filipino guerrillas and Mexican bandidos, the Tweed Ring, earth tremors, the Cross of Gold! Down they spiral into irrational panic, as upward swirl the spooks of terrors past! Chinafyers! Assassins! Jim Crow! The Wild Bunch! Robber barons and longhorns! Black Jack Ketchum, Butcher Weyler, and Rattlesnake Dick! Du Bois! Debs! The

Daltons and Darwin and the lone pray-ree! Amelia Bloomer! Maria Monk! The Grangers and Youngers and Molly Maguires! Flaming crosses! Hookworm! Apaches! Carpetbaggers! Booth and Buckshot and Billy the Kid! Sherman's Bummers! Amputation! Bleeding Kansas! Dead Man's Gap and yellow fever! Humboldt Desert! The Alamo!

  "I REMEMBER!"

  "IT'S SANTY ANNY!"

  "OH LORD, THEY'RE ALL AROUND US!"

  "ABOLITIONISTS!"

  "COMANCHES!"

  "I CAIN'T HOLD ON!"

  "REDCOATS!"

  "THEY'RE BURNING WASHINGTON!"

  "LOOK OUT!"

The shouts of the people spark and crackle in the night air as though to suggest that their own panic might somehow save them, but the sparks give off a lightless light like a child's Fourth of July tin pinwheel, confusing them more than illuminating them, stinging their eyes, pricking their skin, and spiraling them ever deeper into the dark pit of memories and voices in their minds, like an old man driven in his dreams to suffer yet again the terrors of his boyhood passage, the night in the forest, the first wounds, the pangs of birth, the mysterious emptiness beyond conception. Their skin crawls at the chill slithering embrace of spectral Lobsterbacks and Coercive Acts, darkling waters, smallpox, cold-blooded Hessians, and lice! The pitch-black forest of flailing limbs in which they find themselves is alive with dragoons and grenadiers, witches and wolves, hunger, quitrents, mutineers, mastodons, and—obscene and naked, daub'd with various Paints—Hell's swarthy Allies dire, with Visage foul, and horrid awful Grin! their primeval enemy, the bloody Savages, like Fiends of Hell, the very image of the Prince of Darkness—

  "FLAMING EYES!"

  "FACE AS BLACK AS SOOT!"

  "A PAIR OF MIGHTY HORNS—"

  "—AND CLOVEN FOOT!"

  "LEAPIN' LIZARDS!"

  "WE'LL ALL BE KILLT!"

  "EEEEYAA-AA-AHH!"

Meanwhile, over at the Martin Beck, a few candles have been lit and the cast of *The Crucible* is carrying on as usual, playing tonight to an audience of one: the author, slumped gloomily in the back row all by himself, his long legs stretched out over the seat in front of him, no doubt wishing he might address that mob of drunken lunatics outside in the words his character Proctor used a little while ago to the serving girl Mary Warren, discoverer of witches "come," as she said, "to see the great doings in the world": *"I'll show you a great doin' on your arse one of these days!"* Ah well: art . . . not as lethal as one might hope. . . . Onstage now, Elizabeth, Proctor's wife, has just learned from Mary ("The Devil's loose in Salem, Mr. Proctor; we must discover where he's hiding!") that she has herself been "somewhat mentioned" in court, and when Mary has gone, she says quietly to no one in particular: "Oh, the noose, the noose is up!" Her husband, stubbornly optimistic, disagrees, but he is wrong, and deep down, for all the brave face they put on it, they both know it. It is the Deputy-Governor Danforth who has the truth (in effect, he owns it): *"We burn a hot fire here; it melts down all concealments!"* Yes, mister, there is a prodigious guilt in the country—the town waits at the scaffold, and who weeps for these weeps for corruption! The author sighs unhappily, well aware that it was not easy for these people, the people of Salem; for the edge of the terrible wilderness was close by, full of mystery, dark and threatening, the Devil's last preserve, as they called it, his home base and the citadel of his final stand: to the best of their knowledge, the American forest, just over their shoulders and stretching endlessly west, was the last place on earth that was not paying homage to God. Which, he reflects—folding his hands solemnly before his face and wishing that, just for tonight, he might change the ending of his play (what is the power of the author, for Chrissake, if even this is denied him?)—is still true. . . .

"STOP!"

"THEY'RE ALL OVER ME! I CAN'T GIT 'EM OFF!"

"NO-O-OO!"

"LOOK OUT, IT'S—GURGGHH!"

Whoo, it's wilder than ever outside in Hell's Kitchen—which now the jammed-up populace, their Breasts enrag'd still with a mighty Phrensy, take variously to be Valley Forge, Little Bighorn, Transylvania, or Nightmare Alley: the spectral presences, curling up from the bowels of the denuded celebrants like some kind of unspeakable parody of the current baby boom, have proliferated monstrously, assuming invisible but apprehensible shapes more frightening than any that have come before—for the people in their nighttime have passed through their conventional terrors and discovered that which they fear most: each other! Amid a crescendo of ticking clocks, mad diabolical laughter, shattering glass, and recurring notes of impending doo-oom, the eidola of squatters and gooney birds, frat rats and dirt farmers, puritans, populists, and brainwashed vets rise now to intermingle with those of coffinmakers and craven cowards, desperadoes and draft dodgers! What is truth? What is perversity? In the nighttime of the people it's all one! Terrible the grim phantasms of terrorists and traitors, more terrible yet—because beloved, or thought to be—those of founding fathers, trustbusters, first ladies, and village blacksmiths! No longer able even to cry out for help (for to whom can they now cry in such utter dissolution?), the people fall about in sweaty disarray, bodies slapping frightened bodies, chairs scraping and clattering, cameras crashing, as above and betwixt them twist the swollen instable emanations of Jacobins and Rotarians, damyankees, isolationists, abstract painters, Klansmen, foxhole atheists, Two-Seed-in-Spirit Predestinarians, hanging judges and traveling salesmen! There's Ethan Allen! Black Bart! Tom Swift! Bird and Duke and Sitting Bull! Sergeant York! Punjab! Sojourner Truth and Bet-a-Million Gates! And all as big as skyscrapers and scary as hell! Lynched Negroes, still dangling hugely from their ropes like strange bloated fruit, entwine with the gigantic ghosts of radiated Japs and bushwhacked settlers! Oh my God, it's awful! The people thrash about helplessly amid such horrors, their manifold shrieks of terror modulating into a single eerie moan, as around them the restless shades of Joe Hill and Glenn Miller wind and weave grotesquely through those of Sacco and Valentino, Dillinger, Slovik, and Stonewall Jackson!

"Ah, what horrid scene is this, which restless, roving fancy, or something of an higher nature, presents to me; and so chills my blood! Do I see motly armies and painted Salvages spreading desolation thro' the land, dispossessing the free-born of the inheritance received from their forefathers, this goodly patrimony ravished from them by those who never knew what property was, except by seizing that of others for an insatiable Lord—and here, *where Satan's seat was—!*" Thus might the shade of the Reverend Jonathan Mayhew, Poet and Patriot, rightly cry were he to peer down through the darkness with X-ray eyes upon the people locked in this blind desperate battle with their own worst fears and with each other, limbs entangled and hair on end, mouths stretched for screaming and perhaps in fact screaming, no longer distinguishable from one another as Sinclair Weeks here, Patti Page there, but all folded into a single mindless seething mass, jerking and pitching as though being shot through with erratic bursts of high-voltage current. He would discover not so much a violent disorder below him as a kind of frenzied stasis, much like a microscopic pool of excited amoebae, atoms let loose in a walled void, bingo balls in a whirling basket, and so a movement at once fervid and infinitely varied, yet at the same time in a random way rhythmic and predictable, and so imitative of the contained agitation of the universe.

And inevitably, in all this hysterical jangling around, flesh is finding flesh, mouths mouths, heat heat, and the juices, as Satchel Paige would say, is flowin'. The people are no less beset with confusion and panic, horrendous anguish and pain, like to the throes of travail, but they are also suddenly hot as firecrackers—or maybe not so suddenly, maybe it's just the culmination of that strange randy unease they've been feeling all day, ever since waking this morning in their several states of suspended excitation. Now, plunged into a nighttime far deeper than that from which this morning they awoke (or thought they did), the people seek—with distraught hearts and agitated loins—a final connection, a kind of ultimate ingathering, a tribal implosion, that will either release them from this infinite darkness and doleful sorrow or obliterate them once and for all and end their misery. "What indignity is yonder offered to the matrons! and here, to the virgins! O dishonest! profane! execrable sight!" It is astounding to consider how many orifices, large and small, and how many complementary protuberances, soft and rigid, the human body possesses, all the more so when that number is raised to the nth power by jamming thousands of such bodies several layers deep into a confined space and letting everything hang out! Nor in such a wet and wretched nighttime are the people—deprived virtually of every sense but one, frantically giving and receiving with all their gaps and appurtenances, and their minds frozen with delirium, booze, terror, and the seizure of imminent orgasm—limited to other people: no, it's an all-out strategic exchange, and any animal, vegetable, artifact, or other surface irregularity will do! The massa's gone away, and they are really crackin' corn! "Where! in what region! in what world am I! Is this imagination (its own busy tormentor)? Or is it something more divine? I will not, I cannot believe 'tis prophetic vision; or that God has so far abandoned us—!"

"*WAIT!*"

"*VOT'S DOT—?*"

"*NOTHIN' OUT THERE, BROTHER!*"

"*IT'S THE END!*"

"*MY GOD, I'M ABOUT TO—!*"

"*NO. LOOK—!*"

"*AH—!!*"

"*WHA—?!*"

"*THRO' THE MISTS OF THE DEEP—!*"

"OH!"
"SAY, I CAN SEE!"
"I'LL BE DURNED!"
"IT'S A LIGHT!"
"A LIGHT IN THE WEST!"
"THERE IT IS!"
"I'LL BE BLESSED!"
"BUT WHAT . . . ?' "
"IT'S A FLYING SAUCER!"
"IT'S A BOID!"
"ISSA PLENN!"
"NO! IT'S . . . IT'S UNCLE SAM!"

Yes, it is Uncle Sam: as dawn's early light will pierce the deepest of sleeps, so he comes now, that mighty Yankee Peddler, boring an incandescent hole through the black western sky on his return, not from the netherworld, but back from the ridge where the West commences: Yucca Flat, Nevada!—and bearing in his lean gnarled hands a new birth of freedom, a white-hot kernel of manifest destiny: a spark from the sacred flame! Onward he comes, scorching the dropped curtain of night like one of those paper horse-race games torched by the lit tips of cigarettes, leaving a glowing trail behind him which even as it turns to ash seems to let a little light leak through—or perhaps this is an illusion, an afterimage burned not into the sky but into the light-starved retinae of the people wallowing in their nighttime in the Square! Certainly the shock is there, the searing pain—it's one thing to sing about seeing the glory, fellow saints, another actually to have the fucking stuff fry your eyeballs! For a moment Uncle Sam seems to hover flickeringly above them, his craggy features lit eerily from beneath by the fiery glimmer in his cupped hands, his coattails flapping blackly behind him—and then he plummets suddenly down upon them like a falling star! The people, interrupted in the mind-shattering throes of what might have been some ultimate orgasmic fusion, are as yet unable to cope with this new information—they cry out, shield their eyes, and fall back in slippery confusion, tumbling out of some linkages and into others, but generally shrinking back into their old isolate and terrified selves. When they open their eyes again, it is to see their Star-Spangled Superhero standing stark and solemn above them on the Death House stage, cradling freedom's holy light in his outstretched hands and gazing down upon them with glittering eyes sunk in deeply shadowed sockets— weird this light he holds: fierce enough to blind if stared at directly, yet casting no radiance, illuminating nothing except Uncle Sam's hands and face, as though virtually all its light were bent in upon itself! They can sense the tall buildings rearing up over them, the darkened marquees trembling perilously on their thin chains, the statues on the Bond clothing store undraped and tilting dangerously toward each other in a wild monumental grope, horrifically reminiscent of the Rosenbergs' famous moment of unfettered passion up at Sing Sing, but they can see nothing, nothing except the ghastly deep-shadowed pallor of Uncle Sam's gaunt face and the ball of fire in his hands. His mouth opens: they gasp and freeze . . . !

"*In nomine Domini*," intones Uncle Sam gravely in the sudden breathless silence, "*cornbread and hominy, intery mintery cutery corn! do you like jelly, punch in the belly, tumblin' tumbleweeds, tattered and torn! whisko bango poker my stick, een teen tuther futher, sother lother dick! sui filiiquery nickery neck, ite ad crackabone hallibone heck! silence in the courtroom, the judge wants to spit, allie-allie-in-free: you—are—IT!*"

And he slowly opens his great hands and releases the dazzling fireball!

"*Philosophers have explained the world,*" he cries, "*it is necessary to CHANGE the world! So hang on to your hats, folks, cause jist as that old astronomicalizin' Prophet Nate Ames soothsaid nigh onto two hundred years ago, the Coelestial Light directed here by the Finger of God is gonna drive out the long! long! Night of Heathenish Darkness! I shit you not! stand back! it's the NEW New Enlightenment!*"

The little orb of blinding light hovers for a moment on the palms of his hands, slowly expanding, pulsating like a living heart, so bright that even the people with their eyes squeezed shut see it there—then suddenly it flashes outward, cutting through the Square like a sheet of sun, inundating the streets and all the city and nation and oceans beyond with glaring light, with white heat, like some kind of super flashbulb, as suddenly contracts back in on itself, dragging people to their heads, knees, and elbows, and whipping them as in an orange whirlwind toward the stage, and then—WHOOSH!—the darkness lifts up off the Square like a great mushroom cloud, rising high into the lightening sky and sucking all the fears and phantasms of the people's nighttime up with it—and a lot of the people as well, for a foot or two anyway, before dropping them back on the sweaty pavements in an exhausted barebottomed heap. "*Whoopee!*" hollers Uncle Sam gleefully, his blue coattails rising momentarily with the cloud and snapping and cracking fiercely over his head in the purifying storm: "*This here light shall go clean up to Heaven—it'll throw its beams beyond the waves and shine in the darkness there, it'll awaken desires and produce revvylutions and overturnin's until the world is free like what we are! There's nothin' left for us to do but to take 'em all and, in the words of Billy McKinley, uplift and civvylize and otherwise hawg-and-pester 'em till o'er the ramparts we watch they ain't nothin' but congenial Christians, empty shoppin' baskets, and plentya parkin' space! I chant the new empire, and when we Yankees has once sot our souls upon a thing, we always have it, so harness my zebras, gift of the Nubian King, boys: all I ask is a free field and no favor and a mite less indecent exposure! And somebody separate that elephant and jackass there! what're they doin'? That's plumb disgustin'!"*

The lights have come up in Times Square on a scene, as the people now discover, of widespread madness, dissipation, and fever, an inelegant display of general indiscretion and destruction, corruption, sacrilege and sodomy, twisted camera booms, base iniquity, smashed klieg lights and shredded trousseaus, tipped and scattered chairs and pews, incest, desecration, tangled bodies, rampant nihilism, bestiality, liberated freak shows, careless love and cheating hearts, drunkenness, cocksucking, and other fearsomely unclean abominations, all of it liberally sprinkled with soot, snot, and pigeon shit—not exactly Cotton Mather's vision of Theopolis Americana! What a mess! There's whiskey and blood all together, mixed with glass where they lay, not to mention sweat and tears and puddles of cum, vomit and the smashed melonheads of the pageant figures!

Well, an "orful, onnatr'l, and tarifine sight," as Sain't Sut would say, and as if things aren't serious enough, it turns out that while the cops' and secret service's guard and pants have been down, all the pro-Rosenberg lawyers and demonstrators have escaped: Walt Disney's Whale has been spouting them by the bellyful back into the Square, where the scoundrels have somehow recovered their pickets and legal briefs and have nearly reconstructed their Clemency Float! But Uncle Sam, spying them, whips his top hat high into the air and, when it comes down again, plucks an American bald eagle out of it: *"Sic 'em, hoss!"* he cries, and the eagle swoops down on the interlopers, firing off arrows of war into the backsides of the lawyers and lashing the clemency nuts with olive branches. *"I wish to remark,"* remarks Uncle Sam, setting his plug hat firmly back on his hoary brow, *"and my langwidge is plain, that for ways that are dark and for tricks that are vain, the foe's most abominable lop-eared lantern-jawed half-breed whiskey-soaked and generally onscropulous and haughty host do take the cake, if you don't watch 'em! They are disgraceful, depraved, and putrescent, endowed by their*

Creator with certain gangrene hearts and rottin' brains and similar un-
alienated blights, and given to sech public frothin' and fumin' as to
wound and disease the body politic like thorns in the flesh and other
eeroginous zones! But hey! if the Red slayer thinks he slays, boys, he
knows not well the sub-tile ways I keeps whuppin' the she-double-I-it
outen any slantindicular sidewinder what trifles with freedom, swells
the caress of disunion, incites domestical inch-erections amongst us, eats
out our substance, or notherwise bites the hand what lays the golden egg
of peace, property, and the bottomless pork barrel! Whoopee! A nation,
like a person, has got somethin' deeper, somethin' more permanent and
pestifferous, somethin' larger than the scum of its parts, and what this
nation's got is ME! So keep your heads down, ladies, whilst I pours out
my wrath upon 'em like water!"

This bit of positive action and unabashed bullroaring rouses the
people at last from their nighttime stupor, and they suddenly realize
that the Phantom's laughter has ceased entirely, the sky has brightened,
and not only has the Doomsday Clock stopped beating, but the starry
dial atop the Paramount Building still says 7:53! They glance at their
own watches, shake them to see if they're still ticking: yes! the sun
hasn't set after all! Nothing has really happened, *they're still okay!* It's
like coming out of a scary movie—nothing but camera tricks, the
illusory marvels and disasters of Cinerama and 3-D, th-th-that's all,
f-folks! Lights up and laugh!

East side, west side, all around the town, the people stagger to their
feet, grapple with the clothing knotted around their ankles, hobble and
lurch, boys and girls together, toward their proper places, encouraging
each other to shake a leg and making a generally raucous appeal for
national unity. Up on the Death House stage behind Uncle Sam, Judge
Kaufman and his family, Irving Saypol and his prosecuting team, the
Rosenberg jury, Herb Brownell, wives and children and prison officials,
Pentagon Patriots and Singing Saints disconnect themselves from one
another and creep sheepishly toward the wings, squatting and waddling
like ducks, hauling on their pants and panties as they go, while out
front Indians pull up their loincloths, Rat Packers their three-holed
britches, Suffragettes their bloomers.

"That's the style, fella citizens!" thunders Uncle Sam, cracking a
mighty bullwhip like a ringmaster—*"This is the end, so why pretend—*
now's the time to strain every nerve and bend all your energies to keep
well in fronta the mighty struggle for men's minds, hearts, and raw
materials! The untransacted destiny of the American people is to estab-
lish a new order in human affairs, to confirm the destiny of the human

race, and to pull that switch and shed a new and resplendent glory upon mankind! Men's hopes call upon us to say what we will do—who shall live up to the great trust? eh? and who's the yaller low-lived red-mouthed pusley-gutted buckaroo who DARES FAIL TO TRY?"

None dare, of course—except for a few professional troublemakers and close-minded bellyachers, and these the bald eagle, flapping and cawing vehemently, is rounding up and driving toward the Whale's mouth like a cowboy pushing dogies into the stockyard. One the eagle misses is the Rosenbergs' defense lawyer, who, unnoticed in all the excitement, has finally managed to gain a purchase on the edge of the stage. He now draws himself up, lifts one leg over, and gasps: "I demand a reply to my petitions!"

"Very well," says Uncle Sam, and he picks up Betty Crocker's fallen dentures and bites Manny in the nose with them.

Bloch screams and falls from the stage. "What kind of animals am I dealing with?" he rages. "The actions of the Government of the United States in this case reveal to the entire world that the people who are running the Government are much more barbaric than the Nazis when they had power in Germany! I feel ashamed that I am an American today!"

The Square is rocked with hooting and hissing: the people are finding their way back now, getting the feel of things again. "I place the murder of the Rosenbergs at the door of President Eisenhower, Attorney General Brownell, and J. Edgar Hoover!" shrieks Bloch insanely, and the Union County American Legion in hasty assembly demands his disbarment. Bloch is dragged away, his new suit rumpled and his career in ruins, sobbing huskily: "Please tell them I did the best I could for them! Tell them I respect and admire them! Tell them I love them . . . !"

But his words are drowned out by boos, his own histrionics, and sudden laughter, for just as Manny is being stuffed into the Whale's belly, somebody else—looking as miserable as an abused dog in his crushed homburg and dirty socks—is being led out like Jonah by a stiff-backed old lady in prim rimless specs! Who is it? Smokey Bear? The Atomic Bum? No, it's Vice President Richard (Dick) Nixon and his late great Grandma Milhous!

"Everybody's tryin' ta git inta da act!" snorts Uncle Sam, hands on hips, winking down over his nose at the old woman. *"Awright, Granny, send that onregenerit bluebellied tatereater up here where I can take a swat at him with the flat side a the dictates a reason and justice should it come to the raskil's imperdint mind to discomboberate us with any*

more surjestshuns, prayers, or other dierbolical sass!" The old lady returns Uncle Sam's wink and gives the Vice President a whacking high-buttoned boot in his henchbone, sending him flapping forward through the untangling pack-up like a clipped goose trying to take flight. People add their own toes to his general forward endeavor, holding their noses and hollering taunts at him like "Little Dick, he was so quick," and

> "Oh you dirty beggar,
> Oh you dirty crumb!
> Ain't you ashamed
> To show your dirty bum!"

Uncle Sam watches these procedures with a rueful smile, then turns his attention to his kayoed Mistress of Ceremonies, Betty Crocker. He stuffs the false teeth back into her soft gaping jaws and revives her with a splash of six fluid ounces of Tennessee sour mash, observing as he throws that the old girl has taken quite a beating and is probably going to need a face lift once all this is over. Betty rears up, shakes her head, grabs up her rolling pin, smoothes down her skirt, wipes off her jowls with a swipe of her sleeve, snaps her choppers once just to test her grip on them, and then proceeds to lay into every dubious character in sight—not even the bureaucrats are safe, and some Congressmen are seen diving under their chairs. "Hoo-hah!" laughs Uncle Sam, watching her swing away. "I wish the Phantom could see *that!*"

He cracks his bullwhip over Betty's head, snatching a couple dozen silver stars off the shirts of patrolmen and state troopers, then a couple dozen more, converts the whip into a Louisville Slugger and, tossing the badges up in the air, swats them out into the night sky (they seem to stick up there and glitter like something out of a fabulous movie they've all seen but can't quite remember. Graceful is his form, and slender, and his eyes are deep and tender, as with a smile that is childlike and bland, he next turns the whip/bat into a Remington and commences to shoot the stars all down again, knocking them off like clay pigeons—*crack! pop!*—and splattering the heavens with glittering sprays of light like bombs bursting in air! The Singing Saints, their Mormon decorum recovered, zip up and step forward to accompany Uncle Sam's act with their own rendition of "Land of Hope and Glory," but before they can even get as far as the "wider still and wider shall," Uncle Sam—glancing anxiously up at the clock, whose hands have been sliding inexorably up toward eight o'clock—cuts them off: *"Whoa thar, fella patriots! Enough a this high-minded bullshit, it is rather for us to be here deddycated to the great task remainin' before us—thunder is good, thunder is impressive, but it is* lightnin' *what does the work—or as old Ben would say, when there's a great heat on the land in a partickyular region and a passel a clouds comes by full of electrical fire—LOOK OUT BELOW! Yea, it is nigh onto Zero Hour, friends and neighbors! We got a pair of misdemeanin' poachers back there at the settin'-off end of the Last Mile who gotta take their farewell trip to that promised land, gotta pay, as we say, the debt of nature, slip the cable and cock up their toes—and toot sweet! So an end to this foolish hurrahin', the tea party's over! It is time to make room on earth for a little warmth, a little zap of love's bestowin': then nighty-night to them scallywags, cuz it's rubber tire buggy, rubber tire hack, they gotta walk that lonesome valley, and they ain't a—"*

Suddenly, there is a sharp *whirr-CLICK!*, like gears meshing toward some final connection, and then—BONG! BONG! BONG . . . !—all the clocks in New York City, all the clocks in the nation, in the world, strike the fateful hour, making people gasp and bite their fingernails: it is eight o'clock! From the belly of the Whale comes a woman's scream: *"In memory of the Rosenbergs!"*—and the Whale begins to rumble and tremble as though with a fearsome indigestion, an indigestion that sounds like a lot of hysterical amateurs trying to sing "Go Down, Moses!" The people shrink back—

"Hey, no flinchin' out there!" booms Uncle Sam. *"Soft-heartedness, in times like these, shows sof'ness in the upper story!"* He snaps his finger and jabs it at Police Commissioner Monaghan, and George sends his Deputy Patrick Kirley scrambling in to the Whale like a gun-toting antacid to quiet things down in there: one belch and it's over. *"Come on, you doddrabited wheyfaced no-good varmints! Now is the hour! With firmness in the right as God gives us to see to the right, we are gonna drop the handkerchief and light a candle of understandin' in these traitors' hearts which shall not be put out till they've sizzled like a wet cat flung into a kittil of bilin' fat! Huu-u-u WEE! Whilst the stars and stirrups floats in the breezus whar, whar in the name a Jeezus is that miserbul termatis-nosed skaley-heeled rapscallious skonk who will not, with pomp and parade, with shows, games, sports, guns, bells, bonfires, and skeer-provokin' loomynations, lay hold—from one end a this continent t' uther—the hangin' rope!? EH?? Do you hear me, o ye that love mankind? It is time, I say, to loose the fateful lightnin' to reach a fiery rod, and on Death's fearful forehead write the autygraph a God so's any squinty-eyed inimy can read it without his spectacles! So let the burn begin! All I got, and all that I yam, and all that I hope, in this life, I'm now ready to stake on it!"* He takes a final deep puff on his corncob

pipe and—precisely at one minute after the hour—produces his zinger: a huge smoke ring that rises slowly, scaling the cloudy summits of the Times Tower, hovers momentarily up there over its tip, then sinks down over it, unrolling like a condom—he blows at it and it bursts into a spectacular fireworks display, in the center of which, halfway up the tower, is the blazing message:

NOW COMES THE MYSTERY!

He flashes a final salute to his wildly cheering citizens in the Square—"*I got a million of 'em!*" he laughs, tipping his star-spangled plug hat forward on his stately brow in the best Broadway tradition—"*And so now I bid you a welcome adoo, brave Americans all—long may our land be bright with freedom's holy light, you may fire when you are ready, Gridley!*"—and then he disappears, leaving to Betty Crocker the task of setting the final places at the table.

The first of tonight's special guests to appear, introduced by Betty (with a nod to the National Poet Laureate) as "the nation's number one legal hunter of top Communists," is the chief prosecutor in the case, Irving Howard Saypol, now a State Supreme Court Judge—he strides manfully to his front-row seat with all the calm confidence, as Saint Mark would say, of a Christian with four aces, a natural winner, with a big chest, a burgeoning belly, a tough jaw, cold eyes like Uncle Sam's, and a cocked pistol in his hip pocket. He is accompanied by his wife, his children, his chief assistants in the case, Myles Lane, Roy Marcus Cohn, Jim Kilsheimer III, and Jim Branigan, Jr., and all their loved ones. The prosecution team is followed out by the various witnesses at the trial, Betty urging them along like a schoolmarm lining up her kids at the toilet door, everyone from chubby-cheeked David Greenglass, his wife Ruth, and dapper little Harry Gold in his now-familiar pinstripe suit, which prison fare is making baggy on him, to the notorious Red Spy Queen, Elizabeth Bentley, who regrettably is not quite a Blue Angel after all (in fact she looks like a spinster librarian, the kind that tear all the naughty pages out of the books), and Jim Huggins, the immigration inspector from Laredo who helped Morty Sobell across the border. Sobell himself, no longer so tight-lipped as he was at the trial, is kept well out of sight, though his wife Helen has been seen tonight, getting herded into the Whale.

And then the Texas high-school marching band strikes up the theme song (no longer, thank heavens, recognizably Russky) from "The FBI in Peace and War." Saypol, his team, and the carefully developed witnesses got all the headlines at the time of the trial, but of course it was the corps of hard-working agents from the Federal Bureau of Investigation who really cracked the case—men like Bob Lamphere and Hugh Clegg, Dick Brennan and T. Scott Miller, John Lewis, and not to forget Walt Roetting and John Harrington and all the other unsung backstage heroes of the case—and it is these men (some of them holding replicas of John Dillinger's death mask up in front of their faces to protect their secret identities) who now march out as a unit to a thundering ovation, carrying on their broad shoulders like an archbishop or a winning football coach their world-famous boss, J. Edgar Hoover, said by many to be the most powerful man in all America. Hoover—who is still tidying up, rolling down his pantcuffs and tossing what looks like a wig and bits of clothing back to his faithful sidekick Clyde Tolson, standing in the wings—is a little fatter maybe than his comic books like to show, but he is nevertheless a commanding and heroic figure, especially held way high up like that, and whenever he flashes that beloved Jimmy Cagney grimace of recognition, part menacing grin, part sharp-eyed scowl— which he does now, reaching down at the same time to slap the hand of one of the agents supporting him—you'd think from the enraptured roar of the populace out front that it was at least the Second Coming. They pass down through the honor guard to their seats in the special section, exchanging ritual winks with old acquaintances like Dick Tracy and Bruce Wayne, Steve, Daddy, Rip and Kerry, and receiving unabashedly grateful hugs from Miss Lace and Mopsy and Stupefyin' Jones.

It is not easy, needless to say, for anyone to follow such giants, least of all the twelve ordinary middle-class citizens—simple bookkeeper types for the most part, unaccustomed to the public limelight—to whose lot it fell to be the jurors in this historic case, and to whose lot it now falls to come out, together with their wives and children, to do their turn on the stage and step down to take their seats on this one night, like Queens for a Day, with the famous and the mighty. They fumble about in the wings, pretending to be distracted, urging each other to go first, then banging into one another in their eagerness to be helpful, knocking fedoras and glasses off, tripping over each other's feet, apologizing, smiling dismally, some finally backing on as though intending to go the other direction, others stepping out boldly only to freeze in panic when they hit the bright lights, still others getting tangled in the bunting at the edge or stumbling over the electric cables coiling out from under the chair, no one seeming to remember which way they're supposed to go when they get out there, and so in bug-eyed desperation trailing around after each other in a dizzying welter of wrong directions. But Irving Saypol, who can operate with this jury, as Harry Gold would put it, "in the very manner that a virtuoso would play a violin," rises opportunely from his seat in the special section to take command, focusing the jurors' distracted attention and guiding them to their places of honor. Down they come, grateful for Saypol's timely intervention, to the cheers of the citizenry packed up in Times Square, a veritable phalanx of stalwart middle-Americans, whom Brian Donlevy himself would have been proud to have with him on Wake Island and with whom anyone out in Times Square might identify (and who back in the anonymous jam-up does not dream of being up there in the front rows tonight?).

Then, as Betty Crocker solemnly rings her dinner bell three times in the traditional courtroom manner, out from the wings comes the Boy Judge, Irving Robert Kaufman, flanked by two FBI agents and twelve New York City policemen, his pale round face barely visible through all the thick hips and holsters, and followed by his wife, Helen Rosenberg Kaufman, and their three sons. The Judge, swathed in his flowing black robes of office, steps out briefly from under his forest of protectors to thank the FBI for watching over him and to receive, before taking his front-pew seat, a few honors from, among others, his alma mater, the American Legion, the Jewish War Veterans, and the Federation of Women's Clubs. Then, recalling his famous farewell to the jury the day before he laid down the death sentences, he lifts one hand in a gesture both papal and pugnacious, clears his soft throat, and exclaims: *"God bless you all!"*

With all the principals of the case seated, Betty Crocker is left with only two 3 × 5 recipe-sized index cards in her hand. One of course is for the nation's Chief Executive, President Dwight David Eisenhower, who will address the crowd briefly before the executions. The second is for the man she now announces: the country's highest-ranking legal officer, Attorney General Herbert J. Brownell. It is not merely for reasons of protocol that the head of the U.S. Department of Justice has been granted the unique honor this evening of sitting at the right hand of the President of the United States—no, more importantly, it is to make public acknowledgment of the fact that, were it not for this one man, these electrocutions would never have taken place at all tonight . . . if ever. He has overseen the Department's prosecution of the case in the appeals courts these past several weeks, coped with Communist threats and demonstrations, pursued the execution of the death sentences with vigor, skill, conviction, and intransigence, remaining steady as a rock when others in the Administration might have faltered, and even called the Supreme Court into a historic special session in order to

protect the time plan. If any man in America can be said personally to
have shepherded the Rosenbergs to their deaths tonight, it is Herbert
Julius Brownell, and he it is who now, with his wife and children, steps
out on the Death House stage to receive a hero's welcome from the
citizens, this cloud of admiring witnesses, in Times Square. He nods
politely at all the people, now on their feet and giving him a standing
ovation, but it's not the sort of thing that the Attorney General enjoys.

Herb works the anxious-glance-at-the-watch ploy to still the crowd,
then signals for the Singing Saints, who lead the congregated in singing
Irving Berlin's sacred classic, "I Like Ike." And as the chorus mounts to
a thundering climax, into it ambles, in that familiar easygoing yet brassy-
hoofed putting-green stride, grinning affably but shyly, his grandpa's
belly pushing softly against a brand-new single-breasted suit and his
blue eyes twinkling merrily: the 34th President of the United States of
America, Dwight David (the Iron-Hewer) Eisenhower! His left arm is
raised in a friendly open-handed salute to the screaming, stomping,
chanting masses; on his right, smiling graciously: the 30th First Lady of
the Land and the prettiest in a coon's age, the saucy pride of the Hawk-
eye State and belle of officers' clubs these past forty years from one end
of the world to the other: Mamie! The place is going wild! America has
seen nothing like this man since the day it was born—it is indeed, no
fooling, as though George Washington himself were back on earth, alive
and well once more and whacking out bogies at Burning Tree! And who
knows? it may be so! Ike and Mamie bask briefly in the adulation of the
people; then, while the First Lady is escorted by General Jerry Persons
to her place in the front pew, the President steps forward, both arms
raised as though having his chest measured by a tailor, to address the
gathered community, remarking to no one in particular but loud enough
for everyone to hear and smile: "I had no idea that our host had such a
party as this!"

When things have quieted down enough for him to speak, he assumes
a country-philosopher double-chinned pose and, speaking with blurred
haste like a man with a mouthful of saltwater taffy, loose teeth, and a
hundred things to talk about if he could just remember them, says: "My
friends, before I begin the espression of those thoughts that I deem
appopriate to this mo-ment I want to say: this one thing—of course,
huh! there are a *lot* of things in a big country such as ours and the kind
of world, that we are living in that make interesting subjecks, for conversation and very naturally, I wouldn't make a serious decoration on
such a sujject—supject—uh, at this mo-ment but there are a few
thoughts, that crowd into my mind with your permission and I will

attempt to utter them in a very informal and homely way . . ." There is widespread applause at this remark. He tucks one hand awkwardly in his jacket pocket, managing to look bemused, humble, and very important all at the same time. "In many sets—segs—sections of the country in every area, let me say, I have said these things before—and to some of you that are here tonight, some of you here—I hate to be insulting—who I would call contemptries of mine. Whom. What I came to—what I came to repeat—and they are given a new, a sharp meaning by the nature of the tension tormending our whole world and so I don't mind, repeating what I have said as often as I have spoken pubbick—uh, plubicly, about this sub . . . ject. What I should like to point out, and I am talking plain common sense—and let me intercheck, whatever the answer be, let it be plainly spoken, I don't want to sound like Saint Peter. It would be fooling—uh, foolish, to give anything that would appear to be an authoritative conclusion, and certainly I did not come over in the role of a professor to give you a lecher, but I would say this: it is a question that I will not answer, ladies and gentlemen, without a bit more pepprer—uh, pepperation on the thing, of course, I have never thought I had quite all the answers, it's a damn thorn in the side, but certainly, we can hope for the best—the formula matters less than the fete—faith . . ."

Thus he yatters on a moment, telling them how he got struck by lightning himself once back in 1917 and recounting in his own inimitable way the saga of the A-bomb theft: "Finally, my friends, we have here this evening to duscuss with you our problems of keeping the internal house. Uh, secure against the boring of subversies and that sort of thing. Now as late as 1949 certain imminent scientists . . ." But slowly, even as they watch, Eisenhower the happy-go-lucky bumbling oaf gives way to the World Hero, the Man of Destiny: Ike the Divine. Even physically he seems to grow in stature and poise, his voice taking on a new authority and depth as he speaks of the national desire to "stamp out all traces of Communism" and the "power in the Federal Government to defend itself against any kind of internal disease, if it wants to put its heart into it," the loose charming twaddle fading away, and in its stead: his celebrated "Vision of the War between the Sons of Light and the Sons of Darkness": *"The shadow of fear has darkly lengthened across the world!"* he thunders, and in awe they listen. *"We sense with all our faculties that forces of Good and Evil are massed and armed and opposed as rarely before in history!"*

While he lays it on them, smacking his lips and cracking his jaws like a Dallas radio preacher, ten men slip out quietly from the door downstage right, unheralded and unapplauded, to take up their assigned positions for the final act in tonight's program. Four of the men—U.S. Marshal William Carroll, Sing Sing Warden Wilfred Denno, and prison doctors George McCracken and H. V. Kipp—line up just inside the door through which they have entered. The official Executioner, Joseph P. Francel, moves upstage past them into his special alcove, and the other five—Marshal Carroll's deputy Thomas Farley, three FBI agents (technically, the Rosenbergs will be able to confess right up to the last moment, though this is not anticipated; the real hope is that, because God is good, some clue, some word or name, will fly involuntarily like sparks from their charged tongues at the moment of their deaths), and a prison attendant—cross the stage left in front of the electric chair to line up by the disconnected radiator along the wall, just downstage of the Dance Hall door, through which the Rosenbergs are scheduled presently to enter. The prison attendant is carrying a bucket of ammonia with a dark brown sponge floating in it, which he deposits on the floor beside the death chair as he crosses over.

"It is, friends, a spiritual struggle!" the President is declaiming. Dr. Kipp's stethoscope is showing; he tucks it inside his suit jacket, holding his hand over the button. *"And at such a time in history, we who are free must proclaim anew our faith: we are called as a people to give testimony in the sight of the world to our faith that the future shall belong to the free!"* Executioner Francel flicks on the spotlight in his alcove, checks the switches, wiring, ammeters, voltmeters, rheostats, flicks the light off again. *"History does not long entrust the care of freedom to the weak or the timid—we must be ready to dare all for our country! Whatever America hopes to bring to pass in the world must first come to pass in the heart of America!"* The Marshal and the Warden clasp their hands behind their backs, feet slightly apart, a formal at-ease position the others on the stage emulate. Two of the FBI agents tip their heads toward each other. One of them glances at the chair, at the Executioner's alcove, back at the other agent, who nods somberly as though in agreement. *"I know of nothing I can add to make plainer the sincere purpose of the United States!"* the President declares.

The stage lights gradually come up and throughout Times Square the houselights dim, casting the people in soft shadows, as Eisenhower moves toward the prayerful climax of his Vision, asking all Americans to beseech *"Gawt's guidance"* and pray never to be proven guilty of *"the one capital offense against freedom, a lack of staunch faith!"* Whereupon, avoiding the nettlesome dilemma of choosing amongst the various schisms—priest, preacher, or rabbi—imported from Europe, he calls upon his own Guardian of the Harvests, Ezra Taft Benson of the Council of Twelve Apostles, former missionary for both the Boy Scouts of America and the Salt Lake Church of Jesus Christ of Latter-Day Saints, to give the Invocation to the Electric Chair. *"For now, good-bye! It has been wonderful to meet you! I will see you again!"* he says, and steps down to take his seat, front and center, in the pew beside Mamie—what seat there is left: during his address, Joe McCarthy has managed to elbow his way up into the front row in between Herb Brownell and Helen Rosenberg Kaufman, and Ike only has room on the pew for one cheek. A ripple of unconcealed disgust passes briefly over Eisenhower's face as he squeezes into his slot, having to alternate between Herb's lap and Mamie's, but he can't seem to bring himself to ask Joe to move.

The stage lights are up full now in a darkened Square and the Death House set is bathed in a glaring white light as Brother Ezra, in the name of Jehovah, Jesus, and Joseph Smith, leads the people in blessing those whose duty it is "to shed the blood of those who are destined to be slain in consequence of their guilt. . . . For, behold, the day cometh, that shall burn as an oven; and all the proud, yea, and all that do wickedly, shall be stubble: and the day that cometh shall burn them up, saith the Lord of Hosts. . . ." But even before he has finished, another voice can be heard back in the wings, saying: *"Julius, follow me!"* It is not Jesus; it is the young prison chaplain, Rabbi Irving Koslowe. Distantly, like something out of "Inner Sanctum," a cell door rattles open. The antiphon dies away and after a brief gust of anxious shushing, unwinding from the center out to the edge like a dying cyclone, a respectful hush settles over Times Square: they are about to see a man die. . . .

"The Lord is my shepherd, I shall not want," intones Rabbi Koslowe, his voice echoing eerily down the concrete corridor of the Dance Hall, "He maketh me to lie down in green pastures, He leadeth me beside the still waters . . ." Hollow footsteps accompany the rabbi's voice, falling with measured tread like dripping water. It is as though they are all emerging from some deep cave, the steps striking ever firmer ground as they approach, the voice filling out, losing its damp resonance, until suddenly, as the rabbi, fitted out in a black robe, prayer shawl, and yarmulke, and reading from a prayer book held stiffly out in front of him, enters through the door in the corner upstage left under the sign that reads SILENCE, the footsteps disappear and his voice abruptly flattens out, becomes ordinary, muffled, a bit nasal: "He restoreth my soul, He leadeth me in the paths of righteousness for His name's sake . . ." He is followed through the door by two dark-suited prison guards and, wedged between them, a third man, a skinny young scruffy-headed fellow incongruously underdressed in a plain white T-shirt and wrinkled khaki pants and looking somehow like Harry Langdon—maybe it's the white face, the ludicrous flopping slippers on his feet, or perhaps the way he peers around the set in exaggerated astonishment, blinking at the bright lights, his knees sagging when he spies the electric chair: the clown who has stumbled into the wrong room somehow and got mistaken for somebody else who's been expected. "Yea, though I walk through the valley of the shadow of death," says the rabbi, "I will fear no evil, for thou art with me!" The four men pause at the chair. "Thy rod and thy staff they comfort me . . ." The door is closed. No one else has come through it. This then must be that one they have been waiting for: the Master Spy, the Big Thumb, C.C. 110,649, the murderer of millions, the man who, alone with his wife, destabilized the whole world, the mortal enemy of the entire human race—this must be—! A soft gasp of amazement flutters through the Square: he's so . . . so *small!* And young! Julius Rosenberg and Rabbi Koslowe are known to be both the same age, both thirty-five, but the rabbi looks at least a generation older! What is it? the short rumpled hair maybe, the scrawny neck—

"*You have no moustache!*" shrieks a child's voice, shrill and sudden, making people jump. "*What happened to your moustache? You look different!*" The wire-rimmed glasses are gone, too, the patterned neckties, the padded shoulders. . . . "*You must come home!*" screams another little voice. "*Every day there is a lump in my stomach, even when I go to bed!*" The crowds in the Square glance up at the night sky in search of the voices' source, clutch their programs tightly in their sweating hands, edge forward on their seats if they have one, stretch up on tiptoe if not, striving to see what's happening up there on the stage.

The two guards, joined now by the prison attendant who brought in the bucket, have turned Rosenberg around, away from the chair, to face the people out in Times Square. He stands there, fragile and rubbery-limbed, staring chalkily out at all the shadowy multitudes staring back, but either he sees nothing out there, being blind with fear, or disbelieves what he sees. His T-shirt hangs loosely on his softly heaving chest—his little boys have T-shirts like that, too, they've been wearing them in all the photographs, only theirs have DODGERS stamped on them. "Thou preparest a table before me in the presence of mine enemies," the rabbi says, as gently the guards press the prisoner Julius Rosenberg down into the brown-stained oak-and-leather chair. He does not resist; but he does not help them either. His body continues to function, but at some remove from his mind, as though he has already disowned it, while keeping it operative like some kind of visible metaphor for his anguish: not quite real any more, but something to be admired and pitied at the same time. Against their will, the people in fact admire and pity it, even as they fear it: this frailness—the Phantom's last weapon!

The official Executioner comes out of his alcove to help the three prison attendants, as together, like a team of efficient airline stewardesses, they belt Julius Rosenberg in for his execution: chest, groin, legs, arms—he seems to want to sit upright and must be pushed back into the slight recline of the chair. The chest straps are tightened and secured, but still he cranes his head upward. His hands, clenched tightly in his lap as though holding on to something precious, must be pried apart by the four men and forced into the leather straps on the chair arms. His long slender fingers, scratching for a grip, seize on the ends of the chair arms and squeeze till the knuckles go shiny white. "Thou anointest my head with oil," says the rabbi gravely, as indeed one of the guards dips his finger into a jar and slaps a dab of conductive paste on the little bald patch, freshly shaved, at the back of the condemned man's head. He winces like a child shrinking from the cool touch of the alcohol-soaked cotton swab that precedes an inoculation.

"My cup runneth over," continues the rabbi, but his voice seems to be fading, overtaken now by another voice, a woman's, small but resonant and musical, riding in over the goodness and mercy shall follow like descant variations on a plainchant: ". . . *sitting here and fighting for breath in an ever-narrowing circle of tightening time—oh darling, what a ghastly farce we are compelled to endure! I can't believe it yet!*" Not a majestic voice, but sweet and lyrical, the sort of voice one hears in church on the Sabbath singing Gounod's "Ave Maria" or "En Kalohenu" or joining in on the "Alleluia Chorus." In accompaniment, high above the Square on the Roof of the Astor, the lonely bugle grieves. . . . "*I feel so inadequate in the sight of your need! If only I could truly comfort you, dearest one, but I can only sit here and weep bitterly for you and the children and our devastated lives—oh my God, I'm so unhappy!*" The prisoner's canvas-slippered feet are lifted onto the footrest and locked into place. He looks like a seasick traveler being tucked into a deck chair. A guard stoops and rips open a pantleg, which has been previously slit, then sewn together loosely so it wouldn't flap indecorously on the last walk, and rubs in more of the same ointment used on the head. Metal electrodes with wet sponges are attached by the Executioner to these two oiled-up places. "*. . . My heart aches for the children! I looked at my photo of Mike with his hair falling down over his forehead and his tie awry, and thought I should burst with longing!*"

The horrible idea that we may never be with them again drives relentlessly through me and my brain reels, picturing their terror—oh Julie, how greedy I am for life and living . . . !" The prisoner's head is forced back against the leather headrest and strapped in. His eyes are squeezed shut and he is breathing rapidly, his teeth bared. The song that the trumpeter is playing is "Ciribiribin." *"What shall I do? I am lashed by the most tremendous kind of longing! Oh, I love you so very dearly— kiss me goodnight, the way you used to, my dear husband! How much dearer to me you are than you have ever been . . . !"* His eyes blink open momentarily as though for a last look as the leather hood is fitted over his head and then dropped down over his face—but the hood, far from muffling the voice, seems to amplify it. . . . *"How precious were those last few hours I was permitted to spend with you! It is when you cross the distance that separates us and call out your cheery greeting that I come alive and know that I am still my own self and not some fantastic being from another realm! How happy I am then—the very air changes and the heaviness lifts, and the will to live and work and fight is mine! There comes to me such an abiding sense of faith and joy, such a sure knowledge of the rich meaning our lives hold, my heart sings its refrain, 'I am loved, I am loved!' and within me there begins to develop the profoundest kind of belief that somehow, somewhere . . ."* Two of the guards exit, the third returning to his place by the wall. Warden Denno steps out, glances perfunctorily at the straps and connections, then up at Executioner Francel, who nods and returns to his alcove. *". . . I shall find that courage, confidence and perspective I shall need to see me through the bottomless horror, the tortured screams I may not utter, the frenzied longings I must deny! Your faith alone builds my confidence, restores me to my rightful place in my own eyes . . ."* Executioner Francel positions himself before his switch. He moves with the deliberate precision of a man who knows what he is doing. *". . . Then, after you were gone, the loneliness closed around me—it's all so strange without you! Oh bunny dear, hold me close to you tonight, be strong for me—I need you so to be strong for me . . . !"* The Warden raises his hand. Francel grasps the switch, wrapping his hand firmly around the big handle. *"Whatever might be involved, I love you dear one, as I love my very own life! I kiss you good night with all my heart, draw you close into loving—"*

Julius Rosenberg's body is straining suddenly against the straps as though trying to burst from the chair. Air hisses from his lungs. His neck thickens as though swallowing something whole. The leather straps creak and there is a staticky crackling whine in the Square reminiscent of the classic mad-doctor movies—only more close up. The loose clothes flutter and his limbs shake. Greasy yellow-gray smoke plumes from the top of his head like a cast-out devil. Then, abruptly, the whine stops. The body falls back into the chair, limp as a rag. There is a deathly breath-held silence in Times Square. Before it can be broken, the Executioner methodically pulls a switch a second time and again the body leaps from its seat to heave and labor against its shackles. By the time the third charge is delivered, there are still a lot of gaping mouths and bulging eyeballs out front—some of the Holy Six in particular, close enough to smell the smoke, are looking a little green around the gills— but on the whole, the worst is past: they've seen it now and know what to expect. Most of them anyway—some have closed their eyes, a few have turned away. Mamie Eisenhower, for example, is whispering something over her shoulder to Georgie Patton's widow, and seems to have missed the whole thing. Her husband's eyelids have already started to droop, as they always do when his part is over; he crosses his arms and legs, lifting his right ham into Herb's lap, and glances dismally down the row at Joe McCarthy, who, having caught a deep wheezing breath and crossed himself, now uncorks a hip flask and takes a long reviving snort. Irving Saypol sits cool as custard, erect yet relaxed, his long bespectacled face betraying no emotion whatsoever, his assistants Lane, Cohn, Kilsheimer, and Branigan doing their best to emulate him. Judge Kaufman is partly screened by his long-necked wife, leaning across in front of him to whisper with Mamie Eisenhower, but behind her short-bobbed hair, his thick lips have pulled back to reveal the gap in his upper incisors, and there is a tic popping away in the thick white pouch of flesh in front of his left ear. Some of his jurors still seem a bit shaken as well (is this what they voted for?), and G-man Hoover's bulldog scowl looks more like a case of severe heartburn right now than mere righteous indignation, but for the most part the picture is one of a general release from tension with each successive charge, a return, in the words of Warren Harding, to normalcy. The best index of this is the behavior of all the children out front: fascinated by the first two jolts, they are now bored by the third; they squirm in their seats as Julius's body whips and snaps in its bonds, covering up their ears against the crackling whine, asking "What's history?" and complaining that they want to go home or go see Mickey Mouse or use the toilet.

When Francel has opened the switch and the body has collapsed for the third time, the two prison doctors walk over and rip the T-shirt down the front. Dr. McCracken puts his stethescope to the bared chest, nods to the others, and, wiping the sweat from his upper lip with the

back of his hand, says: *"I pronounce this man dead."* Whereupon,
Julius Rosenberg, taking Judge Irving Kaufman and the U.S. Department of Justice with him, enters the record books as the first American
citizen ever executed by a civil court for espionage. More records are set
to be broken when Ethel Rosenberg takes her turn in the chair, but this
one belongs to Julius alone, and, as such things appeal to Americans, it
is duly cheered—less enthusiastically up front, where the disquieting
presence of Death can still be felt like a sticky malodorous fog, more
warmly as it spreads out toward the periphery, traveling like a happy
rumor, merging finally into a drunken exultant uproar out at the far
edges, where everyone is having a terrific time without exactly knowing
why.

Guards unbuckle Rosenberg's corpse, offering the public a quick sensational glimpse of his blue tongue, wildly distorted facial muscles, and
fractured eyeballs, then they heave the sacklike thing up onto the white-
sheeted gurney, grunting as they work. While the cadaver is being
wheeled offstage to the autopsy room, the attendant who brought in the
ammonia bucket mops up the puddle beneath the electric chair and
sponges off the soiled seat, working with self-conscious fastidiousness,
aware of all the eyes upon him. The audience with gentle good humor
applauds him—he smiles sheepishly, wiping his hands on his pants, and
ducks back to his position beside the wall, stage left.

Cecil B. De Mille, meanwhile, using the Paramount Building as a kind
of giant magic lantern, the Claridge Hotel as a screen, has commenced to
project Uncle Sam's documentary film on the Rosenberg boys, the idea
being to augment the pathos (Americans, as he knows, go ape over
sentiment) and to restore a certain monumentality to the event, a bit
diminished by the actual human size of the principals and the loss
during the blackout of the larger-than-life pageant icons—but they are
running behind now with the executions, the Sabbath is rushing up on
them, and so hardly has the film faded into the initial first-reel prison
encounter between parents and children, the littlest son greeting his
mother with "You look much smaller, Mama!" ("No, it is you who are
growing bigger!"), when Rabbi Koslowe's voice can again be heard
down at the echoey far end of the Last Mile, gravely reciting, as cell
doors clang and steps once more approach, the 15th Psalm: "Lord, who
shall abide in Thy tabernacle? who shall dwell in Thy holy hill . . . ?"

Yet, though it begins much the same as the one before, this is, as the
people soon realize, no mere repeat performance—no, this is a true
second act, a topper, they can feel it, even before Ethel Rosenberg has
made her appearance through the Dance Hall door: something very

different is about to happen! Maybe it's simply because she's a woman—it's a rare thing to watch a woman being put to death, Uncle Sam was probably thinking of that when he set up the order; or maybe it's the way they walk this time, the rustling of starched skirts, the click of hard heels coming down the corridor; or the flickering images on the Claridge perhaps, the little Rosenberg boys up there, several stories high, playing horsey on their parents' backs; or David's provocative description, recited by the rabbi but chosen by Ethel, of a citizen of Zion: "He that backbiteth not with his tongue, nor doeth evil to his neighbour, nor taketh up a reproach against his neighbour!" This is not a prayer, it is an accusation! She is challenging them all, just as she challenged the press and public with her defiantly political Death House letters, or the President with her unyielding mercy pleas, or the Judge with heated quotations from Shaw's *Saint Joan:* "You damn yourself," she told him, "because it feels grand to throw oil on the flaming hell of your own temper! But when it is brought home to you; when you see the thing you have done; when it's blinding your eyes, stifling your nostrils, tearing your heart, then—then—O God, take away this sight from me! O Christ! deliver me from this fire that is consuming me!"

By the time they pass under the SILENCE sign and into the heat and stench and glare of the Death House stage, Rabbi Koslowe has moved on to Ethel's second selection, the 31st Psalm: ". . . Thou hast set my feet in a large room. Have mercy on me, O Lord, for I am in trouble: mine eye is consumed with grief, yea, my soul and my belly!" But if Ethel Rosenberg—driving force behind the Master Spy, willing slave of a conspiracy against all humanity, and typist for the Crime of the Century—is consumed by grief, it is not obvious in the way she makes her entrance, walking buoyantly between two white-frocked prison matrons, her hands clasped in front of her, her head held high and her eyes sparkling, her face lit with a serene smile, declaring by her very presence that, unlike Shaw's Saint Joan, she will not be burned offstage—indeed, even had this been the plan, she would not have allowed it.

She is dressed simply in a green cotton dress with white polka dots and loafer-type terrycloth slippers, her hair close-cropped on top, a tiny creature, just five feet tall, pert, full-breasted, and disturbingly pretty, with none of the puffy puckery-mouthed sag of the newspaper photos—maybe it's the haircut, the loose springlike dress, the color in her cheeks; probably, though, it's just her commanding style. There are some out in the audience who have been feeling they've seen all there is to see the first time around—you just plug them in, they twitch and jerk awhile and shit their pants, then you unplug them and cart them off, ho hum—and who have become a bit restless, distracted, looking ahead already to the Bobo Olson–Paddy Young bout to follow, laying their bets, getting into arguments, or else, especially if they've got their kids with them, contemplating the quickest route out of the pack-up—but Ethel's entrance has changed all that. She's got every one of them on the edge of their seats or the balls of their feet. President Eisenhower sits hunched forward, his eyes wide open for a change, and Mamie too is watching now. Vice President Nixon is white as a sheet, gripping the seat of his chair, sweating profusely. Julius shared his terror with them all, and so they were able to sympathize with him, get inside and suffer what he suffered, then survive—but Ethel is insisting on being herself, forcing them to think about something or someone other than themselves, which is both disquieting and exciting. She gazes around the set and out into Times Square with a kind of fierce delight, enjoying what she sees, meeting each of her accusers with a bold steady stare, smiling at the people beyond, daring them all to watch and listen. . . . "For I have heard the slander of many," reads the rabbi, "fear was on every side: while they took counsel together against me, they devised to take away my life!" Her husband's voice enters almost as though, with a flick of her short curls, she has cued it—*"It's the warmth and comradeship of decent people, it is the compassionate heart of good people and the fraternal solidarity of mankind—this is what is really worthwhile and this is what is good in the world!"*—but at the same time, though her lips remain closed in their gently taunting smile, her own voice is present, too: *"All my heart I send to all who hold me dear—I am not alone—and I die 'with honor and with dignity'—knowing my husband and I must be vindicated by history!"* Joe McCarthy is grinning broadly in frank admiration, and even Darryl Zanuck seems impressed. "Let the lying lips be put to silence," reads the rabbi, "which speak grievous things proudly and contemptuously against the righteous!" She has not only stolen the atom bomb—*she has stolen the Bible as well!*

The two matrons accompanying her—Helen Evans and Lucy Many—hesitate. Ethel turns to them, smiles warmly, shakes Mrs. Evans's hand and kisses her cheek, shakes Mrs. Many's hand—they flee, genuinely touched, dabbing at their eyes with clutched handkerchiefs. Then, unassisted, Ethel walks directly to the electric chair and plumps herself down in it with all the familiarity of a daily commuter taking her seat in the subway. Her husband's voice meanwhile, accompanied by friendly street noises from the Lower East Side of their childhood, is speaking of June and love and how happy they were as young radicals, first as lovers and students, then as man and wife. . . . *"I look up at the calendar and*

June 18th catches my eye—how vividly I remember that lovely Sunday in June! We were so full of joie de vivre, so happy and so much in love—I never dreamed I could love anyone so much! Remember the photos from our honeymoon at Spring Glen? In many ways, my bunny, you are prettier and lovelier now even than then!" She shifts her body to make it easier for the guards strapping her in, helping them place the leather bands across her chest and lap, smiling at their embarrassed awkwardness. She is so tiny she had to scoot down in the seat for her feet to reach the footrests and the electrode there. *"And the many wonderful summers we spent together—do you recall our summer vacations with the boys? Can you picture all of us together in the country or at the beach? You carrying Robbie on your back and Michael on my back, and the big race was on. Do you remember the procession when it came time for the little one to be put to bed? You led the way holding his feet. I held his shoulders and Michael marched in the middle with his brother's back resting on his head. By now it seems so far away, but the beauty of it lingers. . . . Gosh, how sad without you . . ."* Up on the Claridge, Julius is zooming the little one through the prison visiting room like an airplane. Ethel tips her head to one side to help the Executioner attach the electrode to the shaved place on her scalp, wincing briefly when the wet sponge touches it. Her husband's voice has begun to whine. . . . *"The days are lonely, sweetheart, and the dark long nights are empty without you. Many times during the day I ask myself over and over why and I have to put it out of my mind because it doesn't make sense. Somehow it seems so long ago that I saw you and everything is strange and distant. An empty feeling grips me and everything seems so unreal and out of focus. Tears fill my eyes as I—"* She shakes her head as though shuddering and interrupts him. When his voice returns, it is once again deep and proud and reassuring: *"You and I must steel ourselves, my love, although our hearts are breaking: the approaching darkest hour of our trial and the grave peril that threatens us require every effort on our part to avoid hysterics and false heroics! We will have to call on the great strength of the solid union of our hearts and souls to find the stamina to face what is in store for us!"* Her smile returns. She watches the guards strap her arms in, flexing her fingers to show them she's comfortable. *"We can face the lies, the pain and even death, as long as we are united in heart and soul, in love and truth. What we are and all that we have no one can take away from us even though they keep us apart and threaten us with death. And come what may I am sure that our name will eventually be cleared. . . ."* She looks straight ahead at all the people in the special section down front as the black strap is placed across her mouth, gazing at them above the leather gag without hatred, without malice, but not letting them forget either what they are doing to her. Her eyes are open and shining brightly as the black leather hood comes down, covering her face. "Be of good courage," the rabbi is saying huskily, "and He shall strengthen your heart." Above her Julius and the boys are looking through a barred window at a tugboat pulling a string of barges on the Hudson River. *"Nobody welcomes suffering, honey, but as long as we do the right thing by our children and the good people of the world, nothing else matters!"* The guards exit. Warden Denno checks the connections. Up on the Claridge, her sons are being taken to a baseball game. Executioner Francel returns to his alcove. *"Oh my darling, how beautiful you look! I want to sit beside you, my love, stroke your hair, I want to look into your eyes while I hold your hands in mine. Ethel, you are just my girl and nothing on earth can change that. I can only say that life has been worthwhile because you have been beside me. Good night, sweet woman! I caress you tenderly and send all my love. I am happy that you have made my life so—"*

There is a sudden harsh metallic rattle, as before, and Ethel leaps against the straps, her body lifting clear of the seat, her dress fluttering as though caught in a wind, her hands balling into fists. Again there's the odor of burning meat and smoke curling up from her scalp, as her body temperature pitches up to 140 degrees. Francel opens the switch and she falls back into the chair like a soft Raggedy Ann doll with its face wiped away. Before the crowds can swallow and catch their breath, Francel pulls the long handle again, holds it, releases it, then pulls it down again, her delicate white throat gorged twice over by the driving current, her body plunging against the leather straps each time, the air filled with a fierce crackling whine: they've heard it six times now, but it's not something you can get used to. Then, as suddenly, it is over. Her body slaps limply back into the chair, all its poise, all its proud strength and compelling tension expunged.

Executioner Francel glances out briefly at the body from his alcove. Then, wiping his hands with a dustcloth, he makes a cursory examination of his switch panel and prepares to shut the system down. A guard steps forward, brushes his hand in front of his face as though sweeping away something unpleasant, and unbuckles the black leather strap binding Ethel's breasts. She's fallen so limp now: she seems almost childlike. While a second guard proceeds to unstrap her arms and legs, the two prison doctors approach, extracting their stethoscopes. Out front, there is a soft rustle and a deep communal sigh, as the people settle back, gazing around them as though in some surprise at finding themselves where they are, exchanging perfunctory but sympathetic church-lawn smiles, murmured remarks, a few whispered jokes—just to loosen up a little—about what they have seen, or think they might have seen. Someone points up at the clock on the Paramount Building and they all watch the second hand sweep past the uppermost star: 8:13. Just in time. The Sabbath has begun. You have to credit Uncle Sam, they all agree. The houselights are already starting to come up. Newsmen have left their places and are running, as they have been assigned to do, toward the bank of telephones inside the Times Tower to cable their stories in, although above them the news of Ethel's death is already being flashed around the tower in moving lights. Up at the far ends of the VIP aisles, Paddy and Bobo are already in their fighting togs, puffing and snorting and punching the air, warming up for the big fight due to begin shortly.

The guard unstrapping Ethel's limbs apologizes to the doctors for holding them up and steps out of their way, leaving one leg still bound. Dr. Kipp routinely rips her dress open down the front, and Dr. Mc-Cracken applies his stethescope to her bare chest. It seems to take him longer than usual. He frowns and asks Dr. Kipp to have a listen.

What's happening? An uneasy murmur ripples through the crowd. Warden Denno and Marshal Carroll look startled. Herb Brownell is on his feet, Irving Saypol as well, Tom Clark, some of the jurors—the President gropes absently for his field glasses and, not finding them, grabs Brownell's elbow instead: what's wrong? The people look up at the images of the Rosenberg boys being projected onto the Claridge, but the film has got caught in the projector, and all they see is a frozen shot of Ebbetts Field with a gaping hot hole in the center, melting its way horrifically out toward the edges—

"This woman," gasps the doctor, *"is still alive!"*

Now they're all up on their feet! This is impossible! Executioner Francel steps out of his alcove scratching his head in stupid bewilderment. "Want another?" he asks, but he seems confused, indecisive. The Warden, too, seems to have lost the initiative, and the doctors, thrown into this ad lib situation, are lost. There's but a moment's hesitation—long enough to reflect perhaps that it's too late, the Sabbath has already begun—and then, as a gaunt hoary figure rises up from the front-and-center section in his familiar star-spangled plug hat to cry, *"A little more grape, Captain Bragg!"*, they all rush forward, led by young Dick Nixon, followed by Joe McCarthy, Herb Brownell, Bill Knowland, Lyndon Johnson, Foster Dulles and Allen, Engine Charlie, and Estes

Kefauver, virtually the entire VIP section, scrambling up over the side of the stage, fighting for position as though their very future depended on it, racing for the switch—it's hard to tell who gets his hands on it first, maybe the Vice President with his head start, maybe Francel himself, or young Senator Kennedy, more athletic than most, or perhaps all of them at once, but whoever or how many, they throw themselves on it with such force they snap the thing clean off! The guard nearest the chair, seeing what was about to happen, has been frantically trying to belt Ethel up again, but he only gets one of the straps done up, and loosely at that, when the charge hits, hurling him backwards off the stage and cutting a wide swath through the VIPs as he flies by. Ethel Rosenberg's body, held only at head, groin, and one leg, is whipped like a sail in a high wind, flapping out at the people like one of those trick images in a 3-D movie, making them scream and duck and pray for deliverance. Her body, sizzling and popping like firecrackers, lights up with the force of the current, casting a flickering radiance on all those around her, and so she burns—and burns—and burns—as though held aloft by her own incandescent will and haloed about by all the gleaming great of the nation—

EPILOGUE

Beauty and the Beast

> "You shall know, my sons, shall know
> why we leave the song unsung,
> the book unread, the work undone
> to rest beneath the sod . . ."

It was her voice. She was singing her poem, the one she'd written when the year began. I could hear her outside the spare-room window . . .

> "Mourn no more, my sons, no more
> why the lies and smears were framed,
> the tears we shed, the hurt we bore
> to all shall be proclaimed . . ."

Ah, tears, hurt: what did she know? I sat inside on the carpeted floor, curled up in the dark, there among all those dog biscuits and blankets, kennels, knitted sweaters, and rubber bones that the American people in their love and simplicity had sent to Checkers, whimpering softly to myself, nuzzling the curtains, scratching my itches, feeling sick and bitter and hairy and abused. I'd worked myself ill over this thing, and where had it got me? Cast out. Disgraced. Triped and fell on and kiked in the side—oh Jesus, I felt a pain all over . . .

> "Earth shall smile, my sons, shall smile
> and green above our resting place,
> the killing end, the world rejoice
> in brotherhood and peace . . ."

521

I hadn't stayed around after for Uncle Sam's new instant-replay gimmick or for the boxing or wedding ceremonies, I'd had all I could take for one night, and besides I smelled too bad—instead I'd dashed off to that country-club boodle banquet in New Jersey, hoping to lose myself in the smoke of old-fashioned backroom politicking. But I hadn't been able to get up any appetite for that shit either, I'd just sat there amid all those beaming fatsos, part of the waxworks, feeling ugly, very low-down and smarmy and ugly, deep in post-crisis fatigue, suffering their smirks and grimaces and thinking: Ah fuck, I've done it again. No matter how many times I warn myself, no matter how many goddamn notes I write myself or how many quotations I copy out, I always forget: the point of greatest danger is not in preparing to meet the crisis or fighting the fucking battle—it occurs after the crisis of battle is over. It is then, with all his emotional resources shot to shit and his guard down, that a guy can easily, if confronted with another battle, even a minor skirmish, blow it.

When I got home I was very sore, feeling restless and troubled. I'd wanted to talk about it all somehow with Pat, but she'd been busy with the girls, still up and overexcited apparently by all the big-city entertainments, and she'd looked completely pooped. Of course, she always looked pooped, it was her way of advertising to the world what a joy it was to be married to me, but tonight there was something zombielike in her eyes that hinted at a final turning-off, an end of the road. She'd only had one thing to say to me all night. That was when I'd collapsed into my seat beside her at the burnings after having had to run the gauntlet of the VIP aisles from the Whale's mouth. I'd been close to tears. I'd wanted her to hug me close and comfort me. Instead, she'd patted my hand absently and, staring blankly up at the electric chair, had said: "That was a nice speech, dear."

Now she'd come into the bedroom where I'd just commenced to get undressed, thinking to take a bath, and had asked flatly: "What does 'I am a scamp' mean, Dick?"

"How the hell should I know?" I'd yelped. I was still very jumpy.

"I don't know. But it's written there on your backside," she'd said.

"What—?!!" I'd turned my butt toward a mirror: sure enough, there it was, in big greasy red letters, still more or less legible though badly smeared. "Ah . . . well . . . that!" A moustache too, stuck there on one cheek, that one I'd bought for a disguise—I'd wondered where I'd lost the damned thing. All the time, feeling it pasted back there, I'd thought I'd somehow fouled myself. I'd snatched it away irritably and pulled my pants back up: "It's, uh, it's my enemies, Pat . . . they—"

But Pat had already left the room: she was back in the bathroom picking up Julie, who'd fallen asleep on the toilet. I'd chased after her, holding my pants up, feeling hurt and misunderstood. Hated even: Jesus Christ, what an anniversary . . . ! She'd brushed past me impatiently, carrying Julie into the girls' bedroom, and I'd followed. Tricia was in there, jumping about in little circles with her hands over her eyes, singing out: "Help, help, the Phantom's got me!" Checkers was bounding at her heels, yapping and wagging his tail.

"Pat!" I'd cried. "Listen to me! It's not what you think!" It had welled up in me: that new fondness for her I'd been feeling ever since the near-betrayal. "I did it for the nation, Pat! For the Party!" I'd be nowhere without her, I knew. She was the only one I trusted, the only one I loved—I *needed* her, couldn't she see that? "I did it for *you*, Pat! For *us!*" But she'd acted like I didn't even exist. I'd recalled suddenly that game we used to play when we were just engaged: "Hey, look, Pat! Rrowf! Snort! Gr-r-roww-ff!" I'd squatted down and hunched my shoulders, roughed up my hair, bared my teeth, and gone lumbering about the room, barking and yelping and rolling my eyes up at Pat and Tricia. If I'd had a tail, I would have wagged it.

"Oh, Dick, grow up," Pat had snapped irritably.

"I don't wanna play monsters, Daddy," Tricia had whined, breaking into tears. "I wanna play Run, Sheep, Run with Mommy!"

"We're not playing anything, young lady. Your Daddy's leaving this room right now and you're going nighty-night! It's very late! Now get your pajamas on!"

"Yarf, Pat!" I'd pleaded, scratching my armpits, bounding up and down pathetically, then rolling around on the floor. If only she'd patted my head, scratched my ears, anything! My elbow had bumped Julie's doll Tiny and it had fallen off a chair, banged its head on the floor, and let out a little crying noise. This had started Checkers barking at me, in turn waking up Julie. "*Gruff! Yip!*" I'd bellowed over her wailing. "*Hrr-r-rowwl-ll!*"

"Now stop that, Dick!" Pat had scolded, her voice cold and angry. "You're going to give them bad dreams!"

Grunting and huffing, I'd lurched for the doll and tipped over a table full of games and building blocks. I'd squatted amid the debris, clutching Tiny. Now everybody was screaming. Because of the doll. Somehow I'd managed to take Tiny's head off. What was happening to me? I'd struggled for words, I'd wanted to tell Pat that she was the only one who could free me from this terrible enchantment, but all I could think of were arf and whine and snarl.

"Get out of here!" Pat had cried. "Right now! *Or you'll be sorry!*"

I'd gone galumphing out into the hallway on all fours, feeling hunted, banging my shoulder—the sore one—on the doorjamb, skinning my face on the hallway carpet. That swarm of black thing was coming down on me again. I could feel it in Checkers's fangs as he growled and nipped at my shins. I could smell it in my skunky armpits and foul breath. And I could see it coming out of Pat's mouth as she passed me to go into our bedroom. What she'd said was: "Put Checkers in the basement, Dick, before you go to bed," but what I'd seen coming out was: "You make me sick." I'd reared up on my hind feet to follow after, but she'd slammed the door in my face. Oh, the bitch! I'd fallen back, howling and moaning like a wounded bear, then had gone lunging about, crashing into things, batting the walls, falling through doorways, ending up finally in a dark corner of the spare room, curled up, pawing my ears in misery, listening to Ethel Rosenberg's aria drifting in through the window on the midsummer-night's breeze, howling along pathetically and thinking: in the end, I'm not hard enough for politics, I don't deserve to be President, I'm too good, the world's not like that, my mother and my grandmother ruined me . . .

> "Work and build, my sons, and build
> a monument to love and joy,
> to human worth, to faith we kept
> for you, my sons, for you . . ."

Well, poor Ethel—let's face it, she hadn't had it easy either. I'd envied her her equanimity at the end: she'd died a death of almost unbearable beauty. In fact, it *was* unbearable—that was probably why we'd all fought our way up to the switch when the electrician bungled it. Ultimately anyway: I'd have to admit that wasn't exactly what was on my mind at the time. I'd been thinking more about just getting the goddamn thing over with. I was hanging on then by the grace of one thought only: that the day had to end, it would all be got past. Had to. Time marches on. Shakespeare said that in some play, I believe. Some tomorrow would inevitably become today and we could start forgetting, that was the main thing. I'd never doubted this until that moment the doctors said she was still alive: then suddenly I'd felt like we were teetering on the brink of infinity. Scared the hell out of me. The rest was simple reflex.

Like the way I'd left the stage earlier on. When the lights went out, everybody had started screaming. It was terrible. Somebody was screaming wildly right where I was! It was me, I'd realized. Christ, I'd leapt completely outside myself! I'd pulled myself together as best I could, swallowed down my yelping panic, groped around in the dark for something to hang onto. What was awful was the terrible *emptiness*—it had felt like there was nothing holding anything together any more! I'd hit upon a chair and sat down in it. I'd felt safer. Thank God for gravity! I'd remembered my pants: I had to get them untangled before the lights came up again. I'd worked one shoe off. Then I'd felt the leather on my butt, the studs, and it had come to me suddenly where I was sitting. For one dreadful moment I'd felt locked to the chair, as though the leather of the seat and the skin of my ass had got interchanged somehow—then I'd ripped free at last, and the rest, as I say, was reflex. The momentum had carried me right off the edge of the stage and down with a bruising splat onto that sea of turbulent flesh below. Don't know who I hit, but it had felt like Bess Truman. I'd pitched and rolled blindly through the turmoil, carried along by the tide. Everything was wet and slippery and violent, with high crests and deep troughs: like rape, I'd thought. I was afraid I was going to get seasick.

Then I'd opened my eyes and discovered I could see after all, even though everybody else in the Square had still seemed to be flopping about helplessly with glazed looks in their eyes, screaming about the darkness. I'd understood this. When I was very young, just a freshman in high school, my father took Harold and Don and me to Los Angeles to hear Dr. Paul Rader preach a revival sermon and give ourselves to Jesus. Mother did not go. I grasped, even then, that this was not her Jesus, not the Jesus I'd grown up with, the Jesus of little boys. This was a ferocious Jesus who lived in a wild place only grown-up men could go to. Or anyway this was the impression I got from my father, who seemed very serious, even frightened. My mother was sad to see us go and I felt sorry for her—it was like some kind of conspiracy against her. At the meeting, everyone became very emotional. My own father became very emotional, in a way I'd never seen before—he cried and seemed to lose control of himself, seemed to *want* to lose control of himself, as though the very firmness of his will—and he was always a very willful man—depended on this momentary release. Harold and Don cried, too. So did I, it seemed to be important to my father that I did so and I obeyed as I always obeyed. And like the rest of them, I walked down the aisle through that dark forest of wild emotions and pledged my life to that fierce Jesus. But all the time I felt as though I were walking in a dream, somebody else's dream, not mine—I didn't really quite believe in what I was doing. It was like being in a play and I could throw myself into the role with intensity and conviction, but inside I was holding something

back. Even as I wept: later I was to recall this scene to help me to weep
on cue in *Bird-in-Hand*, in the back seat of my Dad's car with Ola, up at
Wheeling—but that night I felt guilty about it. I worried that I had not
been completely saved. Grace, I knew, was a matter of luck—after all,
there were peoples all over the world who had missed out, who were still
missing out, who'd never even heard of the name of Jesus, much less had
a chance to be baptized, so grace wasn't a blanket promise . . . and
maybe I was not one of the chosen ones. I wept and knelt and prayed
with the others, but I couldn't really *give* myself to Jesus, not entirely,
not the way the others did. Later, after I'd seen more of the world, I felt
pleased with myself for not having given in. I was proud of my discipline—what my mother called Self-Regulation and Self-Restraint—
and even though I envied my brothers' ability to plunge uncritically out
into Dad's world, I nevertheless felt a notch above them. I felt singled
out, touched by a special kind of grace, a unique destiny: I was God's
undercover agent in a secular world. For such a one, emotional release
was a kind of debauchery. An impiety. My way was harder, but at least I
could see where I was going.

And so it had been there in Times Square: the lights had been snuffed
all right, the marquees and billboards now as dead as the old city
trolleys, but though it had been like peering through pea soup, I could
nevertheless make out what was happening, even if nobody else could. It
was awesome to look at, of course—flesh, as far as you could see, engaged in every grab-assing obscenity imaginable, a frantic all-community
grope that my own privates did not entirely escape—but the dimensions
had taken the excitement out of it. In fact, if anything, it had been
spooky, unnerving: all that desperate weakness, that frenzied vulnerability, everybody screaming and reaching out and plunging haplessly
away in one another—it was like something out of *Fantasia* or *The Book
of Revelation.* I'd bobbed along on the flood, longing for the old bell
tower back home, some place of refuge where I could lock myself away,
think things over, work out the parameters of this new situation, get my
pants back up. Maybe, I'd thought, this is what hell will be like for me:
endless self-exposure. This was a Self that was not in my mother's
lexicon. It was the toughest part about being a politician, the one thing I
personally hated the most. I'm no shrinking violet, I'm not unduly shy
or modest, but I'm a private man and always have been. Formal. When I
have sex I like to do it between the sheets in a dark room. When I take a
shit I lock the door. My chest is hairy but I don't show it off. I don't
even like to *eat* in public and just *talking* about one's personal life
embarrasses me. And now all this today—Christ, I believed in touching

the pulse of the nation, but this was going too fucking far! It was probably a good thing I was all washed up.

I'd beached finally in the mouth of a whale, one of Disney's exhibits evidently. A dismal cavernous maw, dark and foreboding, but under the circumstances I'd found it inviting. I'd dragged myself inside, down the throat, away from the murky insanity of the mainstream out in the Square, clutching my poor bruised nuts and glad of any sanctuary. This has been worse than Bougainville, I'd thought. I'd wished Pat were with me and I'd wondered if I should go looking for her once I'd got my pants on—but then I'd realized I'd already seen her out there, part of her anyway (or was that a dream I'd had? it was all getting mixed up in my mind), it was really my mother I'd wished were with me. Jesus, I'd sighed, crawling along, drawn toward the belly by a distant flickering light, this has been the longest day of my life!

What had I expected to find inside the Whale? I'd seen the film with my daughters, and so had anticipated the craggy cathedral-like walls, the tremulous shadows cast by a lonely lantern, eerie digestive noises. Past that? A little benevolent magic maybe? a touch of the Mission Inn, Gepetto with a stiff drink and fried fish? Probably just a little peace and quiet where, covered in darkness, I could draw myself together, stop gesturing, jerking about, come to rest. What I certainly had *not* expected was to find my grandmother Almira Burdg Milhous sitting there in her rocking chair, gazing sternly down upon me over her rimless spectacles.

"Pull yourself together, Richard," she'd said gravely. "Seek the soul's communion with the Eternal Mind!"

"Grandmother!" I'd gasped, unable to believe my eyes. "My God, what are *you* doing here?"

"No swearing, Richard. And put your trousers on."

She'd sat there in her creaky old chair, gently rocking, her hair rolled up in a tight little bun on her head, her delicate white throat ringed round by a small lace collar, watching me with her sad deepset eyes, a melancholic smile on her lips, as I struggled with my pants, tearing them off, unknotting them, tugging them back on again. "I—I'm sorry, Grandmother!" For everything that had been happening out there, I'd meant, my own indecency included—just seeing her there, quietly juxtaposed against all that madness, had thrown it all into a new perspective: what must she think of us? I'd lost buttons and belt and the zipper didn't work: I'd had to hold my pants up with my hands.

"Where are your shoes, Richard?"

"I . . . uh, must have lost them! I—" But I'd reached the point where I had exhausted all my emotional reserve. Tears had rushed into my eyes, and I'd pitched forward into her lap. I'd wanted to hide myself there forever. "Good old Grandmother!" I'd wept.

"Stand up, Richard," she'd commanded. "Remember the Four Selfs!"

"But why has this happened to me, Grandmother?" I'd wailed. "I've always been a *good* man!"

"Not always," she'd replied matter-of-factly. "What about that time your father caught you swimming in the ditch?"

"The . . . the others dared me!"

"And you used to smoke cornsilks, steal grapes and watermelons, don't tell me you didn't, and you were mean to your brother Donny!"

"He was a smart aleck, he asked for it!" Why was she challenging me like this?

"You were jealous of poor Harold and didn't really care when he died."

"I *did!*" I'd protested, drawing back, and had shed some more tears just to prove it. "And I was *really* sorry when Arthur died!"

The tears were real now, but she'd pressed on mercilessly: "Why didn't you ever have any friends? Why did you go off by yourself at our picnics and not join in the fun? What's the matter with you, Richard? Why have you always been so moody and proud and selfish and stand-offish?"

"I had friends! They voted for me! But in politics—"

"Politics! Yes, I heard about that, too, Richard. All those naughty tricks you played on poor Jerry Voorhis and Mrs. Douglas and that nice Mr. Warren—"

"Nice, my foot! The world is rough, Grandmother, and when they hit you, you have to hit them back, and the best way to do that is to hit them before they hit you! I don't apologize for that—I'm a political animal, Grandmother, and—"

"Yes, and you smell like one, too," she'd sniffed. "You've lost your Quaker spirit, Richard."

"Only on domestic issues, Grandmother! I'm still a Quaker on foreign issues!"

"Drinking, smoking, swearing, cheating, telling untruths and tricking people—tsk tsk! You never talk about God or Jesus any more, Richard —and you play cards and take money from people—"

"Not for myself!" I'd insisted. "I don't take anything for myself!"

"And all those paragraphs about you in the college yearbooks—you wrote them yourself!"

"Not—not my senior year, I didn't, Grandmother!"

" 'Great things are expected . . .' My my! You should be ashamed, Richard!"

"Well, you . . . you have to be conceited in this business . . ."

"And what did you do up in that bell tower all by yourself? You know, Richard, your mother and father used to wonder if perhaps you weren't a bit disturbed. You were a very strange boy. I used to defend you, just as I defended all the boys, but . . ."

"I . . . I like to go my own way, Grandmother, keep my own counsel. That's the way I am, and one thing I always have to be—"

"You used to peek up the hired girls' skirts. You even tried to peek up *my* skirts!"

"I . . . did—?!"

"And you harbored wicked thoughts about little Ola and Marjorie and those burlesque dancers you used to go see with your cousin—"

"That was a long time ago, Grandmother, before I was married. I—"

"Oh yes? What about that secretary at the OPA, that nurse out in the Pacific Ocean—"

"I . . . I was lonely—"

"And this afternoon? Were you lonely this afternoon?"

"Wha—?! How . . . how did you—?"

" 'Oh, Ethel! I'd do anything for you!' Shame, shame, Richard! No wonder they've been punishing you!"

"I . . . I was just pretending! It's true! I'd gone up there to—Grandmother! Why are you writing all this down?"

"Ah . . . the, uh, better to counsel you with, my dear," she'd replied with a faint tight-lipped smile.

It was about this time that I'd begun to recall all those notes to myself about letting down too soon after crisis. For one thing, my Grandmother Milhous was dead, had been for years. For another, there *hadn't* been any secretary at the OPA, that had just been—and then it had come to me, like the punch line of an old joke heard a thousand times over, who it was: *"Edgar! You!"*

"You know, Dick," he'd smiled, chucking me under the chin, "the reason you've never been any good at making out is that you talk too much about yourself!"

"Goddamn you, Edgar!" I'd stormed, slapping his hand away. *"It's been you all along!"*

There were noises out in the Square now and crowds of hostile people were being shoved toward us into the Whale. "Come on, Dick," Hoover had said, smoothing down his heavy skirts, "I'd better get you out of here before the choice between the quick and the dead goes the wrong way for you. . . ."

Ah, why should an honest man enter public life and submit himself and his family to this kind of thing? Of course, a man who goes voluntarily into the political arena must expect some wounds in the battles in which he engages, but it seemed to me I suffered more than I deserved to. Both Pat and I had perhaps what one might describe as an overdeveloped sense of privacy. I know, people in political life have to live in a fishbowl. Every public figure, whose most important asset is his reputation, is at the mercy of the smear artists and the rumormongers, that's politics, but no matter how often you tell yourself that "this is part of the battle," or that "an attack is a compliment because your adversaries never bother taking on someone who amounts to nothing," there are times when you wonder if you shouldn't chuck the whole business.

Ethel's aria had faded and in its place, somewhere in the distance, far beyond the bedroom window, I seemed to hear somebody whistling, and what they were whistling was: "Happy Days Are Here Again!" *My song!* Oh my God! I knew who it was—was he coming here? I shrank back, panting wheezily, my heart in my throat, tears springing to my eyes. I felt like I used to feel whenever I'd hear my old man approaching in a rage, clutching his razor strap. Even if it wasn't for me. Things would sort of light up and get reddish all around me, inside as well as out, and that was what happened now. I squeezed my eyes shut: oh shit, hadn't I suffered enough? And when I opened them again, sure enough, there he was: standing in front of me near the fluttering curtains, his eyes glittering with animal menace, a cold sneer on his lips, the pallid gray light falling through the open window on his goateed face making him look suddenly old and ugly.

"Come here, boy," he said, smiling frostily and jabbing his recruitment finger at me with one hand, unbuttoning his striped pantaloons with the other: *"I want YOU!"*

"But—!"

"Speech me no speeches, my friend, I had a bellyfulla baloney—what I got a burnin' yearnin' for now is a little humble toil, heavenward duty, and onmittygated cornholin' whoopee! So jes' drap your drawers and bend over, boy—you been ee-LECK-ted!"

"Wha—?!"

"You heerd me!" he roared. "E pluribus the ole anum, buster, and on the double!" He dragged me backwards into the light, whipped my pants down, gave my ass a cracking caress: "Ah, an old old sight, you scamp, and yet somehow so young—aye, and not changed a wink since first I seen it! Bless me, you look purtier'n a tree frog on a fence rail with the wind up!"

"Please!" I whimpered. "I can't—!"

"I'll help you," he whispered girlishly, tickling my rectum. "Come on, loosen up, Nick! unlock the ole Snack Shack and impart to me summa your noble spirit, like, eh, like the lady says . . ."

But I scrambled out of his grip while he was fumbling with his braces, bounded back into the blankets and dog biscuits. "My God, you've— gasp!—just killed her!" I cried, cowering in a dark corner. "How can you make fun of her like that, she's not even cold yet—!"

"Cause I'se wicked, I is," he replied with a wolfish grin, flashing his incisors. The air seemed thick with a heavy doggy stink, but I didn't know if it came from him, me, or Checkers's gear. "I'se mighty wicked, anyhow, I can't help it—she's part a me now, both her and her brave engineer, just as much as Pocahontas, Billy the Kid, or Bambi—"

"You didn't have to kill them! You just did it for fun! You're a . . . a butcher! a beast! *You're no better than the Phantom!*"

"Aw fidgety fudge, them two raskils was lucky—"

"Lucky—!"

"Sure! It ain't easy holdin' a community together, order ain't what comes natural, you know that, boy, and a lotta people gotta get killt tryin' to pretend it is, that's how the game is played—but not many of 'em gets a chance to have it done to 'em onstage in Times Square!"

I knew that what he was telling me was the truth—but what about the way I *felt?* He wasn't telling me everything, I thought. . . . "All they wanted was what you promised them, the Bill of Rights, the Declaration—"

"Bah! The wild oats of youth! Listen, bein' young and rearin' up agin the old folks makes you fotch up a lotta hootin' and hollerin' you live to regret—puritanism! whoo, worse'n acne! It's great for stirrin' up the jism when you're nation-breedin', but it ain't no way to live a life!"

"You've . . . you've changed," I said, my voice shaking. "You're not the same as when I was a boy!"

He laughed softly and reached into the darkness to snatch me by the nape in his viselike grip. "You're forty years old, son: time you was weaned!"

"No!" I begged. *"Please—!"*

"You wanta make it with me," he panted, dragging me brutally out of the shadows and spinning me around, "you gotta love me like I really am: Sam Slick the Yankee Peddler, gun-totin' hustler and tooth-'n'-claw

tamer of the heathen wilderness, lusty and in everthing a screamin' med-
dler, novus ball-bustin' ordo seclorum, that's me, boy—and goodnight
Mrs. Calabash to any damfool what gets in my way!" He licked his
finger.

"But you . . . you *can't—!*"

"Can and will, my beauty, can and will! You said it yourself: they's a
political axiom that wheresomever a vacuum exists, it will be filled by
the nearest or strongest power! Well, you're lookin' at it, mister: an
example and fit instrument, big as they come in this world and gittin'
bigger by the minute! Towerin' genius disdains a beaten path—it seeks
regions hitherto unexplored—so clutch aholt on somethin' and say your
prayers, cuz I propose to move immeejitly upon your works!"

"*No!*" I cried. "*Stop!*" But too late, he was already lodged deep in my
rectum and ramming it in deeper—oh Christ! it felt like he was trying
to shove the whole goddamn Washington Monument up my ass! "*For
God's sake!*" I screamed. "*You're tearing me apart!*"

"No gains without—*grunt!*—pains, son," he replied coldly, forcing his
way in inch by inch—or was it yard by yard? Why had I ever doubted
him? "You hanker for the fast track, the—*mmf!*—dust of the arena, the
big leagues—well, these things are what you—*uff! ah!*—pay!"

"I take it back!"

He didn't even seem to hear me. "Maybe, as our Early Warning Sentinels have put it, some healthy tissue will have to—*pant!*—have to be
destroyed—but what the hell, rondyvoos with destiny ain't beanbag!"

"I don't *want* to!" I wailed in agony, twisting and pitching about. "*I
quit!*"

"Jehu Nimshi!" he bellowed. "If you ain't the all-starten skittiest
crittur in all Hail Columbia! I'm bewarin' you, Throttlebottom: I propose to—*fah!*—fight it out on this yere line, if it takes all summer! *Why
are you nervous?*"

"Oh my God!" I wept.

"Ain't you always said: when a man's—*ugh!*—constrained or—*huff!*
—arty-fishal, he don't get through, so be not a—*coo!*—a-quail neither
awestrucken! Thar ain't nothin' to fear but fear itself and a dry hole!
Opportunity—*ungff!*—is a-knockin', boy, but if you're gonna stay all
stobbed up, then by hokey I say—*grunt!*—let's call for a hatchet!"

"*No!*" I shrieked, giving way. And in he came, filling me with a
ripping all-rupturing force so fierce I thought I'd die! This . . . this is
not happening to me alone, I thought desperately, or tried to think, as
he pounded deeper and deeper, destroying everything, even my senses,
my consciousness—but to the nation as well!

"Whoop! clean as a hound's tooth!" he enthused. "Hoo hah! I do believe our form of guvvament, be it ever so humble, is deeply—*oof! ah!*—imbedded in ole Slippery Gulch at last! a miracle of fit and flattery! *Yow! Fooff!*"

Jesus, he was killing me! I'd been right about it all along! It *was* my execution! I was utterly gorged by him, he was slamming away in my belly, my chest, my very skull! I couldn't even breathe! I thought my heart would burst, my eyeballs would pop out! I was screaming and howling horribly but nobody came to my rescue.

"Now—*puff!*—don't be a baby, baby!" Uncle Sam crooned softly, leaning down to blow in my ear. He seemed to be wrapping me round, pressing his flesh against mine, inside and out—I felt like a tissue of pure pain, lodged like a condom between two grinding surfaces. . . . "I know, it—*grunt!*—always hurts the first time—*hoo!*—gettin' exposed like this to a crool invasion from—*pant!*—without and convulsions within, but bear up: heaven holds all for which you—*whuff!*—sigh—so there, little boy, don't—don't cry!" He was breathing heavily now, whamming away like a steam engine—I felt like I was being blown up like a balloon. "We're gonna do—*phew!*—great things together, we're—*nngh!*—doin' great things together right now—we—*yow!*—look out, son, my—*gasp!*—my cup—*oh! ah!*—runneth over—!"

My insides were rent suddenly with a powerful explosion, sending me skidding on my face several feet across the floor, and there was a terrific inundation! I seemed to be leaking at all pores and orifices—I couldn't even scream! Uncle Sam let out a fearsome groan and seemed to fall away—yet he remained inside me, throbbing and exploding. I lay there on the spare-room floor, gurgling, sweating, half-senseless, bruised and swollen and stuffed like a sausage, thinking: Well, I've been through the fire. After this, very few, if any, difficult situations could seem insurmountable if anything personal is involved. Nothing could match this. Nothing could top it. Not without being fatal.

Finally, when I felt able to speak, I lifted my head and asked feebly: "Please . . . ! When . . . when are you going to . . . to get out?" But I saw then that he *was* out. He was buttoning up his striped pantaloons, which were now stained with the lipstick off my ass. Or maybe this time it *was* blood. I fell back, curled up around my pain. Oh my God, so this was what it was like! I felt like a woman in hard labor, bloated, sewn up, stuffed with some enormous bag of gas I couldn't release. I recalled Hoover's glazed stare, Roosevelt's anguished tics, Ike's silly smile: I should have guessed. . . .

"Well, this is the end of a perfect day," Uncle Sam was saying. He